A HILL
Toward Home

ROBERT EARL WINTER

outskirts
press

Outskirts Press, Inc.
http://www.outskirtspress.com

Paperback ISBN: 978-1-9772-3759-0
Hardback ISBN: 978-1-9772-4104-7

PRINTED IN THE UNITED STATES OF AMERICA

CONTENTS

ACKNOWLEDGEMENTS

While the structure of the account of the Civil War has been gleaned from copious reading and research of the volumes listed below, much of the story line has been taken and adapted from family tradition and legend. The characters, other than those historic men and women obvious to the reader, are from either the author's collection of family stories or his own imagination, linking them conveniently to actual persons, places, and events. The names of some of the actual family members have been changed to protect the identity of their descendants, but others may be vaguely recognized by their progeny, with or without benefit of their true names.

There are a few songs written into the story, the source and authorship of which intensive research has failed to identify. These were passed down to me by my father, Rowland E. Winter, a consummate story teller in his own right. I must also register great appreciation to the services provided by Wikipedia, verifying much of the information gleaned from my research, some of which, however, I found to be conflicting as to dates, times, numbers, and even names. In such cases, I used the information that most suited my story line.

Publications and authors which I used in support of my story include: April 1865, by Jay Winik. Dred Scott v. Sandford, 60 U.S. (19 How.) 393 (1857). East Tennessee and the Civil War, by Oliver P. Temple. Generals in Blue, by Ezra J. Warner. Grant Moves South, by Bruce Catton. History of the First Tennessee Volunteer Cavalry, by W. R. Carter. History of the Thirteenth Tennessee Volunteer Cavalry U.S.A. by Samuel W. Scott and Samuel P. Angel. The Impending Crisis of the South, by Hinton R. Helper. The Knoxville Campaign, by Earl J. Hess. Nathan Bedford Forrest, First with the Most, by Robert Selph Henry. Southern Lady, Yankee Spy, by Elizabeth R. Varon.

10,000 Famous Freemasons, by William R. Denslow. Uncle Tom's Cabin, by Harriet Beecher Stowe, and The History of the Nashville, Chattanooga and St. Louis Railroad 1873-1916, by Jesse C. Burt Jr.

Bonnie Evans, an accomplished author, herself, rendered invaluable assistance in directing my path to publication.

My wife, Carolyne Winter, rendered invaluable service in reviewing, correcting and proofing this work, as well as prodding me to continue in the writing when my mind refused to cooperate.

It is to Carolyne that I dedicate the work, as without her encouragement it would still lie unfinished in the bowels of my computer.

FOREWORD

History, like truth, is an entire, seamless, endless fabric. Its beginning stretches back to the time of the first inscribed word or character and reaches forward to most recent moment; now, this very second. History, also like truth, beauty, justice and many other virtues lies principally in the perception of the beholder. Each of us maintains his or her own unique, exclusive view of history and none shares, word for word, fact for fact, the exact perception of anyone else.

History takes three forms; history experienced, history recalled, and history recorded. Experience is transitory and temporary. It is modified moment by moment, by setting and circumstance. It is constantly evolving and with the passage of time eventually becomes history recalled, which, too, is personal and may be only of value to the person who is the central figure; the hero of that particular narrow band of (his)story. It may be shared with others to a limited degree but sometimes even then it evolves with time and takes on a shade often far different from the original experience.

History recorded bears only faint resemblance to the other two forms, but is often the only reference we, in subsequent ages, have to rely on. We often see it written, "history is written by the victor," and that, to a great extent is true. It doesn't mean that there was no history experienced by the vanquished, it only means that it didn't get preserved for posterity.

Fortunately, when a great person or a tumultuous event breaks upon us there are usually enough accounts written by various sources that we can sometimes, with reasonable accuracy, reconstitute much of the original fabric. The American Civil War (or The War Between the States, depending on your version of 'history') produced several such great people and was just such an epoch event, and there is certainly no lack of material from which to draw in reconstructing a personalized experience.

This work tries to present history of the second form; history recalled. It is taken from the other two forms and rewoven. There are admittedly some holes, some patches, and some tears in the fabric. Some of the colors may be a little brighter or a little more faded than the original; the blues more blue and the grays perhaps shaded toward a richer butternut. It is not the 'unvarnished truth' nor is it intended to be, but neither is it a shameless fabrication. The story is taken from some personal family tradition and recall, some local color and legend, and virtually years of research. It is also stretched over a framework of recorded events, which I have used to support my patchwork fabric and give it form.

The unique aspect of the American Civil War was that it was an exclusively American experience involving friends, neighbors and even family members on opposing sides. We can speculate as to the real cause of the war, whether it be states rights, slavery, patriotism, preservation of a way of life, or any of a hundred other reasons but the fact remains that the war was, after all, an inevitable product of a dual system that existed far back into time, even before the American Revolution.

The pleasure of writing a book based on the War Between the States is that it gives the author a purpose to study, review, research, and sometimes vicariously relive the events that made up that strangely fascinating and challenging four-year bite of the American experience. It brings the author into personal contact with those who were involved, if they chose to record their experiences for posterity, and there were many involved in the War Between the States who did just that.

It is said that war often shapes civilizations. This statement may be an oversimplification of real experience. However, we must nevertheless recognize the fact that the Civil War and those who took part in it did, indeed, change the direction of this country, it's attitude toward itself, and its relationship to the rest of the world that could not have happened without it. It was, in every sense of the term, an epoch event, an event of the greatest magnitude that this country has ever experienced. Even the Revolutionary War, changing this land from a colony under subjugation to an independent nation of the first order, only found true meaning when the government of that nation was tried and tested in the crucible of the Civil War.

Individuals, too, were tested and changed by the war. As we study them, we find them changing from indifferent and disinterested men and women to visionaries; people of great strength and resolve. Unfortunately, we also see some of them progressing, or more properly, regressing to brigands and bandits just as readily. I've chosen to ignore most of those; the Quantrills, the Jameses, the Youngers, except to add a bit of flavor to my story and lend contrast to those who exemplified the higher, more virtuous human characteristics that were the inevitable product of the Civil War.

1

PHILIPPI FOOTRACES

Logan's stomach was in tight knots. His brow and palms were soaked with sweat, and his head was pounding. The Spencer rifle in his hands, for all its good qualities as an accurate and reliable weapon, felt as cumbersome as a fencepost. He tried to look down the sights, but his eyes wouldn't focus.

His long-time friend and now supervisor, Sergeant Frank Davis had chosen Jesse Logan, trained him, tested him, lectured him, counseled him, and had now sent him with a squad of supporters out onto this god-forsaken hillside to do what? To shoot some soldiers! To actually try to kill some people that he didn't even know whether they were good or bad people. They just happened to be members of the Confederate army.

His new friend, his 'spotter', and tent-mate, Jimmo Ogilby and he had had long discussions about how great it was not to have to march with the company against the enemy, but to be able to pick them off from a safe distance. Now, that idea was not nearly so attractive, when he was expected to put it into practice.

It was almost ten o'clock, the time he was supposed to start the battle by shooting some enemy soldiers, one of those he could plainly see in the valley below.

"Get a hold of yourself, Logan," Jesse muttered silently to himself. *"Sergeant Davis told you it would be like this and you have to think about your job. You volunteered to be here, remember? You volunteered to be a rifleman and take out the top brass of the enemy, to minimize the danger that our boys would be facing. You volunteered. Volunteered!"*

All of a sudden, the reflections on his situation went out of his head. He heard cannon and rifle fire coming from the hills below him, and knew

General Rosecrans had commenced his attack and he, Jesse Logan, was expected to do his job.

He wiped the sweat out of his eyes and took aim at what appeared to be a captain or major or something. He closed his eyes and squeezed the trigger. The Spencer leaped in his sweaty hands and he opened his eyes. There was so much smoke from the shot that he couldn't even see the officer he'd been aiming at.

Jimmo Ogilby immediately scrambled over to where Jesse was crouched behind a rock, "You hit him, Jesse. You hit him. You hit that captain. You did."

Jesse was anything but happy with the news, but steeled himself for another try. Sergeant Davis had drilled it into the sniper teams that their first shots would cause confusion in the ranks, but the enemy troops wouldn't usually be able to detect the source of fire and the riflemen were to take as many follow-up shots as soon as possible. He settled behind his rock and took aim at a sergeant. This time he kept his eyes open as he had learned to do hunting deer and rabbits. He fired the Spencer and when the smoke cleared, he could see the sergeant was also down with men clustering around him. Logan fired again and hit one of the members of that group. "Remember. These people are a threat to our side; to our fellow soldiers. The goal is to get this war behind us and that's what you're doing right now. The sooner this thing is over, the sooner we can go home."

Jimmo tapped Jesse on the shoulder, "You see that group a little over to the right? There's a lieutenant in with that bunch of men."

Jesse sighted the Spencer as Jimmo watched through a telescope. His next shot dropped the lieutenant. He was no newcomer to firing at live animals, but this was totally different. He wiped the sweat from his eyes and looked for another target.

⸺◈⸺

Jesse had been in the army now for over two months. He, like most of the recruits in the company, was dedicated to what he and his companions called the 'cause of the Union', and had looked forward with considerable enthusiasm to the idea of being a soldier and going to war. He had even taken calmly to the idea that it would be necessary to shoot enemy soldiers, just as he had been expected to shoot hostile Indians whom he and his family had encountered out west back in the fifties. He just hadn't become accustomed to the idea of taking the life of a person posing no immediate threat to one's own safety.

Jesse Logan, Sergeant Frank Davis, James Ogilby, Elijah Hawkins, Abner Thomas, Martin Mason, Shelby Smith, and a thousand other men had joined the federal army at the first call, from Indiana. Jesse had been visiting in Illinois with his brother David at the time, and when the call went out, he lit out for Evansville, Indiana, where it looked as though there would be a good chance of enlisting. They had all mustered in together on a ninety-day enlistment, had taken their initial training and had been assigned to the Sixth Indiana Volunteer Regiment under a captain named Jeremiah C. Sullivan and Colonel Erastus Tyler in General Rosecrans's Indiana Brigade.

Captain Sullivan was a mild mannered, round faced man with a small van dyke goatee. He had been an officer in the navy before he resigned his commission to study the law in Indiana. He was well liked by his troops though they saw him as somewhat bookish for a captain, still they respected his judgment and his position.

The regiment had 'marched off' to the east through Ohio and into Virginia at Parkersburg. Actually, they didn't march much at all, they travelled by river boat most of the way.

Their orders had been to drive the Confederate army from western Virginia, which region was in full sympathy with the Union, much the same as the people of Carter County, Tennessee, where Jesse had been born and where he had been living with his grandmother and grandfather before the war had started. At Parkersburg, they joined with the Ohio Volunteers under General George McClellan, who, as senior general, assumed command of the combined forces. They then continued east through Clarksville, as there had been reports of Rebel forces in the area.

General McClellan advanced his forces along the Northwestern Railway as far as Grafton and as he did so Confederate General Porterfield drew his forces back to Philippi. As McClellan neared the region, he sent Colonel Benjamin F. Kelley and the First Virginia Provisional Regiment (later the First West Virginia Infantry) as an advance guard. On June 3, at Philippi, they routed a small force of Rebels in a night attack and then they rested. General McClellan was good at that, and the men in the ranks appreciated his concern for their wellbeing. His strategy seemed to be one of extremely cautious progress, with ample preparations being made to approach the next encounter with frequent pauses for rest and reconnaissance.

Philippi had been not much more than a skirmish and Jesse's unit was not really involved. He never even fired his rifle, but it was an initiation of sorts and the men in ranks felt a great sense of triumph and a little relief.

It was just as they had hoped. Their "overwhelming strength and superior tactics," as General McClellan had called them, would, "drive the Rebels all the way to Richmond". The skirmish at Philippi was quickly given the moniker as the "Philippi Footraces" because of the haste with which the small Confederate regiment vacated the town.

By this time the ninety-day enlistments were running out and most of the men in the regiment volunteered for a three-year term. General William Rosecrans was still in command of the brigade, but Captain Sullivan was promoted to the rank of Colonel and put in command of the regiment. Lieutenant William Weller was promoted to Captain in command of Company "H", much to the chagrin of First Lieutenant John Goodin, who had ranked Weller by three days.

The recruits were a salty lot at that time. They had been mustered in only a few short weeks before but thought themselves to be soldiers in every sense of the word. James Ogilby was a Scotsman, whose family had immigrated only a few years before the war broke out. They had been sheep farmers, and had left Scotland to try their hand at the rich plains of the American West, which, at the time, took them to Indiana. At home, he was called Jamie, but as soon as he and Jesse met, they hit it off, and Jesse gave him the nick-name of Jim O, or Jimmo, to distinguish him from the dozen or so other Jims and Jameses in the unit. He was a stout young man, with a shock of sandy hair, and a pink face, which lent the impression that he was perpetually blushing. Except, that is, when he actually did blush, at which time his face took on a ruddy glow that was the delight of his fellow recruits who constantly tried to embarrass him.

Jimmo took all this good naturedly, but his immediate attachment to Jesse was a natural buffer, as he was assigned as Jesse's spotter. This gave him and Jesse a certain distinction and an opportunity to work separately from the rest of the company when the snipers would be sent out to the perimeters of the battlefield to harass the enemy. It was a tactic Sergeant Davis had refined to perfection, and worked well in Colonel Sullivan's developing military strategy.

Sergeant Frank Davis had been a private in the war with Mexico in 1846 and 1847, and had fought with valor beside many of the notable officers and enlisted men now holding important positions in both the Federal and Confederate armies. He had stayed in the army for almost twelve years and had risen to the rank of sergeant, but then met a lady who stole his heart and convinced him that he should leave the army and go into business with his father in Evansville, Indiana. They were married, and the shipping business was good in Evansville, but when the war broke out, he couldn't resist the call to arms.

A married sergeant was something of a rarity in the early days of the war, and some said marriage robbed a man of the courageous abandon necessary to carry out orders and lead his men into battle. Frank Davis was never short on courage, and while it could never be said that he avoided risk, the risks he took and to which he subjected his men, were measured, calculated, and precisely managed to get the most out of the opportunity.

Then, "Just think of it as a hill toward home," Davis would say to his men, as they were about to assault an objective. "Just one more hill toward home, boys."

Frank Davis was just as anxious to go home as any of them, but he was also committed to doing a job. Jesse and Frank Davis had known each other briefly a few years back, and had developed considerable respect for each other at that time. It was a fortuitous reunion when they both joined the Sixth Indiana Volunteer Infantry and Davis probably would have suggested Jesse for the rank of Corporal if he hadn't been aware of Jesse's marksmanship abilities.

On the ninth of July, General McClellan had given orders to move out in a southeasterly direction, as the intelligence he had received indicated the Confederate forces, now under Confederate General Robert Garnett, were guarding a town called Beverly, which was a key junction on the Staunton and Parkersburg Turnpike. There were scores of Union-friendly citizens in the area, and the enemy couldn't make a move without the Union Army learning of it immediately.

General McClellan was in his element. He had graduated from West Point Military Academy in 1846, with such other luminaries as Confederate Generals Thomas J. Jackson and George Picket. He had been assigned to General Winfield Scott's staff as an engineer during the Mexican War, and had then left the army in 1857 for a career with the Illinois Central Railroad. His management style was one of planning and preparation, which meant he needed the unswerving support of his staff and subordinates and all the operational information he could obtain on which to make decisions.

General McClellan planned to move the army into Beverly, but the turnpike between Philippi and Beverly was blocked by General Garnett, and the alternate passes were felt to be too narrow and winding to support McClellan's entire column. He didn't feel he could move the entire force at once. Reports from the friendly citizens gave him to believe the Confederates were in the hills around Beverly, specifically Rich Mountain and Laurel Hill, in a chain of hills running roughly north and south and through which the Federals would have to pass to take that valley.

His plan was to skirt Camp Garnett, move south along a small creek on the west side of Rich Mountain, as far as the southern branch of the Parkersburg Turnpike, completely avoiding General Garnett's main force of about 3500. General McClellan would initiate the attack on July 11, at 10:00 AM, if he could locate and confront the enemy. General Rosecrans's forces were to delay a short time west of the ridge, and then to move in as a support force, after the McClellan's Ohio Volunteers had cleared the route.

At the last minute, however a young man, 18-year-old David Hart, familiar with the terrain, had appeared in camp with information that there was an alternate route through Rich Mountain which was passable though somewhat winding and tortuous. Hart told them this route would put them onto the battlefield in a position of advantage, flanking the Rebels who were dug in at the farm owned by his family, and by doing so they would be furnishing valuable flanking support for McClellan's main contingent. They would be facing a force of unknown size commanded by General Garnett. Intelligence told them that on July 9, Garnett had established himself securely on Rich Mountain and Laurel Hill protecting Beverly on the east and north.

Still McClellan decided to attack. On July 10, Leaving General Thomas Morris to confront the Rebels at Camp Garnett, he ordered General Rosecrans and a brigade consisting of the 6th and 13th Indiana, the 5th, 15th, and 16th Ohio, and the 1st and 2nd (West) Virginia Infantries, along with the 1st Ohio Light Artillery, almost 2,000 men, to attack from the south end of the valley. Fortunately for Rosecrans, Garnett had thought Rich Mountain too strong to be attacked and left only 1,300 Confederates under the command of Colonel John Pegram to hold that position.

On the night of July 10, Brigadier General William S. Rosecrans, "Old Rosy", put his troops into action, following the route indicated by the helpful young man. The night was dark and there was a driving rain that made the movement all that much more difficult, but the information was good and the brigade moved into position as planned. Sergeant Davis had sent a detachment of skirmishers, including Jesse Logan, out ahead and gave them instructions to establish a position at a point of visibility and vantage, avoiding the Confederate pickets, and commence a sniping attack at ten o'clock.

"Look for the officers," Davis had told his three sniper teams. "Without officers the men will be in more confusion, and our job will be a lot easier. Take as high a position as you can find, with dense brush or heavily wooded hillsides, and get that first shot off at ten o'clock. We'll be listening for your shot as a signal you're in place. Logan, — are you all right with shooting at somebody? You know this isn't just a target or an antelope. It will be a real person."

Jesse had told Sergeant Davis not to worry, that he would do his job as he had been instructed. He was almost 21 years old, now, and had been over the routine and mental preparation with the sergeant a dozen times but Davis was still undecided as to whether to go out with the sharpshooter team the first time out or not. Through his past association with Sergeant Davis, Logan had developed a deep trust in the older man, and he had every intention of demonstrating that trust.

Sergeant Davis also told the skirmish force to keep as low a profile as possible, as it was supposed to be McClellan's Ohio Brigade that was to initiate the action, and the force under General Rosecrans was to act in support only. The reason for Jesse's ten o'clock opening shot was that ten o'clock was to be the time General McClellan had designated as the time his own attack was to start.

Logan's little squad, consisting of twelve men under the direction of Abner Thomas, a newly appointed corporal, moved out quickly and quietly. The heavy rain, which would make it difficult for them to use their muskets, helped cover the sound of their movement. Jesse was armed with his Spencer rifle, which used metallic cartridges putting him at a considerable advantage, as it was not only more accurate at long range, but less subject to misfire than the regularly issued muzzle-loading muskets loaded with paper cartridges. They trudged along in the rain, not bothering to even communicate with one another, shrouded by their gum blankets, needed to keep them and their powder dry following the directions given by young David Hart.

Corporal Thomas was cautious, but Sergeant Davis's instructions left little to chance. "From here," the sergeant had told the squad, "I want you to go as far as you safely can and work your way north along the eastern fringe of the valley. Stay with the cover as much as you can and well up on the side of the hills. At thirty-minute intervals, I want you to send a man back with progress reports on your movements. I'll send him right back, 'soon as I can, to keep you informed of what's goin' on back here. Logan is to start firing at ten o'clock, sharp, and Ogilby is to stay with him to spot. Give those rifle teams as much protection as you can but for the rest of the squad, your immediate responsibility is intelligence. If you're close enough for them to do their job, you should be close enough to do yours. Remember, men, this is just another hill toward home. If we can take this hill, we'll be that much closer to getting back to our families."

Corporal Ab Thomas and the small force had moved out well before 5:00 AM, just as it was getting light, staying with cover as instructed. They moved quickly away from the main force, soon losing contact with them.

They kept the hillside to their left, ascending steadily, until they had been out about four hours.

The enemy was spread a little higher up the hill than they had expected. They were hunkered down against the rain, and were totally unaware of the approach of the skirmishers, though they suspected and prepared for the main force moving against them from the north, the opposite direction from that which Rosecrans was to use.

Thomas sent the couriers back as directed to report to Sergeant Davis. As the morning progressed the weather began to clear and as ten o'clock approached, they could see the enemy, but Jesse still didn't feel he had a sufficiently commanding position to hit a good target. He suggested they move higher on the mountainside to improve his vantage. The Spencer was good for 1000 yards, but with only open, or 'iron' sights on his rifle, Jesse wanted to get a lot closer than that, or his accuracy would suffer.

"Davis said I should start my firing at ten o'clock," Jesse said to Ab Thomas. "How much time do we have?"

"About ten minutes, yet," Thomas replied, looking at his watch, "We'd better start looking for a good place to set you up."

"There's some rocks and trees on that next rise that I think I can use," Jesse said. "I'd better get up there and set up. Are you going to send a messenger back now, or wait till we get set?"

"I'll wait," Thomas replied. "You move on over there and we'll check the area for pickets." It took longer than Jesse had reckoned to get into position, and by the time he was ready with what he thought were suitable targets, he thought it was well after ten.

The whole thing felt odd. He had never before settled into a take-aim position to shoot at a man, much less one in full uniform. On both trips he had taken across the plains when he was younger, he had been forced to shoot at hostile Indians, but that was on the spur of the moment and necessary to save his life. This was different. Pure and simple, he was bushwhacking.

When they heard the firing from below them, as General Rosecrans had set his troops in motion in spite of Logan's delay, Corporal Ab Thomas was not prepared for Jesse's opening shot. He pulled out his pocket watch, the only watch in the squad at that time, and peered at it, discovering, to his disgust, that it must be well after the ten o'clock start time. His watch had stopped at ten minutes before ten o'clock, and the implications were clear. In his haste to set off on the squad's mission he had forgotten to wind his watch that morning, but had also failed to initiate the sniper fire as directed. He didn't know what time it was but he was sure he had not been able to carry out the sergeant's orders, and he was going to get a lecture when he got back to the lines. He wound his watch and dispatched his ten o'clock courier. The return message would not be a pleasant one.

Presently movement on the hillside below Jesse's position told him that there was a squad of about ten Rebels making their way up the hill toward his position. His first thought was to move out, but then he thought of his advantage. He was shooting down on them; they had to shoot uphill. He had a rifle, they probably had muskets. He could fire seven rounds to their one. He was ensconced in a clump of trees and rocks. They had to range in the open, and did not yet seem to have identified Logan's exact location.

Sergeant Davis had discussed tactics with the men, and had advised them how much easier it was to defend than to attack a position. From experience, Jesse knew the rules of ballistics when it came to shooting down-hill. He set his sights at 200 yards, tracked one of the soldiers who seemed to be out in front of the squad and fired. When the rifle smoke cleared, the man was on the ground and his companions were scattered. The Rebels were well aware of their disadvantage, and it looked as though they were making plans to spread out and surround Jesse and Jimmo, without unnecessarily exposing themselves to the deadly fire Jesse was laying down. He had only fired nine shots but each of them had done damage. He reloaded with five more cartridges in the seven-round magazine of the Spencer.

As he waited and watched, Jesse reflected on his situation. He had been anxious to get into the war. It represented high adventure, and his family in Tennessee had firmly supported the Union cause, encouraging him to go back across the Ohio River where he found there was even stronger Union sentiment. The feelings in East Tennessee were mixed. Carter County, Tennessee, like the several counties surrounding it was a strong Union bastion, but some of the people in the counties farther west, were just as strongly Secessionist. For the last year or so there had been killings and beatings as the tensions of secession had torn the communities apart. Jesse had met several fine young men at school in Elizabethton and other gatherings that had expressed strong secessionist feelings, though he was not sure why. He'd also met some young hotheads with the attitude that they wanted to rebel against something, not sure what, and this was an opportunity to join with others of like mind and "kick some tail".

Slaves in that part of the country were uncommon and mostly an unnecessary burden. Jesse didn't know anyone except a few of the wealthier townspeople, and a friend of his family that was involved in freighting, who owned them. But there was also the issue of what he had heard called "states' rights" discussed. With it went the accompanying argument that if the north were to impose their will in the U.S. Congress, as they often seemed to be doing, there would be no hope for any state to maintain its authority over any of its own business. Jesse thought this was something of a 'straw man' issue, and that the matter of slavery was really the key to all the dissension. Pure and simple, the wealthy wanted to protect their investment and resented any threat to diminish it. They had paid good money to acquire the people they 'owned', and they didn't feel it was fair to have someone just come and take those people from them.

Jesse and Jimmo watched as the little force of rebel soldiers climbed the hill. As they approached within about sixty yards, they stopped, and regrouped. Jesse could catch snatches of what they were saying, even though they were still in the cover of some trees. The word "trap," reached his ears, as did, "sniper, skedaddle", and "captain's orders." It appeared that he had knocked out their leader and the squad was uncertain as to how to proceed.

Presently the rebel soldiers slipped out of the grove of trees on the far side from where Jesse was crouched and made their way hurriedly back down the hill. He was disappointed, but there were other matters to attend to at the moment. Corporal Thomas came over to where Jesse was hidden and encouraged him to go ahead and try to pick off whoever he could in the Rebel squad, but by then Jesse couldn't get off a clear shot.

The forces under General Rosecrans were on the move, coming up the valley from Jesse's right. What a sight! The whole Rosecrans Regiment was advancing in an organized and disciplined manner, and Jesse had never before been in a position to see such a spectacle. He was overwhelmed by the sheer magnitude of the force. A battery of cannon had been set up below where his small troop was located, and had opened up on the Confederate forces. The Rebels were pretty well dug in at the Hart Farm however, and showed no inclination to retreat.

General Rosecrans was now visible in the distance conferring with his staff and giving orders. They had caught the enemy off guard to some degree and though General McClellan may have been able to carry the day with the force he had available, it looked as though General Rosecrans certainly guaranteed the victory. Jesse consulted with Ab Thomas, who had received word from Sergeant Davis to move their position up the hillside if they felt Logan could still be of service as a sniper.

"There's plenty of cover here, Ab," Jesse said, "and I think I can harass them some. Can you scout up the hill for a better spot but leave me a couple of men as protection?" He was nervous.

"Sure," Thomas said, "We're supposed to stay out here till Sergeant Davis pulls us back. 'Got plenty of ammunition?"

"I have about thirty rounds in my sardine can, yet," Logan assured Thomas as he peered into his cartridge case. "If that isn't enough, I'd better not be here."

They both laughed nervously. "Jesse, if you talk to Sergeant Davis, let him know that we were really busy securing our position at ten o'clock, and jus' couldn't get into position to start firing." Ab said with something of a plea in his voice. "I know I'm gonna catch hell for not havin' you start on time."

"I'll sure do what I can, Ab," Jesse assured him, "It was as much my fault for trying to get better position."

"Well, we'll see," Thomas wasn't optimistic.

Jesse and his small support group stayed in the rocks for a short time and then moved farther up the hill and north into a grove of trees that Ab Thomas had suggested, as a confederate battery was trying to identify his position. He fired another fifteen rounds, doing damage with almost every shot, and moving his position periodically to confuse the enemy and avoid detection.

At about four o'clock, the Confederate troops had retired about a mile and Logan's squad had moved their position several times to keep the Rebs under observation, but then they saw that there was a large squad of men starting out in his direction. They kept to the available cover, and though he managed to hit two or three of them, the Rebs kept coming. The Rebels didn't stop to exchange shots, as they knew their disadvantage. They just kept climbing, keeping out of his sight as much as possible.

"The party's getting rowdy and I think it's time to go home," Jesse said to the others. "Here come some guys who can just wreck any event and I don't want to be around when they get here."

"You're right, Jess," Shelby Smith responded, "Just when we were starting to enjoy ourselves these party-crashers show up."

—⚬—

While Rosecrans led his column toward the Hart farm, McClellan had been waiting impatiently to launch the frontal assault on the Rebel emplacement. But McClellan was encountering difficulties. By eleven o'clock that morning his forces were in position, but his artillery placements had not been completed to his ultimate satisfaction. He remained with his advance pickets awaiting Rosecrans' assault upon the Confederate rearguard at Camp Garnett, not realizing the attack had actually begun as planned. The action by the forces under General Rosecrans were beyond some hills and out of range of McClellan's hearing.

General McClellan had held his troops in assault position for almost three hours, making last-minute preparations and "waiting for Rosecrans to attack". When he eventually heard the firing at the Hart farm, McClellan and his troops moved up to the forward picket line, but he could not bring himself to order the frontal attack. He was in a position to see some Confederates making speeches, which were greeted by loud cheers. The jubilant mood of the Confederates seen from that position and the apparent failure of Rosecrans to attack served to convince McClellan that the Confederates had overpowered the Federals at Hart farm.

As the battle for Hart farm slowed toward evening, also learning that the Forty-fourth Virginia (CSA) was posted nearby and considering the exhausted state of his troops, Rosecrans departed from McClellan's battle plan to bivouac for the night at the Hart farm, but he had accomplished his purpose for that day.

Rosecrans's capture of Rich Mountain put the Federals squarely across Garnett's line of retreat toward Beverly and to the east, but General Garnett was determined to continue the fight. Entrenched securely at 'Camp Garnett' at Laurel Hill, he was well protected, but isolated from reinforcement or escape. As General Rosecrans later described it to the Congressional Committee on the Conduct of the War, the key to Confederate defenses in Trans-Allegheny Virginia was Camp Garnett and its adjacent fortifications; Rich Mountain and Laurel Hill. The fall of Camp Garnett would threaten Confederate positions in the Shenandoah Valley from Harpers Ferry to Staunton. It was a text-book example of how military distributions could be positioned to demonstrate the 'domino theory' of defense.

The bulk of the Confederate army under General Garnett was thus bottled up. Rosecrans, having captured Colonel Pegram and the 20th Virginia Infantry on Rich Mountain, had placed the Rebels in a pinch between his and General McClellan's main force, which was dug in at Laurel Hill. General Garnett now had to break out or face capture and total defeat, and he was not one to accept the latter alternative. With Rich Mountain gone and Laurel Hill threatened, Camp Garnett was not the place to be at the time. General Garnett decided his best escape was to try to slip between Rosecrans and

McClellan in an easterly direction. The route he chose would take him to a crossing over the Cheat River called Corrick's Ford.

On the thirteenth of July, General Garnett launched an effort to try to break between the line of General Rosecrans and the force under General McClellan at Laurel Hill and a sharp battle ensued. Jesse was again assigned to act as a sharpshooter. This time he was a little more mentally prepared for his assignment.

The next day, Sergeant Davis called Jesse aside and handed him a beautiful gold pocket watch. "Take this watch." Sergeant Davis said sternly. "I want you to keep it. We need to have at least two watches out there to coordinate our timing."

"Where'd you get it?" Jesse asked. "Where did you get a watch like that, Sergeant? Watches cost money, and I know you ain't much given to throwin' your money around."

"Don't worry about where I got it. You need a watch, and here it is. We can't take a chance on messing up the way we did over on the side of Rich Mountain Thursday. When I tell you to start shooting at ten o'clock, I want to hear a round fly at exactly ten o'clock, and not before, and not after. You're the best shot we have in the company, Logan, and I need you and that Spencer rifle of yours out on the edges of the field to get their attention, and take down their leaders, if you can."

"Well, you know, I did take down that captain. I knew you wanted me to start shooting at ten o'clock. I k - k - killed that captain, then a sergeant and a lieutenant and about ten other Rebs. It was the best I could do at the time." Jesse took the watch reluctantly. "You got it off a dead Reb, didn't you?"

"He won't be needing it," Sergeant Davis mumbled. "You're just goin' to have to get used to the idea that the spoils of war are just as legal down here in the field as they are among the gen'rals and those people in Washington or Richmond. When we were back there at Rich Mountain at the Hart farm, who do you know that had any concern about who owned what part of the ground? When you crossed that little ford in the rain that morning, did you worry about who it belonged to? Private Logan, it is called 'the spoils of war,' and no matter whether we are taking land, cannons, horses, or watches from the defeated enemy, it is all legitimate plunder."

Private Logan hung his head and looked at the watch Sergeant Davis had given him, as he walked slowly back to the tent that he and his bunkmate James Ogilby had called home for the past two days. The watch was quite a prize, probably real gold, with a hunting case that closed over the face of the watch to protect it. It had a beautiful chain to which was attached both its key and an ornate watch fob with some figures Jesse didn't recognize.

It had engraving inside the case which looked quite new, and had most likely been a presentation to the former owner, shortly before he went into battle; his last.

"What've you there, Jess?" Ogilby asked, as Logan approached their tent.

"Hey, Jimmo," Jesse responded, "The Sergeant gave me this watch to keep me in line when we're out on the rim, sniping at the Johnnies. He was a little unhappy with me when I didn't let fly right on time over on Rich Mountain the other day. He thought I should've been able to knock down at least a major or colonel or better when we opened up on them, and wants to make sure I get the next one right."

"It's truly a thing of beauty," Jimmo said, admiring the watch in Jesse's hand, "He's complaining that you hit only their captain, a lieutenant, and a sergeant? He's been telling us that the army can't run without sergeants, and now he complains that you should have gone for a higher officer? Maybe he's just trying to protect his chums from the old army."

The fact that he was good at what he was doing gave Jesse some recognition among his peers. At six foot six inches tall, his size and his pale-colored hair made him stand out in the ranks, and the other members of the company felt they had a celebrity in their midst, and sometimes chided him in good humor about his status.

"They'd make you a general if they thought that you'd keep up popping off them Rebs," Elijah Hawkins joked.

"They couldn't spare him out on the perimeter," Shelby Smith responded.

"Don't let it go to your head. Jesse Boy," Jimmo said, protectively, "But before you get that big promotion, you teach me to use that rifle and leave it with me when you go."

General Rosecrans issued orders the evening of July 12 to have the troops up and ready by four o'clock the next morning. Company "H" was to anchor the right of Rosecrans's Brigade facing Garnett's 4600 troops, and holding one of the forward positions. Their reputation for discipline earned them the distinction of being one of the lead positions in many of the battles. They were up before four o'clock, assembled for roll call and prepared to finish the job they had begun two days previously, or so they thought. Sergeant Davis was explaining the approach he expected the men to use, and was about to dispatch the unit.

Jesse turned to the man to his left, Lige Hawkins, and said in a stage whisper, "He talks like a man in a paper sack suit."

"What are you muttering about Private Logan?" Sergeant Davis had overheard the comment, as Jesse had intended.

"Sergeant Davis, don't you know those Johnny Rebs are shooting real bullets?"

"What do you care for those real bullets, Whitey?" Hawkins joked, "You don't spend enough time out in the open to catch any of them, and if you did get into a shooting match, that Spencer of yours can shoot all day without reloading."

"Well, if I do run out of bullets, I can't just pick up new ones at the corner store, though," Jesse responded, "So I have to be real cautious how many I use."

"What was that comment about a man in a paper sack suit, Logan," Sergeant Davis demanded with his face within inches of Jesse's.

"Sergeant, I was defending your honor just now, Private Hawkins said that uniform you're wearing wasn't fit to drape a potato sack. Well, I 'lowed as how it certainly would do a potato sack proud. But, say there, Sergeant," Logan said pulling his new watch from his pocket, "I do think it's time we got started, don't you?"

"Logan, Ogilby, Mason, Smith, fall out. Company, close ranks, right face," Davis was chuckling when he addressed the squad, "Forward, march, column half right, march." They were on their way into battle, but the men were smiling as they went out to face the enemy. Jesse, James Ogilby, Martin Mason and Shelby Smith were to assume their usual role as a sharp-shooting team.

⸺《◉》⸺

General McClellan, was also preparing to attack General Garnett's position at Laurel Hill. His tactics were much more deliberate than those of General Rosecrans, and his forces were not in place until after six o'clock. As McClellan was placing his units in position to attack and as the artillery was being moved to the knoll to shell Camp Garnett, a cavalryman rode into camp, reporting a Confederate withdrawal. He briefed McClellan on the facts that Rosecrans had sent in the Nineteenth Ohio, units of the Tenth and Thirteenth Indiana and Burdsal's cavalry and had already driven the confederates out of Camp Garnett and had occupied the camp.

There had been considerable distance between McClellan and General Rosecrans, as evidenced by the fact that they had not communicated for two days, but General Garnett had a rather sizeable force to squeeze through the gap between the two armies. This also involved crossing Cheat Creek, swollen by the recent rains, and for this purpose he chose Corrick's Ford. Abandoning Camp Garnett would mean that he would have to abandon a large cache of supplies, but Rosecrans pressed him so hard that there was not even enough time to set them afire. A small group of sick and wounded Confederates were also left at Camp Garnett in charge of a surgeon and a captain who were to surrender the camp at daybreak.

Confusion in the Tygart Valley was rampant with the Rebels clearing the valley and McClellan's Federals not even realizing it. Confederate Officers were issuing conflicting orders and soldiers were running in all directions.

Early in the battle, a civilian, Mr. John Hughes, who was acting as a courier and guide for General Garnett was riding toward the Rebel camp at Rich Mountain to deliver a message when Confederate pickets retiring from the Hart farm, shot and killed him, mistaking him for a Federal. It was a sad affair. Hughes had been a member of the convention that adopted the Ordinance of Secession for the State of Virginia. He was a strong Secessionist, and native of Beverly, but was killed for his service to the cause of secession by one of his own.

No one knew who the enemy was, and it was even difficult for the sniper team to adopt a position from which to harass the enemy.

Jesse had little time to secure a good position and get off any effective fire when he would have to pack up and move to another location. He was having trouble keeping contact with his own company, though his couriers kept up their half-hour trips as well as they could.

At Camp Garnett, some thirty-three Confederate officers and five hundred sixty enlisted men surrendered to McClellan's forces. After receiving the message of their surrender, McClellan ordered his men to load food and provisions in wagons and deliver them to the surrendering soldiers. McClellan then moved his units out, passed through Camp Garnett, and halted briefly at General Rosecrans's camp to speak to the wounded, while ignoring General Rosecrans. He then proceeded to occupy Beverly without opposition late in the afternoon. He left Rosecrans' brigade at Camp Garnett and the Hart farm until the following day when they moved on to Beverly.

By leaving his tents in place and withdrawing silently, General Garnett had fairly well managed to slip past McClellan without detection. Intending to move over the Staunton and Parkersburg Turnpike before McClellan could block his escape route by occupying Beverly. Confederate General Garnett proceeded southward on the pike until he was erroneously informed that the Federals were already in possession of Beverly. He then turned northward from the pike, hoping to evade the Federals and move his troops around the northern section of the mountain range to return to Staunton.

At Corrick's Ford the wagons were momentarily halted. While the First Georgia and part of the Twenty-third Virginia regiments were trying to rescue the wagons from the deep water, Federal troops engaged them in a brief exchange of small weapons fire. General Garnett had returned to the rear guard to check on the action and while directing the Confederates in removing the wagons from the ford, he was shot and killed by a sergeant from the Thirteenth Indiana, leaving the Confederate forces with diminished leadership. They were on their own.

From Beverly General McClellan made good use of the telegraph lines, which he had constructed as his armies advanced. McClellan immediately reported the successes of his campaign. The Federal authorities had been much concerned with his campaign and were elated by McClellan's seemingly easy victory.

Following the battles of Rich Mountain and Corrick's Ford, General McClellan sent to his troops the following message, which was faithfully reproduced by the northern press:

'Soldiers of the Army of the West: I am more than satisfied with you. You have annihilated two armies, commanded by educated and experienced soldiers, intrenched in mountain fastness fortified at their leisure . . . You have killed more than two hundred and fifty of the enemy, who has lost all his baggage and equipage. All this has been accomplished with the loss of twenty brave men killed and sixty wounded on your part.'

In Washington, as a result of the actions at Beverly and Philippi, Representative Thomas M. Edwards of New Hampshire introduced a resolution in the House of Representatives, unanimously adopted, which read in part:

'Resolved: That the thanks of this House be presented to Major General G. B. McClellan, and the officers and soldiers of his command for the series of brilliant and decisive victories . . . achieved . . . on the battlefields of Western Virginia.'

General Rosecrans and his brigade had been instrumental in defeating an army of 1300 Confederates on Rich Mountain and 4600 at Camp Garnett, but when all was said and done, General McClellan, upset over having let Garnett's regiment slip through his fingers, cast about for someone to blame. He was understandably upset but, rather than accept any of the responsibility, he chose General Rosecrans for the object of his wrath. He claimed that he had expected Rosecrans to take the Hart Farm and alert him of his actions. It mattered little that the July 10th agreement had been to launch a simultaneous attack at ten o'clock, and that he, himself, had delayed the movement of his own forces until he discovered that the battle was well underway. George McClellan was a man who wanted to have all the information on all matters laid out right on his desk, and he didn't like surprises. The facts were that Rosecrans's attack was executed as planned, but acoustics got in the way. McClellan didn't accept that as any excuse, and Old Rosy felt the sting of McClellan's criticism.

In his report to Washington, General McClellan took full credit for the victory, and also censured General Rosecrans for failing to follow orders and send a courier to keep him advised. It was General Rosecrans's turn to be furious. Everyone except Sergeant Davis was dumbfounded. They couldn't understand why such a ringing defeat of the enemy should have resulted in censure. Davis took the matter stoically. He had been in the army long enough, even fighting alongside George McClellan in Mexico, to understand the importance of keeping one's superior officer advised. That had not been done in this case. He also knew the technique of some of the officers in the army, especially the ambitious ones, taking credit for all successes and scapegoating their own mistakes, and William Rosecrans was the designated goat.

Earlier in the year, when the war had been considered imminent, Jesse's brother David had purchased a brand new 1860 Spencer rifle against such eventuality as an invasion of Cairo, Illinois, where he was living. When he learned of Jesse's plans to enlist, David gave him the rifle as a gift. The state of Indiana authorized the purchase of firearms from the citizens who were willing to part with them, and eventually paid David the $33.50 it had cost him. So Jesse had been selected as one of Sergeant Davis's designated sharp shooters.

Sergeant Davis's instructions to Jesse were always to work his way out onto the fringe of the battlefield to find a spot where he could observe the enemy's command staff and do as much damage to their top ranks as possible. It was an effective way to demoralize the enemy as well as deplete their upper ranks. It was dangerous business, however, as the rebels were always anxious to knock out the Union snipers to counter their deadly effect.

The Rebs had sharpshooters of their own, and at times there was a spirited exchange between the snipers from the opposing sides. The Spencer rifle was both accurate and well made, and it seldom failed to fire. It held seven metallic cartridges in its magazine drilled through the stock, and a man could get off a series of seven shots in less than a minute, though it sometimes took another minute to reload. The exchanges between Jesse and his counterparts on the Confederate side were greatly tilted in his favor owing to the rapid-fire rate of his rifle. (As the war progressed, a tube to recharge the whole seven-shot magazine was developed and improved the firing rate of the weapon considerably.)

When his skills weren't required as a sharpshooter, Jesse was expected to march and fight with the company, though he was allowed to keep the Spencer as his regular weapon. It was as modern as any rifle Jesse had ever shot, and he protected it carefully, for he knew his position and possibly his life depended on it.

Jesse was also allowed to keep with him a Colt .31 caliber revolver, which he usually kept in his knapsack, but then carried in a holster on his belt when he went into battle. Both he and Jimmo were permitted such exceptions, as they were a team most of the time, Jimmo spotting and Jesse shooting. Jimmo also had a .31 caliber revolver that he had brought from home.

The successes of the campaign by the newly formed Army of the Ohio had attracted notoriety, and several reporters had been visiting in camp to provide their particular publications with first-hand information. It was surprising how fast the reporters gravitated to the scene of dramatic success or equally dramatic failure. One of these reporters was a man with the unlikely name of Monroe Monroe, who worked for a Philadelphia weekly. Monroe fancied himself quite a bird dog, and spent a great deal of his time haunting the troops and hunting for colorful stories.

Logan's involvement on Rich Mountain and later engagements attracted Monroe's attention, and he sent back to his publisher a romantic article on the young man's marksmanship and derring-do. Logan took the flattery in stride, but he also took a lot of good-natured ribbing from the other men in the company. Monroe reported not only his exploits but a detailed description of him and information on the fact that his family was from Tennessee, all of which was picked up and reproduced in publications from both sides of the conflict, including the 'Knoxville Whig', a publication edited by a strong Union supporter from East Tennessee, Parson William Brownlow. The folks in East Tennessee were either proud or disgusted with the story, depending on which side of the secession issue they stood.

Jesse's size, his fair hair, and his proficiency with his rifle seemed to intrigue the news correspondents, and among them they contrived the concept of him as an 'angel of death' to the Rebels, and the sobriquet of "The White Angel" to pin on him. All this notoriety further contributed to the needling he would take from his peers in the company, his publicity in the newspapers, and his own embarrassment.

Later on, the death of General Garnett commander of the Confederate regiment was picked up by another reporter for a northern news magazine, who had been observing the activity from well behind the Union lines, giving Jesse credit. This story, too, was polished and published in both northern and southern papers, and even though Jesse denied responsibility for the death of the confederate general, the reporters ignored his denial.

As a result of the publicity Logan received from the news articles, a gun dealer from Clarksburg contacted Colonel Sullivan and offered to mount a telescopic sight on the Spencer, improving the effectiveness of the rifle considerably. The modification was to be without cost, and Jesse readily agreed. This gained additional publicity when the reporters learned of it and Jesse didn't think he'd ever hear the last of the matter.

Under Sergeant Davis's direction, the company had been quickly molded into a well-trained and disciplined unit. His experience in the war of 1846 and later as he rose through the ranks in the regular army gave him both the skill and the credibility to shape the troops into something more than a uniformed mob. While some of the other companies lacked the sense of discipline to carry out the orders delivered by their sergeants, Company "H" learned from the start to work together, and their proficiency at drill gave them a sense of confidence and pride inspiring them to perform all the better. It also earned them the envy of the other companies, and some key assignments on the field of battle.

At almost twenty-one, Jesse had grown into a rather imposing young man. He stood six and a half feet tall, with curly pale blond hair and blue eyes. His years pitching hay and cutting wood in the Carson Valley, Utah Territory, and later working with his grandfather and Uncle John as a sawyer in Carter County, Tennessee had left him wide shoulders, a narrow waist, and stout arms. He was quiet in manner, but had a devious sense of humor, which he often displayed with jokes and jabs at Jimmo and even Sergeant Davis, two of his favorite objects for such display. Jesse also managed from time to time to break out in song, drawing from those taught him by his Grandfather Kellar, with whom he lived for a time after his mother had sent him east, as she said "for an education."

Near the town of Beverly where Company "H" was camped after their victory at Corrick's Ford, the time passed quickly. General McClellan had given orders to rest the troops after the recent battle but when they weren't repairing their equipment or looking for replacement parts, Sergeant Davis kept the men busy drilling almost all day. The men, proud of their skill and reputation, grumbled about the incessant drilling, but submitted willingly. Sergeant Davis always seemed to have a new maneuver or tactic in the back of his mind to teach them. He worked them on turning, flanking, oblique movements, moving into files of one, two, or four, spreading into skirmish line, forming up out of skirmish line, wheeling in line, and a dozen other drills that they didn't even know the reasons for. He told the troops he wanted them to march wherever and whenever they moved. When two or three of his men were seen walking together, if he was around, he called cadence for them to march to. Discipline, Sergeant Davis told the men, would save more lives than marksmanship and he felt it was his job to get as many of them home in one piece as he possibly could.

The Sixth Indiana was bivouacked in a large meadow in the foothills of the Appalachian Mountains for the time, near the Cheat River. As the brigade rested, General Rosecrans could be seen storming about the camp. Half the time he was consulting with his subordinates, rehashing the victory which had driven the Rebels down into the Shenandoah Valley or planning his next campaign, and the other half of the time he was railing against "That damned little Napoleon" who took the credit for the last victory.

One day Jesse had made his way over to the Suttler's tent to see what the latest goods were for sale. He had heard a soldier in one of the nearby camps playing a harmonica, and was inspired to try one. He had played the fiddle a little, at home in Kellars Crossing, and thought he might see if he could make music on the mouth organ.

Suttlers were a necessary lot and at that point in the war the trade of the suttler was often quite good. They had food, dry goods, scissors, combs, pocket knives, underwear, odd ammunition for the firearms the men were permitted to keep of their own property, newspapers, and a host of such items as the army didn't normally provide. The suttlers usually showed up in the camps one or two days after the troops had settled in for bivouac, and ordinarily attached themselves to the same regiment, if possible. The feeling of customer relations was important even in the situation of war. They set up shop in any kind of structure available. Usually their store was a tent, as command staff got to occupy any buildings available, but there were times when a deserted building also served as the suttler's store.

The suttler that had been with the regiment was a man known only as Mr. Livingston. He was a rather quiet man with calm dark eyes and pale skin. He usually smoked a pipe, and the tent always smelled of the tobacco smoke. He was assisted by a young woman the men knew only as Miss Livingston, and assumed she was his daughter. She was an attractive woman, probably in her early twenties, with abundant brown, curly hair, and an attractive figure, which the boys could only speculate about, as she dressed plainly and modestly, though her wardrobe seemed to be quite extensive. The men also discussed the fact that they seldom saw Miss Livingston in the same dress twice. In fact, they discussed almost every aspect of Miss Livingston's life, presence, character, and being, as she was the closest thing any of them had to female companionship. Not that she was particularly friendly, nor did she show partiality to any of the troops. It was just that she was an attractive young woman, and that in itself was all she needed to be to get their attention.

Jesse had had little business in the store except to buy one of those little round discs with his name stamped on it that eventually became known as a 'dog tag'. They were popular among the soldiers, and as one fellow put it, "If I get blowed up by one of them bombs the Johnnies throw at us, at least there'll be something left of me to bury."

Jesse walked into the suttler's tent and though he could smell the strong odor of Mr. Livingston's pipe, the only person present was Miss Livingston.

"May I help you, Mr. Logan?' the young woman asked in a most cordial manner.

The greeting made Jesse look twice, as to his knowledge she had never so much as noticed his existence or known his name. "We just got in some new stock, and you might be interested in these wool socks."

"Well," Jesse said, "My land, Miss Livingston, you do look nice today. I was just thinking I might get a mouth organ. I heard some of the other fellas playin' theirs and it seemed to me to be a good way to pass the time."

"Do you play?" she asked, still in a most friendly manner. "What kind of harmonica are you looking for? We have several."

"Well, I don't rightly know," Jesse said. "I played the fiddle, some, but I don't know much about mouth organs. I jus' heard these fellas playing them and thought I might be able to."

"Where are you from, Mr. Logan," Miss Livingston asked. "Your accent has a ring to it that suggests you may be from the south."

"I have lived some, over most of the country, but you're right. I was born in east Tennessee and have lived the past four or five years Carter County." Did Jesse notice Miss Livingston stiffen at the mention of Carter County, or was it just his imagination? At any rate, he kept on talking. "My family moved west when I was a little boy, but then I went back to stay with kinfolk, when I was about fifteen."

"I thought so," she said, opening the case of musical instruments, "Where did you live out west, in California?"

The light conversation continued during Jesse's visit to the tent, and when he had purchased the mouth organ, he thought would suit him, he paid and started out the through the tent flap.

"Don't go playing that when you're out at your post looking to shoot those Rebs." Miss Livingston said. "They might hear you and slip over for a visit when you're looking the other way. We wouldn't want to lose one of our best sharpies, Mr. Logan."

"Don't you worry none, Miss Livingston. They say silence is golden, and I believe it when it comes to setting up out there."

"Well, I've also heard that silence is consent," she tossed back at him, "and as you can tell, I'm seldom silent."

"Well, what did that mean?" Jesse mused as he walked away from the tent. *"Sometimes I can't figure women out, and then sometimes I don't even try."*

The success of the Army of the Ohio in the Tygart Valley was widely acclaimed in the north, and especially in Washington. It was really the first good news of the war as such and though small and remote from the centers of population, it was hailed as the harbinger of the way the war would go and 'On to Richmond' was heard frequently and repeated in the press. The prevailing feeling after the news of July 13 was jubilation, and it was with this attitude that the citizens and politicians from Washington went forth to watch the Army of the Potomac, USA chase the Army of Northern Virginia, CSA all the way to Richmond from a small town named Manassas, Virginia, less than a week later.

'On to Richmond' didn't happen. Bull Run, or Manassas as it was referred to in the southern press, was a disaster for the northern forces and the Washington politicos began immediately casting about for someone to blame.

General Irwin McDowell, who had been commander of the Army of the Potomac was summarily removed on July 27, and replaced by General George B. McClellan.

"Little Napoleon" had made his mark with the powers at Washington and had been selected to save the Union.

2

THE EARLY DAYS, WATAUGA VALLEY

J esse Logan had been born in eastern Tennessee in 1840, the youngest of nine children. His father, David, had been a doctor in Carter County, as was his father before him, but his desire had been to move westward, as the country was expanding. Then, in 1843, three years after Jesse was born, Dr. David Logan and his wife Elizabeth, became intrigued by the message and evangelical fervor of a group of itinerant preachers who came through the area. They called themselves "Mormons". These men gave such a glowing account of what they proposed as an ideal life, community, and atmosphere for raising a family, that many of the local folks, the Logans among them, simply sold their farms and homes, bought wagons, and hit the trail for the Mormon settlements in Indiana, Illinois, and Missouri.

Their life was good, at first. Work was available, neighbors shared what they had with each other, and Dr. Logan's talents were in demand. Perhaps it was the fact that the Mormons were too ready to help each other, contributing to the wealth of those who were, as they called themselves, "Saints" or "the faithful", that sparked the resentment among those whom they referred to as "Gentiles."

Unrest developed between the Mormon and non-Mormon communities, which caused the leaders of the church to give serious thought to moving the congregation westward. As this idea began to take shape, the resentment exploded into violence when a number of the opposing factions in the community around Nauvoo, Illinois began taking their aggressions out on each other. Dr. and Mrs. Logan, who had been living in Clinton County, Missouri, had moved their family to Nauvoo, which at the time was the seat of the Mormon activities, and the largest town in the state with about 12,000 inhabitants. They had thought that they would be safer among the members of the larger Mormon population.

Then, one evening in late June 1844 there was a knock at the door of the cabin the Logan family called home. The doctor was asked to come out to help with a number of injuries, which had resulted from a fight among some of the townspeople. That was the last time the family saw their father and husband alive.

Dr. Logan became a statistic, not a very good one, for he left little behind to show for his having lived. He owned two saddle horses, a couple of saddles, and a lot of obligations owed him by the many people whom he had treated with little or no thought of compensation. He had long since sold his team and wagon to a family bound for the promise of a new life in the Kansas Territory.

Dr. Logan also left a wife, Elizabeth, five sons, and four daughters. Jesse was almost four at the time of his father's death. He was bewildered by the events of the time, but was pretty well unaware of the implications, except that he missed his father, terribly.

Eliza Logan stayed in Nauvoo for a short time, then moved back to St. Joseph, Missouri, where she managed to open a boarding house, and with the help of friends, and the efforts of her older sons William and David Jr., kept the little family together, fed, and clothed. Schools were virtually non-existent, but Eliza had attended grammar school in Elizabethton, Tennessee and was a fairly well-educated woman. She encouraged her flock to learn to read and write which they did by fits and starts, none of them achieving much more than the minimum skills necessary to write a letter or read a grocery bill.

Will Logan, Jesse's oldest brother was seventeen when the family returned to St. Joseph, and was a pretty good horseman. He hung around a livery stable that belonged to Mr. Arnberg, and managed to get a job tending horses, cleaning the tack, and sweeping out the barn. St. Joseph was a jumping-off point for emigrants heading west and business was brisk.

David Logan, Jr., at fifteen, through the reputation of his father, obtained an apprenticeship with James Potter, the local saddle and harness maker, and developed considerable skill at the trade, which would serve him well throughout his life. It also provided a small income for the family, helping to keep them together.

Following David in line were Sarah, Brigette, John, George, Jane Ann (Jennie), Mary Louise, and Jesse. Though Jesse was ten years younger than David, they had developed a close relationship. There was a strong resemblance between them, even more so than the rest of the brothers, and they enjoyed a friendship that transcended kinship and bridged the difference in their ages.

By the time Will was nineteen he had had just about all he could take of cleaning stalls and tack, and when the opportunity arose to work as a wrangler with the herd of horses accompanying a company of Mormon settlers traveling west, he took it.

"Willie," his mother had said, "you have a good job here with a solid future, and you're throwing it away to follow along with that Captain Ramsey and his company. You have no idea what you're getting yourself into. And to beat that, you're our main support, here, and with the girls growing up, I need the hand of a man at home to help keep them at home and out of harm's way."

"Mama, David is doing just fine at the saddle shop. He's bigger than I am, and a lot more responsible. I'm just not happy here. The Arksey boys just come back from Utah Territory, and they say there's plenty of work for a man who's good with horses, and land is so plentiful you can just about choose your own section and work it. We've been dirt-poor since Papa died, and I mean to get me a spread where I can maybe send for you and the kids and we'd be set for life."

"Well go then." Eliza had said, "But don't look to have me leave here for any god-forsaken outpost out in that god-forsaken territory you call Utah. I may not be making much at the boarding house, but it's a far site better than risking my life among those savages out west. Your grandfather Henry could tell you it's no fun striking out amongst the untamed Indians out away from civilization, and I don't want any part of it."

Will took his pay from Mr. Arnberg in the form of a horse, got out one of his father's saddles, and left the next day with the Ramsey Company for the promise of the Great Salt Lake and the country beyond.

"Captain" John Ramsey was a leader of the Mormon Church, and rather well to do in his own right. He had outfitted several of the wagons in the twenty-eight wagon train, and had furnished many of the horses and oxen which would be needed to move the train along. Most of the wagons would be pulled by oxen, and the horses would be used to scout, search for food, and communicate with the few forts and encampments along the way. John Ramsey was a serious-minded man, with a rather brusque manner, but was well respected and trusted, both by the hierarchy of the church and by the people. The company had the makings of a successful crossing, and but for the fact that another company had left for the west only a month earlier, there would probably have been two or three times as many wagons in the train.

As it was, with only twenty-eight wagons, Ramsey felt he could move quite quickly, and gain considerable time on the larger, earlier train.

Captain Ramsey had not chosen lightly when he picked Will Logan as his wrangler. The string of horses Will was responsible for consisted of fifteen to twenty horses at any time, depending on the number of members of the company who were mounted. The horses could move faster than the main train, and could often forage for themselves, moving away from the train for short times, grazing along the route, still staying within sight and sound of the company for protection.

The Indians, some of them rather hostile to the idea of settlers taking over their territory, were always in need of horses, and if they could, they would not hesitate to help themselves to this little band or any other they found to be unguarded. Raiding, which the settlers regarded as stealing, was, in the Native American culture, an act of bravery and was practiced freely. Neither did the idea of leaving the bones of two or three dead cowboys to bleach in the prairie sun bother them in the least. It would just mean that there were two or three fewer members of an already unwelcome hoard.

Will knew horses but was also eager to learn about the perils of the plains in the form of raiding parties. He was to work with the wagon boss, Enoch Palmer, a tall, spare man with a ready sense of humor, but just as ready with a musket or pistol to protect the train. Enoch had a full moustache, which Will tried to emulate with only scant success in the two months it took to cross the distance from St. Joseph to Great Salt Lake City. He was anxious to earn the respect of Enoch, and from the time the wagons left St. Joseph, he stayed in the saddle fourteen to sixteen hours a day, keeping a steady control over the herd, and helping where he could. He usually changed horses three times a day, partly to make sure none of them were used too hard, and partly to familiarize himself with as many of the horses as he could.

There was one man in the train, a man named Owen, who owned two of the horses in the string, and let it be known that he didn't want Will or anyone else riding his horses. Other than that, Will had a pretty clear hand at picking the horses he was to ride. The other 'saints' who owned horses in the string appreciated Will's situation, and didn't object to his using their horses, when he needed to.

The oxen attached to the train were either hitched to the wagons, or were led or driven by members of the families they belonged to. There was an abundance of oxen, as well as a few milk cows at first, as Captain Ramsey had anticipated the likelihood of some of them falling along the way, either from exhaustion, or being needed for food. His purpose was to move his company of saints across the prairie as quickly and safely as possible, and the oxen were just a means to that end. The process employed by the pioneers was to travel as far and as fast as the herd of cattle would tolerate during the day, then circle the wagons on a grassy section of land and corral the cattle within the ring of wagons. The cattle grazed the inner circle and the horses were tethered on the outside of the ring, given enough lead rope to satisfy their appetites. With only twenty-eight wagons, the grassland for the cattle was small, so it was necessary to space the wagons as far apart as possible each night and then the families would occupy the spaces with their camp gear, forming a human barrier to complete the circle.

The trip was mostly uneventful. Captain Ramsey's reputation for efficiency was well deserved, as the train gained almost a week on the one that had started ahead of them. Will Logan's reputation as a wrangler was pretty well established, too, and, later on, when he reached Great Salt Lake City with the company, he was put to work at a ranch on the recommendation of Captain Ramsey, and at nineteen, seemed launched on the career of a well-respected ranch hand. It was to be over two years before Will would see his family, again, but he never strayed very far in thought from that "spread" on which he could set his mother and family and be "set for life".

Jesse had been almost seven when Will had headed west and his leaving left quite a void in the family structure. Will had represented the male head of the house, and it took Jesse some time to get used to the idea that he was gone. Losing his father at the age of four and now losing his older brother left a void in Jesse's life. Jesse naturally turned to David as the object of his admiration.

David had a delightful sense of humor, which Jesse as a young boy had taken to and emulated, and in time they had even developed small routines which they often lapsed into as the opportunities presented themselves, to the delight or disgust of their family, depending on the prevailing mood. Eliza often compared them to bear cubs romping in the forest or at other times to members of a team of traveling clowns.

David, working for Mr. Potter in the harness shop, on one occasion had been present when Mr. Potter had been served with a legal document. He came home that evening and, with great seriousness, tried to explain the significance of the matter to the family.

"This fellow came to the shop, today, and served Mr. Potter with a writ," David told his mother at dinner.

"What's a writ," Jesse inquired.

"It's a legal paper that someone in the court writes and then the sheriff gives it to the person it is addressed to who is supposed to do something about it," David said.

"What's 'legal' mean?" was Jesse's next question.

"Legal means 'right' or 'correct' in the eyes of the law, Jesse," Eliza told him.

"How do they know it's right?" Jesse asked immediately.

David: "The fellow that writes it knows how to write it right."

Jesse: "What's the fellow's name?"

David: "His name is Reed Ryder," (joining into the game).

Jesse: "You mean it is Reed Ryder who can write a writ right?"

David: "If Reed Ryder writes it, it must be a written right."

Jesse: "Doesn't anybody read the writ to see if it's written right?"

David: "Yes, there is a writ reader to check up on Reed Ryder, the writ writer and see that the writ is written right."

Jesse: "What's his name?"

David: "Rick Reeder is the writ reader."

Jesse: "So, Reed Ryder, the writ writer writes a writ right and when the writ is written, Rick Reeder the writ reader reads the writ to see if Reed Ryder has written it right."

"Enough, you two," Eliza broke in. "you are going to drive us crazy."

"Mother," Jesse chirped, "You're getting redder and redder. Maybe you have been reading too many of Reed Ryder's writs."

"I said 'enough', Jesse," Eliza and the rest of the family were thoroughly enjoying the banter between the two boys, but she felt it had to stop somewhere. What had started out to be an interesting and informative conversation on the legal system had evolved into a comedy routine between the family clowns.

Often when David would come home from work and expound at the dinner table on some aspect of the harness business, in all seriousness he would express concern over the fiscal implications of the transactions in which he had been involved. He was a good businessman, and didn't hesitate to share his sense of economics with the family, particularly his soulmate, Jesse. At eight or nine, Jesse could not always appreciate the import of David's message, but usually he listened obediently. At times though, when David would launch into a long dissertation, getting wrapped up in the seriousness of his business and how he perceived it, Jesse would get impatient and try to lighten the mood of the conversation.

One technique Jesse used from time to time, to interrupt David's delivery on the importance of economics would be, in a falsetto voice, go, "Cheep, Cheep, Cheep."

This invariably brought peals of laughter from the other members of the family and often a punch in the shoulder from David if he was within striking distance. The family maintained a close relationship, even though their father and oldest brother were no longer with them.

The boarding house was developing into a sound business for the Logan family. Trappers from the upper Missouri Valley in the summer and traders from the same area in the winter spent their free time along the lower rivers, from Cairo to Sioux City, biding their time. For the trappers, winter was their busy season upriver when the muskrat, otter and beaver developed their thick coats, and for the traders it was the spring and summer when the Indians were on the move and the emigrants found need for any supplies they had not brought from the east. The hotels and boarding houses down river were seldom empty.

The traders and particularly the trappers, a breed apart, spoke a language and developed a sense of value far different from their down-river cousins who had maintained the ordered life of a yeoman farmer or shopkeeper. They had learned to survive by their wit and cunning and were often a rough and uncouth lot, though especially deferential to Eliza Logan, whom they regarded as not only a person of refinement, but also a power to be dealt with. Jesse found these people to be a subject of awe and fascination. The stories they told of life in the mountains, usually enhanced and embellished by highly developed imaginations, were the stuff a boy of nine drank in without question. It was all his brothers and mother could do to keep him from sneaking aboard the next up-river steamer to join the throng of trappers when they headed out in the fall, or join up with a trader as he was packing his wares for a trip into the Indian country.

The product of this economic trade was good for the Logan family, and Eliza diligently saw to it that her establishment was as clean and attractive to all customers as possible, though she didn't especially relish the prospect of the trappers coming back into town each spring. They were a dirty lot at first though as the summer progressed, they mostly cleaned up quite nicely.

David also brought home his pay every month, and was learning much about the saddle and harness business. Mr. Potter had no sons, and David had been courting Mary, his only daughter. It looked as though Eliza was going to gain a daughter, but in that happening, she would be losing the benefit of the salary David had been bringing home. If David married, or went into partnership with Mr. Potter, he would be expected to invest in the business to the greatest extent possible, and there wouldn't be anything from that quarter to supplement revenues from the boarding house.

While she wanted the best for David, Eliza knew she was going to have to make some adjustments in her budget to compensate for the loss.

By 1850, Eliza Logan, having established herself in a respectable part of St. Joseph with a large boarding house, also found herself catering to the trade generated by the migration of people moving west to take advantage of cheap land, a new way of life, and gold! The latter dominated the thinking and conversations about town and all up and down the Missouri River. St. Joseph was a jumping-off place for many of the trips west by wagon either to the Oregon country or to California. There were also some Mormon families who had been evangelized in Europe, coming up-river from New Orleans and heading west to the Utah Territory from towns along the river.

That year, when Jesse was turning ten, his older brother Will had come back to St. Joseph and begged their mother to come west. She had told him years ago that she would live out her life in what she referred to as the civilization of Missouri. Over the years, however, Will had come back to St. Joseph on one occasion, and had written letter after letter to his family back home extolling the glories of the new territory. He had made a trip with the Mormon settlers to the Carson Valley in Western Nevada, and had come away as charmed by the country as only an aspiring cattle rancher could be.

Will's glowing accounts of the beauties to behold in the new country, her disenchantment with conditions in St. Joseph, and her desire to see the children who were still at home have a chance at a better life, convinced her. Eliza Logan sold what had become a moderately prosperous boarding house, packed up her remaining brood, and struck out again for a new life in the west.

David, now twenty, had married Mary Potter and was established as a junior partner with Mr. Potter in the harness business. Next in age in the Logan family were Sarah, eighteen, Brigitte, seventeen, then John, George, Jennie, Mary Louise, and Jesse in descending order. At sixteen, John would be the oldest male in the family. He and George, like two peas in a pod, would share the responsibilities of caring for the livestock and driving the team. They would use six horses pulling tandem wagons, as Will felt they would be more valuable than oxen when they reached their destination. David would, of course, stay with the business in St. Joseph. Like the boarding house, the harness shop was prospering with the demand for equipment to help the emigrants cross the plains.

The years since Will had gone west had not much changed the Oregon Trail. The ruts were a little deeper in places, and some new forts had sprung up along the way, but some of the Indian tribes were getting edgy about the constant stream of settlers coming through their territory.

Enoch Palmer was now "Captain" Palmer, and Will had committed to work as Wagon Master for this trip. One of the first things he did when he had gotten back to St. Joseph was to buy one of those Dragoon revolvers Samuel Colt had developed, and which were selling for twelve dollars at the mercantile store. It was a lot of money, but the old flintlock pistols he had been carrying were just not reliable enough for a man in charge of moving a wagon train.

On the way west Will would be fully occupied as Wagon Master. The company consisted of sixty-eight wagons and his abilities, as a wagon master would be sorely tried. Groups of settlers bound for Oregon were mixed with gold seekers and Mormon immigrants. Traders were also taking advantage of the protection of the train, as they had some valuable goods to deliver to both natives and settlers. Travel was slow because of the size of the train, and tempers were often tried.

Jesse was picked to help keep the horse herd in control. Though he was big for a boy of his age, he could not be mistaken for a man on any of the horses he was assigned, so that he was only useful as a second or third wrangler.

The Indian tribes were still inclined to watch for a chance to try their hand at expanding their own string of ponies, and any indication of weakness in the team of wranglers would most likely be exploited. Will had assigned Jesse as a wrangler, partly to act as a backup, and partly so the he could keep track of the boy, whose adventuresome spirit, Will feared, might possibly lead to him getting in trouble.

There was a law forbidding the trading of firearms to the Indians. Though not many of them knew how to operate the flintlocks, they were quick to learn and anxious to try to get their hands on the guns, both as trading pieces and to learn to shoot them and improve their chances in hunting and in battle. The "fire sticks", as the Indians called them were both symbols of prestige and potent weapons. Any brave with a musket was far and away superior to his neighbors in his public image, as well as to his enemies in battle.

Jesse had the smooth-bore musket his father had owned for hunting. Though it didn't have the power the more modern weapons packed, it was accurate enough in the hands of someone accustomed to its peculiar characteristics, and could be extremely effective. Even at that age Jesse had learned the tricks of how to set the flint, the trigger pressure needed to drop the hammer, how much powder to use, both in the barrel and the pan, and just what balls worked the best in the old piece. The old gun had been used a lot, and a slightly elongated ball worked best. Also, since the touchhole was a little burned out, the piece fired quite quickly for a flintlock but was also subject to frequent misfiring. Jesse was careful to keep the barrel from fouling, but over the years, the powder had badly burned out the chamber and the charge and ball tended to rattle unless well packed with soft wadding.

At best, however, a smooth bore flintlock was an awkward piece to be carried by a boy on a horse. Will admonished Jesse daily to take care in handling the musket, and rigged a sling for him to carry it on his back. Of course, this meant that Jesse would have to charge the pan whenever he was to use the musket, and when game presented itself, it was a rare moment that Jesse was able to get a shot off. His skills with the gun were sorely tried, and he was to learn great patience as well as marksmanship.

About the third week out of St. Joe, before they had even reached the Platte River, Jesse was riding a blaze-sided mare named Hannah and was going down a small draw with the herd. There were two other wranglers, and the herd was not over forty head, so the riding was easy. The horses in the string were mostly grazing, and everything was pretty quiet. As he came up the far side of the draw, something caught his eye, just disappearing over the next rise. He thought it may be a buffalo, and he had been given specific instructions not to try the old gun on a buffalo, but, hey, it wouldn't hurt to look,

Jesse dug his heels into Hannah's sides, but the horse let out a low snort and shied sideways. "What's the matter with you, you old sow?" Jesse whispered so as not to spook the game. "Haven't you ever seen a buffalo before?"

Jesse got off and began to lead Hannah, partly because she wouldn't go on her own, and partly to keep a low profile and give him a chance to charge the pan of his musket. He'd gone about fifty yards and was just approaching the crest of another rise along the bank of a creek, when up stepped an Indian, in what must have been, Jesse thought, the ugliest job of war paint he had ever seen.

"Want fire stick," the Indian uttered in a low guttural voice. "Injun want white boy fire stick."

"It ain't no good. It don't work," Jesse said, as loudly as he could. "It's just sort of a look-like fire stick, Mister."

"Want fire stick," the red man repeated, and with that, started toward Jesse who, raising the musket as if to threaten the Indian, stopped him in his tracks.

Jesse didn't know what happened next, but all of a sudden there was a commotion off to his right, and from behind him two shots rang out. He had been holding the musket by his side and as he stumbled backwards, he reflexively raised the barrel and pulled the trigger. The musket fired. The Indian he'd been facing crumpled where he stood, and just behind him by thirty or forty yards, two other Indians on horseback were high tailing it for the north, not even waiting to see what had happened to their companions.

As Jesse had been confronted by the Indian and had yelled loud enough to alarm the whole train, Will had been riding out to see why Jesse had disappeared. The Indian who had demanded Jesse's gun was a decoy, and two of his fellow braves had been sneaking up on foot on Jesse from behind, just over the brow of the creek bank, with the two others on horseback in reserve.

Will had been fast enough with his revolver to shoot the two bushwhackers sneaking up from behind Jesse, and Jesse, through pure reflex, shot his adversary.

Jesse was sick, really sick, right there on the side of the creek. He had certainly been scared, and couldn't have said for sure whether he would have carried out the threat of pointing his musket at the Indian he faced, but there were three shots and three Indians lying on the creek bank. He'd been part of a confrontation that had taken the lives of three human beings, and he didn't feel very good about it.

Will helped Jesse back on his horse, and rode with him back to his mother's wagons. When Eliza found out what had happened, she said nothing. Will had expected a tongue lashing, but she just said nothing. She very quietly took Jesse back into the wagon, washed his face, and then she spoke to him as he hadn't heard her speak in years. She told him he was very precious to her, and that she was happy he was not hurt, and that she didn't care how many other people were hurt or injured or killed. All that was important to her was that her son Jesse was all right.

Eliza had lost a husband in a violent confrontation, and it was almost more than she could bear at the time. She was out here in this strange land against her better judgment. Her youngest child had just shot a human being to death, and her composure was stretched pretty thin, but Elizabeth Logan was a strong woman. This was neither the first nor would it be the last test of her mettle, but she would survive. At forty-three, Eliza had done a lot of living, and had seen a lot of dying, but her strength and a trustful faith in God would take her through more than this in the years to come.

The next day, Jesse was out at dawn, lining up the horse he would use that day. Will came by the herd where Jesse was getting ready to saddle up his horse, and said "Jesse, 'you okay, Boy?" Jesse looked at him and smiled.

"I'm all right, Willie," Jesse said. "I reckon I'll survive."

Then, in a loud voice, Will said, "Yes, Jesse, I guess you will. You take care, son, that 'look-like fire stick' may be old, but it seems to me to be pretty effective in a fight."

After that Jesse was known as the boy with the look-like-fire-stick. Will would have liked to have gotten Jesse a better weapon, but for one thing, they were scarce and expensive. For another thing though, at Jesse's size, the old fowling piece was just about all he could handle without backing up against a tree to shoot.

3

MORMON STATION

ormon Station had been started as an outpost at the foot of the Sierra Nevada Mountains by trackers and scouts, and had been known by various names since it had first been established in about 1847. The town is located at the base of the Sierra Mountains at the edge of a broad valley named for Kit Carson, one of the principal scouts for the survey and mapping party led by Colonel John C. Fremont in 1845 and '46. The outpost and the surrounding valley had been designated by the leadership of the Mormon Church to be the seat of Carson County, which was then the western reaches of Utah Territory, including most of the present state of Nevada.

Several families, evangelized and recruited by Mormon missionaries, mostly from western England, Wales, and Scotland had been selected to continue westward from Great Salt Lake City to assist in establishing the area. Other families, Mormon and non-Mormon alike had followed the lead of these first settlers and had chosen to settle in the Carson Valley and also in Jacks Valley, a branch of the Carson Valley, a little to the north and west nestled at the base of the Sierras. Still other families, passing through toward the promise of California, had paused and put down their roots in the Carson Valley, so lush and verdant was the landscape there.

———◦((◦))◦———

On February 25th, 1849 a company of 250 Welsh "Saints" had sailed from Liverpool for New Orleans on the ship Buena Vista, under the direction of Elder Dan Jones. The company had a safe passage across the Atlantic, but suffered extremely from the cholera while passing up the Mississippi and Missouri Rivers to Council Bluffs, Iowa, where the emigrants arrived on May 17th. At Council Bluffs, they divided into family groups and made their way west, arriving in Salt Lake City during August and September that year. There they wintered over, staying with families in the Salt Lake area, until early spring, when they pushed on Westward across the Great Salt Desert and then along the Humboldt River, arriving at their destination in June, amidst swarms of gnats, mosquitoes, and face flies. The weather had been particularly rainy that year, and the Carson Valley was a virtual Paradise, except for the insects.

Among the company of Saints were Benjamin T. Jones, 43, his wife, Jane, also 43, and their eight children. Ben had been a locksmith in Wales, and was just as skilled as a blacksmith, gunsmith, and even a clockmaker, professions he pursued for the rest of his days in the land where he had chosen to settle. He wasted no time in setting up a shop, using coal to fire his forge when he could get it, but more often using charcoal from kilns which his countryman Owen Richard had started in the nearby canyons against the face of the Sierras.

Ben's principal customers and unwittingly, his source of material for his trade, were the emigrants passing through the region on their way to the gold country, and the farmers and ranchers trying to get started in the valley. There was no lack of raw material for an enterprising blacksmith, for Ben kept his sons busy collecting cast-off iron parts from along the wagon trail collecting them in the wagon they had brought from Council Bluffs. Fixtures, hinges, swivels, wheel-rims, axles, bolts, brackets, and a multitude of other odd parts were the stuff from which Ben Jones supplied anything from door latches to field plows for the citizens of Mormon Station and the settlers passing through.

During the summer of 1850, a family named Eldredge got as far west as Mormon Station with a load of various machines for making handles for axes and hammers. On their way west, the father and bread winner had suddenly been seized with some sort of liver ailment and had died just about the time the family arrived at Mormon Station. Mrs. Eldredge, her five children being between the ages of one and eight years, was desperate. She had accompanied her husband from a comfortable situation in Ohio on the expectation that their life in the west would be even more comfortable. The stories had come back to them in Ohio that the miners in the west were in sore need in the type of tool handles her husband specialized in, and they would have no trouble setting up shop in one of the towns along the western Sierra foothills where demand for their products would be endless.

Ben and Jane Jones adopted the family as best they could and entered into an agreement with Rachel Eldredge to purchase the machinery that she and her husband had brought with them.

Ben set the machinery up, then built a makeshift shed over the cutting equipment to protect it from the weather. At first, he powered the machinery by means of a water-wheel, but after about two years of breakdowns, he acquired a steam engine. The steam engine was hauled over the Sierra Mountains to Mormon Station in pieces by freight wagon, from Stockton, an inland ocean-port in California. He set it up outside the shed, and connected it to the cutting machine by a long flat belt attached to a set of overhead pulleys. The entire operation was located near Ben's fledgling blacksmith shop and power from the steam engine was used in both places. Ben's experience at cutting tool-handles was limited, but his ingenuity was boundless and though the raw material for the handles, seasoned hardwood, was scarce in the local forests, there were broken wagon tongues and cast-off doubletrees to be found along the trails and these he put to good use.

Ben had five sons; twins, Tom and Russel, 21, Evan, 15, Richard, or Dick, as he was called, who was 12, and John, 7. When the boys weren't making their salvage trips out across the valley, they were working with their father or farming and building homes in the area.

Russel Jones by this time had a wife, Mary and two children of his own, so that he, in particular, had to keep up a hard pace to keep his own family fed. It was 'Rush', then, whom Ben assigned to operate the handlery and assist at the blacksmith shop.

It was into this environment that Will Logan, now 23 brought his mother and seven of his brothers and sisters to live, a year after the Jones family had arrived. Eliza Logan still had a considerable nest egg from the sale of her home in St. Joseph, and was determined to use it to the best advantage for the benefit of her family. The Logans, while familiar with the ways and laws of the country, were still at the mercy of the elements, to some extent. Will was the eldest man in the household. Eliza, the matriarch, still in her forties, was new to the life of farming and ranching, and they were, at best, thin on talent.

The Logans met Ben and Jane Jones almost as soon as they arrived in town, and young Jesse, in particular, took an immediate liking to the man. Typical of his Welsh heritage, Ben Jones was not a large man, and was rough in his speech, which was also blurred with a fine Welsh brogue. But his manner was that of a person who could be at once kind and strong, and his talent at his trade distinguished him as one who would stand out as one of the town's most valued citizens. There was that in his bearing, while rough and artless was at the same time so imposing that it was natural to hold him in respect and to anticipate from his words and deeds profound truths and actions. He had a direct manner that was reassuring, and when he looked you in the eye, his own pale blue eyes seemed to penetrate your very soul.

Jesse also took a liking to Dick, Ben's fourth son who, at 12, was only a little older, though somewhat smaller in size than Jesse. The two boys seemed to be of one mind in many of their ways, and while old enough to do considerable work about the shop or farm, were still young enough to be able to make a game out of much of what they were about. They were also able to cause a moderate amount of grief among their elders by the mischief that they could cook up between them. The handlery was one of their favorite diversions. They watched as the sections of wagon tongues were placed in the stocks and within a few minutes were turned out as finished handles for hammers, axes, mauls, and even hoes and shovels, depending on the shaping dies that Rush Jones had placed in the master stock. They helped where they could, preparing the handles, and moving the stock and finished products to be sold in Parkers Mercantile Store that was developing adjacent to Ben Jones' blacksmith shop.

Eliza Logan, realizing the need for adequate lodging for many of the travelers who would perhaps be lingering for a time in Mormon Station, started right away to build a house in a place she expected would become the center part of town. She engaged the services of Ben and his boys, and with her own family, they got a log house up before winter. It wasn't large that first year, but later on it grew, little by little, until Eliza was able to use it for an additional source of income as a boarding house. Even so, it was not an easy life for one who, at seventeen, had married a Doctor, David Logan, who had been a promising member of one of Carter County, Tennessee's leading families, and a respected member of the East Tennessee community. Her life had taken several turns away from that she could have anticipated as one of the belles of Carter County.

Will Logan, having brought the beginnings of a cattle herd with him from Missouri, first turned to farming north of town, but with little time to get in any crops before the seasons changed, he had all he could do to just start a small house garden to keep them through the winter. Even at that, he had to put his brother Jesse and Dick Jones to work, cultivating the garden in the daytime and guarding it from the deer at night.

Ben Jones had brought with him from Missouri some fundamental gun-smithing materials and parts, and soon modified Jesse's old flintlock musket to use the new 'percussion cap' firing system. While the accuracy of the gun didn't improve, he could now load and fire much more quickly and the gun's ignition process was not nearly as likely to fail or foul. It was as though a new world opened up for the young hunter in his ability to get game and help feed his family.

By the following spring, Ben Jones had crafted a large plow from the wheel-rims of wagons left along the trail, and Will Logan put it to good use behind a team of four oxen he had brought from Missouri. The plow was a monster, but with some adjustment, and great effort, Will, with John and George relieving him at times, could plow about an acre a day, starting what was to become one of the best farms in the valley. Even so, Will didn't stay long at the plow handles, and later that year, sold his small farm to John James, who had come west with the same company as Ben Jones. With the small down payment from John and some mighty good negotiating, Will bought a dozen more cattle to supplement his own small herd and went into the beef business. He also had eight good horses, which he had brought from Missouri, and his dream to own a "spread" seemed as if it just might come true. Meanwhile, George had the start of a pig farm, and John was working on a sawmill for the development of the town's building programs. The four girls were fully occupied at home with their mother, helping to run the boarding house.

The summer of 1852 was productive in Carson Valley, and with the farming being good, and the meager income that they obtained from trading with the immigrants, the families of Mormon Station did well. It was a close-knit community, and sharing was one of the hallmarks of the Mormon doctrine, so that even the "Gentile" members of the community managed to avail themselves of the interdependence practiced by the faithful. Eliza was much relieved to find the feeling between the Mormon and Non-Mormon citizens was so much friendlier than what she had seen in Illinois and Missouri, but in time she drifted away from her adopted faith and resumed the old "Covenanter" faith she was introduced to as a girl.

Will Logan had diligently watched as the settlers came through from the east with their small herds of cattle and horses, and when any of them had need of commodities which were available to them in the valley, he made it a point to try to arrange an exchange which would expand his small herd. His brothers, John and George, were just as diligent about farming and building up the herd of hogs, and between the three of the Logan boys, the supply of food in the Carson Valley was slowly increasing. The deer population was not always plentiful, though Jesse, now having an improved firing system on his father's old flintlock, often managed to bring in a deer or antelope, and even, from time to time, an elk. His marksmanship skills had improved over the years, and the family counted on him to help keep meat on the table. The distinguishing feature of the musket was that the shooter was only allowed one shot to bring down the quarry, and to miss that first shot was the end of the game.

Among the workers that showed up in the valley was a man known only as Fall. No one, and in all probability not even Fall knew either his other name if he had one, or even whether Fall was first or last. He was an amiable man, probably in his forties (he didn't know that, either) and well suited for the job.

Fall had no family. Some thought his original family might have been African slaves or an African-Indian mix, but he wasn't sure. His first recollections had been as a part of a family of Indians in the Indian Territory, and for all he knew, they were his family. At any rate, he had been raised by the Indians, lived among them for much of his childhood, and had only taken up with white people when his Indian family had been killed in a skirmish with some bandits. His curly hair and dark skin gave him away as other than pure Indian, though. The settlers who found him in the ruins of his family's camp kept him as one of their own until he was old enough to be on his own. Then he had migrated across the Rockies, into Colorado, and eventually to the Carson Valley, where he found work as a cowboy.

This interesting man fascinated Jesse and Dick. He was kind and considerate toward the two young men and helped them learn the ways of tanning, hunting, fishing and trapping. He spoke a broken English, somewhat akin to the dialect Jesse had heard from some of the Indians around Salt Lake City, and he also taught them a few Indian words and phrases. He rode a mule by choice, and could coax it into some of the more precarious situations where many horses had great difficulty.

One day while they were riding out west of the ranch Dick was on a small horse, he called Tom Thumb and Jesse was on his favorite mare, Sally. Jesse had stopped to get a drink from a small stream and was in the process of overtaking the two other riders when he overheard the conversation between them.

"Why do you always ride that mule, Fall?" he heard Dick ask.

"Him go places horse can't go. Git me to all places I want ride."

"But isn't he kind of slow? It seems like a horse would be lots faster"

"Him pretty fast. Maybe can't outrun some other horse, but him outrun all the cows. 'Nother thing, I like riding mule. Him ride more good, walk more smooth."

"He's so big, though, Fall," said Jesse, who had now caught up with his companions. "Sometimes it looks like you're riding the whole stable."

Fall grinned at the weak joke and shot back at Jesse, "You try him sometime, Jesse. I betcha you never go back to that bone-bag, Sally. I think she not go'n' git you back home, sometimes. If I git on that skinny old horse she fall down, jes' like my name."

"Alright," Jesse challenged, "I'll bet I can beat you to that patch blackberries yonder. I'll give you head start, even."

The three riders struck out toward the blackberry patch, Fall in front, then Dick on Tom Thumb, with Jesse in the rear. By the time they got halfway, Jesse had overtaken Dick and the two boys overtook Fall, finishing in a dead heat.

"Okay, you pretty good on that old mare, Jesse, but you don't worry none about the bears getting her this winter. She so skinny, the bears pass her up and look for acorns and grubs, instead. I think I look in mouth an' see she got any teeth left. Maybe file down so she chew better."

4

SPANISH MARY

In the spring of 1855, a man, an 'apostle' of the Mormon Church, came from Salt Lake City to evaluate the prospects of Mormon Station as fulfilling its intended purpose as the capitol of Carson County, the portion of the territory which later came to be known as Nevada. Elder Orson Hyde, a genial but sincere man of about fifty, traveled over the rough and rugged Humboldt Trail to see for himself and to report back to his fellow apostles governing the Mormon Church, just what this prospective seat of government in the western reaches of the territory consisted of. He spent considerable time talking to the Faithful and Gentile population alike, and after some consideration, proposed that "Genoa" as it was then to be named, would be the County Seat of Carson County.

The post office, which had been established in 1852 had a new sign painted on its front and Mormon Station faded into memory. The town now had a post office, an identity, and, possibly more significant to its growth and prosperity, a bar, which had opened up early that spring, much to the consternation of Elder Hyde.

It was also in the early summer of 1855 that a Mexican family from California had come to the Carson Valley. The man's name was 'Don Teofilo' Vasquez, and his wife was 'Dona Estrella'. They brought with them four children, two drivers for their wagons, and a wrangler for the six or seven other fine, blooded horses they had brought. They also brought with them a young lady of about eighteen who was engaged as a nurse for the children and an assistant to Dona Vasquez. Her name was Maria.

Don Teofilo, was a citizen of both California and Mexico, as he had managed to survive the take-over of California in 1846, and was well established in the cattle business in the San Bernardino Valley. He had visited the Carson Valley years earlier and had been impressed by the richness of the region. He was now interested in starting a business and possibly capitalizing on the opportunity to supply food to the immigrants who were streaming through the region.

Don and Dona Vasquez had come up the Owens Valley in a rather ostentatious coach, with a supply wagon following. The coach was an eight-seater, with ample space for the family and young Maria, as well as the driver. They were seeking lodging for the fortnight or two that they planned to stay, and Eliza Logan's reputation as an innkeeper was well regarded. Even though her home was still not very large, she managed, through some manipulation of her own family, to provide visitors with adequate lodging.

Maria was an extremely attractive young lady with a wasp waist, ample bosom, and flashing dark eyes. She was not too occupied with the chores of tending the Vasquez children to captivate the Logan family with her friendliness, and Jesse, at almost 15 by now, was smitten by her beauty.

Don Teofilo was an engaging sort of fellow, with mutton chop whiskers, and a ready smile. A shrewd businessman, he began a campaign of contacting the local ranchers, including the van Sickles, John James, the Logans, Hampton Beatie, Jacob Winter and other cattlemen in the area. His objective was to either buy out a local cattle operation or else obtain a tract of land, then return to California, and bring his own herd of cattle into the valley.

He had been in the valley but a few days when his plans hit a snag. On this particular day, Eliza Logan had invited Estrella Vasquez to go into town to try to buy some clothes for the children. They took the three oldest with them, but left the infant at the ranch with Maria. On their return, Senor Vasquez's horse was noticed, tied out front of the house, but he was nowhere to be seen. On their entering the house, however, Maria was seen fleeing the bedroom where the Vasquez family was staying, and on investigation, Don Teofilo was caught with his pants down, or to be more exact, with the pants off in a corner, and his ostentatious nakedness showing.

The Vasquez family, including their drivers and wrangler left immediately for California. Maria did not.

Maria's grasp of English was excellent, though it had a distinct musical quality reminiscent of her Spanish heritage. She left the Logan home a short time after the departure of the Vasquez family, and sought work in town as a domestic servant. She did work for a short time for the van Sickle family, but their need for a housekeeper was limited. Soon Maria, who had let people know she preferred to be called Mary, began working as a barmaid at the closest thing the town had to what could be called a saloon. Maria's qualities were such that the wranglers and cowboys, who managed to come to town occasionally, readily sought her company, and she did not go hungry.

If her situation seemed pathetic or regretful, she wasn't aware of it. Spanish Mary was enjoying life, and she let the folks around Genoa know it. She had an exuberance about her that the citizens of the region admired, even if some of them didn't admire her chosen profession. Knowing Eliza Logan and Mrs. van Sickle, Mary made the most of her associations, and with some of the skills she had learned at the hands of Dona Vasquez, she made herself useful as a seamstress or a domestic worker during the day. Of course, she had other pastimes to occupy her attention in the evening and at night, if she chose. She was discriminating in her contacts, if the word could be used in this context, and Spanish Mary became known as a person who was not to be trifled with.

Maria and Jesse had also become acquainted during the Vasquez's short stay at the Logan home, and she immediately took a liking to the tall handsome young man, with his engaging sense of humor. Jesse, at almost fifteen had grown to stand nearly six feet tall, and his blond hair and deeply tanned skin made him quite a striking figure for a young lady to contemplate. Mary's enthusiasm and appearance drew men to her, and Jesse, though strongly attracted to her, dismissed the thought of any romantic association with the girl as exactly what it was; a fantasy. Her level of sophistication placed her far beyond his reach.

Mary didn't leave it at that, though. To her, any man was a conquest, and whenever she encountered Jesse, she flirted shamelessly with him and lost no opportunity in letting him have some sort of exposure to her manifold charms. Whether it was brushing up against him, tantalizing him with her smile, dropping suggestive hints, or flashing an ankle when she knew he'd be watching, Spanish Mary was a master. Jesse responded at first with awkward embarrassment, but as the game warmed, he joined it enthusiastically. Mary's thinly veiled suggestions were met by challenges to fulfill. Her smiles were returned with all the sincere warmth of his soul, and when she approached closely enough, he'd take her hand or shoulder or the back of her neck and draw her closer to his side with what he hoped would appear to be a brotherly hug.

Eliza Logan didn't miss any of the interplay, and at times cautioned Jesse about his manners with women and reminded him that his time to engage the romantic friendship of a young lady was not yet at hand. Jesse's brothers also cautioned him as to the wisdom of creating too strong a bond with a girl whose reputation had been called into question, though they too readily recognized Maria's attractiveness.

The summer of 1855 was a warm one. Jesse and Dick Jones had become quite close and they spent a good part of their time together. The boys worked in the fields of both their families, along the western fringe of the valley, a lush rich grassland which produced hay for the immigrant trade. In the afternoon when it was too hot to put up hay, cut wood, or search the valley for wagon parts for Ben Jones's business, Jesse and Dick sometimes took time to swim in one of the several small creeks flowing out of the Sierras and supplying water to the fields.

One particular fine day the boys took time out to stop at Silver Creek, a short distance from town, retreated up stream to a rather deep eddying pond, and unsaddled their horses for a swim in the creek.

"I can't stay long, Jesse", Dick said, "I have to get back home and bring in the old cow for milking. She wandered away this morning, and I saw her back there on the side of the hill. If I don't start pretty soon, I'll have to drive her so hard she'll hold back her milk and I'll be in trouble."

"Well, I'd probably better get back, too, so we shouldn't stay too long." Jesse replied.

The water was cold and refreshing, and the boys, swimming in the nude enjoyed it immensely. Presently, however, lying in the heat of the afternoon sun on the bank of the stream on their saddle blankets, Dick said, "Jesse, I got to get goin'."

With that, he got up, put on his clothes, saddled his horse, and rode off toward home. Jesse had been halfway dozing on his saddle blanket, and was only remotely aware of Dick's actions, but woke up enough to say, "Well, I'll see you later, Dick, and we can find out what they want us to do tomorrow." With that he lay back down.

Fifteen-year-old boys probably spend about eighty percent of their time thinking about the opposite sex, and the other twenty percent thinking of food. Jesse's thoughts were not on food that afternoon. In his state of undress, without the distractions of any other person about, his thoughts and fantasies were transmitted to his sexual member, which responded appropriately by assuming an erect posture. His admiration of Spanish Mary, though he knew her to be unattainable, nonetheless sparked his state of mind. Occupied as he was in such fantasy, he didn't hear the approach of Mary herself, until he opened his eyes to see her kneeling beside him, naked above the waist.

Mary had been picking blackberries along the stream above where Dick and Jesse had been swimming, and had removed the top part of her dress to enjoy the warmth of the summer sun. She had been attracted by their voices and, ambling down-stream, she peered through the bushes, just as Dick was riding away. She decided it was time to exploit the relationship she had established with Jesse, even if it was only brief. Who knew? Someday it may become an affair leading to something more permanent. He was a member of a prominent Carson Valley family and not at all bad looking.

Jesse, at first, couldn't believe his eyes. Immediately his erection flagged in the presence of another person, but on his looking up at the loveliness of her naked breasts, it came right back up.

When he thought of the fact that Dick had just left and may come back, he again lost his libido, but then as Mary started to pull her skirt down over her hips, here it came again. Second thoughts about her age and unattainability, and the fact that he was naked in front of a person of the opposite sex, caused momentary loss of structure in Jesse's physiognomy, but as Mary slowly revealed herself to him, he lost all inhibition. After several ups and downs, Jesse reached over and pulled her down beside him, and for a very long time they enjoyed each other, thoroughly.

Mary hadn't said a word, but her intentions were obvious. There they lay, or more descriptively, wrestled on that sweaty horse blanket, oblivious to all but their own pleasure. Mary's scant sexual sophistication and her unabashed confidence in her desire and ability to please her partner provided Jesse a half-hour lesson in lovemaking he never could have gained from books or lectures. The time passed without their saying more than half a dozen words, other than the occasional sigh or gasp or uttering the name of their partner. Satiated, they finally lay back, clinging to each other quietly on the blanket.

Presently Jesse rose on his elbow and told Mary he was going to have to leave. He was feeling pangs of guilt, as both his mother and older brothers had warned him sternly against such loss of self-control as he had just displayed, but when he looked at the form before him, he seriously considered revisiting the cause of his guilt, without hesitation. Despite his urgings, he simply kissed her on the mouth, and got up to put his clothes on.

"Will I see you again, Jesse," Maria asked in her lilting voice, pronouncing his name 'Yaysee'.

"I don't know, Mary," he said, "I can't say. I don't know what to say. We shouldn't have done this, you know. We aren't married. What would people say?"

Thoughts were flooding through his mind. This had been a momentous occasion, but one which his upbringing had conditioned him to try to avoid for the next several years. Yet it seemed as natural and as right as shaking hands, or saddling your horse, or kissing your mother goodnight when you went to bed.

That was the wrong thing to think! Would he ever kiss his mother goodnight without reflecting on this moment? Would his mother, out of sheer intuition, sense his recent transgression and know what he had been up to? Would the whole town know that Jesse Logan had been with this girl who at once was the object of his passionate and eternal affection and also the subject of the town's gossip?

Spanish Mary read his thoughts. "Don't mind the others," she said softly, "They don't mean nothing to me." Then, her voice dripped with indignation, "I have to live in this wild country, and I do it the best way I know how. I sew, I help the ladies and I help other people, and I work as a serving girl, and sometimes men want to pay me money to be their friend, but it don't mean nothing to you and me. Remember me, Jesse, I am your girl."

"I've got to go, Mary," Jesse said. "I'll see you around."

"Jesse, I'm your girl," Maria stood, stark naked, feet spread apart, hands on hips, and as beautiful as any Grecian statue, crying loudly as he rode away, "Remember me, Jesse, I'm your girl!"

In the days following, Jesse did remember that vision, and wondered how he could ever leave the arms of so lovely a creature. "Why", he thought time and again, "why didn't I at least go back and kiss her one more time?"

It was only a few days later that Eliza asked Jesse to take her into town the next day so she could buy some dry goods and groceries she needed. They started early in the day as there were chores to be done and Jesse had to get out to his brother's ranch. Will, had asked Jesse to also bring back some feed for the horses, as they were getting low, and he hadn't yet thrashed his own crop of grain for the year.

Jesse dropped his mother off at the general store and drove the wagon on down the street to the livery stable where he bought two sacks of grain and put them in the wagon for the trip home. He pulled the horses up in front of Parker's General Store, and went inside to help carry out the groceries. Eliza was ready for him, pointed to the bushel-basket of groceries she wanted him to put in the wagon, and proceeded to finish her conversation with Mrs. Parker. Jesse picked up the basket and started for the door.

He backed up against the screen door to open it for his mother, and waited. Eliza had not finished her conversation with Mrs. Parker, but when she did, she too started for the door. As she approached, Jesse pushed back against the door and just started to turn. As he did, he came face to face with Spanish Mary, who was just preparing to enter the store.

"Hello, Maria," Eliza said, but Mary said nothing. Her eyes were locked with Jesse's and neither of them moved or spoke. Their lips parted slightly as if to speak, but nothing came out. Gone were the friendly and slightly suggestive exchanges. Gone, too, were the nudging or reaching for one another's hand. The two young people locked on each other's eyes with an expression of having just seen the other for the first time.

Eliza read the message. She had seen that look before between lovers, and it said to her, "If these two aren't sharing a bed somewhere, it is only by the grace of God and lack of opportunity."

Though she had occasionally entertained thoughts of having one of her sons return to her old home in Tennessee, Eliza had held these as only vague and remote desires. At that moment, she started with plans, which would result in Jesse moving back to Tennessee to live with her family, for "a chance to get a better education". Jesse's days in Genoa were coming to an end.

———««(●)»———

Eliza, born Elizabeth Kellar, had come from a family which was German, Swedish and Irish, the first of whom had come to the shores of America over 200 years earlier. The earliest of the Koehllar line coming to America was George, who migrated from Bern, Switzerland, west through Germany, down the Rhine, and Thence across the Atlantic to Philadelphia, where he immediately headed west into the Susquehanna Valley. George had three sons, one of whom stayed in western Pennsylvania, one moving south into Georgia, and one, Henry moving up the Shenandoah Valley, into the Great Smokey Mountains, where he established his family in the business of lumber. His fortunes took him to the Doe River, a tributary of the Holston, in a community occupied by a people who called themselves 'Covenantors', Scotch-Irish Calvinists whose strong work ethic complemented his own. He started out clearing land and cutting logs for his neighbors. He and his sons also cut firewood and sold or traded it for necessities. They then set up a little saw mill for the housing trade, and eventually used their talents cutting and supplying hardwood for the furniture business in Virginia and North Carolina which began to blossom during the early nineteenth century.

The third generation of Kellars, Eliza's father, who was also named Henry, and his two sons, John and Frederick, who with their families, were all in the business of furnishing some kind of wood. They banded together when it was profitable, traded with each other, helped each other, and went their own ways when it best suited their purposes. Though they married local girls without regard to heritage, the family all retained the fierce independence of their German and Scotch-Irish ancestry, and worked the land and forests without aid of slaves whom they considered so much excess baggage.

Henry had told his sons, "If you own a person or an animal, it's your job as the owner to feed, house, and furnish the ordinary necessaries of life for them. It don't make any sense to me to go out and buy something or someone if you don't have serious use for them, 'cause then you own him for life. When he's sick, he's yours. When the weather's too bad to work, he's yours. When he's asleep, he's yours, and when he dies, he's still yours and you've lost on your investment. It makes more sense to hire a man at day wages and pay him what he's worth. Then if he makes mischief or turns lazy, you just go out and hire someone else."

The philosophy suited the Kellar family just fine, and they got along well in the county. Carter County was a mix of folks, a few of whom were slave owners but most were not. They got on as friends and business associates, and never thought much of the difference, until the tension started in Washington and Albany and Charleston, and some of the parts of the country where slaves were an important part of the economy.

Eliza had kept in touch with her family and the family of her husband, David Logan. She had written at least twice a year, and had told her mother, Emmelyn Kellar, that she had someday hoped to have at least one of her sons go back "home" and possibly attend school in Elizabethton, as she had.

⸺◈⸺

That year, Will Logan had accumulated three wagon loads of hides that he tanned and was then looking for a crew to drive the wagons back to Illinois where his brother David had settled with his own harness shop. He had the hides all prepared, and he wanted to get them on the trail as soon as he could before winter came. He didn't know just how long it would take, but estimated about two months. At the suggestion of his mother, Jesse would be one of the designated drivers.

Will had made arrangements with his brother David, and felt that between them they could turn a good profit on the hides. Most of the hides were from cattle, but he also had some deer hides, horse hides, buffalo hides, and a number of bear and beaver buried in the stacks to preserve and protect them. With the help of Fall, who had considerable tanning skills, it was mostly the cowhides and a few horsehides that were tanned. The untanned hides were salted and bound in bales for the trip. It was a smelly mess, and the trip would require considerable dedication and a strong stomach.

It was expected that Jesse could help drive the wagons to Fort Laramie, then take a barge or riverboat down the Missouri River to Cairo. After leaving the hides with David, he would go up the Ohio to the Tennessee River, up the Tennessee as far as Knoxville, and then on up the Holston River to Choates Ford. There he would be within walking distance of his destination, or he could possibly buy a horse from a cousin in the livery business, there in Choates Ford. The way to Kellar Crossing he would have to negotiate on his own, but his cousin, Ozzie Spurgeon, would undoubtedly be able to furnish directions.

Jesse was in quite a quandary. He had fallen head over heels in love with Spanish Mary, but at the same time, at nearly fifteen, love sometimes only lasts a day or two. He was excited about setting out on such an adventure with the eventual objective of meeting the family he'd left some eleven years ago and didn't even remember. He thought it best to avoid Mary as he felt she might make a scene if she found he was going away.

Her last words as he was riding away from that passionate and memorable encounter by Silver Creek still rang in his ears; "Remember, Jesse. I'm your girl." He wasn't quite sure what that meant, but was afraid it might mean that she would kick up a fuss for the whole world to see as he drove with those wagons out of town.

Jesse and Will didn't have much time to map out plans for the trip. The wagons were loaded, and a span of eight horses was secured to pull them in tandem. Sally, Jesse's old saddle horse was sent along to help the men scout, secure food, and go for help, if necessary. Two saddle horses would have been nice, but they didn't have the horses to spare. As it was, Jesse and two other drovers were to handle the job, and were given instructions to take the horses as far as Salt Lake City then trade them for mules, if possible, for the rest of the trip. The mules could not only move at a steadier pace than the horses but trading off the horses would provide fresh draught animals for the trip over the Rocky Mountains.

While Jesse was entrusted with the responsibility of the family's interests, Hoke Blackstone, a sometimes cowboy, sometimes trapper, sometimes carpenter, and an all-time regular fellow was charged with the responsibility of carrying out the day-to-day business of running the wagon train. Eventually, depending on the availability of supplies, Hoke would probably turn right around at Fort Laramie and bring a load of trading goods back to Genoa. The third member of the team was Fall, the dark-skinned cowboy from the Logan Ranch. Will Logan thought he might be of value to the freight wagons if they encountered hostilities from the Paiute and the Shoshone Indians or later the Sioux, which was likely.

—————※(()))※—————

It was August 2, 1855. Jesse was almost fifteen years old, and he was leaving, for all he knew, for good. His life in Carson Valley had been idyllic for a young man in his early teens, but he felt a sense of maturity, as well as a sense of pride at having been selected for the responsibilities of this mission. He also looked forward to seeing his brother and old jousting companion, David in Cairo, Illinois, as well as the family in Tennessee of whom he only had the vaguest memories.

5

THE TRIP EAST

Jesse, Hoke, and Fall would take turns at the reins, with one of the alternates in the wagon seat beside the driver and the other mounted on Sally, the saddle horse they had been assigned, if she held up. Or in the alternative, the third member could ride the seat of one of the other wagons. It was a well, albeit hastily organized team of talent that was to be sent east, with what was hoped to be an entrepreneurial experiment on Will Logan's part. The second and third men were supposed to retain either the shotgun or the musket they had taken along, as the cargo was one that would be attractive, not only to Indians, but also to roving bandits who sometimes frequented the trail.

These little bands of part time outlaws spent some of their time trapping and hunting, but a ready-made shipment of about six ton of hides, already pretty well tanned for market would turn a nice profit in Fort Laramie. Will had heard of these bands, and had cautioned the trio against getting too friendly with the odd 'mountain man' who just happened to attach himself to the train. Except for Salt Lake City, the vast expanse of territory between the Sierras and the Missouri Valley was only very lightly settled and populated. And while most of the odd individuals or small groups of whites were known to each other and to the military authorities and remained fairly responsible, yet there were still those of an opportunistic character who were willing to chance robbery and even murder, if it meant easing their own difficult situation.

Will had also told the group to try to take up with other freighters from any of the forts or small towns dotted along the way. There wasn't much between Genoa and Salt Lake City, and the Paiute and Shoshone Indians were thought to be fairly peaceable at the time, but the company of other traders was a good form of insurance. The Humboldt Valley, through which they were to pass, was mostly occupied by just buffalo and antelope, with a few bands of Indians in the hills or along the banks of the rivers.

Water at that time of the year was in short supply and often brackish, so they were instructed to stay as close as possible to watercourses. This was not always the quickest way east, but would save the horses and ensure the feed and water supply. They would head up the Carson River until they reached a place called Rag Town. They were then to head north until they picked up the Humboldt River, and follow it till they got to a little outpost called Humboldt Wells. At times there were one or two traders or wayfarers there, and at other times, no one. They would then have to head east on the emigrant trail to Salt Lake City. From there the trail was fairly clear all the way to Fort Laramie.

The most difficult part of the journey at this time of the year would be that from Humboldt Wells to Salt Lake City. Depending on conditions, the availability of water at Humboldt Wells would be tentative at best, and this was the time of year it would be at its lowest. From the wells to Salt Lake City, however, water was non-existent, and the barrels had to be well stocked with water for that leg of their journey. To do this, they would have to fill the barrels well before their last contact with the Humboldt River, twenty miles or so before they reached the wells, as the trail left the river.

All three men wore broad hats and clothing that would protect them from the sun. Jesse had with him a carpetbag with all his worldly belongings in it, as he was expected to stay with their family in the east for the next four or five years. Jesse had also acquired a .31 caliber revolver, much to the chagrin of his mother, who didn't favor the use of handguns. She considered them more of a threat to life than a means of protection. She was mollified in this position somewhat though, as it had been a revolver in the hands of his older brother that had saved Jesse's life a few years ago on their way west.

As they left town, Jesse had the revolver in his carpetbag, but before long he had taken it out and stuck in his belt and, as the trip progressed, he put together a pretty good holster out of a piece of the leather in their load of hides. He felt very mature with the gun on his side. Fall and Hoke smiled between themselves at the spectacle of a fifteen-year old boy carrying a gun hung on his belt, but had the good sense to keep their feelings to themselves. Hoke, too had an old Colt Dragoon revolver, which he sometimes carried on his belt, and sometimes left strapped to the dashboard of the lead wagon. Hoke liked to drive, and was the one who spent the most time at the reins. He had a 'soft hand' on the reins, and the horses responded well to his touch.

They left early the morning of August third, and headed north. Their first night they would spend at Eagle Valley, the next night would be at Gold Canyon and then they would travel on northeast along the Carson River.

Eagle Valley, or Eagle Station, as it was sometimes known was little more than a set of ranch buildings among which was a bar and a blacksmith shop. The owners, Abe Curry, John Musser, Frank Proctor, and Ben Green shared the duties of postmaster, storekeeper and blacksmith, along with the running of their small herds of sheep, cattle, and horses. There were, at any given time, a number of cowboys, roustabouts, grifters, and prostitutes hanging around the saloon, as it was also a gathering place for gamblers, a distinction that had so far escaped Genoa.

Jesse, Hoke, and Fall decided to spend the night a few hundred yards past the station, and found a good camp by the banks of the river.

As evening approached, Jesse told Hoke he was going back to the station to look around and Hoke suggested he leave his gun in camp, but Jesse just passed off the suggestion without comment.

After Jesse had left, Hoke said to Fall, "You watch the camp, Fall, I'm going to give Jesse a little backing, just in case he runs into trouble with that-there pistol on his belt."

There were nine horses to feed and tether and a load of hides to tend to, and the three of them could not all be gone from the camp at the same time.

As Jesse approached the saloon, one of the first people that he ran into was a man named Lars, a cowboy he had known from around Mormon Station. They struck up a conversation. "What 'you doin' out on the trail, Jesse?" the cowhand asked. "I thought you was pretty well tied to that ranch of your'n down the valley."

"I got a load of hides to deliver back east, and this is our first stopover on the way," Jesse replied.

"Lookin' fer a little fun, are ye?" his companion asked.

"Not really," Jesse responded, not quite sure of what Lars had in mind, "I just came in to see the sights."

"Well, this is surely the place for some sights. Look over there at that-there lady by the hitchin' post. Ain't she a sight fer sore eyes?"

"Son of a gun!" Jesse exclaimed, "She surely is somethin'. I've never seen anyone in a dress like that. Why, you can see her legs almost up to her knees. I never did see —," his voice trailed off.

The woman looked their way, and started to move toward them. It suddenly occurred to Jesse that he was looking at a 'lady of the night', a term he had sometimes heard in connection with Maria. His thoughts flashed back to Spanish Mary, and he wondered if she wore a dress like that when she was out at night.

"Hello, Slim," the woman said in a friendly voice, as though she had known him for a long time. "'You just in town for the night?"

"This here is Sadie," The cowboy introduced her to Jesse. "Sadie, I want you to meet Jesse. He's a rich cattleman with a load of hides he's takin' back east to sell."

Jesse couldn't keep his eyes from front of Sadie's gown, and as there was almost a foot difference in their heights, just looking at her to converse gave him ample opportunity to let his glance stray. Her bodice was cut low, and he had never seen such a display of bosom protruding from over the front of a woman's dress.

"It's nice to make your acquaintance, Jesse, do you need someplace to spend the night?" Sadie asked. "I've got a really comfortable little place, over here. I'm sure you'll like it much better than camp, wherever that might be, and much, much friendlier"

Jesse's heart was in his throat. He was out here virtually on his own, and this beautiful creature had selected him as an object of her affections. At least, that was what it sounded like. How lucky can a boy get! His first night out and here a full-grown woman walks up to him on the street and seeks his company for the night.

"Better go with her," his friend whispered, "You ain't gonna get a chance like this fer a long, long time, Jesse."

"Yo, Jess!" Hoke's voice broke the spell. "Jesse, we need you back at the camp. The horses are a little nervous this being our first night out, and we 'got to get a early start in the mornin'. An' I'd think we'd ought to spell each other on the watch. We didn't talk about it before you left, but I was hopin' you'd take the first watch."

All of a sudden, Jesse was again the responsible ranch hand that he'd started out to be. Hoke had come into town seeking his help on maintaining a guard over the horses and wagons, and was concerned about the next day's run, as Jesse knew he should be. He reminded himself that it was he who was to be responsible for the family's interests, and the sights of the town had led him astray.

"Thanks, Hoke," Jesse said in his most mature voice. "Yeah, I reckon we'd better be getting back. As long as the horses are fresh and if we can get an early start, we can likely make it to Gold Canyon, tomorrow, don't y' think?" He turned to make his excuses to his new friend, Sadie, but she and Lars were walking off down the road together arm in arm as if they were a twosome and had been intending all along to spend the evening together.

"Who's the whore?" Hoke asked.

"That's Sadie," Jesse said, "Ain't she sumpthin'?"

"She surely is, Boy, she surely is."

———— ((O)) ————

Jesse took the first watch at guard, and at about midnight, he woke Fall. "Nothing's happening, Fall," Jesse said, "Are you gonna be alright for a few hours?"

"Sure, Jesse," Fall replied, "'Not sure we need for us to be out here, but 'don't hurt be safe. 'You have good time in town?"

Jesse laid out his bedroll and lay down. As he was falling asleep, he reflected on the day he had just spent. To his surprise, Maria had not made a scene, nor had she even shown her face on the street as Jesse rode out of Genoa. Then, this evening he had met another beautiful woman, and had been saved from an embarrassing and awkward situation by the timely appearance of Hoke. She too had wandered off without so much as a backward glance. Women were funny. Neither Maria nor Sadie had seemed to give him a second thought, even though he had been smitten by their beauty and charm. Also, Jesse wondered if Hoke had just come into town to look for him and ask his advice or if he had been tailing him to keep him out of trouble.

His thoughts were mingled with the prospects of long days on the road, new adventures, and the meeting of his brother, David in Cairo after over four years of separation. It took him some time to sort out all these thoughts and fall asleep.

The next morning Hoke awakened Jesse and Fall before dawn, and at first light they had the horses grained and hitched to the wagons. They broke camp with only a cup of strong coffee and some biscuits in their bellies and struck out for the east. They moved quickly along the Carson River, which was nothing more than a trickle in places, and got to Gold Canyon just before dark. Gold Canyon was just a dusty little camp, named for a small gold strike in 1849 that had dwindled almost as fast as it had started. It was now another outpost for the Mormon Church to branch out and settle that part of the country, but not as well developed as Genoa. They pitched camp, staked the horses had a bit of supper and slept. It had only been about fifteen miles from Eagle Station but they had been delayed along the way by a broken trace on the harness of one of the wheel horses, and the men were still pretty tired.

Jesse, as before took the first watch, but could hardly keep his eyes open. As they were in a camp that was now populated mostly by the 'saints' of the Mormon Church, they weren't too concerned about thieves, but it was a good habit to get into; keeping watch at night. There was plenty of opportunity to sleep on the trail in the daytime, when the other members of the team were awake and alert for trouble. About midnight, Jesse heard a couple of the horses nicker and rustle around as though there was something or someone approaching. It was time to change watch so Jesse went over to wake Fall.

"Time to get up?" Fall grumbled.

"Shh," Jesse whispered, "I'm goin' out and take a look at the horses. Somethin's botherin' 'em. I think I'll just circle aroun' and see what's goin' on. I think there's somebody out there."

"I come out perty quick," Fall whispered back.

Jesse quietly walked a short distance angling to the right from where he had left the horses and from where the disturbance had come. The sleep was out of him now and he peered into the waning moonlight, alert to any sight or sound.

He had gone just forty or fifty feet through a stand of cottonwoods when he saw the figure of a man standing near Sally, their saddle horse, the only one they had in the string. Jesse paused and watched for a moment. He didn't know if he had been seen, and the man was not moving, so Jesse held his position and pondered his next move.

He slipped the revolver out of his belt, and held it in front of him. The chambers were all capped, so far as he knew. He hadn't checked the gun since early in the day, and cursed himself for his negligence. Caps can easily be knocked off a percussion piece, even if you crimp them with your teeth. His revolver had new nipples on it, Ben Jones had seen to that before he left home, but that didn't mean much if the gun is jarred or scraped. He felt around the cylinder. All the caps were intact.

The man turned and looked around at a sound he detected coming from within the little herd of horses.

"Stand easy, Mister," Fall's voice came from among the horses. "Jes' stand quiet. Not scare horses or me. I scare easy."

The figure started running quickly away from Fall's voice, directly toward Jesse. Jesse knew better than to shoot the man, but felt he had to do something to protect himself and stop the fleeing figure. As the man moved toward him Jesse summoned all his strength and lashed out at the fleeing figure with the gun he was holding, hitting him square across the face. He went down quickly, but just as quickly was on his feet lashing out at Jesse with an energy of one who'd been caught in an act of chicanery and was trying to escape. Jesse had dropped the revolver and was occupied trying to fend off the intruder's attack and recover his lost gun. The stranger was getting the better of his struggle with the boy, when Fall moved in and caught him from behind. With one arm around the man's neck, he applied pressure on the man's carotid arteries, cutting off the blood to his brain. The man fell unconscious at Fall's feet, seemingly lifeless.

Fall had also alerted Hoke, who now showed up with a lantern. The stranger, it turned out, was Lars, the cowboy from Eagle Station. Hoke knew Lars, and had worked with him a time or two.

"Would you like to tell us what ye're doin' out here, messin' with our horses?" Hoke demanded when Lars came to.

"If I'd had a clear shot, you'd be dead," Jesse contributed, though he hadn't really contemplated shooting the man.

They had tied Lars up by the wrists and had tethered him to one of the cottonwoods. He was still dazed, but unhurt, except for the blood drying on his face where Jesse had hit him. Jesse had recovered his gun by the light of Hoke's lantern and returned it to the holster on his belt.

Presently, he spoke, "Who hit me?" was his first question. "I was just riding out from Eagle Station to see if I could find you fellas and maybe get a job riding through the valley with you all. I heer'd the Indians are making trouble up on the Humboldt, and thought you might could use a hand."

"So you left yer horse in town in the middle of the night and come over to talk to our horses and ask them fer a job, I suppose," Hoke said sarcastically.

"I wasn't sure it were you, and didn't want to kick up a fuss till I knowed. I was just looking to see if the horses was yer'n."

"You ain't makin' sense, Mister," Jesse said, "How would you know from lookin' at the horses who we were. You ain't ever seen them horses with us before."

"I see'd you ride out of Eagle Station this mornin'," Lars protested, "and talked to you last night about where you was goin'."

"Then why didn't you ask us this morning instead of chasing us all the way to Gold Canyon?" Jesse countered. "Look, Mister, you aren't making any sense and I think you were just here to steal our horses. I should have shot you a minute ago, but it's not too late. Horse thieves don't last long in these parts, and we don't have either the time or hankering to turn you over to the marshal, if there is one." With that he started to pull his revolver out of its holster.

"Wait a minute, Jesse," Hoke said hurriedly." I been knowin' old Lars fer a long time, and this is the first I he'erd or seen of his stealin' horses. Couldn't we jes' turn him loose and send him off? He didn't take the horses, anyway, and we cain't be sure he was a'gonna."

Jesse was enjoying a little sport at Lars's expense, and knew Hoke was playing along, but there was work to do and this was no time for games. "Lars," Jesse said in what he conceived as his most authoritative tone, "you get on back to town. I don't trust you enough to stay here and argue with you, much less take you on as a hand." With that Jesse turned and walked back toward the bedrolls, still shaking with silent laughter. Hoke and Fall turned the man loose and 'counseled' him smartly.

"You get goin', Lars," Hoke said, "That thar Jesse is one mad cowboy."

"I'm goin', I'm goin'. Thank you, Hoke. You won't see me again, I promise."

When they were sure Lars had gone, Hoke and Fall returned to camp. "Well, that was one for the books," Hoke said, laughing just a little. "It always gets to me a little when I see a man get so scared."

"I know, and I feel bad," Jesse said. "I thought for minute he'd messed his pants."

"He did," Hoke responded. "I smelled it on him. He's probably out there right now cleaning himself up."

"Him deserve what he got," Fall said. "But him be back. We watch. Tomorrow, next day, sometime Lars make trouble. "Not kind of man who walk away from shame. Desperate man sometimes look to take desperate revenge."

"You think so?" Jesse asked. "He got off pretty light for a horse thief. And there's another thing. He knows we aren't asleep on night watch."

"We see."

<hr />

With all the excitement the night before, Hoke still had them up before dawn and on the road as before. There were no more towns, now until Rag Town or even Humboldt Wells, and they were just unto themselves. Jesse thought as he rode along in the second wagon, leaning up against a mound of smelly hides, that nightlife on the trail was pretty exciting. He also thought the days were pretty boring, and went off to sleep. He talked some with Fall and asked how he had been able to subdue Lars, the cowboy from Eagle Station so easily.

"When feller gets a chance, he grab man from back and lock arm around neck," Fall explained. "Then, put on little squeeze, do somethin' to blood runnin' up neck, and put him sleep. When feller wake up, after a minute, him pretty groggy fer few minutes, and lots easier to talk to than before." With that, Fall put Jesse in a position to submit to the maneuver. "Good way to stop fight. You want me show you?"

"Thanks, Fall, I'll take your word for it. I'd just as soon go to sleep the reg'lar way, whenever I get tired. Maybe you can try it on Hoke."

"Ye'r jes' full'a good ideas, ain't'cha young feller?" Hoke responded. "Why'nt'cha let him try it on you, Jess? You look like you could use a little sleep."

"I was just thinking of your welfare, Hoke. I wouldn't want you to get too worn out on the trail so's you couldn't stay awake at night."

"Don't you worry none about me. I'll stay awake all right. It's you who's always dozing off on watch. I never seen such a feller, who could sleep all day on the trail and then have so much trouble stayin' awake at night. Never in my life."

That day and the next and the next were pretty much the same. Toward evening of the third day out of Gold Canyon, they arrived at a small dusty settlement with the hand-painted sign 'Rag Town' alongside the trail. It was populated by perhaps ten people, and was even less of a town than Eagle Station. They stopped at the first shack they came to, which was the home of Asa Kenyon and his family of five, constituting half the population of the town.

There they learned that Lars had given them the correct information about the Indians of the upper Humboldt giving the travelers trouble. The Lakota Sioux had been particularly hostile farther north and it had upset the delicate balance of peaceful relations with the Paiute Indians along the Humboldt Valley. Hoke decided they should take a different route. They would stay with the Carson River another day, then cross the Shoshone Mountains along a trail running almost due east to the Reese River. Then they would head north along the Reese, which joined the Humboldt east of where the hostilities were supposed to have been occurring.

Again, they struck out with very little problem, but the weather was hot and after a two-day ride, they came to the Reese River and found that it was bone dry. In order to keep their load light they had only stocked one of their water barrels, and on the morning of the fourth day in the Reese Valley, the horses were showing the effects of lack of water. That afternoon, Fall was out on Sally, their saddle horse, and returned to the train.

"Water east along mountains," Fall announced. "Not much, but plenty for us, I think. Easy ride across valley."

They headed toward the eastern fringe of the valley, and found a small marsh against the foot of the hills. Hoof prints showed that deer and antelope had been frequenting the spring, but in the hoof prints in the mud, little puddles of water had gathered. Before letting the horses get to the water, the three of them got down and drank from the tiny puddles. The water was strong-smelling of minerals and deer urine.

"Too much piss fer young feller, I think," Fall said to Jesse.

"I reckon I'm just going to have to get used to it, Fall. It's either that or go thirsty," Jesse smiled. He lay face down on the wet ground and sucked the water out of a dozen of the hoof prints. The water wasn't particularly satisfying, but they moistened their mouths and then gave the horses a chance to drink. The horses spent a long time going from hole to hole sucking up the bitter fluid.

"We'll stay here fer the night," Hoke said. "By mornin' there should be a fair amount of water collected, and it'll give us somethin' to go on till we hit the Humboldt. Jesse you get the shovel out of the rear wagon and see if you can scoop out some of these holes fer the water to collect in. Fall, you take a look around and see kin you find any sign of Indians. I'll stake the horses".

They were a little early for an evening stopover, but the horses were tired and by bedding near the spring they could keep the deer away and expect to have a pretty decent drink before they set off in the morning.

Fall came back into camp with the news that there was no sign of Indians in the region.

The trip was uneventful for the next two days until they reached the trail along the Humboldt River. There they found evidence that there had indeed been attacks on the wagons heading west. Broken wheels, disabled wagons, and dead animals dotted the trail, but they saw only two graves and no human remains at all.

"It jes' looks like the Indians are attackin' to get to the stuff from the trains. They don't seem to be tryin' to kill off the settlers, but probably want what's in their loads, and maybe their horses," Hoke observed.

"How do you know that?" Jesse asked.

"The wagons ain't circled like they was making an all-out attack. Thar's jus' a wagon broke down now and then, and not in groups. It's like they set up an ambush along the trail and when a wagon train'd come along they'd either bargain or maybe steal the stuff they were after. People ain't their main target, like they would be if they was tryin' to stop the crossin'."

"Want guns," Fall observed. "Injuns stop wagons to get guns. They maybe kill horse, white men run to next wagon, Injun take guns."

"Yeah, and pro'ly the caps, powder, an' lead is what they want, too," Hoke said. "The white people would be carryin' their guns, but they leave the ammunition in their wagon."

"Maybe both," Fall said.

"What does that mean as far as we're concerned?" Jesse asked.

"I don't know, Jesse, it depends on how they look at us. A train heading east won't be expected to be hauling much ammunition, but then the Indians might not see it that way. I wish we'd been able to bring along more guns. This shotgun won't carry far enough to give us much protection from anyone intent on popping us off from a distance, and it looks like the Indians might be inclined to do jus' that."

Jesse thought about that for a minute. "Hoke," he said after some thought, "We have some lead slugs for the shotgun that we brought for game. Why don't we load with those?"

"That's it, Jess, why didn't I think of that?"

"Jesse got good idea, but loadin' slug slow," Fall said referring to the fact that the guns had to be loaded through the muzzle, and they didn't have the usual paper cartridge for the shotgun ball that they did for the birds shot.

"Well," said Jesse, "I'll get some charges made up ahead, and if we have trouble, I'll load and you fellows shoot. I got pretty good in the old days with my pa's fowling piece."

"'Sounds like a good plan," Hoke said. "I don't think we'll be much of a match for Indians with muskets, but it beats slingshots. If Indians do show up, we'll try to get them in close. Then we can even the odds with our pistols."

As the wagons moved east Jesse busied himself taking apart the paper cartridges of bird shot, and twisting the remaining paper closed, so that he could use the powder charges for the lead slugs. "These won't carry as far as a musket," he told the other men, "But it's better than bird shot."

Following the Humboldt River gave the three teamsters a fairly level trail and the wagon tracks of the dozens before them provided good signs for avoiding some of the steep rocky slopes bordering the river. A problem with the terrain was that it also provided anyone wanting to attack a wagon or a train good access, as there wasn't any way to escape.

They were about a day up the Humboldt River, east from where the Reese joined it, in a section of the river's course where the valley narrows to just enough of a canyon for the river and a narrow trail. At one of the narrow points of the canyon about a dozen Indians came down a little draw on the south rim of the canyon. They rode up to within twenty-five feet of the wagons. Their one musket was loaded and the shotgun was loaded with a slug. All three men were riding the lead wagon with Hoke and Fall in the seat and Jesse sitting up on the front of the load.

"Here they come. They're comin' in close to look us over," Hoke said in a low voice as the Indians approached. He dropped the reins, which he had tied loosely at the wagon seat, pulled out his Colt and stuck it out of sight between his knees. "Talk to them, Fall," he said. "Tell them we're traders with only hides, and not much else.

Fall spoke to the Indians as best he could in their native dialect for a few minutes, and turned to Hoke. "They want hides and guns, both," he said. "Say hides are theirs 'cause they come from their country."

"Tell 'em we came a long way and the hides ain't from around here and they're cow hides," Hoke suggested.

"Tell 'em that already, they not believe," Fall said. "I tell them we talk about it now, fer few minutes."

"We're going to have to take them on," Hoke said to the others. As he talked, he gestured toward the load of hides and fingered some of the various skins, as though he was discussing giving in to the Indians. "They're close in now but when the shooting starts, they'll try to get out of range of our weapons, but still stay close enough to shoot us. This canyon is too narrow for them to circle and we got a little edge there. Still, they may try for our lead horses to pin us down, and then circle us to prevent our using the load of hides as a shield. If you can, Fall, you watch for any of them attacking the horses."

The Indians had come down into the valley from their right, and Hoke was the most exposed, sitting in the driver's seat. They had now begun to spread out to surround the wagon. "Jesse, when we start shooting, you roll off on the left. if you can hit two or three with your pistol before they get going, I'll try to do the same. You try for the ones on the right and I'll go for the ones on the left. There's only about eight guns that I can see so try to hit the ones that are armed with muskets, first. Fall, you go for the one in the middle doin' all the talkin'. They have single shot weapons, and there ain't but about eight shots in the first go 'round. We have thirteen shots between us without reloading, but look out for the spears and arrows, too." As he spoke, Hoke gestured as though he were counting on his fingers, and he pointed at their horses as though he was suggesting a bargain with the Indians.

"Fall, if you can, ask them a question they will have to talk over, like 'what if we trade our wagons for one or two of their horses' or something like that. When you're ready, just real quiet like say, 'time'. That will be our signal to go."

Fall spoke to the Indians again for a few moments, and when they glanced at each other as if to consult, he inserted, in an even tone, "Time".

The three of them sprang into action. Jesse rolled over to his left from where he had been sitting while drawing his revolver, staying on the wagon, and shielding his body with the hides. Hoke, in the right-hand seat pulled out his Dragoon and started firing first. He hit one of his targets, misfired, and hit two more before the Indians could react. Jesse started firing as soon as Hoke's first shot went off, and knocked three braves off their horses before they could lift their muskets. One of the Indians loosed an arrow at Jesse, barely missing him, and Jesse shot and killed him.

The brave who had been in the middle of the group and had been doing all the talking, lowered his musket to shoot, but Fall hit him in the chest with a blast from the shotgun. Of the eight Indians armed with guns, six were down. One of the survivors shot at Jesse, but hit only the pile of hides. Fall grabbed the musket and pulled the trigger. He hit the horse of one of the remaining enemy but the man landed on his feet and fired his musket, hitting Fall in the stomach. After shooting Fall, he immediately reached for a tomahawk and made a lunge for the wagon. Hoke fired at the Indian and hit him in the chest. He grimaced and fell backward in the sand of the Humboldt riverbed.

Jesse had fired four times, and Hoke fired five times with one misfire. There were three of the Indians still on their horses, only one of whom had a gun, which was empty. He had fired the flintlock but it only flashed in the pan and didn't ignite the charge in the chamber. One of the remaining Indians rushed toward the lead horse in the team with spear poised, but Jesse used his one remaining shot, hitting the man in the chest and discouraging any such thoughts as the man got up and struggled back to his horse, but was unable to mount. He fell to the sand, helpless.

Jesse's revolver was empty and he reached for the shotgun to reload it with a round of solid shot that he had prepared, but the Indians had had enough fighting.

As they wheeled their horses to flee, Jesse took careful aim and shot the last of those who had a firearm. The others fled. Jesse's quarry was hit only in the shoulder and knocked off his horse. He tried to remount, but his arm was disabled. He grabbed a spear that had fallen in the fray and rushed toward the wagon. Hoke shot him in the face with his last round.

Two of the Indians escaped. The one with a bullet in his chest lay dying beside the trail. Nine others lay on the ground, dead or so seriously injured that they died shortly. Fall had taken a serious shot in the gut, and was lying on the seat of the wagon, his face contorted in pain.

"Lay still, Fall," Hoke said, gently, "We'll get you to Salt Lake City and they might have a doctor there."

"Don't hold out much hope for old black man," Fall said weakly. "Old black man about done for," and with that he closed his eyes in death.

"He's gone, Hoke!" Jesse choked on the words. "Fall's dead, ain't he?"

"Yes, Jesse, he's gone, but he may have saved our lives. You done mighty good for a kid your age, I want you to know that. You did all you could to save us and the wagons, and I'm real proud of you. 'You got any more bullets in that gun?"

"It ain't that, Hoke, I just did what I had to, to stay alive," Jesse said, looking at his revolver. "My gun's empty. What are we gonna do with Fall?"

"We'd best bury him right here," Hoke said. There's no use takin' him into Salt Lake. It's two weeks away, and they wouldn't do no more than what we can do right here."

They buried Fall along the river bank and placed a pile of stones on the grave. Then Hoke said a few words about Fall, how good a man he was, and how he never hurt anyone except those who did wrong, and other things like that. Jesse recited the Twenty-Third Psalm, which he had learned from his mother.

After they did that, they took the muskets and spears dropped by the Indians and stuffed them into the wagons under some of the hides where they could get to them, if they needed to. The weapons weren't much good. Two of them were flintlocks and badly burned out. Even the percussion locks were in pretty bad shape, but at least they represented protection for the two teamsters, and were not in the hands of hostile Indians.

The horses were spooked, but unhurt. One of the Indians' horses had remained with the wagons when the Indians fled and Jesse caught it and tied it to the rear wagon beside Sally. Hoke and Jesse moved the train a mile or two east and pitched camp early. They unhitched the team, brushed them down and grained them, something they didn't usually do at night, but this wasn't just any night. It had been a tough day. They had to recover a little of their composure, too.

Hoke got out some salt pork and some beans, and after boiling the mess for several hours, they had a supper fit for a king, at least it seemed so to them.

The night watches were longer now with only the two of them but still, the following day, Jesse and Hoke were up again at dawn and on the trail, heading up the Humboldt River toward where they would leave the river and follow the trail to Salt Lake City without benefit of water, except what they could carry. At Humboldt Wells they bade goodbye to what was left of the river, which at that point flowed in from the north. They had stocked their two water barrels with fresh water, against what they calculated would be an eight-day journey to Salt Lake City. They would ration it out to the horses in water bags.

The trail across the Great Salt Desert was long and tiring, but the way was mostly flat. They had chosen a good time to cross. The moon was full and by travelling at night and sleeping during the day, they managed to avoid the heat of the day. The weather was beginning to cool down at night but there had not yet been any rain to soften the soil, which would turn mushy if it got wet. They met one small wagon train heading west, and from them had gotten the latest news from back east, and shared the word that the Indians would be a serious threat.

Hoke and Jesse had time to talk and reminisce over the next few days. There was no threat from Indians or any other source during the long ride. The way was perfectly flat and the only thing they had to concern themselves with was the occasional soft spot in the otherwise endless salt desert. By following the established wagon tracks they were safe enough from such problems. The pull was easy for the horses and they had saved enough grain to keep them well maintained.

"Hoke," Jesse said after about four days had passed since their encounter with the Indians along the Humboldt River, "that little set-to back there along the river reminded me of something that happened to me when I was a youngster." He went on to relate the incident that had occurred back in Nebraska Territory when that Indian had tried to get his musket.

"You really shot one of them Indians?" Hoke asked. "How old were you?"

"I was about ten or eleven, then." Jesse chuckled, "and it scared me so bad I threw up, right out there by the river."

"You better start putting some notches in your gun to keep track of the Indians you've took down."

"I'd just as soon not, Hoke. It ain't my fav'rit' idea of fun."

Their estimate of eight days was accurate. On the morning of the eighth day they pulled into Salt Lake City, pitching camp on the western end of town. Salt Lake City at that time was a bustling town of several hundred people, with farms scattered outside of town. Hoke and Jesse looked to see if they could trade the horses in their team for a span of mules, but there were none to be had at a decent price. The horses were still in fair condition, so after three days to rest and feed the horses up a little, they struck out for the Platte River and Fort Laramie.

They traveled north and east from Salt Lake City into the Wasatch Mountains on a trail called South Pass, to Fort Bridger. It was a steep climb at first but after the second day out the river course became more gradual and the climb easier. The weather was turning cold, especially at night, and there was a stiff wind blowing down the pass that chilled the two teamsters to the skin, so they found some deer hides that had been well tanned, to use as robes against the cold of the season. They spent the first night out of Salt Lake City at a small meadow along the canyon that was South Pass. The grass was good, and water was plentiful, so that even though they were cold, prospects for a successful trip brightened their spirits.

The morning of September first found Jesse and Hoke at their usual chores preparing to move the train on up the canyon to Fort Bridger and east to Fort Laramie, where they thought they would be able to put their load on a packet boat. Their plans were then for Jesse to continue with the cargo to David's shop in Cairo. Hoke would return to Salt Lake City, buy the supplies which Will had given him orders for, pick up a drover, and return to Genoa. Since they wouldn't get paid until the load got to Cairo, Will had given them enough money to cover the cost of the goods Hoke was to buy, if he was careful.

As they headed up South Pass toward Fort Bridger, after several days, the landscape changed from a verdant green with abundant grass and trees to a drier and more barren scene. Along the north side of the valley was a wall of sharp bluffs rising several hundred feet from the valley floor. Occasionally there was a break in the wall caused by a small stream coursing down from the hills beyond the bluffs. Hoke and Jesse could see the green of grass and trees up these little canyons but stopped for the night only once, to avail themselves of the pasture for their horses, as they were anxious to move on to Fort Laramie.

As they were plodding up this long valley toward Fort Bridger, suddenly two figures on horseback rode in alongside the train from one of the canyons and struck up a conversation. They were dressed like trappers, but had no pack mules with them. It was almost as Will had scripted the scenario for them back in Genoa when they were leaving home, giving them warning that there was always the possibility of bandits along the way willing to relieve them of their load.

Without a word, Jesse, his pistol visible on his belt, took the shotgun, climbed down from the moving wagon, and waited until the wagons had passed. Sally had been tied to the rear wagon, and as she passed Jesse, he untied her, tightened the cinch on her saddle, and mounted. He then moved out away from the wagons, but close enough to hear any conversation and to protect Hoke if need be.

As they traveled up the canyon, it occurred to Jesse that one of the trappers was a man he had encountered as a child at his mother's boarding house in St. Joseph. He rode up closer to the man, "Say, Mister, ain't you Mr. Arbuckle? I remember you from Saint Joe, when I was a little boy an' you was stayin' at my mama's boardin' house. I used to try to keep company with you an' some of the other trappers, an' thought I might run off an' go with you when you went back up-river in the fall."

While talking, Jesse managed to stay close by, but a little behind the two other horsemen, and the revolver on his belt obviously gave him an advantage in fire-power over the two men who carried only single-shot, flint-lock pistols,

The man, Mr. Arbuckle, was surprised that Jesse should remember him, and, after a minute or two, admitted that he might remember Jesse as a small, boy. Jesse then kept up a line of chatter that apparently discouraged the two trappers from any nefarious thoughts they may have otherwise entertained, and after submitting to Jesse's diatribe for about thirty minutes, they simply gave a slight wave, turned and rode back down the trail toward Salt Lake.

Jesse rode Sally up alongside the lead wagon. "I reckon those were some of the ones Will was talking about."

"Yes, I reckon so," Hoke answered. "You certainly managed to take their mind off'n their business with your line of chatter, though, Jesse. Did you really know that one when you was a little boy?"

"I did. He stayed at my ma's boarding house for two summers, as I r'member. I think I'll just move out away from the wagon for a while, Hoke. The cover is a little better if those fellers come back. I won't be far. Bridger can't be too much further."

"Prob'ly t'morrow. We'd best keep a good eye out fer them highbinders, though."

Trapping had been a lucrative trade in the area for almost fifty years, but the beaver had diminished and buffalo were not particularly popular with the leather industry. As Will had told them, though, there were still a few vagrant would-be trappers in the mountains, who would not turn down a chance to take in a good load of hides, if they could get them cheap. Shooting the owners and appropriating the hides was about the price they would be willing to pay. When one of the hands has a five-shot revolver, and enough smarts as to threaten the success of their venture as Jesse had done though, the game stakes just got a little too high.

Stopping briefly at Fort Bridger, Hoke and Jesse were greeted coolly.

There had been considerable contention about Jim Bridger's activities about the fort, and the Mormon leadership in Salt Lake had just authorized purchase of the entire village, trying to establish what they perceived as a policy more consistent with the philosophy of the Mormon Church. They knew that Bridger was supplying liquor and guns to the Indians, which threatened travelers and the settlers in the Salt Lake Valley and such conduct needed to be halted. From Fort Bridger, Hoke and Jesse had no more trouble on in to Laramie. The US Army had been active in the region and the Indians were no longer posing much of a threat.

6

FORT LARAMIE

At Fort Laramie, things were in turmoil. Chief Little Thunder, of the Lakota Sioux Tribe had been on the warpath for over a year with the result being that within the past month General William Harney had tracked him down and decimated his tribe of about five hundred men, women and children in a battle at Blue Water Creek. This had all happened just fifty or sixty miles to the east, along the North Platt River. Harney had then sent squads of Dragoons out across the countryside, looking for stragglers and demonstrating the superior strength of the army. One of the squads, under a sergeant named Frank Davis, had arrived at Fort Laramie at about the time Hoke and Jesse had pulled in from the west with their load of hides. The twenty-eight men from the troop were milling about, looking to replenish their supplies, seeking further orders, reliving their recent exploits and creating all kinds of confusion, as only can be done by a troop of soldiers who were pent-up, played-out, scared, and scarred, but ultimately successful and flushed with victory.

Their experience had been one well planned by the general and his subordinates, but the men in the ranks only knew that at first, they were in for a fight, then they were in the middle of a fight, and then at last they had come away victorious, with only five killed of about two hundred men involved and not many more than that wounded. They were then almost immediately broken up into squads and sent out to look for stragglers and survivors from the enemy ranks.

The settlement at Fort Laramie was a small town of about two hundred, used by the army as a staging point for the protection of the upper North Platt River, as a trading post for trappers and hunters, as a stop-off point on the Oregon Trail, and as a place where Indian Agents were sometimes stationed to serve the needs of the local tribes. Hoke and Jesse were regarded as something of a curiosity, as the fur trade had diminished somewhat since the late 1840's, and hides in the quantity they had brought were an infrequent commodity since that time. They talked over the question of whether to sell the hides at the fort or take them all the way to Cairo. Hoke had just enough money to secure needed supplies at Salt Lake City, and the cash could come in handy, especially since there would be no certain method of sending the proceeds from the sale back to Genoa from Cairo. On the other hand, they were sure Jesse would get a better price for the hides in Cairo at his brother's shop, which had been their original plan.

One problem became obvious, however, as soon as they arrived. The North Platt River was nowhere near deep enough at that point to float much more than a canoe, let alone the barge or bateau that would be required to ship the load of hides they had brought. There were several traders at Fort Laramie who would be willing to buy the load of hides right on the spot, but the two westerners were skeptical of the price they would receive as being fair market.

The army sergeant, Davis, finally came up with what Jesse felt was the best solution to their problem. "I'll be going on to Fort Pierre on the Missouri, almost immediately," Davis told Jesse, "and you two men can come along with the troop. It won't be any trouble for either of us and the trip by wagon will be a lot easier than to try to pole a raft down a river that's not much more than a series of mudholes."

"Well," Hoke finally said, "Jesse, maybe you could take the wagons the rest of the way. I kin check around Laramie, an' it could jes' be that I could head back west from here, and you could go on without me. I could take Sally and the Indian pony, and hire out as a drover or wagon master for some of the settlers who have come this far, and at least get them back to Salt Lake City this fall. Then I'll see what the weather looks like, an' decide what's best fer me gettin' home." It was mid-September and a six-day trip back to Salt Lake City, and getting all the way home would be questionable. Their wagons were in bad shape for wear, and would have to be repaired to make the trip back to Genoa, and Jesse could probably sell the team and wagons at Fort Pierre.

So Jesse and Hoke parted company. They had been six weeks on the road together, and had become close friends. Hoke had gained a great respect for his young companion, and Jesse had certainly profited from their association.

The following day, Sergeant Davis assembled his squad, along with a wagonload of their gear, and with Jesse at the head of the train to avoid eating too much dust, they struck out for Fort Pierre. The trip was uneventful, but Davis kept the soldiers busy scouting and there was far more business to hold the interest of a fifteen-year-old than the previous six weeks had provided. On the second day out, the food supply was getting short, the soldiers having had little luck in taking any game. They had stopped for the night and it looked as though they would be eating dried beef and hard tack and the men were complaining. Frank Davis was standing nearby as Jesse was unhitching his team of horses when one of the soldiers walked up and complained to the sergeant as to the lack of food.

"Sergeant," Jesse said, "We've seen plenty of antelope and elk around here in the evenings, why don't you have someone just go out and bag one?"

"Mr. Logan," the sergeant replied a little impatiently, "These men aren't hunters, much. They can ride as well as any Indian and shoot a lot better, but they just can't seem to get the hang of sneaking up on a buck. Do you think you could do any better?"

"I'd surely like to try," Jesse responded. "If I could borrow one of those rifles, I'd reckon I could get something out there."

"You just bought yourself in on a bet, young feller," Davis replied. Then turning to one of the soldiers he said, "Manley, get this young man a rifle. He just told me he's going to feed the troop."

Jesse was a little embarrassed as he could hear the murmur among the troop as Manley selected a rifle from the supply wagon and brought it over to where Davis and Jesse were standing. "Do you want a couple of cartridges besides the one in the chamber?" Corporal Manley asked in a voice suggesting doubt as to the possibility of the younger man's ability to fulfill his mission.

"Well," Jesse said, "I'm not the greatest shot in the world, but if I can't bring him down with the first shot, I don't think he's going to stay around for me to reload. You know, Sergeant, maybe someone could come on out with me with a spare gun and be ready to shoot if I miss."

"Sure, I can do that," Sergeant Davis replied enthusiastically, "I'm sort of anxious to see how you're going to pull this off."

Jesse and Frank Davis left the train for the south and went a short distance over a couple of low hills. Approaching the brow of each rise, Jesse would begin to walk very slowly, moving toward the top of the hill and sometimes getting down on his hands and knees as though he expected to surprise an entire herd. As he got to the top of the hill he'd stop completely and gaze patiently over the landscape for what seemed to Davis like five or ten minutes and walk slowly back and forth just below the ridge-line. Then, satisfied that he was missing nothing, he'd proceed cautiously over the hill, down into the canyon and on toward the next ridge.

At the brow of the fourth rise Jesse stopped and held up his hand for Davis to do the same. Quietly, he moved forward a few steps and pointed to the next rise. Davis looked toward where he was pointing, but could see nothing. Dusk was falling, and there was a virtual hedge of brush and trees along the ridge where Jesse was looking. If there was anything there, it was invisible to Frank Davis. Jesse assumed a prone position raised the rifle and drew back the hammer. At the click of the hammer a buck elk lifted his head, and Jesse fired. The buck dropped and didn't move. Jesse said nothing but jumped up, grabbed the second rifle from Davis's hands, giving him the spent gun and ran full tilt toward the fallen buck. It had been a shot of about two hundred yards, but the Minie ball had found its mark. With a shot to the head, Jesse had both felled his prey and preserved the maximum amount of meat for the troop's table. Running up to the buck, Jesse pulled a knife from his belt, bled the animal at the throat, and immediately started dressing it for them to drag it back to the camp.

Meanwhile, several curious soldiers had ventured out after the hunters, despite admonitions to stay in camp to avoid spooking the game. At the sound of the gun, they came forward and joined Frank Davis as he followed Jesse's footsteps. By the time they got to where Jesse was working over the buck, he'd removed the head and entrails and, standing up, he advised the soldiers they could now help him take the carcass back to camp. They cut a sapling, tied the buck's feet together, and hauled it into camp amid cheering and catcalls. In their absence, the men in camp had placed bets as to the success of the mission and it was now time for the losers to pay up.

The elk dressed out at about a hundred and eighty pounds and was enough to feed the troop that evening. Even so, after having turned for over two hours on a spit over a brisk fire and with thirty hungry men attacking the delicious morsel, there was little left for the coyotes but a few well-picked bones.

The next day, on cue, Jesse was given one of the best Springfield rifles and sent out, this time with another partner, and within the period of half an hour was hailed back in camp with another big buck. In truth, Jesse found the game in the upper Platte Valley much less wary than he'd been used to in the Carson Valley and his proficiency at taking game, he thought to himself, was somewhat overrated.

The following morning, Jesse inquired of the sergeant if he might keep one of the rifles near him on his wagon. Late in the day, as the troop was considering stopping for the night, an elk appeared on the brow of a hill about a hundred yards from the trail. As the elk watched curiously, Jesse drew his team of horses to a stop, slowly got the rifle from behind him, and shot the animal, saving the men from a hike out into the hills. Jesse, having been introduced to the troop only days before, was hailed as the hero of the trip, and the legend of the "Great White-Headed Hunter" was established.

———— ((◦)) ————

Sergeant Davis was heavily occupied with supervising the movement of his men toward Fort Pierre, but from time to time he'd tie his horse to the back of Jesse's wagons and ride in the wagon seat with the young teamster.

"Where'd you learn to shoot like that, young fellow?" he asked as they rode along. "You don't waste much ammunition, do you?"

"I've been doing a lot of shooting with some pretty worn-down guns over the years, Mr. Davis," the young man replied, "and shooting these rifles is like just pointing your finger. It seems as though they just reach out and swat whatever you point at."

"Well, you surely have a knack for shooting, my friend. I'd like to have twenty men in my troop that could shoot like that. We'd never have any more trouble with any of the Indians, I'm sure."

They talked about Jesse's experiences in the Carson Valley and about the sergeant's life since he'd been in the army. He had joined the army from Indiana and had been a private in the war with Mexico. Since that time, he'd been mostly assigned to the Missouri Valley, but had also done a short tour with the garrison at Harpers Ferry, Virginia. He told Jesse he liked the army life, but that his father was getting along in years and he'd been giving some thought to going back to get involved with the shipping business. He just didn't know just what he'd do when this enlistment was up in just a few months, but it looked as though this might be the parting of the ways for Sergeant Davis and the army.

"I have only a short time on this enlistment," Davis told Jesse. "I understand we'll be heading west from here, possibly out to your country. The Indians have been causing some grief down along the Humboldt and even farther south, and General Harney thinks we should send a force down there to deal with them. After that, I don't know what I'm going to do. This thing with my father is pretty attractive. He has a good business going and I'd like to give him a hand. Besides, I think it's time I settled down."

The two of them got along pretty well and Jesse felt he'd found a friend in Frank Davis that he thought he could trust with his life. He found it easy to understand how his men could develop such a strong faith in their sergeant. At thirty-six or so years, Frank Davis showed both character and wisdom. Jesse thought it a shame to waste those kinds of qualities on bills and receipts, but also felt it would be a better way of life for Frank to settle down and perhaps get on with raising a family, something that wouldn't be very easy here on the plains.

When the progress across the hills between Fort Laramie and Fort Pierre was in its fourth day, Sergeant Davis tied his horse to the back of Jesse's wagons and ran up alongside to climb up into the seat next to Jesse. This young man had shown real promise in his ability to handle a large team of horses and his ability to handle himself in situations requiring maturity and composure. He might make good material for recruitment into the army.

"How do you feel about leaving home, Mr. Logan?" the sergeant inquired. "You're going to be a long way off from your family for some time to come."

"Oh, it doesn't bother me too much. I remember my grandfather and grandmother back in Tennessee from when I was small, and I'm sort of looking forward to seeing them. Besides," he said with a mute chuckle, "it was probably high time I left town out there in Mormon Station, anyway."

Sergeant Davis missed the innuendo to the relationship Jesse had shared with Maria, and continued with his conversation. "How big was your family in Mormon Station? Did you have many friends out there?"

"Oh, yes. I have three brothers and four sisters in Nevada, and a brother in Illinois. As for friends, there were several fellows my age that I chummed around with."

"Did you have a sweetheart, Mr. Logan?"

Jesse blushed. He had thought a great deal about Maria while he was on the road, but had dismissed any consideration of her as no more than a passing fancy. Now, however, someone had asked him directly if he'd had a 'sweetheart' and it made him focus on the fact that they had, in fact, been more than casual friends. "I, ah — well, I sort of have a — well, she's not exactly what you would call my sweetheart. It's — well — it's just that we've been pretty close for some time, you know."

"Oh? How close have you been?"

"Well, we're pretty friendly and we sometimes tease one another a little, all friendly like."

Davis could sense Jesse's nervousness and pursued the matter. "That doesn't sound too close. How old is this young lady?" He was expecting a reply citing an age of twelve or fourteen. He was taken aback with Jesse's response.

"She's — I think she's about eighteen."

"And how old are you, Jesse?"

"I'm four — Fifteen, Mr. Davis."

"Fourteen or fifteen, which is it, Jess?"

"I'm fifteen — fifteen." It sounded old to Jesse, as he had just achieved his fifteenth birthday, but he was sure Sergeant Davis didn't think fifteen was very old.

"Are you really sweethearts, Son?" the question just slipped out. He didn't mean to imply a fifteen-year-old could not be romantic with a young lady of eighteen, but the direction this conversation was taking both intrigued and surprised him.

"Well, sir — well, we've been — as I said — we've been pretty close."

In philosophical conversations with Ben Jones, Jesse had adopted what he considered to be a code of honor and felt that it would be a violation of that code to tell anyone about his relationship with Maria or any other woman, but the line of questioning the sergeant had taken had thrown him off balance. On the other hand, Sergeant Davis hadn't intended for the conversation to take this turn, but his interest in this young man had prompted him to ask questions he might have otherwise left unsaid. He felt an admiration for Jesse, but thought too that Jesse may be a little beyond his element with a girl several years his senior. The conversation lapsed for several minutes, but Davis didn't want to just get down from the wagon and suspend the discourse. He thought that if he did, Jesse might feel that he was being judgmental.

Finally, Davis said, "Well, Jesse, did you just ride off and leave this girl without so much as a 'Goodbye' or did you kiss her when you left town?"

"I didn't get much of a chance to say goodbye, I reckon. Anyway, she's the kind of girl that pretty well thinks for herself, and I don't think she's going to shed a lot of tears when she finds I'm gone."

The days were warm for September in the Dakotas, and the two new friends found themselves relaxing on the trail, which was fairly easy at most times. Jesse did most of the driving, but Davis relieved him, occasionally. Their conversation ranged from their families to the weather, to the Indian threat, and Jesse's marksmanship. The flies along the trail were persistent, and at times, bothersome. In the heat, Jesse and Frank Davis both often removed their shirts and were wearing only the traditional short-sleeved long-john underwear, from the waist up. From time to time, a particularly pesky fly would light on Jesse's arm and he was constantly waving them off, having to change hands with the reins. He cursed the pests frequently as they rode along.

"Those are just elbow flies," Frank Davis declared. "They aren't any trouble if you know how to deal with them."

"OK, if you know so much about bugs and the like, Mister Davis, how do you know these are elbow flies?"

"Well, it just goes to prove, don't it? They just land on your elbow, don't they?"

"Yep, I reckon that's right, but what do you mean they're easy to deal with?"

"Well, look at you. Whenever one lands on your arm, you switch the reins, look him over, and wave him off, and he comes back in fifteen seconds and lights on your other arm. Then you have to switch back and shoo him off'n that arm, and every time you pull your arm up like you did just now and look at him, or at least try to, and then try to shoo him off. I'm telling you, these flies are not real bright, and it doesn't take much to outsmart 'em. Watch this." With that, Davis sat motionless for a few moments with his hands on his knees. Presently a large fly landed on his left arm, just above the elbow. Without looking, he moved his right hand slowly over toward his left elbow, and at just the right moment, without even looking at the fly, he swatted it.

He turned to Jesse with a look of satisfaction on his face. "See, Jesse, that's what I mean that they ain't too bright and a feller with a little experience can outfox 'em every time. Remember, there aren't but maybe ten or fifteen of those flies in these parts. It just seems like more, 'cause the same ones keep comin' back. If you swat one you've eliminated that one. Just take 'em out one by one, and you'll get more rest between flies. You just have to be smarter than the average fly, that's all."

Jesse tried the technique. The next fly that landed on his elbow, without looking at it, he imitated Sergeant Davis' movements and, sure enough, he got his quarry. A moment or two later he swatted another one on the other arm. "Say, you're right. They aren't very quick, and if you just move in on 'em, without lookin', you can swat every one of 'em. That's pretty clever."

<hr />

At Fort Pierre, Jesse managed to sell his wagons and the team of horses and spent two days looking for transportation downriver. Davis helped him as much as he could and gave him a few tips on what he knew about the river boat travel and some of the obstacles he could encounter. Then, after he managed to get passage on a small barge from Fort Pierre, Jesse bade goodbye to Frank Davis and settled down to a trip down the Missouri and Mississippi Rivers that was slow and mostly rather boring.

There were only three other passengers, beside the owner, and two crewmembers most of the way to St. Joseph and Jesse volunteered to work the rudder from time to time or pole the banks of the river to keep the barge midstream. One of the passengers was a trader returning to St. Louis and the other two were a man and his wife who had become disillusioned with their trip west, and were returning to Ohio. Jesse whittled, slept, and helped bag game along the shore, when it was available and accessible. He had kept the best of the muskets they had recovered in the fight with the Indians, a flintlock, and used it effectively.

At a place called Springfield in the Dakota Territory a man came onto the barge with two black men with him. He was obviously their 'owner', judging by the way he ordered them about. He had made an arrangement with the owner of the barge to have the two men help pole, and he spared no effort to make them earn the money he'd bargained for their labors. One of the black men sort of reminded Jesse of his friend Fall, and though he didn't exchange any more than an occasional 'Hello' with the two, he felt that when the time was right, he'd like to sit down and talk to them. He was curious about their dialect, which was different from anything he'd heard before, but was nonetheless, if one tuned his ears, easy enough to understand.

The couple from Ohio made some disparaging remarks toward the owner of the slaves, implying that he was some kind of monster in owning two human beings, regardless of their skin-color or level of education. Since Jesse had been a small boy when he left Tennessee, he'd gained no opinion concerning the subject of slavery, good or bad. He'd just never given it any thought. The one person whom he had encountered who was of a dark skin color was his friend Fall, who had been a valuable asset to the cattle business his brother Will was involved in, a resource in the tanning trade, and had sacrificed his own life saving the lives of his friends, an equal in every way to those around him.

At supper one evening, the folks from Ohio, the trader, the slave owner, the barge owner and Jesse were gathered, enjoying the fruits of Jesse's skill as a marksman in bringing down an Elk that had come to the water's edge to drink as the barge had approached. The meat had been brought on board and cooked over an open fire and was very much appreciated by all. As the meal progressed, however, the Ohio man mentioned that he felt it would be nice for the two dark-skinned men to join them for a bite to eat. The idea was soundly and quickly rejected by the boat's owner and the owner of the slaves.

"You don't want them two eatin' with us, Mister," Mr. Hardree, their 'owner' said in an assertive manner. "They ain't too civilized, and you'uns would jes' be invitin' trouble, puttin' them in next to high-class white folks like yourselves at the supper table. They's slaves, Mister, and slaves they's gonna stay. They ain't hardly got out of the ways of the jungle, and I don't intend to give them no uppity ideas."

Not much more was said on the subject, but Jesse was perplexed at the firmness with which Mr. Hardree characterized the two black men as being unfit for association with the other people on the boat.

Mrs. Largan, the lady from Ohio, stopped one morning as she was walking about the deck and engaged Jesse in conversation. She was carrying a small book with her and asked if Jesse was inclined to do much reading. "I find this book to be quite interesting," she said, "and wondered if you might like to read it while we're here together on this boat."

"Well, I do enjoy reading when I get a chance, and I read all the books I could get my hands on back home." Jesse responded. "What's the book about, Ma'am?"

"It's a book about the life of slaves in the south, called 'Uncle Tom's Cabin'. Have you heard of it?"

"No, I don't believe I have. I'd surely like to read it, if you don't mind," he replied.

So Jesse was introduced to the most controversial novel of the day about a matter to which he'd given very little thought in the past. The book was written in a conversational style that Jesse wasn't accustomed to, and was quite captivating for a young man. The dialogue was a little difficult, as the author tried to give to the characters a personality through their manner of speaking and was sometimes difficult to follow. Jesse, having listened to the speech of the two black men with Mr. Hardree, however, was able to identify with the vernacular that the author, Harriet Stowe, had assigned to her characters.

Besides being interesting reading and a good diversion for the lack of activities on the trip, the book delivered a powerful criticism of slavery in general. It also lodged a strong condemnation toward the entire voting population of the United States for tolerating slavery at all, whether they engaged in the practice or simply allowed it to exist in the lives of others. Jesse was dubious, from time to time and from page to page, as to whether such conditions as the author described could actually exist in the world, but was deeply impressed by the message the book conveyed.

At St. Joseph, a large derrick, something similar to what Jesse had seen used for stacking hay, was used to transfer the hides to a larger riverboat, and the last leg of his trip began. This part was a little more exciting, as Jesse had an opportunity to watch the boat's great steam engine propel the boat by means of a large paddlewheel. In fact, the boat was called a paddlewheeler, or sternwheeler, by the passengers and crew. Jesse wasn't very familiar with the means of propulsion, though he'd seen such boats on the river when he was younger, and also the steam engine Ben Jones used at his shop. He watched the wheel and the engine for hours, fascinated by the machinery.

From St. Joseph, the boat moved down the Missouri River at what Jesse thought to be a rather rapid rate, both the current and the paddlewheel moving it along. They stopped at several small towns along the way, on both the Missouri River and also the Mississippi River after the two converged. When they got to St. Louis, the boat stopped overnight. Jesse was tempted to go ashore, but the hides he was taking to Cairo were stacked on deck, and he was uneasy about leaving them unattended. St. Louis was a big city, and certainly deserved exploring, but Jesse stayed put.

After St. Louis, the boat only made three more stops, one at Menard, one at a little place called Neelys Landing, and one at Cape Girardeau. At Neelys Landing, a man got on who intrigued Jesse. He wore a tall silk hat, dressed very nicely, and carried a walking stick. After he had got on the boat and had spent a little time in the saloon, he came out onto the deck, and eyed with interest this young man who by that time looked somewhat worn and threadbare.

The boots Jesse had worn from home were broken out at the sides, and his trousers, already patched, were worn through in several places. Though he had two pair of better pants in his carpetbag, Jesse tried to keep from wearing any but those he had on when he got on the boat. His shirt was also torn and threadbare, and his only coat, a canvass jacket, was so dirt-encrusted it looked as though he had rolled in the mud, even though he shook it vigorously a few times to dislodge some of the dirt. He still had the broad-brimmed hat, which by now was drooping around the edges of the brim and gave him something of a sinister look. He had taken the revolver from his belt, put the holster in his bag and the gun in the pocket of his jacket, but his musket was usually nearby or in his hand. This was not unusual, as fully seventy-five percent of the men on the boat were carrying firearms of some sort.

Jesse was about six feet tall at the age of fifteen, and despite his smooth face and light-colored hair, he looked somewhat older in the clothes he was wearing. His voice had dropped within the past few months, and he tried to speak slowly and choose his words carefully, so that people would not think him ignorant. Aware of his appearance, he tried to stay to himself. He spent most of his time resting near the bundles of hides or watching the paddle-wheel system work, and did not mingle much with the other people on board. He took his meals from a vendor who plied the decks of the riverboat, and he was careful to make the cash he had in his pocket, part of which he'd gained from the sale of the wagons and horses at Fort Laramie, last till he got to Cairo.

The well-dressed stranger looked the tall young man over with interest. "Sir, you appear to have come a long distance, are you a trapper?" the man finally asked from the rail where he had been standing.

Jesse was standing against the deckhouse near where his cargo of hides was stacked. "No, Sir," Jesse replied, trying to speak slowly and deliberately, "I've just come from Fort Pierre, and these are mostly cow hides for the shoe and harness trade."

"You're a rancher, then," the stranger pressed.

"My family is in cattle ranching in the west, yes," Jesse was hesitant to volunteer. He had been warned enough about opportunists trying to take the load of hides away from him, and had experienced such efforts already, and was not anxious to provide any more information than was necessary to maintain a courteous conversation. From his exposure to the river boat crowd of trappers and traders before his family had left Saint Joseph, he had built up a sense of caution toward these sharp and often unscrupulous men. At fifteen, he was well aware that there were people much more experienced than he, and though he was a natural optimist in most events, he tried to look on every stranger with cautious reserve. His family had entrusted him with a considerable responsibility and he had no intention of betraying that trust. The stranger seemed friendly, however, and Jesse was interested in hearing what he had to say. He had seen people dressed as this man was only a few times when he was a small boy. It appeared to Jesse as though the man would have to be somewhat respectable to be dressed so well, yet his assumed caution kept him from getting too friendly with anyone, especially only two days from his destination.

"Allow me to introduce myself, I'm Courtland Rice," the man said, holding out a Carte d'Visite for Jesse. "I'm in the fur and leather business, among other things, and I'd be interested in discussing with you the purchase of those hides. Would you mind if I looked more closely at them?"

"We have the hides consigned," Jesse said, drawing from memory a word he had heard his brother Will use, when they had first started to discuss the idea of shipping the hides east. "I am delivering them to a jobber in Cairo. We've received partial payment on them already, and I'm just finishing up the bargain."

"How very fortunate for you, my friend," Rice said smoothly. "I hasten to point out that of which you must already be aware, that is that hides are commanding a dear price these days, and I trust you have obtained from your client a contingency commitment for just such an eventuality. By the bye, you have me at a disadvantage. With whom have I been having the pleasure of this conversation?"

Jesse didn't know whether he was being tested or whether the man was in earnest, but he had never met a person who had such a grasp of the language and who could use it so skillfully. He felt that he was being hornswoggled but at the same time the words he was hearing, obviously intended to put him at ease, actually had an opposite effect. What Mr. Rice didn't know, and what Jesse wasn't telling him was the fact that the bargain for the hides was within the family, and the dealing was brother to brother.

"My name is Logan, Sir," he finally said.

Rice continued, "Mr. Logan, have you managed to weigh and inventory the hides, yet? Does your jobber have an exact figure as to the weight he is buying? Perhaps you may be interested in, ah — sharing the rich profits he will undoubtedly realize from the purchase of these fine hides, by trading a small portion of your load with one who is willing to compensate you most generously for your trouble. I'd suggest you have there, in the entire pile, somewhere in the range of six or eight thousand pounds. Let us just suppose some of these hides were to — well — to leave the boat between here and their destination, say Sheppards Point, which is just a short distance downriver. You would be the richer by a great amount, and your jobber would be perfectly happy with the remainder, not knowing what you started out with originally. You've heard the old adage, "Where ignorance is bliss, 'tis folly to be wise," no doubt. Your jobber would be perfectly blissful, now wouldn't he?"

Jesse was beginning to enjoy this conversation. Cortland Rice was not only a highbinder, he was also a word merchant. This fellow could talk a snake right out of his skin. He had a way of twisting words that could make a person apprehensive and at the same time relieve his apprehensions. Jesse actually contemplated the results of going along with Rice's scheme, knowing he never would, but the concept was delicious, despite the fact that he would be undercutting his own brother. The conversation continued for several minutes with Jesse beginning to study his companion, enjoying just listening to the music of the man's persuasive diatribe.

"Mr. Rice," Jesse finally said, after five or ten minutes of persuasion, "Let me see if I understand what you're saying. What you really want me to do is to appropriate some of these hides and sell them to you. And I'm to do this at a price which I have no idea whether it is good or bad. I haven't been tracking the price of hides since I brought these aboard the boat and you probably have that figured out. I'd just have your word that the price we'd settle on would be at all fair. Isn't that about right?"

Rice was not to be confounded in his quest. He had met more sophisticated men than this country bumpkin, just wandering down the streets of Saint Joseph or Neelys Landing, or any other town in the west, and his composure would not be rattled by this sort of rebuff. But he was getting a little impatient with the man with whom, he thought, he was going to have to start all over again, on possibly a different tack toward the same end.

"Mr. — ah — Logan, is it? Mr. Logan —," he said, as if turning the name over in his mind. "Isn't there a David Logan who owns a harness shop in Cairo?"

"I believe there is, Mr. Rice, Yes."

"And you're related to him, is that right?" Rice went on.

"Yes, Sir, he's my brother," Jesse said with a slight grin.

Rice was furious. His best manner, his best pitch, designed to persuade the most obdurate cynic to relinquish his wealth had been wasted on this young rascal. And worst of all, the blackguard would have continued interminably to toy with him, had he not detected the ruse. Angry with himself for assuming he was taking this young scoundrel in, Courtland Rice turned on his heel and stalked forward along the deck. After a few paces he turned back to face Jesse to deliver a rebuke, but in the meantime, Jesse had sat down on the deck with his back against the wall of the engine house, his hat pulled over his eyes, as unconcerned with the episode as though it had happened to someone else. Rice stalked away plotting revenge, if in his power to deliver.

<hr />

Toward evening, the paddle-wheeler pulled up at Cape Girardeau, sidling up to a long pier built to the water's edge. Jesse watched over the railing as freight was loaded and unloaded. In the distance, he saw Rice on the pier talking to some stevedores and gesturing toward the boat. Rice glanced up at the deck and caught Jesse watching and immediately turned away from the two men and walked around a corner of the building. In a moment, the two men followed him, but after a short while the two pug uglies came onto the boat and approached Jesse.

"My friend says you got away with some of his cargo back up the river," the shorter one said to Jesse. "He says he don't want no trouble, but jes' wants what he won in that-there game. We tol' him we'd jes' as soon throw you in the river, but all he wants is the hides you cheated him out'a, in that card game, and ever'thin'll be jake."

"Mister," Jesse said evenly, "Mr. Rice is setting you boys up for a couple of suckers. I'm no bluff, and I want you to know I sure ain't played that Rice fella' for the stake of these hides. If that's what ye'r talking about, you can go ask the captain or any of the hands 'bout this pile. I've been carrying this stinkin' bundle of hides all the way from Nevada, and he jes' got on the boat at Neeley's Landing. Check with the purser. I ain't never been in a game with your Mister Rice."

"Mister," the pug was mimicking Jesse, "We don't have to check with the purser, we got the word of our friend, and that's all we need. Move out of the way and let us unload our cargo, else ye're in fer a swim."

"Back off, Mister," Jesse was bluffing, and he knew they knew it. He couldn't go for the captain, as the thugs may be able to get away with part of the hides before he got back. If he tried to resist physically, he'd end up in the river. He needed to attract attention and noise was his only hope at this juncture. He pulled the revolver out of his pocket and fired one round into the air. He felt two or three would have been better, but he couldn't afford to waste the ammunition, in case his try for attention failed.

Immediately, there appeared at the rail above them, the first mate and another deck hand. "What's going on?" the mate demanded.

"Nothin'," the shorter pug responded. "We was jes' havin' a frenly conversation and ol' Willie here pulled out a gun and popped off a cap fer no reason. I think he's a little over excited at all the commotion here at the Cape."

"What happened, Willie," the mate asked Jesse. They had talked before and the mate knew Jesse's name was not 'Willie'.

"A disagreement over the price of hides, I guess, Mr. Staniford." Jesse replied. "These fellows wanted the hides I have here, and they want them for nothing."

"What're you two doing on the boat?" Staniford asked the two ruffians. "The captain told you to stay away from here unless you have business."

"I thought we did have business," the spokesman for the duo said, "I suspect we've been shucked. We'd better go back and talk to the fella that sent us, and get things straightened out."

With that, they turned and started for the gangway.

"I don't think you'll have any more trouble from those two, Jesse," Staniford said. "Did Rice send them up?"

"That's the way I figure it," Jesse responded. "I saw them talking on the dock a few minutes ago."

"Well, the captain has pulled up the plank for the night, and we're going to push off before long. Get some rest. We'll be in Cairo by tomorrow. You've had a long trip. I reckon you'll be a mite happy to see the end."

Jesse propped himself against the stack of hides and fell asleep. He dreamed of home and food, but the smell of the hides kept infiltrating his dreams, and in his dreams he had great difficulty resolving the contrasting smells with what he felt they should have been.

It was early October when the paddlewheeler circled the tip of the Illinois Peninsula at Fort Defiance, steamed a short distance up the Ohio River, and docked at the levee in Cairo, Illinois, the 'City of Cairo', for it had just emerged from the status as a "settlement" along the busy rivers of the west and was well located for the harness trade. The Illinois Central Railroad had just been extended to the city and with its situation at the confluence of two of the country's major rivers, commercial trade went in all directions and it all switched carriers at Cairo. The leather business which David had acquired only two years ago was booming and he was taking full advantage of the opportunities for an aggressive entrepreneur. His shop was on Washington Street, the main street through town, and the tannery was not far away on the west side of the town, away from the docks.

David was at the Seventh Street Pier to meet Jesse, having inquired earlier on the anticipated arrival of the Missouri steamers from upriver. Jesse recognized David immediately, but the same was not so for David. Jesse had been ten years old when he last saw his brother while David had been twenty-one. The years since their last meeting had changed David only a little, but Jesse had grown about eight inches. He had filled out from the work he had become accustomed to, and now, with slouch hat and filthy clothes, he looked anything but what David remembered.

Jesse stood at the rail and watched as the passengers disembarked. After that, the deck hands and stevedores began trucking the more accessible loads down the gangway. Next would come the offloading of the heavier cargo such as the one for which Jesse had been responsible. David had come on deck and was looking for his consigned load and also for his brother. He walked toward the stern, having seen the hides from the dock, but he didn't recognize Jesse.

He approached one of the deck hands and asked," Is there a bill of lading on this stack of hides? I'm expecting a load of hides and I think this may be it."

"You'll have to talk to the purser, Mister," the deck hand replied. "I jus' load an' unload. I ain't got no idea who belongs to what."

"Can you tell me where I can find the purser?" David asked, turning to Jesse. He looked the young man over, and decided he never seen a more disreputable looking wretch, suspecting he was a vagabond who had sneaked aboard and was probably waiting an opportunity to sneak ashore. "Do you know anything of a man accompanying this cargo?" he gestured toward the stack of hides.

"Cheap, cheap, cheap, "Jesse chirped in a falsetto voice as he had done years before at the dinner table or when David was getting too serious over some financial matter.

David, with disbelief written all over his face, scrutinized the man facing him. "Jesse. Is that really you?" David inquired incredulously, stooping to peer under Jesse's hat. "You look awful. You look great. How on earth can you live with yourself in that condition? You've grown. You're filthy! Boy! It is sure good to see you, Kid. Wow! Can we go get a bite to eat or should we unload these hides first? Jesse, you do look good in spite of the seven layers of dirt."

Jesse took his brother by the hand and for a moment they just looked at each other. Then the two of them, the well-groomed merchant and the up-river wretch grabbed one another in a bear hug, dirt and all, wrestling back and forth and almost losing their footing on the deck.

"David, it is sure good to see you. How's Mary? How are the children? Let's get this load on the dock and then we can talk. You won't believe how many people have tried to get this stinking pile away from me in the past two months."

The words tumbled forth from both their mouths, running together, each answering and asking questions at the same time, sometimes hesitating, sometimes blurting out the next thought.

"I'll get the purser if you can get the attention of the rig boss," Jesse suggested. "Do you have wagons?"

"I do, but only two," David said. "We'll have to leave some of them on the dock until I can have them picked up."

"You know this town better than I do, David, but I want to tell you, there all sorts of people looking to get their hands on these hides. Don't you think we'd better put a guard on them?"

David thought for a moment. He'd never picked up such a large shipment before and most of what he'd bought had been delivered to his shop. In deference to Jesse's concerns David agreed to post a guard until he could arrange delivery. They arranged the guard and delivery and headed up Seventh Street toward David's shop.

Since Jesse and the family had gone to Nevada, James Potter had died.

The shop in St. Joseph had sold and David and Mary had moved down river to Cairo, Illinois. David had purchased an operating business in Cairo and was dealing in both retail and wholesale leather and harnesses at the time, as well as having joined into a partnership with the owner of a tannery. The town of Cairo, with a population of about two thousand people and situated at the confluence of the Ohio and Mississippi Rivers was well suited for the business.

Two children, Elizabeth and David III, were now part of the Logan household, Jesse's first niece and nephew.

David escorted Jesse to the shop, introduced him to his assistant, Mr. Cooper, and showed him a little of the operation. He then advised Mr. Cooper of the plans to receive the shipment of hides and he and Jesse went across the street to a hotel to get something to eat and catch up on the intervening years since their separation.

Jesse didn't spend much time at David and Mary Logan's home on Washington Street. After three days he bade his brother and sister-in-law goodbye and boarded a riverboat headed the short distance up the Ohio, and then up the Tennessee River. The trip up-river took almost two weeks to traverse the distance from Cairo to Choates Ford (or Middleton, as it had just been named), Tennessee. There he got in touch with a distant cousin, Osborn Spurgeon, whom his mother made him promise he would visit on his way to Kellar's Crossing. His 'Uncle' Osborn, or Ozzie, as his friends called him, was in the grain and livery business in Middleton.

The family there welcomed Jesse as an established member, and invited him to stay the night with them. At supper time Jesse shared with them his plans, but told them that he thought he should obtain a horse for his own use, since it would probably be an imposition on his grandparents for him to use one of their horses for the next few years.

"Well, Jesse," 'Uncle' Ozzie said grandly, "you've surely come to the right place, I must say. We have horses aplenty, and if you don't see the one you want here, we can surely get it for you. We have anything from the calmest, gentlest nag to the most spirited stallion, and anything in between. What's your pleasure?"

"I suppose that I should look over the pack and see what we can settle on, Uncle. I've ridden some pretty lively horses in the past few years and the last one I rode coming east was the champion nag." He then went on to describe his needs and they agreed to look over the horses available and make a decision accordingly.

The next morning, Jesse, his uncle, and his Cousin Daniel went out to the livery pen and leaned on the fence. There were eight or nine horses in the pen that indeed represented a considerable range of equine types and personalities. One of the horses immediately caught Jesse's interest. It was a young gelding, a blue roan with a mottled grey main and tail and a blaze face. The horse had a look of confidence about him, typical of his age, but stood calmly enough among his companions.

"What would I have to pay for the blue roan, Uncle Ozzie," Jesse asked.

Ozzie glanced over a Daniel with a knowing smile. "I knew you'd pick him." He responded. "That's Max. He's a good looker and he's gentle enough aroun' people and the other horses, but he's never been ridden for more'n about two seconds. He jus' don't like people on his back. I'd recommend you'd take a look at some of the other horses."

Jesse pondered the idea and looked over the herd. "Could I go in and pet him a little?" he asked nodding his head at Max.

"Surely, surely," Uncle Ozzie replied. "Pet him all you want, but don't get too 'ttached to him, 'cause he jus' ain't the type to be ridden. We've been considering letting him go to the glue factory if he doesn't calm down."

Jesse entered the corral and walked over to the roan. While Max displayed some nervousness, when Jesse simply put his hand on his withers and stroked his neck and shoulders he seemed to accept the attention without flinching. Jesse then scratched Max's side a bit, again without any adverse reaction. Finally, Jesse went forward and patted the horse's head caressing his nose and face. Max responded with a nod of the head, rubbing it against Jesse's chest in a gesture of acceptance.

"I really do like this horse," Jesse said to Ozzie.

"Don't get too 'ttached to him, young feller," the older man repeated. "Daniel has been working with him for a couple of months, ever since we got him, and he still can't stay on him. At all!"

At that, Daniel put in, "Cousin, I've tried everything with him and even though he's perfect calm while I'm on the ground, that's where he wants me to stay; on the ground. And that's where he puts me, ever' time I try to get on him. Right back on the ground!"

They walked back to the house and talked a while. Jesse just couldn't get over the idea that Max was the horse he wanted. As they talked, Jesse reflected on his experiences in Nevada and the techniques he had learned from the Indians and some of the vaqueros he knew, and how they trained their horses.

Finally, he asked, "Have you ever tried him with a hackamore?" using a term derived from the Spanish word 'jaquima;' a headstall or halter.

"A what?" both Ozzie and Daniel said in chorus.

Whereupon, Jesse asked to see their tack room and look at their bridle equipment. They showed him what they had and he dug for a few minutes into the array of equipment, coming up with an old bosal. Knocking off the dust on his pants leg, he inquired, "You wouldn't have a hair rope around, would you?"

Ozzie and Daniel looked at each other in wonderment. "What for?" Ozzie asked.

"It just helps keep his mind on business," Jesse replied. "A hemp rope would be just about as good, I guess."

With the hemp rope they supplied, Jesse began tying it in overlapping knots to the nose-piece of the bosal till he was satisfied it would fit Max's nose. He then looped the rope to fashion a set of reins and walked out to the pen to revisit his choice of horse-flesh. Calming Max with soft tones and caresses, Jesse slipped the fixture over Max's nose and ears. Max didn't flinch and Jesse rewarded him with some further stroking and compliments. The saddle was no problem. Max had been through this part before and didn't object. When Jesse was satisfied that the saddle would stay in place under trying circumstances, he led Max out of the pen into an open field of soft dirt. Pulling a bandana out of his pocket, Jesse again spoke in soft, soothing tones to the horse and wrapped the rag around his eyes, just tucking the ends under the cheek-straps of the hackamore to keep it in place.

"Now, Dan," Jesse said in a low tone of voice, "when I say to, pull the blindfold off Max's face and get out of the way."

After checking the stirrups' length Jesse climbed slowly into the saddle. Max swung his head from side to side, but was blind-folded and couldn't decide what he wanted to do next.

"Okay, Dan, pull the rag off."

Daniel trotted gingerly over to the horse, pulled off the rag and leapt back.

Max started to duck his head but Jesse had knotted the rope securely. The hard nose-piece of the hackamore applied pressure on a particularly sensitive portion of the horse's nose, giving the rider more control than would just a bit in his mouth. Max crow-hopped a couple of times, but couldn't get in position to buck with Jesse holding his head up. He danced around, pawed the ground, tossed his head from side to side and made a serious effort to buck without effect. Jesse remained in control.

After two or three trips in skips and hops around the field where the scene played out, and after several efforts to unseat his rider, Max seemed to calm down and accept his fate. Jesse urged him into a trot, then a gallop, and then brought him to a stop, talking to the horse all the while. Max was in a sweat, despite the cool weather and the reasonably light workout.

At that, Jesse climbed down from the saddle, picked up the rag Daniel had dropped, and rubbed Max vigorously about the neck, shoulders, and face, still talking to him.

"I think I'll take him, Uncle."

They agreed on a price for the horse and saddle. The hackamore was free. Jesse worked with the horse the rest of the day and stayed again that night with the Spurgeon family.

He struck out on the last leg of his journey on October 23 on a cold clear morning. He headed south along a rough road that his uncle had pointed out to him, through Carters Station. There he stopped to visit some of his father's relatives, the family of Josiah Logan, a blacksmith, and his wife Ella, whom he'd known briefly as a boy, and had his noon meal with them. After dinner, Jesse got on his horse gingerly. The saddle he had purchased was an old one and he hadn't ridden for several weeks. He was a little sore from the morning's ride and from the previous day's workout.

Later in the day he stopped at the home of Doctor Pleasant Logan, another uncle in Elizabethton and then continued south along the Doe River. After a short ride he dismounted in front of a large home along the Little Doe River that had been indicated to him as the home of Henry and Emma Kellar. They were waiting for him. His mother's letters had preceded him, and his grandparents had prepared themselves to receive the boy who had bid them goodbye eleven years ago.

7

KELLARS CROSSING, FALL, 1855

The Kellars received Jesse most warmly. They were anxious to see him, as his mother had written over the years of the progress that her family had made, but Jesse, the youngest was an unknown ingredient in the family mix. The girls had established themselves with the business of the boarding house. Will, David, George and John were successful in their established fields, but Jesse was as yet an unproven member.

Jesse sensed this, and set about immediately to prove himself as a contributing member of the family. The primary qualities he had to bring to the bargain were his youthful strength and endurance, and an abiding sense of humor. He brought with him, also, a certain sense of equilibrium that complimented their own with respect to the matter of human servitude. He'd been ruminating on the incident involving those two black men back in Nebraska and was unsettled by the whole issue of slavery.

It was common knowledge within his family that one of their ancestors, a man from London, had been "transported in lieu of execution" from English jails and had served a fourteen-year term of servitude — slavery — when he arrived on American shores. He had accepted this obligation and from it found a sense of strength and equanimity, which the family had maintained through the generations. One was no less human for his or his family's having served another, nor to them did slavery imply some divine plan for the subjugation of one man, or race of men, by another. It was purely an economic phenomenon.

In the Utah Territory Jesse had lived and worked with a race of dark-skinned people who, while perhaps not the equal to their lighter skinned neighbors technologically or culturally, they were certainly an intelligent and independent people. At times they constituted a threat or physical challenge and at other times a resource for assistance and strength. From their association with the Indians around Mormon Station the Logan family, and Jesse in particular had learned a great deal. Jesse had learned how to stalk game, how to survive the fierce storms that occasionally swept down out of the Sierra Mountains, and how to tan the hides of the game they had taken, a skill upon which his old friend Fall had expanded and the family had made use of just recently. These and other valuable lessons, if nothing else would, afforded these people a level of respect — stature not enjoyed by the African people in the east, but denied them, Jesse thought, only because their captors kept them in a condition of subjugation. Through all this, his friend Fall had been an intermediary and interpreter.

Jesse had not received much of a formal education, but he was a student of human behavior and a willing one at that. He studied, he explored, he analyzed and he asked questions. He had received some literary education from his mother, who had saved the family bible and other books on their way west, and he and his grandfather Kellar seemed meant for each other intellectually. From the time Jesse stepped through the door of the Kellar home, he and Henry Kellar, who had been named for his own grandfather, had a relationship and an exchange of views that challenged them both.

His grandfather, while perhaps taller, reminded Jesse of Ben Jones for whom Jesse had developed such an attachment back at Mormon Station. Their personal qualities were similar and they even shared some similar mannerisms. His grandmother was simply an older version of his mother, and Jesse would sit sometimes in awe of the characteristics these women shared. Their calm sense of determination, their caring concern for their friends and family, their composure, their grace, their generosity, and a host of other qualities set them apart from the norm as a source of strength for their families.

The public schools in Tennessee were developing gradually under the urging of Governor Andrew Johnson, and Jesse was enrolled in school in Elizabethton as soon as he arrived, in keeping with his mother's wishes. He was started in what was liberally termed the seventh grade but because of both his size and his level of intelligence and knowledge he was pushed forward quickly. Though he felt awkward at first because of his size, he was soon placed in the ninth grade, only one year behind his peers of the same age and a year later was advanced to the group about his own age.

In the ninth grade he was to encounter a teacher who would make all grade level designations immaterial. Mr. Putnam nominally assigned to teach mathematics, literature, and history took it upon himself to further Jesse's learning through all the subjects available. Mr. Putnam lived in Doe River Cove, only a short distance from Kellars Crossing, was a friend of his grandparents, and took a keen interest in Jesse's education. After the first few months at Grammar School in Elizabethton, he assumed the responsibility to provide tutoring for Jesse that allowed him to gain sufficient education even beyond the necessity of attending formal classes.

Meanwhile, John Kellar, Jesse's uncle who had taken over the family business from his father, took Jesse into the family hardwood and lumber business, complimenting the education he was gaining through the services of Mr. Putnam. The business was thriving in the Great Smokey Mountains. The completion of the Virginia and East Tennessee Railroad around 1850 had established the region as a source for the hardwood required for the furniture businesses in Virginia and North Carolina. There had even been some small shops set up in Johnson and Sullivan Counties for the production of furniture, but since it was cheaper to ship milled lumber than finished furniture, these shops were not particularly profitable.

While he knew East Tennessee as the place of his birth, Jesse did not begin to appreciate the character of the land and its people until those few short years he spent there in his late teens. The people were so committed to their surroundings that he found it difficult to believe that his father and mother would uproot themselves to travel west. As it was with Jesse's family, the people of East Tennessee were an unpretentious but intelligent breed. They were gifted and amiable people, but far less ambitious in their pursuit of wealth than their lowland cousins. While not particularly rich by contemporary standards, they were well enough to do without being given to extravagance, well-read without intellectual snobbery, and well-bred while sufficiently settled in their surroundings to entertain plain tastes.

As Governor Andrew Johnson, himself a tailor by trade, often phrased it, the yeoman or 'mechanic' class, the people who owned their own farms or small businesses or who worked for others for wages, were deprived of a fair chance to win a decent living by the fact that they were actually in competition with the slave. The Kellars owned their own mills and many of their forests, and sought help from no one except their own friends and family, and occasionally from neighbors whom they hired by the day. At times, Henry Kellar hired freed black men or even slaves from his neighbors, paying the day rate of ten cents to the owner. Actually, slavery was just too cumbersome a policy for Henry Kellar.

The United States and particularly East Tennessee were experiencing dynamic and mystifying changes and inventions in the 1850's, and in his discussions with Grandpa Kellar and also with Mr. Putnam, Jesse was intrigued by the intellectual challenges with which they tested him. The question of government as a component of freedom was the subject of discussion more than once. The "Republican Experiment" as Mr. Putnam called the young country had to function by popular consent of the people, but to do so, the minority, no matter how tempestuous, was required to accept the will of the majority, no matter how benign. When a law was passed by the legislative process, it became the rule to which all were expected to adhere. The executive officers of the state or nation were authorized to enforce those rules and the judicial officers decided on disputes and misunderstandings.

According to the lessons taught in his history classes, the young man learned that slavery had been practiced in all ages in almost all countries, over the course of centuries. It had been a practice from as far back as biblical times to take prisoners during times of war and conscript them into a work force for service to the victors. Little by little, however, this practice was being abandoned, except in some of the more primitive countries of the world — and in the southern part of the United States of America. In the United States, however, there were many people who disapproved of slavery, even to the point of agitating for its abolishment. As time went by, the influence of these people became a point of contention and even in the secluded regions of East Tennessee, their voices could be heard and their influence felt. Even in East Tennessee, the events that eventually produced the Civil War were swirling around them.

The Missouri Compromise, which, in 1820, had been hailed by southerners as a permanent solution to the 'slave state' question, had been nullified in just the past year by the Kansas-Nebraska Act, which had been passed through Congress, also with the strong support of the southern states. Now, states when chartered by the federal government could select their own status as a slave or non-slave state. As a result, emigrants poured into any territory that was destined to become a state, and whoever got the most voters — slave or non-slave — into the state at voting time, won the prize. As it was easier for people unencumbered by slaves to pick up and move to the new territory, the slave-holding interests in Kansas lost the political race.

⸻ ((●)) ⸻

There was also one other citizen of East Tennessee, actually Greenville, that distinguished himself, and made a deep and lasting impression on Jesse, not for his cultivated and sophisticated manners, for he was only an amateur at that, but for his concern for the common man. He was the 'statesman tailor', the 'orator mechanic', the Governor. Andrew Johnson, who had pulled himself along by his own efforts, and established himself as a model for all young people in that part of the state, was an unabashed advocate of solidarity with the Union. And though he owned slaves himself, Johnson was critical of that institution as demeaning to the progress and dignity of the free working man, dark or light, who wanted to improve himself through his own effort and acquired skills.

Governor Johnson's daughter, Mary was married to Dan Stover, a neighbor and good friend of Henry Kellar. The governor took frequent opportunities to visit his daughter and in doing so, spent considerable time in conversation with Grandpa Kellar, whom he found to be a stimulating advocate for the cause of the union and opposed to slavery. Johnson, though a plain and simple man, was a veteran debater and often included Jesse in these discussions much to the young man's pleasure and enlightenment.

Johnson had entered Congress from East Tennessee back in 1843 and one of his first efforts when he had got settled in his small rooms in Washington was to sponsor a Homestead Bill. The measure would offer land in the unpopulated parts of the country to anyone who would live on it and work it for a time. The time required would be nominally four to five years, whatever kind of a compromise Johnson and his fellow supporters of the concept could hammer out at the time the bill came to a vote. It was a measure crafted to work for the small yeoman farmer, and was opposed by many plantation owners, including those supporting slavery. The opponents simply felt that the working class, the 'uneducated rabble', if you will, were not the sort of people who should be trusted with either land or the voting privilege that land ownership brought with it.

Elected to the office of Governor of Tennessee in 1852, Johnson was a Democrat in every sense of the word. He favored public education for all, gradual abolition of slavery, homesteading, and the dignity of the 'mechanic' or 'yeoman' classes as the foundation of democracy. While Grandpa Kellar was ordinarily a Whig in his political leanings, under the influence of Dan Stover and Andrew Johnson, he occasionally 'kicked over the traces' and voted Democrat, especially when Johnson was the candidate.

Amidst these challenges to his thinking and reasoning, Jesse watched and evaluated the hostility that seemed to be gripping the nation, but particularly East Tennessee.

His associations with the people his own age were most pleasant. A young man a little older than Jesse, Tom Singleton, adopted Jesse as soon as they met. The school year had already started and once Jesse had adjusted to the class level at which he was to be placed he encountered Tom, who was to make him feel much less like a stranger in his own land.

Elizabethton, where Jesse was enrolled in school was about an hour's ride from Kellars Crossing, and Tom lived in Doe River Cove, almost as far and on the same road as Jesse had to travel. The first day Jesse attended the ninth grade, after he had obtained the books he was to use and had been dismissed for the day, he left the schoolhouse and walked over to where his horse was tied. He adjusted the cinch, mounted his horse, Max, and turned in the direction of home. Tom had been waiting for him, and immediately fell in beside Jesse on the road toward home.

"That's a pretty good looking horse you've got there," Tom commented. "I haven't seen him around here before. Did you bring him from your home?"

"No," Jesse chuckled, "home for me is a lot further than my old horse, Sally could make the trip. I just bought him in Choates Ford when I got off the boat. That's a pretty good looking horse you're riding, too."

"Oh, he's alright. I have another horse at home that I usually ride, but he was out in the pasture this morning and I didn't want to go after him. This one's 'Rack'. He's actually my pa's horse. Where'd you come from?"

"I came from Utah Territory, actually Carson County, or Nevada they seem to have named it for whenever it becomes a state. It's clear west of here about two thousand miles."

"Wow! That is really a long ways. How'd you get here?" Tom was impressed.

Jesse went on to give him a brief description of the trip he had just completed, and he was surprised himself at the various means of transport and the change of scene he had gone through. He omitted the encounters with some of the people he'd met along the way, as he thought it would sound as though he was trying to impress Tom, which was not the way he wanted to approach a new friendship.

"That's really something," Tom was still impressed. "Were you born out there in that country?"

"No, I was actually born right here in the Watauga Valley, I think it was not far from where I'm living now. My father and mother decided to move west when I was little, and I'm just coming back here after," — he thought for a moment, "after about eleven or twelve years, I guess."

The conversation continued over the course of the ride, each young man exploring the other's character and personality. Presently, Tom asked, "Do you hunt, much?"

"I sure do, whenever I get the chance," Jesse responded enthusiastically.

"We've got plenty of game in these parts, deer, 'coons, foxes, squirrels.

"That sounds great. When do you go?" Jesse asked.

"Well, we'll be going out after deer as soon as the first snow falls. The leaves are down and they're out browsing right now. Haven't you seen any yet?"

"Just a couple of doe and their fawns the other day."

"Well, the bucks are out there. I saw a big six pointer yesterday."

"Do you take the does around here?" Jesse asked. "I know some places they don't hunt does 'cause it knocks down the herd."

"We don't usually take the does, but if we do shoot one, we don't just leave her there. She's still food for the table."

"I used to be pretty good hunting deer. They were a real nuisance around the crops back home and my brother used to make me stay out at night and early in the morning to keep them out of our fields. We'd take the does, bucks and all. One would do just as much damage to the hay crops as the next, and they play the devil with corn."

"That's the same around here. We can ask Mr. Frye out on Laurel Fork Road if we could hunt his field. I'm sure he'll go for it." Tom suggested.

"Is it that the big house on the right about a quarter mile before you get to Kellars Crossing? He does a lot of business with my grandpa. I'll stop and see him on my way home. When should we go?"

"Right after the first snow. We can go out before, but it's easier afterwards. They're easier to see. But you check, anyway, OK? Tell him there'd be maybe three or four of us."

By this time they were in Doe River Cove, at Tom's home, and he stopped in front of his house. "It was good getting to know you, Jesse," he said. "I'd been wanting to meet you ever since you got to town. You let me know what Mr. Frye says. 'See you tomorrow."

Jesse gestured his goodbye and turned his horse toward Kellars Crossing. A few minutes later, he stopped at the Frye home. Mr. Frye was out in the field just before you get to the house.

"Mr. Frye," Jesse said, "Hello, I'm Jesse Logan. I just live over at Kellars Crossing."

"Yes. I know your family. What can I do for you, young feller?" Mr. Frye was happy to take a break from taking up the winter squash.

"Mr. Frye, Would it be possible for a few of us fella's from school to hunt your place for deer when the snow comes?"

They went over the particulars of the proposal and agreed the boys would be allowed to hunt. Mr. Frye went on to another subject. "I knew you pa. He was a good doctor and we surely hated to see him and your ma leave the valley. They were fine people. It's nice to be able to meet one of their young'uns."

"Thank you, Sir. It's nice to meet you, and it's nice to be back here in Tennessee. It's a real pretty part of the country. I liked Nevada, but this is pretty, too."

"You're a big'un. How old are you?"

"I'm fifteen, Mr. Frye," Jesse said.

"You look some older, except for the yeller hair. You must get that from your ma."

"You knew my parents?"

"My boy Peter sparked your ma, before your daddy came out from Jonesborough and stole her away."

"No fooling! It's hard to think of my folks as anything but, well, just my folks, but I'd like to hear about what they were like when they were young. I hardly even remember my Pa. But, anyway, I'd better be going. I told my grandma I'd be home by sundown, and it's getting on past that by some little bit."

The next day, Jesse caught up with Tom just as he was leaving Doe River Cove for school. "Tom," he said, "Mr. Frye said it'd be alright to hunt his place, but my grandpa said we could hunt his place, too."

As they rode toward Elizabethton, a third boy joined them. Jesse had not met him before, but it appeared he was on his way to school, also. "Jesse, do you know Eli Morgan?" Tom asked as the boy rode alongside.

"Nice to meet you, Eli," Jesse said. "I'm Jesse Logan."

Eli was a sandy haired youth, perhaps a year older than Jesse. He rode a mule, and his hair wanted combing, but he had a ready smile and from atop his mule he reached out his hand toward Jesse. "Good to meet you, Jesse. Where 'you from?"

It was a standard question. It seemed that the people of the valley, while not unfriendly, were curious about newcomers. It was not an easy society to break into because there weren't many people coming to the region and the folks just weren't accustomed to the experience of accepting strangers. The families of those who had settled there went back many years, and very few new people now sought residence in the mountains.

When Jesse told him how he happened to be there, Eli didn't say anything, but pulled a stick of dried meat from his pocket and offered it to Jesse. Jesse took it and nodded his thanks. This was acceptance, he supposed.

"Jesse and me are thinking about going hunting on his Grandpa's place after the first snow, Eli. 'Want to come along?" Tom asked.

"Be just fine with me, Tom," Eli responded. "Alright with you, Jesse?"

"Just fine. What kind of rifle do you shoot?" he asked.

"I got a old musket that shoots perty good," Eli replied. "It ain't much, but it's good enough to shoot those durn abolitionists that have been stirrin' up all the trouble up here. I heard they's been down t' Knoxville in numbers that'd make your head swim. You know that-there Governor Johnson and Judge Hyder and some of those buzzards have been just itching to free the Niggros and have us all go to work for them!"

Jesse wondered why such a subject had popped up in the midst of a friendly conversation, but he maintained his silence on the subject.

"Why're you bringin' that up, Eli? Tom said impatiently. "What did the slaves ever do for you? Your family ain't got any."

"I just don't like anyone coming in here and telling us how to run our own lives," Eli complained. "It's hard enough with all the stuff we got to do to satisfy the gov'mint without them durn ab'litionists coming around setting up new rules we have to live by. What about you, Jesse? You're from out west and come to take up livin' here. How do you feel about freein' the Niggros?"

"It seems like they're human beings, just like the rest of us and I'll be durned if I can figure out why one man should own another. It don't make sense to me. It really doesn't. A few months ago, I was working with a dark-skinned sort of man who I think was probably Negro, and he not only saved my life, he died doing it."

"What are you trying to feed us, Jesse? Are you sayin' some Niggro got hisself killed jes' tryin' to save yer life? Where was that at?" Eli demanded.

"I'm just telling you, I had a friend who was a black man and he got shot in a fight with some Indians but first, he killed some of them and probably saved my life. That's what I'm sayin'."

"Jesse Logan, the great Indian fighter? You want us to believe you're some kind of Davy Crockett out there killing bears and Injuns like some kind of heero?"

"Eli, I don't care what you believe. It don't matter whether you believe me or not. What happened, happened, and whether you believe it don't change anything." Jesse was getting a little upset at himself for getting drawn into the discussion and for giving the impression that he was bragging, or worse yet, lying about his exploits 'out west'.

"Jesse Logan, the great Indian fighter," Eli shrieked. "Him get great wampum. Him kill many braves with bare hands. 'Great Indian fighter. Ugh."

"Jesse, did you really get into a fight with Indians?" Tom asked.

"I'd rather not talk about it, Tom," Jesse said, upset with himself for mentioning the matter.

Eli Morgan was one grade behind Jesse and two years behind Tom, but they saw him occasionally between classes and whenever he saw Jesse, he broke out in some kind of mock Indian dance or made some other ridiculous comment to tease Jesse. Soon it was as though the element with which Eli associated, his brother Arthur and a few others, developed an alienation and polarity with those students Tom, Jesse, Paul Venable, Adam Gainfield, Alf Gahagan, and a few other friends that chummed around together. Also, they agreed to some extent along the lines associated with the principle of secession and, to some degree, slavery.

———————————————

Another of Jesse's classmates in the ninth grade was a young man named Sid Coster. He was pleasant and somewhat comical in his manner, but usually showed himself to be a solid thinker on the subjects they encountered in school. He had a good grasp of arithmetic and reading and was also good in history. He and Jesse studied together quite often, as Jesse felt he needed someone with a good grip on the basics.

Sid was somewhat divided on the principles of secession. He supported the idea of the Union staying together, but was disturbed at the direction he saw some of the northern abolitionist groups moving. He felt they were going to take control of the federal government and make it difficult for the slave states to survive and handle their own affairs, including slavery. He was a supporter of slavery, though Jesse did not know why, since his father was a teamster, owning his own wagon, eight or ten good draught horses and but two slaves. Of the latter he complained regularly that they were of no value to him, they just didn't understand the fine points of the drayage business. It was often these two, Joshua and Simeon that Jesse's uncle, John Kellar, hired for day work in the lumber mill or in the forest. Jesse wondered first, how they could be expected to qualify in a commercial enterprise as they were absolutely without any education, and secondly, why Mr. Coster didn't just sell them.

Sid was patient in his explanation of the situation with his father and the slaves. "You have to understand, Jesse," he'd say, "ownin' slaves in this part of the country ain't just for the benefit of the work you can get out of them. There's a certain 'social standing' that goes along with owning slaves. If you ain't got any slaves and jus' works fer a livin' day after day, people looks down on you jus like you was no better that a Niggro, yourself."

At the same time, knowing Henry Kellar's opposition to slavery, Sid tried to be somewhat circumspect in his explanation, not wanting to appear to be critical of Jesse's grandfather. "You know, Jesse, we need them and they need us. Why, where would these poor iggern't people be if they didn't have us white folks to look out for 'em?"

"They'd be back in Africa where they were before some of our people stole them, Sid, that's where they'd be."

"Now, you know that's not so, Jesse. They was mostly captured by their own people and sent over here to America. At least they've been given a warm place to stay and are fed pretty good. In Africa they'd probably all be dead or put in chains."

Jesse grinned at the image that the comment conjured. "And what makes you think American chains are better to a black man than African chains where he'd be among his neighbors, friendly or otherwise, Sid? I tell you it probably don't make a whit of difference to him, except over there he's more likely to escape and get back to his own people. And another thing, I don't think it does any of us any good to lord it over another person, just because he isn't of our color or race. God just didn't make us that way."

"There you go, Jesse. What do you know about any plan God has for them or us? Don't you think it's just possible that God put us here to protect them dark folks? After all, those people had just as many centuries to develop learning and culture as our kinfolk did, and what good did it do them? I think maybe God put us where we are to bring these people out of iggernce and give them some learning."

"Then why ain't we doing it, Sid? What learning have we given the black people? How much can your pa's slaves read or write?"

"Well, that's another question, Jesse," Sid became defensive. "If we eddicated ours, they'd get uppity ideas and run for the north, and then my pa 'ud not only be out the price of two slaves, he'd be criticized all around for breakin' the law. You see, these laws against eddicating the slaves are made for good reason. If they git too smart, they go running for the north and agitate the abolitionists up there. And you know yourself there's a whole bunch of them northern agitators that'd like nothing better than to come down here and tell us how to run our business. There's enough of that going on already, what with that Senator Sumner and his like."

"Just you think on this, Jesse. Suppose God had wanted them black folks to be independent. Just suppose. Isn't it possible He put them in this country to try a little experiment? Over in Africa they're just huntin' an' fishin' an' fightin' with each other, an' not learnin' much at all. Then He puts them here to try to see what would happen to them if they was exposed to the culture of the white races an' He finds out it just ain't working. He lets us go ahead with keepin' them safe from each other by providin' homes for them and havin' them pay their keep by workin' fer their masters. Doesn't that make sense?"

"It might, Sid, if there wasn't some of those same Negro people who had been given a chance at an education and raised in the north or west and made fine responsible people, hard working and God fearing, and them just as much the same blood as the folks we see down in the south who are supposed to be so backward they can't find their way from the house to the barn."

Mr. Putnam saw all that was happening, and though he maintained a strict neutrality on the question of slavery, he managed to spend extra time with Jesse to give him the benefit of additional tutoring to advance him in his schoolwork. By the time Jesse completed his first year at Elizabethton, he was well abreast of his age group in learning and was taking classes with Tom, Paul and Sid.

Jesse and Tom and one or two other boys did go hunting that winter, and were successful in bringing down ample game to assist the food supply for their families. The musket Jesse had brought with him on the trip from Utah was one of those taken from the marauding Indians on the Humboldt River. It was even decorated in a manner typical of the Indian customs but he kept it at home, always careful to borrow a gun from his grandfather or Uncle John when he went hunting. Never, for a long, long time, did Jesse make reference to his experiences out west.

History is replete with examples of rural, mountainous regions exercising fierce independence from the prevailing attitude of their surrounding lowland compatriots, and East Tennessee was no different. Parson W. G. Brownlow, Editor of the 'Knoxville Whig', while he maintained a position of favor toward slavery, provided a great inspiration to the people of the region in the cause of the union. So did Andrew Johnson, who had been recently re-elected as Governor, though he was a Democrat, an avowed adversary of Parson Brownlow, and owned a few slaves himself. Both Johnson and Brownlow were citizens of East Tennessee and their membership in opposing political parties and parallel positions on slavery and the union was just one example of the political potpourri that existed in the region.

The idea of slavery, as Henry Kellar had discussed, was not very attractive to the people of East Tennessee, and the idea of seceding from the union simply to preserve an unpopular way of life was particularly unpleasant. Though the records are mixed, and it cannot with accuracy be determined, it has been variously estimated that during the war which was to ensue, the people of East Tennessee, though it was eventually identified as a 'Confederate state', furnished between thirty and forty thousand troops to the cause of the Union. Since very few of the troops formed up into discreet East Tennessee units, the number is lost to history. Even so, there stands a testimony to the commitment of these people who were willing to defy the authority of their state to preserve the Union and their reverence and veneration for the "Old Flag."

On the other hand, there were still those in Carter and Johnson counties and the other East Tennessee counties who, for whatever reason, strongly supported the cause of secession, and expressed themselves by harassing the people whom, they claimed, were legitimate targets. History gives us dozens of incidents wherein small bands of these 'home guard' terrorized neighborhoods and towns in the name of secession. It may be speculated that these roughneck bands or those similar bands from the opposing viewpoint were no more than ruffians and thieves acting under color of devotion toward one side or the other. Depending on one's ultimate perspective or the cause for which they or their friends were aligning themselves, it may also be argued that they were just patriotic privateers, doing whatever they could to further the cause of 'freedom' as they themselves defined the term.

Tensions grew through the next few years and debates and canvasses were conducted contesting the comparative merits of both issues. Among those exponents there was Andrew Johnson, accomplished apologist and the idol of his party, and there was also Representative Thomas A. R. Nelson who was a prominent Whig leader and was elected to Congress from the First District of Tennessee. He was a lawyer of high attainment, distinguished for native ability, learning and eloquence, and a strong advocate of adhering to the cause of unity among the original states.

In addition to these two distinguished gentlemen espousing the cause of the Union were William B. Carter, his cousin Nathaniel Taylor, Connally Trigg, Oliver Temple, R. R. Butler, John Baxter and many others. The question of 'Separation, or No Separation' was thoroughly discussed throughout East Tennessee.

Andrew Johnson and Thomas Nelson were regarded as two of the ablest representatives of the two old parties, and they made a joint canvass of East Tennessee in behalf of "No Separation," and, later, "No Representation" in the Confederate Congress. It is not strange that these two distinguished citizens, having boldly espoused the cause of the Union, should attract attention, and wield a great influence in molding the sentiment of the people of East Tennessee.

Young people usually adopt the political perspective of those they admire and particularly those they are close to. Jesse's family was unanimously against both secession and slavery, the former strongly and the latter firmly but not especially passionately. The philosophies instilled in Jesse by people such as his grandfather, Mr. Putnam and Governor Johnson led him to the conclusion that slavery was unfair to both master and servant. It imposed an imbalance of competition on the economy and it denied to the indentured the dignity extended to others in the same society.

In 1857 there was an incident, which seemed to focus and underscore the disdain some of the people of the region shared against the institution of slavery. Eleven years earlier, in 1846, a man from Missouri, a slave state, took with him when he traveled to Nebraska, his servant, a black man named Dred Scott. Nebraska, still a territory, was governed by Federal law, which prohibited slavery. Scott escaped from his 'owner' and tried to claim his freedom in the "Free Territory", but was captured and returned. Then, in his behalf, locals from the territory, abolitionist in sentiment, assisted him in suing to nullify the return on the grounds of federal law prevailing in the territory, which did not recognize slavery.

The case rose ponderously to the Supreme Court and there, based on the United States Constitution, Dred Scott made history. The Fifth Amendment of the United States Constitution prohibits any person being deprived of life, liberty, or property "without due process of law". In this case, Supreme Court, under Chief Justice Roger Taney (he preferred that the name be pronounced 'tawny') held in its decision that a law that simply prohibited slavery in a territory, did not rise to the "constitutional level" necessary to "deprive" Scott's master of the ownership of his "property", namely Dred Scott. The decisions further held, essentially, that all blacks, slaves as well as free, were not, and could never become, citizens of the United States. The court also declared the 1820 Missouri Compromise unconstitutional, thus permitting slavery in all of the country's states and territories.

Newspaper articles on both sides of the issue proclaimed the fairness or unfairness of the decision. The Albany, New York Evening Journal, a newspaper of decidedly Republican stripe, declared in an editorial March 7, 1857 "It is no novelty to find the Supreme Court following the lead of the Slavery Extension party, to which most of its members belong." Then, on March 9, it followed up with "... a new shackle for the North will be handed to the servile Supreme Court, to rivet upon us." On March 10, they again complained, "Judge Taney requests the American people to believe that the framers of the Constitution did not know their own minds." And, "... the half million of men and women paralysed by the atheistic logic of the decision of the case of Dred Scott...." that the decision was, "... a blot upon our National character abroad, and a long-remembered shame at home."

And on March 19 the Journal editor, Thurlow Weed further pointed out, referring to the members of the Taney Court that, "Five of its nine silk gowns are worn by Slaveholders."

Some of the pro-slavery newspapers were equally strident in their support of the Supreme Court decision. The Richmond, Virginia Enquirer, on March 10, opined that justice had been ultimately upheld ... "in contradistinction to and in repudiation of the diabolical doctrines inculcated by factionists and fanatics; and that too by a tribunal of jurists, as learned, impartial and unprejudiced as perhaps the world has ever seen."

The Enquirer toned down its rhetoric by March 17, in its editorial, still supporting the idea that slaves were merely 'property', saying simply, "If they would let us alone and leave slavery to the states, and to the same protection and privileges enjoyed by all other property under the Constitution, the agitation of the question would come to an end on the instant". But, it seems, the slavery question was not just left to the states. The Supreme Court decision left the door open to allow slavery throughout the nation and the abolitionists were enraged.

Even the Charleston, South Carolina Mercury, situated in that hotbed of hotheads said, on March 27, ". . . we shall acquire, by the decision of the Supreme Court, not one right more than they granted to us before . . . not one foot of slave territory more than we would have acquired without It." Fine sentiments, but once the Roger Taney bell had rung in favor of universal slavery, it would be highly unlikely that the question would ever come to an end, and it was clear to many that slave territory could now be spread across the nation.

Meetings among the opposing partisans were frequent, and though they seldom went to the extent of turning neighbor against neighbor through violence, the attitudes of the opposing factions were well and widely known.

"The worst of it is," Grandpa Kellar maintained, "in a way, Taney is right. The Constitution is the highest law we have in this country, and anything that runs contrary to that law loses its effect. If — and I say this with all due reservation, — if we are to regard black people as property, then what they said and did was proper. The contradiction most people see in the argument is that people, black or white, ain't just property. That same Fifth Amendment to the Constitution forbids 'any person' from bein' deprived of their liberty, but that's another question."

"But, why, Grandpa," Jesse would argue, "when the same government that makes the law is the government that wrote the constitution, then why can't an anti-slavery law hold up?"

"Jesse, this is certainly a lesson in civics," Henry Kellar responded, and went on to explain the order of America's laws and their application to each other. "The thing that scares me is that this decision, carried to its ultimate conclusion, can spread slavery all over the country and make a shambles of our state system of government."

"And here's the rub," he chuckled, "the 'states rights' advocates down here in the south are applauding this decision, but you can see that what it is, is a real blow — a real severe blow — to the sovereignty of our states. Now, any law that any state passes can be struck down by a majority of them 'Justices' in the Supreme Court and states' rights don't mean a hoot. It's a two-edged sword, Jesse, my boy, but many of the so-called supporters of states' rights are so caught up in the "victory" that has been won for slavery, they don't fathom the deeper implications of the issue."

Jesse wasn't sure he understood the implications at all. The situation, in his mind, boiled down to one thing; slavery. If it weren't for the abolitionists in the north agitating for the control or elimination of the slave-holding oligarchy in the south, the slave states would have no issue such as 'States Rights', at least not to the extent that they would threaten to split the nation. On the other hand, if it weren't for the 'peculiar institution' being maintained in the south, there would be no reason for the abolitionist movement to exist.

In his Social Studies lessons, Mr. Putnam had tried to explain the comparative types of government popular at the time throughout the world. The United States of America, he explained were a collection of states, or at first colonies, that the people thereof decided to combine into a common country they called a republic, or more precisely, a 'democratic republic'.

"We the people of the United States of America, in order to form a more perfect Union, — the Preamble to the Constitution begins," Mr. Putnam had reminded them. "Not 'we the people of the State of Virginia, South Carolina, New York, etc., in order to form a more perfect combination of countries", but — in order to form a more perfect UNION! Then they went ahead and wrote a constitution for a republic based on democratic ideals. What does that mean — a democratic republic?"

Sid Coster raised his hand. "It means we have a nation where the people vote for its legislators and then the legislators make the laws."

"Is everybody happy with that description?" Mr. Putnam asked. No one spoke. "Is what Mr. Coster just said satisfactory to your understanding of what a democratic republic is, Mr. Singleton?"

Tom Singleton squirmed in his seat and grinned, "Yes, Sir," he replied. "That's what I think."

"Do you agree, Mr. Logan?" Mr. Putnam asked of Jesse.

"Well, yes, Sir," Jesse replied, "Except not all the people vote for the legislators, I don't think. The Indians don't vote, and the Negroes don't either."

"You're right, Mr. Logan," Mr. Putnam responded, "and neither do our women, but that's a different issue for a different time. The description Mr. Coster gave was right out of the book. Someone has been doing some studying, I think."

Jesse, who was sitting behind Sid, nudged him with his foot and whispered, "Toady, Coster," in a teasing voice.

Mr. Putnam couldn't hear what was said, but he didn't miss the implication. "Mr. Logan, perhaps you'd like to explain to the class what it means to disobey the laws of the country." Jesse looked blank.

"I mean, Mr. Logan, what happens to a person or a group of people that go against the laws that the people, through their legislature, have passed."

"I don't understand what you mean, Sir," Jesse mumbled. "I guess they go to jail, or to court, or something like that."

"But, Mr. Logan, just suppose the legislature of a state passes a law that — for instance, — assigns a certain tract of land to the construction of a railroad and a town through which this railroad is to be built takes over the land for the construction of a town hall. Can the state government demand that the building be removed?"

"Yes, Sir. I believe they can."

"Of course they can. But what if that town, or their elected counsel, scratches its collective municipal head and says, 'We want that town hall right where it is and we're not going to move it. We'll just form our own state and those fellows can just build their railroad around our state.' What would happen then?"

"Wouldn't a town or place like that have to get approval from the government of the state or of Washington to do a thing like that?" Logan asked, trying to envision a town scratching its head.

"Precisely, Mr. Logan, precisely. 'We the people of the United States of America' — have created a system of government that is set up to deal with problems like that. Does anyone here remember what we learned about the Whiskey Rebellion? What was that all about, Mr. Logan?"

"Sir, I missed that one," Jesse said, raising a chuckle from his classmates. "I think that was the time my Uncle Earnest set up such a fuss at Aunt Edna for hiding his jug." at which the class broke out in uncontrolled laughter.

"But I think, Sir," he was trying now to recover the teacher's good graces, "that was back in about 1790 when some farmers got upset with the central government. They decided to try to act like a separate country, I think, and refused to go along with the tax the government was putting on whiskey and some other stuff they were producing on their farms. I guess they actually tried to secede from the Union. President Washington called out the Militia and settled things down. My grandpa told me that the farmers all moved to South Carolina." The last comment was directed at the neighboring state, which some of the local folks, in a good-natured way, accused of being radical secessionists, and drew another laugh from the class.

"Mr. Logan, you certainly have a way of rewriting history, but your premise is essentially correct, and actually, the leader of that rebellion, Mr. David Bradford, did move, but it was to Florida. Florida was, at that time under the control of Spain, as you know, and he escaped to avoid capture and possible prison. And incidentally, Mr. Logan, it was in 1794, not 1790, but it happened over a period of years, not unlike what we see here in the south, over a different matter. Many of the citizens' grievances were real and very important to them personally, but the result was that the rule of the majority of the people of the country was upheld by the executive branch of the government. The revolt was subdued and the people were obliged to take their complaints to the government through peaceful means, rather than through the precipitous process of secession."

————)(◉)(————

There was something else of significance that happened with respect to Jesse's education that year. A man named Hinton R. Helper wrote a book called 'The Impending Crisis in the South'. Mr. Helper was a North Carolinian and his book was an emphatic but pathetic cry for a correction in the economic policies in the south, particularly their dependence on slavery. In its first chapter, the author provided statistical evidence ascribing to the institution of slavery, between the adoption of the Constitution in 1789 and the time his book was written in 1857, a depressing effect on the economic prosperity of the slave states. He showed by a statistical comparison that one region of the United States (the north) had managed "to rise to a degree of almost unexampled power and eminence", while the other, the southern states, had actually sunk into what he described as, ". . . a state of comparative imbecility and obscurity."

While written in a somewhat antagonistic voice, the book powerfully demonstrated that a heavy dependency on slave labor was probably the worst thing that could have happened to the south with respect to their economic growth vis-a-vis the northern states. It robbed the south of the very people that were the strength and support of business progress, the inventor, the skilled craftsman, the private entrepreneur, the yeoman innovator. There was simply no room for such people among the oligarchy of the south, and if they wished to pursue their chosen field, they had to move to another country or to a northern state. The slave owner, from the porch of his mansion, sipping his julep and gazing over his vast holdings, had no use for the tinker, the watchmaker, the silversmith, the inventor. The plantation owner was too caught up in maintaining status quo to concern himself with industrialization or technological development.

Governor Johnson had all but memorized the book, using its arguments to prove his contention that the working, or 'yeoman' classes in the south were suffering by being deprived of the training needed to sustain a technical work force. He contended that the slave owners were more inclined to have technical work, such as blacksmithing, carpentry and masonry, as well as the newly emerging trades of electricity, machinery and plumbing done by poorly trained but cheap slave labor, than by skilled 'mechanics'. He went on to repeat points made in Helper's book that the south was suffering from a lack of manufacturing skills as a result of those goods being more readily and often more cheaply available from the neighboring states to the north, who utilized 'paid labor' and were therefor able to also make use of their abilities to read, write, and utilize mathematics, something that the 'Southern Oligarchy' denied their slaves.

In his book Helper claimed unswerving allegiance to the south, but felt that the institution of slavery was creating an absolute dependence on the services supplied by the north and the southern states were slipping into an abyss of reliance on others to provide the necessities of life. "We want Bibles, brooms, buckets and books, and we go to the North; we want pens, ink, paper, wafers and envelopes, and we go to the North; we want shoes, hats, handkerchiefs, umbrellas and pocket knives, and we go to the North; we want furniture, crockery, glassware and pianos, and we go to the North; we want toys, primers, school books, fashionable apparel, machinery, medicines, tombstones, and a thousand other things, and we go to the North for them all." He wrote and went on to say "All the world sees, or ought to see, that in a commercial, mechanical, manufactural, financial, and literary point of view, we are as helpless as babes."

Governor Johnson further contended that education, one of his strongly emphasized programs was also suffering under the slave economy. According to his claims, rich slave owners were providing no education for their slaves, which was not unexpected but which spread the needs for education over such vast geographic regions that it became too expensive to maintain schools in the small local communities. He also pointed out that many were inclined to send their own children to private schools, have them tutored, or send them north for an education. They would rather do this than have them attend school with the children of the poorer working-class whites, a class that H.R. Helper referred to as the "second degree of slavery", making the public schools less economical since there were not enough children to justify their existence. Jesse, both from personal contact with Governor Johnson and from his own education and observation, was deeply impressed by these arguments.

"We're fortunate, here in the Watauga Valley," Mr. Putnam advised the class, "that we have so few slaves in our community that the education system is able to function, since the children of school age are also those who are being sent to school by their parents. Imagine, if you will, a community that is composed fifty percent black people, people who, by law, are not able to send their children to school. That would mean that there would be only half as many students in this school and we would be hard pressed to justify keeping the school open."

During the election year of 1858, an Illinois lawyer named Abraham Lincoln, whose distant cousin, Mordecai Lincoln was a magistrate in nearby Greenville, summed up the feelings of many in the region. In one of his speeches reprinted in Parson Brownlow's newspaper, Mr. Lincoln challenged the position of many of the "Mugwumps" who seemed to feel that there was no philosophical conflict with the idea of having some states with laws condoning and some outlawing slavery. And yet in the middle of all this stood the decision of Chief Justice Roger Taney and the United States Supreme Court allowing a slave owner to maintain 'ownership' of a slave whether he be in either class of state or even in a US territory, all of which Congress had declared to be free from slavery. Lincoln, in his speech was quoted, "A house divided against itself cannot stand. I believe this Government cannot endure permanently half slave and half free. As I would not be a slave, so would I not be a master. This expresses my idea of democracy."

This was, perhaps, an abstract concept, and bore little relevance in the minds of the people with slaves of their own, except that later it became a point of contention implying, at least to the slaveholders, that Lincoln was actually in favor of a split between the North and South. They considered the institution of slavery to be a 'sacred right and duty', and considered their slaves to be legitimate personal property first, and incapable of caring for themselves in any event. The statement, however, provided a rallying point for the pro-slavery interests a scant two years later when that same Abraham Lincoln was elected President of the United States. But in 1858, with little more than a second thought on the subject, Jesse, relying on the intelligence and sophistication of the public figures with whom he had the closest association, found slavery a thoroughly unattractive institution.

It was in this framework that he developed his thinking as a young adult. It was also within the framework of this mindset that he watched national events unfold. The caning of radical abolitionist Senator Charles Sumner by equally radical secessionist Representative Preston Brooks on the floor of the US Senate occurred in May during his first year in school at Elizabethton. It made him wonder what was wrong with some of his southern neighbors. In October 1859 a Kansas farmer named John Brown staged a raid on the Federal Arsenal at Harpers Ferry, Virginia, ostensibly hoping to foment a rebellion among the Negroes and Jesse also had to wonder about the judgment of some of the people opposing slavery and their sense of reason. Also, in 1859, Governor Johnson was replaced by a new man, Isham Harris, whom Grandpa Kellar claimed was likely to lead the state on a closer road to secession, should the issue come to that point.

Discussing these conflicting issues of logic with his grandfather, Jesse found that Henry Kellar was no more help in explaining some of the vicissitudes of human nature than anyone else.

"Jesse," Grandpa Kellar would say, "sometimes I say to myself 'Well —,' and then sometimes I just don't know what to say. The best thing for us to try to do is to maintain a good relationship with our neighbors and let them big-wig greenhorns fight it out among themselves."

They laughed together at the foibles of humanity, but the underlying uncertainties made both of them uncomfortable.

In 1860, the presidential election year, four principle candidates were on the Ballot. The newly formed Republican Party named as their candidate Mr. Lincoln. Grandpa Kellar, ever the faithful Whig, supported John Bell, who was not only a Whig, but the only truly national candidate on the ballot. The Democrats being spilt over slavery, elected two candidates, one from the north and one from the south, and in splitting their vote, lost them the election. Other parties, Free Soil, Abolition, Know Nothing, and some other minor factions also fielded some candidates, but were not of any major consideration. John Bell was from Tennessee and was considered by many to be the only candidate who could hold the country together, but the Whig party had lost its former glory and power, and the competing passions of abolition and secession so polarized the nation that his message was lost in the clamor. Bell, among the four major contenders, ran dead last.

So it was that Abraham Lincoln was elected President of the United States and rumors of secession were touched off like fireworks in the south. On December 18, 1860, Senator Johnson delivered his 'Save the Nation' speech in Congress that placed the issue of secession in perspective, giving what many believed good reason for the states to stay together. Nevertheless, two days later, on December 20, the South Carolina Legislature voted to secede from the United States, and the talk around the Watauga Valley was that other states would do the same. On January 9, Mississippi passed a resolution of secession and on January 10, Florida followed suit. Alabama did the same on January 11. It seemed as though many southern states were competing to be the first and fastest in the race to secede.

Among some about the valley there was even talk of Tennessee seceding from the Union. To Jesse this was inconceivable. It didn't make sense to him that a few diehard secessionists as was the case in Carter County could influence the political situation in Tennessee to the point of seceding from the United States. The results of the surveys done by Andrew Johnson and Thomas A. R. Nelson seemed to prove the loyalty of the people of Tennessee to the "Grand Old Union", with all it stood for. In Jesse's mind, with all the trials and suffering his ancestors had experienced, and the commitment the people about him had to the cause of unity, Tennessee could simply not turn its back on the grand republic.

He argued the issue with Sid Coster a time or two, and the discussion always turned out the same. Jesse brought up the argument that if the southern states, six of them by then, were to try to survive on their own, the North, with its overwhelming technological apparatus and its greater population, would bury the south economically and even militarily. Sid claimed that the North was not all that interested in what happened south of the Mason-Dixon Line, and the passionate commitment that the southern people had to their regional interests would prevail in any conflict.

Grandpa Kellar, who had been watching the political situation as much as Jesse, along with their friend Dan Stover, who lived over in Carter's Station, often had occasion to talk to Senator Johnson and the information he passed along was not encouraging for the Unionists of the valley. Having become U. S. Senator in 1859, Andrew Johnson had become one of the nation's leading speakers in staunch support of preserving the Union.

As a senator, though, he had also been in close touch with some of the other political leaders in the country, and he conveyed the impression that secession, if not imminent, was going to be seriously contested throughout the next few months.

———◦((◦))◦———

In the midst of all this difficulty, toward the end of December in 1860, Jesse, having completed his course of studies with Mr. Putnam, was considering returning to his home in Nevada. He broached the subject with his grandmother and grandfather.

"Jesse," Grandpa Kellar said, "as much as we have grown together here and as useful as you have become to us, it seems to me that it is time you gave some thought to getting back to your mama and family in Nevada. You got a good education as your mother wanted. You've spent the last five years here and we've enjoyed your company, but the letters from home tell us you could be useful there, too. What you could do is head back to Cairo and see your brother David and analyze the picture from there. I think you belong out west. While we'd dearly love to have you and your entire family here in the valley maybe that's not in the plan. It is your choice. I've told you many times, 'you have to play the hand you've been dealt'. No one else can play your hand for you."

In January 1861 the Georgia Militia seized the federal arsenal and garrison at Fort Pulaski, and Jesse felt, as did many in his circle of friends and family that war was closing in on them. He decided to follow his grandfather's advice. The rivers were still open and if he set out right away, he thought he could reach Cairo before any of them froze. He said a hurried goodbye to his friends and headed for Middletown where he would catch the down-river boats to Cairo.

Tom Singleton came out to the house to give Jesse a hand in packing up his meager belongings and then rode with him to Middletown to take Jesse's horse back to Kellars Crossing. As they left Kellars Crossing, Jesse's family was out in front of the old house to bid him goodbye. He came out of the house with most of his belongings, his jacket buttoned up to the neck against the cold.

"How come you don't button your jacket straight?" Tom asked when he saw Jesse.

Jesse looked down at the front of his jacket and found that, in his haste, he had secured the front of the jacket one button away from correct. "Oh, it fits me better this way," Jesse said in good humor. Then, pulling his pants around to the side and affecting a limp as though he had one leg shorter than the other and dragging one foot behind him, he made his way over toward Max, his horse, and attempted to mount. Max, though the two of them had been inseparable for the past five years, had other ideas about letting this strange creature near him and began backing away. Amid the laughter of his family, Jesse straightened his trousers and jacket, stood straight, and walked over to Max, calming him with a few gentle strokes to the neck and some soft words. He then secured his saddlebags, mounted the horse and turned toward the north, the road taking him through Doe River Cove, from where he would go north to Middletown on the Holston River.

As the two old friends rode toward Middletown, they did a lot of talking about all sorts of subjects.

"Jesse," Tom asked when they were not more than a mile out of Doe River Cove, "Did you really get into a fight with some Indians where one of your friends was killed?" The concept had been weighing on Tom's mind for over four years and he wanted to resolve any doubts.

Jesse chuckled, "Tom, you've had that on your mind for all these years, haven't you? Why didn't you just come out with it before now?"

"Jesse," Tom responded, "You were so mad at Eli when he jabbed you about being in a fight with the Indians that I was afraid you might take my head off if I mentioned it."

"I know, I know. That first day I met Eli, I really took a liking to him. And then when he got all over me about my getting into a fight with some Indians, I was mad at myself for bringing up the subject in the first place, let alone the way he dogged me about it ever since." He then related to Tom both the incident he was involved in when, at ten years of age he had shot an Indian warrior and again in his sixteenth year when he and Hoke and Fall were heading east with the load of hides and he was in an actual gunfight.

Tom was incredulous. "Jesse, how did you feel when that all happened."

"I threw up, the first time," Jesse laughed. "The second time it was pretty clear in my mind that I was going to have to do some fast shooting or all three of us would be killed. I tell you, Tom, life was cheap out there along those wagon roads among the Indians, the trappers, and the highwaymen, 'specially if it was someone else's life. You know, I couldn't think of anything — past getting the odds against us cut down to somewhere near even. When that happened, the Indians scooted just like they did when my brother rescued me the first time."

Tom said no more on the question, but was obviously turning the matter over in his mind.

"What're you planning to do, Tom," Jesse asked presently. "I know you've been working with your pa on the farm. Is that going to be your life's work or are you planning something else to do?" They had talked these matters over in the past but had never reached resolution.

"Well, you know," Tom announced after a long pause, "one thing I'm thinking about doing is I'm going to join the Masons".

"Hey, that's right. Your twenty-one, now, and they'll let you get into the Masons, won't they?"

"I made an application with Sheriff Simerly last week, and they're going to vote on me tonight. I'm kind of excited. 'You ever think about joining?"

"Of course I've thought about it. My grandpa and Uncle John are both Masons, but I'm only twenty. They say you have to be twenty-one."

"That's right. That's right," Tom said. "Well, maybe you can join a lodge where you're goin' and then someday we can sit in lodge together."

"I don't even know if there is a Masons' lodge in Genoa," Jesse mused. "I'll have to check on that."

"I think we're goin' to have to join the army, from what people are saying around here," Tom ventured after a while.

"I'd be leaning to doin' that, anyway. How do you reckon to go about it?"

"I think I'd go see Judge Nelson or Senator Johnson or some such as them," Tom replied. "There's a Colonel Something-or-other over In Johnson County or — you know, Dan Stover — might give me some advice. I hope it don't come to that, but if it does, I'm ready."

"Me too," Jesse said. "I'd hate to miss something like that. Just think — you get to travel all over the country and you even get paid for it. Maybe they'd even send us to Mexico."

"What for? The fight would be right here." Tom scoffed.

"Yeah, I guess you're right. I can't see how they could have a war right in our own country. Who would be doing the fighting?"

"Well, for starters, I bet that Eli and Arthur Morgan and maybe Sid Coster and some of those fellows would sign up with the secession people, and try to get Tennessee out of the Union like Alabama and Georgia and South Carolina."

"I guess so."

The conversation lagged and then started again along the way, and presently they arrived at Middletown. Henry Kellar had given Jesse $40.00 for his horse and another $40.00 just for good measure. Nothing had been said about compensation for the work he had done over the years or the board and room he had enjoyed. Those matters were not addressed among family. It was taken for granted that they were just part of the bargain. Jesse paid the $1.00 for his boat fare and turned back to Tom.

"Tom, I never thanked you for taking me on — sort of under your wing when I first came to town. That was one of the nicest things anyone ever did for me."

"Jess, I just thought you needed a friend about that time, and anyway I was sort of interested in seeing what you were made of."

They both looked at each other for a few seconds and then Jesse picked up his bedroll and carpetbag, turned and went up the gangplank onto the boat. He found a spot on the deck where he could settle down for a few days, then turned and waved at his friend.

"Good bye Tom. I'll look you up if I get back this way," Jesse didn't want to appear as though he was about to cry. He felt worse about leaving Tom than he did when he had left Genoa, five years earlier.

"'So long, Jess. If I come out west, I'll be looking for you."

"That's where I'll be, Pardner," they both laughed.

The boat had been about to push off and as soon as Jesse was on board, the crewman pulled in the plank and they left the dock.

8

CAIRO, ILLINOIS

From Middletown, the boat that carried Logan to Knoxville was a flat-bottom affair, as there were rocks and sandbars to negotiate and the water was not consistently deep enough for anything with a draught over about three feet. At Knoxville, he changed to a larger boat, a steam-driven, flat bottom sternwheeler that carried about seventy-five passengers and considerable freight. By the time the boat left Knoxville, a drenching rain had begun and Jesse was forced to spend the major part of his day inside the large cabin that was provided for the convenience of the passengers. The atmosphere in the cabin was close and uncomfortable, as most of the men and a few women smoked either pipes or cigars. He tried to spend most of his time toward the rear of the lounge as there was an open area on the afterdeck, but there he encountered such a splash from the paddlewheel that he had to wear a heavy coat.

Among the passengers with whom Logan embarked at Knoxville was a fellow who was well dressed and appeared to be a rather prosperous businessman. Jesse couldn't help thinking back to the days about five years ago when he was travelling east and encountered the fellow Rice, who tried to talk him out of some of the hides he was bringing with him, or as Jesse thought to himself with a wry grin; *"The man literally tried to swindle me out of my skin(s)."*

As the days wore on, he had occasion to talk to the fellow from Knoxville, and found him rather civil and friendly. The man, Mr. Wilkins was the name he used, seemed to always carry a book or newspaper and spent much of the time reading. He was not opposed to conversation, however, and on occasion offered Logan the newspaper he'd been reading. The headlines seemed to be all about the idea of a pending conflict between some of the southern states and those who adhered to the Union.

From Knoxville, owing to the rain that continued for several days, the Tennessee River was clear all the way to its mouth where it emptied into the Ohio just upriver from Paducah, Kentucky and, except for the occasional stop along the way to discharge or pick up freight or passengers, the boat made remarkably good time. Mr. Wilkins was an engaging conversationalist and spoke to Jesse as an intellectual equal, asking his opinion on several matters, some of which Jesse had never really considered up until that moment, though he did share what he had learned from the study of the book by Hinton Helper.

A native and current resident of Knoxville, Mr. Wilkins told the younger man that he was on his way to Clifton, Tennessee to negotiate the purchase of some horses, and even tried to persuade Jesse to join him in returning the horses to Knoxville, an offer, while attractive, Jesse declined.

During his conversations with Mr. Wilkins, Jesse got the firm impression that he disapproved of the idea of secession from the Union, even to the point of considering moving his business north, but that he would be loath to relocate, as he was a Tennessean through and through, and the goodwill he had developed over the years he had been in business meant a lot to him. Logan found that the man was well acquainted with Parson Brownlow and some of the other notables that had canvassed the state opposing disunion. Wilkins considered himself a particular friend of Judge Thomas A. R. Nelson the prominent Whig leader and in his conversations with Jesse quoted him liberally.

"There are many wise and serious truths pointed out by my friend Tom Nelson," Wilkins said to Jesse one day as they stood by the rail of the paddlewheeler. "For instance, many use the excuse that their allegiance is to some such state or other and so, if their state were to secede from the union, they would support her. Felix Zollicoffer, my old friend and, in my opinion, a very bright and well-intended man, is one who takes this line of argument. But I want you to tell me, young man, why must I support a state that goes against my concept of honor and justice? Why is it that the state of Tennessee, carved out of territorial fabric, and a creature of the Federal Government, should presume to consider itself free to secede from the very government that spake her into existence? Other states, Louisiana, for example, purchased with legal tender only fifty-seven years ago under the administration of President Jefferson and existing only by the generosity and suffrage of the Federal government in Washington should be able to conjure up legal basis for secession from that same government? Also, why is it that I am condemned by many for my fidelity to the Union when all I am doing is supporting and defending the very same feeling of those counties or region or city where I was born and raised and who share my devotion to the Union? Why is it a damnable offense to refuse to adhere to the attitude prevailing among those from the western part of the state when I am a native of East Tennessee? If you can answer these questions you will have my undying and unwavering respect."

Jesse admitted that he was at a loss to comprehend the contradictions in the reasoning of some of the protagonists of secession and slavery and that his family was of the same mind. He noted that some of the men that his grandfather did business with and dealt with socially or as members of his Masonic lodge were divided along the lines of loyalty to the Union and that he felt there was an inconsistency in their argument for secession.

"Please don't tell me your grandfather discusses politics in his lodge, Mr. Logan," Wilkins said in exaggerated earnestness.

"Oh, no, sir," Jesse hurriedly assured him, "but the same fellows that meet in the lodge on Monday are friends on Tuesday and they don't seem to hesitate to talk politics then."

Wilkins laughed, "I was just joshing with you, Mr. Logan. I'm a Mason myself, and while we avoid subjects such as politics and religion within the lodge, we have no such restraints on our conversations at other times."

"I wonder if you'd tell me, Mr. Wilkins, and this is something I've always been curious about, where did Masonry come from and what is it all about. I'm too young to join a lodge, as yet, but when I turn twenty-one, I fully intend to, but all I'm ever told about the organization is that its whole purpose is just 'to make good men better'. What does that mean? Was it always like that?"

"No, no it wasn't, my friend. Masonry is a conglomeration or collection of great truths handed down through the ages and polished by time and usage to its present situation of simply an organization of good friends, or as we call ourselves, 'brothers'. Many years ago, or so it seems — no one really knows — there were builders and craftsmen who organized into groups to construct great buildings, some of which took decades to complete. These craftsmen became fast friends and apparently became so attached to each other that they would do just about anything to help a brother in distress. It literally became a family, or a series of small families, sometimes scattered about the countryside and sometimes gathered in lodging quarters near where a cathedral or castle was to be built. Then, in time, some great men, philosophers, writers, noblemen, and such took an interest in the great fraternal and noble spirit of these little groups and asked to be accepted as members, not to engage in the skilled work — for this would have taken years of apprenticeship — but as 'adoptive' or 'speculative' Masons. The working masons had developed such a high reputation for honor, fidelity, and loyalty that men like Isaac Newton, Francis Bacon, and Christopher Wren sought acceptance, just out of admiration for their principles. Isn't that remarkable, that some rusty, dusty old workmen should be so highly respected, that their 'Lodges' — as they came to be known — were thought worthy of the admiration of many of the great thinkers of the day?"

"I reckon it's no different, today," Jesse said thoughtfully. "Many of the Masons I know are really fine men — some rich and some not so rich — but all decent God-fearing men and well respected in their community."

"Well, Mr. Logan, it really is a little different today. The original purpose of lodges; that of housing and providing support for stone cutters and such — no longer exists. Freemasons, as we know the term are simply an assemblage of the latter category — those who seek fellowship and enlightenment. You say that you're not a Mason today, but you've taken the first step necessary to be made a Mason, and that is the earnestness of purpose to assume the standards and principles that Masons believe in. When you achieve the age and make the decision to become a Mason, try to let me know about it and I will make every effort to attend your conferral."

"Thank you, sir. If I can, I will."

At Clifton Jesse bade goodbye to the man he'd come so much to admire and continued north for two more days. He changed boats at Paducah, Kentucky and boarded a large sidewheeler for the rest of the trip to Cairo.

A 'Constitutional Convention' was called in early February in Montgomery Alabama for the purpose of establishing a government termed "The Confederate States of America" Tennessee did not send official representation, but did have a number of 'observers' at the convention. On February 8, the delegates finished with the drafting of the constitution, and on February 22, Jefferson Davis was sworn in as President of the Confederacy. Jesse read about all this on his way down river, and when he stepped off the riverboat on which he had completed the last leg of his journey at Cairo it was as though the whole country was talking about the southern secession.

The State of Tennessee voted in February 1861 by a majority of 68,000 to 59,000 not to secede from the union. Even so, following a call on April 17 from President Lincoln to furnish troops for the Federal army Governor Isham Harris replied, "Tennessee will not furnish a single man for purposes of coercion, but 50,000, if necessary, for the defense of our rights and those of our Southern brothers."

Thereafter he formed a "Military League" which established a relationship with the Confederate government, then forming up in Mobile, Alabama. Prominent citizens of the entire state, but principally East Tennessee were outraged, but the force of the government under Governor Harris moved steadily toward secession, until on June 6, the legislature ratified a motion of secession. Governor Harris issued a proclamation on June 24, 1861 severing relationships with the Federal Government.

———————

In late January, when Jesse got off the boat at Cairo, David was at the dock, waiting for him. David had with him his two children, Elizabeth, now nine, and David, seven. It was a Saturday, and the children were not in school. They were bundled against the cold, as the winter had begun in earnest in southern Illinois. They went directly to David's home on Walnut Street, not far from his shop on Washington Street, but in a neighborhood with many fine homes and shaded yards, though the trees were now quite bare. Cairo was growing as a commercial center, and David's business was growing with it. Leather for the expanding trade to the west was an important commodity, and David's business was prospering.

David, now thirty, was an honored and respected member of Cairo society. He and Ralph Cooper had joined together as partners during the mid-fifties, and were doing well. Ralph was a skilled tanner and cutter, and David was adept at management and marketing. They had also taken on several skilled employees including two former slaves who were valuable in the business. David was the manager of the partnership, and the knack he had developed for the handling of money since he had worked with James Potter, his father-in-law, put the business on a firm footing.

Mary had prepared dinner for the family, and after she saw to it that the children had taken off their heavy winter outer garments, she gathered the family in the dining room and seated them for the noon meal.

"David, would you say grace?" Mary asked quietly when they were all seated around the table. David nodded and looked about to make sure everyone was ready with heads bowed.

"Father," David intoned, "we thank You for the food You have provided for us, and for all the blessings of the day. We pray You will be with us and guide us in all our endeavors, both in these troubled times and in the days to come. Bless the hands that have prepared this food, and keep us mindful that it is You, Who are the source of all our blessings. We thank You for the safe trip of Jesse, and pray that You will be with him as he returns to our family out west." Then, thinking he was getting a little too wordy and that some of the family may be getting hungry, David concluded quickly, "We ask this all in Your name. Amen."

"That wasn't your usual blessing, Daddy," young David piped up.

"Well, Son, this isn't a regular day," David replied. "This is only the second time since you were born that we've seen your Uncle Jesse, and I wanted to make sure I covered all the important issues with God."

The conversation at the dinner table was congenial, if somewhat intense. There was much to talk about. The family in Nevada, insofar as David knew, was well. Will had established himself in the Carson Valley as one of the leading cattle producers. George was farming a large acreage in the Carson Valley, and John had gone to work with three other men, building bridges and viaducts throughout the territory. With the discovery of gold and silver in the past couple of years, the demand for these services had boomed, and John was doing extremely well.

"What will you be doing, now, Jesse?" David inquired after a time.

"I just don't know, David," Jesse replied. "I want to go back home to Nevada, but this talk about war and secession and all that has me wondering whether I should have stayed in Kellars Crossing. Grandpa and Grandma are getting along in years, while Uncle Fred and Uncle John and his two boys are all that's left, besides the Kellars over the hill in Cedar Mountain."

"Why don't you stay a month or two with us, help out at the store, and when spring comes, things might settle down a bit?" David suggested.

"You know, that was what Grandpa suggested, and, as a matter of fact, I'd be kind of anxious to learn a little about the harness and leather business." David had developed the trading part of the business from that which Jesse and Hoke had started back in 1855, and the arrangement had profited both David and Will. It was an interesting and profitable business, and Jesse was thinking that he might even work his way into it with his brothers. If a war were to start, there would be plenty of demand for harnesses and saddles from the government.

It didn't turn out as they had speculated. Talk of war had intensified, and Cairo, at the confluence of the Ohio and Mississippi Rivers was second only to St. Louis as the seat of rumor and consternation in the area. Just across the river in Missouri, there were skirmishes and hostile words between the forces supporting secession and those preferring to stay with the Union. In Saint Louis, the tensions between Governor Claiborne Jackson, a staunch secessionist and Captain Nathaniel Lyon, who commanded the local garrison, were the subject of much discussion and speculation.

Then, in April, there came a request for 75,000 ninety-day enlistments to 'suppress the rebellion' from the new president, President Lincoln. This resulted in Jesse's decision to leave Cairo for Indiana, where there seemed to be a good chance of his joining the army. He recalled the conversations he'd had with Tom Singleton, and the challenge of serving in the interest of maintaining the Union was irresistible.

When David heard that Jesse was determined to go into the army, he took him aside.

"Jesse, I don't know whether this is the right thing to do, but it seems to be right for you. I'd be inclined to do the same thing if I were in your shoes. You're young, single, and without any set direction in your life. I don't think this thing will last, but you never know. The people we talk to around here are all of the opinion that the southern states are being led along by a bunch of radicals and are caught up in this secession thing without due thought for their future. The north has all the industry and commercial strength, and the south seems to have the great share of farm products like cotton and hogs and grain. One thing they don't realize, though, is that these things are also starting to develop out here in the west. With things like this new reaper that that fellow McCormick has come up with, the use of slaves will become less and less profitable, and a country relying on a slave economy will be poorer than a church mouse in twenty or thirty years. That's the way I see it, anyway."

"Grandpa Kellar used to say about the same things as you just did, Dave, and in school we studied some statistics by a mathematician named Helper, that seemed to show that slavery is already actually hurting the economy in the south," Jesse said. "Grandpap thinks a man or even a country that depends on a slave economy is in for a bad surprise in a few years. Anyway, I just hate to miss the chance to serve my country and, in the process, maybe see some of the country I'd never in this world get a chance to see on my own. I'm glad to see we agree on that."

"One other thing, Jess," David lowered his voice. "You know that rifle I've got, the breech loader we've been taking out for target practice."

"Sure I know it. You said it is a Spencer, or something, didn't you?"

"Yes, that's the one. I've only had it a short time, since that fellow from the east came through selling those things."

"So, what's your point?"

"I want you to have it. I think you'll be able to take your own rifle with you, and I hear the government will even buy the thing from me and let you keep it. That's what I heard down at the dock last week, anyway."

"Dave, I can't believe it. I just can't believe this. I — well, I just can't believe it. You want to give me that rifle? That thing really shoots. What will you do, then? What if the war comes here to Cairo and you don't have anything but that old musket to shoot?"

"Well, you're real good with the thing, and I thought you ought to have it."

The conversation continued for a few minutes, and Jesse agreed to take the rifle with him. If the army wouldn't allow him to keep his own weapon, he'd see to it that the rifle was returned to David. And so it was settled.

Jesse took a steamer upriver to Evansville, Indiana and enlisted in the army.

One of the first people he met was Sergeant Frank Davis who had rejoined the army as soon as the call was sent out and was assigned to Company "H", Seventh Indiana Volunteers. This was the man with whom Jesse had developed such a close friendship back on the trail from Fort Laramie to Fort Pierre, and it was a happy reunion. They had little time to reminisce about their intervening years, but Jesse did learn that Sergeant Davis had, indeed left the army, after marrying a girl he'd met out west. He and his wife had two children, a girl and a boy. Like Jesse, Frank Davis had been anxious to serve his country in what appeared to be not much more than a brief skirmish, despite the posturing of the politicians on both sides of the secession issue.

Jesse asked about the possibility of keeping his own personal weapon. Within two days, Sergeant Davis came back with the answer that this would be all right, and he proceeded to check Jesse out on the use of the weapon.

━━━━●((●))●━━━━

Back in Cairo, David Logan received a letter from his brother confirming that the rifle would remain in his hands, but he promised David to return it as soon as possible. David was gratified. It was as much a gesture of brotherly love toward his younger brother, but he thought, also that it may be instrumental in making things a little safer for Jesse.

Then, in early June, David was in the store when a rather plain looking soldier came through the front door, asking about wholesale sales of harness and equipment for the local garrison. He explained that he had the authority from Army Headquarters to purchase materials as needed and wanted to know how much David thought he could supply. It was not your usual request, and the man, while well-spoken and very cordial, was not one who, as David surmised, would inspire confidence in his authority to make a large-scale purchase. David was a businessman, however, and until the soldier proved otherwise, David decided he would take him at his word.

The first request was for one hundred fifty sets of draught harnesses, for which the soldier furnished full design. It was not the largest order David had ever filled. He had once negotiated with the City of Saint Louis, and had won the bid for two hundred sets, so he had set up a series of jobbers who could help him fill such large orders, fashioned to his design. It had helped put him into the upper strata of the harness business. It was unusual, however for a man to walk in from the street and ask for such a large order. He negotiated a price, which both men found fair, and promised a response within the week as to whether and when he could fill the order.

A day or two later, the officer was back. This time, it was saddles. He wanted forty of the newer style saddles that the army was then using. David again quoted a decent price and committed to the delivery, contingent upon supply. The soldier thanked him and left the store.

Ralph Cooper was in the store at the time and came over to David after the man had left. "Who is that fellow, David?" Ralph inquired.

"I don't know his name, but he sure seems to have the power of the army behind him," David replied. "He talks as though he can buy the whole business, but he surely isn't what you would call a pillar of confidence and command."

The next day, the same soldier came into the store, but did not give any indication that he wanted to buy anything. He just seemed to be looking about as though he was interested in the harnesses and other tack, particularly a set of saddlebags.

"Not going to buy anything, today, Sir," David inquired.

The soldier smiled and mentioned to David that he'd been in the harness business before the war, and was interested in comparing prices and policies and such. He was very soft-spoken. He seemed to show a considerable knowledge of the harness business, though he admitted that he didn't particularly care for the business.

"I suppose I'm fortunate there was a war, if you can consider such a thing as good fortune. The smells and atmosphere of the harness shop where I worked were — well, unpleasant to me. I've always been uncomfortable with the idea of killing animals for their hides or for food, and I find the business of running a tannery absolutely repulsive, even though I understand the necessity of it all. Nor am I opposed to the consumption of meat for food, you understand. It's just the killing and the blood and the smell that puts me off."

"This is the strangest sort of person to be an officer in the army," David thought to himself. *"How can anyone so opposed to killing resign himself to the necessity of battle and the carnage that accompanies all phases of war? What will happen when he's in charge of a group of soldiers and an enemy shell explodes nearby? Will he be able to function as he should or will he faint or run or get sick or something?"* Questions ran through Logan's head as to how the man had obtained any rank in the army. He guessed that it must have been a result of some considerable political influence, as there was not much of the soldier in the appearance of the man.

David and his strange guest discussed the harness business at great length. It turned out that this man was also devoted to horses, and from what David was able to observe, he handled the horse he rode with such a gentle hand and skill that he was able to take it places that a horse would ordinarily balk at or shy away from.

"I'm from an old leather monger family," the soldier told David, "and although I was never particularly good at business, I'm still drawn to the whole concept of the leather trade. My father owned a harness shop when I was growing up and I actually joined the army — I suppose, anyway — to avoid going into business with him. Then when I got out of the army in 1854 and for a number of years afterward, I tried several different trades, but ended up back at my father's store. When the war started, I joined again in order to get away from the store, I suppose. That was last April." The idea of his having joined the army twice to avoid the harness business seemed comical to him and he grinned widely when describing his situation. He had a youthful face, and David estimated his age to be no more than thirty-five, just a few years older than David himself.

Over the next few weeks the soldier, David learned that his name was Sam, came into the store on several occasions, and they got to be pretty good friends. David told Sam about his younger brother. He even bragged a little about the episodes when Jesse was obligated to use a gun to save his own life at a very young age. He also told Sam of Jesse's ability as a horseman, which piqued Sam's interest. He told David how fond he was of horses, and that he had excelled in horsemanship at West Point.

They also discussed Jesse's short stay at Cairo only a few months earlier. David described Jesse as an excellent horseman and expressed the hope that he would make a contribution to the northern cause. Sam and David conversed at length about their interests and aspirations. It appeared that Sam had few of either, but David nevertheless found him to be an amiable and courteous conversationalist.

As the time passed, Sam came into the store on several occasions, and once or twice David showed him the newspaper articles he had found describing Jesse as the 'White Angel'. David let Sam know that it was the Spencer rifle he had given Jesse that had contributed to his reputation.

"I thought you said he's a horseman," Sam commented.

"He's good at horsemanship, all right," David responded, "but he also learned to shoot back in Nevada and in Tennessee where he was raised.

The fact that Sam had attended West Point puzzled David even further. Sam just didn't seem the 'soldierly' type, and he certainly didn't fit David's concept of a West Point graduate.

One day David's curiosity got the better of him and, as discretely as possible, asked Sam if he had ever been under enemy fire, thinking perhaps that he had been in some minor skirmishes with Indians out west, or something of the sort.

"Yes, yes I was," Sam responded with a smile. "Back in the forties, I was with General Taylor in Mexico and we actually did quite a bit of fighting." He went on to tell of his adventures in Mexico, including what he seemed to feel was a rather humorous incident, when he and his men had hoisted a small cannon up to the steeple of a church and held off an entire regiment of Mexican troops.

"General Taylor thought so much of our ingenuity that he put me in for promotion to Captain. I was really flattered, but one of my sergeants, a man named Stance, thought he should have gotten credit for the trick. He steamed and stewed about that for the rest of the war. I've been in command of a company of the Illinois Volunteers in Missouri these past few months, also, David. And don't you recall last August, when our troops took over Paducah, Kentucky? I was in charge of that excursion and I think I may just be in for some fighting quite soon again."

It seemed to David that perhaps he was underestimating this man, but he still had his doubts that Sam would ever stand up to the test of a really sever battle.

One day late in October, Sam came into the store for some personal items, and mentioned to David that he was preparing to take a force down river from Cairo. It seems he had gotten clearance from his superiors to engage the enemy at Columbus, Kentucky and Belmont, Missouri, just across the river from Columbus. He said he didn't want to waste any time in the process as the clearance might be withdrawn at any minute. He seemed a changed man. His eyes were bright and he even walked with a brisker stride than David had remembered from previous visits. David was flattered that Sam confided in him his plans to engage the enemy, as he felt it was probably a violation of military protocol to share such information with civilians. Sam purchased some saddle soap and some liniment for his horse. Then, more as an afterthought, Sam bought the pair of saddlebags he had been admiring. When he reached into his pocket for his purse, his surprised look told David he had forgotten to bring it.

"Forget your purse, Sam?" David inquired. "That's all right, I'll trust you till you get back."

"I'm sorry, David. I guess I rushed off in such a hurry I forgot to bring it. May I sign a chit? It'll only be a few days so far as I know." Sam apologized.

"We'll just let it ride, Sam. I trust you."

"No, let me sign a chit. In this business, you never know if there will be a tomorrow. At least if I sign, you'll have a claim against the government in case I don't make it back."

David made out a bill for the merchandise and Sam signed it, thanked David in his usual courteous manner, and left the store. After he'd gone, Ralph Cooper came in from the back room of the store.

"Did you ever find out what that fellow's name is, David?" Cooper asked. David picked up the receipt and examined the signature. He had never known Sam's last name. It was hard to make out, but appeared to be 'Grant'. The cordial unassuming soldier that David had spent so much time in casual conversation with over the past four or five months was U. S. "Sam" Grant, commander of the Cairo garrison.

9

THE ARMY OF THE OHIO SUMMER 1861

D uring those earlier days of summer, the battles of Philippi, Rich Mountain and Laurel Hill established the Federal presence at Beverly, and from there, General Rosecrans took the initiative to move the Army of the Ohio slowly south. His objective was to drive the Confederates out of the Alleghanies of western Virginia. The region had a significant advantage for both North and South, as the Federals could use the mountains as a staging area to launch offensives into the Shenandoah Valley all the way from Harpers Ferry to Staunton and beyond. There were even plans, according to George McClellan's reports, to move south and east through Lynchburg or Charlottesville and eventually into Richmond.

On the other hand, the Confederate forces needed the region as a means of cutting off the movement of supplies and personnel by the Union between east and west. The Staunton-Parkersburg Turnpike was built to provide access from the Shenandoah Valley of Virginia to the Ohio River, and was completed in 1848. It crossed high mountains and deep rivers, no insignificant engineering feat, and opened up large sections of western Virginia, first to settlement and transportation of products from the region's rich coal deposits, and now to the movement of the materiel of war. The Baltimore and Ohio Railroad also traversed the region as an artery for trade, and was vital to the war effort. Could the Confederacy but secure western Virginia and then perhaps a corridor north from Wheeling to Lake Erie, a distance of about a hundred miles, they could cut the Union in half, greatly complicating their communications and transportation.

General Rosecrans, though he hadn't enjoyed the fame and fortune of receiving the credit some thought he deserved in the conquest of the region, was still a vital player in the game of war, and he was committed to that role.

The Army of the Ohio, after a brief bivouac along the Tygart Valley, began to move south. By August 20, a small force was detached and sent out to reconnoiter the Rebel position at a place called Hawk's Nest, but were sent scurrying back with two or three minor wounds as opposed to the same suffered by the Rebels.

Company "H" had been attached to the Seventh Ohio Regiment under the command of Col. Erastus Tyler and in late August, Colonel Tyler took the regiment south and encamped at Kesslers Cross Lanes. On the morning of August 26, Jesse, having been recently promoted to Corporal, was assigned to picket duty with a squad of 20, and was deployed out along Gauley River. Duty was dull, but Jesse tried to keep the men alert by any means, as it was only a week since there had been an encounter with the Rebels quite near their current position.

They were standing four-hour watches, and it was approaching noon, the time for relief of the watch. Jesse sent two of the men back toward camp to locate and guide in the squad coming out to relieve them.

Jesse looked at his watch. It was ten minutes to twelve, and he was getting hungry. James had just come toward him to inquire about the time, when a shot rang out and Jimmo collapsed.

"I'm hit, Jesse," Jimmo gasped. "I think I'm shot."

"Where, where is it, Jimmo?" Jesse said anxiously.

"It's in my back, I think. It doesn't hurt, but I can't stand up."

Jesse dropped to James' side just as a second shot rang out. He heard the bullet clip the branches over him where he had been standing. Jesse looked in the direction from where the shots had come, but could see nothing. After a moment of scrutinizing the brush and trees, Jesse saw the movement of a man across the river. With careful aim, he squeezed the trigger of his Spencer. The figure collapsed. Other men could be seen moving through the brush, but with the telescopic sight on his rifle, it was difficult for Jesse to track them in the foliage. He picked up Jimmo's musket, cocked it and aimed at the moving figures. Another shot exploded to his right, Martin Mason, one of the members of his squad had come to check with him, and another of the gray clad figures fell. Jesse fired and knocked down another of the Rebels, and knew from the firing that the rest of his squad had been alerted and were holding off the Rebel advance. About that time, the relief squad from camp had moved into place, and was taking up position. Jesse turned his attention to his fallen companion.

"Lie still, Jimmo. We'll have you back at camp in a few minutes and the surgeon will have you fixed up in no time." Jesse knew he was stretching the truth. A shot in the middle back was serious, and he didn't know whether his friend could be saved or not.

"What happened?" Jimmo asked.

"There was an advance squad of rebels that moved in on us," Jesse said. He wished he had been more alert and seen them before his squad was spotted.

"Those bloody, blighted, blimey, blackguards have done me in, Jess." Jimmo was not one particularly given to strong speech, and Jesse had never heard such language from him. "Did you get any of them?"

"Of course we did, Jimmo," Jesse assured him. "The fellows are still firing at them and I don't know how many have gone down, but I do know of three for sure."

"Bloody, blinking, blighters." James exclaimed again. Jesse took this for a good sign, as at least Jimmo was strong enough to deliver plenty of adjectives toward his attackers.

"Lie still, Pal, I'm going to see to the skirmish. I'll be back in a minute and check on you." Jesse was unsure as to whether to try to pick James up and try to take him in, or to leave him momentarily to make sure his troops were in place.

"I'll be alright, Jesse. You go check on the troops."

Jesse moved to his left, where the shooting seemed to be the heaviest. He knew he was needed, both to coordinate the fighting and for the firepower he could deliver. In heavy brush, while it was hard to follow a moving target, the sight on his Spencer could pick out a gray uniform that was often invisible to the naked eye, if the owner stood still for a moment. He found two of his men and asked as to the progress.

"Where are the others?" Jesse asked.

"Over there," Marty Mason responded, pointing to his left. "The Rebs seem to be moving north along the creek."

"You two go back and find Ogilby, back where we were earlier," Jesse directed. "He's shot and can't move. Carry him back to the infirmary and have him looked at. I don't know if there's any hope. He's shot in the back, right at the waist, as far as I can tell, but I don't want to guess." Jesse couldn't continue.

Two of his men headed back toward where Jesse had come, and Jesse moved toward the direction they had indicated.

Otis Brown, a corporal from the Company "B" was in charge of the relief squad, was just a few yards farther along the river bank, and Jesse caught up with him.

"What do you think we ought to do, Logan," Otis asked. "I don't have any idea of the numbers. The firing from their side is not real heavy, but it may just be an advance."

"Let's hold our position and send a runner back for orders," Jesse said. "I've lost one man down, and have sent two more back with him to camp. Have we lost any others?"

"No. I don't think so," Brown replied.

"How many do you have?' Jesse asked.

"I have eighteen and myself. "

"That makes thirty-five of us, with my three out of commission and a messenger going back. Do you have any one you think will give a good report? Maybe you ought to go back, Otis. You have as much information as anyone. I'll take the squad."

"Sounds good. What do you want me to tell them?' Brown asked.

"Just tell your sergeant what's happening, and make sure you get the word to my sergeant, Sergeant Davis, "H" Company. Tell them we're holding for now, but we'll roll it up if it gets too hot. Get going. I'll have to get these men spread out. How many rounds do they have?"

"My men have twenty rounds, each."

"That should be enough to hold the line. If command wants us to stay here, have them send someone back immediately with instructions and reinforcements. Good luck." Jesse turned his attention to the men at his left who had begun firing faster in the past two or three minutes. The fire from across the creek was also intensifying.

Looking off to his right in the direction from which the Rebs had just come across the Gauley River, Jesse could see a force of Confederate soldiers crossing the stream. With careful aim, he fired his rifle twice and two Rebels fell into the water. He fired twice more with similar effect. There was a momentary pause in their progress, but the gray uniforms kept coming.

"Fall back!" Jesse shouted to the men of the 'Ohio' that he could see on his left. "Form up fifty yards to the rear, on that little rise. We've got heavy opposition to our right." He heard the command being passed and could see several of the men moving toward the rear. Jesse aimed again at the column of gray approaching, and fired twice more. His rifle was empty with the last shot and he didn't stop to reload. He got back to the small assembly and called them into formation in a column of four. As soon as he got a solid count, he gave the order to move.

"Right face. Forward, march. Column right, march. Quick time, march." Jesse had drilled men very little since his promotion to Corporal, but the time he had spent in drill with Sergeant Davis had been implanted in his mind. Also, the men in the squad were not very particular at that moment whether their squad leader was good or not with his commands. Their interest was to get back to the line as quickly as possible, but they were becoming seasoned, now, and it seemed most appropriate to follow orders and there was a feeling of confidence by staying together and moving as a unit.

Jesse was met at camp by the men of the Seventh Ohio with his own company forming into battle line on the right.

Sergeant Davis had been informed as to the activity back near Gauley River and was quick to commend Jesse on his action.

"How's Jimmo?" was Jesse's first question.

"He's back at the infirmary right now," Sergeant Davis informed him. "We can check on him later."

"How did he seem when they brought him in?" Jesse persisted.

"It was hard to tell," Davis evaded the inevitable. James Ogilby didn't appear to be well at all when he was brought back from the river. In fact, he didn't appear to be alive, but Davis had ordered him sent back to the field hospital, anyway.

"Do you think he's going to make it?" Jesse wouldn't give up.

"Corporal Logan," Sergeant Davis was not inclined to let the matter dominate his thoughts at the moment, "The doctor will do what he can for Private Ogilby, and we have other matters to think about right now. Take your position in the ranks."

It was too late. In spite of the earlier warning Corporal Brown had provided, the Rebels were moving in on the small Union force quicker than they could take a defensive position. With stubborn determination, the gray line moved in on them.

Most of the men of the Union brigade fought kneeling as they fired, many of them behind trees, stones, and whatever cover they could get, but there were considerable groups that stood. Occasionally one of these groups, which had endured the storm of missiles for moments without perceptible reduction, would try to push back toward the Rebel line, but in a matter of moments many of the men of the group would be down. There was no visible movement of the enemy, no audible change in the roar of the firing, yet the men in blue virtually collapsed as a man, either dead or wounded.

No command to fall back was given, none could have been heard. Man-by-man the survivors drew back among the wounded, some of whom could drag themselves back, or the shirkers whom no one could have dragged forward. The psychology of a soldier is often odd and inexplicable. Today's skulker may be tomorrow's hero. A man feeling his fate is sealed may abandon hope and charge recklessly, or he may try to hide behind the nearest tree.

As the disorganized groups fell back, they were attacked by a flanking force of the enemy moving through the field in a direction nearly parallel with what had been the Ohio's front but the sergeant commanding that portion of the line sensed the threat and repositioned the Union force. Green as they were, the Yankee soldiers responded smartly to their leader's orders and held stubbornly.

Just twenty-five minutes had elapsed since the enemy had attacked at the Gauley River but was now slowing its advance. The Yankees were forced step by step to fall back. Colonel Tyler sent down orders for the brigade to retire, and they continued to move back reluctantly.

The losses were unbelievable. The entire loss was over a hundred men in the Ohio brigade in less than an hour of actual fighting.

Once clear of their encampment, the regiment took up a position on a heavily wooded rise, where they remained through the night with pickets liberally placed holding the Rebels at bay. When daybreak came, they found that the Confederate force had mysteriously retired on their own, after having stripped the Union camp of all food, ammunition, medical supplies, and anything else they took a fancy to. When the regiment returned to camp, they found it completely ransacked. The federal forces had suffered one of its most serious defeats of the campaign, with 245 killed and wounded. James Ogilby was among the dead.

On Sept. 10, General Rosecrans brought 3 brigades south from Clarksburg to the support of Colonel Tyler who was moving against the Rebels at Carnifex Ferry. He advanced against Confederate Brigadier General John Floyd's camp, but was halted by darkness. The next day Rosecrans opened up with an artillery barrage that finally, after a half day of shelling, convinced Floyd to retreat, with losses which Union command estimated at 250. The cannon barrage had been awesome and the effects of Corporal Logan and the other Union snipers sent out to harass the enemy also took a severe toll. Those left in the Union camp could do nothing more than cover their ears for a period of about four hours the evening of the 10th, and the next morning, when they moved toward the Rebel position, they were overcome with the carnage. For the rest of the day they did nothing but bury the dead.

Jesse was numbed by the experiences of the past few weeks. He had lost a friend for whom he cared like a brother. The love he had felt for Jimmo was strong, though they had only known each other for a few months. They had shared their food, their tent, their fears, and their desire to see the war come to a quick end. They had laughed together and shared each other's concerns for their families. Jesse had relied on James for his wisdom, courage, and an uncanny ability to spot the enemy approaching when they had been out on post as a sniper team.

And now, the task of burying the dead of the enemy, who had fallen to the cannon fire from the Union batteries, was almost more than he could bear and the thought that he had been a contributor to the destruction weighed heavily on his conscience. These were all James Ogilbys to someone. They each had a family, friends, loved ones, perhaps a pet dog at home, a horse, dreams —.

"Corporal Logan, come on back here. I want you to give your report to the Colonel," Sergeant Davis was calling Jesse from the far side of a small clearing. "Colonel Sullivan has to submit his report, and would like some information on this action."

Jesse walked over to where Sergeant Davis was standing, but was having a hard time collecting his thoughts.

"Are you alright, Logan?" Davis asked.

"What does the colonel want to know, Sergeant?"

"He's putting together his report on last night's action and would like to hear from some of the men in the ranks as to what they saw. He finds it a little peculiar that the Rebs just stayed and took our shelling. Did you have any opportunity to talk to any of the wounded Rebels you brought back to our lines yesterday?'

"Just that one lieutenant I told you about. He was saying they were expecting General Wise to move up from the south and flank us, but he didn't show up. That's about all I know."

"Jesse, go talk to the colonel and then why don't you go back to your tent and relax for a time. You look like death warmed over."

"Yes, well, maybe I will, Sergeant. I've seen enough killing to last me a lifetime, and somehow I don't think I've seen more than a small start of it."

"I think you're right, Jesse. I think you're more right than any of us know."

After a brief conversation with Colonel Sullivan, Logan went back toward the tent he was now occupying by himself, and on the way, he passed Mr. Livingston and Miss Livingston moving goods into the suttlers tent that they had recently set up.

"How do you do Mr. Logan?" Miss Livingston asked. "I'm sorry to hear of the loss of Private Ogilby. I know you and he were close friends."

"That's kind of you to be so understanding," Jesse replied. "Yes, we were good friends, even though we'd known each other for only a short time. It seemed as though we'd been friends for our whole lives. This whole mess can really be depressing. It puts a whole new light on this idea of fighting, when a person so close to you gets killed."

"Would you mind helping me with some of these boxes?" Miss Livingston asked after a few moments of reflection. "Unless you have something else you must do."

"Not just now," Jesse said. "An' I'd be happy to help you."

For a period of about an hour, Jesse helped carry the suttler's boxes from the wagon and stack them in the tent as Olivia Livingston watched, gave him directions as to where to put them and talked. It took Jesse's mind off the war for at least a few moments.

It seems Miss Livingston was from the Frederick, Maryland area before the war, her family having been in the mercantile business. She was vague about the details, but told Jesse that Mr. Livingston had some friends in government who advised him that there would be a great need for people with merchandising experience to assist in the supply of non-issue goods, and in the process, maintain a good livelihood for themselves.

"An' have your plans succeeded?" Jesse asked her.

"To some extent," she replied, "but it is something one must pursue diligently, with little time for themselves, and there are certainly risks of various sorts involved.

"Something like being in the army, itself."

"Well, we have a little more control over our lives than you do. By the way, what made you join the Union army? You were living in Tennessee when the war started, as I understand. Why didn't you join the southern cause?"

"Lots of reasons, I suppose. My family is not particularly in sympathy with the idea of slavery, and we are dead-set opposed to secession, and we could see trouble brewin' with those of the neighborhood who weren't of the same mind. I was on my way back to my home in Nevada when the call came out for ninety-day volunteers, an' the idea of the adventure of it all, an' fighting for a good cause while getting paid intrigued me. Some of my ancestors came to this country over two hundred years ago, and the idea of bustin' up a nation they worked so hard to build really bothers me. I think we should try to work this thing out rather than just kick the bucket over and start fightin'."

"You know, Miss Livingston," Jesse continued, "When the recruitment call came out, the whole idea was that we would get the thing over fast and go back to whatever we were doin' before, an' I didn't want to miss the opportunity to take part in somethin' so grand. Now that I've seen the elephant and realize this is a big country and there are a lot of people on both sides fightin' for what they think is right and aren't likely to go home without defendin' their ideas, I kind of think my ideas on the war have changed. Even so, I'm not gonna go home till the job's done. Does that make any sense?"

"Did anyone ever mention to you the idea of states' rights, Mr. Logan?" Miss Livingston asked. "This seems to be a very important issue to some people. Being from Maryland, we have there a similar mix of sentiments as your family in Tennessee, I'd guess, and one of the things that arouses the anger of many of my old neighbors is the idea that the northerners, or the westerners, or newspaper people, or anyone else can tell us what we can or cannot do with our personal property, when the state of Maryland has nothing to say on the matter. Eighty years ago, your ancestors and mine struggled, fought, and won the right of self-determination. And scarcely seventy years ago our grandfathers wrote a Bill of Rights, part of which says people can't be deprived of their property without legal process and just compensation. Now it's all out the window because some politician in Washington or an editor in Albany wants to change the world."

"I've heard that line of reasoning, Miss Livingston, and I know there are people in the north that seem to be just agitating for the sake of making a point. I also know of people in my home town who own slaves and treat them like they were family. But it still seems to me that there are some people that have no particular problem with the idea that people, albeit black people, are the subject of ownership by other people. And when, I might ask, does the "black line" stop? Suppose my fifth great grandmother was a Negress. When does my family tree go from black to being white?"

"For me," Jesse continued, "I find this sort of foreign to the idea of liberty. What seems to be liberty for one person isn't equally distributed, is it? And another thing, you know this is supposed to be a representative form of government where the majority opinion prevails and the remedy for unpopular laws should be the subject taken up in Congress rather than in the battlefield. Don't you agree?"

"Well, Mr. Logan, I do agree, but in this case, the weight of representation seems to be favoring the abolition interests, and now with that Mr. Lincoln in office, I have to wonder if the people in the south aren't doing the right thing for their own interests, just as their grandfathers did in 1775. What do you think of that?"

"OK, let's just say that secession from the nation is one of the rights a state enjoys. I don't think so, but let's just say it is. Now — we have eleven states that have established this as their option if they become unhappy with the state of affairs in the country. What happens next year or the year after when Georgia and Florida decide they should resume slave trade with some Caribbean countries, and there's no law allowing it?"

"Slave trade was abolished in 1808, Mr. Logan, and the constitution of the Confederacy also prohibits it."

"But what would happen if they did try to start it up again.

"The Confederacy has declared it illegal, and illegal it should stay. Everyone knows we have enough black people to satisfy that need."

"You haven't answered my question. What would happen," he recited in a deliberate manner, "to a state that decided to resume slave trade?"

"I told you, it's illegal. Don't you understand illegal? There's a law prohibiting such things."

"Well, yes, but I'm a rich land owner from Georgia. Or — here's a better one — maybe I am from Texas and there aren't enough slaves here in Texas and I also want to open up a new piece of land. Anyway, I think I'd like to have a few more slaves and they're too expensive here in the good old C S of A. I decide to make a case of it with my neighbors and secede from the Confederacy."

"Well, I guess you could do that."

"And now, those folks back in Florida and Georgia see what is happening in Texas and they want to secede and start their own country, too. Can they do that, Miss Livingston?"

"I see where you're going with this, and I know that this is an argument for forcibly preserving the Union, but what rights does a person have in a small state, if they can't secede?"

"What, I ask you — what is the root cause of people wanting to 'assert' states' rights; of wanting to secede? What has started all this turmoil over states' rights and the pursuit of those supposed rights? What is at the root of the disagreement?"

"The Radicals up north want to impose their will on the people of the southern states and we don't think that's right. It's not just slavery; it's all sorts of things."

"What sorts of things, and why are there abolitionist radicals?"

"Well, everything. First, they abolish the slave trade and now they want to do away with slavery, itself."

"So it's all about slavery, then. Isn't it?"

"Mr. Logan, I didn't call you over here to be lectured. I just wanted some help, and here you are imposing your northern philosophy on me and I don't appreciate it. That's just the way the southern people feel when you abolitionists come down here and try to take over."

"Hey there. Remember me, the country boy from Tennessee? Miss Livingston, I have traveled some and I've seen some places and people who have scraped and scrunched to stay alive and all without the help of slaves, and I just don't see the need, for one thing. And, for another, I don't see the need to degrade one person or race of people just so someone else can get rich at their expense. And, for another thing —."

"Two things are enough, Mr. Logan. You've made your point. I don't know how this discussion got started, but when we first started talking, I was against slavery and disunion, too, but then I found myself defending them. How did you manage to get me into such a position? I thought I was pretty well informed on the subject of states' rights, but you seem to focus on what appears to be the central issue," she said with some concern in her voice. Then, more cheerfully, "I'm going to have to do some thinking on the subject. Come back next week and I'll beat you into the ground with my superior reasoning and logic."

"I feel you're already pretty well informed on the subject, and have done a lot of serious thinkin' on it," Jesse smiled. "Believe me, Miss Livingston, I'm no crusader. As I said before, I got into the army mostly because I just wanted to be a part of the great adventure and because the argument of preserving the Union was more appealing than the alternative. But now that I'm here, I'm going to stick it out till the end. Besides, where else could I meet such pleasant company?"

"You don't really have any deep conviction about slavery, then, do you?" Miss Livingston said, ignoring Jesse's compliment. "You know, even your friend Professor Brownlow and his 'Knoxville Whig', while he proclaims loyalty to the Union, still favors slavery, and says so in many of his articles."

"That's Parson Brownlow," Jesse said softly.

"Whatever he is, he still says he favors the continuation of slavery or at least some kind of subjugation of the dark races. How do you feel?"

"I don't necessarily agree with everything Parson Brownlow or anyone else has to say, no matter how strongly they may believe in their position. I have to go along with the position my grandfather has often expressed on the subject. My Grandpa Kellar was a hardnosed, hardworking, independent Pennsylvania Dutchman who shied away from the ownership of other people, not necessarily because of some noble principle, but because he knew he could do better without them. My Grandfather Logan was a doctor like my father, and I don't know if he owned slaves or not, but I don't think so. Most of the people where I lived had no need for slaves. As far back in my family as anyone can remember, we have lived by our own skills and hard work, and depended on no one to do our work for us. It's just not something we needed. The only person in my family who had anything to do with slavery was a great, great grandfather who was a slave, himself, and that was back in the early seventeen hundreds."

Miss Livingston studied him intently for a moment, feeling it was highly unlikely that he should have any African blood in him, with such fair coloring.

"No, no, my ancestors were not Africans, Miss Livingston," he said with a smile, reading her thoughts, "One of my ancestors was sent from England when they cleared out some of the jails over there. As they put it at the time he was 'transported in lieu of execution'. He spent a number of years in servitude to pay for his passage and work off his sentence, but it was slavery, nevertheless, and I'm kind of proud of that little bit of family history."

Miss Livingston smiled at her having been so transparent as to let Jesse know what she was thinking, but she also welcomed his sharing some of his family skeletons with her. She was not the kind of person who warmed readily to people, but she felt an attraction to this man who showed her such honesty and warmth.

It was light work and Jesse welcomed the diversion from the gruesome task he had just left. The company was pleasant, and the time passed quickly. When they were done, Miss Livingston invited him to share a drink of water from the canvas cooler they kept close by. Seated on some high stools that were just outside the tent, Jesse's attention was unavoidably drawn to Miss Livingston's figure, visible in form through the light dress and only one or two undergarments she had been wearing during the process of unloading the wagon.

Miss Livingston smiled. "Keep your eyes to yourself, Mr. Logan," she said, demonstrating the fact that she, too, could read thoughts. "You wouldn't make a very good card player. Your thoughts are written all over your face."

Jesse blushed brightly through his summer tan, but he managed a smile. "Please, Miss Livingston, I suppose I was being a little transparent," he replied as evenly as he could. "But on the other hand, I think I should advise you that your charms are so apparent as to defy oversight."

"That will be quite enough," she said in assumed indignance, rising from the stool and putting down the cup of water. "I think you had better be going before one of us says something that will lead somewhere neither of us intends to go."

"Speak for yourself," Jesse responded, warming to the contest.

Miss Livingston's face softened to something of a pleading smile. "You have been most gracious to help me with the boxes from the wagon, and I have enjoyed the lively conversation you furnished, but now I must get back to work with unpacking, and really must ask you to leave."

"I don't know what happened to my manners, Miss Livingston," Jesse apologized, "I don't usually carry on this way. Still, I must tell you this before I go, and I don't wish you to take what I say as disrespect, 'cause that's not the way it's intended. But there's a warmth about you that I sensed the first moment I came into your tent. I don't know if it's just my imagination or admiration, or if everyone else senses this, this — aura, some sort of magnetic field that surrounds you. Has anyone else ever mentioned such a feeling?" He stood as if to leave.

"It's time you left, Mr. Logan. Whether the question was offered in disrespect or not, is not important. It was presumptuous and impertinent of you to pose it, and you will certainly not receive an answer from me to such a transparent appeal for my favor," she said in a tone of genuine indignance. Whereupon, she tossed her head and walked past Jesse toward the tent. As she stalked away, however, she made sure she brushed close enough to Jesse to give him a good dose of the 'aura' he had just described. Jesse's sense of desire was immediately aroused as she walked by and he felt a strong impulse to grab her by the waist, but he held himself in check. This was neither the time nor the place to make a scene, but he couldn't help thinking — even hoping that there would be such opportunities in the future.

Inside the tent, Olivia Livingston smiled to herself at the scene she had just provoked. She felt a strong attraction for this man, but her circumstances prevented her from displaying any such thing. Still, she was pleased that Jesse was so strongly moved by her presence.

————))((————

The Seventh Ohio Volunteer Infantry, to which Company "H" was then attached, made steady progress south, fighting all the way, with few breaks. The country through which they were passing was of mixed sentiment toward secession, with the unionists in strong preponderance, and the feeling they were fighting on friendly soil helped both their spirit and their progress. Jesse's assignment for the most part, when his sharpshooter skills were not being used, was as a scout and courier, as they were entering country with which he was as familiar as anyone in the regiment. Jesse was now assigned Elijah Hawkins as a spotter, and they also formed a scouting team with a squad of anywhere from two to eight others from the company. Lige Hawkins was not the lighthearted humorist that Jimmo had been, but he was friendly, outgoing, and very observant. Jesse felt he would be a good partner. He was a man of medium height, with curly brown hair and hazel eyes. He was three or four years older than Jesse, and showed considerable wisdom for his age. He was a good spotter and kept Jesse well informed as to their surroundings when they were out in the brush and Jesse was preoccupied with his peering for long minutes at a time looking for enemy soldiers.

The army pushed their way down through McDowell County where they stopped for a few days to regroup and plan their progress. The duty was fairly easy, as the citizens in the region were mostly friendly and offered whatever assistance they could to the Federal army, both as a unit and to the men individually.

They had good rapport with the people of Coalwood, near where they were bivouacked those few days in September, and on occasion the men were allowed to attend church and social functions in small numbers. Colonel Sullivan had given orders that the men were not to abuse their welcome by overwhelming the people of the town with their numbers or with any action that could be considered offensive.

The people of the town were most gracious. They often invited one or two of the men of the regiment to take Sunday dinner with them after church, and Jesse had been honored on one occasion by such an invitation. While the menfolk of Coalwood treated Jesse with great respect and camaraderie, because of the notoriety which he had been given in the newspapers, the young ladies for the same reason kept him at a distance. It was hard for a woman to become friendly with a man who had the reputation of a hired killer. Jesse was well aware of his reputation, and while he tried to demonstrate courtesy, affability, and decorum, he received no attention from any of the ladies of the town, except one.

Daisy Morton, a buxom and slightly forward young woman went out of her way to attract Jesse's attention. Jesse was not particularly attracted to Daisy, though she was quite pretty and had a most gracious manner. Her assertiveness told Jesse she could probably be a little overbearing and perhaps a trifle unreasonable if the occasion turned against her. Also, she reminded him a little of Sadie, the woman from the streets of Eagle Station years ago.

Daisy's father was a member of the unofficial militia of McDowell County, and he too sought Jesse's company as a 'fellow soldier'. On a Sunday in mid-September, Judson Morton invited Jesse to dinner and he accepted not yet knowing the relationship between Mr. Morton and Daisy. On arrival at the Morton home, he was greeted at the front door by a maid and escorted into the parlor. Morton, his wife, Daisy and two younger boys were seated around the room as a reception committee.

"Come in, my boy, come in." Morton greeted him, rising and extending his hand. "I want you to meet my wife and my daughter, Daisy. And these are my sons, Jesse, like yourself, and Arthur. Folks," he said addressing the family, "this is Jesse Logan, or more popularly known in the newspapers as The White Angel."

Jesse blushed and hoped it wasn't too obvious. "How do you do, Ma'am?" Jesse said to Mrs. Morton. "Miss Daisy, it's so nice to see you. Hello, Jesse, Hello Arthur." Jesse extended his hand to greet the two young men who both rose, took his hand self-consciously and bowed slightly as they did.

"Mr. Logan has graciously agreed to take dinner with us today, and I'm so honored that he did. He has quite a name as a, ah — as a significant force against the Secesh, and the papers have been making a big thing of it. Would you mind telling us how many of those rascals you've killed off so far Mr. Logan?"

"I ah — I wonder if it might be better to discuss this at some other time, Mr. Morton," Jesse protested. "I'm sure the ladies would be more comfortable if we were to take up the weather or something — probably anything."

"Nonsense, Mr. Logan," Morton insisted, "This is something all of us are interested in. I hear you're from just down the valley out in Tennessee, too. Carter County, isn't it?"

"Yes, Sir," Jesse said, glad for the redirection of the conversation, "I'm from the Watauga Valley, just out of Elizabethton."

"That's down in Rebel country, isn't it?" Morton asked. "How did it happen you're with an Ohio unit?"

"I was visiting with my brother in Illinois when the war broke out and joined the closest unit I could find at the time."

"A real patriot you are, Logan. 'Just couldn't wait to get into the fight, now, could you? I bet you have killed more Rebs than any other soldier in the army, haven't you?"

Jesse smiled a half-smile, sorry that he had accepted the dinner invitation. Looking at it from where he was standing at the time, joining the army didn't seem like it had been such a great idea. He wasn't really prepared for the likes of a Judson Morton. This man's enthusiasm for killing, Jesse thought, could only be enjoyed by someone who had never engaged in the activity.

"I never gave the matter all that much consideration, Mr. Morton,"

Jesse protested. "Having to engage the enemy is just a part of the job, and I happen to have been selected for a job that I really don't take much pleasure in. I joined the army mostly because if I didn't it would be as though I wasn't doing my share to get this thing over. And also, I wanted to try to preserve the Union, but if I didn't have to kill another soul in this cursed war, I'd be just as happy."

Jesse smiled apologetically. He knew he was not living up to what the Mortons, or at least Judson Morton, expected of him. Mr. Morton apparently expected a swashbuckling, swaggering guerilla fighter with twin revolvers and an Arkansas Toothpick at his belt.

"We all do what we can to get this thing behind us. My sergeant, who I feel is one of the most peaceful men I've ever met, tells us every time we go into battle, he says, 'Just think of it as another hill toward home,' and that's the way I like to look at it. I don't have any taste for killing other people. I'm just a man out there doing my job, and that's the job they assigned me and every hill we take is just another hill toward home."

Then, "Boy! I really got wound up. I didn't mean to give you folks a speech, and you can see I never trained to be a preacher. I hope you'll forgive me for carrying on like that. I didn't think I was so used up by the war to go on so in front of such nice folks who were so considerate and caring as to invite me into their home. Can you forgive me for getting on so?"

There was silence in the room. Five sets of eyes were fixed on his, and Jesse felt more vulnerable than he had out along Gauley River last month when the gray coats were shooting at him. Then Mrs. Morton started clapping softly. Then Daisy and the boys joined in, and soon the whole family joined in the applause.

"I think that was a most gallant and commendable speech, Mr. Logan," Mrs. Morton offered. "Don't you Daisy?" But Daisy was still spellbound by Jesse's little speech.

"Come on in and have dinner, Son," Mr. Morton clapped Jesse on the shoulder. "You really are a patriot, and a modest one at that. Boys," he said, turning to the two behind him, "I hope you're paying attention to this man. He's not only one of the best soldiers we have in the army, he's also the kind of a man who speaks his mind and makes sense when he does it."

Daisy sidled up to Jesse on the other side from her father and slipped her arm into his, completing the short trip into the dining room as a threesome. Jesse felt as though the Morton family had officially adopted him. He wasn't sure if that was good or bad.

After dinner, Mrs. Morton announced the family was too full to move, and suggested Jesse and Daisy go for a walk on the town. The boys insisted they were not full at all, but Mr. Morton let them know that they were fuller than they thought, and advised them to let Jesse and Daisy go out on their own.

Jesse didn't quite know how to handle this courtesy. He felt he had met his old adversary Cortland Rice, and was being hustled into something he wasn't prepared to deal with. With appropriate decorum, however, he thanked Mrs. Morton for dinner and held the door for Daisy. She looked more fetching after a relaxing dinner, and he thought to himself that he just might enjoy the rest of the afternoon.

Coalwood was a town of perhaps six streets, and a couple couldn't walk far without retracing their steps. In order to satisfy what he judged an appropriate time to be occupied by a stroll, Jesse suggested they take some time on one of the park benches that lined the town square. Daisy agreed. The weather was warm, and the shade of several large oak trees was most welcome.

Seated on the bench in the presence of about fifty-percent of the town's citizenry, Daisy decided Jesse was in fact the man to whom she wanted to surrender her heart and apparently her reputation. First, she turned in his direction and got close enough for him to feel her heart beating, which it was doing with reckless abandon.

"Can you feel my heart, Mr. Logan?" she inquired. "I don't know what's happened to me. I feel faint, and have no idea why. Here, do give me your hand. I must know if you think my heart is racing out of control." Taking his hand in hers, Daisy placed it against the center of her chest, then moved it a little to the side and down.

Jesse could see the next move coming and quickly jerked his hand away. "You know, Miss Morton, I do think we should be getting you back to your home. It may just be that you've caught some kind of fever that has started your heart racing." He started to stand up, but immediately thought better of it. Close contact with Daisy even out in public had had an effect on his libido and he found it inadvisable to stand up. He slid away as far as he could from the girl and regained his composure. Then he stood, extended his hand and helped Daisy to rise. When he did, Jesse glanced up at the people along the walkway, and as he did, he locked eyes with Olivia Livingston. Miss Livingston, in one of the loveliest dresses he had seen her wear, eyed him scornfully. Then her face broke into a faint smile. She turned and was caught up in the Sunday crowd strolling through town.

Jesse was disgusted with himself, but he didn't know why. Miss Livingston had given him no reason to believe that he was special to her, and though he had found her attractive and had enjoyed a little flirtation, they were no more than acquaintances at this time. Why did he concern himself that he'd been caught, — if that was the right word, in the presence, if not the clutches, of another woman?

Jesse and Daisy walked back to the Morton home, in what seemed to be something of a strained silence. It made Jesse apprehensive, as he knew the soldiers of the regiment had strict orders to treat the citizens with the utmost respect and to comport themselves as gentlemen at all times. The scene on the bench in the town square was not what he would consider gentlemanly conduct.

Finally, he spoke, "Miss Daisy, are you alright? Your color seems to be returning, and you are looking quite well."

"Mr. Logan, please don't speak to me another word. I was deeply offended by the liberties you took with me there in the park, and I shall not forgive you. Not in the least."

"I do apologize if I've done anything to offend you, Miss Morton," Jesse's apology was genuine, though he was fully aware of the fact that he was probably sorry for something totally different from that which she had constructed for him.

"I said 'don't speak to me,' Mr. Logan, and I meant it."

They were in front of the Morton home by then and Daisy flounced up the walk and into the house before Jesse could even hold the door for her. She slammed the door behind her leaving Jesse on the front walk in bewilderment.

He turned and walked the mile or so back to camp and immediately sought out the counsel of Sergeant Davis. He laid out the matter to Sergeant Davis, sparing nothing, and said, "Sergeant, I know we are supposed to act like gentlemen in town, and I thought I was doing pretty well, but this thing turned on me like a cornered bear."

Davis could hardly keep his composure, and Jesse read his thoughts.

"You think it's funny that your dumb country cousin corporal gets himself into these scrapes, don't you?"

"Jesse," Sergeant Davis finally said through gritted teeth, "I've seen you as cool as spring water in the face of fire, and you handle yourself with confidence and composure when dealing with men, but I think I should tell you — no — order you, 'stay away from women!' I want you in one piece through the end of this-here war, and you aren't going to survive if you don't keep away from women."

"Sergeant, I'm not asking you for any advice to the lovelorn. I'm telling you all this so that you won't be surprised when Mr. Morton comes storming into camp with the sheriff, tomorrow with a warrant for my arrest. I have a feeling that lady is going to be gunning for my hide."

"I know, Logan, I know. Was there anyone around that you know of that can support your story?" Davis asked.

Jesse thought for a moment. "Miss Livingston, the suttler's daughter was over on the side-walk when it happened and may have seen what went on."

"Get her! I want to talk to her as soon as possible."

Jesse left the tent and headed for the Suttler's tent. Miss Livingston was just inside the tent, talking to a soldier from Company "C". She saw Jesse come into the tent and immediately flashed a wonderfully winning smile at the other soldier. Jesse's heart hit the floor at the display of friendship with the other soldier, but his mission at the moment had nothing to do with Miss Livingston's emotions, or so he assumed.

"Miss Livingston, could I talk with you for a moment?" Jesse said urgently.

"In a moment, Corporal," she replied indifferently, "Mr. Pierce and I are conducting business."

But the other soldier was finished with what he had to say, despite her fetching smile, and turned to walk out of the tent.

"Are you sure you won't reconsider?" Miss Livingston asked sweetly.

"Ma'am, I only come in here to bring in that bucket of apples. What's there to reconsider?"

Miss Livingston had been caught in her own little game. There was nothing going on between her and Private Pierce, and she was just trying to get Jesse's goat.

Without so much as a blink, she turned to Jesse. "Yes, Corporal Logan, what can I do for you?"

Today I was in town with a lady and we were sitting on a park bench in the square. Did you see me there?"

"I don't recall, Mr. Logan, what time was it?"

"It was about two in the afternoon, I think. Don't you recall seeing me? I saw you there in town and you seemed to be looking straight at me. Please think."

"Why is it so important that I saw you in town with a pretty girl?"

Jesse's defenses went up. "I didn't say she was pretty, Miss Livingston. Please don't create something out of nothing. You did see me there with that lady, didn't you?"

Miss Livingston's face flushed as she realized her composure had cracked a bit. She had twice displayed evidence of her feelings and it was not what she had planned. "I do remember seeing you there in town, yes." She had to recover her credibility and still not let Jesse know she was at all upset by the incident. She continued defensively, "I was just walking in the town and happened by the square where you and that woman were."

"Did you see what happened?"

"What do you mean?"

"I mean," Jesse was getting exasperated with her evasiveness, "Did you see when we sat down and she kind of got close to me?"

"It seemed that you were just as close to her as she to you. You certainly didn't move away from her until the last moment."

"Miss Livingston, I was just trying to be nice to the girl. Her father had invited me to dinner today, and I didn't even know he had a daughter. Then they sent us out to walk around town and when I suggested we sit down on the bench she went after me like a robin on a junie-bug. When I pulled away, she acted like she was really insulted and I do think she's going to complain to her father that I was impolite or something."

"Did she project an 'aura', Mr. Logan?"

"Be reasonable, Miss Livingston. I could get into a whole lot of trouble over this. I went to Sergeant Davis and told him what happened and when he got back up off the floor after half laughing himself to death, he told me to bring in someone who saw what happened and could give a little support to my story. I'm afraid her father might make trouble with the colonel."

Olivia Livingston was relieved, amused, and agitated at the same time. She wanted to laugh from the relief in discovering the true situation between Jesse and Daisy, but she certainly wasn't going to laugh and have Jesse mistake her mirth for ridicule of his situation. She smiled, even a little warmly. "Of course, I'll come over to Sergeant Davis' tent and try to help straighten this thing out. It's the least I can do, — telling a little lie for a friend."

The last was said in jest, but meanwhile, Frank Davis had stepped through the tent flap and had overheard that portion of the exchange. "Will it be necessary for you to lie, Miss?" he asked. "If that's the case, I had better not talk to you about this matter."

"Oh, Sir, no, Sir," she said hurriedly. "Please, Sergeant, I was just having a little fun at Corporal Logan's expense. I saw everything that happened in town today, and I assure you, Jesse was nothing but a gentleman. He extricated himself from a difficult situation by the most appropriate means possible, and did nothing to bring discredit on the army. The young lady was most forward with him as I saw it, and has nothing to complain of as to the way she was treated, at least in my presence."

She had called him by his first name, and Jesse felt a rush of pleasure at the sound of it. It seemed everyone was enjoying this incident except him, but the sound of his name from the lips of a woman to whom he was becoming so attracted, relieved his discomfort immeasurably.

"Corporal, I want you out of here for a few days. The telegraph is down and Colonel Sullivan needs a courier for communication with Regiment. They are either over at Lewisburg or up at Carnifex Ferry. Go to Lewisburg, that's about forty miles. If General Rosecrans isn't there, he will still be at Carnifex, but I think the telegraph is up between the two. Wait for a reply, and then get back here as fast as you can. There are two or three horses available at Quartermaster. I want you to mount up and get on the road as quick as possible. Any questions?"

"No, Sir. I hear the road to Lewisburg is open and clear, right now. I should be able to reach there by this time tomorrow. Sooner if I can change horses somewhere."

"I'll leave that up to you. I'll give you a voucher for whatever you need. Get your gear together and be ready to go in fifteen minutes. I'll meet you at my tent."

With that, Sergeant Davis turned and left the tent. Jesse and Miss Livingston were alone in the suttler's tent.

"Thank you for bailing me out of that scrape, Miss Livingston," Jesse said simply, "You were most helpful. When I saw you standing there on the street, I was a little embarrassed, but I'm certainly glad you were where you were."

"I was so intrigued by what was happening there, and in broad daylight. Miss Morton has a reputation for being somewhat forward, but this was ridiculous. From what I saw, she almost attacked you, and you seemed to have been taken by surprise. But, tell me, Mr. Logan. You never answered my question as to whether Miss Morton projected an aura about her."

"You just won't let up, will you?" Jesse said fiercely, but in good humor. "The last time we talked about this subject, you dismissed me rather shortly, and I'm certainly not anxious for us to part on such an unpleasant note this evening. I think I'll just not mention it again." With that, he smiled at her and turned as if to go.

"Jesse," she said the name for the second time, "I owe you a hug. You have been abused enough for the day, and I wouldn't want you riding off in a bad mood. It might distract your thoughts from your mission." With that she moved around in front of Jesse, who was facing toward the door of the tent and put her arms around his neck.

It was all Jesse needed. He held Olivia close to him but instead of just a hug, he kissed her passionately on the lips, two or three times. He held her closely for a few moments, then stepped back. "That was some aura!" Jesse said breathlessly.

"You said you weren't going to mention it again," she whispered. "I only offered you a hug, and you stole the rest."

"Well, I owe you, Miss — Olivia, I'll pay you back when I get back from Lewisburg."

Miss Livingston was silent, but her eyes let Jesse know she might be holding him to his promise.

Jesse left the tent and went over to the quartermaster's tent, where there were two horses standing, both saddled and ready to go. Jesse ran his hands over their legs, checked their hooves and shoes, and picked the chestnut gelding.

"You seem to know what you're about, at least with horses, Corporal," Lieutenant Goodin was standing nearby, watching the selection process.

"No sense starting out with one that won't take you all the way, Lieutenant."

"What were you doing over in the Suttler's tent just now, Logan?"

"I had some business to take care of with Miss Livingston, Sir. It appears I'm going to be away for a day or two, and I wanted to thank her for some help she had given me earlier today."

"Oh? What kind of help did she give you?"

"She just provided some information the Sergeant needed on a report he was working on and I thought it would be good if I thanked her for her help." Jesse began to sense some antagonism on the part of the lieutenant, and he was walking a fine line between insubordination and giving out information that might get Olivia or himself in trouble. Lieutenant Goodin had a reputation for being a 'stickler' for discipline and Jesse didn't want to get on his bad side.

"Why should you thank her for help she gave the sergeant, Corporal?" Goodin was going to get to the bottom of the matter. He had eyes for Miss Livingston, and did not intend to broach any competition from a mere corporal.

Just then, Sergeant Davis came out of his tent. He had overheard the conversation between Jesse and Lieutenant Goodin, and wanted to avoid any friction.

"Excuse me, Sir," Sergeant Davis interrupted, "Logan, it's time you got on the road. Is that the horse you are going to use? He's only been rested for about a day since we used him last, and that was all the way to Lewisburg, too."

"He looks better than that other one to me, Sergeant. The bay has a little tear at the right front fetlock and his right rear shoe looks a little loose. I won't ride him too hard till he's had a chance to warm up."

"Alright, then, Logan," Davis replied. "Did you get all squared away with the people over in the suttler's tent?"

"Yes, Sir. Miss Livingston said she'll be there all evening if you need any more information."

Jesse took the envelope from Sergeant Davis, mounted the horse, and saluted Lieutenant Goodin, who returned the salute carelessly. Logan then went over to the mess tent and obtained some provisions he thought he would need and rode off into the gathering dusk. Olivia had been watching the activity from within her tent. She had noticed the attention Lieutenant Goodin had been paying her, and was not particularly interested in him. She hoped there would be no tension between the two men.

Olivia had let the friendship between herself and Jesse progress much farther than she had intended, but at the same time she enjoyed his company. He was a gentleman in every sense of the word, but was not backward in expressing himself. Also, she sensed in his presence a feeling of warmth and comfort. It was almost as though he projected a kind of — aura.

<hr />

Later that evening, Olivia went to the tent occupied by regimental command and sought out Colonel Sullivan. "I have a sufficient store of goods to justify a trip down into Confederate territory, Colonel, and I do think it's time I paid a visit to our sources in Richmond, if you think it appropriate. It's been almost two months since I visited our contacts there, and my curiosity is getting the best of me. Is it possible for me to secure transportation to take enough stock to justify a trip?"

"Certainly, Miss Livingston. I've established a source in town that will supply whatever you need. How large a carriage do you think the trip will require?"

"It won't be much, Colonel. I just have two cases of percussion caps, several boxes of medical supplies, about a hundred pounds of writing paper, some quills, and some ladies' undergarments. Oh, and I have some small note paper that I thought might be attractive, and some other small stuff. If I could get a small spring wagon with a canopy or folding top, that should be sufficient."

"Very well," the colonel responded, "when would you like to start?"

"As early tomorrow as I can, if that would be alright."

"I'll have a rig here in an hour, Miss. Will that be satisfactory?"

"That will be fine, Colonel. I think I can be in New Castle by late tomorrow, and then it should take me another three or four days to get to Richmond. It will be an endurance test, but I think I can be back in about two weeks."

Jesse was back in camp late Wednesday afternoon. He reported to Sergeant Davis and immediately returned to his tent. The nights were beginning to get cool. There was definitely a feeling of fall in the air. Jesse would have liked to have gone over to the Suttler's tent, but felt it was too late. Sergeant Davis had said there might be an order to move, depending on the Colonel's interpretation of the orders that Jesse had returned with. Jesse slept soundly. The ride had been without incident but any ride of a hundred miles over a three-day period was tiring.

The following morning, Jesse rose at dawn, and was out in front of his tent when 'Assembly' sounded. The men fell into formation on the parade ground. It was just as Sergeant Davis had predicted, but the move would not begin until the following day. The men had one day to gather their gear and be ready to move out. The rest of the day would be committed to cleaning up the campgrounds. Jesse was detailed to take out a perimeter picket. He assembled the twenty-four men he was assigned and they moved in formation toward their detailed position. As they left camp, Jesse cast his eyes toward the Suttler's tent, but there was no sign of life at that hour.

By about 1:00 that afternoon, Jesse's detail had been relieved and they returned to the camp. As soon as he was free, Jesse high-tailed it over to the Suttler's tent. He planned to pay Olivia back for the kiss he had 'stolen'.

As he walked into the tent, Jesse could smell the strong tobacco smoke from Mr. Livingston's pipe. He went in and looked around, but Olivia was nowhere to be seen. Finally, Jesse went over to Mr. Livingston and inquired, "Is Miss Livingston here? I was anxious to hear from her how her interview with Sergeant Davis went." He was hesitant to disclose to her father any of that which had occurred between them on Sunday.

"She had to leave for a few days. She'll probably be back next week or so," Mr. Livingston said casually. "She didn't say anything to me about any interview, so I don't think I can help clear the matter up."

"Well, it wasn't that important, I reckon. I can see about it some other time." He left, wondering why Olivia had left without telling him. This was the second or third time she had just disappeared for several days at a time, and Jesse was curious. *"Remember, the girl has no commitment to me and is under no obligation to tell me anything,"* Jesse thought to himself.

10

EAST TENNESSEE

Tazewell County, just to the south of where the small brigade had been encamped, was found to have a stronger Secessionist element than that which the men had become accustomed to farther north. They were confronted by resistance, not only from the Rebel army but also from the citizens, who were nowhere near as cordial as were their neighbors to the north.

The discussions among the men around the campfires had taken a turn. They now discussed the fact that, for the past eight months they had been welcomed at every town and crossroad they came to, and the sensation here was different in this part of the country. People they encountered here were much more sullen in their manner. While they still came out of their houses to watch as the men marched through town, the smiles were now replaced by looks of curiosity or even suspicion or hostility. Flags had disappeared, the confederate Stars and Bars being discretely kept in concealment and there were very few Stars and Stripes showing at all.

Resistance was still to be found, and Jesse and his new partner, 'Lige' Hawkins were still in use as a sharpshooter team, as were several other members of the company, but now he had to be even more careful. Though the use of the sharpshooter was mainly confined to the rural areas, except in special situations, the people of the region would sometimes harass the teams, signaling their positions to the Rebels and even shooting at them from the surrounding hills. It was often necessary to take a support team out to protect the sharpshooter, and in the process they were much less successful. Invariably when Jesse and Lige were in a vantage spot, local citizens managed to signal their position to the enemy, which often resulted in a lively response from a Rebel battery.

Jesse was also getting low level harassment from Lieutenant Goodin.

Though Sergeant Davis had tried to allay the concerns of the lieutenant when he had seen Jesse at the door flap of the suttler's tent, seemingly enjoying a conversation with Olivia, Lieutenant Goodin suspected Jesse as being Olivia's reason for her coolness toward him. Consequently, he took every opportunity to see to it that Jesse not only toed the mark as to his official duties, but also that he was going to get no opportunity to be in company with Olivia without close observation by the lieutenant.

As the unit entered Tazewell County, they received intelligence that a sizeable Confederate force was forming in the next range of mountains through which they would have to pass. Jesse and Lige were sent out with a team of six to scout the Rebel positions, and were given instructions to try to avoid any fire, but to return and report only, if possible.

They were both armed, Jesse with his Spencer rifle and his revolver, and Lige with a rifled musket and the Colt Pocket Revolver that had belonged to Jimmo before he died. Jesse had long-since given up his objections to the use of property that had belonged to men who had died, either friend or foe.

As they climbed the low hills at the foot of the mountains, they moved slowly and cautiously. While the region was only sparsely populated, they still suspected they were being watched, even though they could see no signs of the enemy. Lige had brought with him a small telescope Sergeant Davis had assigned him, and he used it frequently.

"I don't like this, Lige," Jesse said, "It's spooky. It's almost like we were the honored guests at a surprise party, and the only problem is that the surprise will be one we don't like."

"I know it. It's like there's a Reb behind every rock until you get there, and then he's gone. How many other scouting teams did they send out?"

"There's three teams in all. We're on the far right, which makes me feel a little better. I keep thinking it's the team in the middle that's going to get the big surprise."

"That's Bert Manson and Billy Miller. They're pretty sharp. They should be able to stay out of trouble."

Jesse scanned the scene to his left. "There they are, over on that second ridge. Boy! They sure are visible from here. I hope there's no Johnnies up the hill watching."

As Jesse spoke, he swung the telescope of his rifle toward the hill above the two other scouts, and jerked to a stop. "Hey! Take a look, Lige. 'You see the fellow on the ridge, just to the right of those rocks and the two lone trees?"

Lige took out his glass and sighted it as Jesse rested his Spencer in the fork of a tree. "Yeah. I see two of them, and there's something glinting in the sun just to their left. There's another one. He's got a scoped rifle like yours and it looks like he is sighting in on Bert and Billy. You'd better take them out, Jesse."

No sooner had Lige made the comment but Jesse fired the Spencer. One of the soldiers, a distance of almost four hundred yards, threw up his arms and fell to the ground. Jesse took aim and fired again before the soldiers on the hill could tell where the firing was coming from. Another Rebel soldier fell, but about that time there were about twenty of the Rebel skirmishers along the ridge and they began firing at the other scouting team as fast as they could reload. Jesse took careful aim and fired again, dropping a third member of the Rebel force. Lige fired once, but his musket didn't have the range to do any damage.

"We'd better get out of here," Hawkins said anxiously. "We weren't even supposed to get into a fight."

"Well, anyway, we found the Johnnies and we can all get back to our line standing up," Jesse said, starting back down the hill. By this time, the Confederate skirmishers had spotted him and Hawkins, and they were taking ineffective fire. Like Lige's musket, the Rebel firepower was insufficient at that range and they moved quickly and with less caution than when they had approached.

"Hold it right there, Yank," a voice came from their left from behind some dense bushes. Neither Lige nor Jesse hesitated. They had been trained, drilled, and schooled by Sergeant Davis to react immediately if confronted by anyone hiding in ambush, not to look, not to turn, not to even show any response other than to take cover or run as fast as they could from the threat. Jesse dove for some rocks to his right, and Lige started running a zigzag pattern toward the brow of a little hill about ten yards distant.

A shot rang out that sounded to Jesse like the report of a lightweight squirrel rifle. The shot had been aimed at Hawkins, who gained the top of the rise and threw himself on the ground behind it. Another shot hit the ground near where he had disappeared, kicking up dirt and rocks. That sounded like a musket of a little larger caliber.

Before the attackers could reload, Jesse stepped from behind the rocks and fired into the bushes three times in close succession with his rifle and a voice rang out indicating someone had been hit by one of Jesse's shots. Encouraged by Jesse's response to the attack. Lige rose and ran to his right, attempting to flank their enemy, firing his revolver as he ran.

"Hold it, Yank, hold it, we ain't got no more bullets. We're through. Hold it," came a cry from the bushes.

"Come on out of there!" Jesse ordered from the protection of the rocks, and two men in rough clothing emerged from the foliage. "You, too! Come on out of there!" Jesse bluffed, not expecting anyone else to emerge. To his surprise, one more, a younger man came out of the foliage holding in his left hand a rifle, which he dropped as soon as he was clear of the bushes. His right arm hung limply, blood dripping from his fingers.

"Check the bushes, Lige," Jesse called.

"I did. There's no one else in there, Corporal," Hawkins said, emerging at about the same point as the three others.

"So, what d'we have here, some guerillas or are you fellas spies? You're not in uniform, so you must not be soldiers. Check them for weapons, Private."

Hawkins did as Jesse directed, but found nothing in the way of additional weapons.

"Did you men leave any weapons in the bushes?" Jesse demanded.

The three looked at each other, and two of them said with wide eyes, "Oh, no, Sir, no Sir."

"Don't give me that 'Who-struck-John.' When I ask you a question, I expect a straight answer. What's in the bushes?"

Hawkins had ducked back into the bushed and presently emerged with two muskets. "They had tossed them farther back into the brush, I guess."

"Private," Jesse said, "discharge that unfired rifle back toward the hills and throw them off into the brush. No, on second thought, I think we'd better take them with us so they can't use them again if they come back here and find them. Give them back for these fellas to carry." When this had been done, Jesse continued, "Alright, you three bushwhackers, move. That way toward that bunch of trees."

"What you gonna do with us?" one of the three inquired, nervously.

"What were you gonna to do with us?" Jesse responded, angrily.

"We was gonna to turn you'uns over to th' legal authorities."

"Well, I'm the legal authority, here, and I'm still thinkin'." As Jesse followed the three men, he noticed that the clothing of one closest to him, the man with the injured right arm, hung a little odd. He reached out with the barrel of his rifle and struck the man's chest, the place that seemed responsible for the distortion. There was a distinct sound of metal against metal.

"Hold it, Mister," Jesse said to the man. "Move away from those two other men. Now just stand still with your hands out where we can see them. Drop that rifle."

The man didn't hesitate, but did as Jesse said and stood with his hands out away from his body.

"Check the bib of his overalls again, Lige," Jesse said.

Hawkins did as he was told and found a small side-hammer revolver in an inside pocket of the man's overalls.

"You should'a used it on 'em, Nate," the older of the three growled.

"I couldn't get to it right smart," Nate said. "I think my arm is busted."

"If I'd of had that gun, you'd be a dead Yank," the other man glared at Jesse.

"You're just sayin' that to make me feel good," Jesse said lightly, and ordered the man to pick up the empty rifle he'd been carrying. "C'mon, you three, get movin'. We ain't got all day."

Hawkins moved over close to Jesse and in a low voice apologized. "I'm sorry, Jesse, I just missed it the first time, I guess."

Jesse put his finger to his lips, gesturing for silence. "We can talk about it later."

"We can talk about it later," the ringleader of the three prisoners squealed, mimicking Jesse. "We can talk about it later in bed, you queer bugger."

"Shut up, Ben," Nate said harshly. "You're gonna get us into all kinds of trouble we ain't already in."

"We can talk about it later, sweetheart," Ben squealed in a sing-song voice, even louder than before. Meanwhile he was lagging behind the other two, apparently trying to create a distraction slowing the party, in hopes of allowing capture by an advance of the Rebel army.

"Move it, you," Hawkins ordered, prodding Ben in the ribs with his musket.

Ben, who had also been given an empty rifle to carry, lashed out with the gun, striking Hawkins in the side of the head, causing him to stagger sideways and fall to his knees. He then raised the rifle intending to use it as a club against the Union soldier as the other two prisoners moved as if to attack Jesse. Jesse pulled his revolver from his belt holster and fired at Ben hitting him in the head and turned it on the other two who stopped dead in their tracks.

"You killed him, you killed him. He warn't nothin' but a plain civilian and you killed him," Nate exclaimed.

"And I'll do the same for you, if you don't shut your trap. I don't want any trouble with you men," Jesse said in an even tone, "I'm sorry this here man had to die, but he started something that isn't going to stop till you're either dead or locked up. You're going back with me, dead or alive, and it's your call. Now, Nate, you pick up that gun that Ben had and you two throw those guns over in that canyon. Now start moving. I'm in a hurry, and I won't stand still for any more delays. Move!"

In half an hour they were back within the Union lines. The others had already returned and reported, and the regiment was forming for battle.

Jesse turned his prisoners over to the Provost and reported to Lieutenant Goodin. It seemed that Jesse towered over Lieutenant Goodin by about ten inches and this fact alone seemed to agitate the lieutenant no end.

"I thought your orders were not to engage the enemy, Corporal," were the first words Lieutenant Goodin spoke.

"Lieutenant, there was a sharpshooter drawing a bead on two of our men and I didn't feel I could just stand there and let one of them be killed."

"Corporal, you are not paid to think, to feel, to guess, or to speculate on the actions of the enemy. You are paid to obey orders and your orders were to avoid encounter. Am I making myself clear?"

"Yes, Sir." Jesse responded obediently.

"Do you know what the penalty is for disobedience to direct orders in time of war, Corporal?" Lieutenant Goodin demanded.

"I know it's pretty severe," Jesse said, searching his mind for what may be the appropriate penalty for saving the life of at least one of his companions, killing three or four of the enemy, and bringing in two prisoners.

"You're right. It's pretty severe, possibly as severe as the firing squad, if the consequences are such as would call for it."

The voices coming from the tent had attracted the attention of Colonel Sullivan, who wandered over and stepped into the tent.

"Lieutenant, have you obtained from this man his estimate on the strength of the enemy?" Colonel Sullivan asked.

"I was just about to ask him that question, Colonel. You see, through Corporal Logan's dereliction, he and the other scouts were unable to get into any sort of position to complete their assignment. By his negligence, he alerted the enemy to his and our presence before they could make an observation."

"It was the report of four of the other men in the team that they had already been spotted and by his quick action he probably saved the life of at least one of his comrades, Lieutenant. Did Corporal Logan also tell you that he probably saved the life of his partner as they were bringing in their prisoners?"

"No, Sir, the corporal has not been very forthcoming with any information at all from this sortie. He seems to be keeping a lot of information to himself, though I'm not sure why,"

"What's the conversation about the firing squad? I heard you mention a firing squad as I came in," Colonel Sullivan inquired.

"Sir, it was just a casual discussion about the possible ranges of punishment that could conceivably result from various forms of misconduct on the part of the soldiers, —."

"Lieutenant," Colonel Sullivan interrupted, "I wonder if you'd mind checking on the readiness of the company. It seems to be the intent of command that we take up a defensive position today and then tomorrow be prepared to assault the hill these men were scouting earlier. You might check with Colonel Tyler on that, too, if you will. I'll complete this interview."

Turning to Jesse, Colonel Sullivan resumed the interview. No mention was made of the admonition to avoid hostile encounter when they had been dispatched. The Colonel seemed satisfied that his men were disciplined enough to take appropriate action when they were sent out on scouting missions.

———⊂«◎»⊃———

The following day, the regiment was up before dawn preparing to assault what was expected to be a rather substantial Rebel entrenchment along the opposing ridge and flanking a low pass. Company "H" was to be held in reserve, but Jesse, Lige Hawkins, Martin Mason, and Shelby Smith were to work as a sharpshooter team off the left flank of the assaulting force. They had familiarized themselves to a small degree with the terrain, and were to start at four o'clock to try to get into a vantage position before the assault began. Their orders were the same as on previous battles; stay as high above the lines as the topography would allow, try for the upper level command personnel, and evacuate quickly if it looked as though the enemy was moving their way, as their usefulness would be nullified if their location was detected.

At four o'clock they moved out. It was November and the light didn't come until almost seven, but there was enough of a moon for them to pick their way among the trees and rocks without attracting attention. One of the first things they encountered on their way across the valley was the body of Ben, sprawled along the side of the trail.

"My head still hurts from the blow he gave me," Lige said softly.

"He was one of the orneriest men I've ever had the pleasure to meet. I wonder what they'll do with those other two," Jesse said in reply. Nothing more was said for the next half-hour or so. They climbed steadily, moving more to the southwest from where they had seen the pickets the day before. They could always circle back if they went too far to the south, but if they didn't go far enough, they'd walk right into the Rebel camp.

By daybreak, they had ascended the mountain about as far as they remembered the pickets to have been. They stopped for a breather and a drink from their canteens, and communicated only in whispers, hand signals, and facial expressions. There was no sign of the enemy, and they were wondering what to do next. They decided to move slowly up onto the next ridge and then northeast along that ridge at least as far as where they had seen the pickets. Their progress slowed to a crawl, for that is precisely what they were doing much of the time. They stayed with brush, trees, rocks, and the shelter of any irregularities in the land that they could find, only edging out from their concealment occasionally to check for the presence of the enemy. They were hoping the Rebel force had fled south, and they could return to their lines with the glad news. Such was not the case.

At about half past seven, after they had climbed well up the mountainside, Jesse, crawling forward from their sheltered position, spotted movement in the small valley near where the pickets had been, and shielded by the ridge where the firing had come from the previous day. He motioned to Hawkins and the others that the enemy was in sight and for two of them to move about some to check for pickets in their area and for one of the men, Smith, to return to the Union lines and report. Jesse would wait until the Rebels were alerted to the approach of the Union advance, pick a target and try to knock out their top staff. After about ten minutes, Hawkins came back with information that the immediate area was clear of hostiles.

They had waited a full half-hour when activity in camp told them the Federals had been detected coming up the hill. The Rebels had an excellent position, and Jesse watched with concern, as he knew his comrades were in for a tough fight. He had decided which tent belonged to the commanding officer but it was facing away from him and he only caught brief glimpses of the commander, whom he thought to be a captain. This seemed about right for the size of the Rebel force, judging the Confederate strength to be about 250 to 300, as opposed to their Tyler Brigade of almost 1000. It was little consolation that they outnumbered the Rebels, though. The defensive position of the Confederates was formidable.

Positions were taken along the token breastwork at the ridge. There wasn't much need for breastwork as the Confederates would be firing down the hill at the Federals and the advantage was in the elevation.

Jesse soon saw his chance. There was a captain, two lieutenants and a sergeant in conference and they began wandering slowly toward the line. His vision was obscured occasionally by trees, but if they would just move another twenty feet, he'd have a clear shot. After an agonizing delay, the four men moved into the clearing.

Jesse fired and the captain fell. He fired again and hit the sergeant. The two lieutenants had moved back toward the shelter of the trees, with one still barely visible through the trees and Jesse fired again. The Lieutenant also fell to the ground.

Jesse had given his position away and he signaled Marty and Lige to move. They crawled back from their vantage point, stood up and ran for the ridge above them. The Confederates would be sending out skirmishers to look for them, but it was least likely that they would be searching the mountains above the camp. It didn't appear that there was any cavalry attached to the Rebel company, and Jesse felt better about that. There were only three saddle horses tied near the command tent, and no one had yet thought to use them to search for the snipers. He felt that would change when they calmed down long enough to map a plan.

Shouting could be still heard coming from the camp, and the confusion was complete. "Where did those shots come from?" "Why didn't we have some pickets out?" "How badly is he hit?" "Lieutenant Nelson, we need you at the front. The Yanks are coming up the hill like a bunch of rats."

Jesse, Marty, and Lige were lying on their stomachs on a small ridge above and behind where the Rebel line was deployed. "Do you ever get to ride much, Marty?" Jesse asked with a raised eyebrow.

"I'll tell you what. I haven't ridden a horse for a couple of months and I'm just itching to get back into the saddle," Mason replied.

"What about you, Lige?"

"Any time'" Lige responded.

"What do you think our chances are, Marty?"

"About fifty-fifty, I'd say."

"That's about what I was thinking. That's good enough for me, how about you fellas?"

Both of the others nodded their assent. Logan held up his hand for a moment, and as quickly as possible, recharged his rifle. "I think we'd better make it down the hill on this side of the tent and then if we slit the back of the tent and go for the horses that way, we'll have the best chance of getting as far as we can without being seen."

"I'll do the cutting. You'll have all you can do with that rifle and your pistol." Mason said.

"Let's go," Jesse said softly.

The three men ran as quietly down the hill as possible and up to the back of the tent. There they were completely shielded from sight. Mason had pulled a knife from his belt and quickly slit the back of the tent. Even the sound the knife made against the canvas was lost in the commotion. They slipped into the tent which was unoccupied, and over to the front flap. Jesse peered through the tent flap. The field was clear, and Jesse motioned Marty and Lige out of the tent. It was only about ten feet to where the horses were tied at a makeshift hitching rail. The other two men led the way and Jesse covered their movement.

They managed to untie the horses and get partway into the saddle when a shout rang out. "There they are! They got the horses! They're getting away!"

Jesse took two shots with his rifle and ran for the third horse which Marty was holding by the reins. Hawkins fired his revolver at the man sounding the alarm, which caused him to duck behind a tree and the three were in their saddles by then. In an instant they were urging their mounts at a full gallop toward the place from which they had first been firing. Bullets clipped the trees around the fleeing men, but none of them were hit. They dodged trees and bushes as they sped southwest along the low valley, and were soon out of sight of the rebel camp.

After about three hundred yards at full gallop, the three men slowed their mounts to a trot. "Well, boys, what do you think of that for adding insult to injury?" Jesse asked.

"I can't believe we got away with it, Jess," Lige gasped.

"Well, maybe we haven't, yet, but so far we have managed to give them the slip. I suggest we go back to the lines. We've done about all the damage we can for one day."

They rode back down the hill following the same path that they had climbed earlier that morning. "It's sure a lot easier going down than it was up," Marty observed.

"That's because you're horseback, you crackpot," Lige countered. "Do you reckon they'll let us keep the horses?"

"Not if Jesse's pal Goodin has anything to say about it," Mason quipped.

"You mean old "Blotchy?" Lige chided.

"You had to bring up that name, didn't you?" Logan scowled at the others. "That rat is no pal of mine. What do you suppose makes him so mean?"

"I think he was born that way." Lige observed.

"I think he practices at night in front of a mirror, just being mean," Marty offered.

"Well," Jesse responded, "he certainly has it down to an art. He's almost perfect at it, for my money."

They made their way back to their lines and Jesse went immediately to Headquarters tent and submitted their report to Lieutenant Goodin. "I thought your orders were to take out some of the Rebel Officers," Lieutenant Goodin said after they had made their report.

"Sir, I did mention, didn't I, that we took out a captain, two lieutenants, and a sergeant before we were spotted. It was only in an effort to escape their patrols that we captured these horses." Jesse reminded him.

"Corporal, you have a peculiar way of disobeying orders and trying to make it look as though whatever you do is justified by the fact that you did it because it was so heroic. It's as though you had no alternative but to play your silly little games of capturing civilians or horses or some other thing we have no use for and you want us to applaud you because you're so big and brave. I'm getting a little tired of your going off and fighting your own little war and leaving the army out of your plans."

Jesse was speechless. He was getting a little agitated himself, but anything he said at this point could be taken as an attempt to justify his actions, and would just anger Lieutenant Goodin all the more.

"Now, just what would you like me to do with these horses, Corporal?" Lieutenant Goodin demanded.

Under other circumstances, the question would deserve a calm and rational answer. In this situation, the question begged for a very irrational reply, and Lieutenant Goodin realized it. Jesse said nothing, but though his eyes were downcast, the shadow of a smile on his face gave him away.

Lieutenant Goodin's face turned a beet red, leaving blotches of pale skin here and there. The redness proceeded well up beyond his receding hairline, causing his light brown hair to appear to stand out from his head. Jesse had heard others in the company refer to Lieutenant Goodin as "Old Blotchy" and he now knew why.

"I've had about enough of your insubordination, Corporal," the lieutenant steamed, "I'm letting you know you'll be on report to Command for this offense, and may consider yourself confined to camp unless otherwise instructed. Dismissed!"

Jesse saluted and left the tent. He was in a foul mood, wondering what he could possibly do to satisfy this man.

"What's up, old man?" Hawkins asked as he fell in beside Jesse on his way back to their tent. "You look as if your whole world had come apart."

"You know, Lige, this would be a pretty good war if it weren't for that snake."

<hr>

Their first encounter with hostile forces after they left Tazewell County was near a town named Broadford along the upper Holston River. Jesse was not prepared for the feeling of nostalgia and homesickness when he learned the name of the river which was the same Holston that flowed through Tennessee just a few miles from his home. The knowledge that he was so near Carter County gave a new meaning to Sergeant Davis' expression about 'a hill toward home'. The valley was at the foot of the Clinch Mountains, and it was over those mountains the regiment was to travel. The morning was damp and a low fog shrouded the valley, with pockets of more dense fog along the river. The valleys up the side of the mountain could also be seen to have what looked like rivers of fog hanging in them. It gave the scene a surrealistic appearance, and lent the impression that they were entering a wonderland, where a man could encounter any sort of unusual happenings.

As usual, Logan and Hawkins were sent forth, this time with a contingent of 24 skirmishers to reconnoiter and locate the enemy. They moved slowly and quietly through the valley, and then Jesse and Lige separated from the vidette, and went seeking an appropriate site to establish themselves for their assigned duties as a rifle team. They would set up along a ridge and direct their fire at the Rebel force that had situated itself and dug in on a low range of mountains just south of Broadford. As was their custom, they took with them a courier, Jim Owens, who would, after the team was set, return to Brigade and let Sergeant Davis know of their position.

The ridge they had to settle for was not much higher than that where the Rebels were entrenched. They were in a small grove of pine trees surrounded by large rocks and were well concealed, but after a few shots they would have to move once the Rebels figured out their position. The occasional fog came in and then left the little valley, but Jesse could nevertheless pick out his targets.

Owens had left them only a few minutes when the first opportunity presented itself. An officer — possibly a Captain — had moved out to supervise the setting up of a battery about 150 yards from their location. Confederate pickets had been sent out but had not approached close enough to cause the snipers any concern.

Jesse took aim and fired. The captain had been in the midst of a small group of men, and as Jesse fired, he moved slightly to his right so that the ball missed him, but caught a sergeant in the chest. He dropped on the spot, and the others in the group scurried. Jesse was getting used to the scene, and levered a new round into the chamber as quickly as possible. The weather was still so foggy that the smoke from his rifle did not show to his adversaries and the report from the rifle resounded from all sides, so they didn't have any notion of where the shot came from.

The captain was huddled behind a caisson, and Jesse's next shot was not going to be easy. He waited, anticipating the captain's sprinting for cover, but knew he should not wait too long, as it was as much the psychological effect that he was trying for, than to select any particular person. Logan had found that if he chose one person to fire at, to the exclusion of all others, he was often disappointed, as invariably the person would take adequate defensive actions and many other opportunities were missed.

Moving his attention up and to the left, he spotted another sergeant and squeezed the trigger. The sergeant fell mortally wounded and Jesse looked for another target.

Scanning back to where the captain had been, he found him still hiding behind the caisson. He sighted and fired, hitting the caisson and probably sending pieces of the bullet into the clothing of the captain, which, Jesse thought with satisfaction, would give him his share of excitement for the day.

Jesse was looking about for signs he had been spotted when he heard Lige's voice. "Hello Lieutenant, what can we do for you, Sir?"

Jesse turned. It was Lieutenant Goodin on a horse, one of those they had captured a few days earlier, approaching their position as calmly as though they were sitting around camp. "Lieutenant Goodin, Sir, it would be better if you weren't quite so — ah — so visible. We have a pretty secure position, here, but I've fired three shots and the Rebs are going to be looking for us. You're in danger here, Sir."

Actually, Jesse was more concerned that the lieutenant would 'sell' their position than his concern for Goodin's safety. He had no love for Lieutenant Goodin and it seemed as though the lieutenant had developed a personal dislike for Jesse.

"I just came out to see how you were doing, Corporal, and here you are making me feel unwelcome," Lieutenant Goodin complained in mock humor. "I've been observing your performance for some time, now, Logan, and I'm impressed at how well you're doing. You're a remarkable young man. You know horses, you're an excellent shot, you're well regarded with the press, and you're popular with the ladies. Incidentally, the sheriff of McDowell County was at headquarters looking for you the day after you rode off to Lewisburg. I told him you were not available and he seemed quite satisfied."

"Thank you, Lieutenant, I'm much indebted to you for that."

"Think nothing of it, Logan, what are friends for?"

"Lieutenant, you really should dismount, Sir. The Rebels will have my range here before long, and you're quite visible up there on that horse," Jesse admonished again.

Hawkins had been scanning the countryside with his glass, and broke into the conversation. "He's right, Lieutenant, those fellows can be pretty cagey when they want to and we've just popped two of their men. They won't be taking that lightly."

"Only two? I heard three shots." Lieutenant Goodin acted surprised. "You know, I'd like to try my hand at shooting that fine rifle of yours, Logan," he said as he climbed off the horse.

"Of course, if you like, Lieutenant, but don't you think it would be better if we were to do that at a less dangerous time?"

"Nonsense, Logan," he responded, "I think I'd like to be able to do some damage to the enemy, just as my brave and gallant men have done for the past months."

"Well, if you insist, Sir. Why don't you come over to this side of these trees? The Rebs are visible from here."

"I can see them quite well from over here, thank you," Goodin said, taking Jesse's rifle.

"But Lieutenant, the cover is better behind those trees," Jesse cautioned.

"Even if they knew we were here, they still couldn't hit us from this distance." Lieutenant Goodin was unimpressed with the caution Jesse was displaying. "It's best in these situations," he said knowingly, as though he was instructing the other soldiers in the art of sharp shooting, "to get the very best vantage possible, and fire from a position of rest, as provided by this rock."

Lieutenant Goodin had assumed a position of good visibility covering the front line of the Confederate camp, but he was exposed to his right rear, where the Rebels had deployed twenty or twenty-five pickets through the woods. The Rebels had started firing sporadically from their line of breastwork, and the sound carried up the hill, but at the time there was still no indication from below that their little sniper team had been located. Jesse and Lige were keeping to cover, however, while Lieutenant Goodin had taken up a position with his rifle resting upon a rock quite visible from anyone above them.

"Sir, if you would permit me —."

"Corporal, I know what I'm doing. You may not realize it, but I'm a pretty good marksman. I was near the top of my class at military school. There's an officer there beside that caisson, and he's about to —." Goodin fired the Spencer, completely missing his target.

"What the —? What's wrong with this rifle?" Lieutenant Goodin stepped back and looked down at the rifle in his hands.

As he stepped back a shot rang out from a grove of trees above them. Goodin threw the rifle in the air and toppled over backwards, blood gushing from the right side of his face. A Rebel sharpshooter had taken a position far enough to the rear to draw a bead on the lieutenant. The bullet struck Goodin near his right eye and tore through the side of his face, breaking his jaw, exiting near his chin and lodging somewhere in his chest.

Jesse had been crouching near the lieutenant and was in a position to catch the rifle as it fell. He immediately spun around, looking for the sniper.

"Lige, did you see where that came from?" Jesse whispered.

"I think it was from over in those trees on that far rise," Hawkins said hoarsely. "That man was crazy standing up there like that."

"Lige, take his horse and see if you can decoy that sniper. He may think there were just two of us and that you're getting away. Make it fast, and stay as low as you can."

"Okay. I'm on my way."

"Good luck, Buddy."

Hawkins sprinted out of the grove of trees where they were ensconced, made his way to the lieutenant's horse and jumped on. He wheeled the horse as though to return to the Federal lines and started off at a gallop. Up the hill, where Jesse suspected the sniper had been, two men stepped out of the trees to get a better view and a shot at the fleeing horseman. It was all Jesse needed. Before the Rebel rifleman could get a bead on Hawkins, he fired and the Rebel rifleman collapsed. Jesse levered another round into the chamber of his Spencer, took careful aim, and shot the spotter. He then ran in the direction he had seen his partner riding. The woods were sure to be full of pickets attracted by the shots, and it was getting a little too warm to stay around.

Lige had ridden only a short distance and stopped. When Jesse came running up, he was smiling. "It worked, it worked, I got the two of them," Jesse laughed, then he stopped short. They had been instrumental in four or five human deaths, and he had found himself in a state of jubilation.

"Lige," Jesse said, sobering," this is no business for normal people."

"You know what, Jesse, in this war there are no normal people."

"We're going to have to get him out of here," Jesse said, nodding his head in the direction of the fallen lieutenant. "We can't just leave him there. He might not be dead."

"Yeah, but then again, he might, and we're all going to be dead if we don't skedaddle. Whatever he got, he asked for. No one can be that stupid and expect to live through this war."

"I don't know, Lige, if we can get him out of sight, maybe the regiment can come up and save him. I don't see but a hundred and fifty or two hundred Rebs standing up to our side, especially with as much damage as we've done to their command staff. Listen, you take the horse and get back to the lines and report on the strength of this bunch of Greybacks and I'll see what I can do for Old Blotchy."

"Nothin' doin', Jesse. If you stay, I stay. Let's get to it."

After waiting some fifteen or twenty minutes, they made their way back to the place where Lieutenant Goodin had fallen and found him lying in a pool of blood from the wounds he had received. Jesse leaned over him and tried to find signs of life, but if the lieutenant had any pulse at all, it was too weak to detect.

"Jesse, I'll look to the lieutenant and you keep an eye out for the Rebs," Hawkins said. "From the firing down there, it looks as though they may be in retreat. But we'd better take care. If they find us here, they'll know it was us 'shot those two sergeants."

The Confederate company offered little resistance to the advancing Bluecoats, as they were seriously outnumbered. They retired east along the ridges from where they had come just a few days earlier, the three men hidden in the rocks managing to escape detection. Hawkins took some water from his canteen and, with his handkerchief washed the wounds about Lieutenant Goodin's head.

"Jesse, I think he's alive," Lige said after a few minutes. "I don't know if what we did saved his life, but I do think he's still living, at least for now."

They could see the Tyler Regiment off through the trees to the east, in pursuit of the fleeing Rebels, and it looked as though the three of them might be left behind, an unpleasant prospect for two soldiers and a half-dead lieutenant.

"Lige, I'm going to ride over and get help. Those fellows are going to miss us completely if we don't do something. You stay with the lieutenant and keep him comfortable."

Jesse had no sooner mounted up when a shot rang out from the direction the Union regiment had been coming up the hill. Colonel Sullivan had sent out videttes to pick up stragglers, and they had mistaken Jesse for a fleeing Rebel. Jesse tumbled off his horse and grabbed his rifle from the scabbard, but when he saw the blue jacketed soldiers, he lowered the rifle.

"Hey, hold your fire," he yelled. "We're "H" Company, Seventh Ohio. Give us a hand. We've got a wounded officer here."

The troop moved up to where Jesse and the two others were, and their sergeant came over to Jesse. "We never expected to find anyone from our side up here. How'd you get here so fast?"

"We're a rifle team and this is our lieutenant 'come out to check on us. He's hit bad, and needs to get to the hospital."

"You're "H" Company, huh? And that's Old Blotchy Goodin, ain't it?" the sergeant said in a disgusted manner. "Well, I'd just as soon leave him here for the buzzards, if it was my call, but if you want to keep him alive, I reckon I won't interfere. I do question your sanity, though. You won't get a better chance to get shed of some baggage than you got right now. If you want to leave him layin' right where he is, I'm deef and blind and so's my whole troop, Corp'l."

Jesse smiled at the implication that Lieutenant Goodin's reputation was not confined to "H" Company, but he had committed himself to saving the lieutenant's life if he could and was not inclined to retreat from that position. "Thanks for the offer, Sergeant, but I reckon we're going to try to salvage what's left of him," he said. "I didn't realize he was so popular outside his own company."

"He's one Yank I wish was workin' for the Rebs. Matter of fact, I ain't so sure he ain't," the sergeant growled. Then turning to the squad that was following, he yelled, "Stretcher!" Presently, two soldiers came up with a stretcher and lifted Lieutenant Goodin onto it.

When he was moved, Lieutenant Goodin moaned and opened one eye. "What happened?" he mumbled, then closed his eye and seemed to slip back into unconsciousness.

"He's alive," both Jesse and Lige said without enthusiasm, then Jesse said, "I want to thank you, Sergeant. I know he's less than Mr. Popularity around camp, but look at it this way. If we save him now, he may take a bullet for one of us some other time."

"Well, now, that's a happy thought," the sergeant responded, looking sideways at Jesse. "You jus' made my day, Corp'l. I'll write that one down in my diary fer my daily meditation."

The regiment moved easily through western Virginia and presently found themselves in Hawkins County, Tennessee. It was January, by this time, and while they were somewhat extended from the main forces' winter encampment in Nicholas County, Virginia, the Confederate forces seemed to be posing little resistance. By this time US General George Thomas had assumed command of the Army of the Ohio, under which they were assigned, and he had directed General Buell to make every effort to invest eastern Kentucky. Confederate General Crittenden, in charge of the region for the South had drawn off many of the troops occupying East Tennessee to counter a buildup of Federal strength farther west.

Jesse was beginning to feel at home. Carter County was only a few miles to the southeast, and while the weather was turning cold, the reception from the people of the area was anything but cold. The people of eastern, Tennessee were overjoyed at the presence of the Federal troops in their part of the country. Upon the urging of Senator Andrew Johnson, General McClellan, and even President Lincoln, relief from the oppression that southern sympathizers had been heaping on them, was now in sight, and they knew, now the tide had turned.

<hr />

In June of 1861, Rev. William B. Carter, for whose family Carter County had been named, risked his life to make his way through the battle lines and travel to Washington to present in person to President Lincoln the plight of the people of East Tennessee. His visit and the persistence of Andrew Johnson resulted in directives being sent to General Winfield Scott to, "... send an officer to Tennessee to muster into the service of the United States 10,000 men, to receive pay when called into active service by this department. ... All the regiments aforesaid will be raised for service in East Tennessee and in adjacent counties in East Kentucky ..."

There was no doubt that the president was aware of the problems of the loyal East Tennesseans, but being aware and taking steps to relieve the problems were two different things. Priorities must be considered in their proper order, and even though the people of East Tennessee were beleaguered by the presence of the Confederate forces, the strategic importance of the region was greater for the South than it was for the North.

Jesse's Grandfather Henry Kellar had been able to keep his Union sentiments from affecting his livelihood as he, at the suggestion of his sons John and Fred, had gradually altered their lumbering operation to the milling of railroad ties in anticipation of the need for improved transportation in the region. Before the outbreak of the war he had also bought some equipment for the production of wagon wheel spokes to be made from the oak and ash from the nearby hills. His business prospered, though there was a growing uncertainty as to the means of payment received from the sale of his products. The State of Tennessee, now committed to the Confederate cause, had begun issuing currency, or script, promising full faith compensation when the difficulties surrounding their forming a new nation were settled, as had several of the other states involved. While there was uncertainty as to the validity of this sort of money, it was the only currency available and the Kellars used it as the availability of Federal greenbacks diminished.

The states had also issued instructions to the local banks to impound any Federal currency that turned up and send it to Nashville for "exchange for like value" in Confederate money. In areas such as East Tennessee, northern portions of Alabama and Mississippi, and parts of Louisiana, this policy was viewed as a ploy to penalize those loyal to the old Union by stripping them of any Federal money they might have and replace it with worthless script. Such was the feeling in Carter County, but if one was to stay in business, one had to play along with the local authorities. Where a person stood on the issue of who was right and who was wrong on the matter of secession was certainly a product of their view of slavery.

Henry and Emmelyn Kellar had received several letters from Jesse, informing them of his joining the Union Army and later a little of his activities, assuring them he was safe. Beyond that they knew very little of his activities or sentiments toward the war, except to read articles in the newspapers as to the 'depredations and atrocities' attributed to the "White Angel" as he was named by the press. Henry Kellar, a dedicated Whig and Unionist learned to keep his sentiments to himself, except in very close and guarded company.

Nevertheless, Henry was widely identified as a Union sympathizer and treated accordingly. The Loyalists embraced him, the Secessionists tolerated him, and the neutrals, if there were such in Carter County, accepted him.

East Tennessee was considered by the new Confederacy much like South Carolina was by the old Union; a thorn in their side. The region was important for its agriculture, its lumber, and as a strategic route for the Virginia and East Tennessee Railroad for movement of materiel of war between the east and the west, but its people were almost unanimous in their opposition to the cause of secession. A force of the Confederate Army, and some irregular 'militia' units, were maintained in the region to protect the rail lines, prevent invasion by the northerners, and also to recruit the local eligible males for military service. With few exceptions, the latter effort was largely ineffective, the young men of military age avoiding the recruiting efforts as much as possible.

In August, 1861, Felix Zollicoffer, who had been a strong voice for preservation of the Union, but then proclaimed his allegiance to the state of Tennessee, had been made a general in the Confederate Army of the Tennessee. From Knoxville he issued a proclamation, addressed to the people of East Tennessee and trying to explain his position toward their intransigence. Though the states alliance with the Confederacy had been engineered primarily by the machinations of Governor Isham Harris, Zollicoffer argued that the "ballot box had prevailed" in the decision as to whether to secede, and had decided the issue for one and all. It was now expected of all Tennesseans of whatever sentiment to abide by that decision.

He went on to note:

"All who desire peace can have peace, by quietly and harmlessly pursuing their lawful avocations (sic). But Tennessee, having taken her stand with her sister states of the South, her honor and safety require that no aid shall be given within her borders to the arms of the tyrant Lincoln."

"Can there be recreant sons of Tennessee who would strike at their brothers while thus struggling for Southern honor and independence? or who would invite the enemy over the border to inaugurate war and desolation amid our own fair fields? ... If any, it were better for their memory had they perished before such dishonor. Let not the Union men ... be carried along by excitement or passion into so deplorable an extreme."

The proclamation was the subject of much discussion and consternation. Henry and his friends, those of strong Union sympathies, cussed and discussed Zollicoffer's proclamation endlessly.

"That snake," Jeremy Gainfield exclaimed. "He was all for the Union back in '59 and '60, and here he is telling us we'd be better off dead than to stay with the Union. He's a fine one to talk about strikin' at yer brother, when he's turned his back on ever'thin' he stood fer back then and joined the army of the bunch that's tryin' to break up the Union. And fer what? I tell you, it's all about slavery."

On November 8, there had been an organized effort by loyal Unionists to disable the transportation system of the region by burning several railroad bridges from western Virginia to Alabama. This included the bridge at the town of Union, (formerly Middletown and recently renamed Zollicoffer), along the Holston River. Then, on November 9, there had been a great gathering of about 1500 Unionists in Elizabethton and just down river at Taylor's Ford, anticipating investment by the Union Army, from which the East Tennessee Brigade (USA) was formed. All this activity, despite a contingent of Tennessee State Militia (CSA) under Captain David McClellan, was evidence of the strong Union sentiment in the area, and the feeling that they would be liberated from their Confederate agitators.

When the Tyler Regiment entered Hawkins County in early January, they were met by such a display of welcome, they could have imagined the war was over and they were marching home victorious.

━━━━━◄(●)►━━━━━

Confederate General Braxton Bragg had pulled most of the Confederate forces westward to counter the threat from General Fremont and Colonel Grant. The Confederate presence in the Watauga Valley was greatly diminished and the tensions in the area relaxed. Captain David McClellan's Confederate militia cavalry unit, Company "B", headquartered in Greenville, was about all that was left from Sweetwater to Bristol, Virginia, except for a few bands of irregulars.

Sergeant Davis went to the colonel and asked permission for Jesse to take a month's furlough, as they were within but a few miles of his home, with very few hostiles in the area. Colonel Sullivan consented, and Jesse was on his way to Kellars Crossing.

The homecoming celebration Jesse encountered was more than he could have anticipated. He was welcomed by family, friends, strangers, dignitaries, and everyone else with an interest in the Union cause in general and of Jesse's part in the war in particular. Parson Brownlow from Knoxville was in the area and visited the Kellars' home to wish Jesse well.

Even though the Federal forces were still some miles distant, the presence of a member of the Union Army and a native son at that, was cause for celebration. Grandma Kellar and the ladies of Kellars Crossing prepared a meal fit for any major feast, and served it up at the work barn at the Kellar mill. The weather was cold, but there was little snow on the ground, and the barn had solid sides to cut the wind. The event was held during mid-afternoon, so the cold was almost negligible.

The atmosphere was festive, and friends with whom Jesse had worked and attended school, church, and social functions all greeted him warmly. Several of Jesse's close friends had done much as he had in the early days of the war, and had joined other units of the Federal army. Other friends had gone the Confederate army, too, so the feeling, while warm, was also sometimes tentative. His old and dear friend Tom Singleton was still living in Doe River Cove and was working at the mill and was also at the party, thus far having avoided the Confederate conscription because of the need for the mill's products by the government.

Also visiting the gathering and paying their respects to the local hero were such notable Unionists as Colonel Dan Stover, Major Elijah Simerly, Captain John Helton, Lieutenants Will Jenkins and Henry Pierce, and a host of other members of the loyalist East Tennessee Brigade. These were men who had chosen to stay in East Tennessee and form up the nucleus of a resistance force, and were widely recognized for their valor and commitment.

More than once had Jesse's exploits as a sharpshooter been noted in the press and the local papers had missed no opportunity to mention that he was from Carter County. It was a truly hero's welcome.

Tom Singleton wasted no time in greeting his old friend. It had been barely a year since they had seen each other, but much had happened in the meantime.

"You've made quite a name for yourself, Jesse," Tom said as soon as they had greeted each other.

"Tom, I don't know what they have been writing in the papers but I'll tell you, most of it is made up. Some of the stuff they've been claiming to be my work, I wasn't even near where it was happening."

"Well, when you left last year, you didn't say much about getting into the army, and I was all enthusiastic about joining, and here we are. I've been training with the militia, but I'll tell you, the Secesh make it awfully tough on us. We're not strong enough to make much trouble for them, and when we do try to make trouble, they take it out on the townspeople and anyone else they think is sympathetic with the Union cause. Up until now, I haven't been able to leave town to get up into Kentucky where most of our people have gone to join up. I think I'll join, now that the Union army is in East Tennessee and we're pretty well safe from the Rebs. I don't know if you heard about the bridge that some of the local people burned over at Zollicoffer back in November, but since then the Rebs have made life miserable for anyone they think might be anyway connected with that little party."

"I heard about it. Were you in on it?" Jesse asked in a tone of confidentiality.

"No, I wish I had been, but they kept it pretty well under wraps till the night it happened. We still don't exactly know who did it. 'You know Dan Stover over there?"

"Sure I do. Was he one of them?"

"I don't know for sure, but word has it that he was one of the leaders." Tom confided.

"I'd like to go talk to him. That's really great of him to come to this thing. I've got an idea it could be dangerous even being seen at a gathering like this one. If there's anyone here who's friendly with the Rebs, the word will get back and everyone's neck'll be in the noose. I don't even know if I want to be seen with the likes of you renegades," he said jokingly, "It could ruin a man's reputation."

Jesse and Tom walked over to where Dan Stover and Elijah Simerly were standing and talking. Tom introduced Jesse to the two men. "Dan, Sheriff, I'm sure you remember our local celebrity and fellow soldier, Jesse Logan. Jesse, I guess you know Colonel Stover and Sheriff 'Lige Simerly, or should I say Major Simerly?"

"Lige will do just fine, Tom. Hello, Jesse, I see you're a traveling man."

Jesse had heard the term before, but its significance escaped him. "No more than I have to, Sheriff," he said.

"No, I mean you're wearing some jewelry I recognize," Simerly said.

Jesse was confused. He wasn't wearing any jewelry except his watch. He looked down at the watch fob where the three other men had fixed their eyes. "Oh, this. My sergeant got this off a dead Reb in that battle up at Rich Mountain and he gave it to me so I could keep track of the time."

"Do you mind if I take a look at it, Jesse?" Dan Stover asked.

"Not at all," Jesse handed him the watch. "It has some engraving on the inside of the cover. It belonged to a Confederate soldier." Though he had gotten used to the fact that sometimes it was necessary to appropriate the property of the fallen enemy, now he felt a closeness to the former owner of the watch, and wished he could give it back.

"It belonged to an 'Alfred Stearman, of the Seventh Virginia Vols, CSA'. He was the Master of Mountain City Lodge. It looks like the members of the lodge gave it to him when he joined the army," Stover said somberly, and handed the watch back to Jesse.

"I'd sure like to get it back to his family," Jesse said. "I didn't recognize the figures or the significance of the engraving."

"Then you're not a Mason, Jesse?" Elijah Simerly asked.

"No, Sir. Tom and I talked about joining a lodge, but I was too young before I left last year, and haven't had an opportunity since then. I'd like to join a lodge one of these days, though."

"Tom, would you get the particulars on this man and turn them in to Steven Venable before Monday night?" Stover asked. "We'll have that lodge so loaded up with Union men, old Turner Carnahan will have a fit."

"'Glad to, Dan," Tom replied enthusiastically. "I'll get him signed up right away." The conversation went right past Jesse, but he got the idea that the three other men were discussing making him a member of their Masonic Lodge.

The following Monday evening, dinner was served at Kennedy Masonic Lodge in Elizabethton, and the gathering of thirty-five or forty men enjoyed a peaceful evening. Nothing, Jesse thought, could beat the fellowship he was enjoying at that moment.

Jesse was to spend almost five weeks in Carter County. He had been allowed from January 10th to February 11th and he was going to make the most of it. Recruiting for the Union was high on his list of priorities, but it would be necessary to have any new recruits make their way back north into eastern Kentucky, to contact an established garrison and be mustered into the Federal army.

Toward the end of his furlough, the last Saturday night he had left of his leave, a party consisting mostly of young people whom he had gone to school with gathered at the home of Paul Venable in Elizabethton. It was a small group as care was given not to encourage attendance by any of the Confederate sympathizers in the region. Steven Venable, Paul's father had a fine home in Elizabethton, and after having met Jesse at the Masonic Lodge, he was easily talked into allowing the party at their home. His wife, Nan and their daughter Lily would act as hostesses, along with some of the other girls in their late teens and early twenties.

While the party did not seem to gain the momentum of the welcoming party at Kellars Crossing, nevertheless it was a great success, as the tension associated with the occupancy by Rebel troops was minimal. As the party progressed, Jesse felt more and more like the Jesse Logan of the late fifties. Friends he had not seen for over a year were at the party, and there were some faces he was only vaguely familiar with, one being Lily Venable, Paul's sister.

Lily was just eighteen. While Jesse recalled having met her when he was younger and he and Paul were in school together, he had only vague memories of this young woman from his earlier days in Carter County. She was two or three years younger than Paul and had been something of a boisterous young woman, more interested in horses than she was in socializing with her classmates. As Jesse recalled, she had a favorite horse she liked to race, but the horse was also temperamental and not suited to racing. In fact, he remembered her having been thrown from the horse several times, resulting in some fairly serious scrapes and bruises.

Logan found that Lily had matured considerably in the past couple of years and had become something of a beauty, though she had also retained the appearance of a person used to being outdoors a great deal of the time. She had a direct, often disarmingly abrupt way of talking, and was obviously at ease with everyone at the gathering. They talked at great length and while she didn't seem at all ruffled by the publicity Jesse had received as a local hero, he, on the other hand, found her to be quite a charmer. While Lily didn't demonstrate any discernable attraction toward Jesse, she certainly didn't shun him, and he spent as much time at her side as he could without appearing to ignore the other guests.

It was about eight o'clock when Jesse left for the evening. He walked to the door with Lily, and as he was leaving, he asked her if he might write her some letters when he left Carter County with his regiment. Other men in the regiment had regular correspondence with girls back home, and Jesse felt it would be very pleasant to be able to write to a pretty girl. Though Jesse was strongly attracted to Olivia Livingston, he was never sure of where he stood with her. She had not been with the regiment very much since he'd made that ride to Lewiston and when she was there, she often seemed preoccupied with her work. Besides, it wouldn't hurt to have a choice. Probably nothing would come of either association, anyway.

Lily said she would be delighted to correspond with Jesse if her parents approved, and she thought they would.

"If you write me a letter and don't hear back from me, you can assume my parents disapprove," she said jokingly. Much would depend on the nature of the political situation in the valley, and the question of the mail getting through.

Jesse was to have only two more days in the valley. On Monday he would be going to the Masonic Lodge and would be getting his 'Third Degree' as they termed it. After that he would be a full-fledged Mason. He looked forward to the event, as it would then give him the standing to attend any lodge in the country and enjoy the company of some highly respected and notable men. He had heard that Senator Johnson was a Mason, as was General McClellan. Jesse thought it would be nice to attend a lodge meeting and sit next to the general and just call him 'George', or 'Mac' or something equally casual. Governor Isham Harris was also a member of the fraternity, and Jesse thought it might be nice if he could talk some to him.

The events of the evening having drawn to a close, the guests bid their goodbyes to the hosts and left the Venable home. He rode the five miles or so to Doe River Cove with some of the other young men in the group in a surrey that Tom Singleton's family owned, but then was obliged to walk the short distance on to Kellars Crossing.

One of the members of the Carter County Militia, Captain Dan Ellis, had been a neighbor of the Kellar family in the Watauga Valley and was widely recognized, and widely sought by the Confederates, as a scout, guerilla fighter, and organizer for the cause of the Union. Captain Ellis, with Colonel Dan Stover, Sam Cunningham, Harrison Hendrix his son, S. H. Hendrix, and about twenty others had planned and executed the bridge burning at Zollicoffer the night of November 8, the preceding year, on the Virginia and East Tennessee Railroad. They had done so in coordination with intelligence from the Union forces that there would be a Federal force entering East Tennessee from the north, and the burning of the Zollicoffer Bridge, along with several others on the rivers of the region would disrupt the Confederate response to the invasion. The burning of the Zollicoffer Bridge resulted in a frenzy of arrests, accusations, and orders from the Confederate government all leveled against the unionists of the region. The burning and the resulting retaliation galvanized the conviction of many of the rest of the citizens of the region and converted many to the Union cause, swelling the ranks of the unofficial and lightly armed militia.

Numerous influential citizens had done what they could to petition President Lincoln, General Sherman, General McClellan and anyone else they could get to listen to their entreaties to send troops to the area to hold the Rebels at bay. General George Thomas, who was now in command of the Army of the Ohio and stationed at Fort Dick Robinson, Kentucky, started to move into the region to lend his support to the beleaguered East Tennessee Regiment, but was called back after only two days enroute. The Federal Government was well aware of the plight of these loyal Unionists, but unfortunately the region was not sufficiently important to the strategy of the Union Army at the time. The only reason anyone could give for occupation by the northern army was the disruption of Confederate rail communications and the region's possible relief from the ravages of hostile forces.

One civic official of a town near Knoxville, Mr. Madison T. Peoples had written to Confederate Secretary of War Judah Benjamin on November 20, 1861:

Sir: In my opinion there is not a Union Man in Carter County who is not involved to some extent in the rebellion. Many of them were drawn into it by wicked leaders and some have hastily repented, but many others will seek the first favorable opportunity to repeat the experiment.

... Even now our most quiet and law-abiding citizens have been shot down in cold blood from behind coverts by the tories (sic) and proof can be made that they have been tampering with the slaves.

... If we are invaded, every Southern man will be taken prisoner or else murdered in the night time.

The "rebellion" Mr. Peoples was referring to, of course, was the resistance the people of Carter County were offering to the cause of the Confederacy; the "law-abiding citizens" were his description of the supporters of the Confederate cause.

———— ⸭⟪❂⟫⸭ ————

As it turned out, though the Confederates were pulled farther west at the time, still the small Union regiment in Hawkins County, Tennessee was about all that were to venture into East Tennessee for some time to come.

General Thomas had authorized the Tyler Brigade to act as an expeditionary force making their way the fifty or so miles south from McDowell County, Virginia to test the defenses in East Tennessee. Confederate General Wood immediately called upon the Army of the Tennessee, CSA, to provide reinforcements to drive the Federals out of the region. East Tennessee was too important as a source of food and also for its railroads to the west for the Rebels to give up to a token force of Yankees. Tyler began to feel the pressure immediately and knew he'd extended his regiment too far. It would be necessary to pull back.

Orders were given that on February 14 the Tyler Brigade would execute an orderly retirement. Jesse would receive his 'Third Degree' at the Masonic Lodge, on the 12th, and be able to get back to the regiment in time to return to McDowell County.

11

LIBBY

"Let's shoot him," Eli Morgan growled, glaring at Jesse as though he had just identified the cause of mankind's misery. "I been knowin' this buzzard sence we was whelps, and I say he don't deserve to live. This cussed furiner was nuthin' but trouble when he first came to these parts, and he ain't been nuthin' but trouble sence. I heer'd he's the one who's be'n snipin' a lot of our off'cers out on the front lines, all up and down the Alleghanies."

"I say we string him up," Eli's brother Arthur said. "We hain't hung anybody 'round these parts lately, 'specially since we ain't caught up with all them unionists who burnt the bridge down on the Holston, and I wouldn't be surprised ef he was one of 'em."

"Them Kellars is jes' too big fer their britches, anyhow," Mac McMurray joined in. "That man's Oncle John beat up my pa right smart back afore the war, and Pa hain't got over it sence."

Jesse had been on his way home from the party at the Venable home and had not been prepared to meet up with the likes of this little band of 'home guard' who were farther south that they usually ranged. Guerillas were nothing unusual in East Tennessee. Both Union and Secessionist sympathizers had formed up into loosely knit groups, partly for protection from each other, and partly, as they expressed it, from patriotism, and sometimes out of pure orneriness.

The burning of the Zollicoffer Bridge had been the start of it. The railroads in the region and especially the East Tennessee and Virginia, which were partially supported and relied upon by trade from the Kellar mills, were virtually immobilized by the burnings, and then by the continual sniping at construction crews sent to rebuild them. Now the woods were full of renegade bands of both stripe, often wreaking as much destruction on their own people as on those of the enemy. The Union regiment in

Hawkins County hadn't intimidated everyone, and the rumor was that the Confederates were rushing to push them out, anyway.

"Hain't anybody got a rope?' Eli asked.

"I got this yere lead rope fer my horse," Mac stepped up.

"Well, ain't that jes' dandy?" Eli snorted. "That thar rope won't string up this yere long necked sucker. Hain't anybody got a rope we kin use to stretch that neck of his'n a little longer?"

"Well, we kin tie it around his neck and lead him down to old man Frye's place. I know he has enough rope," Mac responded.

"Yeah, but we'd best not let old man Frye in on our little game. Him and Logan's Grandpap are pretty tight, and he'll set up one helluva fuss ef he finds out what we're a'doin'," Arthur cautioned.

"Well, let's git goin'," Eli said, "We'll think of something. We might just shoot him after all."

"Hang him. Hang him," Albert Coster kept up a chant. Albert was not too bright, and the little band just kept him around to do their heavy work, and also because he'd probably kick up a fuss if they left him home. "Hang him. I hain't never seen nobody git hunged."

"Shut up, Albert," his brother Sidney, snapped. "You'll jes' git us in all kinds of trouble wif yer big mouth. You boys better mind yer se'f, too. We ain't in sech friendly country, here, and we could jes' as easy git shot, ourselves, ef one of them unionists hears us." Sidney said in a stage whisper directed at Eli and the others.

Eli Morgan claimed a relationship to John Hunt Morgan, who also ranged the area farther north, but John Morgan didn't admit kinship if there was any. John Morgan was trying to maintain the image of protector, and Eli and his band had developed the reputation of spoilers. Eli, at twenty-three, dreamed of, or to put it more accurately, salivated at the idea of gaining the stature of John Hunt Morgan.

"Come on, Mr. Yankee sharp shooter," Eli said in a falsely solicitous manner. "We're going to see what ye're made of. Maybe Sidney's right. Shootin' you would make too much noise and we jes might cut yer throat to save time an' trouble ef we cain't hang you. 'Too bad fer you, you ain't got yer good friend the Indian killer with you jes' now," he said referring to the old antagonism between him and Jesse regarding Jesse's friend, Fall, back in 1855 on the trail through Nevada.

It was well after eight o'clock in the evening and the moon had just started to show through the trees as they dragged Jesse down the road toward Doe River Cove and what they recalled as a farm belonging to John Frye. Frye was a respected farmer in the valley, and as he didn't own slaves himself, he opposed secession, but not particularly vocally. He had an interest in a small store in Doe River Cove, and tried to maintain neutrality in the conflict that was rampant in the region.

Looking up the road toward Elizabethton, Jesse saw what he thought was a pair of horsemen coming their direction. Jesse had a rope around his neck, but wasn't tied at the hands or feet, and was able to move freely. He didn't know who the horsemen were, but felt his chances couldn't be any worse with them than by staying with this band of cutthroats.

"Shoot. Shoot!" Jesse yelled as loud as he could toward the horsemen. The horsemen quickly dismounted, and when the others turned to see whom he was shouting at, Jesse kicked out at one of his captors, grabbed the rope from the grasp of Eli, knocked Albert into the road against two others, and ran for the woods.

Eli, who had an old pistol, recovered his balance and fired at Jesse's fleeing figure, as did Sidney Coster, but Jesse anticipated the shots, and was weaving as he ran. It was too dark for Eli to reload and get off another good shot, and he gave up.

The two riders, a Confederate lieutenant and a corporal, weren't sure what the firing was all about, or if they, themselves were being fired on. They held their weapons at ready, but didn't shoot, as the gunfire didn't seem to be coming their way.

"Hold your fire, there," Lieutenant Arnold shouted. "What are you men firing at?"

"We jes lost a prisoner, Cap'n," Eli called back. "We was bringing him in fer you'uns, so's you'uns could turn him in."

Eli didn't know whether he was addressing a southern or northern soldier, or even what rank he held, but he was covering all his options and was trying to avoid specificity until he found out. "We thinks he's a deserter, and you'uns probably got a price on his head."

As the two groups cautiously closed, Eli and the others could see they had encountered Confederate soldiers, and Eli was relieved that he had given the lieutenant the benefit of a promotion.

"Sure, enough, Cap'n. That feller was Jesse Logan, who used to be from these parts, but turned fer the north and snuck back here to stir things up, I reckon."

"I'd heard Logan was in this area," Lieutenant Arnold said, "and you're right, mister. I'd like to get my hands on him. Do you men think you can get him back?"

"We'll surely try," Eli replied. "We knows this here country like a gopher knows a garden, and we'll bring him in fer you ef'n we kin."

They spread out and moved into the woods, but Jesse, who had moved quickly at first when the confusion was greatest, was creeping ever so quietly, now, and was well ahead of the pack. His footprints in the light snow he'd managed to confuse by several double-backs, and he was well out of range from detection.

He took his time, moving only when he was sure there was no one nearby and cautiously made his way back to the road. He then headed south toward Kellars Crossing, and the safety of his pro-union neighborhood. He traveled quietly along the road, making no sound except the occasional crunching of snow underfoot for a period of five minutes. Suddenly, Jesse heard from about fifteen feet away the unmistakable click of the hammer of a carbine being cocked.

"Hold it there, Mr. Logan," a voice sounded out of the darkness. "Just hold yer hands out away from yer body so's I don't have to shoot you."

The voice gained a body in the form of the rebel corporal, who had lighted a match and was holding it over his head. He had left his horse with the lieutenant and had made his way quickly down the road toward where they felt Jesse would go.

The soldier's voice was familiar and when Logan managed to get close enough to identify the man he stopped in surprise.

"Adam Gainfield, what are you doing in a Rebel uniform? You were always a pretty clear thinker in school and were all the time arguing against secession and the like, and here you are. What happened to you Adam? What happened?

"I ain't goin' to discuss politics with you, Mr. Logan, I'm just here to take you in. Now you turn around and start moving, please."

Logan could see Gainfield was nervous and trembling visibly. The carbine he carried was shaking in his hands and as Logan had heard him cock the weapon at their initial encounter, he was concerned that the man might discharge the carbine from sheer trembling.

"Corporal, I respect your decision to join the Confederate Army, or any army you choose, but now that I'm your prisoner, don't you think it would be safer if you let the hammer down on that carbine? You remember when we used to hunt together on my grandpa's farm, we always tried to keep the hammer down until we had reason to shoot. Believe me, you don't have any reason to shoot me. Honest!"

"Don't bother to talk to me Mr. Logan. I'm in the army of my choice for my own reasons, and I don't need your advice. You jus' keep movin'. Don't stop, don't turn around. Don't talk. Just keep movin'."

Gainfield was under a lot of pressure, Logan could tell. He and Jesse had been good friends in school, and he had been the last person Jesse would expect to ever join the Confederate Army — voluntarily.

"Adam, they conscripted you, didn't they?" Logan asked as he trudged slowly north toward Doe River Cove. "You got trapped and had to go into the army, didn't you?"

"Mr. Logan, I told you to keep ye'r mouf shut, and I meant it. There ain't no point in tryin' to talk me out of anything."

By this time, they had reached the spot where the lieutenant and some of Eli's gang had convened.

"Lieutenant, look what I got here," the corporal cried when they were within earshot of the lieutenant and two members of the renegade band. "I found him down the road, just like you said."

"Are you Jesse Logan?" the lieutenant asked, when Jesse was close enough to be seen. There was no chance of mistaking Jesse's tall frame and shock of pale yellow hair by the light of the lantern the lieutenant had lit. "We've been looking for you, Logan. There has been quite a story going around about your marksmanship down in Virginia, and our informers let us know you'd come up here. I suppose you've decided to join us for a while. Is that how it is, or did you come up here to stir up trouble, as these men are saying?"

"Sir," Jesse said evenly, "I don't think this is the time or place to discuss my political leanings, and down there in Virginia I was just doing the job I was given. We all have a job in this war and I've been doing what I was told. You're doin' the same, and to the best of your ability, I reckon. As for bein' up here in Carter County, I was furloughed to visit my family, and that's what I'm doin'."

"Logan," Howard Arnold was impressed by Jesse's calmness and courtesy, "From what I have heard, you're pretty good at what you do, and there has been quite a stir around these parts when the word was out that you were back. I'd judge your marksmanship is something you learned here in the hills, but it wasn't too wise of you to come back. Every patrol in four counties is alerted for your capture. I won't quibble with you as to the propriety of what you're doing or what I'm doing. My job, as you put it, is to take you in, and your job right now is to stay alive. Do you understand me? In this case we could just as soon hang you for a spy. You do understand me, don't you, Mr. Logan?"

By this time, the entire band of Eli Morgan's 'home guards' had returned to the road. "Hang him. Hang him!" Albert cried. "I hain't never seen nobody git hung'd."

Eli Morgan chimed in, "Cap'n, we kin git a rope, right quick, and save you the trouble of a'takin' him in."

Eli was getting under Lieutenant Arnold's skin just a little. His obsequious manner was irritating, and his addressing Arnold by the improper rank when his rank insignia was quite obvious was annoying. "Sir," he said, addressing Eli, "You flatter me. I'm a lieutenant, not a captain, and my orders are to take this man back to Elizabethton. I'm grateful to you for trying to capture him, but my orders are to bring him in, and that's what I intend, unless he tries to escape."

"Does we git a RE-ward, Lootinent? We'd be happy wif a little compensation fer the danger we ben through bringin' this here buzzard to justice." Eli persisted, anxious to acquit himself with his fellows, and make the best of a sour situation.

"I'm sorry, but there is no price on Mr. Logan's capture, and besides," he twisted the knife a little, "If I recall, it was my corporal who effected the capture after you had allowed him to escape."

"Lootinent," Eli was seething at the rebuff. "Lootinent, thar's five of us here and thar's jes'two of you'uns," he said with understated threat in his voice. "I'd hate to be on that end of the odds wif a prisoner who's showed he kin make the kind of trouble this feller has. Ef you'uns don't want to string this booger up right here, I'd suggest that mebbe you he'p pay us'ns fer our trouble and expenses."

With that, the lieutenant and corporal, who had remounted, with Jesse tied and held by a rope to the corporal's saddle, separated slightly, still facing the little band of renegades. Suddenly Lieutenant Arnold spurred his horse forward into the midst of the group, knocking the thugs helter-skelter. Eli's pistol went flying, as did the musket McMurray had been holding. Jesse kicked at Sidney Coster and knocked his pistol into the darkness. The other members of Morgan's gang dropped their guns, as the soldiers covered them with their revolvers.

"Sir," Lieutenant Arnold maintained his composure, "The penalty for lynching a prisoner in the hands of the military is death by hanging. I'm sure you didn't intend such an offense, but let me suggest that it would be best for you in future, if you measured your words more carefully, so that they not be taken as a threat. Let me also suggest now, that you gently kick those guns over into the brush there, and walk off down the road. 'That direction." He pointed north.

Arnold turned to Jesse after the little mob was out of earshot, "Thank you, Mr. Logan. Your bravery won't get you a parole, but it may have kept you alive for a day or two."

"That's my job, right now, I think you said, 'Cap'n'." Jesse smiled.

Lieutenant Arnold, having aspirated a bit of saliva, was coughing and laughing at the same time, and it was a few moments before he gained his composure. "You are a cool one, Logan," he said, "I'm not sure I could be so calm in this situation."

"Lieutenant, I assure you I'm much calmer now than I was when those 'home guards' had a rope around my neck. Prison doesn't look nearly as bad when you view it from that perspective. Their options were shooting me, hanging me, or cutting my throat and they didn't even ask my preference."

"Home guard, eh?" Lieutenant Arnold joked. "I think a more appropriate description would be 'cut throats' as that was one of their suggestions, wasn't it?"

As they talked, the trio had started north down the road toward Elizabethton, where their unit was stationed, and where they had a lockup for captured Yanks and runaway Rebels. The following day he could be questioned and then delivered to the nearest permanent prison, probably in Chattanooga.

Custody of prisoners was tenuous in these parts, as the Smokey Mountains were crisscrossed with competing forces from both sides, but Jesse's local reputation had made him a most desirable prize. It would be particularly important for the Confederate forces to take Jesse in, unless, as Lieutenant Arnold had said, he made an effort to escape in which case he would be killed. The Rebels did not want this man to return to the field. He had cost them dearly in reputation and personnel losses, particularly at the command level, and with his being from Carter County, it was something of a propaganda coup to have him in their custody.

Vaguely aware of his celebrity status, Jesse was simply intent on first, staying alive, second, escaping from his captors, and third, getting back to his company. His life had taken on a new perspective, since he had come home to Carter County.

As he sat in the little jail at Elizabethton, he was wondering what was going to happen to him the next day. Lieutenant Arnold had mentioned the possibility of his being hung for a spy. Though Jesse knew he wasn't a spy, it could certainly have been a good excuse for the Rebels to get rid of him. It would not be the first time one side or the other had used such a flimsy notion to eliminate a man whom they didn't want around, and East Tennessee was just the sort of country that inspired acts of retaliation sometimes based on flimsy notions.

The strongly unionist regions of Carter and Johnson Counties and their companion counties, including those just across the line in western North Carolina, coupled with the mixture of sentiments farther west, made for a boiling cauldron of unrest. At times, the slightest incident, such as a theft of livestock, the burning of a building or the capture of an enemy agent could trigger an outbreak of violence by either side. Just such a riot had occurred in Knoxville and to a lesser extent in Elizabethton in early June of 1861 when the state legislature had voted for secession against the previous vote of the people to remain with the union.

The Confederates had a tenuous hold on the area around Elizabethton. That may change tomorrow. Lieutenant Arnold, in charge of the Elizabethton outpost knew all this, and he wanted Jesse taken to Carters Station as quickly as possible. There was a stronger jail and a squad of about 35 soldiers there, even though the political sympathies of that town were strongly unionist. At first light, he detailed a squad to remove Jesse to the larger jail, where he was again held overnight and questioned briefly.

Jesse's life was something of an open book in this region. Having been born here, spending his latter teenage years here and now returning with some notoriety to the region, he was rather well known. The press from both sides of the rebellion issue had magnified Jesse's reputation, and deaths of many Confederate officers and especially of soldiers from East Tennessee were often attributed to Jesse Logan, whether he had been anywhere near the battle in which those men were killed or not.

The East Tennessee and Virginia Railroad ran from Chattanooga through Knoxville, then northeast to Roanoke and on to Richmond, and at the time the road was open and trains were getting through. It was the best chance the Rebels had of getting their prisoner to Richmond with the least chance of incident. Lieutenant Arnold assigned a sergeant and a private to the detail with strict security instructions and also instructions to telegraph their progress both back to Johnson City and forward to Richmond, the clearing house for military prisoners. The trip took two days, and was without incident.

The squad arrived at Richmond late in the evening on the second day, and were met by an ambulance, which was to transport them to the prison. As the trio arrived at the train station, the sergeant checked the manacles on Jesse's wrists and put a rope around his waist. The train depot was only a short distance from the jail, but as they got off the train a small crowd gathered immediately and assailed Jesse with vulgarities and taunts. The bystanders gave Jesse every vile name they could think of, only because he was a Yankee.

When they had gone a short distance, the private who was assisting in his movement to the jail said loudly to some of the crowd, "This here is the famous White Angel who's been killing so many of our boys back up in the Alleghenies."

With those words as a signal, the crowd grew ugly. The three men could hear a low roar starting in the rear of the group, and growing in volume and intensity.

"You ignorant fool," the sergeant hissed at the private. "You're going to get us all killed. Why can't you keep your big mouth shut? Run up to the door of the jail and tell them we're here and need to get inside fast."

The private turned pale and with eyes wide and a scared look on his face, he jumped down from the wagon and sprinted forward to the door of the jail. Pounding on the door, he summoned two guards from inside the jail. They stepped outside and leveled their shotguns at the menacing crowd, who faded as fast as they had formed. Apparently, this had not been the first such incident. The idlers along the Richmond streets seemed to take pleasure in watching for Yankee prisoners, and when they saw them, they treated them like something less than human. Jesse and his captors hurried inside the jail with the crowd still murmuring taunts and threats.

The Henrico County Jail had been taken over recently by the Confederate Government as a receiving station for war prisoners, captured Confederate deserters, political prisoners, and spies. The prison population was growing daily and there were few alternative facilities in which to house prisoners. Jesse was thrown into a small holding cell with about ten other prisoners, still wearing his blue uniform.

It seemed odd to Jesse that there wasn't even an interview with a jail official when he was put into the cell, but thus it was for about six weeks. He was absolutely ignored by the jail staff, except to be fed with the other prisoners twice a day.

Late in March, a group of soldiers assembled the prisoners in groups of twenty or thirty, shackled them as well as they could with the few chains at their disposal, and marched them the short distance to a three-story brick building at the corner of 19th and Cary Streets. There was a sign on the front of the building that read "Libby and Son". The prisoners were told this was to be their new home until the end of the war. The prospects were not inspiring. The few prisoners Jesse had come to know at the jail he'd just left were not in the same group as he was, and the men he was with were all strangers to him. They stood about with a kind of dull curiosity etched on their faces, accepting the inevitable, but wondering if this place could be any worse than the one they had just left

A heavyset man sporting a pair of mismatched revolvers and a Bowie knife attached to his belt greeted them at the door. He identified himself as 'Commander' Ross, announced that he had been expecting these prisoners, and that they were to make themselves comfortable, laughing heartily at his own joke. He directed the soldiers to escort the prisoners to one of several rooms, about 45 feet wide and 85 or 90 feet long. There they were released from their chains and allowed to walk about the room.

After three days, Jesse was summoned into the office by Ross, who, as it turned out, was simply the clerk assigned to maintain the prison records. "Are you Jesse Logan?" Erasmus Ross asked not looking up from his desk.

"Yes, Sir," Jesse replied politely, realizing that while Ross was merely a clerk, he still had the power to make life difficult for any prisoner, and Jesse had had enough of notoriety by this time, anyway.

"So you're the White Angel we've been reading about." Ross looked Jesse up and down. "Why don't you jes' fly away, Angel?" What's keepin' you here, 'somebody jes' clip your wings?" He laughed at his own little joke. "Major Turner wants to see you, Logan. He's likely wondering the same's I am, what's all the fuss about this here White Angel?"

"Believe me, Mr. Ross," Jesse replied, "The newspapers have blown this thing all out of proportion. I'm just a soldier doin' his job, same as you."

The flattery of calling Ross a soldier was not without effect. It was apparent that Ross, a civilian employee, would have liked to be considered a soldier, but it appeared that he was not enrolled or accepted as such. Jesse didn't care. He would treat the man with as much deference as he had to, to maintain his respect. As Jesse and Ross were talking, an officer walked into the room from an adjacent office. Ross came to attention, turning to face the officer. "What can I do for you, Major?" Ross inquired courteously.

Major Thomas Turner as commandant of the prison, was a man a few years older than Jesse, with dark hair and gray eyes. He was a thin man and wore a full-dress Confederate uniform, complete with forage cap, even in his office. He stood and walked with a stiff, formal stance earning him the sobriquet of 'Broomstick' Turner, as distinguished from his first assistant, Lieutenant Richard Turner, who was roundly disliked by the prison population and soon became known by the prisoners as 'Dirty Dick'.

"See to it that these prisoners are thoroughly searched and accounted for, Ross," the major said stiffly. "You never know what the civilian jails have allowed to get through. These men may have any and all sorts of weapons and contraband on them." He eyed Jesse up and down as though he was some sort of strange animal.

"What's the name of this one, Ross?" he asked haughtily. "He looks like some kind of scarecrow."

"This is — ah, Jesse Logan, of the Seventh Ohio Volunteers, Major," Ross said looking at his records. "He's the one they call White Angel."

"Well, well, well. So we have a celebrity in our midst. Ross, see to it that you have as much information on these men as you can get. You never know when we may have an escape risk on our hands. I want this prison to be the best example of security in the system. General Winder gave us clear instructions that we were to be the future clearing house for the facilities in the Richmond area, and we have an obligation to see to it that these rascals aren't out to create trouble. Where are you from, Soldier?" he said, turning to Jesse.

"I'm from Tennessee, Sir," Jesse responded formally, immediately regretting the disclosure, when he could just as easily have said he was from Illinois, or even Nevada.

"Tennessee? What are you doing in a Union uniform?"

Jesse knew he was going to have to handle the question with discretion. Regional loyalties were important to the people of the South. Even though Tennessee had voted early on to remain in the Union, the actions of the governor had placed them in the Confederacy, and the rest of the southern states simply accepted the fact that if you were from a Confederate state, you were, by definition, a Rebel.

"I'm from East Tennessee, Sir," he said, trying to evade the obvious, "but I was up north when the war broke out and I just joined up figuring it was going to be a short war."

"How would you feel about joining the glorious cause of rebellion and fight for independence, Mr. White Angel?" Major Turner inquired.

"I'd surely have to think that one over," Jesse evaded. "I don't think that idea would set too well with the Federals, if I ever got captured. Isn't there something about getting shot as a deserter if you do that?"

"Well, you think it over, Mister. The people of Tennessee would be mighty proud to have you fighting for their side." The officer turned and walked back into his office. The interview was over.

"Jes' now you're goin' back to the lock-up, but I'm goin' to call the guards an' they'll search you good." Commander Ross advised. "If you have anythin' on you what you ain't supposed to, or somethin' they might take a likin' to, they'll make life a little harder than it already is. If you want, I'll hold anythin' like that, an' git it back to you when I kin. You maybe are thinkin' 'Why trust this feller,' but I'm tellin you that givin' somethin' like that to me now is a heap better than lettin' them guards find it on you. What'll it be? I'll keep it fer ye', I promise."

Jesse was suspicious. The few dollars he'd had in his pocket had been immediately seized by the Rebel soldiers in Elizabethton. The one item he still had in his pocket was the watch he'd received from Sergeant Davis back at Rich Mountain, and he'd developed quite an attachment to the watch, hoping someday to return it to the family of the southern soldier to whom it had belonged. There was some logic in Erasmus Ross's reasoning, but Logan had been a prisoner of the Confederacy now for over six weeks, and still had the watch. If he gave the watch to Ross, he might have a chance of getting it back. If he had it seized by the guards, his chances of ever seeing it again were probably somewhere near zero. He pulled the watch and chain out of a pocket and gave it to Ross.

"This may not be anything, Mr. Ross, but my sergeant gave it to me and I'd like to get it back to the family of the man who it belonged to, if I can find them. He died back in one of the first days of the war."

"I'll hold it fer you, Logan. Believe me." Ross said in a friendly manner, then he turned and opened the door to the hallway leading to the holding 'tanks'.

Jesse was searched thoroughly and escorted down a long corridor on the first floor of the building and shoved back through the barred door from which he had come earlier. There were about eighty-five prisoners already in the large, barn-like room, and most of them were simply milling about or talking to one another. Two or three were sleeping on the bare floor without benefit of pillow or blanket.

"How does anybody stand it in here?" Jesse asked the man next to him.

"What are our choices, friend?" the fellow replied. "Believe me, none of us would be here if we had someplace else to go," he said with impeccable logic, and then asked, "Where 'you from?"

"I'm from Tennessee," Jesse replied absently. He had learned that such an answer invariably drew some kind of curiosity, but to tell anyone he was from Nevada was not much better.

"What are you doing in here?" his new friend asked, "Are you some kind of a political prisoner? I thought they sent those people over to Castle Godwin or up to the third floor."

"No," Jesse told him, "I'm just as much a unionist as you are, I reckon, but I just happen to have been raised in East Tennessee."

The two men talked for the remainder of the afternoon, joined by others, all trying to adjust to their situation.

The following morning, Jesse was again called to the commandant's office for questioning. Though he had no particular information to provide the confederate authorities, he was a rather notorious prisoner in the eyes of the Rebels, and he was grilled at length about his status as a southerner in Federal uniform. He explained the fact that his original home, or homes had been in Nevada, and this seemed to appease the authorities, somewhat. After an hour, he was returned to his housing unit.

His size was also something of a curiosity, and where ever he went, the guards seemed challenged by his height and treated him roughly. The first man he had met, when he was thrust through the door on the night of his arrival at Libby was named Wilfred Williams. He was from upstate New York, and had been captured at Manassas. He had been at Henrico County Jail about six months when Jesse arrived. He was a friendly sort of a fellow, and he and Jesse talked for hours about their homes and families. Willie, as he was called, had been a cavalryman with the Second New York and had been shot in the right hand, causing the loss of two of his fingers. The wound was a clean one, though it had not been treated, and Willie kept it wrapped with strips of cloth he had obtained from the Sanitary Committee, and it seemed to be healing quite well.

The guard, Amos Straught, was as close to a friend of the prisoners as it was possible to find among the security personnel, and the prisoners treated him with great deference. They tried not to let any of the staff know there was anything but hostility between him and them. They also maintained discipline when Straught was on the floor, as they were anxious to keep him in good graces with Major Turner.

Jesse spent his days trying to think of something besides Olivia Livingston. He thought of some of the other people in his life, Lily Venable included, but most of his time he spent thinking of Olivia. His comment to Lily about writing her a letter passed through his mind, and one day, he obtained a small piece of paper and an envelope from the Relief Commission that came through occasionally, and wrote Lily a letter. He didn't have much hope of ever mailing it, but just writing to her made him feel better.

Dear Miss Venable.

As you may have heard, I have become a prisoner of the Secesh, and have been put in prison. The life is not a pleasant one here, but I am all right. I hope you are the same. There is very little to do at this place, which is called Libby, and is located in Richmond. I have never been in Richmond, before, but this is not exactly what I would think of as the best way to visit this big town.

There are many intresting things happening here, not the least being the manner in which the guards calculate new ways to make life difficult for us prisners. Nearly every week some new restriction is imposed. Southerners on sentry duty make nothing of watching for an excuse to pass out unusual and uncalled for disciplin. Security has become so tight that one day, one of the guards shot another one who had stuck his head out of a window. The rules are that the prisners aren't to put any part of their bodies out of a window, and will be shot at if it happens and the guard that was shot just forgot the lessons that we prisners learnt so well.

I think you ought to know how much I enjoyed seeing you at the social your Pa held at your house last January. It had been about a year since I saw you last, and it was nice to make your acquaintance again.

Well, this is not a very big piece of paper, and I have to figure a way to get it into the post. I like writing to you, even though you may not be able to write back. I don't think the guards let any mail come to us, because I surely haven't seen any come in.

Your willing and obedient servant,

Jesse Logan.

As Jesse was sealing and pressing the envelope flat, 'Commander' Ross happened to open the door to the 'tank' as their quarters were known. Jesse was kneeling on the floor which was the only flat surface available on which to write a letter. Ross walked the few feet where Jesse sat and put a foot on the letter. "What have we here, Mr. Angel?" Ross demanded in a demeaning tone.

"I — I was just writing some notes, sort of, and thought I'd maybe mail them, or keep them to give to a friend, if I ever get released." Jesse stammered.

With no little effort, Ross bent down and picked up the letter.

"How'd you expect to get this little love-letter mailed, Logan?" Ross inquired, looking at the name on the envelope. "You know we ain't lettin' pris'ners write outta here."

"I was kind of thinkin' I'd get you or one of the other officers to mail it when things ease up. Some of the other prisoners said that sometimes there are some letters that are allowed to go out."

"'Can't do it, Logan," Ross's reply was quick. "Y'know I can get in all kinds of trouble, if I get caught doin' such thing."

"How could you ever get caught, Mr. Ross?" Jesse asked. "It's just a matter of carrying the letter out of the prison and leaving it at the post box."

"For one thing," Ross said, "that letter would never go through the lines. And for another, sometimes we get searched when we leave this place to make sure we ain't carrying out no food or nothin' we could he'p feed our families."

"How in the world do they expect any of you guards to use the food for your families? It makes us sick, and I'm sure your children wouldn't last a day if they were to eat any of it."

"Well, when the food comes in here is not all that bad. Hit's the cookin' and waterin' it down that makes it so bad. Two of the guards were caught just the other day carrying out food. They're up in County Jail, right now, just waitin' for a court martial."

Jesse persisted. "It's only a piece of paper, Mr. Ross. Here, look here," he took the letter back, "I've got it all folded up and pasted together, and it won't have to go through the lines. It's to someone here in the south, up in Tennessee." Whenever he referred to his home, it was 'up' as everyone in the Smokies referred to the rest of the world as 'down'.

"Forget the letter, Logan," Ross said, snatching it out of Jesse's hand and putting it in his pocket. "Better you not get caught with it on you." He turned and left the tank.

———•((◍))•———

Time at Libby passed slowly. Jesse had spent the last part of February and most of the month of March at Henrico County Jail and most of April at Libby. He was getting to feel like one of the fixtures at the General Housing Dormitory where he was assigned. The other prisoners had accepted him, and most of them had become rather friendly. As the days passed, Major Turner seemed to begin taking an interest in Jesse, and had called him into the prison office more than once to question him. One day, Turner questioned Jesse about his reputation for marksmanship.

"I understand you were quite the sharpshooter out in the Allegheny country," Turner commented casually.

"I was just doing the job I was assigned to do, Major," Logan said, trying not to agitate the officer or create a situation that would give the confederate authorities reason to harbor ill feelings toward him. "I was a pretty fair shot back home, and I had a really good rifle, and the combination gave them a reason to think I could work as a rifleman, I reckon."

"I fancy myself something of a marksman, also, Logan, and I'd like to discuss some of the techniques you were using and maybe pick up some pointers. Maybe you could teach me a few of your tricks."

"If there are any tricks involved in this conversation," Jesse thought to himself, *"the major is the one using them to gain some kind of an admission."* He knew better than to trust an officer who just 'called him in for a friendly discussion'. That just wasn't the way the war worked.

Major Turner continued, "What would you suggest would be the best way to improve one's score at the targets, Logan? I'm firing a rifled musket, a Springfield, and I keep a pretty small pattern at fifty yards, but when I go much beyond that, my pattern really spreads out." The question was innocent enough.

"Sir, those Springfields are not always as accurate as a lot of people think. I'd suggest you first look at the rifle, and satisfy yourself of its accuracy. Make sure the barrel and action are well fitted to the stock. Then use it a few times from a really solid bench rest, and see what kind of a pattern it gives you. After that you can work on your own techniques, — your stance, breathing, posture and that sort of thing — and try for improvement there. I can work with you on those," Jesse suggested in a noncommittal manner. His suspicions were still aroused, but the conversation was not about him, and he thought he could steer clear of incrimination, if he was careful.

The conversation continued for the better part of an hour. At first Jesse was cautious in giving the major any information he thought could be used against him or his companions in the prison. As time went on, however, it became clear that there was a real interest on Major Turner's part in improving his own abilities to handle a rifle.

Presently Turner rose and announced, "Logan, I'm going to take you out with me tomorrow and we'll put your theories to the test." He turned to Commander Ross, who had come to the door, and had heard part of the conversation, "Ross, clear my calendar for tomorrow and have a couple of horses brought around at eight o'clock in the morning. I'm going to try my hand at some of Mr. Logan's techniques."

Jesse was dismissed and returned to his quarters. He kept his experiences with Major Turner to himself, and wondered silently where the events of the day would lead him. It was certain to be more interesting than the existence to which he had been subjected these past several weeks. The thought still haunted him, though, that his close association with the security staff of the prison was a dangerous road, and he would have to be constantly on guard against compromising himself or his fellow soldiers.

Later in the afternoon, some people from the Sanitary Committee came through the prison and delivered some minor luxuries to the prisoners. A woman who apparently had a medical background examined Willie's hand, and she applied a clean bandage to the wound, already healing fairly nicely. Willie had lost the two last fingers of his right hand, and it was the subject of considerable humorous conjecture as to whether such a wound would keep him out of the war if he were to be exchanged. Another of the women, a Miss van Lew, took an interest in Jesse.

She approached him at a time when she was unobserved by the guards and in a low voice, said, "Mr. Logan, we are going to try to get you out of this place as quickly as possible. We feel your life is in danger, and it would be an easy thing for the Rebels to have you killed trying to escape or something. Be careful. Don't take any chances, and also, don't do anything out of the ordinary for a prisoner of your status."

With that, she was gone. Jesse had no opportunity to inform her of his pending assignment to go with Major Turner to the Confederate firing range. She summoned one of the guards and had him open the door of the tank and left while the other members of the committee were still talking to various prisoners. One of the guards walked over to Jesse.

"What did you say to 'Crazy Bett' that made her take off out of here so fast, Logan?" The name Crazy Bett had been one Jesse had heard discussed from time to time, though he hadn't associated it with a particular person. It had been ascribed to someone who had the reputation of being eccentric to the point of lunacy, but whom the authorities allowed into the prisons as harmless enough. Jesse was turning over in his mind the combined and conflicting facts of her having recognized him, and warned him of danger and at the same time being regarded as an eccentric.

"She just said something about the fact that there wasn't enough blankets in here, and I told her we was alright for the time, since it gets too hot in here anyways," Jesse responded. "After that she just turned around and scooted. I don't know what got into her head, Sir."

The evening meal that day was better than usual. The gruel was reasonably flavorful and there were a few beans distributed to each prisoner, though they were hardly soaked enough to soften them up for eating. There was also a slice of bread to sop up the gruel. As he ate, Jesse reflected on the warning "Crazy Bett" van Lew had delivered. It was obvious she knew who he was, and when she had addressed him, she seemed anything but crazy. The advice made sense, as it was evident the guards regarded Jesse with suspicion and hostility reserved for special prisoners. Her advice posed a particular problem in as much as she had warned him against any unusual activity. At the same time, he felt it would be unwise to refuse to go out with Major Turner the following day, as that in itself might raise suspicion.

The following day, as planned previous to Miss van Lew's visit Logan was called to the office of 'Commander' Ross. "The major says you and him are goin' out to do some target shootin'," Ross said in a low voice.

"That's what he told me yesterday," Jesse responded.

"Jes' a friendly word of advice, Logan. Don't try anything funny. The major isn't as bad a shot as he'd like you to believe, an' shootin' a big-time pris'ner would be a feather in his cap. Keep close and don't turn yer back on him."

Jesse felt a chill run up his spine. He remembered the advice Elizabeth van Lew had given him and was stunned that Ross showed a similar concern. He stared at Ross for a few seconds before responding. "Thanks, Mr. Ross. Thank you. I'm much obliged."

Major Turner, a corporal, and Jesse left the prison and, crossing the Mayo Bridge over the James River, went out to the countryside where there was a target range set up for militia practice. The major was dressed in his most resplendent uniform, in keeping with his custom, but the soldiers at the target range took little notice of him, as he was a common sight at the place. He and Jesse spent over an hour going over the elements of ballistics and marksmanship with some practice firing on Major Turner's part. When they had finished, they prepared to return to the prison.

"I'm quite pleased with the improvement in my use of the rifle, Logan," the major said with obvious satisfaction in his voice. "I appreciate your help."

Jesse was gratified that the session had gone so well and that there had been no adverse incident to mar the event. "I think you're making good progress, Major," he said. "If you'll just keep up the practice, and give mind to those little suggestions I made, I think you'll find you'll do quite well."

"Logan," Turner said, after some hesitation, "Have you given any thought to the suggestion I made some time ago about joining the cause of secession?"

"Yes, Sir, I have," Jesse replied, still trying to dodge the issue, "But I'm really concerned about being treated as a deserter by the Yanks, if I was ever to be caught."

"That'd be no problem, Logan. We'd just keep you here in Richmond and you'd never be exposed to capture."

"You mean take an assignment as a guard at the prison?"

"That's right. You'd just be working here for me."

"No, thank you, Sir. The life of a prison guard isn't for me." Jesse knew the conversation was going nowhere. Even if, in his wildest moment, Jesse thought of defecting, he knew there would be no guarantee of his staying in Richmond even if he wanted to. It puzzled him that the major would even bring the matter up. He thought about the warning he'd received the day before from Elizabeth van Lew and also from Erasmus Ross, and wondered what was going on in the major's head.

The Mayo Bridge across the James River was a few blocks west of the prison, and Jesse was grateful for the extra time out of the prison and having crossed the river, they were riding rather briskly down Cary Street toward the prison when Jesse noticed three women walking toward them on the sidewalk. Women out walking during the day in Richmond was not unusual, but these three were dressed in high fashion, something out of the ordinary for the conditions at that time, and one of the women was Elizabeth van Lew. Trying not to stare, Jesse observed the three with some curiosity when it struck him that one of the women with Miss van Lew was Olivia Livingston. He suppressed an urge to hail her, and though it appeared that she had noticed the group he was with, she gave no indication of recognizing Jesse. In fact, it was apparent she studiously avoided looking his direction after a first glance.

Jesse kept his composure, and rode on with the major and the corporal who was with them to guard him, but his mind was racing.

"What is going on?" He was thinking. *"How did Miss Livingston get to Richmond? What is her business here? How is it that she was dressed in such fashionable clothes when she seemed purposely to dress so plainly back at camp? Was he dreaming? Perhaps this was not Miss Livingston at all, but a twin."*

Presently they were back at Libby and dismounting. Major Turner, the formal appearing commandant of the prison, one whom Jesse was inclined by nature and warned by the other prisoners to avoid, was not such an unpleasant person after all. He had his human side, and Jesse thought the day had not been wasted. It may just be that his contact with the major would ease the tension between the guard staff and the prisoners, if anything could.

That evening, Jesse kept to himself. When questioned by the other prisoners as to his absence, he replied he'd been called out for some drudgery duty outside the prison. He had some thinking to do.

Several days later, the Sanitary Committee again visited the dormitory in which Jess was staying. 'Crazy Bett' was with the committee, and in the course of her rounds came unobtrusively up to Jesse.

"What were you doing out on the street the other day?" she demanded maintaining a friendly smile, but delivering the question in a distinctly insistent tone. "I told you to keep a low profile and not to do anything out of the ordinary."

"I'd made a commitment to the commandant the day before to give him some advice in target shooting and I could hardly claim that something had come up that changed my plans, now, could I?"

"Mr. Logan, I repeat, your life is in danger. If the southerners get an excuse, they will not hesitate to shoot you, and I'm of the opinion that you were allowed out and given a horse just to tempt you to try to escape. Now, please —."

One of the guards had approached where they were standing, and Miss van Lew immediately changed the subject, while maintaining the same friendly attitude. "I'm going to see to it that you get a pair of sox, and I want you to promise me you'll wear them faithfully. They're good for your feet, you know."

With that, she joined the other members of the committee and they left the prison. Outside, the seven members that were on that day's visit parted and went their own separate ways. Elizabeth van Lew returned to her mansion on Grace Street, where she was greeted at the door by Olivia.

"What happened," Olivia demanded, without so much as a greeting.

"He said he'd agreed to go out of the prison for target practice with the commandant and, of course couldn't back out without arousing suspicion."

"Well, I suppose that's right. Did you tell him that they had just taken him out for target practice, with him as the target?" Olivia wasn't joking.

"Yes, I did, and I admonished him to be careful and not to do anything out of the ordinary."

"Telling Jesse Logan to avoid the extraordinary is like telling the wind to stop blowing, I'm afraid," Olivia mused.

"You love him, don't you, Libbie?" Bett ventured.

"Did you tell him I'm here, Betsy?"

"Libbie, he knows you're here. He saw us together the other day."

"But did you tell him we're working together?"

12

VISIT TO LODGE #19

few days after their trip to the target range, Major Turner called Jesse into his office. "Logan," he said, "I need some errands run and since you're one of the ablest of the prisoners and undoubtedly know little of the layout of this town, it appears to me that you would probably be the least risk to try to escape. Besides, your appearance makes you an easy and likely target for the military patrols hereabouts, and your uniform hasn't quite taken on the — ah — the dilapidated appearance of some the others. You have also, I might add, shown us some degree of cooperation with the staff, which I'm willing to reward by giving you this — ahhh — this little freedom for the period of an hour or so."

What Turner hadn't said was that it was the custom in the prison to use the newest 'fish' to run errands since they hadn't yet developed close associations with their fellow prisoners, and were much less likely to have contrived any contraband excursions or smuggling attempts. The staff would pick a newer prisoner at random and send him on the errand without warning. It was possible that his confidence in Logan had increased somewhat after the day together at the target range, but it was also possible that he was being set up for an escape attempt. Jesse reflected on the warnings he'd received from Elizabeth van Lew and gave second thoughts to accepting the errand, but to do so would probably arouse suspicion with the major. It was truly a game of chess, but Jesse accepted the challenge.

The excursion Turner dispatched Jesse upon, that of going to the Richmond and Danville Railroad Station, a matter of six or seven blocks, and picking up some blankets, was nothing more than a test. Jesse gave considerable thought to the reason for the errand, but he was happy to have another opportunity to leave the prison, even if for a brief time. He did wonder, however, why there were blankets coming to the prison, since there certainly were none issued to the prisoners. It was late May, by then, and he had not seen more than a dozen blankets among his 'room mates' since he had arrived.

He went to the rear of the building escorted by the guard, Amos Straught and was given a handcart and a note with the directions written on it, as well as a pass signed by Major Turner. Then he was let out through the rear door and directed to the train station, which was on Broad Street, to pick up a bale of blankets which had come in from the south.

Richmond was a city laid out on a number of low rolling hills along the north side of the James River. It was a picturesque town, with modest shops, stores, and a few hotels sometimes arranged side by side with larger factories and warehouses.

He felt a little foolish pushing a handcart through the streets of Richmond. It occurred to Jesse that in normal circumstances there would have been some kind of delivery wagon arranged to accomplish this sort of task. However, he also noticed that there were a number of other people, mostly black men, pushing handcarts through the streets with all sorts of goods on them. Horses were in short supply and apparently it was becoming the custom to walk wherever one went and also to push a handcart if the occasion called for it.

Cary Street where Libby Prison was located runs roughly parallel to the James River. When Jesse got to the front of the building, he proceeded west in the direction he was instructed to go. When he got to Pearl Street, he stopped and pulled the note out of his pocket. He proceeded another block, and there on his left was the railroad depot. He went to the freight area, which was bustling with activity, and presented the claim slip he had been given to a man who appeared to be in charge.

"What's this?" the dock man asked.

"I'm from over at Libby and they sent me for some freight; blankets, I think," Logan replied.

"Oh, ye're one of them Billy Yank prisoners they're usin' fer t'do th' niggers' work up there," the dockhand commented, casually and without particular rancor.

Jesse bristled, but held his composure. Work was work, so far as he knew, and wasn't apportioned by race. After a slight hesitation, he smiled disarmingly. "Mister," he said, "I'd do a mule's work, if I had to, I'm so happy to be shed of that place for a few minutes."

"It's that bad, is it?" an agent from inside the depot had stepped out onto the dock and picked up the conversation. "You don't look like you've been too badly abused, from the looks of you."

"I was just locked up a few months ago, and I suppose I've not gotten that 'Libby glow' about me, yet," Logan tried to treat the subject lightly.

"How's come you're down at Libby, 'you some kind of a big shot?" the agent seemed aware of the reputation of the institution for security.

"Well, I don't exactly know about that," Jesse said, evasively, "I was just a corporal in an Ohio regiment, and drifted a little too far over the line one night."

The agent looked Jesse over curiously. "You're that sharpshooter they've been writin' about in the papers, aren't you? What happened? It was only a few months ago they caught up with you and locked you up and now they put you out on the street, walking around Richmond like just another citizen. No offense to you, you un'erstan', but I just can't get it in my head how the gov'ment thinks. Who's the head of that prison where you are, now, that Major Turner? If the newspapers knew he was sending the White Angel out on his errands without a guard they'd have his head."

"You know," he went on, "I have a friend who's a guard down at the Prison, Amos Straught, do you know him?"

Jesse nodded and the clerk continued as though he wasn't even waiting for an answer. "I've asked old Amos, 'what're you fellers doing down there at that prison? It seems like the only ones who know what's going on down there are you and the rats and bed bugs.' Amos just laughs and says 'Fred,' he says, 'the bed bugs probably know more about the business than I do'."

With that, 'Fred' laughed uproariously at his own joke. Jesse laughed too, though he wasn't quite as amused at the joke as was its author.

Jesse was a little uncomfortable discussing matters in the prison. If the social situation was anything here like it was up in Tennessee, one's opinions were better kept private or they would be spread all over town before morning.

"Are you pretty good friends with Mr. Straught?" Jesse asked.

"Oh, yes, we're good friends. I see him in lodge a lot. Are you a Mason?"

"Well, I sort-of am. I got my first two degrees in Elizabethton, up in Tennessee last January, but I don't think that makes me a full-fledged Mason, does it?"

"Oh, you got your second degree?" Fred asked, demonstrating an increased level of curiosity.

"Yes, that was it. It was my second degree. I took my first degree the week before."

"Well, I'll tell the fellers at the lodge you're down there at Libby. Maybe some of us can help to make life a little easier for you. Are there any other Masons in there?"

"I haven't thought to ask," Jesse said apologetically. "Since I haven't yet got my third degree, I guess I'm not too familiar with what goes on. Isn't that kind of the way it is?"

"You've got it," Fred replied. "You'll learn all that as time goes on. Well, congratulations on getting your first two degrees, anyway. We'd better get you loaded up. C'm'on back here."

Jesse and Fred walked back into the warehouse and Fred selected four large bales of blankets.

"Here are the blankets, but I don't think you can tote them on that handcart. Are they expecting you to make another trip?"

"If you had a rope I could borrow, I think I could get the whole load in this trip, Then maybe I could get the rope to Mr. Straught and he could give it back to you when he sees you at, ah — at the lodge."

They tied a light rope around the four bales and they fit precisely, if precariously, on the handcart. Logan took the handles and stood up.

"This is going to be just fine," he said. "Who should I tell Mr. Straught to give the rope back to?"

"My name is Fred Hatrack," the clerk said. "What is yours?"

"Oh, I'm sorry, my name is Jesse Logan," Jesse said, putting down the handcart and extending his hand.

Fred Hatrack took his hand and shook it warmly. "It's been nice meeting you, Jesse," he said. "Perhaps we'll meet again under different circumstances. You'd best be getting back to the prison. The bed bugs will be waiting for you. But, you know, I still can't figure out what our gov'ment is doing. For the life of me, I sometimes think that one hand doesn't know what the other hand is doin'. How is it that the same army, supposedly, that captures a high falutin' soldier like yourself and puts him in a high security prison, turns around and lets him wander the streets of the capitol city all by hisself only a few weeks later? Does that make sense to you?"

"Mr. Hatrack, I'm not in the business of trying to figure out gov'ment, but if I was, I guess I'd just be shakin' my head like you, right now. I'll see you later, I hope."

Jesse took his load of blankets and returned to the prison, which was now downhill from where he received the load of blankets and was an easy trip, except for the curbs. He managed to stay pretty well to the center of the streets to avoid such obstacles. Amos Straught met him at the rear door. "I didn't expect you back so soon, Logan," Amos said. "That's quite a load. Where did you get the rope?"

"A friend of yours leant it to me, Fred Hatrack."

"Oh, you ran into Fred. I should have expected he'd be working there, today. I should have told you to look for him."

"He said I could leave the rope with you and you'd get it back to him at lodge. He says you and he are both members of the same lodge of Masons. You know, I got my first and second degrees in Elizabethton last January," Logan said tentatively, wondering if he should share the information with Straught.

"Well, congratulations. I didn't know that. I knew there was some reason why I liked you," Straught said amiably. "I'm sure there are other members of the 'craft' in here, but I've been a little hesitant to check about, as I don't want the commander to get the idea I'm too friendly with the prisoners. It wouldn't work to the benefit of either me or you."

"I understand. I'll keep it to myself," Jesse assured him.

<hr>

"Lilly, there's an interesting looking letter for you from Richmond," Steven Venable said to his daughter on his return from the Post Office.

"For me, Daddy? Oh. I think I know who it's from," she said looking at the envelope. "Do you remember Jesse Logan, the boy from Kellars Crossing who was at that party in February?"

"I remember him well, Honey. He was picked by the Secesh the night of the party, as I recall. I was afraid they wouldn't let him live, to be quite honest, him such a 'notorious' example of our East Tennessee youth, and all."

Lilly had opened the letter and read the first few lines. "He's at a place called Libby Prison, of all names. He says he's all right. Can I read it to you?"

"If you like," her father replied. Then, as Lilly read the letter, Steven Venable began reflecting on his association with Jesse. Venable was the Secretary of Kennedy Masonic Lodge in Elizabethton, and had participated in the awarding of the masonic degrees Jesse had been a part of. The members of the lodge had hoped he would have been able to receive his third and final degree before he had to return to duty or even in one of the traveling 'service' lodges that followed some of the fighting. His capture by the Confederates had interrupted that, though. But it seemed to Venable that Jesse had been anxious to complete the three degrees, and a thought ran through his mind that it would not be out of the question if a Richmond lodge were to confer the third degree.

In East Tennessee, Masons were Masons, and it didn't much matter whether they had aligned themselves with the Confederate or Union cause, they were still friends, and would try to remain so. Steven Venable had a friend, John Dove, who was secretary of Randolph Lodge in Richmond. A letter to Dove would, at least, satisfy his curiosity.

"Don't expect many letters from that young man, Lilly," Venable said. "I understand the prisoners are restricted from writing letters. He doesn't say how he was to have gotten the letter out of the prison, does he?"

"No, it doesn't say, Daddy. "Do you think I should write back to him?"

"Not right away, Darling. Let me see if I can open up communications with Mr. Logan another way."

Steven Venable owned a hardware store in Elizabethton, and though he tried to keep his Union sympathies private, he was nonetheless identified with the northern cause. The following day, he visited a friend at the local bank, Turner Carnahan, a man who was known to be in sympathy with the south, but not vehemently so. The two men were both members of Kennedy Lodge, and this year Carnahan was 'Master'.

"Turner, I have a problem," Venable said after they had gone into Carnahan's office and the door was closed. "You remember that young man we gave the first and second to in January?"

"You mean the Yankee soldier, Steven? Yes, I remember him. They caught that young fellow and sent him away, as I recall."

"That's my problem, Turner. The man is in a prison in Richmond and I think it would be nice if we could arrange with Randolph Lodge down there to give him his third degree."

"You have word from this young man, do you?"

"Well, keep this in all confidence, if you would, but my daughter received a note from him yesterday, telling her of his whereabouts, and though he didn't say anything in the letter about his activity in the lodge, we at least know where he is and that he's all right. John Dove is Secretary of Randolph Lodge, down there and I thought I'd write to him and see whether they're interested. If they're anything like we are right now, they have their hands full with degrees and such, but well, who knows? They may just do it for us. I thought I'd better pass the question by you, as Master, and see if you thought it would be all right.

"You've got my stamp of approval, Brother. I think it would even be nice if someone from our lodge could go down to Richmond and sit in on the degree. That's not likely, though, with your people out there stirring up all this trouble."

"Well, you rotten old buzzard. What do you mean, 'my people'? Those are your men all over the country terrorizing us honest citizens."

"Oh, I forgot. It was last January that it was your people." Carnahan countered. "This month it's my people restoring order."

"You just wait, Carnahan. You'll get yours. When I'm anointed king, the likes of you'll be run out of town on a rail."

"You'd do that to the Master of your own lodge? What kind of brotherly love is that?"

"I'll give you a dose of brotherly love," Venable said, with a smile, doubling up his fist and shaking it at Carnahan. "But in the meantime, you think a letter to John Dove would be in order?"

"I think it's a great idea, Steven. How's the wife?"

"Sarah's fine, and Abbie?"

"She's just fine. Will you be at lodge Monday?"

"Of course, is there anything I need to put on the agenda?"

"Well, you will note the letter, won't you?"

"Yes, I'll write it right away and get it into the agenda, Turner. Thank you."

"It will be interesting to see what they do with the letter," Carnahan said, escorting Venable out of his office. "See you Monday."

The two men shook hands and Steven Venable left the bank. When he got back to his store, he went into his small office, closed the door, and stared for a long moment out the window.

Kennedy Lodge, #163, F&AM
Elizabethton, Tennessee
May 18, 1862

John Dove, Sec'y
Randolph Lodge #19 AF&AM
Richmond, Virginia
Dear Bro. John.
Recently we had the pleasure to initiate and pass a young man who was assigned to the Federal forces then occupying this region. Since that time this man was taken into custody by the Confederate Army and sent as a prisoner of war to Libby Prison in your city.
The man, Jesse Logan, was at the time quite anxious to complete his degrees. Of course the process has been interrupted so far as Kennedy Lodge is concerned, but it has occurred to me that it may be possible for him to receive his third degree at your hands, if you were so inclined.
I imagine this sort of degree would be something of an exception for yours or any lodge, to raise a man, admittedly of a different political stripe, and one who at the time is in a prisoner of war facility. It may

even bring with it a bit of interest from the brethren, prompting further fraternal communication.

I might also add that Bro. Logan enjoys some little notoriety, he having received the attention of the press as a very skilled sharpshooter. Inasmuch as we avoid taking up political subjects in lodge, I doubt that this will cause a problem, but I hasten to make note of the fact to avoid any possibility of contention and embarrassment in your lodge.

I attach a copy of Bro. Logan's petition, and also of the minutes of this lodge for the day of his passing to the degree of Fellow Craft, both copies under lodge seal.

Please let me know if there is anything further you need in this matter. I remain, sincerely and fraternally, yr. obt. svt..

Turner Carnahan, W. M. Kennedy Lodge, #163 F&AM

by Steven Venable, Sec'y.

Randolph Lodge #19 in Richmond held their regular meetings on Wednesday nights. The Monday before their regular meeting, John Dove, Secretary of the lodge and a member of almost fifty years, went to the post office, as was his daily custom. In the mail he found the letter from Steven Venable. He went immediately to the Confederate Garrison on Grace Street and contacted Colonel Robert Reynolds, who at the time was serving as Master of Randolph Lodge.

"I have the strangest communication I've ever received from a Mason," he told Reynolds. "It's from a brother I know in Tennessee who's the secretary of Kennedy Lodge in Elizabethton. It seems they've conferred the first two degrees on a fellow who is now over at Libby Prison, as a prisoner, and are wondering if we would confer his third degree. What do you think?"

"They want us to what? To confer a 'Third' on a Yank that's over at Libby?" Reynolds asked incredulously.

"That's right, Bob. He was given his first and second a few months ago and he'd like to continue, I guess. They sent along a copy of his application for membership to their lodge and a copy of the minutes of his second degree, both under the lodge seal. They must really want this fellow to get that degree."

"This is lunacy. How could we ever do such a thing?"

"Well, you know, Fred and Amos told us last week of that young man over there who is a second-degree Mason and was out of the prison on some errands recently. They both know him. Amos let him out under orders from the commandant and the fellow was sent up to the railroad station to pick up something or other for the prison. They were both impressed by this fellow and sort of hinted about the same thing Brother Venable has asked about in his letter."

On Wednesday night at Randolph Lodge the subject was brought up under 'new business'. After Dove read the letter, the group of forty or so members, many in uniform, sat silent for about thirty seconds. It was as though they were each trying to comprehend what was being asked and there was some small degree of murmuring among them, discussing the question among themselves. Presently Amos Straught stood up and asked permission to speak, which is the custom in most Masonic lodges.

"Yes, brother Straught," the master responded, whereupon Amos described his dealings with Jesse, related that Jesse had expressed a desire to further his degree work, and recommended in favor of the request.

Others members seemed to have reservations, but finally the Master spoke. "I know we are all concerned as to whether it's appropriate for us to confer degrees on a man who would be considered an adversary if we were out on the battle line, but remember, we are all committed to the principles of brotherly love and relief. Let's make our decision based on those principles, not on our feelings toward the government that this man is working, or had been working under. The fact that he is a committed soldier in the service of a country opposed to ours doesn't alter the fact that he is a brother Mason and a request has been made that we are in a position to act upon without any injury or inconvenience to ourselves. Brother Amos even said that Logan himself had expressed a desire to obtain his third degree."

When it was obvious that the Master did not opposed the request but even spoke in support of it, several members stood and discussed the logistics of such an effort. The question was then called and ratified and the date set, provided Jesse could be produced on the night assigned.

Three weeks later, at about five o'clock in the afternoon, a uniformed corporal appeared at the front door of Libby with signed orders to take Logan out of the prison for a period not to exceed eight hours. 'Commander' Ross examined the document, questioned the corporal to his complete satisfaction, called for a guard and gave instructions to bring Jesse up to the office. Jesse was beginning to show the wear and tear of prison life by then, as the uniform he had been brought in with was still on his back and becoming badly worn and torn in a few places. Even though he had managed to wash it once, it was filthy at the time he was called in to the office and weeks of starvation diet and the occasional work detail were showing, both on him and his uniform.

"Logan," Ross said, "this man has orders to take you out with him on some sort of an assignment. Corporal," he said turning to the soldier, "what is this assignment you're taking this man on at this hour of the day?"

"I just got this from my sergeant, Sir," the corporal said noncommittally. "He didn't say what it was all about."

"Alright, just so's he's back at the time stated here on the order, Corporal," the clerk said officiously. "We can't have these people running all over the street unaccounted for. And remember, there's a curfew at dark, so's you'd better have him back by then or risk the both of you being shot."

"Yes, Sir, thank you, Sir," Corporal Stapp said appreciatively.

Erasmus Ross put the release order in his desk. He had a feeling he would not be seeing Jesse Logan again for a long time, if ever at all, and if that were the case, he would need the order to vouch for the fact that he had adhered to protocol.

Corporals Stapp and Logan walked out the front door of Libby and headed up Nineteenth Street toward the Masonic Lodge. Again, Jesse had serious reservations about the process, but was also fascinated by the intrigue of the situation. The admonitions of Elizabeth van Lew surfaced occasionally in his mind but were quickly suppressed. Fred Hatrack was waiting for them at the door of the Masonic lodge and looked at Jesse's filthy clothes.

"Brother Logan," Hatrack suggested after looking Jesse over, "why don't you step in here and wash up? We have some other clothes for you to wear temporarily during the ceremony of your degree."

Amos Straught also met Logan and tried to make him feel at ease, as did the Master, Colonel Reynolds. And with that, he was taken into the lodge and participated in the degree ceremony.

13

RICHMOND, VIRGINIA AT NIGHT

After the lodge meeting, the members of the lodge adjourned to an adjoining room where a modest spread of cakes and coffee had been prepared. The atmosphere was convivial and Logan was indeed made to feel a part of the organization. He had been given a random collection of clothes that it was suggested he wear while an effort was made to have his uniform washed.

Politics were not discussed, at least in his immediate presence and his national loyalties were assiduously avoided. Nevertheless, the spirit of the meeting was warm and friendly and, while he was regarded as something of a curiosity, it was more owing to his size, his youth, and the fact that he was from another part of the country than anything regarding his choice of government.

John Dove, who had lost his wife a few years previously had been known to have been showing an interest in a young lady about half his age and was receiving some friendly advice and chiding, over the way she should be treated. He and Jesse were seated next to each other at the table and Jesse was drawn into the conversation. By tradition, politics and religion were subjects to be avoided in Masonic meetings, but matters of the heart, though handled circumspectly, were not.

Amos Straught was needling Dove about his ability to keep up the pace of courtship with this younger woman. "Brother Logan, what do you think of our venerable secretary trying to keep up with this young girl? Maybe we should introduce her to you or Brother Stapp, you fellows being young and, I assume unattached, you may strike a spark of affection in her, while I'm afraid Brother John has about struck his last spark."

"Don't be too sure of that, Mr. — uh, oh — Brother Amos. I've known some pretty furious December-May courtships in my time back there where I come from."

"Yes, yes, we've heard of some of those great romantics up there in the Great Smoky Mountains. Some of those fellows are reputed to maintain their virility for decades, but we're down here in the Tidewater and somehow haven't been able to keep up the pace. I don't know about Brother John, but I have trouble even keeping up with the lady I'm married to, and as beautiful and vivacious as she is, she's not what you'd call a child."

"Well, I can't speak for David, but as for me, keep me out of this combination. For one thing, I'm a little — well — indisposed at the present time, and for another, I can't think of a single friendship I've entertained with the fairer sex in the past few years that has brought me anything but trouble, trouble, trouble. The reason I'm enjoying your hospitality right now is owing to my friendship with a young lady I wrote to back in Tennessee. But that has been more fortuitous than disastrous, I think." And with that introduction, Logan went on to relate how he had come to be where he was, both as to his capture and his relationship with Randolph Lodge as a result of his friendship with Lily Venable, whose name he was careful to omit from discussion.

His account drew considerable laughter from those around him.

As he prepared to leave after the meeting of the Masons, Jesse started to look for the clothing he had worn when he was brought to the meeting. Removing the jacket he had been given, he looked about. David Stapp, the corporal who had brought him from Libby came up to him and in a friendly manner asked, "What can we help you with, Jesse?"

"My clothes, my clothes," Jesse said, looking about the small room where he had been prepared to receive his Masonic degree. "The clothes I had on when I came in. They aren't much in the way of appearance, but they're all I have."

"Brother Logan," the master of the lodge said, overhearing the conversation, "the clothes you came here with were pretty terrible. Those clothes you have on are yours, to do with whatever you choose. They are but a motley supply of odds and bits gathered from several members of the lodge, and scant use to any of us. I apologize for the way they fit you, but as you can see, your proportions are a little different from those of us who contributed to the collection, and as you see, most of us are wearing uniforms you'd best not be seen in. Further, I fear, our Tiler gathered up your old clothing and, if I'm not in error, they are still quite wet. They were, ahh — not in very good condition, but I'll have them for you in a few minutes." Then, a few minutes later, one of the members brought out a wet bundle of what had been Jesse's uniform,

"Thank you, Colonel — ahh — Brother Reynolds, "But surely, I owe you something in the bargain. Not to offer any disrespect, but I'm sure that many of the members here are as badly used by the fortunes of war as I am. Yet, as you know, I have nothing to give in exchange. Nothing."

"So I expected to find you, my friend. Part of the value of any bargain is the spirit in which it is given, and we want you to know that you have given us a great deal of pleasure this evening in agreeing to participate in these ceremonies. To be able to confer a third degree on a fine young man and a brother in need, such as yourself, is suitable compensation for the small tribute of clothing you have received. But the hour is late and our members must be getting along. I'll see you to the door."

With that, the Master escorted Jesse to the door of the lodge and wished him good night.

Jesse was a little puzzled. "Might I ask which direction I should take to return to my ahh — quarters? Would it be out of line for me to ask if one or two of the other members may be going that direction? I understand there may be soldiers on the street enforcing a curfew. Besides that, I'm out of uniform."

"Brother Logan," Reynolds responded, "You are now a fully vested and qualified Mason, and it would be presumptuous for any among us to now try to direct your ways, unless we perceived them to be in error, which I don't see as the case." And with that, he changed the subject of the conversation. "We would be pleased to have you consider Randolph Lodge your home, and we invite you to return at your earliest opportunity. Or, if you should choose to visit another lodge, be sure to be prepared to demonstrate those words and gestures we showed you this evening, so that you might be properly recognized. Also, if you should find yourself in trouble, and communicate that with a fellow Mason, he will, so far as he is able, relieve your distress. Good night, my brother."

Colonel Reynolds had been escorting Jesse toward the door, and on, "Good night," closed it behind him.

Finding himself in the middle of Richmond in the middle of the night, in the middle of a war in which he represented the enemy, in clothing that would brand him a spy, seemed to Jesse the height of irony in an already dreadfully ironic situation. *"They'll hang me. That's what they'll do if the Confederate soldiers catch me. The whole thing has been nothing but a plot to get me into a compromise for an excuse to kill me. Miss van Lew was right."*

"What sort of lunatic fate was it that snatched a man out of the relative security of a prison, where he had a chance of parole or exchange, and deposit him on the street, late at night in the middle of the enemy capitol on a collision course with certain death? What sort of friends were these who

engineered his predicament, and where had his sense of self-preservation been when he agreed to participate in the night's activities?"

Some of the last advice he was given was to turn to a brother Mason for relief if he was ever in distress, yet it was just such a group that had put him in this condition of dire distress.

Without reflecting further, Jesse knew that he must do whatever he could to stay alive, and the most logical thing he could do would be to get back into prison. He started off in what he thought was the right direction to return to prison, but the thought of voluntarily going up to the door of Libby Prison and asking to get in just didn't set right. *"That is really not the sensible thing to do, except, perhaps, as a last resort,"* He said to himself. *'What if I'm not caught? What if I can stay out of sight, and slip out of town and make it back to the Union lines."*

It was a long-odds chance. First, he didn't know the city, except for his brief trips to the train station or other places he'd been sent on such errands. Second, he wouldn't be familiar with the countryside, even if he got out of the city. Third, was the question of whether it was better to try for the Union lines or head for Carter County?

Fourth... *"Play the hand you're dealt..."* the words of Grandpa Kellar came back to him, *"No one can assume tomorrow's going to be any better than today."*

"Let's take first things first," he said to himself. *"That means stay out of sight and stay alive until you can figure a plan."*

As he started hesitantly down 18th Street Jesse stopped and contemplated his situation.

"You look lost, Brother," a shadowy figure stepped out of a doorway behind the Masonic lodge building and Jesse's heart froze. "Can I be of assistance?"

"Whoa! Is that you, Mr. ahh — Fred, is that you?" Logan ventured.

"Yes, Brother Logan, the Master asked me to offer you aid. In the lodge, our ancient landmarks prevent us from discussing our political situation, but we all sensed your dilemma, and are anxious to give you a hand. Brother Reynolds, being a Colonel in the army is also constrained from assisting you outside of the lodge, but he wanted to see that you were well cared for. He asked me if I would mind giving you a little guidance and I told him I'd be happy to. I lost a son in this war just four months ago, and you remind me a great deal of him. He only lived a short time after we gave him his Master Mason's apron, and I'd like to think perhaps we can do a little better by you."

"I'm sorry," Jesse said, not wanting to explore the subject further, but Fred Hatrack didn't stop there.

"He was up in Morgan County with General Jackson," he went on, "and I'm told he was working as a sharpshooter, but some of — ah — some of the enemy got around him and tried to capture him. He was killed in the fight."

"I'm so sorry, Fred," Jesse said again, "I don't know what to say. I've worked as a rifleman, too, and I know the dangers of the job. So Brother Reynolds knew the danger he was placing me in, but apparently he felt the risks were worth the effort."

"Yes, he's a military man, though he's attached to headquarters here in Richmond at the present. Some of us decided, just since we met with you, that it wouldn't do to return you to Libby unless you really want to go back. Jesse, I'll be honest with you. You're what they call a high-profile prisoner. There's talk around the lodge that the authorities would like to get you into a position where they could justify killing you. Now, here we are on opposite sides of a war, but are obligated by our vows as Masons to protect each other. In Masonry, we talk trust and we talk tolerance. We don't talk politics, but we just thought it would be better to get you out of town and on your way, as best as possible, toward home."

Jesse's chances of survival looked about ten times better at this moment than they had five minutes ago. Fate had not been so cruel after all.

Fred Hatrack continued, "First we'd better get out of sight. My chances of survival at this moment are not much better than yours. There's a 'shoot-to-kill' curfew in effect. It's relaxed a little when there's a meeting such as ours going on, but the time for the relaxed regulations have about expired. Come on over here out of sight."

"Please understand that, as was mentioned earlier, none of our actions this evening were meant to trifle with your feelings, but we want to let you know in no uncertain terms that this is a drastic departure from custom. It'll probably not happen again in this or any other country, ours or yours."

The last comment hit its mark. Fred Hatrack was convinced there was a distinction between the Confederate States and the United States of America, which was totally different from Jesse's attitude toward the subject, and what he had been fighting for. His companion and now protector was just as convinced that though they were brothers they were citizens of different countries. The man's son had died for the concept. There would be others in the coming months from both sides who would continue to die, but Jesse was being released from prison in this man's 'country' because of a bond of fellowship Jesse had only been able to guess at before this moment. He was prompted to ask of this new friend how he perceived the question of slavery as being the issue that divided the country, but knew this came too close to a forbidden subject of discussion. Neither did he want to challenge the man's loyalties or his patriotism. This was neither the time nor place for such a discussion.

Their escape from the city was tortuously slow. They were near the east end of the city and Jesse wanted to go west. Though the regular troops that usually populated the capitol city had been drawn out to counter a serious threat by the Federals down toward the tip of the James Peninsula, there was still quite a cadre comprised of old men or men that had been injured in the war, who looked as though they meant business. If there was a shortage of arms in the south as Jesse had been informed, it was only apparent so far as the style of weapons he saw. There were Kentucky rifles, fowling pieces, flintlocks, and any variety of muskets and pistols. There were also pitchforks and clubs in the hands of some, but they were all accompanied by someone else with a gun.

Jesse and Fred hid themselves in every conceivable place they could hide. Fortunately for them the economies of the war had necessitated strict restraint on the use of gas for the street lamps, and the darkness was their friend. Fred knew his way through the streets of Richmond, and he also had a pretty good idea of the routes of the patrols.

What he didn't know was that only a few blocks away was the home of Elizabeth van Lew, a sanctuary for fugitives from the custody of the Confederate government. Fred was not privy to such intelligence. Erasmus Ross could have been helpful, had his help been sought, but he wasn't among the men who were at the lodge that evening.

By dawn, they had reached the western outskirts of the city. Fred showed Jesse to a deserted shed west of the city, on the edge of a tobacco field that didn't look as though it had been planted for some time.

"I'll be back to check on you later," Fred said. "I'll try to rustle up some food, but it won't be much. Stay here today Jesse, and when I come back, about the best I can do will be to give you something of a map and send you off. I'll give you the names of some brothers out north and west of town who, I'm sure, will help you along the way. If you keep off the roads and watch for patrols, you'll probably be able to make your way north to your lines, with luck. Remember, Son, if you think you're in trouble, don't hesitate to give that signal we showed you."

With this, he demonstrated the 'help' sign that Masons are taught. "It has kept more than one man alive, and it don't cost you nothin' to give it. If Leo had given it instead of tryin' to fight his way out of trouble, he might just be sitting in one of those jails up north —." His voice trailed off.

"Thank you, Fred," Jesse shook the man's hand. "And thank the brothers at the lodge for me. I didn't get much of a chance to express my appreciation, especially to David Stapp, If I don't see you by about sundown, I'll just strike out on my own. Don't worry none about the food. I'll be all right, I'm sure. You've done enough for me to last a lifetime."

"You know, Jesse," Fred mused, "We never even talked about whether you wanted to go back to Libby or head out of town. I reckon this is what you wanted to do or you'd have told me."

"You get out of here, you old scoundrel," Jesse chided. "You knew all along I'd never go back to that place if I had the choice. By the way, though, if you were to come across some trousers about six inches longer could I prevail on you to bring them out to me, please? I look like a yahoo in a street parade in these duds. If anyone was to spot me, they'd know for sure that I was wearing somebody else's clothes."

"I'll see what I can do, Brother Logan," and Fred was gone off along the trees at the edge of the meadow.

Jesse looked around the shed. It looked as though it had been a drying shed for the tobacco that had been grown in the nearby field. There were a few stray leaves of dry tobacco lying around, but the place smelled musty. It must not have been used for a long time. With as little sound as possible, Jesse found a corner where he could sit and sleep and still keep an eye on the door and the town of Richmond beyond the field. There was no closure on the doorway, and after a little reflection he was concerned that he may be seen, so just as silently, he got up, slipped out the door, and crept into the sparse growth behind the shed. It was June and the weather was warming, and he certainly didn't need the shelter of the building. He felt lots safer out in the open on the edge of the woods but he knew he should remain close so that he could get the food and directions Fred Hatrack had so generously promised.

— ((●)) —

Jesse woke with a start. He heard voices coming across the field toward him. It sounded like a group of boys coming toward the shed that he had vacated earlier that morning. He was glad he didn't have to try to escape from the shed now, as the doorway faced the direction from which they were coming. Jesse tried to hug the ground closer, and looked for shelter farther into the sparse growth from where he was lying.

"I was over here las' week," one of the voices was saying, "and there's some t'bacca leaves still in there."

"Did you bring the matches, Gordy?" another voice inquired.

"Sure did," Gordy responded, "How are we going to get the t'bacca into these pipes, though?"

"We kin just ruffle 'em b'tween our fingers," someone said. "I've tried it afore with this old dry t'bacca, and it works jes' fine."

Logan felt he was well enough out of sight, but when the boys got into the shed, he continued to slip farther into the woods. The woods were not particularly dense, but the boys were preoccupied with their prank, and he was not too concerned about being seen.

There were five of the boys, and they were apparently busy with their business of preparing the tobacco for smoking. Soon Jesse could smell the smoke they were so intent on experimenting with, and he felt a little more comfortable, as he didn't think any of them would be going outside where they would be seen from across the field smoking the corn cob pipes they had brought. He was wrong about anyone coming out of the shed. One of the boys had to relieve himself, and had slipped around the back of the shed to make water. As he came around the corner of the shed, Logan was still on his feet in a crouched position and the boy spotted him.

"Hey, what you doing out there, Elmer?' The boy apparently mistook Jesse for one of his own.

"I'm in here," Elmer responded from inside the shed.

"Then who's that out in the woods?" the first boy yelled.

The boys, in curiosity, came pouring out of the shed and looked in the direction their companion was pointing. Jesse had fallen flat, but knew he'd been seen. He felt that he had a start on the boys and in the best of conditions could escape them. This was not the best of conditions, however. They probably knew the country better than he did, and were also probably in much better shape. He assessed his options for a moment and decided there weren't many. If he stayed put, the boys could overpower him and return him to town. It was just the sort of adventure teenage boys in a war-minded town might seize upon. He didn't think he could talk them into thinking he was just another vagabond, as such men were either considered deserters or escapees, but if he ran there would be no doubt in their minds.

"What you all hollering about," Jesse stood up and shouted. "Cain't a man git a little rest. I reckon I drunk a little too much at that-thar party last night, and was jes' sleepin' in the woods." He had made signs as though to move toward the boys, but kept his distance. "That-thar t'bacc'y smells real good. 'Got any fer me?"

The boys felt no fear for this rather simple looking fellow and they started to move toward him. After all there were five of them, and they were feeling a little heady from the effects of the tobacco, anyway.

"You don't look like you been to no party," one of the boys challenged him. Ye're stickin' out of them clothes like you was some kind of scarecrow."

"That's 'cause I had to leave in a hurry and got someone else's pants," Jesse dodged with a chuckle, "I reckon their owner is still lookin' fer 'em."

"Say, one of them prisoners over't Libby slipped out last night, and they say he was 'bout seven feet tall. That ain't you, is it, Mister?"

Jesse didn't have a chance to answer. When the boys had come running out of the shed, someone had left something burning in the dry tobacco scattered on the floor. The shed was on fire, and Jesse was the first to see the danger.

"Fire!" Jesse shouted. "Get some water."

The effect was immediate. The confusion was beautiful. The boys turned and ran for town and Jesse turned and ran for the woods. As he made his way deeper into the woods, he cursed his own carelessness. *"I survived for a year by being able to keep my head low, and in the last six months, I've been caught twice because I wasn't paying attention to the basics. If those boys had been Rebel soldiers I'd have been shot."*

There was no water nearby, and by the time the panicked boys got to town, a matter of only a few minutes, the shed was an inferno. They had to report the fire, but they would also report the hobo they had seen in the vicinity of the shed and in the process, blame him for the fire.

The conclusion would be, of course that the man who the boys had seen, the man who 'started the fire', was the same man who had somehow escaped the custody of those who had signed him out of the prison. Corporal Stapp was pretty well beyond reproach, for he had, ostensibly anyway, simply been following orders, and 'Commander' Ross had in his desk, a copy of that order that was written in such vague terms that it would be impossible to trace.

Jesse headed west. He didn't know where the Union lines were, from where he was, but he knew where Kellars Crossing was, and it seemed like the safest bet, right now. He moved west and south through the woods, till he came to a river. Tired and hungry, he rested beside the stream, but he reflected on the old tales he had heard that bloodhounds lost scent of their quarry in water. He decided to cross the river.

He was a good swimmer, and he didn't hesitate to strike out. He still had his old uniform bundled in a cloth bag that the Masons had given him. The water was deep, but it didn't appear to be very fast, and the opposite shore was only about 40 yards away. The river was flowing east and Jesse wanted to go west, but right then, putting space between himself and his pursuers was foremost in his mind. He tied his shoes around his neck to give his feet the freedom to help him swim, and waded in, trying to hold the bag with his clothes in it above his head. Slowly he made his way out into the stream, but all of a sudden, he lost his footing and was plunged into deep water, losing the bundle of clothes. He started after the bag of clothes, but the current pulled it too far from his grasp and he decided against swimming downstream any further. As it was, the current pulled him along, but he managed to make his way slowly across the James River. He crawled out on the south side of the river and decided he'd better continue walking until his clothes dried. He kept his shoes tied around his neck, as he wanted to give his feet a little relief until he needed the shoes for rougher ground.

Jesse ambled along, trying to look like he was just another southern soldier on his way back from the front. He knew there were many deserters on both sides, and he felt he would draw less attention if he stayed in the open with the roads, at least for now. He didn't know how much of a search the Confederate authorities would make for his capture, but he knew the farther he got from Richmond, the less likelihood there would be of suspicion and arrest.

The approaching evening found Jesse near a grove of trees, and he ventured into the woods for cover. On entering the woods, he was struck by the similarity between this grove and several in Carter County. The trees were all about the same age, five to ten years old, being a regrowth of forests, which had been there decades ago. At home in Carter County he had seen the younger boys climb the saplings up to a height of about twenty feet, and then, by swaying back and forth, making their way from tree to tree without touching the ground. Even at that time, he had thought this would be a good way to make his way through a wooded area without leaving a scent on the ground.

"Why not try it?" Jesse thought. "I think I may have a little time, and if I take some evasive maneuvers like this, I may just save my skin."

He put his shoes back on his feet, climbed a tree near the road, and started it swaying. He was surprised at his ability to cover the distance from tree to tree in a short period of time, probably almost as fast as he'd be able to walk. He'd gone about two hundred yards when the forest suddenly played out. It wasn't far, but it may be enough, at least to throw any dogs off the track. He hadn't heard of the rebel authorities using dogs, but it wouldn't hurt, anyway. Jesse climbed down out of the last of the trees at the edge of the wood.

"Where 'you headed, young feller?" a voice behind him demanded.

"Oh, great!" Jesse was disgusted with himself. "Caught again."

"Well, Mister," Jesse responded evasively, "I thought I saw some nuts up that tree, yonder, and climbed up there to get them."

"There ain't no nuts in these trees, 'specially in the spring. "You from around here?"

"No, Sir, I'm on furlough from my unit headed home to see my grammaw." Jesse lied, trying to assume the best local accent he could, which he had picked up when he was living in Tennessee.

"Where's that," the farmer persisted, "Where 'you headed fer, is what I asked you in the first place."

"I'm tryin' for Tennessee," Jesse told the truth. "Just up over the Smokies and down the Holston River."

"You got a fur piece to go. Why don't you take the cars?"

"The cars ain't runnin, regular, and 'sides, I ain't got much money. I need to git there as quick as I kin, and the cars ain't all that reliable. Another thing, I heard General Banks is over in the valley, and he's been tearing up the tracks."

"Ye're a skinny one, I reckon, when was it you ate last? 'You want some supper?"

"I hain't too hungry, but if you had a ear of corn I could take with me, I'd be obliged," Jesse was not too anxious to stay for dinner.

"Come on in and I'll see what's on the stove. The Rebs come through here yistiday and about cleaned us out." The statement was curious coming from a southern farmer. It seemed he would have said 'the army' or 'some soldiers', but not 'the Rebs.'

"For sure, I wouldn't want to do you out of any of your food," Jesse protested. "I know it's been tough this past year, and things are pretty lean as it is".

"Ef ye're on yer way to see yer grammaw," the farmer said emphatically, "and need a bite to eat, I'll see that you git it. You kin even stay the night if ye're a mind."

"I couldn't stay," Jesse said quickly. He worried about folks talking to each other and giving away what progress he had so far made. "I really have to git goin'."

"Are you on the run?" the farmer eyed Jesse suspiciously. "Are you sure you ain't on the skedaddle? Listen, Son, I hain't got too much use fer the Rebs, no how. My onliest son, Caleb was conscripted into the army and was captured by the Yanks. Right away he turned to fight fer the north, and I'm jes' as happy, even though it means he'll be shot fer a deserter if he's ever caught by the Rebs. I never did go with this secession stuff, and I'll not turn you over ef ye're a'runnin from the army, and that's a fact."

Jesse just looked at the man standing there defiantly before him. This was a powerful admission to make to someone whom the man had just met and who, for all this man knew, Jesse was a genuine Confederate soldier.

"I'm a Yankee soldier, and I just escaped from Libby." Jesse blurted out. "I got away night b'fore last, and I'm trying to get home to Carter County, Tennessee. I'll be seeing if I can rejoin my company from there."

"Git inside," the farmer motioned toward the house. "I don't know ef they'll be out after you, but we'll do what we kin to throw 'em off the track. I was a'wonderin' what all that climbin' through the trees like a squirrel was, and I reckon I should 'a' known I had a Yank on my hands. Let me shake your hand, Son."

"Mama," the farmer called when they got into the house, "Could you fix supper for my Yankee friend, here? This here young man jest let hisse'f out from Libby Prison down in Richmond, and he's hungry. Son, this here's my bride of thirty years, Dorothy, or Dolly, I calls her, and I don't know yer name."

"My name is Jesse, Ma'm, and I'm pleased to meet you. You don't know how pleased I am." Jesse said.

"I'm proud to meet you, too, Mr. Jesse," Dorothy said. "Horace, kin you kill us a chicken?"

"Please, please don't go to that kind of trouble," Jesse was serious. "You know, if you had a little bacon and p'tatoes, I'd be grateful," he said.

They argued, briefly about supper, but Jesse won. He knew there would be some bacon about, and he certainly didn't want to put them to the expense of killing one of their chickens. It probably would have been one of their last, if the Rebel soldiers had been through that recently.

Ham, potatoes, eggs, and fresh greens. It was a supper fit for a king, and Jesse felt just about like one, that evening. It had been the first solid meal he'd had in about five months, except for the cakes and coffee he'd had at the Masons' lodge.

He scrubbed himself with hot water and some strong brown soap that his hostess had provided, and went off to bed. He slept in the shed out behind the house, just in case of a search, but he slept like a baby and woke the next morning refreshed.

Horace was chopping wood when Jesse emerged from the shed, and when he saw Jesse, he said, "Son, our boy Caleb is jest about yer size, and there's a old pair of his pants jest inside the door of the shed. Ye're welcome to them. Y'won't stick out quite so far on yer way back to Tennessee."

"That's probably a pretty good idea," Jesse said, "If you don't think he'll miss them, I'd be obliged. I'm out of uniform anyhow, and could be shot as a spy if I'm caught. At least some clothes that fit would make it a little less obvious that I'm on the run."

"When you see them ye'll understand what I mean when I say he'll be happy to part with 'em. Ma stitched 'em up a bit, but there's not much left to patch."

Horace was right. The trousers looked like a patchwork quilt made into a pair of pants, but they fit, and Jesse knew he'd be less conspicuous as he headed west.

After breakfast of bacon, eggs, and coffee made from roasted peanuts, Horace offered to take Jesse in his wagon for a way, but Jesse thought it better that he travel alone. He had been lucky so far, and though he was grateful, he didn't think it would be wise to stay with these fine people too much longer, or expose Horace to the hazard of being identified as a Union soldier if they were stopped.

Before he went, Horace took Jesse aside and showed him a cupboard in the barn where he kept a little extra food, a musket, and some blankets. It was concealed behind a panel in the wall of the barn, and was indistinguishable from the rest of the structure. "If ye're ever through this way and need a place to stay, feel welcome to use this fer a night or two," Horace told Jesse in a fatherly manner. "Even if me and Dolly ain't home, don't mind. Just feel free ef you need to. I keep it fer Caleb ef he ever comes this way and needs hidin'."

"You know what?" Jesse replied amiably, "I surely don't plan to pass this way again, but I'll keep it in mind. I'd like to come back and see you folks whenever the time is right, though. You've been awful nice to me."

He got directions, offered his profound thanks, and bade goodbye to his hosts for the night. He headed west on the road, coming to a small town named Moseley, where the road intersected the railroad. A small train was just pulling out of the station, heading west, and Jesse just couldn't resist trying his hand at 'hopping the cars'. The train seemed to be carrying mainly lumber, but there were also some railroad rails, a cattle car, and some cannon apparently headed for the Shenandoah Valley or even farther west to Tennessee. There was also one passenger car toward the front of the train, and Jesse chose to avoid it, catching a car toward the rear. There were no attendants nearby when he climbed aboard, and he made himself as comfortable and inconspicuous as possible on a flat car between piles of lumber.

The train gained speed as it left the yard, and soon they were traveling at a good rate through the Virginia farmland though the road was rough. They went through such places as Amelia, Jetersville, Farmville, and Appomattox Station, and when the train was approaching Lynchburg, Jesse got off. He had seen the sign along the track, and had heard of the town, which he decided must be rather large, and possibly a dangerous place for a Yankee soldier to be caught.

It was getting on toward night, and he thought perhaps he could move around the town in the dark and catch the cars the next day. Traveling on foot wasn't easy. Dogs barked, soldiers were on patrol, curious citizens seemed to be everywhere, and he had only the vaguest idea where he was going. It reminded him of that comment his grandpa Kellar used to make when he faced some kind of a dilemma, "Well, what next?" he'd comment to Jesse, "Like old br'er rabbit used to say, Son, 'If it ain't a dog, it's a man with a gun.'"

Jesse was thinking that he now knew just how "Poor Br'er Rabbit" felt.

He stayed with the outskirts of town along the southern edge, and managed to make pretty good progress in a westerly direction. Though he couldn't tell what direction he was heading, he felt that he would come to the westbound tracks in time, and wait there for an opportunity to hop another train. After about an hour, he crossed a small stream and was confronted by a board fence that seemed to stretch off to his left for some considerable distance. Peering through the spaces between the boards he could see that the fence surrounded some kind of large building; a factory or a warehouse. If he got over the fence, he could probably make his way across the yard of the building and avoid an additional hike of what looked like half a mile or so. He made his way along the fence looking for loose boards and also to check for guard dogs. It was now well after dark and the building seemed to be empty of all but possibly some guards.

There didn't seem to be any dogs in the yard, and though he did see an occasional man patrolling the outside of the building, he thought he could avoid him. Finally, after waiting until he was sure all signs of life had subsided, Jesse found a loose board in the fence and crawled through. Inside the yard, he slipped between some wagons parked about, and also some machinery he didn't recognize. Curiosity got the better of Jesse, though. He crawled over to one of the machines and examined it as best he could in the dim moonlight. He still couldn't figure out what the machine was. The one he was closest to was about seven feet high and just about as wide both directions. It was made of steel, and consisted of a framework on which were mounted two or three belt-driven mandrels. There were cutter heads mounted along several of the mandrels, and the realization gradually sank in as to what the machine was. It was a larger version of the machine his old friend Ben Jones had bought from the young widow in Mormon Station, the one for cutting the shape of axe handles. This one was for cutting the shape of a rifle stock. He had never seen one of the machines before, but its use was clearly that of a rifle-stock cutter.

Exploring further, Jesse found other discarded machinery, which indicated the building was a huge gun factory, right there on the outskirts of Lynchburg. Jesse stood for a moment and pondered his situation. This was an opportunity to strike a blow for the North, if he would be able to set fire to the factory, but he was without means to get the fire started. If there were gunpowder inside, he could possibly ignite it by striking some of the black powder between metal surfaces, but he'd have to be awfully lucky to escape with his life.

The scene was quiet, so Jesse decided to crawl in closer and investigate his chances for setting this thing afire. He spotted a large door that looked as though it was in frequent use, and crept in that direction intending to try it. As he approached, still concealed among the wagons parked nearby, the door opened and a man stepped out holding a lantern. He was one of the watchmen, and he peered around in the darkness, not particularly suspicious, but nevertheless doing what he was supposed to do.

Jesse froze. The guard turned, latched the door, and started off around the building on his rounds. As soon as he was out of sight, Jesse ran to the door and tried the latch. It wasn't locked, and he was able to open it and slip through, closing the door behind him. The inside of the building was pitch black, but Jesse was able to make out a dimly lighted area in the far interior of the factory. Making his way toward the light was a slow process. Jesse began to wonder why he had chosen to get involved in such a harebrained scheme, when he didn't have even the remotest idea of his chances of success. Nevertheless, he moved closer to the light to see if there was any chance of his using it to pursue his cause. Along the way his hand closed on the handle of a large wrench, which he picked up in case he encountered anyone.

The light turned out to be a lantern sitting on a small table near where there sat another guard, reading a book. As Jesse approached, the man heard the sound of his foot scraping on the wooden floor.

"You back so soon, John?" the man asked turning slightly, and as he turned, Jesse swung the wrench at his head, knocking him unconscious. He collapsed without uttering another sound.

Jesse knew he would have to work fast before 'John' came back into the building. He looked around, and found a set of keys, searched the unconscious figure on the floor and pulled a small side-hammer revolver and a folding knife from his pocket. He then took the lantern and began to search the building for explosives. He felt it unlikely that the production of both arms and powder would be carried on in the same building, but it was possible that there would be a store of powder for the purpose of testing the guns. He moved as fast as he could toward the rear of the building for a place to start searching. From the size of the building and the direction John had taken, Jesse judged he would have about ten or fifteen minutes to clear the building.

Gradually a new idea formulated in his mind. It bothered him to have to take the life of the man on the floor. It looked as though there were only two guards on duty, and if he could disable them both he could take his time destroying the factory. He went back found some heavy twine, and tied the unconscious man securely, dragging him over between some boxes where he wouldn't be seen if 'John' were to return unexpectedly. He then picked up the wrench he'd used against the guard and made his way back to the door where he had first entered. He turned the lantern down to its lowest flame and placed it out of sight.

He didn't have to wait long. After only a few minutes Jesse heard the rattle of the door latch and John entered the darkened building. When John had closed the door behind him, Jesse spoke.

"Put the lantern down, John, and just hold your hands out away from you," Jesse said in a low voice. "Don't turn around. I'm holding a gun at your back."

"Alex, what are you up to?" John said, turning slightly, but when he saw Jesse with a wrench in one hand and a gun in the other, he carefully turned back around and put the lantern down. Jesse had drawn back his hand to strike out at John, but relaxed when he saw this wouldn't be necessary.

"We don't want to hurt you, so just start moving toward the guard station and I'll tell you what I want you to do," Jesse said. "You won't get hurt if you do what I tell you to. First, real slow, now. Take the gun out of your pocket."

"I don't have a gun, Mister, John said.

"I'll tell you what, John. We've been watching this place for several days, and I'm tired, nervous, and really cranky. If you don't pull that gun out of your pocket right now, I'm going to whack you with this-here wrench and knock you silly. Then we won't have to argue." With that, Jesse cocked the hammer of his revolver, the sound having an electrifying effect on John, who reached into his pants pocket and produced a small Colt revolver.

"Put it on the floor very gently and move away from it," Jesse advised in the same low tones as before. John did as he was told, Logan eased the hammer on his gun down, put it in his pocket and picked up the Colt.

"How's come you to know my name?" John summoned the nerve to ask.

"Like I say, we've been studying this setup for quite a time," Jesse lied, "and we know quite a bit about you and Alex. Just keep moving, but not too fast."

Jesse had picked up the lantern John had put down, and was following him toward the guard station, leaving the other lantern near the door of the building. When they got to the guard station Jesse showed him where Alex was lying and told John to drag him out of the building. Alex, however, had regained consciousness, and with help, walked toward the door as instructed. Jesse picked up more of the twine and also a little cloth sack, with what appeared to be the lunch that one of the men had brought to work, and followed the two guards toward the door.

"I want both of you to stop at the door. Alex, you set over there against the wall and turn around facing it. John you turn around and put your hands behind your back." Jesse had cut a length of the twine, but couldn't think of a way to hold the gun and tie the man's hands.

"You'd better lie down on the floor, John, I don't want to have to knock you out or shoot you, if I don't have to," Jesse advised. With that, he managed to tie John's hands securely, and proceeded to gag both men. He then checked Alex's bonds, searched the two for any other weapons, and tied a noose around each man's neck, connecting them with about two or three feet of the twine.

"Now, let's take a little walk," Jesse said, helping them to their feet. They walked out of the building and around to one side where Jesse guessed there were no neighboring houses to register an alarm. He then sat the two men down, tied their feet, and then tied their elbows back-to-back. Satisfied, he went over to the fence and kicked out two boards. When he had made a hole in the fence big enough to scramble through, he said in a low voice, "'You out there, Willie? It's okay, there was only just these two. Keep an eye on them. I'm going back inside."

Jesse then returned to the factory and set about looking for the powder he suspected was there. He found a small supply of gunpowder near the front of the building. It was not much more than he thought he would need to run a trail to the outside yard for safe ignition, so he found a can of Kerosene and proceeded to douse as much of the flammable material as he could readily find. He then laid a trail of gunpowder out the door as far as it would go, lit it with the flame from his lantern, and headed toward the hole in the fence. He didn't pause to admire his handiwork, but made his way west from the scene as quickly as he could. Even so, the fire spread quickly and Jesse had no problem finding his way for the next twenty or thirty minutes. He had plenty of light. As he made his way west from the conflagration, he could hear a loud bell, signaling a fire alarm.

John and Alex were lying about fifty feet from the building, but as the flames mounted, some of the wagons and other equipment in the yard began to burn. As people arrived to fight the fire, the two men were able to attract enough attention to be rescued, and were able to avoid injury, except to their pride and the lump on the side of Alex's head.

———————·«(●)»·———————

The destruction to the factory was almost complete. Some of the equipment in the yard was saved, but most of that was badly worn and had been set outside to be refurbished or repaired. The Fire Brigade responded and did what they could to suppress the flames, but they were understandably cautious. Knowing the factory was making firearms, they were concerned about further explosions.

In questioning John and Alex, the military authorities secured the description of the only perpetrator who had been seen. They suspected from the account of his actions that there were other members of the sabotage ring who were working in concert with the man setting the fire. The whole operation, at least as Alex and John described it, showed considerable planning in the manner in which it was carried out. There was also the question of the manner in which the perpetrator had made his escape, removing boards from the fence at a particular location, which he seemed to have determined beforehand, and ostensibly speaking to an accomplice outside the fence. The garrison investigators checked the area outside for hoofprints and found none, mystifying them still further.

14

NEW CASTLE

After leaving the burning building Jesse looked into the bag which he had taken from the guard station to see if it was actually a lunch bag as he had suspected. It was.

He examined the contents and found a fried egg sandwich, which he devoured immediately. There was also a small cake of what appeared to be cornbread, which he put in his pocket for future consumption. He then continued west around the southern fringe of Lynchburg, eventually encountering the railroad that he felt would take him toward Roanoke and the Shenandoah Valley. It was almost dawn when he spied a train preparing to leave the yards in the direction he wanted to go. Again, avoiding the passenger cars, Jesse hopped a car carrying horses, but in rethinking this choice, he made his way toward the rear of the train, again selecting a flat car loaded with cannons. As before, there were no guards on that portion of the train and he guessed it was carrying no ammunition.

He had retained both the guns he had taken back at the rifle factory. One was a five-shot .32 caliber Bacon, and the other a .31 caliber Colt. Neither had extra ammunition and though he thought about throwing one away as excess baggage, he felt it would be safer if he kept them both. Neither gun was particularly powerful and were probably only useful so far as their ability to threaten. He had learned over the years that the threat of force was often more potent than its actual use.

As he rode along, he reflected on the past few days. Colonel Reynolds, the Master of Randolph Lodge had been instrumental in Jesse's escape from prison, and now, after only a few days, he had caused a fire which must have burned a large part of that gun factory. He was a little bit ashamed of his having committed such a brazen act of sabotage, when all that the members of the lodge had expected was that he would just return to his unit and resume his army career. Well, "C'est le guerre", as he'd heard Mr. Putnam say, 'those are the fortunes of war'. With that thought, Jesse went to sleep.

He awoke as the train was pulling into the rail yard at Roanoke. It was midday, and he had been lulled to sleep by the movement of the train and the warm weather. He slipped off the flat car as the train slowed, and strolled casually toward some other cars waiting in the yard, hoping to appear as an unhurried hobo should anyone be watching. He was sure that the combination of his escape from Libby and the fire at Lynchburg would place him high on the Rebels' wanted list, but to act in a furtive manner would surely put any observer on guard.

Hiding amongst the freight cars randomly parked about the yard, Jesse contemplated his next move. He had only eaten the egg sandwich in the past two days, and he now consumed the piece of cornbread. He was feeling some pretty severe pangs of hunger. Here in the southern Shenandoah, food should be fairly plentiful. The region hadn't been particularly subjected to the demands of either of the warring armies.

With no money, Jesse would have to beg, work, or steal to get food. He felt working would be the preferred option, not that he was feeling particularly industrious at the time, but it was just that the risks were less than the other two options. He walked out of the rail yard by way of the tracks heading west, looking for an opportunity to ask someone for the opportunity to do some work. Even this contained some risks, as there weren't supposed to be any strangers wandering about these days. You were supposed to be in the army or working at some war-related job.

Coming to a small farm, he could see some hogs in a pen toward the rear of the dooryard. There was a man of about sixty-five feeding them. Jesse decided to approach him.

"Mister, would you have any work a man could do for maybe a meal and a place to sleep?" Jesse asked, approaching the man, "I'd be glad to help with the chores or do anything you need done."

"I got plenty of energy to do the little bit around here," the man replied, "But if ye want to stay a few days I thinks the Massa may have some plowin' to do."

"Well, I was trying to get up the valley to Tennessee, and I was kind of in a hurry, but if you do need help, I'd be glad to spend some time staying around here and helping out."

The man eyed Jesse for a moment. "Ye're tryin' to get up the valley, are ye?" he asked. "What's so important up there?"

"I jus' wanted to see my kinfolk before I had to go back to my company," the answer was truthful enough without giving away his Union loyalties. "I got separated a few days ago and am just now tryin' to catch up with my unit."

"How'd ye do that?"

"I was on the train and I overslept my stop," Jesse knew the conversation couldn't go much further without the farmer getting suspicious.

"I don't think the Massa'd have no work you'd be good fer," the man finally said, "If you cain't find yer railroad stop, you prob'ly couldn't find which way the horses was headed. You better be on yer way, I reckon."

"Could you spare a few ears of corn fer a hungry man?" Jesse decided to try Plan B.

"Well, I reckon I could spare couple o' y'ears." he dug into a burlap sack standing nearby and handed two ears of dried corn to Jesse. "Here, this won't ruin me, I don't s'ppose. Kin you make it a'right on this?"

"I really appreciate this, Mister," Jesse said. "That's awfully nice of you." Jesse shucked off a few kernels and put them in his mouth. "That'll hold me for a couple of days. Thanks."

Then, as an afterthought, Jesse turned back to the man, "How far is it to Lewisburg, Mister," he asked.

"It's about a two-day trip by horseback," the man said, "But you'll have a tough time making it in less than four, on foot, an' the country gets purty steep. Another thing, that's Union country, an' they're a mite unfrien'ly up there, I'd think."

"Oh, that's right. I reckon I'd forgot about that," Jesse responded. "Thanks for the advice. Have you lived in this part of the country very long?"

"Well, I was borned right hy'ere, right on this farm, an' I've lived hy'ere all my life," the man responded.

"Do you have a family here?' Jesse asked, looking around to make sure he wasn't observed.

"My missus died a few years back and my chilluns all be'n sold." The man said sadly. "I jus' got me to worry about, now, and waitin' fer kingdom come, unless Mister Lincum kin git us'ns freed, but that don't seem likely, do it? I don't know why I'm tellin' you this, sence you're bein' a so'jer in the army."

"Can I tell you something, something that could get us both in trouble if you were to let it out to anyone?" Jesse said in a low voice. "I'm a Union soldier, mister, an' to my way of thinking, Mr. Lincoln is a lot closer to givin' you your freedom than a lot of people think."

The man's only response was a surprised expression, and he continued with his chores for a minute or two before he again looked up and examined his visitor, somewhat dubiously. "You don't look like no north'n so'jer," he said, looking Jesse up and down. "What would a Yankee so'jer be doin' in them rags ye're wearin', an' in this part of the country?"

"I just escaped from prison an' I'm tryin' to get back to my company," Jesse explained. "If I can get back to Lewisburg, I think that's where my company is."

"Come on in the barn, wif you, den, So'jer," the man exclaimed in a low voice, "I got some chicken stew you kin eat quick. Den you bes' be gitten' on yo' way."

When he left the barn of his new friend, Jesse turned northwest. His recollection of the region told him that he was closer now to where he thought the Seventh Ohio would be than to his home in Carter County, and he was getting tired of running. It was worth a try.

He found the road to New Castle, which he thought would then take him on to Lewisburg and his old unit. He was refreshed from the sleep he'd had on the train, and could eat the corn the farmer had given him while continuing on his way. It required putting a few kernels of corn in his mouth and holding them until they softened, and then they could be chewed and swallowed. There was water in the creek beside the road, and he felt he could get to New Castle by morning.

Actually, it was well after noon, two days later when Jesse found himself on the streets of New Castle. He was tired and footsore, and was beginning to feel that it didn't make much difference whether he got back to the Seventh Ohio or any other unit or even whether the Rebs picked him up. The corn he had gotten from the farmer was gone, and he was just plain used up. He was just about to sit down by the side of the road when he saw a man on a horse approaching him. Out of the corner of his eye Jesse saw the man coming and turned away, suspecting he had been recognized, or at least that the man was going to question Jesse about his presence.

"Say, young feller, don't you ever stay where you belong?" Dan Ellis fired his opening question at Jesse.

Logan looked up and just stared, not fully comprehending that this was truly his old friend and neighbor, the man who was so sought after by the Confederates for his role in the resistance of East Tennessee, and for his ability to slip unnoticed between the northern and southern lines. Finally, reality set in, and Jesse regained his speech.

"Dan Ellis! You old son of a gun! What in the world are you doing so far from home? 'Just out for a ride?"

"Jesse," Dan said, getting down from his horse and throwing his arms around the younger man, "Aren't you a sight fer sore eyes! 'Last we'd heard you'd be'n throw'd in prison down in Richmond, and never thought we'd ever see you again. How did you ever get here?"

"Dan, it's a long story, but I'm thinking we'd better get to someplace a little less public. I don't think this is the town where we'd want to be drawing a crowd."

"Yes, I reckon you're right, Jesse. Come with me. I know some people who are a little friendlier than the rag-tag rabble you usually meet on the streets of these Rebel towns."

They went west on the main road through town and turned into a side street. Behind the store building on the corner, Dan tied his horse and went through the back door. "Bert," he called out to the proprietor. "Hey, Bert. Are you here?'

A small man came from the front of the store and greeted Dan.

"Bert, this here is Jesse Logan, lately returned from the bowels of Libby Prison and widely noted for his skill with the Spencer rifle. He's lookin' for a ride home."

Jesse was quick to explain, "I'll tell you what. I'm not so anxious for a way back to Doe River Cove as I am to get back to my old outfit. The only thing about it is that all my gear, my Spencer, my pistol, and all my uniforms and equipment are at Kellars Crossing. If it weren't for them, I'd get straight back to the old Seventh Ohio."

"Nice to meet you, Jesse. How's come you're from East Tennessee and are fighting with an Ohio regiment?" Bert asked. Bert was a smallish man, in his late fifties, with thinning gray hair and a small goatee. The store he owned was Bert Oakley Dry Goods, but he dealt in everything from food stuffs to farm machinery. He was popular with the townsfolk of New Castle, only because he kept his political opinions to himself, and provided an unbelievable selection of hard-to-find necessities of life. He was the ideal contact for a Union spy or scout, as the case might be, and he was one of Dan Ellis' main contacts in the region. Bert's outgoing nature and small stature labeled him as anything but an 'enemy agent' in this small, out-of-the-way town in southwestern Virginia.

"You fellows are going to have to excuse me for a minute. I have some paying customers out front, and I shouldn't keep them waiting." With that Bert returned to the front part of the store.

"So, how did you get yourself out of prison, Jesse," were Dan's first words.

When Jesse began to describe his experience with the Richmond Masons, Dan hung on his every word, and when Jesse had finished, he laughed incredulously.

"I was at the lodge in Elizabethton the night Steven Venable told us he was going to send that letter to that Richmond Lodge to see if they would put on your third degree. We never, ever suspected that the thing would turn out like it did. Why, you're only about a week out of prison, aren't you?"

"Just about," Jesse responded.

"Jesse, that's the funniest thing I ever heard," Dan Ellis was still laughing.

"Well, I'll tell you. When I got set out on the street after the lodge meeting, I wasn't laughing," Jesse chuckled. "I was giving serious thought to going back to Libby and turning myself in." He then told Dan of his experiences with Fred Hatrack and with Horace and Dorothy and his treatment at their hands.

"I don't know if people like that will survive the war, living in the midst of such strong secessionist feelings," he said to Dan.

"I don't know, either, Jesse," Dan responded, "but I surely hope they can."

They talked for ten or fifteen minutes and presently Bert came back from the front of the store. Dan told Bert about Jesse's experiences and they all enjoyed another laugh. They also agreed that this was one of the most profound, and perhaps the more bizarre, examples of the benefits of being a Mason that they had ever heard of.

Finally, Dan said, "Well, Jesse, what's your pleasure? Do you want to go back to Carter County or on up to Camp Dick Robinson? That's where I think your old company is, right now, although Stonewall Jackson has been pulling everything the Union has to give down out of the hills. He's just giving old J. C. Fremont fits. The Federals never know where he's gonna turn up next. That's why I came down the valley, but I haven't been no help in tryin' to keep track of him. No help at all."

Bert agreed. "Jackson was through here about a month ago, and then he turned up at Winchester and Front Royal, just knocking our people silly. He's sure some kind of a general, I'll tell you."

Bert then changed the subject, "If you need a gun to get you by till you get back to your regiment, I might have an old revolver or two tucked away for just such an occasion. It'll give you a little protection on the way and they'd issue you a rifle when you get there."

"You don't understand, Bert," Dan said. "Have you ever heard of the White Angel?"

"Isn't he that Yank, the one who was so sharp with the sniper rifle a few months ago?" Bert asked. "What ever became of him?"

"This is him, Bert. Jesse's the one they called the White Angel."

"Come on, Dan, let's not get off on that subject," Jesse admonished. "I hate that name. Half the things they claimed I did, I wasn't even in that part of the country. It was just the imagination of some over-enthusiastic reporter that got this whole thing started."

"It don't matter, Jesse, you're still him," Dan said with a grin. "Just like Robin Hood, you've got a reputation for better or worse, and people are going to play it up till who-knows-when. It's kind of like the things I'm supposed to have done like getting people and supplies and stuff through the lines. Every time someone slips across, they pin it on me. Bert knows that ain't always the case, don't you Bert?"

Bert assumed a shocked look. "Why, Dan, you just told me last week you weren't getting enough credit for all the things you do for the Union, and you thought you ought to hire a publicity man to see that you got all that was coming to you."

Dan and Jesse laughed over the little man's humor, and then Jesse changed the subject. Pulling the two revolvers out of his pockets, he passed them to Bert. "If you had something a little larger caliber, Bert, I'd make you a trade, two for one."

"Well, let me see what I have," Bert responded. He went to a cupboard next to the wall and moved it aside. Taking up two floorboards, he rummaged about in a space beneath the floor. "I have this .36 Remington and a 32 caliber, S and W, 'Old Army'."

Jesse looked at the two and chose the Smith and Wesson. "I'll take this one. It's a little easier to carry and I like the idea of the solid cartridges."

"You know, Jesse, there aren't many of these guns around. Word has it that they were making these or something a lot like them down at Lynchburg up until a couple of days ago, but someone got in and burned the factory down. The papers say it was a big Union sabotage ring. Anyway, they just burned it to the ground," Bert expounded.

"Humph. What do you know about that?" Logan grunted, checking the Smith for bullets. "Bert you wouldn't have a few extra rounds for this one, would you? And I was wondering if you might have a pair of pants that would fit me. I'm tired of looking like a clown from the waist down."

Bert went back to the space under the floor and pulled out a box of bullets for the revolver. "Use those sparingly, Jesse, There's not a lot of them around."

"Now, would either of you know where a man could find a horse at little or no cost?" Jesse inquired.

"We'll have to give that one some thought," Dan responded. There's a man north of town who can maybe help us on that. How's about some food, Jess? How long's it been since you ate?"

"I had a couple of ears of corn that lasted me through the last two days, but to tell you the truth, my stomach thinks my throat's been cut, Dan. The big hungries have finished off the little ones and are about to start gnawing on my backbone. I could surely use some grub, all right. One other thing, Bert. You wouldn't have a pair of socks I could talk you out of, would you?"

Bert went to the front of the store and came back with a pair of wool socks, a small bag of pecan nuts, a quantity of dried beef, and a pair of pants. "This ain't much, but it'll keep the hungries away. Take 'em with you. You can pay me when the war's over."

Jesse changed pants, thanked Bert, and left by the back door. "It'll attract less attention if we both just walk separately for a ways, Jesse," Ellis said, "and then you can get up behind me. I may know a farmer out a little way who has an extra horse. We might talk him out of a bite to eat, too."

General Thomas "Stonewall" Jackson had penetrated the area southwest of New Castle, the month before, and then had moved through to the east and north toward Winchester, where he defeated General Nathaniel Banks. He then returned back up the Shenandoah Valley toward Harrisonburg.

With the Confederate army thus engaged, and the country between New Castle and Lewisburg fairly clear of any serious threat, Dan and Jesse had little trouble traveling through the countryside. However, when they reached the home of Dan's friend, Lawson Pearce, where they hoped to find a horse for Jesse, they were disappointed. When Jackson's army had come through the region, they confiscated every horse, cow, pig, sheep, chicken and rabbit they could find. They had done no damage to speak of, but to replenish their food supply and horses they had recently lost, they stripped the countryside of all livestock, leaving Confederate currency as payment. Lawson Pearce had lost three horses to the expedition, and was left with little to eat and nothing with which to plow his land to raise anything.

After they'd had some of the biscuits and gravy provided by their host, and over Pearce's objections, Dan Ellis unsaddled his horse, tied it behind the Pearce home, and he and Jesse said their good-byes and struck out on foot. Jesse was footsore from his long trek from Richmond, but was so impressed by Ellis' generosity that he said nothing at all about the matter until they were well away from the Pearce farm.

He finally said to Dan, "That was really nice of you, Dan, but won't you

---

be needin' that horse? You have a pretty important part in this war. You take a lot of people through the lines, you carry messages and mail, you scout for the North, and I don't think anybody could complain if you kept your horse."

"Jesse," Dan said, "think about it this way. We can do what we have to do, move along the road and get from place to place without a horse. Sometimes, when we want to duck into the brush, a horse is even a hindrance. Lawson can't plow, haul a wagon, help his neighbors, or anything else without a horse. That's number one. Number two, whenever you can help a friend without doing serious injury to yourself, you'd better do it. Someday it'll come back to you. You can count on that just as sure as you can count on the sun coming up tomorrow."

Jesse had been on his feet for about thirty-six hours by then, and he felt like he was ready to collapse. Dan realized his plight and encouraged him on. "If we keep going just a little farther, Jesse, I think I know of a place we can stop, and get some sleep for the night. Can you stick it out?"

They moved on northwest toward Lewisburg. The countryside was becoming decidedly less populated. Suddenly, just as the sun was a couple of hours above the horizon, a deer ventured out across the road in front of them. Dan quickly raised his rifle and fired. The deer dropped and the two men rushed forward to subdue it. Dan's aim had been good, and the deer had been hit just behind the shoulder.

"This is the place, Jesse. Here's where we eat supper and bed down for the night," Dan said with his usual sense of assurance. "I didn't know it would happen so soon, but I figured we'd bring something down for our supper."

Dan Ellis had developed a wide reputation as a man to be trusted and relied upon for assistance. He was also known for his ability to move quickly through the land and take people from place to place with a minimum of bother and baggage. Jesse was beginning to understand why he had such a reputation. He was a hard driver when he needed to be, a kind friend when kindness was most appreciated, and above all, Dan was resourceful.

"You had no more idea than I did about a 'place to sleep', did you, Dan," Jesse chided.

Dan just laughed, "Let's just say I've been this way before, Jess."

Dan had a sheath knife that he sharpened on a stone he carried in his knapsack. They prepared the deer for cooking and built a fire. They rigged a spit and suspended the deer over the fire, turning it occasionally for a period of almost three hours, keeping the fire burning brightly for light, heat and to completely cook the venison. When it was done, Dan laid the meat out on the hide, which he had cleaned and scraped on the bank of the nearby stream. Except for one of the hams, he cut the meat into strips. The meat would keep the two men in food for the next few days, if they were careful, and when dried it would be less likely to spoil. The ham he had saved was for their supper, and they finished it off, leaving nothing. Then they skewered the remaining meat and suspended it over the fire keeping up a low fire throughout the night. The next morning, after a good night's sleep they stuffed the dried meat in their pockets and in the knapsack Dan was carrying, and started west.

They had only gone a few hundred yards when they heard the sound of a horse approaching them from the direction of New Castle. Ducking into the brush, they let the horse approach and saw that it was Lawson Pearce. Dan called to him and Lawson stopped, getting off his horse.

"Dan, there's a couple of men from the East Tennessee Militia down in New Castle looking for you. They say they need to have you back in the Watauga to help pilot some people through to Kentucky, and it sounds like Dan Stover particularly needs to get a holt of you. I don't know how they got through, but they seem to be in a hurry and want to know if you can come back as quick as you can. Bert sent his nephew up to my place, and I came as fast as I could. You'd better take this horse back, Dan."

"Lawson," Dan said, "I'll do better on foot back as far as New Castle. I'd rather not be on horseback with the fuss that Ol' Stonewall set up in these parts. I heard from Bert that there's still a regiment of Rebel Cavalry in these parts, an' I think walkin' is better than ridin' right now. I'll git back to town and see what I can do. Jesse, maybe you'd better stay here in New Castle with Bert and Lawson unless you'd like to try to make it to Lewisburg on your own."

As they walked back toward New Castle, they began to prepare for Dan's trip back to Carter County, dividing the venison. They went over several possibilities for Jesse's course of action and Jesse decided it would be better if he headed north toward Lewisburg to rejoin his regiment. He was concerned though, that the two 'messengers' were a Rebel trick to try to capture Dan Ellis so they agreed that he'd go back to New Castle with Dan, clear up that question and then proceed north.

When they got to New Castle, they went immediately to Bert Oakley's store. They separated and Jesse went up to the front of the store as Dan went around to the rear. Jesse paused as he approached the front door, but Bert was near the door and opened it, motioning Jesse inside.

"They're out back, Jesse," Bert said. "It's two men from Elizabethton."

"Are you sure they're okay?" Jesse asked in a low voice. "These aren't a couple of bushwhackers, are they?"

"No, I don't think so." Bert responded. "They are in too much of a hurry, and seem to be pretty sure of what they're talking about."

"Dan went around to the back, and I'm going to keep out of sight, if I can, to keep him covered. What's the best way back there so's I won't be seen right away?"

"Just come through here," Bert said softly, "and stay behind those boxes you see over by that door." He pointed the way to the rear door.

Jesse did as he was told and as he crept silently back toward the rear of the store, he could hear voices coming from the back room. One of the voices was clearly that of Sidney Coster, who was one of the 'home guard' who had been in on Jesse's capture back near Doe River Cove in February. Jesse couldn't believe it, but the other voice sounded like that of Tom Singleton. Jesse couldn't make out what the two were saying, and he moved in closer to hear better.

"We'd better be moving away from here. The Rebs are going to smell a rat and figure us fer unionists if we hang around here much longer," Sid was saying.

"We don't even know if that boy caught up with those fellas. He never did come back to let us know," Tom agreed.

"Come on, Tom," Sid said urgently. "This is too scary fer me. We better tell this feller we're gonna hide somewheres out of town and come back later. I don't like this at all."

Jesse sensed the two were authentic, though he couldn't imagine Sidney Coster in any role than that of a Rebel guerilla. He stepped clear of the boxes just as Dan Ellis came through the back door. Tom and Sid both looked toward the door as Dan came in.

"Tom, Sid," Dan exclaimed, "what's going on?"

"Dan Stover wants you back in Tennessee as quick as you can get there," Tom began. "The Rebs are building a big force in Knoxville, we're trying to put the regiment in shape, and he also needs to get someone through the gap into Kentucky to notify them of what's happening up there. Things are coming apart at the seams, Dan. You can't believe the time we had getting here."

"There's a friend of yours who had a hard time getting here, too," Dan said. "He's standing right behind you with a gun in his hand, ready to shoot you down if you make a wrong move."

Tom and Sidney turned to see Jesse's huge frame standing in the doorway to the front part of the store. Jesse was still puzzled by Sid's presence there, and had only just then lowered his revolver.

"Jesse," Tom exclaimed. "Jesse Logan," he repeated in a hushed voice, suddenly realizing they were not in friendly country. He rushed over to where Jesse was standing, ignoring the gun in his hand, and grasped Jesse by the shoulders. "Boy, am I glad to see you! How did you get out of prison?"

Sid, who had hung back when Tom had rushed to Jesse's side, went over to where Jesse and Tom were standing and held out his hand. "Jesse," he said, "I owe you a big apology. I just found out what I should have know'd all along, and I want you to know how happy I am to see you safe, and how sorry I am that I had any part in gettin' you throwed in prison."

The two men related some of the events that had transpired since Jesse had been sent to prison in Richmond, including the death of Sid's brother Albert for some supposedly 'disloyal' actions against the Confederacy. Albert was not very bright, and when he told some of the Northern sympathizers about the gang's part in capturing Jesse, Evan Stance got some other secessionist 'home guard' together, dragged Albert out of his house, and hung him by the neck. Stance's comment when Albert was being dragged from the house, was that Albert wanted so much to see someone hung that he could experience it for himself and see how it felt. Sidney had switched sides over the incident, and now he was as sought after as Jesse or Dan Ellis.

The four men left Bert's store individually and went out to Lawson Pearce's farm. There they discussed their possible course of action. They decided Sid and Dan would take the horses that Sid and Tom had brought with them and return to Tennessee. Tom and Jesse would strike out west on foot and try to tie up with the Union Army, Tom being anxious to enlist anyway he could. He was embarrassed at not having gotten into the army, even though he had been a member of the irregular militia in East Tennessee. Still he would like to be able to work with Jesse in the Seventh Ohio. They said their good-byes, Dan Ellis giving his best advice to Jesse and Tom for their journey, and parted.

Tom had a musket, an old flint-lock pistol, and a knife, which he had brought from Tennessee, and Jesse had his revolver. They went only a few miles into the hills toward Lewisburg when darkness overtook them, and they bedded down for the night.

The following morning, they were both awake and up before sunup. They chewed some of the jerky and headed northwest, staying with the Lewisburg road.

Tom and Jesse discussed their experiences since they had last seen each other, and generally enjoyed the morning. When they had gone about four miles toward Lewisburg, they spotted a wagon approaching from the west over a rise in the road a quarter of a mile west. Hoping they had not been seen, they ducked into the underbrush and waited. As the wagon approached, they could see that it was a rather large freight wagon, painted with someone's name on the side. As it got closer, Jesse recognized the wagon. It was 'Livingston Mercantile', the suttler from his old brigade. The team of four horses was driven by Mr. Livingston, himself, but to Jesse's consternation, the seat beside him was empty.

"Mr. Livingston," Jesse greeted him, stepping out of the brush beside the road, "it's nice to see a friendly face in this strange land. Where's your daughter?"

The "friendly face" was implacable as ever, with the familiar tobacco pipe clenched in its teeth. If anything, Mr. Livingston looked puzzled.

"Where's Miss Livingston?" Jesse repeated the question.

"Oh, her," Livingston realized what Jesse was saying. "She's in the back of the wagon, getting some rest." He had pulled the horses to a stop.

Feeling the wagon stop and hearing voices, Olivia climbed from the rear of the wagon and over the seat to find out what had happened. Seeing Jesse, she smiled but showed no sign of surprise, nor did she display any emotion other than her usually cordial manner.

"Well, Mr. Logan," she said, "Haven't you been the busy one? It's so nice to see you."

Jesse had an inkling of what she was referring to, but he held back any but the most noncommittal comment. "I reckon you've been busy, yourself, Miss Livingston. It's been quite a space since I've seen you, almost six months, I seem to recall." Then he remembered his friend Tom, who had stepped to the side of the road beside him.

"Miss Livingston, Mr. Livingston, I'd like you to meet my friend, Tom Singleton, from Carter County, Tennessee. Tom and I are heading back for Lewisburg to see if we can't connect with the Seventh Ohio again."

"You'll not find any but a small garrison at Lewisburg, I'm afraid," Olivia responded. "Colonel Sullivan has pulled them back to Meadow Bluff. We're without a regiment, and thought we'd go down the valley to try to drum up a little business."

"But this is Rebel country. Don't you think they might deal a little harshly with people from the Northern Army?" Jesse asked.

"We've run into this sort of thing before. A suttler is a suttler, and the Rebs treat us almost as well as the Yanks, except that they give us Confederate money for our trade. That doesn't spend quite so well where we usually obtain our wares." Miss Livingston said with a smile. "We prefer Yankee money, but we survive on either side of the line."

"So I'm told," Jesse said knowingly, but again he didn't pursue the matter.

Olivia smiled again and continued, "Mr. Logan, since your old unit is now quite a distance from here, what do you plan to do?"

"I'll tell you what. I'm open to suggestions about now," Jesse sighed. "Tom and I have been wandering these parts for a couple of days, now, and our plans seem to be subject to change, almost hourly."

"Was Mr. Singleton with you at Lynchburg?" Olivia asked.

Jesse was surprised at the question. He had told no one of his burning the gun factory at Lynchburg, and though Olivia had reached the right conclusion he sensed that it was still only speculation on her part.

He maintained his composure and with a sly smile, he responded smoothly, "No, Tom wasn't on that train. He came here on foot." His eyes pleaded with her not to pursue the matter, and she nodded slightly and lowered her eyelids to show she understood.

The conversation drifted to conjecture as to what the two men would do, now that the nearest Union regiment was probably two hundred miles away, but Tom and Jesse reached no conclusion.

"Why don't you trail along with us for a ways?" Miss Livingston finally suggested. "You won't be any more obvious than you are right now, and at least we have some provisions we can share with you."

"I'm sure Mr. Logan would like to move a little more quickly than he would with us," Mr. Livingston spoke for the first time during the conversation.

"Nonsense," Miss Livingston cut him off sharply, "Mr. Logan won't be able to move any faster on foot than he can with us. With the load we have on the wagon, it's necessary for one of us to walk part of the time, anyway, and this will give us someone to walk with."

It seemed odd for Miss Livingston to speak so sharply to her father, and Jesse had the impression that this was not just a daughter consulting with her father over business matters. It seemed these two were more like business partners than father and daughter, and there seemed to be a little tension between them just now. More than ever, Jesse suspected that this was more of a business than a family relationship. Be that as it may, he was looking for the opportunity to get Olivia aside and find out how much she knew about his recent activities.

"I'd welcome a chance to walk along some with you folks, if it wouldn't be an imposition. How about you, Tom?"

Tom was out of his element. He'd been at a loss to try to keep up with the conversation, and, except for an immediate infatuation with Olivia, he wasn't following what was going on at all. At Jesse's question, though, he responded quickly, "Sure. I'd really like to stay with the wagon for a time. At least until we can come up with a better plan."

"Excuse me, a moment," Olivia said, ducking back into the enclosure of the wagon. After a few seconds she reappeared and climbed easily down, walking over to where Tom and Jesse were standing.

Mr. Livingston didn't say another word. He just flicked the reins and with a clicking sound he made with his tongue he urged the horses into a brisk walk. Tom, Olivia, and Jesse fell in behind the wagon, and they were again headed east.

"Do you ever get the feeling you've been this way before, Jesse," Tom asked with a smile.

"I'm going to know this road pretty well after a few more trips," Jesse responded.

Olivia provided most of the conversation, telling the two men what she could of the matters surrounding the Seventh Ohio. She didn't speak of her being in Richmond, however, and Jesse thought it better to wait to talk about that encounter. Neither did they talk of what he had done in Lynchburg, but he did tell the others about his experiences with the boys in the tobacco shed and the couple who had been so kind to him and who had a son in the Federal army. He also told them of his meeting with Dan Ellis, and how it was pretty much an answer to prayer.

Jesse was having a very enjoyable time of it with two of his best friends and nothing more to worry about than getting back to his old unit. He knew that this would take time and diligence and that he would have to rely on some of the ingenuity that Dan Ellis had displayed in slipping across the lines. Nevertheless, he was determined to make the most of his situation. As they walked along the road behind the wagon, Jesse was entirely at ease. He tried to make both Olivia and Tom comfortable and to give them a better feeling for the friendship that he felt toward both of them.

"Miss Livingston is from up in Maryland, Tom. She and her — father," Jesse stumbled a little on the word, "have been the suttlers for our brigade ever since we came into the war. Why, I was there when she came to the brigade and checked in with General Rosecrans. I'll never forget when she went up to the general and introduced herself. The general looked at her and, just going along with the regulations, he asked her if there was any way she could identify herself. Just as cool as you please, Miss Livingston pulled out a mirror and held it up to her face, and says, 'Yep, that's me, all right.' The general just didn't know what to say, so he let her go ahead and set up their tent."

Olivia took a swing at Jesse with a clenched fist, but Jesse had anticipated her reaction and moved out of range.

"Also," he continued, "she doesn't like me for some reason. I can tell 'cause she's always trying to hurt me." He then turned on Tom.

"Miss Livingston, Tom was my best friend for the best part of the last five or six years. When I started school, he was always there to support me whenever I needed him. He's not real bright, though, as you've probably already found out, but I want you to know he's well connected in Carter County. When I was there last January, he had a job with the sheriff. They put him down by the courthouse with an empty gun and told him to keep the lions from terrorizing the town. When I went to see him, he told me what he was up to and I said to him, 'Tom, there ain't been a lion in Carter County for as long as anyone can remember.' Tom just looks at me and says, 'See, I'm really taking care of business.' He was real proud of that job."

Jesse was in his element. As they walked along that dusty road with the flies buzzing their lazy accompaniment, Jesse broke into song.

I live up on the hill, right by the cider mill,
    My name is Joshua-a-a-ay Ebenezer Fr-y-y-ye,
Now, I know a thing 'r two, you can bet your neck I do.
    You cain't fool me, 'cause I'm too durned sly.

I hitched up the old mare, 'drove her to the county fair,
    'Took first prize on a load of summer squa-a-a-rsh.
I went back up the hill, stopped by the cider mill,
    'Got drunker than a durned fool, by garsh.

Along come a dirty crook, 'said "Let's see your pocket book.
    Won't you give me two tens for a five?"
I said, "Why you poor fool, I'll go get the constabule,
    And have you arrested just as sure as you're alive."

I live up on the hill, right by the cider mill,
    My name is Joshua-a-a-ay Ebenezer Fr-y-y-ye.
Now, I know a thing or two, you can bet your neck I do.
    You cain't fool me, 'cause I'm too durned sly.

Jesse's humor was infectious. The three friends were having an enjoyable afternoon of it and all three were better for the chance to relax. As they followed a respectable distance behind the wagon to avoid the effects of the dust it generated, the conversation drifted from subject to subject. Jesse related some of the details of his experience in Richmond when he was virtually released from captivity by his new-found friends, the Masons.

"Don't forget, old pal," Tom reminded him, "I was the one who got you interested in joining the Masons in the first place."

"That's right," Jesse admitted, poking Tom in the ribs, "it was that day when I was about to get on the packet boat at Union that we were talking about joining the Masons. Of course," he said turning to Olivia, and in a taunting voice, "Tom's so much older than I am that he was able to get in the Masons before I was even eligible."

Without responding to the comment about their comparative ages, Olivia asked, "What is the reason you two wanted to get into the Masons? What is it about the Masons that's so attractive to men?"

"Well," Jesse said, "you just have a chance to meet a lot of fine fellows and you do it on a basis of equality and friendship, no matter what their station in life is, or your own. There were several members of the Confederate army in the lodge at Richmond the night I got my third degree, and they all acted just like brothers to me."

"He's right," Tom commented, "The night we voted on letting Jesse into the lodge, there was the mayor of the town and even Felix Zollicoffer, who was a general in the Rebel army in that area at the time. Anyway, Jesse, you knew General Zollicoffer had been killed, didn't you? And another thing, the people of the town of Union renamed the town after him."

"No, I'm sorry to hear about General Zollicoffer, but he wasn't too popular around the valley after he turned for the Rebs, except maybe in his home town," Jesse said. "But, you know that town was pretty much owned by David McClellan, commander of the 'B Company' of the 'Home Guard'."

"That still doesn't answer my question," Olivia persisted. "What's so great about Masonry that you wanted to join in the first place? What does it accomplish?"

"One of the principles about Masonry, as I'm told," Jesse answered, sobering just slightly, "It's a moral discipline that teaches by — by allegory and example. It takes good men and makes them better for the experience"

After a moment's pause during which Olivia looked intently at Jesse, she said in an even voice, "When is it supposed to start working on you, Jesse?" Whereupon Jesse reached out and grabbed the girl by the shoulders and wrestled her about in a playful manner, but released her almost immediately, stepping away and blushing from the rush of adrenaline he sensed from the brief contact.

Olivia sensed the feeling as well, and pushed at Jesse. "I'll ask you to keep your distance, if you don't mind, Mr. Logan. It's bad enough having to walk these dusty roads in the heat of the day without some big brute coming along and mauling me for simply offering an innocent question about his life."

Tom went on to relate a little more of the matter concerning the death of Sidney Coster's brother, and how it changed Sid to a staunch Unionist. He also told a little more about the vote in the Masonic lodge after Lily Venable had received Jesse's Letter.

"Who is Lily Venable?" Olivia asked pointedly. Tom was quick to answer.

"She's a really pretty girl in Elizabethton that Jesse was writing to from Prison," he volunteered.

"Don't make it sound like something it isn't," Jesse defended. "I met her at a party, and when I got to prison, I found the chance to write a letter and have it mailed by a guard, and I just happened to have her father's address. It isn't hard. It's '4 Johnson Street, Elizabethton'. It was the only address I could remember." He expected some sort of cool response from Olivia, but her next question he was not prepared for.

"Wasn't that Erasmus Ross who mailed the letter for you?" she asked

Jesse stopped and stared at her. "What is going on in that head of yours?" he asked after a few moments. "I can't believe some of the things you're coming out with."

"Then it was 'Rasmus, wasn't it?" she persisted. "Jesse —," she hesitated for a moment, then addressed her next comment to Tom. "Mr. Singleton, could you just go on ahead for a few minutes? There's a matter I have to clear up with Jesse, and I'm not comfortable discussing it in another person's presence until we can agree on a few things."

"Sure," Tom said quickly. Though he'd been struck by an arrow from Cupid's bow when he first saw Olivia, he'd been quite aware there was more to their conversation than he could track, and was happy enough to move out of earshot. His infatuation with Miss Livingston was obviously pointless. If she wasn't in love with Jesse, which was a distinct probability, she was at least so preoccupied with her business with him that she hardly knew that Tom even existed.

When he was well ahead of them, Olivia turned to Jesse, who was only too happy to get to the bottom of some of the mysteries surrounding this woman.

"Well," he said expectantly, "I'm all ears, Miss Livingston, if that's your name."

She lowered her eyes and smiled. "How did you know?" she asked.

"The old man gave it away when we met him this morning. He didn't have any idea who I was talking about when I asked about his daughter. Who are you? Who is he? What were you doing in Richmond? How did you know I burnt down that gun factory? How did you know about Ross? What the heck is going on, here?"

In response, Olivia reached into her purse and withdrew a gold watch on a chain. It was the watch Jesse had entrusted to Erasmus Ross at Libby Prison. "I think this is yours, Jesse. This may explain a little of what I've been up to. Though it was fortunate for you that the Masons let you go from Libby, Erasmus Ross could have made it a lot safer and easier."

Then, as quickly as she could, Olivia told Jesse that she was working as an agent for the North, but keeping a line of information going for the South to maintain her contacts. She was keeping herself in the good graces of the southern authorities by selling to them small manufactured goods, medical supplies, percussion caps, and particularly stationery supplies that were virtually impossible to obtain by any means but the underground market. She'd been in Richmond communicating with some people she knew who were influential there and from whom she obtained considerable information. Her loyalist contacts in Richmond were mainly organized around Elizabeth van Lew, who posed as "Crazy Bett" in order to further her service to the Union. Erasmus (or 'Rasmus) Ross was one of her confidential contacts, though he had told her he had not expected Jesse's escape to occur in the manner it did. As it happened, Jesse's escape in the way it did, made it much easier on Ross, as he could not be implicated in the escape in any way.

The matter of Jesse's burning the gun factory in Lynchburg was mostly conjecture on her part, simply putting the facts in order and knowing there were no other Union agents in the area at the time. She also relied on the description the two guards had provided of the 'ringleader' of the responsible gang of 'saboteurs' and the knowledge that Jesse would be the kind of man whom she thought would be just reckless enough to do such a thing on his own initiative. His reputation with the Seventh Ohio made her think immediately of him when she had heard of an 'organized band of saboteurs' working in the Lynchburg area.

The conclusion she was approaching was that she wanted Jesse to join with her. She suggested that together they could do much more for the cause of the Union than he ever could by sitting on some lonely hillside waiting to kill or be killed.

They had stopped walking and were standing face to face. Jesse glanced up at the wagon ahead of them, wishing they were out of sight. He wanted to grab this woman again and hold her very tightly.

"Logan," Olivia said sternly, "you get those thoughts out of your head this instant. I said I wanted to be your partner, not your mistress."

"If you're so good at reading minds," he said tauntingly, "you know I'm not going to say yes to your first suggestion, but mark my word, Livingston, if that's your name, one of these days, you'll get what's coming to you."

"My name isn't Livingston," she said, "if that's important to you. It's Abernathy. What is it you think I have coming that I have to be so afraid of?" she responded, testing the territory.

"Who said you had to be afraid? And Livingston will do just fine. I've gotten used to it. It's that second suggestion that intrigues me, the one about the mistress. Besides, I owe you a kiss. You remember — the one you accused me of stealing back last December. I still owe you for that, and I'm not one to ignore my just debts."

"So, why aren't you going to agree to my proposal to join forces and scout for the north?" Olivia asked, adeptly changing the subject.

"I'd be out of my element, I'm afraid, Olivia. You know your business. You've developed the right contacts, and I'd be so easily recognized I'd be more of a hindrance than a help to you, I'm afraid."

"Jesse, we could work that out. Mr. Livingston hardly knows what I do, and I really need a partner. He's been a little unhappy with me lately, and I'm afraid he might say something or do something that will ruin my cover," Olivia persisted.

"He doesn't know you're a spy?" Jesse was incredulous. "What does he think you're doing when you leave camp for weeks, visiting sick relatives?"

"He thinks I've gone back to buy more stock for our wagon or sometimes to sell to other suttlers some of the stock we have. He's a true neutralist in this war. He's not the curious type and doesn't ask questions. He appreciates my help, so he says, although he's a little upset with me because I am not always at the tent when he needs me, but he's happy enough to have me around when I'm there. He's not my father, as you may have suspected."

"Are you sweethearts?" Jesse asked as impartially as he could.

Olivia didn't answer immediately. She looked calmly at Jesse for a few moments and then said, "You have no business asking such a question, Jesse, but the answer is 'No', if that makes any difference to you. He's my mother's uncle."

It was Jesse's turn to remain silent for a moment. He studied the girl before him, and wondered if she was lying to him, both about her relationship with Mr. Livingston and also about her activities as a spy for the North. He didn't have the answer to either question, but decided he'd better play this one straight. His emotions were mixed toward this 'Olivia Livingston'. He felt a powerful attraction toward her, but wasn't sure she could be trusted. The incident in Richmond was still fresh in his memory but the fact that she told him she was a spy for the Federals didn't make her a spy, though her association with the van Lew woman, and the matter of her bringing him the watch, certainly gave strong confirmation of the idea. Still the credibility of such an idea was subject to question, so far as he could see.

"Olivia, it does make a difference to me. You have no idea how much of a difference it makes to know that you are not committed to anyone. Even so, I still feel that Tom and I had better find a Federal regiment to hook up with," Jesse finally said. "He expects it, and I feel there's more I can do in the army than on my own. Can I think about it for a day or two?"

"Certainly," Olivia replied. "Let's move along and catch up with the wagon."

"Before we do that, Libbie, there's something I still need to get straight. I told you many months ago that I feel a strong attraction for you, and I'm not the kind of man that lets things like this go by without notice."

As Jesse was speaking, Olivia had turned and walked over to the side of the road where there was a large rock. She waited for Jesse to follow her and, using his arm to steady her, she stepped up on the rock, putting her at about eye-level with him. She then turned and when Jesse paused in his little speech, Olivia put her arms around his neck and kissed him passionately.

"There, now, we're even," she said in a lilting voice, stepping down from the rock.

They caught up with Tom and the wagon and in the course of conversation Olivia and Jesse let Tom know some of what they had been discussing. Jesse filled him in on some of the details and Tom seemed to understand that he was in the company of people who were more than participants in this war. They were people who could make things happen.

"Jesse," Tom said after a time, "If you feel you'd do better by working with Miss Livingston, don't let me stand in the way. I can either tag along or find a regiment to tie into on my own. I can even head back to Tennessee and fight from there, if that works out best."

"Let's sleep on it tonight, Tom," Jesse said, "things may look different after we give it some thought."

By this time, they were back in New Castle, and Jesse decided to check in with Bert Oakley, but he felt it would be better not to let Olivia know of Bert, at least for the present. He had quietly cautioned Tom against revealing the fact that Bert was an active Union agent and after the wagon had gotten some distance past the store, he excused himself from the group. Tom and Olivia were in conversation, and his leaving didn't seem to create any concern on her part. Jesse walked back to Bert's store and went inside. The store was empty of customers and Bert was standing behind the counter.

"I sure didn't expect to see you back here so soon, Jesse," Bert greeted him.

"My plans sort of changed, Bert. I ran into that suttler's wagon you saw go by a minute ago, and they say there's not much going on up at Lewisburg. What have you heard?'

"That's probably right, I'd reckon," Bert said, "General Fremont is out trying to catch up with old Stonewall Jackson, and I'm sure he's pulled everything he has out of the hills. You're going to have to go a long way to find a Union regiment, right now."

About that time, the door of the shop opened and Olivia entered. "Miss Mansfield," Bert Oakley exclaimed. "How nice to see you. I saw a wagon pass a few moments ago and wondered if it was the one you mentioned you had been using. Ahh, — Miss Mansfield, do you know Mr. Logan? He was just passing through town and I suspect he was also with your wagon."

It was an awkward moment for Bert Oakley, as he was simply not sure when talking to 'confidential agents' whether there was any association between them or not. He considered Jesse to be a confidential agent, or 'spy', at least for the present, and he had known Olivia for a number of years, and had dealt with her as an agent several times in the past, under the name of Olivia Mansfield. He had often been one of her suppliers of material for the Rebel market, and she, his.

"Yes, Mr. Oakley," Olivia replied quickly, "Mr. Logan and I have worked together from time to time." Then, turning to Jesse, she said, "Mr. Logan, we missed you back down the street, and I guess we had similar interests in getting in touch with Mr. Oakley."

Jesse smiled broadly. "Miss Mansfield," he said, emphasizing the name, "it seems I just can't keep anything from you. I wasn't aware you knew Mr. Oakley," and then as something of an afterthought, "I wanted to come back and get in touch with him. In our business, I think it's important to keep our local contacts advised as to our whereabouts and particulars as to our mission. Don't you?"

Olivia returned his smile. "I think that's a most important thing to do when we are in hostile country. One never knows when the need will arise when we need their help." Turning to Bert Oakley, Olivia continued. "Mr. Logan and I were discussing the possibility of working as a team, to try to make our mission more effective, Mr. Oakley, what do you think of such an idea?"

Bert did not miss the innuendo in the conversation between Jesse and Olivia, but it seemed to have been offered in good humor, so he ignored it as banter between friends. "Miss Mansfield, I think that's something you two have to work out for yourselves. I'm sure there's times when a team would be really effective, and then, again, working alone is also a necessity from time to time. I'm just here to help, whatever you decide."

Bert continued, "Jesse and I were discussing the movement of General Jackson and General Fremont, just now. I don't think there's going to be much action in these parts for some time, unless the Federals get going on controlling General Jackson. The news I get is that he can pretty well come and go, as he wants to, without any interference from either General Fremont or General Banks. The word in this neck of the woods is that General Jackson is using General Banks as his own special supply department. They're calling him 'Commissary Banks' around here."

"I know. General Jackson and his 'foot cavalry' are so hard to track, I've been at a loss to follow their movement, much less provide any useful information for the Federal forces," Olivia complained. "This is one of the reasons I would like to team up with Mr. Logan. It seems to me that a couple, perhaps in a horse-drawn carriage, could move about more quickly and less conspicuously than I can with my partner Mr. Livingston."

"Quickly, yes. Inconspicuously, I'm not so sure," Jesse said, slowly. "Listen. How do you think the military authorities on either side of the battle lines would regard a man of obviously eligible age traipsing about the country in a rig with a pretty lady beside him? We'd be stopped at the first garrison we came to. Besides, I'm an escapee from a Confederate prison, a citizen of a supposedly southern state, and I'm also a member of the Seventh Ohio Regiment, and here without uniform or papers, all of which would subject me to detention and possibly execution as a spy. This is all against me, not to speak of the reputation I've been given by the press as a threat to the Confederate cause."

It was about noon. Olivia could see she was going to have to compose a new argument if she was to persuade Jesse to join her in her enterprise. She turned to Jesse and said, "Perhaps we should be moving along. I'm sure Mr. Livingston wants to establish himself somewhere he can do some business with one of the armies."

"Why don't I talk with your partner? Maybe we could do a little business between the two of us," Bert said to Olivia.

"Miss Livi —, ah," Jesse started to use the name Livingston, but caught himself. The only problem was, he couldn't remember the name she was using in her contact with Bert Oakley. He continued in spite of his blunder, "I'll run back and get the other two and have them come back for a few minutes." With that he left the store and started after Tom and Mr. Livingston.

As Jesse left the store, he spotted Mr. Livingston's wagon parked under a tree at the side of the road and moved in that direction. Suddenly, just in front of him, a squad of four Confederate cavalrymen came out of a side street and turned up the street toward the wagon. So far, they had not observed Jesse, who moved over against the building to his right and remained out of sight.

The soldiers stopped near the wagon and began to talk to Mr. Livingston and Tom, who was seated on the wagon seat to his left.

"What're ye selling, old man?" the corporal inquired in a friendly manner.

"Just about anything a soldier needs," Livingston responded amiably.

"I could use some chawin' t'baccy, fer sure," another of the soldiers said.

By this time the soldiers had moved a little beyond the wagon and out of Jesse's sight, and thus hidden, he moved closer to be able to hear the conversation.

"Is that all?" Mr. Livingston inquired. "It ain't hardly worth my time to dig in this here wagon just for some t'bacco. Ain't there anything else some of you need to give me reason to get down off this wagon seat?"

"How about this fer a reason?" the corporal said, pulling a revolver from his belt holster.

"Say, Mister," Jesse could hear Tom's voice, "Take it easy. My friend just wants to be sociable and you're getting' all whipped up over nothing."

"Say, Mister, yerse'f. I'll show you who's getting whipped up. Who are you, the mayor in this-here town? You best keep yer fool tongue inside yer head or I'll take and tie a knot in it fer ye." Then he said to one of the other cavalrymen, "Zim, keep an eye on these two. We're goin' around and see what this-here old drummer's got in his boodle."

With that, three of the soldiers dismounted and started around to the rear of the wagon, tying their horses to the left-rear wheel as they went. Jesse had ducked behind the tree near where the wagon was parked, and remained out of sight.

The idea of having the Rebel soldiers opening his stock uninvited, and also of losing a sale, even one in Confederate currency, was more than Mr. Livingston could tolerate and he was concerned that the soldiers would take whatever they wanted.

"Now wait just a gol'durned minute, you three," he yelled, jumping down from the wagon seat and hurrying toward the rear on the opposite side from the soldiers. "I'll get you what you need, but I got a business to run, here, and you don't have no call to get uppity. What do you need? I'll git it fer you." He had moved too fast for Zim to stop him, and Zim was occupied with a man holding a musket, anyway. He had pulled out a revolver of his own and was pointing it generally in Tom's direction.

As Mr. Livingston moved around the wagon, he caught sight of Jesse, who by this time had drawn his own revolver, still staying out of sight of the Rebel soldiers. Without acknowledging Jesse, he moved to protect his stock of goods in the wagon. He reached the rear of the wagon just as the three soldiers were about to pull open the door, and having pulled off his jacket and grabbing a short staff, which he carried along the side of the wagon, Mr. Livingston tried to block the soldiers' access.

The act of his using a staff against them was all the prodding the soldiers needed to take out their aggression on Mr. Livingston. The corporal, who had been doing most of the talking up until that point, struck out with the revolver in his hand, hitting Mr. Livingston in the head and knocking him down. He had cocked his revolver, however, and the shock, or perhaps a light trigger-pull, caused the gun to go off, firing harmlessly into the air.

Jesse was prepared for the worst, however, and on hearing the gunfire, he stepped out from behind the tree and began firing at the soldiers. His first shot went low, striking one of the soldiers in the upper leg. The next two shots he raised, striking the next one in the chest and the third in the head, killing the two of them instantly. The first soldier went down, but managed to pull his pistol from its holster and fire at Jesse, missing him, but hitting Mr. Livingston instead. Jesse fired one more time killing the third soldier. The fourth man, Zim, was confused, but instead of holding Tom at bay, he started toward the rear of the wagon, whereupon, Tom cocked his musket and shot Zim out of the saddle.

Jesse saw Zim fall, and immediately went to Mr. Livingston's aid, but he had been hit in the chest and was apparently dead. Tom, meanwhile, jumped down from the wagon seat and ran to the rear, grabbing the revolver Zim had dropped, since he had no idea of what to expect when he got around the wagon.

"Jesse! It's you! What happened?" were Tom's first words. This was the first time he had been in a shooting battle, and he was rattled.

"I reckon we got into a gunfight with some of the Rebel army and came out on top," Jesse said, trying not to sound too excited, "But pardner, we have some work to do to get out of this town, now that we've showed our colors. Grab one of those horses and mount up. We'll take a chance on not being caught and ride back to Bert's store so we can tell Olivia what happened. Then we'd better skedaddle. The people of this town are going to be after us, you can bet on that."

The two men scooped up the revolvers of the fallen soldiers and stuffed them into the saddlebags of two of the horses. They then jumped on the horses and started west toward Bert Oakley's store as people started to emerge from the stores and side streets to see what had happened.

The horse Logan had chosen had other ideas. Logan had had a chance to watch the four horses ridden by the Rebel soldiers, and picked one he felt would serve him best. It was a big bay gelding with a lopsided blaze on his face and looked to be quite young, though well built.

Sometimes a horse, sensing a different rider from the one it's accustomed to, just has to try them out like a new pair of shoes. This horse was just such an animal.

As soon as Jesse got on his back, the big gelding pitched and plunged as though it was the first time he had ever been ridden. Logan knew better than to try to get off and change horses. He used all the skills he had learned as a boy and guided the bucking horse down the street, digging his heels into the horse's sides and hanging on. Presently the horse realized he was not accomplishing much toward throwing this rider and he changed to a gallop as Jesse had intended. Tom followed. The horse was in good condition. He had done what he could to test the skills of his rider and was apparently satisfied. He never gave Jesse any trouble after that.

From the front of the store, Olivia had seen the activity at the rear of the wagon, and knew the implications. She also knew she should not be identified with Jesse, as he would likely be considered a thief trying to hold up the wagon of Mr. Livingston. As Jesse and Tom came riding back toward her, she threw her hands up in alarm and screamed as though her very life was threatened. She then turned and rushed back into the store.

Jesse read the message. He turned to Tom and motioned him onward, and together they galloped out of town back along the road toward Lewisburg. This was essentially the direction Jesse had planned, and anywhere other than New Castle was better than staying and waiting to be caught as thieves and the killers of four brave Confederate soldiers.

Olivia, after she saw the two men ride out of town, went to Bert and told him of the incident. "Mr. Oakley, Mr. Livingston has been shot, and our wagon is down the street under a tree. I think I'd better go and see if I can help. I'm going to run down the street and see what I can do. Jesse and Tom have ridden out of town toward Lewisburg and I think there are two or three Confederate soldiers lying in the street, either dead or badly wounded. It'll probably look as though Jesse and Tom tried to rob the wagon and got into a fight with the Rebel horsemen."

"Go ahead, Miss Mansfield, I'll close the store and come on down and give you any help I can. Go ahead."

"Call me Miss Livingston when you get down there," Olivia flung over her shoulder.

She hurried down the street and when she got to the wagon, she saw that her worst fears had materialized. A crowd had gathered around the scene, but she could see her uncle on the ground, as were four Confederate soldiers, grouped around the rear of the wagon. She immediately pushed through the crowd and knelt beside Mr. Livingston. She took his head in her lap and tried to revive him, though the wound in his chest told her he was most certainly dead.

Olivia began to cry, moaning softly, "Oh, Father, Father, why did this have to happen? Please Father, don't die. Please don't die."

A man came up to her and asked, "Is this your father, Miss? I saw what happened. Those soldiers came up and it looked like they were checking on the one of the hobos that was up there on the seat with your father. His partner came up the street and hid behind that tree for a minute and then when your father came out to help with something around back, he jumped out from behind the tree and shot them all. 'You know who that feller looked like? I think he was that White Angel they been talkin' about in the papers, the great big one who escaped from prison a couple of weeks ago. 'Big and white headed. I seen him walking up the street a few days ago, and I says to myse'f, 'That there looks like that White Angel,' and I reckon he was. Lord, but could that man shoot! Them soldiers didn't have a chance. Are you goin' to be alright, Miss?"

Olivia was sobbing softly, now. She had placed Mr. Livingston's head gently on his folded jacket, and had stood up. "Yes, thank you, Sir. I think I'll be all right, but I don't know what will become of me or what will be done with my poor father's body. You see, we were fleeing from the Yankees. We're from Falls Church and they took all we had when we were away and I can't go back." Meanwhile, she was thinking, "*Jesse was right. Any association with him would certainly spell trouble for me. I wouldn't get ten miles without someone spotting him and trying to take him in or kill him.*"

"Is there an undertaker here in town?" she said to the people in the crowd. "I'd just like to see my father get a decent burial and try to get back to my people."

About that time, Bert Oakley stepped through the crowd and took Olivia by the arm. "Miss Livingston, what happened?" he asked.

"Oh, Mr. Oakley, Something terrible has happened. My father has been shot, and I don't know what to do. I just don't know what to do." She turned and buried her face in Bert Oakley's shoulder. "I was just asking if there is an undertaker here in New Castle."

"Now don't you worry, Miss," Bert said reassuringly. "We'll certainly help you all we can. You don't have to worry about a thing. We'll take care of everything, won't we Abner?" he said looking toward the man who had identified Jesse.

The men of the town had gathered and were looking to caring for the fallen soldiers. A doctor had appeared and examined each of the dead men in turn. "Somehow it looks like that man must have been shot by one of the soldiers, from the way he was wounded," he said pointing to Mr. Livingston, "and that man was shot from behind, like as if someone from the front of the wagon shot him." This time he was pointing at the fallen soldier named Zim.

"Now, that ain't the case, Doc," Abner said confidently. "I was watching the whole thing from my store, and it was that white-headed feller that shot him and all of the soldiers."

By this time, a town marshal had entered the group and the whole discussion started over again.

"Sheriff, can I take Miss Livingston's wagon back to my store and care for her horses?" Bert inquired of the marshal. "I'll care for her this evening and have my sister put her up for the night, if there's anything you want to talk to her about."

The marshal agreed that the wagon would be of no further value in the matter, and Bert climbed into the seat of the wagon. The officer helped Olivia as she climbed up into the wagon seat with Bert, who then turned the wagon back toward his store. When they were out of earshot of the crowd, Bert said quietly to Olivia, "Well, Miss — ahhh — Miss Livingston, what are you planning to do with this here great big wagon?"

"Mr. Oakley, I just have no idea. It would be totally impossible for a woman to go from camp to camp in a suttler's wagon, even if I was able to handle the horses. The role of a suttler's daughter was ideal for getting about, and now I'm going to have to dream up an entirely new personality to give me reason to move from place to place. I know, now, that Mr. Logan was right about an association between us being counterproductive. Were you there when that man you called Abner said that he thought Mr. Logan was the White Angel?"

"No, I hadn't got there to hear that. Do you think Mr. Logan is the White Angel?" Bert asked tentatively, wondering how much Olivia knew about Jesse.

"Yes, he is," Olivia confided, "and we should try to keep him out of New Castle if we can. He's pretty easy to spot, and I don't think he'd live long in this town."

15

LEWISBURG

Jesse and Tom were headed northwest again, toward Lewisburg. Bert had advised that there would probably not be much of a garrison there, as according to the information he had received, Colonel Sullivan had virtually evacuated those works two or three weeks previously. Nevertheless, Jesse felt that there would be at least a token force at Lewisburg from whom he could gather some direct information. He and Tom had little of their own possessions with them. The jerky they had prepared was mostly in the Wagon that had belonged to Mr. Livingston, and they had fled with such haste that they had not taken anything but the Rebel equipment that was with the horses. After they rode about ten miles, they moved their horses off the road a short distance and examined the stuff in the saddlebags.

In addition to the revolvers they had snatched up from the fallen soldiers they had about two day's supply of food. The horses they had taken from the fallen Confederate soldiers were both in excellent condition, indicating the Rebels had been detached from the fighting troops for several weeks and were able to fatten their horses on feed from local sources. Each saddle had a breech-loading Sharps carbine in a scabbard, and about twenty rounds of ammunition between the two of them. Both the saddles and the rifles were of Federal issue, apparently having been captured previously by the Rebel soldiers.

"Well," Tom said, "it looks like we're just trading equipment from army to army."

"There's a lot of that going around," Jesse said, "especially with old Stonewall Jackson. I wish we had that man on our side. He is one General who really knows how to fight. Speaking of fighting, though, Tom, you did good for yourself back there. How'd you get the drop on that one soldier who was guarding you?"

"I didn't," Tom replied. "He got excited and was heading back toward the back of the wagon when the shooting started. I guess he forgot all about me. All I knew was that Mr. Livingston went back there in a blue fury and I figured he was getting the short end of the deal. When I heard the shooting start, I shot that feller Zim out of not knowing what else to do. I got it into my head to jump down and get his pistol if I could, but you'd already took care of the other three boys."

"For a man who hasn't been in much of a fighting war, Partner, you do real good. If we get back to the old Seventh Ohio, I'm going to ask to have you as a regular roomie."

"I don't reckon I need to tell you that after the fighting stopped I was scared so bad I was shaking in my boots. I remembered the story you told me about the time you shot that Indian who was trying to get your gun away from you when you were a young'un, and I think I could have done about the same thing you did; — throw up."

"You did good, Tommie. When it mattered most, you did the right thing, and that's what staying alive in this war is all about."

The two men got back onto the road and continued west toward Lewisburg. The conversation ranged from the war to home, to Olivia and Lily and to the days they were in school together. When night fell, they took to the woods and found a small clearing where they tethered the horses, cooked up some salt pork and beans and slept.

The following day they arrived in Lewisburg and rode to the small encampment left there by General Tyler, who, now under the command of General Fremont, had vacated the town except for a small holding force.

Jesse didn't recognize the sentry, but identified himself and asked to see the commanding officer. He was escorted to the tent of Lieutenant Frank Davis, who hailed Jesse as a long-lost son and immediately sat him and Tom down to hear what had happened to Jesse to bring him back to his old regiment. Lieutenant Davis also called in Sergeant Lige Hawkins to get some of the details down for a report to General Tyler. It was like old home week. Lige, Lieutenant Davis, Tom, and Jesse spent a good part of the afternoon bringing each other up to date on their part of the war.

After a few minutes' discussion, Lieutenant Davis looked Jesse in the eye and said, "Jesse I'm going to ask you a straight question and I'd like a straight answer."

Jesse was surprised at the comment, as the discussion had been cordial, but direct until this point, and he wondered at such a comment. "Sure, go ahead, Sarge, — er, Lieutenant," he stammered.

"If you don't mind, Jesse, for the purposes of this conversation, I'd prefer you'd call me 'Frank'. I haven't quite got used to the 'Lieutenant' thing yet, either. He fumbled with a pocketknife and then continued. "Before Miss Livingston left Lewisburg, we had some interesting news that she gave us a slant on, that I've been turning over in my mind. You are the only one who can clear up a big question."

Lieutenant Davis cleaned a couple of his fingernails with the pocketknife and then went on. "About two weeks ago there was a big fire in Lynchburg in a gun factory that the Rebs tried to downplay, but the word that got out was that it was the work of a big ring of Union agents, one of whom was a big tall yellow haired fellow who seemed to be the leader. The only thing about it was that Colonel Sullivan, who was here at the time, and who is pretty well informed as to the undercover operations around the country, let it out that there aren't any such agents working in that area right now, and the description fit only one man that I know of. Then I got in on the tail end of a discussion between Miss Livingston and the colonel where she implied the fire was your, — was your doing. How's about it, Jesse, what can you tell the old 'Sarge' about this mystery?"

Jesse had been traveling with his old friend, Tom, and, while sharing confidences, he had told Tom about the fire in Lynchburg. "That Miss Livingston is truly a remarkable woman," Jesse began, evading the subject at hand. "She can make more out of nothing than any ten people I know."

"Then she was wrong?" Davis asked quickly.

Jesse gave a half-smile and glanced sidelong at the lieutenant. "That's not what I said, Frank. I just said she could put together the most implausible facts and come up with a conclusion that may not seem logical, but turns out to be the truth. Yes, I was the 'ring of enemy agents' that pulled off that big fire. Heck! I was just messing around, trying to give the Rebs a hard time, and I guess I cleaned out the canebrake. The reason they thought it was a big gang was that when I was talking to them, I was trying to get those two guards to believe I wasn't alone so's they wouldn't try to take me apart. The whole thing started as kind of a — 'what-if' — sort of thing and went downhill from there. I was just wandering through the countryside and that confounded factory jumped out and got in my way. So, I burnt it down. Don't ask me how Miss Livingston got wind of it, though."

"You mean that one of the biggest news events of the week was just sort of a flight of fancy with our ace rifleman out for a stroll?" Lieutenant Davis asked the question in a lilting voice, as though he was reciting a piece of poetry. "Jesse, you big oaf, you seem to do more damage to the Rebels by accident that most men do on purpose. I'm surprised you didn't steal one of those fellow's horses, just to add insult to injury."

"I would have, if I could," Jesse laughed, "I was so tired of walking and riding the cars by then I would have stole a jackass, if I could have found one."

"Well, I'm surprised. It seems like where ever you go, you manage to snatch someone's horse," Frank Davis said to Jesse, then turning to Tom, asked, "Was he like this when you were in school together, always coming up with a horse when he got tired of walking?"

"When I first met Jesse, he had one of the best horses in the Watauga Valley," Tom replied with a smile. "He said he bought it in Choates Ford, but now I'm not so sure he didn't just steal it off some poor fella."

"Jesse, speaking of horses," Davis then said, "I need a courier to get down to Romney or Winchester and find General Tyler and Colonel Sullivan. I have tried to contact them by telegraph, but either the lines are down or they're just not responding to my messages. We're pretty secure, here, but I'd like to find out from the general whether we are to stay put or try to expand our field of operation. We have had dozens of the local men come to us and try to join up with the garrison, and I feel we could be more effective if we increased our forces here and worked the countryside for Rebel patrols. By the way, that pretty little girl you left in Coalwood was asking about you. She had heard you'd been captured and felt so sorry for you that she came up with the real story on how much a gentleman you had been and that the little episode that Sunday had all been a big misunderstanding."

"Daisy Morton," Jesse reflected, "I hadn't given that problem much thought. I reckon I'll just try to stay as far from Coalwood as I can for a while."

"So who's Daisy Morton?" Tom demanded. "You seem to collect the girls as fast as you do horses, and all of them pretty good looking as far as I can see."

"Being good looking, are you talking about the girls or the horses or both?" Lieutenant Davis asked.

"Both, as I see it," Tom replied. "He never seems to lack for either."

"I told Jesse back in September or October that he should stay as far away from women as possible, and it looks like he just ignored my good advice. Anyway, Jesse, not to change the subject from your favorite topic," Lieutenant Davis continued. "But I'd like you to get up the valley to see if you can't catch up with General Tyler and get me some word as to how we are supposed to proceed on this garrison business, whether he wants us to expand or just hold on. I have some other papers I need to send him and some for Colonel Sullivan. He's the main intelligence contact for this part of the country, you know. The corps is at Romney, right now. I think."

Jesse spent the rest of the day preparing for his run to Romney. He drew a new uniform and checked out his equipment. He would keep the horse he had acquired in New Castle, as the animal had proven to be a stout and dependable mount. It would be a ride of three or four days, partly through hostile country, but if he would try to stay as much as possible within the part of the state controlled by Union forces through Philippi and Grafton, he would not expose himself unnecessarily to the enemy patrols. On the other hand, if he went straight east to the little town of Clifton Forge and then angled north along the foothills it might be easier to locate the Federal forces and shorten his trip. He opted for a compromise. He would head east just a mile or two, then head north along the Greenbrier River to its head and then follow the headwaters of the Potomac River north to Romney and try to reach General Tyler that way.

Lieutenant Davis had a considerable sheaf of papers he wanted to send to Colonel Sullivan. He had obtained applications for service from about seventy-five potential recruits and was seeking permission to process them, as well as provide a record of their enlistment to Regiment. He also had what he believed to be some confidential information of which he felt Colonel and General Tyler should be informed, including the intelligence Jesse had provided on the Lynchburg incident.

Also in the sheaf of papers, was a recommendation that Jesse be promoted to the rank of lieutenant, based on his prior duty and the contribution he made to the Union cause in destroying the Lynchburg gun factory, and a pending need in the company for a second lieutenant.

Jesse's route took him through the Potomac Valley and he enjoyed the trip thoroughly. While he had been advised of its urgency, he was also cautioned to remain clear of Confederate patrols, as the information he had was not only unique, but also highly confidential and could be compromising, if it fell into the hands of the enemy. His ride from Lewisburg was a mixture of Confederate and Federal territory, and his contact with the people along the way was a reflection of their sentiments. In his new uniform he represented himself simply as a Union soldier trying to get back to his regiment. The citizens he encountered who were in sympathy with the South let him pass unmolested while those favoring the union fed him and allowed him to sleep in their barns or sheds.

Arriving at the garrison at Franklin in early June, he found the garrison nearly as depleted, as was the one at Lewisburg. Portions of General Tyler's brigade had been occupying the camp, but had been pulled out for a move east in response to General Fremont's orders to intercept General Stonewall Jackson's move down into the valley around Winchester. The command of the small remaining company was in the hands of Lieutenant Goodin recently returned from his convalescence from the injuries he had received in the Clinch Mountains. Jesse reported to the commander's tent curious to see what had been the result of Lieutenant Goodin's injuries, and also what the Lieutenant's reactions would be seeing Jesse back from his imprisonment.

On entering the tent, Jesse found the light somewhat lower than he expected, and it took him a few seconds for his eyes to adjust. The figure of Lieutenant Goodin was visible in silhouette against the opening in the back of the tent. He rose in response to Jesse's knock on the tent pole and invited his caller into the tent in a low voice.

"Lieutenant," Jesse opened the conversation in the customary manner, "it's Corporal Logan with some papers for the General. I understand the Brigade has moved out, and I felt I should check in with you to see if there is anything you can tell me about their whereabouts and to see if you had anything to be delivered to Command." His large frame so filled the front opening to the tent that he was obliged to stoop in the doorway, but he managed a salute, which wasn't returned.

"Corporal Logan, if you're looking for General Tyler, you've come to the wrong place. He has relocated to Harrisonburg. If I have any documents to be delivered, I'm well staffed with couriers, and the telegraph is working well. Where are you coming from that it's so important for you to by-pass a first lieutenant and report to Brigade?"

As usual, Jesse was baffled by Lieutenant Goodin's line of thinking. Instead of his simply responding to the obvious situation and working toward the best ends of the army, Goodin chose to focus on protocol, without addressing the larger matter of running the war.

"I'm carrying a dispatch from Lieutenant Davis at garrison in Lewisburg, Lieutenant. I thought I might find General Tyler and Colonel Sullivan here at Franklin. The dispatch I have is sealed and I have orders to take it as quickly as possible to Brigade. I thought perhaps you could help me, but also that you may have something here that I could help with delivering."

"You're repeating yourself, Corporal," Goodin replied testily. "Why can't you get it into your head that there is a chain of command through which orders and dispatches pass? As I outrank Lieutenant Davis, I'm instructing you to turn the dispatches over to me for review. I'll decide what information is to be passed on to Brigade."

The implications were obvious. Jesse had been given a direct order to deliver the dispatches in his possession to Colonel Sullivan and General Tyler. Now he was being given a direct order to give the sealed orders to a senior lieutenant. One way or another, he was going to disobey an order. Davis would be easier to deal with, as his relationship with Jesse had been cordial and often friendly. Goodin, on the other hand, seemed to be looking for ways to discredit his subordinates, but especially Jesse Logan. Disobedience here would most certainly result in some sort of discipline. He'd already been through that discussion with Goodin at another time. The thought of having had the opportunity to let this man die back on the side of Clinch Mountain flashed through Jesse's mind.

"Lieutenant, I'll have to go out and get the dispatches from my saddle bags," Jesse said in what he tried to make out as a disarming voice. "If you'll wait just a moment, I'll be right back."

He turned and made his way out of the tent and walked toward his horse. He turned to look back at the tent and saw that Lieutenant Goodin had emerged from the front of the tent and was standing watching him walk away. The Lieutenant's old injuries were visible, even from twenty or so paces. His face was a distortion of its former appearance. His right eye drooped horribly, and it appeared that he might have lost the use of the eye. The scars from the bullet were still quite red, and the right corner of his mouth was scarred so badly that it pulled the mouth to one side. Jesse was shocked by the sight, but merely turned and kept walking toward his horse. He glanced from side to side to see if there would be any obstruction to an escape if he tried to make one. His horse was not particularly fresh, but he'd have to do what he could with surprise.

As he approached his horse, a distance of perhaps forty yards from the command tent, his actions betrayed him and Lieutenant Goodin sensed his intent. "Stop that man," he shouted to anyone within earshot, "stop him, he's getting away." And with that, he turned and entered his tent to get the revolver he had left inside.

Jesse leapt on his horse and spurred it toward the road leading out of camp. No one had responded to Lieutenant Goodin's shouts, as the men about the camp were in various stages of their normal routine, and no horses were available. Lieutenant Goodin came out of his tent with his revolver in hand but Jesse had managed to position his escape to put some trees between himself and Goodin and was all but out of sight when the lieutenant managed to get into any position to fire his weapon.

"Sergeant!" Goodin shouted, "Get up a squadron of men and go after that soldier. He's a thief. He stole some orders intended for this command and is a danger to the Union. I want him back, dead or alive."

By the time a squad could be assembled, Jesse was well on his way toward Harrisonburg. While his horse was a little worn from the trip from Lewisburg, he had not ridden him hard up until that time, and with care, he felt he could outdistance or out-guess his pursuers.

16

THE SHENANDOAH VALLEY

Spending one night on the road, Logan finally found General Tyler's Brigade camped just south of Harrisonburg, and located Colonel Sullivan's tent.

"Corporal, I see from this report that you've not been idle," Colonel Sullivan said after reading some of the reports Jesse had brought him. "In spite of the fact that we had you shown on the books as missing and captured, you seem to have been busy. We did have some unconfirmed intelligence reports that had suggested that you were responsible for that fire at Lynchburg, and Lieutenant Davis's report seems to confirm that. Meanwhile, as you are so equipped and we can't seem to keep you away from horses, I'm going to detach you from your old company and assign you to headquarters for courier duty until such time as General Tyler is able to act on Lieutenant Davis's recommendation. You know, we have a vacancy at adjutant in the regiment, and I may keep you here for now."

"I wouldn't be too comfortable placing you back with "H" Company." Colonel Sullivan continued. "As you know, we have Lieutenant Goodin temporarily in command up there and though he probably owes you his life and for some other reasons I won't pursue I'd think you'd serve the army better at headquarters. By the way, Logan, just yesterday I received a dispatch over the wire that you were to be arrested as a deserter and spy. It was from Goodin at Franklin. What did you do now, that incurred his wrath?"

"I found myself caught between conflicting orders, Sir, and chose to follow the orders of Lieutenant Davis, counter to Lieutenant Goodin's order. It involved the delivery of these papers."

"I'll be honest with you, Logan. Lieutenant Goodin goes by his own interpretation of 'the book' and it's my impression that if you ever read the book you wouldn't find it to your liking. You seem more inclined to think on your feet, or in the saddle as is more your case, than you do to follow convention. Besides, as a lieutenant you'd have to work so closely with Lieutenant Goodin that you'd probably end up in a personal shootout."

"I don't understand, Colonel, what does working as a lieutenant have to do with anything?

"Oh, Davis didn't tell you? Well, he's recommended you for a commission as a lieutenant. I expected he'd discuss it with you, but it all depends on how General Tyler looks at it, anyway. It may not be fait accompli, in any event. I've submitted Davis's name as a candidate for promotion to captain, and there'll be an opening for his old spot. It may as well be a man who's proven himself in the field as you seem to have done."

"Thank you, Colonel. I don't know what to think. I was just getting used to being back in uniform and looking forward to getting together with my old company. I'll do my best, though, if that's what it comes to."

"I know you will, Logan. And by the way, if all indications play out, I should be seeing Brigadier before long, effective back to April. What do you think of that?"

Jesse's thoughts were not of Colonel Sullivan's promotion, or even of his own. He was reflecting on the fact that he was in the presence of a high-ranking officer in the US Army, discussing matters of this level at all. It was a thoroughly flattering experience. It reminded him of the days in Watauga Valley when he and his family were guests at the home of Dan Stover. Dan's father-in-law, Governor Andrew Johnson was present and they discussed the politics of the nation, and Jesse was treated as though he was truly a member of a social order that deserved the respect of such highly placed people.

"General, Sir! Man, oh, man. Well, you deserve it. You're doing the work of a general, and it's only fitting that you get the recognition and rank."

"In the meantime, Logan, I'm going to use you, as I said, as a courier, but when not so employed, I want you to report to Colonel Sam Carroll. He's commanding a brigade that you'll find camped just south of here along the river. Here, I'll write a note of introduction for you, letting Colonel Carroll know what this is all about and asking him to put you to work with one of his cavalry units."

After Colonel Sullivan had scratched out a brief note he gave it to Jesse and pointed out the road that would take him to Colonel Carroll's camp.

Jesse found Colonel Carroll commanding a brigade of cavalry in General Shields's division. They were camped along the bank of the Shenandoah River, just to the north of Port Republic. He was greeted, questioned briefly about the message that Colonel Sullivan had written, and was referred to Lieutenant Barnes.

"You're a temp, are you?" Lt. Barnes asked, alluding to Jesse's status as a detached courier. "Well, Corporal, we can put you to work as long as you're with us, anyway. I'd like to have you check in with Sergeant Joe Stout, and draw some ammunition and equipment from Quartermaster. You'll be needing plenty of supplies. We'll be going out before daybreak, tomorrow, and I don't quite know how long we'll be out."

"Yes, Sir," Jesse said, saluting the lieutenant and, turning on his heels, he headed for the nearest camp to inquire about D Company.

"You'll find Sergeant Stout's troop over to your right there, Soldier," Lieutenant Barnes shouted after Jesse, "and in the Cavalry, we don't go around saluting every brass bar we see. We'd just as soon not call attention to rank. It can be dangerous in combat."

"Alright, Lieutenant, thanks," Jesse replied in a little more casual tone, "thanks a lot."

Jesse rode his horse, Bob, as he had named him, a short distance to the south and found Sergeant Stout overseeing the farrier who was trimming the hooves of one of the horses in preparation for tomorrow's ride. He advised the sergeant of the orders he had received and asked him if he would be able to draw equipment and rations.

"This is your first tour, is it, Logan?" Sergeant Stout inquired, looking him over from head to toe and noting his newly issued uniform. "Where did you get the stripes?"

"I did some time with the Seventh Ohio before coming over here, Sergeant," Jesse replied. "I brought my own horse, this time, though, and the colonel wants me to do some courier duty. He told me to check in with you until such time as I was needed."

"Well, let me tell you a little secret, Corporal. In the Union Army, all the horses belong to Uncle Sam, and when it comes time for you to mount up you'll take the horse you're assigned. That horse you're riding looks to me like the one I'm going to be using tomorrow, and maybe we'll see if we can find you a nag to haul you around. For your first time out, I'll probably use you for holding duty if we have to fight dismounted, and that's if we can find you a horse at all. The cavalry uses its horses up pretty freely, and since you're just a displaced straw-foot, I'm sure you won't mind staying on the ground. Or maybe we can check with the artillery and if they have a spare nag maybe you can use it."

Jesse was getting the runaround, and he knew it. The only thing he didn't know was how to get out of losing his horse without harsh words or whining to the colonel. He knew he'd be expected to have a sound horse if called upon to do courier duty, and he was confident in Bob's ability to take him wherever he wanted to go. He'd cared for the horse carefully and had become somewhat attached to him since he'd taken him from the Rebs at New Castle. He just didn't want to give him up.

Smiling his most disarming smile, Jesse tried reasoning with Sergeant Stout. "The only thing is, Sarge, when they call me out for courier work, they don't expect me to show up on foot. I've pulled a few runs before this, and I know what Command expects when they call you out. They want a man on a horse and that doesn't mean some old nag. I'd sure be grateful if you'd let me keep old Bob. I've had him, now, for several weeks. He never has been the property of the government"

Sergeant Stout's authority had been called into question, by a green corporal in a bright new uniform and sporting a southern accent at that. "I've heard about enough from you Corporal. I got your message, and you ain't moved me at all. I told you that this here horse belongs to the gov'ment and I'm going to ride him tomorrow. Now get your gear off'n him so's I can get old Pete here to check him over. For all I know, he might have ringbone and colic. You're bunking with Tipton, over on "B" Street. You 'n' him should get on just fine, you both bein' transplanted 'Southerns'. I don't know but what you might just be a spy."

Jesse took his saddle, bridle and saddlebags off Bob and started hiking toward what he assumed was B Street. It was a row of tents, set up for double occupancy, and spaced perhaps two feet apart. Soldiers were lounging, cleaning tack, cooking, talking, gambling and just killing time along the "street". He looked into the eyes of those who were conscious of his passing, to see if there were any he may recognize. There were none. "Where might I find Tipton?" Jesse inquired, still demonstrating his disgruntled mood.

"Over h'yare," a voice came from a few feet away to his right, "Ah'm Tipton."

Sergeant Stout had good reason to think Private Tipton was a Southerner. In five words, he branded himself as such. Jesse turned and found looking back at him a young man almost as tall as he and perhaps twenty pounds lighter, in spite of the weight Jesse had lost during his stay at Libby. "Ah'm Cale Tipton, wha'd'you need?"

"I'm supposed to bunk with you, Tipton. I'm Jesse Logan," Jesse softened his attitude, knowing this man was not the cause of his state of mind. "I just got into camp and I reckon you got an empty spot in your tent they want me to fill. Man, you and me, we're going to fill up the tent, the two of us," he said, grinning as he looked Private Tipton over. "You say your name is Cale? I'm, Jesse."

"Pleased to meet you, Jesse, c'm on in. Set down and rest ye'r hands 'n' face," he said, using an old hometown term Jesse was familiar with from back up the valley. Jesse couldn't help liking the young man, with his southern accent and easy manner, and he almost forgot the unpleasantness he'd experienced with Sergeant Stout a few minutes earlier.

"Well, I'm pleased to meet you, too, Cale. Where do you come from?" Jesse caught himself using the same question often asked of him when his accent was noticed.

"I'm from Moseley, down near Lynchburg," the young man replied, and before he could say anything further, Jesse grabbed his hand and shook it hard, taking "Cale" by the right shoulder with his left hand in a gesture of recognition and friendship.

"You're Caleb Tipton, from down at Moseley," Jesse said in obvious pleasant surprise. "I know your ma and pa. I slept in your barn a little while back and wore your old worn-out pants when I was on the run from the Rebs. Your pa is Horace and your ma is Dolly, aren't they?"

"That's right. How'd you know them?" Cale asked in obvious surprise. "How'd you happen to be in Moseley?"

Jesse told Caleb about his adventures after leaving Libby, and a little of how he happened to be where he was. They talked for several minutes and then Jesse said he was going to have to check in with Quartermaster and draw his supplies. After drawing enough equipment to supplement what was in his bags, Jesse returned to the tent he would be sharing with Caleb.

"Do you know what horse you're riding tomorrow, Cale?" Jesse inquired.

"We'll be getting our assignments pretty quick," Caleb responded. "We usually ride the same horse every assignment, but Sergeant Stout sometimes changes the pairing when a horse gets hurt or when a rider is down for any reason. We'll go on over if you're ready and check on our mounts for tomorrow. Then we better check them over and make sure they're sound. The blacksmith tries, but it ain't him that has to ride 'em."

They went to the ring where the horses were tied and contacted Saddler Sergeant George Buckelew who presented a list that Sergeant Stout had prepared, and which showed the assignments for the following day. The horses were well fed and some of the other men were grooming their mounts for the ride. Bob, the horse Jesse had ridden from New Castle, spotted Jesse and nickered his greeting. Jesse found a small bucket of grain and went over to acknowledge Bob for his friendship. He rubbed Bob's neck and scratched him between the ears, receiving a gentle nudge in the chest from Bob's head.

Jesse's name didn't show on Sergeant Buckelew's list. There were, however, two mounts at the end of the list which were unassigned.

"The sergeant must have made this out b'fore he knew you was goin' to ride tomorrow," Caleb observed. Them two horses at the end of the list ain't what I call the best of the bunch. That one," he pointed toward a smallish bay horse, "that's Lister. He kind of runs sideways like a dog. And the other one, Heck, can be a little mulish when he takes a notion. He's tends to shy at pert' near nothin' at times. You have to be on your guard ridin' him or he'll dump you when you're least 'spectin' it."

"I could buy the notion that the list was made up before I got here if it weren't for the fact that the sergeant's assigned himself the horse that I rode in on," Jesse retorted glumly. "He made sure that old Bob was on the list and that he's the one riding him."

"Well, maybe we'd better go check with him, Jesse."

"Yeah, I reckon so. There's no sense in jumping to conclusions, like I've already done," Jesse growled. "I better hold onto my tongue until I see what he has in mind."

"Jesse, I've found Sergeant Stout to be a perty fair man, and that's comin' from a man who h'ain't been too well taken up around h'yare. You know 'bout my turnin' fer the north, and that don't set too well with some people. Stout don't cut me no slack, but he treats me fair enough," Caleb maintained.

"I know, I know, Cale. I'm just sore at losing my horse. I captured him from the Rebs; 'stole him fair and square, and he's taken me everywhere I could have asked for the past couple of weeks. We've become pretty good friends."

"I could see he likes you from the way he acted when we walked up," Caleb observed.

Jesse and Caleb went over to Sergeant Stout's tent where the sergeant was standing out in front arranging his tack.

"Sergeant," Jesse began, "I don't see a mount assigned to me for tomorrow. Should I take one of those unassigned at the bottom of the list?"

"Logan, you aren't familiar with the Cavalry drills, and I want you to stay in camp tomorrow. You can be of some help to the Quartermaster if we have to move, but to take you out on your first day with the unit is just askin' for trouble. We'll most likely engage the enemy tomorrow and I'm afraid you'd be more of a hurt than a help. You'll get some drill and some action soon enough. Have you ever been in a fight? I mean a good shootin' war with real bullets."

"I've been in some skirmishes, Sergeant," Jesse said noncommittally. "I was with General Tyler in that campaign through the Alleghenies last year."

"Can you shoot a rifle, Corporal?" the sergeant asked.

"Yessir, that I can do," Jesse replied with warming enthusiasm. "I worked as a rifleman during the Allegheny Campaign."

"Well, we lost one of our best riflemen last week, but I still have his rifle. Do you think you could do any good in this country?"

"I'd surely like to try, Sergeant. Could you send Tipton out with me as a spotter?"

The sergeant thought a moment. Two southerners with a long-range rifle and a telescope, out away from the controlling influence of the company seemed a little risky. These men were both enlistees with the Federal Army, but Logan especially hadn't proven his loyalty and Tipton was regarded as a true Virginian, even though he was wearing a blue uniform.

"I need Tipton with the troop, Corporal. Maybe the idea wasn't ripe for pickin', yet. I think I'll just assign you to camp 'til we can get a little more trainin' into you. I'll assign you the rifle, but I want you to stay in camp. You're a courier, anyhow, and the Colonel might just call you out." It didn't make much sense to question the man's loyalty inasmuch as he had been accepted and assigned as a courier, but Sergeant Stout wasn't in a reasoning mood, just then. He'd made his decision and was going to stand by it. Somewhere, Jesse supposed, he'd read that this was the mark of a good leader.

"Okay, Sergeant, could I pick up that rifle? It may take a few minutes to get used to it, from what I've seen before."

Sergeant Stout went over to Quartermaster and got the rifle. It was a Merrill breechloader, and a more complex piece of machinery Jesse had never seen. It fired a paper cartridge, and in order to load, it almost had to be disassembled. Jesse hadn't ever encountered a Merrill before, but he didn't complain. He'd become accustomed to working as a rifleman, and was anxious to learn the intricacies of the new weapon.

"Give me a few minutes, Sergeant, and I'll have this thing ticking like a clock," he said cheerfully.

Sergeant Stout didn't have much confidence in either the rifle or in Jesse, and he felt better about leaving both in camp.

———— ((•)) ————

The brigade to which Jesse had been assigned was part of General Shields' division under Colonel Sam Carroll. They had been sent to support

General Tyler in taking Port Republic, where it was thought General Stonewall Jackson was camped. General Shields was camped thirty or thirty-five miles to the north, and General Fremont was situated about twenty miles to the west. The weather had been rainy, and the ground was wet, but the skies were clearing and General Shields had ordered Sam Carroll's brigade to attack Port Republic the following day.

The next day, June eighth, dawned clear. The troop was awake at about four in the morning to prepare for the day's ride. Jesse got up with the rest of the company and went to where the horses were corralled to assist as needed. Caleb secured his mount and led him out of the ring, as did about half of the company, a few at a time. Sergeant Stout had put his lead rope on Bob and was leading him out of the ring when Jesse went over to him and spoke.

"Sergeant, that horse is a mite skittish with a new rider 'til he gets to know him," he said. He knew if it appeared that Bob was a rogue, he might just be put down, but he didn't want Sergeant Stout to have to find it out for himself or he'd lose him for sure. "It took me and him a little time to get used to each other, and I wouldn't want to see you get hurt."

With a knowing smile, Sergeant Stout replied, "Logan, I like this horse, and I been riding since I was a little kid. I've taken on some rough ones, and haven't ever been thrown. Never."

In Nevada there was an old saw that the only man who'd never been tossed from a horse was pretty short on horse-riding experience. It got into a couple of the songs they used to sing about, 'There's never the horse that couldn't be rode, and never the rider that couldn't be throwed'. Jesse decided to button his lip and wait.

Sergeant Stout saddled Bob quickly and with considerable expertise. He checked his cinch, tugged at the straps of his bridle to see that they were sound, lifted his foot into the stirrup and climbed on.

It was like a scene from some comic rodeo. Bob lifted his head to see who was in the saddle and with no more than a pigeon hop, he ducked his head and lurched skyward. Sergeant Stout was just about to reach for his gloves when the lid blew off his nice peaceful ride. As though it had been orchestrated, the sergeant kept on going up when Bob came down, but he then came down just a few feet away, striking his shoulder on the wheel of a wagon and collapsing into a heap on the ground. He rolled over on his back and passed out from the pain. It was quite obvious his shoulder was broken, and Jesse couldn't even guess what else was the matter with him.

Lieutenant Barnes had seen the activity, and cursed angrily. Stout was one of his best sergeants despite his tendency to be a little insensitive, and he didn't have a replacement. His concern for Stout's welfare was certainly a factor in his being upset, but he'd been given orders to ride and Colonel Carroll was not the kind of man to excuse non-performance simply because of an injured sergeant. Barnes looked about for signs of authority and the only set of stripes he could see at the moment were those on Jesse's arm.

"Corporal, you're going to have to take the squad. Mount up and get the men into columns of four. Move! Do you have a horse?"

"I'll just take this one, Lieutenant," Jesse said climbing into the saddle on Bob's back. "He'll do just fine."

Barnes was about to shout a warning at Jesse's foolishness in mounting the horse that had just thrown a man who claimed to be a good horseman, but when Jesse settled his large frame into the saddle, Bob stood like a pet. Aside from having his legs drawn up from the stirrups being a little short, Jesse looked quite at home and Bob was as calm as Jesse was. After a minute in the saddle, Jesse dismounted, adjusted his stirrups, and climbed back on. He rode Bob back to his tent for his equipment and was ready to go.

Lieutenant Barnes and his company of about forty cavalrymen were at the van of a mounted unit that was to charge Port Republic and drive out what was thought to be a small advance of General Jackson's forces. They took the road into town at a fast trot, and routed the few skirmishers they encountered. Their orders were to take a small bridge, the only bridge across the North River, thus allowing General Fremont to come across to their aid, if he was able to get there in time.

Token firing told them the town was, in fact, occupied, but they didn't encounter any serious resistance for the first half an hour or so. They drove off a small force of Confederate infantry holding the bridge, and posted a guard on the bridgehead. Things didn't remain peaceful for long, however, the troop encountered heavier fire as they proceeded into the town, and presently Lieutenant Barnes gave the order to dismount. Firing was coming from the west end of town, and Colonel Carroll halted the troop and called for artillery to clear the resistance.

As the two cannons that the colonel had called up unlimbered, the enemy opened up with three cannons of their own and almost immediately, a company of Rebel infantry began moving in on them from the west. The Federals were plainly outnumbered and no match for men unencumbered with horses in the confines of a town. Jesse turned to Lieutenant Barnes and recommended withdrawal. Barnes agreed and had the bugler sound retreat. "B" Company was given orders to cover the withdrawal of the main body, and Jesse was left in charge of the troop. Lieutenant Barnes headed back to where Colonel Carroll was supervising the brigade and informed him of his decision to withdraw.

"The men are taking heavy fire, Colonel," he shouted over the noise of the cannon and rifle. "I've given them orders to withdraw and regroup. I left instructions to form up at the foot of the bridge. I don't think we should give up this bridge. It may be our only means of crossing North River for some time to come."

"You're right, Lieutenant. Get the men formed up back here as quick as you can. I'll try to get up some reinforcements."

Lieutenant Barnes started back toward the company, but found himself cut off by the Rebel infantry. Try as he may, his route was blocked from returning to his company.

At the same time, Jesse and his small troop of cavalrymen were virtually surrounded and fighting for their lives. They were equipped with single-shot breech-loading carbines, and although they could reload more quickly that the enemy, they found themselves seriously outnumbered as well as surrounded.

"Mount up, men," Jesse commanded in as loud a voice as he could muster. "We're leaving town." Drawing his revolver, he led the men south on a small side alley and then east through the scattered houses that made up the town of Port Republic. Shooting from the back of a moving horse was not as easy or as accurate as from the ground, but the entire company had drawn their revolvers in response to Jesse's action in drawing his. The combination of their fire was enough to cause the enemy soldiers to seek shelter, and the troop was successful in escaping without casualty. They made their way east, but well past the small road that led to the bridgehead the rest of the brigade had been guarding.

The Rebels were moving in force after them, and little by little, they pushed Colonel Carroll and his brigade away from the bridge and toward the east and out of town. Jesse had led his troop a little to the south, but when he saw the blue clad cavalry, he assembled his men and caught up with the larger body. Lieutenant Barnes spotted him riding up.

"How did you do, Corporal? Did you lose any men?" Lieutenant Barnes asked hurriedly.

"No, sir, we got out alright. Some of the men said they saw General Jackson down at the end of the street though, Lieutenant," Jesse said breathlessly.

"That must be the reason the Rebs put up such a fierce fight. Corporal, one of our batteries is still in there. Can you take your squad and pull them out? Do you know where they are? They're on that little knoll just south of the bridge we were holding."

"We'll do it, Lieutenant," Jesse responded confidently, then shouting as he had heard Sergeant (now Lieutenant) Davis do, "Company "B", form up."

The company responded to his command and they headed north toward the river. Reaching the river, the troop turned west and Jesse held up his hand for them to halt. "Men," he shouted, as he turned in the saddle and pulled from his saddle-bag an extra revolver, one that he had captured in New Castle, "we're supposed to head back into town and rescue a battery of artillery that's just west of that bridge we saw earlier. We are going to have to move fast and I don't know what the Rebs have posted since we left. Does everyone have his weapons loaded?"

A few clicks were heard as the men checked their arms and Jesse continued, "It's about half a mile back into town and I'm not sure of where we'll find the battery, but we have to try to get them out, with or without the cannons. Any questions?"

On Jesse's command, the troop started out in a column of four and headed back west along the river. As they approached the town, they were shielded by a grove of trees that lined the North River. As they emerged from the grove Jesse urged them into a gallop and they began a wild shout as though they were pursuing a fleeing quarry. The small squad of men attending the battery was pinned down and holding off about twenty of the enemy that had partially surrounded them. Jesse's troop met little resistance from the gray-clad forces as they approached them from the rear. They rode up the low knoll, gathered the nine Federals on their horses and rode back to the east, firing and screaming as they went. They were forced to abandon the cannons, but won the gratitude of the artillerymen they had rescued.

When the small force returned to the main body, Colonel Carroll was conferring with Lieutenant Barnes.

"How did we manage to get these men out, Lieutenant?" the colonel inquired.

"Well, sir, I knew they had been left back there at the bridge without support, so I sent Corporal —," He couldn't remember Jesse's last name.

"Corporal Logan," Colonel Carroll furnished.

"Yes, sir, Corporal Logan, — back to see if he could get them out. Unfortunately, I see we've lost the guns." Then turning to Jesse, Lieutenant Barnes inquired, "Corporal, did we lose any of the men from the battery, or any of yours, for that matter?'

"We lost the artillery sergeant, Lieutenant, and I think two of the soldiers were slightly wounded. We didn't lose any from our squad, though. I'm afraid the sergeant was dead when we rode up."

It was an uncomfortable situation. The entire cavalry unit of perhaps three hundred men was cut off from the main army, and they were not strong enough to attack the buildup of infantry Stonewall Jackson had assembled at Port Republic.

"We'll move north along the river," Colonel Carroll ordered. "From there we can either find our division or cross the river at a low spot if we can find one. Captain Forbes, have your unit scout in front. Lieutenant Barnes, you take up the rear and be on the lookout for the Rebel horse."

Orders were passed and the unit struck out for the river. After dispatching most of his men to scout to the rear, Jesse was riding with a small contingent from "D" Company when Lieutenant Barnes rode along beside him. "That was a nice piece of work back there, Logan," he began. "How'd you manage to get the men out of that trap? I tried to get back to them and found Rebels at every corner and corncrib."

"You've heard that necessity is the mother of invention, Lieutenant? Well, let me tell you, desperation is necessity's grandma. We just took out our revolvers and 'started for the door', shooting at anything that moved. I've carried a revolver all through the war, so far, and I'm convinced that it doesn't usually do much damage, especially firing from horseback, but it surely does help to distract those people who are trying to shoot at a fella. It really gives them something to think about when they're trying to reload those old muskets"

"By the way, Logan, I heard from the colonel you're up for a promotion. It that so? You're good on a horse, I'll tell you that, but there must be something besides horsemanship that helped convince command you're ready to take on the job of a lieutenant. What did you do?"

"I don't know, Lieutenant. I got lucky a couple of times this last year, and one time I managed to burn down a gun factory in Lynchburg. I was just running from the Rebs and the way things turned out I was at the right place at the right time. It's all a matter of luck."

Lieutenant Barnes looked at Jesse as though he'd just seen him for the first time. "You're the White Angel, aren't you?" he said in disbelief. You're the fella the papers were writing about last summer and then the Rebs made a big noise about capturing you without firing a shot."

"Well, Lieutenant, let me tell you." Jesse said matter-of-factly, "They fired several shots at me, but they missed."

By this time, they could see the main body of horsemen were stopped and could also see a Federal army of foot soldiers and wagons at the point where Colonel Carroll had pulled up. Lieutenant Barnes halted the troop and announced he was going to ride ahead and find out what the next move would be. They had encountered General Tyler and he was conferring with his staff as to the best position to take should they be attacked.

Meanwhile, some of the scouts Jesse had sent out to the rear were back with reports of the Rebels building in strength to the south and west. Jesse rode forward with this information and gave it to Lieutenant Barnes. General Tyler, who hadn't seen Jesse since they were at Coalwood, almost a year ago, recognized him and greeted him warmly. "Well, Mr. Logan. How in the world have you been since your little love affair back up the valley? It seems to have inspired you to greatness." He chided Jesse about the incident with Daisy Morton. "Gentlemen, are you acquainted with the latest member of the army to enjoy the rank of lieutenant? Let me be the first to congratulate you, Lieutenant Logan."

Jesse blushed a bright crimson, but maintained his composure, climbing off his horse and going over to where the general was standing. "Thank you, Sir," he said, taking the general's outstretched hand. "It was really that I was trying so hard to run away from that young lady up in Coalwood that I made it all the way to Richmond before I realized what had happened," poking fun at his own situation.

General Tyler smiled and turned back to the situation at hand. The intelligence Jesse had brought convinced him to seek defensible ground and he chose a spot that extended from the Shenandoah River on the right to a high, flat mound called Lewiston Coaling on the left. It gave the Federal force of 3000 troops a line of about a half-mile that seemed adequately defensible. General Tyler had only the advance contingent of General Shield's brigade, and felt that when the rest of the army moved up he would be able to attack the southerners and drive them off the plain.

The cavalry were to remain in reserve with orders to form up on the left In support of the artillery that General Tyler had posted on the coaling. Facing that side of the line on their left was a tangle of woods and brambles, with the balance of the field quite open giving the Federals a clear line of fire.

They dug in for the evening and waited. Jesse dry-fired and practiced reloading his Merrill rifle in anticipation of using it the following day.

The troop was up the following morning before dawn. It appeared they may be used as ground troops, and while the wisdom of utilizing Cavalry in that manner was widely questioned — especially among the members of the Cavalry — orders were orders. The imminence of Jesse's promotion qualified him for command duty, but his expertise with a rifle placed him in demand at this particular time as a sharpshooter, so his assignment was uncertain. He talked to Lieutenant Barnes and got permission to post on a small rise facing the woods opposite the artillery position. Billy Barnes went out with him after they had notified Colonel Carroll of their whereabouts.

The company was without a captain at the time, and Barnes was in command of about eighty troopers. They were without a sergeant with the injury of Sergeant Stout, and Jesse would fill that post when needed.

They found a convenient spot in a rock outcropping and settled in.

"Incidentally," Barnes remarked, "my name is Billy, Jesse, and my friends call me BK for Billy Kendall. So you were with the Seventh Ohio?"

The conversation focused mostly on Jesse's expectation of BK to act as a spotter, an essential member of any rifle team. When he had gone over the basics, they began the process of watching and waiting. Jesse knew he would have to modify his style of shooting, because of the slower reload time of the Merrill rifle. He discussed this with BK, who understood he'd have to be doubly alert for both potential targets and for potential threats to their own safety.

"When you were over at the Seventh Ohio, did you know a lieutenant by the name of John Goodin?" BK asked.

"Sure did. He was my First LT," Jesse responded noncommittally. It wasn't a good idea to spill your inner sentiments about a person until you knew what the next question was going to be. "Why do you ask?"

"Just wondering. I knew John was with the Seventh, and wondered whether he was still around. We're cousins. He's from Ohio, and I'm from Pennsylvania, and I met him a couple of times when we were kids, but I haven't seen him in many years. How's he doing over there?"

"Well, I just saw him over at Franklin last week. He's in charge of the garrison there until we, or they, I guess it is, get called together. He's doing okay, I reckon, but I have to tell you, Billy, him and me, we weren't particularly close. There was this girl that he had his eye on and I'd been seeing her some, and well, you know —," Jesse went on to relate a little about Olivia as the suttler for the regiment, and how he felt that John Goodin viewed him as a threat to any relationship with her.

"To tell you the truth, BK, I don't think she had anyone in mind for a friend among the troops at the Seventh. I've seen her since then, though, and I tell you, she is one good-looking woman. I don't blame Lieutenant Goodin for trying to shine up to her. One other thing; Goodin took a shot a while back, and is just getting over it. He was out with me on a setup, and a Reb took a shot at him. The bullet took him in the side of the face and passed through into his chest. His face got pretty badly beat up, but he's back at it, now. I guess he's okay, but he still shows some scarring." Jesse didn't go into the particulars as to how John Goodin had acted unwisely standing up in the clear in enemy territory, or how Jesse had very likely saved his life."

"Was that the little love affair General Tyler was talking about back there the other day," Billy Barnes inquired, "the one that got you in trouble with John Goodin?"

"No," Jesse laughed. "That was all about a misunderstanding I got into with a girl whose father invited me to dinner, and it looked like she thought I was dessert."

"What did you think of John personally?" Lieutenant Barnes persisted.

"Why do you ask? I told you we weren't too possum, but I featured him as just another officer, trying to do a tough job." Jesse evaded Barnes' question.

"I got the impression that he was something of a hard case, and sometimes went a little past the mark in dealing with the men in the ranks. He got his commission because of my father, who is John's uncle. My pa is Colonel Jeremy Barnes, who is on General Halleck's staff, and from what I remember of John, he's not one I'd pick for an officer. For one thing, he had some really strong Secesh leanings before the war, and for another, he has one gosh-awful temper. When we were kids, I saw him just take and rip a cat's head off just because the cat scratched him. And I don't mean that it was an instantaneous reaction. He stalked that cat for two days."

Jesse paused in thought for a few moments. "You know, BK, he does show something of a temper. I thought it was just me and his suspecting me of courting that girl." Then he continued, "So your pa's a big 'greenhorn' on General Halleck's staff. How's come you're not sitting pretty in some cushy job back behind the lines?"

"My pa told us he'd get us into units where we could count for what we had in us, but he's not one to hoe your row for you. As far as he's concerned, you'll do it on your own. If you see John again, you might tell him I'm up for captain here. That'll make his day, I'm sure."

BK's last few words were drowned out by a report from Jesse's Merrill. He'd been gazing over the scene before them, and while BK's attention was diverted by the conversation, Jesse's was not. A gray-coated soldier had emerged from the thicket they were facing, and Jesse picked him off at two hundred yards.

"Look sharp, BK. They're gonna be coming out of those woods any time. They know we're out here, now, and are going to be looking for us. Stay down, or better yet, get back to command and let them know what we're about. Tell Colonel Carroll the Rebs are likely setting up some cannon in that grove over there. Stay low, and congratulations." Jesse was giving instructions to the lieutenant as though he was the man's older brother. BK didn't object. He just slid out of the rocks they were hiding in and, using the rocks for cover, ran the seventy-five or eighty yards back to a grove of trees behind which his company was stationed. Rifle fire was building to their left. And the Rebs, as Jesse suspected, had set up a battery in or behind the thicket they'd been watching.

Jesse strained his eyes for movement in the thicket, but saw none. The rifle he was using was deadly accurate, but slower in reloading than was his Spencer. He had to adjust his rhythm to compensate, and he needed to be on the alert as he reloaded. An enemy soldier could cover thirty or more yards in the time it took Jesse to reload.

In just a few minutes, the Rebel battery started firing, giving indications of seeking his position, and Jesse decided to move back. He left by the same route as had BK Barnes had, and in a minute or two came running into the headquarters area set up by Colonel Carroll.

"Oh, you're back, Logan," Colonel Carroll exclaimed as Jesse came in. "I was just about to send someone out after you. We're to move back, but stay in support, for now. This doesn't seem like a typical 'Stonewall Jackson' skirmish. The Rebs are too slow." He didn't elaborate, but Jesse sensed that General Jackson was not close up in this battle, as there wasn't any enthusiasm in the Confederate attack. There had been an intermittent rain over the past several days, and the ground around Port Republic was sodden. This may have explained the slowness of the Rebel attack.

All of a sudden, the roof fell in. A barrage of Confederate shells rained down on their position as fast as their cannon could reload and fire.

"Sound 'retreat', Bugler," Colonel Carroll shouted over the sound of the exploding missiles. "We've got to move back! Barnes, get your men mounted up, and stay within hailing distance." He then shouted orders to his other commanders to form up to the rear, but to try to avoid being backed against the river. The Shenandoah was swollen by the recent rains and virtually impassible by foot or horseback. "Where the hell is Fremont?"

General Fremont was enroute their location from Cross Keys, but was too late to help. As his great army approached the battlefield tenuously held by the forces of General Shields and Colonel Carroll, he found the North River Bridge in flames and his only access to the battlefield was cut off. He could only watch from the west bank of the Shenandoah, as General Jackson drove the Union forces northward down the valley.

Jackson had scored another victory through cunning, surprise, and the generous help of Mother Nature.

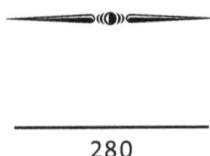

On June 26th, General John Pope was placed in command of what was then the Army of Virginia, USA, and General Fremont was sent east to assume a position under General Pope, but at that, Fremont resigned his commission.

General Lee, assured that the Shenandoah Valley was fairly safe, and concerned for the safety of the Confederate Capitol, called General Jackson east to Gordonsville, giving the Federals in the valley only slight rest, but leaving one of Jackson's most trusted subordinates, General Richard Ewell for the Federals to contend with.

17

RETURN TO LEWISBURG

After the battles along the Shenandoah River had subsided General Tyler marched his demoralized army as far as Franklin, sending a detachment south to garrison at Lewisburg, and went into bivouac for rebuilding his forces. The command of the Army of the Potomac was now under General Pope, who would no doubt, have some ideas of his own as to how the army was to be deployed, but without General Fremont, General Tyler was going to have to straighten this mess out by himself, not that he or anyone on the staff felt that General Fremont had taken a strong hand in the order of things in the army.

Jesse would be assigned again to the Seventh Ohio at Lewisburg, under newly promoted Captain Davis, and second in rank to John Goodin. It was not an assignment Jesse relished, but when he explained his objections to Frank Davis, Davis had objections of his own.

"Logan," he explained, "Maybe you never noticed it but Lieutenant Goodin, for all his faults, is a survivor. Anyone else screwing up so regularly would be cashiered, court martialed, and drummed out of the army. Why is it, do you suppose, that John Goodin hasn't suffered that fate?"

Long pause —, then, "Henry Halleck," Jesse said in a low voice, as though to himself.

"Ho, ho, _ho_, I believe you're onto something," Davis said with mock surprise. "Logan, I think you've gained a little understanding of how the system sometimes works. Goodin's uncle is General Barnes, assigned to General Halleck's staff, and while he is an upstanding soldier and a good administrator himself, he has also seen to it that his son and nephew have been afforded opportunity to prove themselves, if they are capable. Goodin will never go anywhere in this army, but his situation is such that he hasn't quite done anything bad enough to get kicked out. His transgressions have been more of a personal nature, and he hasn't kindled the wrath of enough of the top command to warrant discipline. Now, I'm pleading with you, Lieutenant. Stick with me in this thing so that "H" Company can accomplish something in this war, and we can go on home with our heads held high. Colonel Sullivan, when he was promoted, passed along to me the job of intelligence gathering and transmitting up the line, and I need your experience and that of Miss Livingston in the intelligence field to help me with my job."

"What are my choices, Captain?" Jesse asked. "I'm a shave-tail lieutenant. This is my first assignment, and you're an old friend that I would go to the end of the earth for, anyway. You don't give me much of an out. What you said about Goodin's not going anywhere is obvious from the fact that you've been promoted over him. And while we're on that subject, I'll betcha he's not too happy about that."

"He hasn't said anything to me, but he's let it out that he's going to take over command when I buy the farm. You'd better watch your back, too, young fellow. I think he has it in for both of us. You didn't do the army any favors when you plucked that guy off the mountain last year, you know."

Jesse grinned. "I've been taking guff from all sides from the minute I made the decision to save his life, but let's look at it another way, Captain. Suppose he hadn't died back down there on Clinch Mountain. Suppose — just suppose he was conscious enough to hear what was being said about him out there and that he'd lived anyway. Our troops came up that hill soon enough to save him, you know. Where would that have put me with regard to failure to assist an officer whose life was in danger? How does that load fit your gun?"

It was Frank's turn to grin. "I know, Jesse, we can what-if this thing to death, but it doesn't change anything. So, that's where it stands. You'll stay and help out, and we'll see what comes of it all. Remember, Jesse, it's just another —."

"— Just another hill toward home," Jesse chimed in. "It's nice to be back working for you, Captain, even so. And, at least I got to spend a couple of weeks in the Cavalry. That was something."

Jesse left the small house that Frank Davis had commandeered as a headquarters building and started toward the company street, just as a suttler's wagon pulled into the street. The wagon was familiar, but it had a sign on the side that Jesse wasn't prepared for. "Bert Oakley Enterprises", it read. Sitting in the driver's seat next to Bert was Olivia Livingston.

Jesse's heart did a flip. It had been less than two months since he'd seen Libbie, but his leisure thoughts had been of little else. She'd kissed him just before their last parting and that kiss had borne fruit in the form of fantasies of spring blossoms and soft sunshine with two lovers, arm in arm on peaceful country lanes and in grassy meadows. In his dreams he'd introduced Libbie to his grandparents and his mother, and they were enthralled by her charm. He'd showed Libbie his brother David's leather shop and Will's cattle ranch in Nevada. All in his fantasies.

Bert and Olivia hadn't seen Jesse yet, but they stopped a short distance from where he was standing and got down out of the wagon to go over to Captain Davis' headquarters to secure permission and a location to set up.

"Hello, Miss Libbie," Jesse said as she rounded the back of the wagon. "I see you got yourself a new partner."

"Well, Mr. Logan," Olivia exclaimed, softly. "Well, Mr. Logan. Well —," and she rushed into his outstretched arms, holding him tightly for a little longer than convention might allow. When she stepped back Jesse could see tears welling up in her eyes, and he felt quite a lump in his throat, also.

Jesse's uniform jacket, while quite new, nevertheless showed signs of his old corporal chevrons having been removed, as the fading of the material was less pronounced where the chevrons had been. He hadn't obtained any lieutenant's bars, yet.

"Whatever happened to your corporal stripes, Mr. Logan?" she asked pointedly. "Did you get demoted?"

"Well, maybe in one sense," he replied. "It depends on whether you rank a lieutenant lower than a corporal. Some people do, you know."

"Lieutenant," Olivia mused with her mouth pulled sideways, fighting back more tears. "Lieutenant Logan. It has a nice ring to it, I think."

Meanwhile Bert Oakley had been standing beside Olivia for a brief time, but after shaking Jesse's outstretched hand, he muttered something about seeing about a place to set up and went into Captain Davis' house. Presently Bert came out of the house and approached Jesse and Olivia. "Captain Davis says there's a house just a little way down the street where we can set up. I'm going to take a look at it, and by the way, Jesse, congratulations on your promotion. Nice work, Son," and with that, he got back into the wagon and headed up the street, stopping near a house that had been damaged by cannon fire, but was still quite useable.

As Jesse and Olivia started slowly moving after Bert, walking closely and talking quietly, Lieutenant John Goodin suddenly appeared in the street, almost blocking their path.

"Well, well, who do we have here?" Lieutenant Goodin inquired with assumed joviality. "The great new lieutenant seems to have won the lady's heart, from the looks of things. It's a shame those of us who occupy those lowly positions of just having to do our daily humdrum job of fighting the war aren't blessed with sufficient charm to be noticed by the fair damsel. The 'heero' returns and claims her hand in a trice and the rest of us are relegated to live out our lives in abject boredom and oblivion, without so much as a smile from the comely wench."

Jesse was offended by Goodin's tone, but chose to overlook any insult, implied or inferred.

Olivia was shocked at the appearance of John Goodin, and saddened by the grotesque distortion of his face. He tried to smile, but his face was so scarred the smile became something of a sneer. His manner, obsequious and patronizing, was nevertheless threatening in its import, and the distorted leer that his face portrayed didn't help the situation. She instinctively moved a little, as though to hide behind Jesse, who loomed over Lieutenant Goodin anyway.

"Oh, oh. The lady is even offended by the appearance of the scorned suitor," John Goodin continued, referring to all present in third person. "There's no reason to seek refuge from his presence. He's only a harmless derelict, adrift on the sea of life, with no direction and no one to cling to. A poor hapless creature scarred and scorned by the world, spiritually and physically, as well as socially. Fighting for his country, he bears the scars of battle proudly, but is so manipulated by his surroundings, and indeed by his inferiors, that he is cast into the cauldron of the damned for eternity."

"Lieutenant Goodin," Jesse finally said, "I'm not sure what you're talking about, but it sounds like something out of Shakespeare. What is it you are looking for?"

"Looking? Looking? It's good that the brave hero addresses the poor derelict by his honored title, but the object of the happy couple's scorn seeks nothing more from this encounter than that which is rightfully his. The lady knows whereof I speak."

"Lieutenant Goodin," Olivia found her voice. "I'm not sure what you're talking about, either. Are you all right? Are you well? I'm glad Lieutenant Logan managed to save your life, but you're not making any sense."

Slowly, Olivia's sense of indignation was becoming aroused. This man had done his very best to overcome her earlier revulsion of him by various means, and had failed. Now he seemed to come at her expressing pathos and vying for her sympathy while, at the same time, claiming she owed him something and tacitly threatening her for withholding whatever it was that was supposed to be owed.

"Lieutenant," she said in a new and defiant tone, stepping out from behind Jesse, "you've gone quite far enough. You've been injured, and I'm abjectly, — no, profoundly sorry for that, but you're not the only one who has suffered in this war."

"I just lost my partner, my uncle," she said, "to the cause of the Union, and we've all lost many dear friends to the war. You've been wounded, but you're alive, and your wounds will heal. But at the same time, you've got to turn loose of the idea that anyone owes you anything, or this world will get the better of you, war or no war."

Goodin was taken aback by her defiance. He'd perceived her as a friendly, if somewhat retiring person over the months he had known her. She had allowed this impression to prevail rather than offend him, but now, it seemed her facade had been taken for submission and she intended that impression to change. She also had a motive in projecting the impression of submission. Previously, she didn't wish to arouse Goodin's animosity for fear he would vent his aggression toward Jesse. Jesse was now in a position to neutralize any hostility on Goodin's part, and Olivia was tired of playing games.

"You were plenty nice to me when I was the only officer in your life, Missy," Goodin had dropped the third person routine. "Now that there's another lieutenant to run to and hide behind, you're going to toss me aside, especially now that I'm ugly to look at. Well, I'll tell you a little secret. He won't always be there, as far as you're concerned. Don't come running to me when your big, brave 'heero' sells you for a Daisy Morton or runs off to help the Rebs, or maybe just doesn't come back at all, one day. No Ma'am, don't come to me. I covered for him when the sheriff came around looking for him when he was playing around with that Morton girl, but I ain't going to do it again."

John Goodin stalked off, his face flushed and the veins along his neck bulging with anger.

Jesse and Olivia looked at each other, worried a little for the safety of the other, but they were so happy and relieved to be together again, the concern faded and they turned and walked on toward where Bert Oakley was transferring his goods to the little house he had adopted.

Bert and Olivia had established a partnership. It was a good one, as now there would be no need for Olivia to conceal from her partner her secret activities. Captain Davis had taken over where Colonel (now General) Sullivan had formerly been working as an intelligence contact for the brigade, and Jesse was recognized as an aid to Captain Davis in this regard. He also had developed some independent contacts of his own, but his main job was as adjutant to Captain Davis.

Company "H" had been deployed with General Tyler's Brigade, and now that they were consolidated at Lewisburg, they were being used for some forays into the countryside recruiting, information gathering, and also in response to reports of Confederate activity in the area. Lewisburg was a town of about a thousand people, where the company had been garrisoned, up until the time they had been called out by General Fremont to try to combat the presence of General Jackson in the Shenandoah Valley.

One of the intelligence contacts Jesse had been able to develop was the owner of a small hotel in Lewisburg. Bert Oakley, who had known of the man's Union sympathies for some time, had introduced them. John Pryor had a wife and three children, the oldest being Jane, twenty, then Harold, seventeen, and the youngest was another son, James, fifteen. While John's commitment to the Union cause was considered solid, Jesse and Bert had their doubts about the loyalty of his three children. The boys were inclined to associate with a crowd of young men who were secessionist in their leanings, and the daughter, Jane, was rather quiet, showing no inclination one way or the other. She helped at the hotel with her mother and pretty well kept her opinions to herself. John, however, was useful inasmuch as his business kept him in touch with all kind of people moving from place to place in the area.

Jesse had been allowed to keep his horse, Bob, and used him extensively, maintaining a constant presence wherever his company was assigned. The sorties they ran were of a duration of two to ten days at a time, and they began working well as a unit. From time to time, the company had captured several horses, and there was talk of their becoming a company of Mounted Infantry, which gave incentive to their activities.

Lige Hawkins was Jesse's first sergeant, and others of the old company were still with the unit.

Now that Frank Davis was Captain, he provided a brand of discipline similar to the old army and what was seen in the various regular units to be found in several parts of the army. His feeling for the welfare and comfort of the men in rank was translated into a determination to maintain discipline. It made for a better trained company and, as he put it, was, "designed to keep the men alive."

In early August, Captain Davis ordered Jesse to take a squad south toward New Castle in search of a contingent of Rebel cavalry known to be operating in the area. His squad would consist of twenty-four men, all mounted on horses they had captured. They would be gone for a period of seven or eight days, and would have to live off the land, to a certain extent.

Jesse went over to the house Olivia and Bert were using as a store and broke the news to Libbie. She was saddened by the news, but wished him God-speed, and kissed him lightly on the cheek.

As he was about to leave the store, Jesse turned back to Olivia. "Will you marry me, Libbie?" he asked.

Olivia was surprised by the question and didn't answer for a few moments. "Jesse, I don't think we should even discuss such a thing at a time like this. We're both vulnerable and anxious for the safety of each other, and I think your proposal was more of a reflection of the times than of a deep desire to be married to the likes of me."

Jesse smiled, "Marry me and find out," he said mischievously. Then sobering, "I love you very much, Libbie, and I think we belong with each other."

"I think a great deal of you, too, Jesse, but we're in the midst of battle and uncertain of what will happen to us from day to day. Give me some time to think about this. As they all seem to say, 'this is so sudden'."

Jesse smiled again. "I know we couldn't do it today, but please do give my words some serious thought. There's a chaplain at the garrison, now, and we could get him to perform the ceremony. We both deserve happiness, and nothing would make me happier than to be married to you for the rest of my life."

"However long that might be." He thought to himself.

"I'll certainly give it some thought, Jesse. Now you'd better go steal some horses, or whatever you do on these sorties. You aren't going down to Coalwood on these trips, are you," she said with a smile.

"See," Jesse responded in kind, "if we were married, you wouldn't have to worry about such things."

Jesse's ride took him almost as far as Coalwood and he had to rush the mission to get back in his assigned time. Their main purpose was to scout for Rebel troops and to capture Rebel horses, if possible. Prisoners weren't a consideration, but they were ordered to bring back any Confederate soldiers they might capture, if they could do so without impeding their primary mission. There seemed to be a sizeable Rebel presence in the region, situated in small squads around New Castle. It was probably members of that regiment that Jesse and Tom Singleton had encountered that fatal day in New Castle.

Logan's orders were not to kill anyone outside the line of battle. Scorched earth was not an option in the valley at the time, as it might be later, and it was the policy to try to win the local population with reasonable treatment. If they took any horses from the local citizenry, they would pay well for them in Federal greenbacks and at the same time, try to avoid crippling the ability of the people to farm their land.

They were successful in obtaining seven horses from a Rebel camp, which they raided early one morning, scattering the few soldiers who were there at the time.

Three days later, on their return through some low mountains along the western side of the valley, the troop was peacefully proceeding with their captured horses on lead lines. Their route was along a lightly used wooded farm road through the gentle rolling countryside. They were close enough to Lewisburg to be able to get back by nightfall.

Presently, at about noon they saw, running off to their left, what appeared to be a smaller side road or lane, which, Jesse thought, may lead to a farmstead.

"Lige," Jesse said to his sergeant, "you stay here with the main troop and start cooking dinner. I'm going to take some men with me and check out this road. I shouldn't be too long, but if we don't get back in half an hour, send someone out there to check on us."

Then he turned to Martin Mason, and three of the other members of the troop and directed them to accompany him down the long lane. Martin was now a corporal, and the other three men, Billy Miller, Ezra Reynolds, and Fred Dobbs had been with the company for a considerable time, also.

"I want to go up this little canyon and see where this road leads. It looks like there might be some easy pickins up there for horses or cattle, and we're close enough to Lewisburg to be able to herd some stock back to the garrison, if we find anything."

"He's still thinkin' like a cowboy," Martin said in a low, but audible tone of voice to the other men. "Jesse, can't we just be soldiers for a while, without havin' to go out and rustle cattle everywhere we go?"

"Don't complain, Marty. I don't hear you belly-aching when you get to eat a good piece of beef or pork. Where do you think those things come from, the suttler's wagon?" Jesse responded in good spirits.

They followed the lane for a distance of about 400 yards and came upon a clearing of about an acre, where there was a small house situated. It appeared deserted.

"Marty, I'm going on out there to see what's down this other old lane. Billy, you come with me. You other men might check around through the yard and sheds, and see if you can find any signs of life. If we don't come right back, come on out there, if you don't find anyone here."

Jesse and Billy Miller proceeded past the sheds, along a fenced lane and around a small hill. There, screened by the hill and some oak trees, they found a large barn. It was built against the side of the hill, and had a heavy stone foundation on the two downhill sides. The foundation enclosed the first floor of the barn, where the horses or cattle were supposed to be housed, and the upper level of the barn, wood framed, was where hay was stored and fed through a chute to the livestock below. The doors of the lower part of the barn appeared to be locked from the inside, but as they approached, their horses, sensing other horses inside, whinnied in recognition.

"I think we have signs of life, Bill," Jesse whispered. "Try those doors, but be as quiet as you can. If they're locked like they look to be, there may be someone inside."

Suddenly, a window of the upper level of the barn flew open and a man, whose bare head and shoulders appeared through the window, shouted, "What are you men doing out there? I thought I gave orders —," whereupon, seeing Logan and Miller in Union uniforms, he immediately withdrew his head and slammed the window shut.

"Get the others, Miller," Jesse hissed. "I'll cover the escape till you get back." Then, banking on the chance that the man inside had not seen the limits of his manpower, and shouting as though he were in command of the entire squad, he ordered, "Corporal, I'll take two men and cover the back. You three men take cover and stay low. Don't fire until I give the signal."

"You, inside," Jesse bluffed, riding around to the back side of the barn where there was a door serving the upper level, "come on out of there with your hands in the air. Make it slow, 'cause my men get real nervous at sudden moves." He dismounted and quickly tied Bob to a fence rail, well back out of the way. There was only silence from inside the barn, and Jesse strained to try to figure out where the men or man inside would exit. He took up a post near one corner to try to cover the two doors, one on the upper level and the other down on the stable level, hoping for the early return of the rest of the squad.

Jesse could hear voices from the inside of the barn but couldn't make out how many or what they were saying. One of the voices, however, sounded like that of a woman and he suspected he had come upon a hayloft rendezvous.

Inside the barn, Colonel Jedediah Abernathy, CSA and Miss Jane Pryor quickly put on their clothing. Slipping over to a stairway near the hay chute in the floor of the loft, they descended to the lower level where their horses were secured. Colonel Abernathy drew the bar from the inside of the stable door, and quietly laid it aside.

"You give me a minute or two to get back up there and be ready to slip out the back door, then you open this door and call out to those men out there," he whispered. "They won't harm you, and if they hear you down in front, it may draw them away from the back so's I can get out of here with my skin."

"What do you mean, your skin?" Jane whispered indignantly. "You been talking about marrying me now for ten months and taking me south, and now all you can think about is your skin. Jed Abernathy, I got a family back in Lewisburg and they got a good reputation, and here I am with the likes of you and all you can think about is putting me out in front so's you can save your own hide. I'm skeered, Jed. Even if they don't hurt me, my name is ruin't. You jus' get up there and shoot them Yankees, and get me out of this mess. Get us both out of a mess!"

"Corporal," Jesse yelled, "Get that torch ready. If those men in there start anything, we may have to burn them out."

Presently, the lower door creaked open and a young woman appeared.

"Hello, Hello," the voice of Jane Pryor queried the unseen squad surrounding the barn. "May I come out, please? I'm not armed, and I can't hurt anyone. Please can someone help me? Please."

Jesse suspected a trick. He pulled back out of sight and waited. He turned to cover the door leading from the upper level of the barn, and just as he did so, the figure of a Confederate officer emerged from the upper door.

"Hold it right there, Romeo," Jesse said quietly.

Jed Abernathy didn't hold it. Hearing Jesse, he snapped a quick shot at him and sprinted for the woods. Jesse stepped away from the barn and leveled his revolver at the fleeing figure. He fired one shot and Colonel Abernathy fell with a bullet just above the left knee. He rolled over and raised his revolver toward Jesse, but Jesse fired again, this time striking the colonel in the right shoulder, disabling his gun hand.

"If you want to keep this up, Johnny, I can smash your other arm an' leg," Jesse advised. "It's up to you, though, we can quit any time."

"I quit, I'm done," the officer gasped. "Please, no more. I'm your prisoner," but with that, he fainted from the pain.

The other four men in the squad had been only a short distance away from the barn when the shots exploded, and they hurried forward to find Jane Pryor just standing desperately at the door of the barn, screaming. Jesse and the Rebel officer were out of sight behind the barn. Corporal Martin Mason vaulted off his horse, rushed up to the hysterical girl and demanded, "Where are they? Where's the lieutenant?"

"I think they're out back," she sobbed. "Oh, please don't hurt him, please."

"Billy, you and Fred see who's inside there. Ez, you come with me," Marty snapped. "You men be careful."

Martin and Ezra Reynolds went to the rear of the barn just as Jesse was walking toward the fallen colonel. The first thing he did was to kick the colonel's revolver out of reach and then kneel beside him. Colonel Abernathy was groaning softly, and Jesse rolled him over on his back to try to ease the discomfort of the wounds and to check for additional weapons. He motioned for Martin to fetch his canteen and held it up to the other man's lips, whereupon Colonel Abernathy came to. He drank a few drops of the water and then turned away.

"You'll live, Mister, but I don't know if they'll be able to save your arm," Jesse said gently. What's your name and company?"

"I'm Colonel Jedediah Abernathy, Sixth Virginia Volunteers," the soldier said, and who might you be?"

"We're from the Seventh Ohio Volunteers, and I'm Lieutenant Logan. I don't have to ask what you're doing out here, but I'd be curious as to where your regiment is. I didn't think there was any large bodies of Rebs out in this region since Stonewall Jackson went east."

"I'll thank you to keep a civil tongue in your head when addressing a superior officer, Lieutenant," Colonel Abernathy had regained his composure. "It's none of your business what I was doing here. I happened to have some important business of a confidential nature, and what you have witnessed here should not mislead you into the impression that there was anything inappropriate going on."

Jesse was sorely tempted to make further light of the situation, but his experience so far in the business of gathering intelligence told him to hold his tongue. "I apologize for giving you the impression I was being disrespectful, Colonel, but you must admit that we did find you in something of a strange situation. And before you tell me you saw us coming and ran into that barn to hide, remember your first words to us when you stuck your head out of that window were given as though we were under your command and you didn't have any clothes on, so don't try to tell me I didn't see what I saw. But now, tell me, can you ride?"

Abernathy glanced about him, wondering where his revolver was, but not seeing it, he replied, "Yes, Lieutenant, I believe I can ride. Where do you propose to take me?"

Fred Dobbs and Billy Miller had searched the barn and found nothing unusual but the two horses belonging to Abernathy and the girl, Jane Pryor. She was standing near the door of the barn and Fred Dobbs approached her.

"Aren't you Miss Pryor?" Fred asked the girl, knowing the answer.

"Yes," she sobbed, "and I'm so frightened. That man in there asked me to come all the way out to this place on the promise that he would be able to help my father and mother with their business, and then he got me into that big barn and tried to have his way with me."

"Golly, Ma'am, when you were coming out of the barn before, you didn't sound like someone was after you, and you were begging us not to hurt him. You say he was abusing you? How did you meet him?"

"He's a friend of my father, and although he's an officer in the Southern Army, he's really on the side of the North, or so I thought."

"What's his name?" Fred was not making sense of this conversation, and began to suspect the girl was covering something up.

"His name is Je', Je', Jed something, I think." she said, trying to think of something logical to say that would make sense and still exculpate her from suspicion. "I don't know his last name, but I think my father does."

"When did you talk to him that he coaxed you to come all the way out here to this lonely place? Do you know the people that live here?"

The questions were coming too fast. It was obvious that, as innocent as Fred's manner had been, his line of questioning was going to trip her up if she continued. Jane broke down and sobbed; her last line of defense.

About this time Billy Miller brought the horses out from inside the stable, and Corporal Mason came down from the back of the barn. "The lieutenant wants us to saddle up and try to get back to garrison, tonight. He doesn't want to leave the girl out in the country, and he thinks the Reb colonel should be got back to a doctor as soon as we can do it."

At the last utterance by Mason, the girl screamed and began sobbing all the more.

"I'm sorry, Miss," Mason apologized. "I think he'll be okay, but he is going to have to be looked at by the doctor. Was you sweethearts?"

Jane Pryor didn't respond. She had already implicated herself beyond extrication, and knew anything she said would only make things worse.

It was well after noon by this time and Sergeant Hawkins began to be concerned for the safety of Jesse and his squad. He started to send some men back to find them but by then the small squad and their prisoner were just coming out of the lane from the farmhouse.

Colonel Abernathy was able to ride, awkwardly, but without assistance, and Jane Pryor had mounted her horse, though she remained mute through the entire process.

It was almost dark when the squad reached Lewisburg. Held back by the necessity of supporting Abernathy and leading his and the other captured horses, they arrived quite a bit later than they had anticipated. Captain Davis and John Pryor had ridden out to meet them. Pryor had gone to the garrison, concerned about his missing daughter, and they had ridden out together. When they had closed enough for John Pryor to recognize his daughter, he rode forward anxiously and asked for her welfare.

By this time, Jane had stopped her sobbing, but had said little. At one point, just before they reached Lewisburg, she rode to the side of Colonel Abernathy and, in a whisper, warned him that she was not going to allow her name to be besmirched and might even just lie to protect herself. Abernathy said nothing. He had troubles of his own.

John Pryor asked if he might take his daughter home, and quickly departed with the young woman. The Rebel colonel was immediately taken to the infirmary where the doctor examined his wounds. Jesse went to headquarters and sat down with Captain Davis and Lieutenant Goodin.

"You came back with all your men safely in tow, and brought us a few horses to fatten our string," Davis said in satisfaction. "Eight horses in all, wasn't it?"

"Yes, Sir. Eight, including the Rebel colonel's," Jesse responded. "We came across a small squad of Rebs down just north of New Castle, and saw signs of several others, but they managed to elude us. They were in camp when we rode in on them, and ran like rabbits. We got seven of their horses there, but I think that was a much larger squad from the looks of the camp. I reckon the others had left earlier that morning. You know, Captain, those four Rebs that Tom Singleton and I met up with in New Castle last summer must have been part of that same regiment."

They discussed the rest of the excursion, and then turned to the subject of their captured officer. "He's a Confederate raider," Captain Davis said. We knew him to be working in this area, but we didn't know his name and this is the first close encounter we've had with him. If my information is correct, he's been in command of that small detachment you came across, but has other troops in other parts of the country. That's too high a rank to just be over a squad of thirty or forty men. Lieutenant, I think you've struck a serious blow to the Secesh cause. What do you think, Lieutenant?" the captain said, turning to Lieutenant Goodin.

Goodin did not appear to be paying particular attention to the conversation, and responded somewhat absentmindedly when addressed by the captain. "Oh, it looks to me like he did just that, Captain," he said quickly. "Good work, Logan."

"I'm not so sure we just broke up a tryst, out there in that barn though, Captain," Jesse said advisedly. "Why would Jane Pryor venture two hours' ride out into the hills just to meet a lover? Do you think she's part of a ring? How'd they make the arrangement for her and him to be at that particular place at that time? Does he get in close enough to Lewisburg to make that kind of contact?"

"I don't know, Lieutenant," Captain Davis said. "It's something we're going to have to think about, though, isn't it? Well, you're going to have to get busy on your report, I think. When I've had a chance to read it over, I'll be in a better position to speculate."

"Lieutenant," he said to John Goodin, "would you go on over and see to it that the saddler has enough equipment for those new horses, and have him submit a requisition for sufficient supplies to provide for them, if you feel it's necessary. Check on the prisoner too, if you will."

Then, when Goodin had left, Captain Davis turned to Jesse. "That Pryor girl has been something of a mystery to me lately but I think Goodin has eyes for her, and I don't want to say too much with him around. He isn't always the epitome of discretion where women are concerned. What I think I might do is ask Miss Livingston to go into town and nose around a bit. If I can get her to engage that Pryor woman in an 'innocent conversation', we may get closer to what's happenin' around here. Not just between Abernathy and Jane Pryor, but maybe where he's been gettin' some of the information he's been workin' with these past few weeks."

The next day, Captain Davis and Jesse sat down with Olivia in the captain's office and went over the events of the preceding two weeks. The fact that a colonel of the Confederate Army was in the region was indication that a considerable force of Rebel troops was scattered about in small bands. As a woman of about the same age, it was thought that Olivia could engage Miss Pryor in conversation and perhaps find out what the plans were in the Rebel high command and where some of the security leaks were occurring. Jesse described the scene and conversations he had had with those involved, and his impressions based on what he had observed. Olivia listened attentively, quickly scribbling notes as the conversation progressed.

"You say the Colonel was naked when he stuck his head out of the window to yell at you, Lieutenant," she said, savoring with a slight smile the word 'lieutenant'.

"I don't know about his being completely naked, Miss Livingston. I only saw the part from the arms and shoulders up when he was at the window, but that part was bare, and I don't know of anyone who takes off his shirt for just a casual intelligence-gathering conversation. Also, when Miss Pryor came out of the barn a few moments later, the men saw her and mentioned that she was very emotional. She was asking about the colonel's welfare, and appeared to have hay in her hair that she was picking at. This all leads me to the conclusion that there was some intimate contact there."

"I'd have to agree," she responded. "It's good to know all these details. It makes it easier to talk to her and gain her confidence. I'll not bring these things up unless I find it necessary. Incidentally, I don't believe you told me the name of the man she was with. Do you have that?"

"Oh, yes. I thought I had given it to you. It's Colonel Jedediah Abernathy. He told me he's from the Sixth Virginia Volunteers, but I don't have any — any — are you alright, Olivia?"

Olivia had dropped her pencil and put her hand out as if to prevent herself from falling. Then, regaining her composure, she looked about for her pencil and picking it up from the floor, proceeded to write. Her hand was noticeably shaking, though, and after a few moments, she excused herself and walked toward the suttler's building. Jesse went after her.

"Olivia, what's the matter?" he asked. "You don't look well. Are you all right? What happened?"

"N, n, no, I'm all right, I think," she said in a low voice. "I guess it was just too warm in there for me. Please excuse me. I need to get a glass of water."

"You looked like you'd seen a ghost, just now. Is there anything I can do?"

"Jesse, I said I'm all right," she said impatiently. "Now please, let me alone. I just need some air. I'll be fine."

———————«(●)»———————

Colonel Abernathy had been removed to a vacant hay shed near Lewisburg where an infirmary had been set up by Captain Holcomb, one of the regimental surgeons. There he was placed on the makeshift operating table that had apparently been the door of the shed.

Abernathy was a handsome man of about thirty-five, six feet tall, with sad, blue eyes and dark curly hair, rather striking in appearance, and ingratiating in demeanor. His smile and friendly manner masked a quiet determination to escape at first opportunity. He knew General Ewell and General Lee depended upon him, and he didn't intend to let them down.

The need for Dr. Holcomb's services had been light for the past few days, and his attention had been primarily directed to tending the needs of the sick and wounded from the battles in New Republic and Cross Keys, in which the Seventh Ohio had been only minimally involved.

The shot to the colonel's right shoulder had broken the humerus bone near the joint, and had then passed through the shoulder, exiting cleanly. The shot that struck him in the left leg was imbedded in the flesh, but had not broken any bones. Doctor Holcomb worked quietly, expertly examining the shoulder wound, evaluating the likelihood of his having to amputate the arm. As time was not a pressing consideration, he decided to try to set the arm and avoid amputation.

"I think I'll be able to save this arm," Holcomb said, "But you may not have the full use of it even when it heals. You're lucky that soldier wasn't using a rifle. That .36 ball didn't do as much damage as one of those others would have."

"Doctor, I don't consider myself lucky in any event, whatever that man was using. I simply should have been more patient, and it could have been him lying here." His thoughts were that he would have preferred to have 'that man' lying in a grave by now, and he kicked himself mentally for being so careless. He was especially upset over his having disclosed his presence in the first place, mistaking Logan and Miller for some of his own men. *"That woman,"* he thought, *"what was her name? — Jane Pryor, was the cause of my downfall. I should learn to keep my peter in my pants and all this wouldn't have happened."*

"If you wrap it tight, I think I can move about alright, and as there are apparently no provisions for prisoners here, I reckon you'll have me removed to a place with a lock-up. What do you think of the wound in my leg?"

"I think we can patch it up, but you won't be running any foot races for a time. It appears the bullet struck the bone and angled up a bit into the thigh, and I'll have to dig to remove that one."

"Doctor, I appreciate all you are doing to help me. I know you're not inclined to save limbs in these situations, and you could have just left me a cripple."

Doctor Holcomb bristled a little at the suggestion that he ever, ever did any less for a patient than he could, given the conditions and equipment at hand, but he knew that both sides of battle passed along horror stories about the indifference of the other.

Presently, Colonel Hughes came through the door of the 'infirmary' and inquired as to Colonel Abernathy's condition. Assured of the Rebel soldier's chances of recovery, he introduced himself, pulled up a chair and sat down.

"Lieutenant Logan tells me you're attached to the Sixth Virginia, Colonel. I didn't know they were in this area."

Abernathy smiled through clenched teeth. It was typical of the Yanks to send in an interrogator at just such a time as the doctor was performing a painful procedure and the prisoner's resistance was at a low ebb. Jed Abernathy had been captured before under similar circumstances, and had survived by pure grit. He'd also escaped from the Yanks under just such severe conditions, and he was determined to do it again. The best thing about being wounded, if there was anything good at all, was that his captors underestimated his resilience and might possibly give him a modicum of freedom in his movements about the camp.

"Colonel," Jed said as calmly as he could, "There are probably many things you don't know about the movements of the Sixth Virginia, and I assure you, you'll be no wiser for having had this conversation. I don't want to upset either you or the good doctor, but my inclination is to give you no more information about myself than you already have. Now, if you'd like to talk about my condition, the weather, the idiocy of the high command, or any of those important matters, I'll be glad to accommodate you, but don't ask me about the activities of me or my unit, please."

Sam Hughes, when he heard a colonel from the Confederate army had been captured was anxious to interview him. The fact that the company doctor was treating the man had little to do with his coming to see Abernathy, but it didn't discourage him, either. One of the main reasons he wanted to talk to Abernathy was that they could converse as soldiers of equal rank and the Rebel might be more at ease.

Colonel Hughes wasn't to be discouraged. He just changed direction. "Where are you from, Colonel," he asked in a genial tone. "I understand the Sixth Virginia Vols are from the northern part of the state. I'm from Tuscarora, myself," he lied. Actually, Hughes was from Pennsylvania.

"Are you, now?" Jed Abernathy responded, still wincing with pain as Captain Holcomb began probing his leg wound for the buried bullet. "And why is it you didn't stay loyal to your native state and go with the South?"

Hughes shook his head. "Well, I was in the army at the time, and felt it my duty to remain loyal to the cause of, well, shall we say, the Union. Are you from that area?"

Abernathy wasn't falling for the line of interrogation and to divert its direction, he pursued what he perceived as a point of vulnerability in Sam Hughes' characterization of his 'duty'. "You really feel that it was your duty to go against everything our grandfathers fought for back in 1776? My grandfather was with Greene at Guilford. He was proud of the fact that he and his fellow patriots asserted their rights as human beings to throw off the yoke of oppression and launch a new nation. Look at the proud history of our founding fathers and tell me that any part of this country doesn't have a right to freedom, the same as they did then."

There was sweat standing out on his brow, both from the pain and the fervor of his feelings on the subject of the south's right to rebel, and Colonel Hughes could see that his questioning of this man was going nowhere. Nor would it favor his tactics if he argued with Abernathy on the subject. He stood up.

"Colonel," he said, "I don't want to upset you. It doesn't do your condition any good to carry this on in confrontation. You have some good arguments, but this is not the time to argue. Perhaps we could resume the discussion at a later time."

"Any time, Colonel," Abernathy said with a grimace. "You know I'm right, and you also probably know that I enjoy winning as I've done just now —. Any time."

As Colonel Hughes left the infirmary, Captain Davis was approaching.

"Oh, Colonel," he said. "I was going in to check on the Rebel prisoner, but I see you've been in there already. How is he doing?"

"He's a tough nut, Captain. I didn't even manage to get a word in edgewise, he was so intent on preaching the cause of secession. The doctor has managed to save both his arm and his leg. But, you know, I've just been thinking. It's surprising to me that Logan didn't kill that man. I thought he was supposed to be a pretty good shot."

Davis smiled. "Colonel, — Logan is a good shot, and we have the prize to prove it. Anyone else would have drilled that rascal, but Logan saw his rank insignia and knew he was worth more to us alive than dead. That man has a lot of valuable information in his head, and it wouldn't do any good to let it die with him. Did you question him at all as to his reason for being in this area?"

It was Colonel Hughes turn to smile. "Captain Davis, it's going to take a better interrogator than I am to get anything out of him. He could see me coming at every approach, and checked my every move. He's a smart one, he is."

No lockup was available at the garrison, and the town jail was not deemed suitable for holding a prisoner of this caliber. A small stable at the rear of the house that Captain Davis occupied was hurriedly reinforced for a jail, but it was not well built in any event. General Tyler had ordered Abernathy's relocation at headquarters at Grafton or Franklin as soon as he was considered capable of making the trip, but that would be nearly a hundred miles.

————))(()((————

Later that day, Olivia sought out Jesse in private. Her manner was depressed, and Jesse figured it had something to do with the shock she had registered when they were talking about Colonel Abernathy.

"Jesse, I — ah — I —," she began, hardly knowing how to start the conversation.

"What's the matter, Libbie?" Jesse asked. "What on earth is going on? Come on, you can level with me. What is it? What's been bothering you?"

"Jesse, I have to tell you something, and I just don't know where to start. It's something awful, and I don't want it to affect our friendship, but I don't see how I can help it."

"Olivia, is there someone else in your life? Is that what you're trying to tell me? Has something happened between us? Have I done something wrong? What is it?"

"Jesse, 'you know that man you captured the other day, that Colonel Abernathy?"

The thought struck Jesse like a thunderbolt. He recalled a conversation they had months before on the road between New Castle and Lewisburg, just after Jesse had escaped from prison and she had mentioned her real name. "Olivia! Colonel Abernathy is your what, — your brother? Your uncle?"

"Jesse, Jedediah Abernathy is my husband."

Jesse was dumfounded. He couldn't believe what he was hearing. His world for over a year had been slowly but surely building around this woman and the thought that they could someday be married had become central in his life. Never had she led him on, but neither had she given him the idea that she was anything but a single woman. She had showed affection, but at times she had demonstrated that affection in a somewhat sisterly way, rather than that of a sweetheart. He had no reason to be angry, but he had every reason to be bewildered and even a little distressed.

"Jesse, let me explain. It was —,"

"Olivia, there's nothing to explain. If you're married, you're married. I don't reckon there's much about that that needs to be explained, is there?" he said with his head down.

"Jesse, can we talk this thing over rationally?' she demanded, grasping his arm. "If you want to write me off as a low down, no-good, lying, deceitful harlot, go right ahead, but there's more at stake here than our relationship. You have in your custody a high-ranking Confederate officer, and I may know more about him than anyone else in this garrison. I might even be able to help you get some good information from him. Don't you think we ought to talk about a strategy?"

"Does she mean she'd turn in her own husband? How can I rely on anything she'd have to say?" Were the first thoughts that entered Jesse's mind, but then he somehow recalled some of the advice Henry Kellar had given him. *"Never speak or act in haste or anger. Look before you leap and listen before you talk."*

"You're not making sense, Olivia, but keep talking. I'm either going to hit you in the mouth, or kiss you in approximately the same place, and I haven't yet made up my mind which it's going to be."

Olivia relaxed a bit. This was the Jesse she knew, — the man who could be both humorous, threatening, and logical at the same time. "First, I have to tell you how this all came about, so you'll understand my thinking."

"I was fifteen when I met Jed Abernathy. He was an itinerant peddler and preacher, and had come to Frederick County with his little side show and stopped for a time to put on a sort of revival. I was absolutely moonstruck. All the ladies from miles around flocked to the meetings he held, and they all came down in front to be 'saved' just to have his hands laid on them. Oh, he was so handsome." As she said the last, Olivia's eyes became misty and a smile played about her mouth.

"He was twenty-nine and I was — as I told you, fifteen. For some reason, he picked me out of the crowd of giddy, giggling women and asked me to stay after the meeting. We went for a long walk in the moonlight and he convinced me he was salvation itself. He seduced me, Jesse. I can't apologize or rationalize. I thought I was in control of my emotions, even at that age, but the man is a spellbinder."

"Somehow, Olivia, I can't picture you as anything but in complete control of your emotions. It's a real revelation to find that somewhere back in time you were just a little vulnerable."

Olivia ignored the comment. Jesse had no idea how committed she was to him, and how she so often longed to yield to his touch, but was restrained by the ghost of Jed Abernathy. "My father discovered our little secret even before Jed got out of town, and saw to it, 'shot gun style', that we were married, and that Jed took me with him as his wife. Papa even went so far as to follow us for a time to see that Jed didn't desert me."

"We traveled through the state of Virginia, mostly, down into Richmond and west to this part of the country, and as far south as Elizabethton, in your part of Tennessee. I won't go into the details of our relationship, but I will say that we were the picture of wedded bliss when we were near a town and people, and when there was no one around, I was subjected to a clear understanding of Hell. When I was about five months pregnant, we got into a fight and I lost the baby as a result of the beating he gave me. I left him in New Castle and stayed a time with Bert Oakley and his wife, Varna, before she died. Then I moved to Richmond and Elizabeth van Lew took me in for a time. I was eighteen when I returned to Frederick County. By that time, my father had died and my mother had gone to live with her uncle and aunt, Beth and George Livingston. You knew Uncle George. He was my partner until he was killed in New Castle."

"So that's how you knew the suttler's trade, and were so familiar with the people in Richmond," Jesse mused.

"Partly, yes, and that's how I knew Bert Oakley and then Betsy van Lew," she supplied, and then continued. "I didn't have any idea that Jed Abernathy was anything but dead, Jesse. I didn't even know he was in the army, much less which one. And when you said his name yesterday, I was shocked, to say the least. I prayed it was a different Jedediah Abernathy, but I saw him when they were moving him from the infirmary, and sure enough, that's my long lost, loving husband."

Jesse took Olivia in his arms, kissed her lightly on the forehead, and held her closely for a long time. "How do you think we should proceed, Libbie? Do you want to confront Abernathy, or keep your presence here a secret? Did he spot you when you saw them taking him to the lockup?" Though he felt great compassion and affection for this girl, his mind was racing ahead, trying to map a direction for dealing with the present situation.

"I don't think he saw me at all, and my personal preference is to stay away from him if I can. It all depends on you and Captain Davis and how you feel we should go with this. How long he is going to stay here is also something we have to think about. I'm not going into seclusion for the likes of that scoundrel. You can bet on that."

They talked for a time about Abernathy, his background, his prejudices and aspirations, and anything either of them could think of to create some kind of conversation starter. Olivia expressed a wish for the fact that she was married to remain secret, unless it would be absolutely necessary for the security of the regiment.

"I'll go talk to Captain Davis and Colonel Hughes," Jesse finally said, "and I'll see what they plan to do with him, but I'll keep your name out of it. It's my understanding that they want to move him as quickly as possible, but I think we should get as much information as we can from him while we have him here. I don't see what it would serve to have you confront him, or even let him know you're in the neighborhood."

―――――««O»»―――――

Jed Abernathy had been placed in the stable behind Company "H" headquarters, and a twenty-four-hour guard had been ordered. Lieutenant Goodin had been placed in charge of the detention and was entrusted with the only key to the huge padlock that was used to secure the door. The cell was a boarded-up horse stall. It was comfortable enough, and accessible to the doctor, as needed, but there was only one key and John Goodin had it. The guards posted at the door had instructions to let no one near the stall, other than Doctor Holcomb, Lieutenants Logan or Goodin, Captain Davis, and Colonel Hughes, and any of those were required to contact Lieutenant Goodin if they wanted to enter the cell.

Abernathy took the whole scenario in good humor, or at least as good as he could muster with a broken arm and badly wounded leg. He expressed amusement at the deference afforded him and chided the guards at the level of security he was subjected to. His manner and conduct were so accommodating that he soon became friends with many of the guards, who stood four-hour watches at the direction of Captain Davis. He claimed he was being given such royal treatment that he may just turn for the North, if they would promise to treat him as well as they had so far.

Jesse and Olivia told no one about the relationship between her and the Rebel colonel, not even Bert Oakley. It was something of a risk keeping the information from Bert, as it had been he and his wife who took Olivia in when Abernathy had abandoned her. Nevertheless, he was not much involved in the activity of Abernathy and his commitment to Olivia was such that it probably wouldn't have made any difference if he'd known.

After Abernathy had been in the lockup three or four days, Jesse went in to talk to him. He had to get the key from Lieutenant Goodin, but the visit was approved by Colonel Hughes, as Goodin well knew.

"Colonel Abernathy, I'm Lieutenant Logan," he said. "Perhaps you remember me from the day you were captured. I know it was not one of your better days, but I'd like to discuss with you the reasons you're here in the valley. We've heard there was a rather high-ranking officer in the valley who's been doing some recruiting. How's it been going for you?"

"So, you're the Yank who engineered my downfall," Abernathy responded with a wry grin. "I'd be lying if I was to say I'm glad to meet you. If I'd had my druthers, we'd still be strangers, but that isn't to be, I reckon. What've you got on your mind, Lieutenant?"

"Oh, I was just wondering how you're feeling, and then, as I said, I was also wondering how the recruiting business was going."

"Of course, you prob'ly know the recruiting was just going great until you showed up. Why, we've picked up almost six hundred new recruits in the past month, and that's just from the hills. We haven't even got down into the valley, yet."

Jesse knew this was a gross exaggeration. He had been working the hills, most of which were strongly pro-union, and had solid information that the

Confederate effort had netted them something in the range of twenty to twenty-five new recruits, even as far south as New Castle. He let the subject pass, however, as it wasn't material to his purpose. The two men sparred for a time, with little information passing between them, but Jesse could see it was having an effect on the colonel. He was showing signs of tension. Logan didn't volunteer the fact that it had been he who was responsible for the death of four of Abernathy's men in the fight in New Castle.

"Would you like a drink of water, Colonel?" he volunteered. "I'm kind of thirsty, myself. By the way, you don't know it, but we've met before. When I was young, my grandpa took me to a camp meeting down in Elizabethton, and you were the main speaker that night. I went down in front and you took my hand, put one hand on my head, and gave me a blessing. I want you to know that the memory of that little meeting has stuck with me my whole life. I've got to say — you're one of my heroes. I truly admire a man of God, and you made a great impression on me that night."

Abernathy was taken aback. He couldn't remember Jesse at all, but for all he knew he was telling the truth, otherwise, no one here knew that he had been a preacher before the war. He turned the comment over in his mind. *"Was this a trick on this Yankee lieutenant's part, or was it perhaps the chance I've been looking for to work out an escape plan. This man is clever, but also, he appears to be in dead earnest and possibly somewhat naive. But how would he have known I had ever been a preacher and in Elizabethton? If I could just manipulate him a little, I could at least find some common ground and give myself an opening to execute a plan to escape."*

His whole manner changed. Again, he was the circuit rider, the itinerant preacher, the spellbinder, who could convince his flock to change their ways and accept the paths of 'the faithful'.

"So you remember me, young man. What was your first name?" he asked in his most solicitous manner.

"It's Jesse, Sir. Jesse Logan."

"Yes, Jesse, I do remember you. You had a thick head of blond curls, and were wearing bib overalls, as I recall," he said shooting in the dark, but on pretty safe ground. "You were with your grandpa, a white-haired man of about, — about seventy, and I do believe your grandma was there. She was wearing a calico dress."

Jesse was overtly impressed. He'd have to have been sixteen or seventeen at the time Abernathy was in Elizabethton, but he let the colonel continue with his contrived fantasy.

"Jesse," the colonel went on, "do you think we could kneel for a moment of prayer?'

"Oh, no, Sir, not now," Jesse quickly responded. "If we was to kneel down here and the captain or one of the guards was to catch us, I'd be drummed out of the company right smart. The captain, he isn't a bit of a God-fearing man, and I'd catch all you-know-what as sure as you're born. But I'll tell you what I'll do. When I go to bed tonight, I'll surely say a prayer for your safety and for your healing. I'm told they'll be sending you up north in a few days and I'd be worried about your injured shoulder and leg. I'm awfully sorry I was the instrument of your capture, but what we all have to do is work these things out between us and God, and if we've done anything wrong, we have to ask for forgiveness. Ain't that right, Colonel?"

He hoped he hadn't overplayed the role of an adoring apostle.

Abernathy mused almost silently, "Forgive us our debts as we forgive our debtors. That's right, Jesse, if we've wronged another person, we have to make it right with them, or God won't forgive us. Besides, I believe I've pretty well established an — ah — an understanding with most of the guards and I don't believe they'd turn you in for such a display of piety. You do understand that, don't you, Son?"

"Yes, Sir, I think I do. But Colonel," Jesse went on, "what was it that made you decide to get into the army from being a preacher? Being a colonel is a pretty high rank. You must have shown some real spark to get that high in just these few short months we've been at war."

"Son, I was up in around Leesburg, and I felt the call of the cause of freedom. I organized a couple of companies of volunteers for that glorious cause, and the government saw fit to appoint me as their colonel. It was the least I could do for my fellow Christians fighting for what they know is right. You know our fathers and grandfathers fought for the cause of freedom; the freedom to exercise our own free wills when it comes to government affairs, and that's my message, pure and simple."

"You certainly make a powerful case for the South, Colonel. Have you been involved much in the fighting?"

"You know, Jesse," Abernathy continued ignoring Logan's question, "the South has every reason and right to secede from an overly dominating government today, just as our forefathers had in 1776. There is nothing in your constitution that places one state government under the control of another, and fighting for our freedom is in our blood. It was Patrick Henry who proclaimed that 'the tree of freedom must, from time to time be nurtured by the blood of tyrants and patriots,' and I'm willing to apply that principle to my own life and am prepared to die for that noble cause."

Logan scratched his head without saying anything. *"He's close,"* he thought, *"but if Mr. Putnam heard him say that he'd have him write a hundred times that that little line was a quote from Thomas Jefferson."*

Abernathy, impressed by his own eloquence, went on to describe some of the battles in which he'd been involved, and the fact that he'd been captured once before, but had escaped. He stopped short of explaining how he'd managed the escape, but let Jesse know it was under very strenuous circumstances. He appealed to Jesse's 'Christian spirit' to consider giving him some freedom of movement about the camp.

Jesse told him that while he favored such a policy personally, he felt it too soon to consider it. He explained that there was quite a stir about the camp because of the presence of such a high-ranking officer, and that he was considered something of a celebrity, but reminded the Rebel colonel that he, himself had just admitted he was an escape risk.

Finally, Jesse got up to leave. He never brought up the compromising situation the colonel had been caught in when he was captured, and was surprised Abernathy hadn't made any excuse for his conduct. His strategy was to let that subject wait for another time, ostensibly giving himself time to reflect on Abernathy's 'message' as to his reasons for taking up the southern cause. The meeting, after Jesse had broached his knowledge of Abernathy's past, had been amiable, if not totally forthright.

The guards had been instructed to remove themselves when anyone was interrogating the colonel. They'd been talking in subdued tones to avoid the guard overhearing the conversation, but now raised their voices a little, to give the guard notice of Jesse's intention to leave. Jesse called for the guard and left the stall, locking the door behind him.

"You don't have to lock me in, do you, Lieutenant? Abernathy called after him. "I thought we'd, well, — built up a bond of trust."

"Colonel, you've described to me in very understandable terms your ability and inclination to escape, and I don't want that responsibility on my head. Lead us not into temptation, Colonel," Jesse responded with a smile. "You wouldn't want me to get in trouble, now, would you?"

"All right," Abernathy replied good-naturedly. "I'm sure we can discuss these things at some later time."

Over the course of the next few days, Jesse devoted much of his time to 'making the colonel comfortable'. It was a dance. Jesse was trying to get as much information on the activities of the Rebels in the upper Shenandoah Valley as he could, and Abernathy was, so far as he could discern, winning a convert to his 'cause' and improving his chances of escape. It was a tedious and trying exercise, for both men, but Jesse had the upper hand. Olivia was verifying much of the information, using Jane Pryor and other sources, while Abernathy could only hope his efforts were producing results. Abernathy became defensive a time or two, as when Jesse brought to him an actual list of the twenty-seven recruits who had gone to the Confederacy, and when that happened Jesse backed off, trying to keep the relationship on a friendly basis. At times Logan managed to get the colonel into discussions about the activities of government, but was seldom able to get him to open up about matters of troop placement, strength, strategy, or where the headquarters of his unit was located. At one point, Logan inquired about the colonel's family, marital status, children, and home life, but Abernathy claimed he'd never been married.

Meanwhile, Abernathy, supposedly unknown to Jesse, was courting another potential convert. Well aware of Jesse's success in having captured Abernathy, and seeing him attending the Rebel's needs on a continuing basis, John Goodin decided to try his own hand at the game of intelligence. If he could possibly win Abernathy's confidence and get some important information, it would not only improve his standing in the eyes of Command, but he might just be able to discredit Jesse in the bargain.

Jed Abernathy was a willing partner. He played Goodin's game with enthusiasm. Sensing the simmering disdain Goodin had for Jesse, he sought every opportunity to drive the wedge deeper. He also knew that John Goodin was keeping to himself their association, and wasn't likely to be passing along any of the information he was being fed, useless though it may be. In other words, if he had given Jesse anything useful, which he didn't think he had, there would never be a verification of information between the two lieutenants. Also, he knew that Lieutenant Goodin had the key to his stall. If he was to make his escape from the stall by means of the door, it was in John Goodin's power to permit or prevent it.

John Goodin, contrary to orders, had carried a written message or two from Abernathy to Jane Pryor, whom he was trying his best to impress. He didn't know why she was important as a contact, but felt it was not important for him to question Abernathy's motives. He felt that the fact that he had her identity as a first little piece of information and a start in the intelligence chain, he might later use it as leverage to extort additional information from the colonel. Though he had read the notes, it profited him not at all. The notes from Abernathy were in code and misleading, and were intended only to test his reliability and to place him in a compromise with his commanders.

The friendship between them matured over the course of the next few weeks, while Abernathy's physical condition steadily improved. Goodin shared with the colonel his disdain for Jesse Logan and the fact that Logan, "strutted about the camp," as a big hero, attracting the admiration of a young woman, an "Olivia", the regimental suttler's daughter. Abernathy sensed some degree of jealousy on Goodin's part over that relationship.

"John," Jed said after he felt that their relationship had been pretty well established, "you know I've been having some conversations with that Jesse Logan. I want you to know, as a friend, that man is no ally of yours. I've been leading him down the primrose path. He hasn't learned anything from me that I didn't want him to know, and everything I've told him is bunk."

"I can tell that you're a man of honor, and I don't mind sharing some of my past with you. You and I are head and shoulders above these mutts and mongrels you have around here in the uniform of the US Army. Even Colonel Hughes is a mutt in my book. You seem more high-born than all these other Yankees, and I think you can understand the cause I've been fighting for is the right one, after all. What do you think would become of these poor dark folks if we were to just turn them loose on society? It would ruin the country, yours and mine, and it would be the ruin of them, too. The south is determined to keep them in their place for as long as it takes to educate them, breed them up, send them home, or whatever is best for them. People in the north don't realize that we're working for the best interests of those dark folk, you know. We should let the north go on its own way and let those of us who understand the problem handle it properly. Don't you agree?"

"You know, Colonel," Goodin said, "Those are my sentiments, exactly. I've never been much in favor of turning those people loose on society, and I tried for the life of me, even before the war, to make people see it that way. I don't have anything against the south for wanting to go their own way. I joined the army to please my father and uncle, who is a big greenhorn in the top command in Illinois. I just don't understand why we can't just call this thing off and go home. It would sure save a lot of money and a lot of lives. You and I have both suffered miserably in this fight, and I'm ready to call it quits. You know, these scars I am burdened with are the work of none other than Jesse Logan. It was in trying to help him learn his job that I was shot and disfigured."

"John, I just wish I could get out of this mess and go back home and work for peace. You know, I was pretty influential back home, and I think I could make those folks listen to me, and also get the word out to the Federal government to back this thing down. The only thing is, we have to get rid of Lincoln. He's the big fly in the ointment. If it weren't for him, I think everyone would stop the fighting."

"I know, I know. I've thought the same thing. He has everyone believing he's the great leader, and he's just a big ape. He has no more brains than that Jesse Logan. They're two of a kind, big and dumb and pig headed." The two men laughed at the comparison.

"John, I have an idea that would get me out of here, get rid of Logan, and maybe get you a promotion for bravery. What do you think?"

"I — ah — I don't know, — ah — Jed. What are you talking about, — you get out of here? You want me to help you escape? How would getting rid of Logan get me promoted? I could get in a whole heap of trouble if you escaped. They hold me responsible for your security here. Both Davis and Hughes made it real clear that I'm the one who has all the responsibility for keeping you in security, at least until you're transferred to Franklin."

"Just hear me out, John. Then, if you don't like the plan, no more will be said. I like you and the way you do business, and I think this plan will serve you well. That ape, Logan is no friend of yours, I can tell you that, and the sooner you get him out of your life, the better off things will be for you. I have an idea that my escape could be seen as resulting from Logan's negligence, and elevate your status in the eyes of the Union command. Just listen to me."

Abernathy laid out an elaborate plan whereby Lieutenant Goodin and Jesse would both come into the stall where he was being held, after dismissing the guards, who at any time were instructed to leave the area for the sake of confidentiality. Once inside, Goodin would let Abernathy snatch his gun, shoot Jesse, and escape, after, "knocking you out, with a blow to the head." Goodin would then, "regain consciousness," sound the alarm, and chase Abernathy, who would have already made good his escape. Meanwhile, Abernathy would give John the name of one of his confederates in Lewisburg, one who was instrumental in helping him escape, and John would be able to have the accomplice arrested for aiding the 'escape'.

"How would that help me get a promotion though, Colonel?" John Goodin inquired, whereupon, Abernathy became noticeably agitated and accused John of selfish motives and lack of foresight. Goodin was confused and embarrassed at not fully understanding the plan but agreed to it if Jed thought it would work. By now, Goodin was seriously compromised by his having carried messages from the Rebel to his outside contacts, and was committed to the game, whether he liked it or not.

"How do you propose to get past the soldiers and guards outside the shed?' Goodin inquired, finally. Though he did not fully understand the plan, he felt it might just accomplish several things that would favor his interests.

"We'll do it at night, but before the camp retires completely. I'll tell you which day we have to carry it off. It has to be a day when one particular guard is on duty. This fellow will do anything I tell him. He's so stupid, he thinks I walk on water," and with that they had another good laugh. "You just leave that part up to me," he confided.

Goodin left, his head swimming. He was now so deep into a nefarious obligation to the Rebel colonel that to proceed with such a plan was probably his only recourse. To get rid of Logan would be reason enough to go along with the plan, but to be a hero in capturing one of Abernathy's outside contacts would not only put him in line for a promotion, but also perhaps help him win the favor of Olivia, especially with Logan out of the way. He mulled the idea over in his head. It was too good to pass up. The more he thought about it, the more he liked it. He went back to the stable again the next day, dismissed the guards, and went into Abernathy's stall. They talked over the plan again, with Jed giving him the name of his outside contact. It was John Pryor, Jane's father. At last Goodin thought he understood the purpose of his carrying the notes to Jane.

That information, of course, was completely false. John Pryor was loyal to the Union.

⸺⫸◉⫷⸺

For Jesse's part, his relationship with Olivia had stalled! How could it be that a woman so desirable, one with whom he was so infatuated, and who, on two occasions he'd had the pleasure and privilege of kissing so tenderly, actually shatter his fondest dreams? He was dumbfounded and distracted. Nevertheless, he steeled himself and continued to perform as before, trying to put the problem out of his mind. He was now a commissioned officer in the United States Army and had a job to do. Neither would he let his feelings interfere with the responsibilities of interrogating the Rebel Colonel, and continuing communication with Olivia was required to confirm some of the information he was gaining in his contacts with the colonel.

Olivia could sense that Jesse's attention toward her had changed, but wisely decided that she would let the matter rest. She had known all along that she was legally trapped, and had dreaded the day when her secret was revealed, as it had just been. Olivia quietly prayed for some sort of resolution to her dilemma, but nothing seemed to present itself.

Jesse's interviews with Abernathy lagged. He was aware that Lieutenant Goodin was spending quite a bit of time with Abernathy, contrary to orders. He shared the information with Captain Davis, but they agreed to ignore that matter, hoping that Goodin would, or could produce some positive results.

One day, having neglected his assignment as Abernathy's interrogator for a few days, Logan got the key to his cell and went in for a questioning, though he didn't have anything particular in mind.

"I want to see my wife," was Abernathy's opening demand. "There is a camp-follower here in the garrison, who happens to be my wife. I demand that you bring her here to me so I can discipline her and send her back to her people. It's my privilege and duty as her husband to correct her conduct and send her away."

"Who are you talking about, Colonel," Jesse asked, uncertain whether the Rebel had any positive information as to Olivia's true identity. "Is it that Pryor woman? She hasn't been anywhere near the camp."

"There is a woman here in camp that uses the name Olivia something-or-other, and she is actually Olivia Abernathy, my wife. I want you to bring her here to me, Lieutenant Logan, immediately!"

Logan was irritated at being addressed in a such a demeaning tone by a prisoner of war, but he maintained his composure. "Well, Colonel, first of all —,"

"I demand to see my wife, Lieutenant," Abernathy said, louder than before. "You've been hiding her from me, haven't you? You've been intimate with the wife of a superior officer. I thought more of you, despite the fact that you're nothing but a damn'd Yankee, and here I find you sporting with a married woman. A fine Christian you are, Logan! A fine upstanding Christian!"

"What's your angle, Colonel? What is this tirade all about? You told me a couple of weeks ago that you'd never been married, and here you suddenly tell me you want to see somebody who you claim to be your wife, and don't even know her name. When I caught up with you, you were rolling in the hay with a single woman, and now you want to act out the part of a righteous husband."

"Logan," Abernathy said, again deliberately omitting any reference to Jesse's rank, "you have been a thorn in my side ever since I got here. You have been stringing me along with that song and dance about being a God-fearing man and for no reason other than to get intelligence information from me. Now the charade is over. You get out there and fetch me my wife."

It was a battle of wills. Abernathy, the older man and holding a higher rank, was testing the resolve and resilience of this man whom he had come to assume may be somewhat inclined to honor his demands. Logan, on the other hand, had no problem resisting the older man's demands, but had been stalling to see if there might be some way of using the Rebel's outrageous behavior to secure some additional information.

He finally decided he was wasting his time. "Colonel, I'd like you to consider this one question. If there were a woman in this town in whom I was romantically interested and I found she was your wife, how long do you think it would take for me to figure a way to quietly snap your neck?" With that, Logan turned and left the cell.

━━━━●((◦))●━━━━

Jane Pryor was a disgraced woman in her family circle. Deny as she may any indiscretions with Abernathy, it was common knowledge that she had ridden almost ten miles from town to meet him and had been caught in a hayloft with him. Abernathy had been seen around the outskirts of Lewisburg for several weeks before his capture, but had never been identified or caught. It was well known that he was scouting the area with several of his soldiers, and yet he was able to avoid capture until now, and he also had been able to establish contact with several southern sympathizers in the region.

The notes John Goodin had been passing to her, she took to a man who owned a grocery store at the south end of town. She didn't ask any questions. She was in enough trouble as it was, but she was also in love with Jed Abernathy, and was desperate to see him released. After she had delivered one of the notes, written in code, to the grocer, Josiah Stepney, he related to her that Abernathy was soon to be 'released' and would contact her as soon as he was out of harm's way. She was ecstatic.

Her father, meanwhile, embarrassed by her behavior, nevertheless tried to reason with Jane, and explain to her that Abernathy had simply been using her. He ordered her, in very direct terms to have nothing more to do with Abernathy or anyone he was associated with. Grudgingly she agreed, but the notes kept coming and she delivered them dutifully, father or no.

Olivia had also been visiting Jane. As women of about the same age, Jane was able to relate to Olivia, particularly when Olivia confided that she was 'in love with a man whom she thought could never care for her', and how she often felt that 'the world was conspiring to prevent her happiness'. She used many of the feelings she had experienced as a younger woman, the desperation, heartache, hopelessness, and despair she had known, and related her thoughts to those Jane was experiencing.

Jane took Olivia into her confidence. She was at a point that she felt she had no one to turn to, and Olivia represented a kindred spirit who offered no advice, no judgment, no reprisals, just a kind, willing listener, ready to hug her, hold her hand, and be a friend.

Without a second thought, Jane told Olivia of several contacts, including Josiah Stepney, who Jed Abernathy had guided her to and who, she thought, was working to help free him from his jail.

Despite the intrigue of the drama she was involved in, Olivia's days had lost their luster. Her friendship with Jesse had suddenly become nothing more than a working relationship, and the marriage to which she was bound would not go away. She found no compelling purpose in making one of her periodic expeditions to Richmond, as her supply of contraband was insufficient to justify such a venture. Business in the suttler's store was slow as there were stores in Lewiston that could supply much of the merchandise she ordinarily dealt in.

A day or two after Jesse's confrontation with the Rebel Colonel, he went to the small house Olivia and Bert were using as a store. It was after regular business hours, and Jesse went to inform her of the matter of the Colonel's demands.

Jesse knocked at the closed door of the store and Olivia answered it almost immediately. "Why, Lieutenant Logan, what a surprise. What can I do for you?"

"Olivia, I have to talk to you. Something has come up that you should know about. Night before last I went to talk to the colonel and he immediately started ranting about wanting to see 'his wife' to discipline her as to her conduct, and on and on. He really got loud and demanding. I don't think he really has any firm belief that his wife is in camp, but he has a first name only, and seemed to assume that it is actually someone here in camp. He's been talking to John Goodin, and probably got some information from him or one of the guards."

"Come on inside, please, Jesse," she said. "I don't think we should be discussing this out here on the porch."

Jesse glanced over his shoulder, "What will the neighbors think, Ma'am?" He inquired in his customary humorous manner, "Is Bert here?"

"No, he's gone down to New Castle for a day or two, and 'the neighbors' can think whatever they want to."

They went inside the store, and then went on into the living quarters Olivia occupied. "Jesse, what's this all about? I have no interest in anything that man says. He means nothing to me, and I don't dance to his tune. What did he want?"

"He just went on, as I say, about wanting to see his wife. I get the idea he was just angling for some sort of advantage to devise an escape plan. He accused me of intimacy with you behind his back, or something like that."

"Alright, what did you tell him?"

Jesse grinned, "I told him to carefully consider his accusations, because if I were romantically interested in a woman whom I thought to be his wife I'd probably be looking for a quick way to do him in."

"Would you really do that, Jesse?" she asked softly. By this time they were standing face to face, not more than an inch apart. "Would you really 'do him in' just so you could have me all to yourself?"

Jesse's heart was pounding. His free testosterone had immediately concentrated in his lower groin.

"Olivia," he said taking her hands in his, "you know you're making things awfully hard for me, don't you?"

⸺⸺◈⸺⸺

John Goodin turned the escape plan over and over in his head. It was a good plan, but he felt he could improve on it, giving himself an even better position in the eyes of the army. Also, he thought to himself, *"What if Abernathy, after shooting Logan would turn the gun on me?"* Somehow it occurred to him that perhaps, just perhaps, Abernathy wasn't being completely honest as to his full intentions. *"If the Reb really had some help from the outside, he wouldn't need me around, and if I was able to tell them who his outside contacts are, he'd be better off if I was dead."*

If he could simply go with Logan as planned into the stall, let Abernathy get his weapon and shoot Logan, then he, John Goodin, could overcome Abernathy and come out a hero without being 'knocked out' and without the risk of betrayal on Abernathy's part. To do that, he would need some guarantees, first; that Abernathy wouldn't be fast enough with Goodin's gun to shoot both Logan and him, before he could overcome the colonel. And second, he would need a back-up gun to get the drop on Abernathy. 'Good plan!

"Wait a minute! Wouldn't it be better if the gun I let Abernathy snatch from my belt had only one round in the cylinder? There would be a shot for Logan, and I'd have some assurance that I could 'recapture' Abernathy with no trouble. Suppose Logan weren't killed, (Abernathy would be using his left hand) well, that's a chance I'll have to take. I'd still come out the winner

and would likely attain a better standing in the eyes of Colonel Hughes, whether Abernathy knocks out the competition or not. Then, if I have to shoot Abernathy to keep him from escaping, well, all the better. I might just shoot him anyway."

John Goodin, making sure his regular revolver was loaded with only one ball, dug out the little boot gun he kept in his bag, saw that it was loaded, and waited. For two days he went to visit the prisoner, 'but the time was not right'. Finally, on the third day after they had spoken of the plan, Abernathy announced that that evening they would pull it off.

"Do you have your revolver loaded, John," he asked. "What if Logan objects to your bringing it with you into the stall? He doesn't ever bring his in when he comes to see me."

"Don't worry. I'll tell him I will be only a minute, and if he kicks up too big a fuss, we'll just call it off and work out a new plan," Goodin said casually, trying to sound as though he was prepared for any eventuality. "I'll insist, but we can work out something else if he gets too suspicious. I know that snake pretty well, and we don't want to give him any cause to be on his guard if we can avoid it. I don't want him bringing his gun inside. He's got a reputation of being a pretty good shot. I want all the stakes to be on our side for this game."

"Alright, you may be right. We have to play this thing down as though it's just routine."

That evening, Goodin went to Jesse's tent after he was sure Jesse had removed his gun belt. "I say, Logan, that prisoner wants to talk to you. He just asked me to fetch you about something. He says it's really important."

"What now?" Jesse muttered. "Does it have to be tonight? I was just going over to talk to the captain. Well, I guess that can wait. If Abernathy has anything important to say, it would be better if I'd talk to him first."

They went to the shed where the prisoner was kept. Billy Miller was the guard whom Goodin was supposed to 'dismiss', but Goodin knew Jesse would be suspicious if that happened, and simply ordered him to step well outside the shed, as usual. Goodin's hands were shaking as he unlocked the stall door.

"You ought to leave your weapon with Miller," Jesse admonished.

"I would, but I won't be staying inside with you two, so it'll be alright for now," Goodin had worked out an answer, but stepped inside, anyway.

"Colonel," Jesse began, "Lieutenant Goodin said you had something to tell me."

Immediately Abernathy jumped to his feet and started ranting about losing confidence in Jesse and the fact that he'd expected better treatment.

He brought up the matter of wanting to see 'his wife', complained that the guards were mistreating him and that it was all Jesse's fault. His tirade was an effort to create sufficient distraction to be able to get close to Goodin to get his gun. Jesse, who had walked well into the room, became immediately suspicious. Goodin was not even supposed to be involved in any interrogation, and yet, here he was, and still armed. Logan began moving in John Goodin's direction to prevent Abernathy from getting too close, but when he did, Lieutenant Goodin moved farther toward the prisoner. Suddenly, obvious to Jesse that it had been planned, Abernathy grabbed Goodin's gun with his left hand, pushing him away. He cocked the revolver, a little awkwardly, and fired in John Goodin's direction, hitting him in the lower left side, and then turning the gun on Jesse. John Goodin didn't have a chance to get the boot gun out of his pocket, much less cock or fire it. He collapsed immediately.

Jed Abernathy smiled, "Logan, I'm glad you're a good Christian, because you're about to meet your maker, and I'd hate to see a nice fellow like you go to Hell."

Jesse had instinctively jumped back, but now he was looking at the business end of the stolen gun. The light of the two lanterns in the stall showed bright against the front of the cylinder of the revolver and he could see that all the chambers of the gun were empty. His expression of alarm turned to relief as he smiled back at Abernathy, "Colonel, give me the gun. Neither of us is going anywhere. The gun is empty. Your friend double crossed you."

Abernathy drew back the hammer and pulled the trigger. "Bap!" The cap fired, but there was no powder in the chamber.

He tried it again. "Bap," it went again.

Colonel Abernathy raised the gun as if to use it as a club, but Jesse charged with his shoulder, knocking the colonel against the wall of the stall. Abernathy screamed from pain as his right shoulder struck the wall. He doubled over holding his injured shoulder with his now empty left hand. As he did, John Goodin rolled to one side and pulled the boot gun from his jacket pocket. Jesse caught the action out of the corner of his eye. The only move available to him was to kick out at Goodin's wrist, sending the gun flying. It bounced against the wall and landed a few feet from where Abernathy was huddled. Goodin and Abernathy watched helplessly as Jesse went over and picked up both of the guns, just as Billy Miller rushed through the door of the stall.

"This little escapade must have taken you two several days to cook up, Preacher," Jesse said a little sadly. Then, addressing Miller and taking the key from Goodin's pocket, he said, "Miller, we'd better get this man to the infirmary," pointing to Goodin.

"What about me? I've got an injured shoulder," Abernathy cried.

"First things first, Colonel. We'll get to you in good time. You won't die. Billy, maybe you'd better get some help. I'll watch the prisoner."

When Miller had left, Jesse turned to Abernathy. "Whose Idea was this, Colonel? What did John Goodin offer you to make you fall for such a scheme?"

"Apparently there's some girl he thinks you have eyes for, and he talked me into getting you out of the way so's he could have her to himself."

"Then why'd you shoot him instead of just shooting me? You didn't know he'd short-loaded that revolver, did you? Where's your sense of loyalty, Colonel? You were going to get us both out of the way, but you suspected Goodin was carrying that hideout pistol and you weren't taking any chances. Isn't that right?"

Abernathy hesitated, a faint smile playing across his lips. "Sounds like you got everything figured out, Lieutenant. So, what're you gonna do, shoot me?"

"You don't know what a good idea that is, Reb," Jesse replied in disgust. "You just don't know how good that sounds about now, but no. I'm not going to shoot you. You've been more helpful to us than you'll ever know, Preacher. We've nailed down five of your contacts, including Mr. Stepney, who was waiting for you this evening, and that fellow Forsythe, the court clerk, and three others. They'll be charged with spying and conspiracy to aid an escape, with you and John Goodin, and will probably be hung."

Jesse was bluffing. Only Stepney and Forsythe were in custody. They had been identified through the efforts of Olivia, and picked up on unspecified charges outside the camp earlier in the evening, leading an extra horse. Several other conspirators had been identified and would be sought in the next few days, provided they didn't flee south.

"You really did get your friends into some hot water, Colonel. We didn't know what those two were up to this evening when we picked them up, but you just completed the puzzle."

There were three soldiers beside Sergeant Hawkins who had just come into the shed. Hawkins came over to Jesse and asked what had happened.

"I want you fellows to see to it that Lieutenant Goodin is well cared for. We're going to need his testimony to help convict those other conspirators. If he dies, then the only one we can hang will be this one here," he said nodding in the direction of the colonel, "and he's the one we need the most."

After the stretcher had left bearing Lieutenant Goodin, Jesse turned to Colonel Abernathy. "Now, you try to get some rest, Colonel. The doctor will be busy with Lieutenant Goodin and probably won't have time for you for a few hours. We'll let you know when he can see you."

"Lieutenant, I'm in severe pain," he said in despair, "isn't there another doctor nearby?"

"Colonel, I have a lot of work to do, and I don't feel I can go chasing down another doctor at this hour of the night. I'll talk to the captain, but I'm afraid you're just going to have to be patient." His mood was sour by this time. This man had just tried to kill him in cold blood, and was now begging for mercy, and Jesse had work laid out ahead of him that would probably take till morning to complete.

Without another word he left the stall, locking it behind him and pocketing the key.

18

GREENBRIAR RIVER

The transportation squad was on the trail at 6 o'clock in the morning. Lieutenant Logan was nervous about their chances, but he felt the preparations had been satisfactory and the secrecy had been adequately maintained. He and Sergeant Lige Hawkins had discussed the trip at great length, and Logan was confident in Lige's ability to handle the details of the one-hundred-mile trip. They had secured Abernathy by leg-irons, and two pair of modified shackles on his wrists, necessitated by his still-disabled and painful right arm. Dr. Holcomb examined the arm the night before, and pronounced it sound, but Abernathy complained, nevertheless that the 'positioning' of his arm was causing him great discomfort.

Hawkins would be mounted, as would seven others in the squad, with four men occupying the seats of the two wagons they would use. One of the wagons was a spring wagon, fitted with a canopy and an extra seat in the rear bed. The other wagon was a light cargo wagon, used for supplies, food, grain for the horses, and personal items such as bedding, rain gear, and extra clothing. The men were armed with shotguns and carbines, about equally distributed among both those on horseback and the men on the wagons.

The route the squad would follow would be north along the Greenbriar River almost to its source, which would put them onto the Parkersburg-Staunton Turnpike. A branch of the turnpike would then take them to Grafton where the Seventh Ohio was headquartered. It was a tortuous and winding trail, but Captain Davis felt it would be safer than any of the more eastern routes, vulnerable to Confederate attack.

The trip started well enough, but about ten miles out, up the Greenbriar River, the cargo wagon broke a wheel. Sergeant Hawkins was familiar with the area, having made several scouting expeditions through the region, and promptly persuaded a local farmer to lend him a larger wagon, and the trip continued, albeit at a slightly slower pace.

After the convoy left Lewisburg, Lieutenant Logan returned to Company "H" Headquarters to catch up on his reports and, about noon, he went into town to the hotel operated by John Pryor, and ordered lunch. Pryor was in the hotel office and observing Jesse's presence, joined him with a plate of pot roast of his own.

"Hello, Lieutenant, I see you got Abernathy on the road at last." Pryor remarked.

Jesse looked surprised. "Word certainly travels fast here in Lewisburg," he replied. "We only just sent him off and already the whole town knows about it."

"Lieutenant, there were two men in here last night and I overheard a conversation that could only have meant those two were well aware of your shipping him out today, It was that Cartin fella an' another guy, and when they looked over and got the idea I was listenin', they just got up and scooted out the door. It's the way the acoustics are in this room, when someone sitting at that table is talking, an' —," Pryor went on, but Logan wasn't interested in acoustics. He immediately stood up, finished his coffee, dropped a half-dollar on the table and left.

"John, I have to go. 'Sorry." Logan said, as he left the hotel, got on his horse, and headed east, passing the compound where Company "H" was bivouacked. He stopped at the access road to the compound and hailed a sentry. Returning the man's salute, Logan said, "Soldier, would you get back to Company "H" and tell the captain, Captain Davis, that Lieutenant Logan has gone to try to catch up with the transport detail? Tell him I just got some news that might jeopardize our security, but I think I can head it off. 'Got that?"

"Yes, Sir. Are you Lieutenant Logan?"

"I am, and it's kind'a urgent, so please make it quick."

"I'm on my way, Lieutenant," and turning to another of the sentries, he told the other man to notify their corporal of his mission, and started off on a run toward Company "H".

David Cartin and his partner Joseph Levelton, who was a 'confidential agent' with the Confederate Army, left Lewiston shortly after the squad transporting Colonel Abernathy pulled out of the garrison. They trailed the convoy for a mile or two to determine the route they would take. Satisfied the squad would be following the Greenbriar River, they settled on a plan. There were too many of the Federal soldiers to try a head-on attack, so they decided on one of their other prepared plans. They would wait until the squad stopped for the night, and, when the soldiers were watering the horses, Cartin would frighten the horses when they were at the river, to create some confusion, and Levelton would help free Abernathy.

The plan was 'Number 3' on a list that Jane Pryor had obtained from John Goodin weeks earlier. The only trick was to communicate to Abernathy which of their four prospective plans they would try. The two Rebels planned to overtake the wagons, signal Abernathy as to their choice of escape attempts, and ride on ahead, keeping in remote touch with the transport squad.

———⋯((◉))⋯———

After exchanging wagons with the farmer and promising to return the man's wagon as quickly as possible, Sergeant Hawkins and the transport squad proceeded on a rather dull journey, encountering hardly anyone on the trail except two riders who showed little interest in the group of soldiers, but in passing the ambulance, both of the men surreptitiously displayed three fingers. Abernathy nodded.

The wagon train had progressed about twenty-five miles up the Greenbriar River when late-afternoon, one of the traces on the freight wagon broke, delaying the progress, even further. Sergeant Hawkins, again, was prepared for such minor inconveniences, and had two of the soldiers who had skills in such work, repair the leather trace.

By that time, the men were ready to call it a day, and Hawkins agreed. They selected a small field about seventy-five feet back away from the river and prepared to settle down for the night. This involved simply unhitching the horses, taking them down to the river to drink, and tethering them about the grassy field for the night. They would grain the horses the next morning before setting off again for the north. Any of the soldiers not involved in tethering the horses were to prepare the potatoes and salt-pork for the evening meal. One man, Paul Kingly, was detailed to guard the

Rebel colonel. Two-man teams were assigned for guard duty throughout the night, in three-hour watches.

———⫸⫷((●))⫸⫷———

Like Lige Hawkins, Jesse Logan had spent weeks scouting the region, mostly south of Lewisburg, but enough of the time north of the town to have a working familiarity with the country and be aware of a few short cuts that the wagons couldn't negotiate. Also, his horse was faster than the wagons could travel, and he thought he just might be able to catch the transport squad before nightfall. He urged Bob into an easy lope the first half-mile, then slowed to a fast walk, taking advantage of as many of the short cuts as he could remember, and when it was advantageous to follow the primary road, he did so, keeping up a fast pace. By late afternoon, as he was descending from one of his short cuts, Bob was tiring, but presently, he nickered, as though sensing the presence of other horses.

At the same time, Jesse could hear voices up-river a short distance. There seemed to be a great deal of shouting and confusion. He dismounted, tied his horse to a tree, and proceeded cautiously toward the noise. He had gone only a short distance when, through the underbrush ahead of him, he saw the figure of a man wading across a small stream that flowed into the Greenbriar River. It was Abernathy! The Rebel colonel was without shackles, and well out away from the squad with no guard, apparently having escaped his captors. He seemed to be looking for an accomplice, as every few steps he would stop and search the surrounding woods, but he had not noticed Logan, standing only ten or fifteen yards up the hill. Logan backed cautiously behind some dense brush and waited. It seemed as though the colonel might walk up the hill to where Jesse was concealed, but after a few steps, he altered his direction more on a line parallel with the Greenbriar River, and proceeded slowly, walking without any sign of a limp.

Jesse had left Bob tied only a short distance from where the colonel was walking, and he knew, though Abernathy still had the injured shoulder, that he would probably be able to mount the horse and escape. He started down the hill after Abernathy.

Logan's movement through the underbrush alerted the Rebel, but he simply stopped and inquired in a hushed voice, "Is that you, Levelton?"

"No, Colonel," Jesse said, now approaching the colonel within a few steps, "it's only me; Jesse Logan."

Abernathy was surprised, but was not without recourse. In escaping from his guards he had slipped into the underbrush when Private Kingly was distracted by noises along the river. Then, when Kingly had pursued him into the woods, Abernathy had managed to pick up a fallen tree branch and disable him, whereupon he snatched a bowie knife from Kingly's belt before rushing on into the woods. If he could get close enough, he could draw the knife and use it against Logan who, unaware Abernathy was armed, had not drawn his own weapon.

As the two men closed on one another, Abernathy said in a resigned voice, "Well, Lieutenant, I suppose my efforts were —," whereupon he suddenly drew the bowie knife and lunged at Jesse. He still had the injured shoulder and had to use his left hand in the assault, but was close enough so that Logan didn't have time to draw his revolver. Logan avoided the thrust, however, and spun the colonel around. He seized the colonel's left wrist and wrapped his right arm around Abernathy's throat to apply the 'sleeper hold' he'd learned from his old friend, Fall.

Properly applied, the 'sleeper hold' maneuver will interrupt the blood-flow in the carotid arteries, cutting off the oxygen to the brain and rendering the subject temporarily unconscious. Improperly applied, it can fracture the hyoid bone in the throat, causing swelling of the larynx and a deprivation of air to the lungs, resulting in strangulation and death.

Logan did it wrong.

The colonel fell at Jesse's feet, unconscious, but then, after about thirty seconds, his eyes opened wide in horror. He gasped faintly and held a hand to his throat, his lungs striving desperately for air.

Then his eyes closed.

Logan waited a moment, then bent down and shook the man's shoulder. There was no response. He walked over to where Bob was tied and got his canteen. Returning to the prone body he splashed a little water in the man's face. No reaction! Abernathy was dead!

Jesse was bewildered. Fall hadn't mentioned that a person had to use extreme caution in applying the hold, and Logan couldn't quite grasp the enormity of what he had done. His intent had been to disable the man, even though Abernathy's obvious intent had been more lethal. He stood and thought for a moment, suppressing a strong urge to say something like, *"By the way, Colonel, I took your suggestion and slept with your wife, the other night."*

Jesse got back on his horse and rode toward the commotion along the river. As he approached, two Union soldiers came riding in his direction, looking for the escaped prisoner.

"Lieutenant Logan," one of the horsemen said in surprise. 'Where did you come from? That colonel, the one we were taking to Grafton, he escaped!"

Logan held up a hand to stop the progress of the two soldiers. "He's back there on the ground, just across that little creek. You'll find him. He's just back there a ways," thumbing in the direction from where he had just ridden. He then rode on into camp and sought out Lige Hawkins, who was trying to control the pandemonium.

Hawkins saw Jesse coming and looked momentarily deflated. He wasn't one to try to dodge responsibility, however, and approached Jesse directly. "Lieutenant, I don't suppose I need to tell you what just happened. I know we talked this thing over and over, and I thought I had it under control, but that rascal got away. He said he had to take a crap and slipped into the woods when some kind of a commotion started down by the river. Somehow he got away. I have a search going, and we arrested the guy that started the big fuss down there, but I still don't know how he did it."

"Call off the search, Lige. I killed him." Jesse said with resignation. "I didn't mean to, but I caught him out there in the woods and killed him."

In the process of the search two of the other soldiers located Joseph Levelton lurking in the underbrush, and recognizing him from their earlier encounter that day, they brought him in to be questioned. They escorted him to where Sergeant Hawkins and Lieutenant Logan were talking.

"Who's this?" Hawkins inquired.

"Sergeant, this man is Joseph Levelton. He was riding with that fella Cartin, back down there just outta Lewisburg. We remember him from when they passed us down there. I was kinda watching them when they rode by us, and both of 'em, when they went by the ambulance where that colonel was ridin', they gave a funny kind of a sign, with three fingers they held down by their leg. Both of 'em."

"This man doesn't know what he's talkin' about," Levelton said in a dismissive tone. "I got a bum lef' hand an' my little finger curls under like that all the time. I was jes' ridin' along wif' that other fella. I don' know what he was doin' here. I jes' met up wif' him back down the trail and we d'cided to ride together."

"Then what were you doing with Cartin when I saw you two men at the hotel last night?" Logan demanded, bluffing.

Levelton looked bewildered. He was trapped. He didn't recall having seen Logan or anyone else in uniform at the hotel, yet he was confronted with the truth, and didn't know which way to turn. Denial would be risky. Silence would be inculpating, and if Logan had actually seen the two men together, it would have been at such a distance that he wouldn't have known what their conversation had been all about. Levelton decided to try admitting the meeting as a casual and accidental encounter.

"Oh yeah, I did run into that fella las' night at the hotel, an' then we run into each other this mornin' an' reckoned we'd ride t'gether," Levelton explained.

"Lock him up, Sergeant," Logan ordered. "We've got ourselves a lynching and a conspiracy. When I caught Abernathy out there in the woods, the first thing he did was to call out Levelton's name."

Levelton, who was standing unsecured this whole time, suddenly turned and started running toward the river, but immediately tripped over a half-buried log behind him. The two soldiers who had been instrumental in his capture fell on him and wrestled him into submission.

The leg irons that had been used on Abernathy were now used to secure Levelton and Cartin leg-to-leg, and Sergeant Hawkins, having used two pair of manacles to make Abernathy a little more comfortable, had just enough to restrain the wrists of the two conspirators.

⸻ ⸱«⟨●⟩»⸱ ⸻

Dinner was consumed, horses were tethered, guards were scheduled and assigned, and everyone was made comfortable for a night's rest. The two prisoners were anchored at one edge of the clearing, with guards stationed nearby. Campfires were positioned randomly around the field, and Jesse found enough spare bedding to make a reasonable bed on the ground near Hawkins and one of the fires. He lay down, but couldn't sleep. Reflections of his activities and emotions of the past few days drifted end-to-end through his mind for about an hour, before he got up and went over to the campfire where Hawkins was sitting.

"Quite a day, Lige," Jesse said quietly. "I was nervous about this whole thing, this morning, but I suppose, all-in-all everything turned out okay."

"Me, too, Jesse," Lige Hawkins responded. "There I was, worrying about the break-downs we were having with the wagons, and, if it hadn't been for Bromfeld and Anderson, spotting the little signals between Levelton and Abernathy back on the trail, and your having spotted them at the hotel las' night, we'd be scratching our heads as to what happened."

Logan held his finger up to his lips, "Shhh, I wasn't even at the hotel, last night. That was a bluff but it worked! I just got that news from John Pryor.

He saw these two with their heads together at the hotel last night an' told me about them."

Hawkins put his hand over his mouth, looking surprised, but immediately changed the subject. "It looks like what happened back there was that those two came riding past us on the road just out of Lewiston, and made some kind of a sign to let Abernathy know what they were doin', an' all. Then, when we stopped for the night, he complained about having to take a crap, an' we took the irons off him. In the meantime, Cartin was down by the river an' scared the horses we'd taken down there to water, an' Abernathy made it into the underbrush fast enough so as Kingly missed him, completely, an' I reckon he knocked Kingly out an' stole his knife, when Kingly went out after him."

"So, that's where he got the knife he came after me with," Logan speculated. "You know, Lige, I was really ashamed of myself for killing him, but when you think about it, he prob'ly got what was comin' to him."

19

CORINTH 1862

The following morning, Logan and Sergeant Hawkins again discussed their next move. Abernathy was dead and they had two new prisoners; David Cartin and Joseph Levelton, to deal with. They felt it was best to take them on to Grafton and turn them over to General Tyler for disposition. They had spent a great deal of time on the detention and questioning of Abernathy and, in addition to the dispatches that were to be delivered, it seemed a better idea than to take the two conspirators back to Lewisburg. Lieutenant Logan and three of the men would deliver them to Grafton with their report and Sergeant Hawkins would return to Lewisburg and report to Captain Davis, and also return the supply-wagon they had commandeered along the way.

Cartin and Levelton were put into the ambulance and shackled, and Logan and the three soldiers started north with them In custody, a two-day ride. The trip was without incident, except for the fact that Cartin seemed willing to cooperate with the lieutenant's casual but persistent questioning and provided considerable information about the Rebel activities. After being reminded they were not only spies, but were also implicated in the lynching of a prisoner and in an excellent position to be hanged, if convicted, Cartin became a virtual songbird, but Levelton remained mute. When they stopped the first night, Logan spent several hours questioning Cartin and taking notes. He was forthcoming in such information as numbers, command, recruitment efforts, and even knew a little of the plans General Braxton Bragg had for invading Kentucky.

When the squad got to Grafton, Jesse went directly to regiment headquarters to submit his report to General Tyler, who greeted him warmly.

"My, you came on up here in good time, Lieutenant," General Tyler remarked. "I didn't expect to see you for two or three days." Logan didn't quite understand the implication of the comment, but went on to discuss the subject of the death of Abernathy and the capture of what appeared to be two conspirators in his escape attempt. He reluctantly discussed his part in Abernathy's demise, though he didn't feel he was in any way subject to criticism, except that Abernathy was the husband of a woman for whom he felt considerable affection.

After discussing the report for a few minutes, General Tyler reiterated the fact that Logan had been expected at Regiment in response to a wire that General Tyler had received from General Jeremiah Sullivan requesting Logan's services in western Tennessee.

"General Sullivan lost his adjutant recently and was authorized to name a replacement. It appears you're the man he chose for the job. Orders are written and all you have to do is head on up to the railroad station and catch the next train heading west. I assumed you were here in response to the wire I forwarded to you down in Lewisburg, but I reckon it missed you. Are you willing to take the job?"

The idea took Jesse completely by surprise and at first, he didn't know how to respond. So far as Jesse had known, General Sullivan had been with General McClellan on the campaign on the James Peninsula, but now it appeared that he'd been with General Halleck and General Rosecrans fighting along the Mississippi River.

The wire had probably just missed him when he struck out for the north to catch up with the squad transporting Abernathy. He'd been out of touch with headquarters for three days, and it appeared that there had been a lot going on while he was thus engaged. He thought of Olivia and the fact that he'd not even said anything to her about his going off after the transport squad. Now he was being asked to leave the regiment for good and wouldn't even have a chance to say goodbye.

"Well, General," he said after some thought," I kind of hate to leave my old regiment, but I know General Sullivan really well and would be happy to go to work for him."

"You should know, Lieutenant," General Tyler broke Jesse's train of thought, "that the assignment to adjutant carries with it a promotion to captain. That was included in the wire I sent."

Jesse was shocked and a little embarrassed. The events of the past year and a half passed before his eyes. He'd joined the army to take part in what he perceived as an adventure and a chance to see some of the country. Now he was torn between love and duty in the purest sense of the term. Promotion hadn't been at all on Jesse's mind when he joined the army, but as his term of duty and his experience progressed, he had visions of the service he might be to the army if he were given an opportunity to advance in rank. Now the chance presented itself and he was hesitating. *"What would Olivia recommend? If she were standing here right now, what would she say?"*

There was no doubt in Jesse's mind that Olivia would tell him to go. She was as committed as he was to getting this war behind them and perhaps, just perhaps, the promotion would put him in a position to do some good. Besides, Logan thought the news of his promotion would be good news to Olivia, just because it was a promotion.

"Of course I'll go, General," he said with what he hoped was the voice of certainty.

"I thought you'd say that, Logan. In fact, your orders are already cut and you'd have to refuse to obey a direct order if you hadn't. Congratulations, my boy, you won't regret this decision, I'm positive."

Jesse wasn't so sure. He hurriedly penned a note to Olivia and placed it in an envelope, which he then put into the bag that was to be returned to Captain Davis. Frank would certainly be able to explain to Olivia the urgency of the situation and the opportunity for Jesse to further his career. Meanwhile, it was necessary for Jesse to draw an extra uniform and secure captain's shoulder bars to replace the lieutenant's bars he'd been wearing. He also had to draw new equipment. Except the tack he'd had for his horse and the weapons he was carrying when he rode out of Lewisburg. He was totally unprepared for such a trip or assignment.

————)((•)) ————

It was a three-day trip for the two soldiers who had accompanied Jesse to Franklin to get back to Lewisburg. In the meantime, Captain Davis had let it be known in camp that Jesse was not to be returning to Company "H", and the reasons. At first, Olivia was shocked and a little angered that Jesse would ride off on this wild goose chase without even telling her about it. It was typical Jesse Logan, thinking in the saddle. It had got him in trouble with Lieutenant Goodin when he'd been a corporal, but with all his shortcomings, he usually came out on top.

"Please, don't take this so hard, Miss Livingston." Captain Davis advised her. "I got this wire from Regiment at Franklin last Monday, and it was primarily addressed to Lieutenant — or now Captain Logan, ordering him to Franklin to take a new assignment as adjutant to General Sullivan. I didn't realize that his presence here at Lewisburg was of such interest to you. He did send along a letter which will probably explain his situation better than I could."

Olivia opened the letter.

Dear Miss Livingston,

This letter will probably come as something of a surprise to you. Believe me when I say that the content and import hereof was as much a surprise to me.

I left in something of a hurry, last week, after finding out about plans on Col. A's part to escape from the escort we had sent along with him to Hdq. at Grafton. The information came by way of J. Pryor when I stopped to see him. I caught up with the escort that night, only to find that Col. A. had indeed escaped, but only made it so far as the river, a few yards from their camp, and died in his attempt to flee.

I know this will come as a shock to you, and I've tried to think of a gentle way to tell you, but the only way I could think of was by this missive.

Two confederates of the Col., Mr. David Cartin, and Mr. J. Levelton were captured during the escape attempt and I continued on to Franklin to deliver them to Hdq., where I met with Gnl. Tyler. He advised me our old friend. Gnl. Sullivan had offered to have me assume a position with his staff, and I was in no position to refuse.

Olivia, please be happy for me. While I grieve at the prospect of not seeing you for a time, remember that I've expressed my feelings toward you over and over, and I assure you they haven't changed. Had I found a better way to handle this problem (that of not seeing you again for who knows how long) please believe I should have done so willingly. You are constantly on my mind, and I shall return as soon as I have a chance and perhaps we can marry as I have asked you to do repeatedly in the past and by this letter, I am again asking you to be my wife.

Time is short. I must be preparing for the trip west. Please know you have my warmest regards and ardent feelings.

Your obt. servant.

Jesse Logan, Capt., USA

Olivia was still stunned, but her dismay was now mixed with pride. The man she had fallen in love with as a corporal was now a captain in the United States Army, and the marriage that had festered so bitterly in her heart for so many years no longer held her in its clutches. She was a free woman.

Lieutenant John Goodin, slowly recovering from his wounds, was heartened by the news that Jesse wouldn't be returning to Lewisburg. Not only would he have Olivia to himself, now there would be no Jesse Logan in the company to provide damaging testimony in any trial he might be put to. Goodin realized that his family connections would be limited in protecting him from prosecution, and though the fact that Jesse had been promoted to the rank of captain was certainly a bitter pill, his transfer out of the Seventh Ohio was some relief. He wondered at his good fortune.

Included in the wire Captain Davis had received were the final orders to pull the garrison back from Lewisburg to Franklin. The regiment was being reassigned to Winchester, as there was need to consolidate forces in such a way that they would be available to protect the capitol. The urgency so apparent on the part of the president to occupy the East Tennessee area was again put aside for more pressing business.

⸺◄(●)►⸻

The day after Jesse had delivered the prisoner at Grafton he left for the west. He rode his horse as far as the station where he caught a train for Louisville, Kentucky. There was a stock car assigned to the transportation of horses on the train and Jesse unsaddled Bob and loaded him onto the car. Since Jesse had obtained the horse at New Castle, no one else had ridden him, at least not for long, and they had become constant companions.

The trip to Corinth, Mississippi, where General Sullivan was stationed was fairly smooth, except that on the second day, just after the train had left Louisville, Kentucky, it was halted at the Green River, Kentucky, by a bridge that had been destroyed by a Confederate raid. The Federals were back in control of the track, but the raid had done its job. The bridge had been almost a quarter of a mile long and over a hundred feet high at the center, and it would be some time before the supply line it provided would be restored to service.

It was necessary for those who could and who wanted to proceed, to get off that train, cross the river by whatever means they had at their disposal, and then get onto a second train waiting on the other side. Fortunately, the trains both carried ramps to facilitate the unloading and loading of the horses, and Jesse's crossing of the river was considerably less inconvenient than some of the other passengers.

Captain Logan arrived in Corinth, Mississippi on September 29, 1862. On his arrival, General Sullivan immediately set about preparing to integrate him into his command and to engage in the planned activities of the Army of the Mississippi, though no one seemed to know what those plans were.

General Halleck, who had been General in Chief of the western forces, had thrust aside his Field Commander, General Grant and assumed for himself the role of Field Commander just after the Shiloh battle in April. Halleck then proceeded to combine all forces available to him until they numbered over a hundred thousand for an attack on Corinth, which occupied the entire month of May.

General Sullivan had been reporting to General Rosecrans, who had been assigned under General Pope, but General Pope was no longer in command at Corinth. In June, he'd been sent east to reinforce General McClellan. General Rosecrans was now in command of the Army of the Mississippi under General Halleck, but there had not yet been any orders defining his assignment there.

Then on July 11, 1862, shortly after he had marched, or more appropriately, dug his way into Corinth, Halleck had been reassigned to a position in Washington leaving General Grant again in overall command in the west, but without official orders to that effect.

No one knew what his specific authority was and all of the commanders seemed to be holding their positions by default.

Like General Pope before him, General Rosecrans was in command, tentative though it might be, of the Army of the Mississippi. General Grant was in command, so it seemed, of the Army of the Tennessee and as he ranked the other generals in the field, assumed his old position as Field Commander, providing overall coordinated command over those two armies.

General Buell, also junior to Grant was in command of the Army of the Cumberland when it had been with the combined army under General Halleck, but had then been sent back to the east to occupy Chattanooga in July. The army of 120,000, which General Halleck had under his command when he entered Corinth in late May, now totaled just over 50,000, and they were dispersed over a wide landscape, protecting bridges, railroads, towns, and supply dumps. General Halleck, when General in Chief, had first carefully gathered to his command all the forces available to him, and then, just as deliberately, systematically stripped the army of over half its strength, and had left no orders as to where they were to go or whom to fight.

When he got to Washington DC, it wasn't long before General Halleck, who earlier in his career had been given the sobriquet "Old Brains" was given the new nick-name: "Old Wooden Head", especially in the west where he had reigned in disorder and had left a trail of confusion in his wake when he departed.

And, to make matters worse, on October 2nd, Colonel Phil Sheridan, commanding a small cavalry detachment, rode into camp with the information that a large force under Confederate General Earl Van Dorn was moving on Corinth from the west. Van Dorn had a deserved reputation as a fierce fighter and an excellent strategist, and there was a general furor over the need for preparations to meet the attack.

The Secesh army had thrown up some fairly elaborate defenses before they had evacuated Corinth in May, and General Halleck had made grandiose provisions there to accommodate his one hundred twenty thousand troops before he was summoned to the east. These last defenses were too vast to man with the small army now at General Grant's disposal, and Grant was then required to see to it that strong works were erected to protect only the vital portions of the city from Rebel attack. He left General Rosecrans with what was left of the Army of the Mississippi at Corinth and had set up his own headquarters at Bolivar, Tennessee, some forty miles to the north and central to the support of Memphis and Jackson, as well as Corinth.

General Rosecrans, always the strategist, deployed his forces wisely. He had devised a plan he would use against the Rebel attack, until General Grant would be able to reinforce him from Bolivar. The army would first occupy the old Confederate defenses, those farthest out from the center of the city, then fall back as necessary to the intermediate line erected by General Halleck and as a last resort, occupy the inner line built under the direction of General Grant. If properly executed, the strategy would gradually sap the strength of the attacking forces as they approached through the maze of abatis and trenches, giving the blue-clad soldiers the advantage of a defensive position three times. Numerically, the forces of the two armies were about equal. The Confederates had the advantage of fighting on their home ground, aided by the sympathetic townspeople, but the Federals had the advantage of defensive entrenchment and the fact that the town of Corinth was nearly deserted.

Rosecrans's front was to be manned by three divisions under Generals Thomas J. McKean on the left and Thomas A. Davies in the center. The Third Division of the Union forces, under Brigadier General Charles Hamilton was positioned at the right of the battle line on that morning of October 3rd, with General Sullivan's Second Brigade positioned at the right of the division, anchoring the line on the far right. There were six regiments and two batteries assigned to General Sullivan that day and Jesse's job as adjutant promised to be a demanding one.

The main attack came at about 10:00 AM and was mostly directed at the left and center of the line leaving General Hamilton to swing his division to his rear in support of the center of the line, which the Confederates were pressing hard. As Adjutant under General Sullivan, Jesse was to maintain contact with the other divisions along the front line as well as General Rosecrans's headquarters and communicate with his own brigade.

Fighting the first day was so intense that the front was forced in several places, but Old Rosy's plan of ordered retreat was effective. The Federals knew what was expected of them and they performed in good order. Little by little, the Union soldiers fell back deliberately, bringing their wounded with them and taking severe toll on the advancing Rebels. When he was able to approach the front, Jesse tried to occupy positions of advantage and to familiarize himself with the lay of the land as the troops fell back. On several occasions he was threatened by the sound of the bullets singing their deadly songs as they flew about him, and once his saddle was struck by a bullet just in front of where he was sitting. Carnage was taking its toll on both sides, but Jesse thought the Rebels, fighting valiantly for every inch of the field, were suffering greater casualties than were the northern troops.

At about eleven o'clock, Jesse was delivering instructions to the 10th Missouri to fall back to the secondary line. As he approached, he watched as Captain Jamison, commanding Company D, in Colonel Holmes's Regiment was struck by a cannon ball as he was dismounting from his horse. The ball hit him in the left shoulder, taking the arm and part of the left side of his chest with it. He stood for a moment, looking down at the place where his shoulder had been, then simply closed his eyes and collapsed beside his horse, who stood calmly, as though waiting for further directions.

One of his men walked over and took the horse gently by the reins and led him away. Another man tended to the fallen captain and, seeing no doubt that Captain Jamison was dead, covered him with a tarp, for the time being. There had been no lieutenants in the company since Island Number

10, and Jesse assumed temporary command of the company. The men took their orders from Jesse just as well as they would have from their former captain, and the battle went on.

He reassembled the company at the Halleck line and reported back to Captain Jamison's immediate superior, Major Horney what had transpired.

"Thank you, Captain," Major Horney responded, "is there a lieutenant attached to that company?"

"The men tell me they have not had any lieutenants for several weeks, since Island Number Ten, Sir," Jesse responded, "they're over beyond those burned out buildings to your left. I suppose I could go see what they need and let you know."

"No, you'd better check back with General Sullivan. I'll take care of Company D," he said, and Jesse was relieved of command as quickly as he had taken it.

As evening descended, the entire blue line had fallen back to the inner defenses. The fighting died at dusk and the troops went into a nervous bivouac. There was no doubt that there would be fighting the next day and the Sullivan Brigade would be a part of it.

Jesse reported back to Colonel Holmes and General Sullivan. He had never been an observer in a battle before and the experience was entirely different from that of being a participant. Watching the fighting, he had been moved several times to pull his carbine from its scabbard and join the men in line, but he'd been given strict orders against such action. His job was to deliver messages and make observations, and fighting was denied him, at least for that day.

The fighting on October 3rd forced General Hamilton's division back into a part of the city that was mainly industrial and well back to the defense lines set up by General Grant. The troops were mostly seasoned veterans by now. They had been involved in the battles at Shiloh and Island Number 10, the occupation of Corinth under Halleck, the digging of Corinth defenses under Grant, and now they were fighting for their position under General Hamilton and General Sullivan. After assisting in the repositioning of the Brigade for the fight the next day, Logan spent some time just riding from campfire to campfire, getting to know some of the soldiers.

"Them Rebs ought to be pretty well used up after today, Cap'n," one of the men with the 10th Missouri said to Jesse. "We're gonna whup 'em good tomorrow. We're jes' gonna whup 'em. You'll see."

"I like your confidence, Soldier," Jesse responded. "They're a tough bunch, though. I want you men to talk low, shoot low, and keep your heads low. There's no fight left in a dead soldier, and I want them to be dead Johnnies, and not dead Yanks."

"Cap'n," one of the Missouri troops responded, "I never thought I'd be confused with them as are called Yankees, but here I am in a blue uniform and fighting for the Union, and I reckon that makes me a Yank."

"Well, I'm born and mostly raised in Tennessee, and I reckon I'm just as surprised to be a Yank as much as anyone," Jesse responded with a smile. "But then, I'd never have believed just a couple of years ago that anyone would be crazy enough to start this war."

"Well, don't you worry none about us, Cap'n. We'll be ready fer 'em tomorrow and they'll be gone before nightfall. You just watch".

Jesse wasn't so sure. As he rode out among the men he inquired as to the units and hometowns of the soldiers. They were mostly from Illinois, Iowa, Wisconsin, and Missouri, but there were also some men from Tennessee, Kentucky and even Mississippi, who had volunteered within the past few days and weeks, still loyal to the Old Flag. Those from southern states were warmly welcomed by the northern men, both for the fact that it confirmed their feelings toward the union as well as for the fact that they represented reinforcements.

With the men from Tennessee, Jesse enjoyed a special bond even though they were from the western part of the state. He told them where he was from and of the fact that he'd been acquainted with Governor Johnson. Spending some time with the troops, he expressed great admiration for the state's Military Governor and assured the Tennessee boys that they were among friends. The fact that he was now a captain didn't diminish the feelings he had for the men in rank, but he was well aware of a deference they seemed to show him, even though the concept of rank was a somewhat new idea among these volunteer soldiers.

One of the men from Tennessee Jesse found to be particularly nervous. He'd joined the Union Army only a month ago and though he'd been involved in the battle for Iuka and now having been fighting along with his unit all day, he showed signs of nervousness and Jesse wondered how well he'd hold together the following day. He stopped and spent some time in conversation with the man. He was a good-looking young man, with brown eyes and straight brown hair and the smallest face Jesse could ever remember seeing on a man. It was the face of a small boy, inconsistent with the man's size. He seemed conscious of the fact that his face was so boyish and tried to conceal it with a growth of beard that was only marginally successful. His name was Thresh Curry, and he told Jesse he hailed from River Bend, Tennessee. He had joined the Confederate army under pressure from the folks in his hometown, but his enlistment had, or so he thought, been for a twelve-month duty. Then, when his year was up, President Davis had signed into law the Conscription Act, which extended all enlistments indefinitely. This so irked Curry and some of his friends that after Shiloh, he deserted and went over to the Federals and joined the 10th Missouri, the handiest unit to him when he passed through the lines.

"I didn't want to be a Rebel in the firs' place," Curry explained to the Union Captain, "and when they told me I had to stay with that unit until who-knows-when, I just upped and snuck off. Or to put it more like it was, I stayed behind when them other fellers in my company snuck off."

"Have you written home, yet, soldier?" Jesse asked out of pure concern for Thresh' peace of mind. "How does your family take to your fighting for the union?"

"No, I haven't, Captain," he responded, "For one thing, I cain't read nor write, and for another, they don't know where I am. My folks is mostly Secesh, 'cept for Grandpap, and they wouldn't be too proud hearin' I joined up with the Yanks. Grandpap and me was pretty possum, allus fishin' and one thing and another, and he'd shine up 'ef he knowed I was in the ranks of the Union, but I don't know how to tell him. He'd shine up for sure, he would."

"If you'd give me his name, I'd see if I could get in touch with him and let him know you're all right, Private Curry. Then maybe he could let the rest of the family know, kind of easy like, without telling them where you are."

"Oh, I reckon they suspect, right enough, and if Grandpap was to tell them he knew something about me, they'd know for sure." He paused for a few seconds, then went on. "Well, what the heck. My folks know I'm sour on secession and 'got no use for them big plantation lords. If you'd show me some of the writin' I think I can put together a letter to Grandpap."

The two Tennesseans sat down together for the best part of an hour by the glow of the campfire and composed a letter. It only consisted of a few lines, but when it was finished, Thresh couldn't have been more proud. "Captain," he said, "I'm much obliged for all your help. If my kinfolk hears from Grandpap that I'm fightin' for the north, they'll take it a lot easier than if'n I'us t' jus' tell 'em straight out in a letter to my ma or pa. Grandpap'll put it to 'em so's to make it sound like I 'us doin' the right thing."

"Do you have any brothers and sisters, soldier?" Jesse asked.

"Yes, sir, I got two sisters and three brothers. One of my brothers is fighting in the Rebel army, and the others is too young to be in the army, jus' yet. I don't know how they'll go when they come of age."

After checking one last time with General Sullivan, Logan took to his tent to try to get some rest. It had been a hard day and the following day would not be any easier, but he couldn't sleep. He tossed and rolled in his blankets for a time, then, after a short nap, he was up and out among the men. Many of them were as wakeful as he, and though they conversed among themselves in low tones as they tried to respect the needs of those who were able to sleep, not many rested that night.

As the first light of dawn appeared, the Third Division was called into formation in readiness to attack the enemy lines. It was General Hamilton's policy to attack first, if there was any possibility of doing so, and this was the opportunity.

"It's going to get a little noisy in a few minutes, men," Logan advised those about him. He was on his horse and ready to lead the fighting among the 10th Missouri when Colonel Holmes rode up.

"Captain, I admire your enthusiasm, but I think you're expected at General Sullivan's headquarters. Major Horney and I will manage quite well, I assure you."

Jesse was embarrassed. It was true, as he'd done the day before, he'd been so caught up in the enthusiasm of the preparations that he'd forgotten he was an adjutant and expected to be at headquarters.

"Thank you, Colonel," Jesse said with a sharp salute and a wry smile. "Does it show too much? The fact that I'm eager to get back into the fight? I don't cotton much to war, but I've been talking to the men for most of the night and they're such a brave and gallant lot, I can't help picking up some of their enthusiasm." With that he turned his horse toward the rear and rode back to headquarters.

"Captain Logan, where have you been?" General Sullivan asked with no little impatience in his voice when Jesse rode in and had dismounted.

"Sir, I'm afraid I got a little caught up in the enthusiasm your men showed for the fight this morning. They are really a great group of fellows, and they think a lot of you, too. I've a feeling this is going to be a good day for the Third, General."

When the Confederates came, and they came early and in great force, the Third Division, again posted on the right of the federal line had all it could handle for a time. CSA General van Dorn's strategy, however, was to attack mainly at the center and left of the Union line, and General Rosecrans had wisely reinforced the center with a fresh division under General David Stanley. The Confederates were systematically driven back, and out of town and by noon were in retreat toward the west. A count of casualties showed the loss to the southern army was over 4500 killed and wounded, as to compare with about half that number from the Yankee troops. General Rosecrans' strategy had worked. The battle to save the important railroad at Corinth had fallen in favor of the Union, at least for another day.

Many of the men and officers of General Hamilton's division wanted to pursue the enemy and try to destroy him in detail in flight, but General Rosecrans felt that the men were too used up to do any more fighting that day. Jesse, Colonel Holmes, Major Horney, Captain Rice of the 24th Missouri, and several other officers from the Second Brigade went to General Sullivan and urged him to petition General Rosecrans to allow them to chase the retreating Rebels, but to no avail. His mind was made up, and their orders were to care for the dead and wounded and regroup their various commands.

Dead and wounded lay over a field of several miles in each direction and in spite of their desire to pursue the fleeing southern army, they conceded that it would be days before either side was in any condition to mount a force for further fighting. The pride and relief the men and officers displayed in wake of the victory was more of calm resignation than of elation. They savored the victory, but with only a sense of grim determination and the knowledge that the next battle could easily go the other way. The balance of forces had been about equal going into the fray, and it was only the tactics of the commanders that turned it for the north. The Rebel troops had fought with superb gallantry, and the men in blue gained a new respect for their opponents.

This was a war like no other in history, and the soldiers on both sides seemed to know it. They talked to each other from time to time in the same language and for the most part in the same terms and vernacular. When they were close enough to communicate with the soldiers of the enemy and were not shooting at each other, they were exchanging stories and gossip like the neighbors they truly were.

One of the psychological principles of warfare is to 'dehumanize' the enemy. It's a technique used in all armies at all levels, unconsciously or otherwise, to desensitize the soldiers to the act of taking the life of a fellow human being. The terms 'Billy Yank', or 'Johnny Reb', Blue Jacket, Grey Back, Secesh, and Nigger Lover were all terms applied to the enemy, one or the other, to strip the opposing soldier of his identity and make the act of killing less atrocious. In this war it was hard to do when the 'Johnny' of today was your neighbor or your cousin or your brother, just yesterday, but it went on just the same.

The next day, October 5th, the day after the southern army had left the field, Jesse was on a mission which took him across a part of the battlefield for which there had been such viscous contention the day before. His route took him past a relief squad of Union soldiers trying to select and collect the wounded from both sides who were the most likely to live, given prompt medical attention. Private Curry, the lad with the boyish face, was among the relief squad, hatless and with tears streaming down his face. He spotted Jesse coming his way and turned his head to hide his grief.

Logan rode over to where the man was hunkered over. "Soldier," he said, recalling his own sense of dismay and grief on a similar situation just after such a battle back in Virginia, "you can't let this thing get to you. I know what you're going through, Thresh, and I can feel for you, but you've just got to close your mind to the pain these fellows are feeling right now. You have to keep your mind on the fact that you're doing a job. Your job is saving lives, and if you let your feelings get in your way you're not going to do as good a job as you've been sent out to do. You have to think about stuff that will keep your mind off the troubles these men have right now. Drink lots of water, and stay as much as you can near some smoke drifting through, like that over there." He pointed in the direction of some burning debris. "The smell of the smoke will overpower some of the other smells."

The advice was well intended, but the mention of drinking water and the overpowering odor of the dead men and horses set off a reaction in the young soldier and he turned away from Logan and vomited, retching for two or three minutes before regaining his composure. In the meantime, the sight and smell got to Jesse and he leapt off his horse, anticipating his having to throw up, also. He managed to keep his breakfast down, but nausea swept over him for a moment before he, too recovered his presence. He walked over to where Thresh was standing and put his arm around the younger man's shoulders.

"Come, on, Curry," he said in a half-jovial manner, "I know it's wretched out here, but you'll feel better, now. Just do like I say and try to keep from thinking about anything but doing your job. Now, you'd better get back with the other men or they'll think you're trying to get out of work."

The other members of the squad had moved away from Thresh and Jesse and were trying to maintain their own composure, but the act of compassion on the part of this Union officer was not ignored. The men in the ranks were hungry for any small act of kindness and appreciated it when an officer took the time to give attention to the welfare of the men.

—————≡«(●)»≡—————

At sundown, after a long day of regrouping and reorganizing, Jesse had a chance to secure his sleeping tent and store his belongings. He then sat down with General Sullivan and Colonel Sam Holmes and two other officers for a briefing on what more was expected of him after his first exposure to battle after being promoted.

They spent the better part of an hour with maps and reports with Colonel Holmes conducting much of the briefing. Finally, they got up, went over to a cook tent and got some coffee. On returning to the command tent, the mood relaxed somewhat and General Sullivan took time to bring Jesse up to date on what had happened since they were together in western Virginia. He then waxed into a discussion of the war in general and some of his observations on how it was being conducted.

"In the first place," General Sullivan said as they drank the strong hot coffee, "I was with General McClellan down on the peninsula during that campaign, and from where I sit, General McClellan never should have left northern Virginia to sail all the way down to Hampton Roads. It looked to me as though top command, — General McClellan — was just using that as a means to stall for time and avoid a pitched battle. We were in the best position possible to simply push south and assault Richmond from where we were situated. And secondly, we needed a cavalry. He simply doesn't seem to understand cavalry. I've been with General Rosecrans, now for several months, and I wish to tell you that there is a man who understands the use of cavalry. I know he hasn't done everything right at every turn, and I felt yesterday that we should have at least formed up a regiment and gone after the Rebs, but that's not my point. My point is that the Army of the Potomac could use a man like Rosecrans or that man Grant. They know how and when to fight and they understand the value of the cavalry."

"Then there's General McClernand who's been with us here for a time, though he's not with us just now. He's been doing some writing in the papers about the conduct of the war. While he's not too keen on General Grant either, he makes some good points about how McClellan — General McClellan — should have just gone straight south and taken Richmond in a fair fight. To be truthful, though, you know, I don't know how this McClernand keeps from getting bounced out of the army with some of the stuff he's writing, but some of the things he says are right on the money."

Jesse said that he had heard General Grant had a reputation of being a hard fighter and the war in the west seemed to be going a lot better than it was in Virginia. In Virginia, it seemed, whenever the army pushed south, the Rebels would slip around and threaten Washington from the Shenandoah Valley and the campaign would fall apart from fear of the capitol being attacked.

"That man, Bobby Lee has a flair for keeping the Army of the Potomac off balance," Jesse observed. "Between him and General Jackson many of our brigades were just shuttling back and forth, half the time looking for the Rebs and the other half of the time looking to stay out of their way." With the last statement, he chuckled as though he'd offered a profound and novel observation on the war.

General Sullivan agreed and then made another observation. "Remember, though," he said, "with the occasional rare exception, none — none of the fighting has been on northern soil. The newspapers and many of the 'Peace Democrats' condemn the fact that the Federal Army doesn't seem to be as committed to winning this war as the Confederates are, but where has all the fighting been done? On southern soil, that's where."

"Remember what we talked about when we first mustered in? It's easier to defend than to attack. The same principle holds true for a campaign. When we enter what has been termed 'Confederate Country' the people are hostile and the enemy has a tactical advantage as to both the local people helping him and his familiarity with the geography. Our job is made much harder by these two factors and also by the fact that it is necessary for us to maintain a supply line, sometimes a line of considerable length. That's where General Forrest and Colonel Morgan are really hurting us, of course, but even so, we've kept the war on their soil and on our terms. You recall when we were over in the Appalachians, Mr. Logan. The people were in support of the Union, and our job was made much easier."

Though he didn't offer any argument to the general's last statement, Jesse wasn't too sure he was entirely accurate in his assessment of the fact as to the fighting being all on southern soil and on northern terms. Only a few days earlier he'd had to climb off the train at Munfordville, Kentucky and resort to riding his horse for a couple of miles across the Green River because the raiding Confederates under General Bragg had destroyed the railroad bridge. Kentucky was supposed to be under Federal control, or at the least, neutral.

General Sullivan went on, "There is another consideration in this — this thing about who has the best fighting force, and the superior top-command. I'm not berating anyone in our government, but that man Jefferson Davis has his hand on everything that's being done in the south. You see, he hasn't had a government long enough for the politicians to become entrenched and influential. Mr. Lincoln, on the other hand, is so hog-tied by politics that many of our generals just aren't qualified to handle their jobs. They were assigned by a process of patronage rather than by qualification, me as much as anyone, although I did have some previous military experience. You'll see what I mean as this thing goes along. You'll see."

"Do you remember when we were mustered in? Many of us were all too anxious to get into the army and see the country and send the Johnnies scooting back to Richmond during our ninety-day enlistment. It was a glory road! A glory road! The men joined just so they wouldn't lose out on the glory. Aren't I right, Mr. Logan? The same thing can be said for the generals, my friend."

General Sullivan's eyes were bright as he was speaking. His round face glistened with sweat in the light of the lantern and his goatee bobbled defiantly as he spoke. He was talking with such intensity that he seemed transformed into an orator. Jesse was impressed with the fervor with which the general spoke. He'd formed an early impression of General Sullivan at the time they first met as that of a rather sophisticated and possibly stuffy lawyer who had joined the army to further his career. He later gained new respect for the man when he found he had been a midshipman in the Navy and had served six years before entering the field of Law. Now he found himself forming a new impression of the man; that of a committed patriot and one who was in the war for the service he could be to his country.

General Sullivan was in a mood of mixed dismay and anticipation. "There's something else I see happening, here, gentlemen. Here it is, the fifth of October in an election year, the first national election of Mr. Lincoln's term of office. What does that tell you about how Washington sees what is happening in the field?"

"Well," Colonel Holmes offered, "for one thing, Mr. Lincoln is trying to play it to look as good to the people — the voters — as he possibly can."

"Exactly," General Sullivan ejaculated, "and for another thing, he's trying to make all of the Republicans who are in command of forces in the field to look good at home so that their Republican friends will be elected, or re-elected as the case may be. Or, if the general officer happens to be of another political stripe, he urges him on as quietly and as gently as possible because, when all is said and done, it's a Republican war with a Republican at the top. So, if our sins are embarrassing or our wins are laudable, they are still Republican wins or losses with the president's party gaining or losing in the process. Mark my words, though, gentlemen. There will be some changes after November, and I feel they will be for the better. Because — if the general is — ah, is — a laggard or if he goes off in some direction that doesn't contribute to the success of the campaign, his days are numbered. Numbered, my friends!"

General Sullivan then turned to the subject he had touched on earlier. "I received orders today, gentlemen, to the effect that we, that is this regiment is to move east and try to capture, or at least neutralize Bedford Forrest and, if possible, John Hunt Morgan. We'll talk about it further in the next few days, but for now, suffice it to say that we'll be moving out within a fortnight. See to it that your men are prepared. We'll be living off the land to a large degree and moving fast. That's all for now, but, Captain Logan, I'd like a word with you, if you don't mind."

After the other officers had left the tent, General Sullivan turned to Jesse. "Captain," he said in what seemed to Jesse like a strained voice, "I need to explain to you in no uncertain terms that your place of assignment, your duty station, is at brigade headquarters, here, with me. You are not an infantryman, you aren't a company commander, you are the adjutant to the brigadier general and you are to stay within hailing distance of the command headquarters at all times except on specific assignment or when you've been relieved. I appreciate your desire to work with the men in the ranks, but your job calls for you to be at my side at all times. This is your first assignment, and while it is understandable that you, ah, — you — or I suppose I should say — that I haven't made clear my expectations of you. I think you must understand the need for such a position as an adjutant, and why you were chosen for this job. You've distinguished yourself in the field and have shown a great capacity for initiative and independent thought. These qualities will place you in good stead as my aid, but don't let your independence get the better of you and lead you away from doing what is expected of you. Have I made myself clear, Captain?"

Jesse, appropriately chastised, assured the general that his mistakes of the past two days would not be repeated. Lieutenant Goodin had criticized him when he was a corporal for going off and "fighting his own little war," and he knew of his tendency to take matters into his own hands at times. Teamwork and discipline were essential to the success of the operation. He was well aware of this, and was determined to do the job assigned him to the best of his ability.

"Thank you, Captain. If there's nothing else, you may go."

The next day, Jesse reported to the command tent and found General Sullivan studying a set of maps with Colonel Holmes. As expected, orders had been received from General Grant for General Sullivan to take his own brigade and those of Colonels John Fuller, Adolph Englemann, and Cyrus Dunham and to move north toward Jackson, Tennessee to protect the Union supply lines. Grant had received intelligence that Confederate General Pemberton, in charge of the defense of Vicksburg had requested General Forrest to disrupt the railroads supplying the Yankees with food and war materiel and the attack was likely to be directed just north of their position at Corinth.

General Sullivan confided in the few officers in his cadre that he was only too happy to be moving away from what he termed a potential 'hornets' nest'. To chase after General Nathan Bedford Forrest, however, was much like chasing a swarm of bees. In the first place you never were to know where he would turn up next, and in the second place, if, by some chance, you were to catch up with him your chances of coming away from the encounter unscathed were low indeed.

Forrest had been a successful businessman up until June 1861, when he joined Captain Josiah White's Tennessee Mounted Rangers (CSA) as a private. By October that same year he was a Lieutenant Colonel, and a full Brevet Brigadier General by March of 1862. He gained a reputation across the state of Tennessee and with his close associates as a fierce fighter, a stern but compassionate disciplinarian and a tactical commander beyond belief. In fact, almost everyone in Tennessee, with the exception of the commanding general, Braxton Bragg, had gained the highest regard for Bedford Forrest as a force to be dealt with. Bragg, on the other hand, wrote him off as a partisan ranger, with more luck than skill and more bluff than courage. Since Forrest had entered the army from civilian life and had never had more than a year of formal education, none of which dealt with military tactics, Bragg reasoned that he could not possibly be qualified to lead even a squad, much less a cavalry regiment.

In a contest only a few miles southeast of Nashville early in November Forrest, with a troop of just over 3000 men had engaged General James Negley's brigade of about 12,000. Forrest had so outmaneuvered the Yanks that Negley was sure he had faced an army of "... no less than 25,000," and "... respectfully suggested," that Union command, "... exercise extreme caution against Forrest's cavalry", which he estimated at over 5,000.

20

BEDFORD FORREST

General Grant, now the Field Commander for Federal forces in the west had been in constant consultation with the high command in Washington. There had been a growing awareness that the Mississippi River should be cleared of Confederate resistance, but now it was deemed absolutely essential to the Union strategy to open up the river, and to do so it would be necessary to neutralize that 'Gibraltar of the West', Vicksburg, Mississippi. Whereas General Halleck, before him had felt it necessary to conquer and occupy the entire region of West Tennessee, Mississippi, Louisiana and Northern Alabama in detail, Grant's strategy was to conquer armies and strategic emplacements without necessarily tying up troops by occupying each town.

This would allow his forces to operate more freely and control the region as necessary but without committing soldiers to garrison every town and crossroad. Railroads, on the other hand, were going to have to be protected by roving patrols to avoid guerillas such as Forrest, Morgan, and Quantrill from disrupting transportation.

Vicksburg, Mississippi was of such strategic importance, however, that it was vital to the whole war, and must be brought under Federal control. Under General Halleck, during the previous summer Federal naval forces operating on the Mississippi River had tried to conquer that town, but failed. Vicksburg was impregnable, at least from its position on a bluff so high above the river that the Federal naval guns were hardly capable of firing at such a high angle, doing very little damage to the deeply entrenched fortifications there.

Vicksburg would have to be taken by land forces, but this would require huge amounts of materiel and supplies to be brought in from Columbus, Kentucky, two hundred miles to the north through country that was in great part, in Federal hands, but populated by people mostly loyal to the

Confederacy. The Mobile and Ohio Railroad ran south from Columbus through Jackson, Tennessee, where it joined the Mississippi Central Railroad. The Mississippi Central then went south to Jackson, Mississippi, and from there a spur went west to Vicksburg. It promised to be a rather simple and direct assault, if only the supply line could be kept open.

The Confederate authorities recognized the value of Vicksburg and were determined to hold it at all hazards. General John Pemberton, commanding general for the Army of the Mississippi, (CSA), requested from General Bragg a fast moving, hard hitting strike force to disrupt Grant's supply trains and harass the Federal forces generally.

Brevet Brigadier General Nathan Bedford Forrest was selected for the job, and was assigned a brigade of just over two thousand troops to accomplish this. It was a rag tag army, composed largely of raw recruits, and recently conscripted deserters leavened by a few of Forrest's "Old Battalion," veterans of several battles, and braced by an unswerving loyalty to "Old Bedford", whom they admired a lot, but mostly feared. The brigade was armed with a variety of weapons, almost none of which had been issued by the government and very few of which fired ammunition that was in any way standardized. There were muskets from every known source, flintlocks with and without flint, shotguns, Belgian rifles, Kentucky rifles, fowling pieces, and whatever else could be brought from home or acquired in raids on Federal forces. The men were well mounted because at that time southerners, by definition, were well mounted, but some of the mounts were mules and plow horses. While not fast, these mounts were reliable for the purpose of traveling, and when crossing a swollen river, the rule was 'the bigger the better'.

Forrest had no problems recruiting. One of the complaints often heard from other commanders was that many of their deserters ended up in Forrest's Cavalry. Occasionally, General Bragg would give Forrest orders to identify any deserters he could find and return them to their old unit. The results were always the same. Forrest would complain that he was being stripped of his most valuable men, but would follow the orders. The men would be sent back to their old units and at first opportunity would 'desert' again and return to Forrest. He was a disciplinarian but knew how to make a soldier feel like a soldier. His method of fighting instilled in his troops a spirit of belonging to something grand and they felt they were making a difference in the war, rather than being just another rail in the fence.

In anticipation of the raid, Forrest sent out a small squadron under the command of Lieutenant Farley Austin to prepare some small flatboats or pontoons to facilitate the crossing of the Tennessee River. The river cuts the state of Tennessee in two, running almost straight north and south, and leaves the western quarter of the state isolated during the rainy months, if ferries and bridges are unavailable, as in this event. This made it extremely difficult to move troops into West Tennessee, a problem readily anticipated by Bedford Forrest. If the river was intensely patrolled by the Union navy, it would be almost impossible to cross, but that was not the case. Forrest knew the difficulty the Federals would have defending the entire length of the river and with adequate precautions and a little luck, he could get his small force across. Once across the river he would be able to obtain provisions and recruits along the way.

The twenty-one-year-old Austin, a native of River Bend, a little town just across the Tennessee River and a few miles to the east from Clifton, was well suited for the job. He was the son of a planter, bright and industrious, and thoroughly familiar with the river in that area. Clifton, Tennessee was situated on the east bank of the river opposite a point of land created by the river's making a sharp horseshoe bend that looped to the east. The peninsula thus created on the west side of the river measures about seven or eight miles from east to west and at its western or narrowest neck it is only about two miles across. The eastern side of the river is composed of rich rolling hills with an occasional stand of large trees, Elm, cypress, poplar, and water maple sometimes sixty or seventy feet tall and offering concealment along the river bank. It was in one of these large groves that Lieutenant Austin selected a site as his boat-building station.

The squad of men that had been sent out with Austin was comprised of a cross section of boat builders, roustabouts, lumbermen, and teamsters, with a sergeant, forty-eight-year-old Isaac MacLean, who had been with Forrest in his earlier years as a slave trader. They took with them what they considered to be the necessary supplies and tools to build flatboats from native materials felling and sawing the logs, joining them by means of mortises and pegged joints, and sealing the seams with tar. Only the tools, ropes, and tar were taken from the Quartermaster. The other materials would be acquired on site. Forrest had decided on the use of the flatboats as a pontoon bridge would be too hard to conceal from the river patrols.

The squad left LaVergne, Tennessee on November 20, a clear cold day, in high spirits bound for Clifton. On arriving there they moved to the north, down river to the grove that scouts, with the advice of Lieutenant Austin, had selected. They set out immediately felling trees, building a sawpit, trimming and sizing logs, and cutting planks. With plans in hand they moved quickly selecting the various dimensions of planking, cutting joints and preparing pegs to secure them. As the boats took shape, they also set up a fire-pit and cauldron to heat the tar, to be ladled into the joints between the planking to provide watertight seams.

As the squad worked, after only about four or five days, three boys in their early teens happened by on a makeshift raft composed of boards lashed to molasses barrels. When the boys came abreast of the boat building operation, their curiosity took over.

"Hey, what're you fellers doing?" Abel, one of the boys called as they beached their craft and scrambled ashore. "What's goin' on, here?"

Lieutenant Austin, the only member of the squad in a recognizable uniform was nearby when the boys beached the raft. He'd been briefed on the possibility of such interference and approached the boys immediately. "What're you young fellers doing out on the river at this time of year?" he asked. Where'd y'all come from? Ain't that raft a mite unsteady to haul you'uns out on this here river in the middle of winter?"

"Oh, we do this all the time," Abel responded. "We're out looking fer stuff the yanks throw overboard or to look out for them gunboats they send up here sometimes. Say, you look like a army officer, are you on the run from the army?" he asked bluntly.

"Boys, I'm going to tell you something, but you have to keep it under your hats. I'm a officer in the army of Jefferson Davis and Gen'r'l Bedford Forrest, and you're going to have to swear by the flag of the C S A (drawing out the letters for emphasis) that you ain't a'gonna tell anyone what you know. Kin I trus' you'uns?"

The boys were wide-eyed at the reality that there was a Confederate officer in their midst and he was seeking their confidence. They readily agreed that they would be willing to be sworn to secrecy and allegiance to the flag of the Confederacy. Abel Curry, his brother Luther, and their friend James Taylor all put their left hand on the flag and, raising their right hands, took a solemn oath.

The boys also agreed that they would scout for the Confederate soldiers, both in their present situation and also when the Bedford Brigade came to the river and at whatever other times they were needed. For the rest of the day they helped with the menial chores attending the boat building operation and tried to make themselves useful. They helped dig the fire pit the soldiers were going to need for heating the tar, collected brush and tree trimmings for the fire, helped move the logs required to roll the boats to the water, and were generally useful about the camp.

At about three in the afternoon, Jamey Taylor said, "We're gonna have to get on home to make it before dark, boys, let's get goin'."

"How do you get back up the river with the current this strong? Lieutenant Austin inquired. "You men must have come a long way. As I recall, except for Clifton, there ain't much population above here all the way to River Bend."

"That's where we live." Abel volunteered, "We jes' driff with the current as far as we want to, and then when we git down to where the river crooks back, jes' over the land from River Bend, we pull the raft out of the water and take it apart. Then we roll the barrels across the spit back home and use 'em ag'in th' nex' time we need 'em."

River Bend was on the first turn of the river going into its horseshoe bend and the boys had devised a labor-saving technique of polling down-river a distance of about ten miles and returning overland for a distance of about two.

"If we can," Luther Curry volunteered, "we gits a wagon or finds someone who'll carry us across the spit, but there ain't many a horse left in this country, what with the Yankees stealin' 'em. But also, sometimes our men needs 'em fer to fight them Yanks."

"How do you get the deck back across the spit?" Lieutenant Curry inquired. That's a pretty heavy piece, 'specially when at least two of you'uns is a'rollin' the barrels."

"Oh, we got a hand truck. That-there deck is the door off'n our grandpap's barn, and we has to git it back, 'cause one of these days he's goin' to want to hang it back on the barn."

"Well, I want to thank you boys for your he'p, today. And don't forget you've got to keep this thing a secret. I know the people hereabouts are good loyal citizens, but jes' in case there's a Lincolnite among 'em, I want you to be ca'ful and don't tell no one about what we're doin' here. Also, we may need your he'p gettin' a rope across the river in a few days, to fetch these boats across. Will you'uns be back?"

"Oh, you can count on us, Lootenant," Abel assured him. "We cain't come back t'morry, 'cause we need's one day fer to git our raft back home, but Saturday we'll try to git back here then."

On Saturday, the three boys were back, bright and early. They had been questioned at home as to their extended absence the previous days, but they had settled on the excuse that there was an abandoned wagon on the riverbank around the horseshoe bend and they thought they could salvage most of it.

The first two of the flatboats were fairly well along, and except for some finishing touches and tarring the seams, were ready to put into the water. A path to the water's edge had been cleared and the roller logs put in place with the boats positioned on the first few rollers. The fire pit had been finished and a fire had been started in it. The soldiers had the tar, fifteen blocks of it, loaded on a wagon and proceeded with it toward the pit. They would get the fire as hot as possible, then when the flames subsided, they would put the tar in cauldrons in the pit to heat, while trying to avoid contact between the tar and any of the fire. It was a touchy operation, as there was a need to keep as much heat in the pit as possible, but they could not bring the fire into contact with the tar, especially when it got warm enough to ignite. Small amounts of tar could be lighted without great hazard, but in large quantities the tar was dangerous and could even explode. After the pouring process was finished, they would melt out the remainder of the tar and clean out the cauldrons.

For early December, the weather was exceptionally warm that day and the tar was a little hard to handle, as the blocks were quite soft on the outside. The men with the tar wagon backed the wagon toward the pit preparing to roll the blocks off onto a plank floor they had prepared just above the fire. It had been Lieutenant Austin's intent to only haul one or two blocks over to the fire at any one time, but Sergeant MacLean was anxious to get on with the job and without consultation, brought the whole load.

Someone wasn't watching. The fire pit had been dug at the bottom of a steep slope and as the men rolled the first of the blocks off the wagon, the weight of the load shifted. The wagon tipped backward, dumping most of the tar blocks onto the plank floor, which, having been built on a considerable slant, angled down toward the fire pit. There had not been adequate preparations made for such an occurrence. The blocks of tar started rolling toward the fire, resulting in shouts from the sergeant and men, scrambling among the men and boys, and panic among the horses, who were already spooked by being so near to the fire and backing toward the fire pit. When the horses bolted, the few blocks of tar left on the wagon slid off, flipping several of the first blocks into the air and landing them in the fire, where there were already several blocks starting to burn. In the confusion, all but one block of the tar found its way into the fire or near enough to be ignited by contact with the flames.

The horses and wagon were quickly removed from the area and a fire brigade from the river was formed, using all the men and boys available. Water didn't do much with respect to the burning tar, but the fire brigade did manage to eventually quench the fire burning in the pit. The tar pretty well burned itself out after about an hour of drenching with water from the river, creating a muddy mess all the way from the river to where the fire pit had been, near the boat-launch rollers. The blocks of tar weighed over a hundred pounds each and the heroics of the men only managed to save three blocks.

The fire was a disastrous setback. The boat-building operation was three days ride from LaVergne one way, and time was an essential consideration to the success of the operation. General Forrest was expected in three or four days and he was the kind of commander who expected results. It was no consolation that one of his best sergeants had been too hasty in hauling the tar to the fire pit, all would be chastised, and worse yet, the success of the raid was threatened. Forrest's style and technique were to make every man feel himself to be an integral part of any program and the entire squad was demoralized by the fire and resulting loss of most of the tar.

After a brief counsel, Lieutenant Austin decided to try to float the boats without caulking the seams. The result of that effort was also a minor disaster. The boats, made of wet, heavy planking that had just been sawed from fresh trees could hardly float their own weight, let alone bear the weight of horses, wagons, or soldiers necessary to ferry them across the Tennessee River. Caulking was essential to the floating of the boats, and tar was essential to the caulking process.

One of the Curry brothers spoke up. "My grandpap has 'bout this much tar in his barn back home at River Bend," Abel said, tentatively.

"Well, whyn't you say so earlier?" Lieutenant Austin demanded. "We can buy it off your grandpap, if'n he'll sell it, and if'n he won't sell it to us we'll jes' buy it anyways. This'll settle it fer us, and we'll only be about a day behind schedule."

"Only one problem," Abel replied. "Grandpap is a Lincolnite an' he won't take kindly to our usin' the tar fer our side. I know he'll kick up a fuss and he'll be a'tellin' some of his frien's what's a'happenin'. Do you think that's all right, Lootenant? How're we gonna git aroun' it?"

"What does your grandpap know about what you've be'n doin' here?" Austin inquired. "Have you said anythin' to him about your bein' away over here?'

"I think we said something when we saw him yisti'day, but we tol' him we're trying to wreck out a wagon that's stuck in the bank. That's all he knows, I think."

The other boys agreed. The secret was secure, so far as they knew, but all agreed that to take the tar out of Grandpap Curry's barn would certainly raise his suspicions. There was no concealment of the fact that Grandpap Curry was a loyalist and the boys had shown their secessionist inclinations. The family's ties were close, but loyalties to one cause or the other ran high. Abel and Luther even disclosed the fact that their older brother Tressider, whom they called Thresh, was away in the Union army and the family was divided on even that issue along political lines.

"Is there anyone else in River Bend that you know of that has any tar," Austin asked. "Anyone, that is, that ain't a Lincolnite?"

The boys didn't know of anyone. "Grandpap was workin' on the turnpike over 't Sugar Creek a while back and that's where he got all that tar. And now he's just squirrelin' it away agin some time he thinks he'll need it. He's funny like that. He'll jes' set somethin' in his barn an' think on it fer years, thinkin' he'll use it sometime."

Eldon Curry had already noticed that Abel and Luther had been away from home for quite a time. Even though that in itself was not particularly notable, he also noticed that they had been especially secretive about their actions for the past few days, especially with respect to the raft that he'd helped them contrive some time back, and had helped them return from the north river bend from time to time when they had taken it that far down stream. He wasn't too concerned about his grandsons, though. They were both good boys, even though they showed signs of Secesh leanings. It was not surprising in this day and age, what with the pressure they got from their friends. Anything that smacked of exercising one's independence or rejecting authority, these days, was fair game for young men, and trying to argue to the contrary only reinforced the feeling among boys that age. And then there was that devil Forrest who so captivated the imagination of the younger generation that it was a wonder any of them continued to hold for the Union.

Eldon decided he'd just bide his time and see what developed. At least he had been able to help bring Thresh to a respect for the old flag, and this was some consolation. He'd received a letter from Thresh just a week or so ago, and was gratified to hear where he was and also that he was safe. He said that a Captain Logan had helped him with the letter and was proud to be able to write home. Grandpap had needed help reading the letter. He had shared the letter with the two younger boys, including the fact that Thresh was in the Federal army, but Abel and Luther acted disgusted by the information. Their older brother, Edmund was with General Bragg in Middle Tennessee, and they tended to support him. Thresh was more introspective and deliberate by nature than his older brother and didn't relate as well to the younger boys.

———⟫⟨⦿⟩⟪———

The problem now facing Lieutenant Austin, Sergeant MacLean, and the others at the boat-building site was how to get about 500 pounds of tar from the barn of Eldon Curry to their hands with the least delay and also with the least repercussions.

The rebels could just go take the tar by force. The boys discouraged that idea and Lieutenant Austin wasn't inclined to go against their wishes, as he needed their co-operation on this and other matters. Also, such action might result in the use of deadly force, which would arouse the friends and neighbors.

If Grandpap Curry was not informed of the 'removal' of the tar from his barn and discovered it in anything resembling a short time, he'd be sure to kick up a fuss. If his generosity was imposed upon to give or to sell the tar to some "needy down-river boat builder" or "someone who needed it to patch a roof", he'd be a little more inclined to consent, as long as he didn't learn the real purpose of the use of the tar. If that strategy were discovered he'd not only kick up a fuss, he'd get to the Federals with the information. It was decided that the safer course was to steal it and risk his finding out, either early or late. The Curry boys felt they could engineer a theft when Grandpap was away from the farm and by the time he found out about it the boats would be finished and the Forrest Brigade across the river.

They decided to concoct a scheme to lure Grandpap away from home for a short time and secure some of the tar onto their handcart to haul it across the narrow peninsula of land. The loot would then be loaded onto the raft that they would guide upstream to the grove where they were building the boats. It sounded foolproof, but it all hinged on their ability to get Grandpap away from the farm and then to get that raft in shape to haul about 500 pounds of tar.

The first part depended on the Curry boys. The second part could be dealt with by building up the raft to ensure its seaworthiness in transporting the tar. To accomplish this, it was decided to take the two molasses barrels from the boys' raft and lash them to a stripped-down wagon bed, creating a raft that was a little more stable and would float the entire cargo of tar. The process could always be reversed to restore the raft to its original character to allay any suspicions that might arise when Grandpap next saw it.

So it was decided. The three boys were delighted to be such an important part of a scheme that would help their 'cause' and Lieutenant Austin was relieved that his plans would not be significantly delayed.

That afternoon, after redesigning the raft, six of the soldiers towing a rope for the return trip the next day, were ferried across to the west side of the river and put ashore opposite the grove of trees. They would camp there that night and the three boys would take the raft to their usual landing place. Early the next morning the soldiers would proceed on foot to the spot where the boys usually landed the raft. There they would wait for Jamey Taylor to guide them to the Curry farm with the handcart, haul the tar across the spit of land and manually pull the raft upstream to the construction site.

Lieutenant Austin would stay at the grove and continue construction of the second boat. This was Friday, December 12th. Forrest was expected on Monday or Tuesday.

As the boys approached the landing with their reconfigured raft, they didn't see Grandpap Curry who was coming down the road to give them some help in getting it home. He didn't know what to think when he saw the newly rebuilt craft that they guided into shore, but he proceeded on down to the river to help. As he approached the landing, the boys were intent upon concealing the raft in some underbrush by the bank, and still didn't notice his presence. Their conversation, however, was anything but that of three boys who had just freed up a wrecked wagon.

"What are we goin' to tell Gran'pap to git him away from home, t'morra," Luther was asking. "We can't jes' say 'Hey, Gran'pap, we wants you off'n the farm so's we kin steal some of yer tar'. Now that's a fact."

"I got a idea," Abel replied. "We kin tell him we run into old Mrs. Judkins and she asked us to tell him her brother is sickly."

Then what happens when he finds out we lied, Mr. Smart Alek? What happens when he gits to Mrs. Judkins' place and finds out her brother Is fit and healthy?"

Grandpap stepped on down to the riverbank as the boys turned back from hiding their raft. He'd only heard a portion of what the boys were saying, but his curiosity was aroused by the activities and conversation. "What are you boys jabbering on about?" he asked. "What's this about Mrs. Judkins' brother? Is old Henry on the bottle ag'in or somethin'? An' what's this about stealin' some tar?" he asked in a jovial tone.

"W — well Gran'pap," Abel stammered, "we got this here old wagon out of the riverbank up there a piece, and thought we oughter tar the seams some so's we could jes' use 'er like a boat without usin' them barrels. We saw Mrs. Judkins over near the river a while back and that's what she suggested, that we tar up the seams, and we knew maybe you'd let us have some of that tar in the barn. We asked her about her brother, but she said he's jes' fine, and not sick at all."

"Boys," Eldon Curry said, brightly, "That looks to be a pretty good wagon body, but you know it's goin' t' be a mite heavy to carry across the spit ever' day or two. Maybe I could jes' buy it off'n you and we could work out somethin' that'd make it easier fer you'uns to work yer way back home ever' night or so.

An idea occurred to Abel Curry and he brightened immediately. "Gran'pap, there's the rest of this wagon and some more parts, yet. They's, jes' up the river a ways. Could you come on out and help us one of these days so's we could bring the whole mess in and maybe have mor'n one wagon. Maybe there's a handcart over there, too. At least, anyways I think there is, ain't it so, Lute?"

"Yeah, I don't know what all's up there," Luther joined in the deception, hoping to divert his grandfather's attention to the earlier conversation.

"Where's my barn door?" Grandpap asked bluntly. "If'n you young'uns carried this yere wagon bed home, you must'a left my barn door back there. H'it's getting'on winter an' I'm gonna be needin' that-there barn door. I don't want you young'uns leavin' pieces of my barn all over the countryside."

"Oh, we jes' forgot it, Gran'pap," Luther said hastily. "We kin bring it home the next time we're over there." The boys were getting deeper and deeper into the deception and they realized they'd have to be very cautious to keep the game up.

Eldon Curry was getting curious. "Kin I take a look at that there boat of yer'n, boys, or are you gunna keep it a secret from your old gran'pap?" Seems it's a perty good wagon bed fer havin' been buried in the mud. Where d'you s'pose it come from?"

The boys were caught on the horns of a dilemma. They had put the converted wagon bed and the molasses barrels together with some of the rope supplied by the Confederate troops, and the generous supply of new rope would be hard to explain away. But Grandpap Curry had to be dealt with, and to put him off would be to justify any suspicions he might be entertaining.

They weren't the only ones facing a tough decision, though. Eldon Curry had already begun to suspect some subterfuge and he was now giving thought to backing away from his line of questioning to see if he could get to the bottom of the mystery without disclosing his suspicions. He changed his tack, "Well, boys, maybe it's a'gittin' a mite late fer us t'git to pullin' that-there raft out'n the bushes right now. Why don't we wait till t'morr'y to go look fer that stuff? Oh! But I got some business with a feller over 't Judkins Corners t'morr'y and I cain't he'p you'uns until next week."

"That'd be jes' fine, Gran'pap," Abel said quickly. "We'll jes' leave 'er there till you gits back." The other boys joined in agreement.

The four walked on back home to River Bend, each keeping up their end of the conversation without disclosing their own secrets or secret suspicions.

The next day, after Eldon Curry had struck out in the direction of Judkins Corners, some eight miles from River Bend, the boys headed immediately for the north bend of the river where the raft was tied. It didn't occur to them to suspect any deception on the part of their grandfather, even though he was accustomed to ride the family mule on such trips, and today he went on foot. Eldon's path to Judkins Corners was in a similar direction to that the boys took across the neck of the peninsula and after going about a mile he just waited in concealment along the trail until the boys passed and then fell in some distance behind them. It was not difficult to keep contact with the boys from a suitable distance as their voices carried well, even though the morning was drizzly and damp. Presently, however, he heard adult voices in conversation with the boys and he found the group had reversed course and was heading back his way. Ducking into some heavy growth beside the road, Eldon Curry waited for the group to pass him. It consisted of the three boys and six men, some lightly armed, and pushing a handcart. The men and boys were now talking in hushed tones and obviously concerned about being detected. They would pause at the turns in the path and four of the men were occasionally sent out as scouts to warn the group of any onlookers. Though Curry's concealment had been hasty it was good enough so that the soldiers didn't spot him.

As they approached the Curry farm, the soldiers stopped about a hundred yards from the barn, seeking the cover of some blackberry vines. After a short time, Sergeant MacLean and one other soldier, accompanied by Abel, crept toward the barn and went inside. They returned a few moments later with a block of tar between them, slung from a pair of poles. Shortly, all the soldiers proceeded cautiously and quietly to the barn and came back with blocks of tar until Eldon reckoned that five blocks of his tar had been removed from the barn and placed on the soldiers' handcart. He felt betrayed by the boys and was sorely tempted to reveal himself and challenge the group, but his curiosity and sense of self-preservation restrained him. These were Rebel soldiers and his Union sympathies were well known about these parts. It could be dangerous for him to reveal himself, let alone try to stop an act of theft in the process.

The squad trailed off toward the river where the raft was tied, the boys walking along as though part of the plan, which they were. Eldon followed at a safe distance as far as the landing and remained out of sight. They put the tar into the makeshift boat and with Abel and one of the soldiers aboard poling to keep from hanging up on the bank, the others manned two towropes, pulling the raft upstream toward where the soldiers had been camped. The riverbank was unpopulated and they encountered no one on the way.

When they got to the temporary camp on the west side of the river, they pulled from the water the end of the rope that they had submerged across the river the day before, and tied it securely to the raft. Then, on a signal from the west side of the river, the soldiers on the opposite side proceeded to pull the raft across, and once more Lieutenant Austin had tar for the seams of the flatboats.

Having two of the proposed three boats almost finished, Austin made the decision to forego any plans to build the additional boat, as his supply of tar was limited and his deadline for completion was fast approaching. The planking for the decks was adequate and General Forrest was expected on about the fifteenth of December, only one day away. Details had to be attended to and the boats prepared for use.

On December 15, Forrest and a brigade of just over two thousand cavalrymen, along with cannons, horses, and wagons arrived and carefully proceeded to cross the Tennessee River. The crossing took two days, in increasingly heavy weather and was accomplished some four or five miles downstream from where the boats had been built, protected by picket lines stretched up and down the river to guard against the possibility of prying Union eyes.

Eldon Curry, avoiding the pickets, watched the crossing.

The boats held up fairly well under the abuse of the brigade, and after the crossing was accomplished, they were hidden in a small creek that emptied into the Tennessee River. Forrest, after seeing to it that his return passage was assured, moved his brigade north and west some eight or ten miles away from the river and set up camp. There the soldiers built fires, checked their equipment, stood inspection, and warmed themselves for the first time in three days. The equipage for the raid would not be extensive, as General Forrest knew that he'd have ample supplies acquired from the local folk, including forage for his horses.

Grandpap Curry had not been very comfortable during the previous several days either, but wasted no time making his way to Judkins Corners, where he knew there was a garrison of Union soldiers. It was not the only notice of the crossing that the Yankees had received, but it was the most recent and the most accurate in terms of actual numbers. Curry had broken into short pieces, little sticks that each represented one hundred Rebel soldiers, and was sure that the number of Confederate soldiers that had crossed in Forrest's brigade to be no more than twenty-two hundred. However, he also speculated that there may have been some recruiting done along the way thus far, and the numbers could have increased only slightly in the two or three intervening days.

———— «(●)» ————

General Sullivan had been given the assignment to go after Forrest with the positive injunction that if he could not be captured or killed, then at least he was to be pursued closely and neutralized as a threat to the Union's communications lines. Even that would be found to be an impossibility. By November 10, the brigade under General Sullivan was moving out toward the north, with upwards of two thousand men and a small support train. It was felt that there would not be a need for a particularly large supply train, as the purpose of the mission was to protect the Mobile and Ohio Railroad, necessitating their being within a day's ride of the road at all times.

General Grant had also sent out with them a brigade of Cavalry, under Colonel Robert Ingersoll. The cavalry was to be used as a scouting arm, as General Grant didn't feel he had sufficient cavalry of his own to go up against Forrest's brigade of anywhere between three and five thousand, depending on which estimate one believed. He also sent General Mason Brayman and a brigade of almost fifteen hundred soldiers north from Bolivar to join up with the Sullivan Brigade at Jackson, Tennessee. The Sullivan Brigade camped along the way north, with Colonel Ingersoll's cavalry running scouting missions daily, camping wherever they could find forage for their mounts and sending couriers back to report. At times, Logan accompanied the cavalry and at other times, he stayed with General Sullivan. He'd been admonished once to either stay with the Brigade or secure permission to do otherwise, and the lesson stuck. By November 24, the reports started coming in to General Sullivan's headquarters with the information that Forrest had crossed the Tennessee River near Clifton.

Colonel Ingersoll was immediately sent out from Jackson with a force made up of troops from Illinois and Ohio with two companies of recruits from West Tennessee to try to intercept Forrest at Judkins Corners. Ingersoll set up on the edge of town, entrenched to receive Forrest head-on.

Forrest did not like the head-on idea, though, and demonstrating dutifully on Ingersoll's front to keep him occupied, he sent his main force around to the right. The Tennessee troops in Ingersoll's unit, green as they were, realized that if captured, they would be fodder for conscription into Forrest's brigade. They fled as soon as threatened, opening up Ingersoll's left to attack. The Tennessee troops escaped, Ingersoll did not. He was ingloriously captured with 150 of his men and two fine three-inch Rodman rifled cannon which he'd brought along.

Forrest chased the remainder of Ingersoll's regiment almost to Jackson and there played some cat-and-mouse with the Sullivan Brigade, but shortly retired. One of the peculiar characteristics of General Forrest was that he not only knew when and where to attack, he knew when to retire, and this was the time. He had no ambitions to capture great numbers of the Federal army. That would only slow him down. His mission was to harass and destroy communications, and a prolonged battle against heavy odds was not the sort of battle he was interested in. Forrest was a gambler, but he always knew the odds, and if they were stacked against him, he just left the game to others and moved on. He even released the small company of men captured with Colonel Ingersoll, after relieving them of their arms, horses, and gear, as well as the Rodman cannons and all the money Colonel Ingersoll had lost in a friendly game of four-card draw during the three days he was a guest of the Confederate government.

While demonstrating around Jackson for the period of two or three days and destroying the railroads leading all directions from town, Forrest then proceeded north. He was like a will o' the wisp, a virtual ghost, except for the damage he caused to the transportation and communications in the region. His attacks would be masked by feints and demonstrations, sometimes thirty or more miles from his objective, sometimes on just the other side of the town.

Though the local folk were of mixed loyalties, the ones that were pro-Union were seldom bothered by his presence and the secessionist sympathizers were so caught up in the romance surrounding his being there to liberate them that they rushed to his aid.

Chasing him was difficult. As he moved through the countryside his troops and their horses consumed so much of the provisions that were locally available that they virtually cut a swath through which pursuit was all but impossible. At best, to try to follow Forrest through the countryside in this manner proved to be so slow as to be senseless, as he could move quickly and skim the provisions available and his pursuers would have to pause continuously to restock their supplies from the meager gleanings he'd left behind. If, in the event the defending force happened to get in Forrest's front in large enough numbers to be a threat, Forrest simply redirected his attack toward some other target, of which there were plenty.

His numbers were almost always exaggerated. Though people like Grandpap Curry provided a fairly accurate count, there were those like Colonel Ingersoll who estimated, after his capture and release, that Forrest had no less than 5000 troops mounted and ready for duty. Though Ingersoll was most likely exaggerating Forrest's numbers, at least partially to rationalize his own surrender, General Sullivan chose to accept the numbers provided by a professional soldier and responded accordingly. He was reluctant to confront Forrest with anything less than four or five thousand in the open, but, since it was his duty to protect the railroads, he chose rather to place small, strongly entrenched garrisons at 'strategic' points along the railroads. This type of defense was made to order for an offense like Forrest's. With a feint at the enemy's front, he'd flank him from the side or rear. The Union commander being committed and immobile, Forrest, with skill and bravado, could usually convince him of his being surrounded by the overwhelming numbers already warned of by General Sullivan. After capturing such a garrison, Forrest's subordinates would then make elaborate demonstrations to convince the prisoners of their great numbers and then eventually release them to be returned to General Sullivan with stories verifying his most dire suspicions.

Captain Logan could not come to grips with the idea of the great numbers reportedly attributed to Forrest's brigade. He'd been at Judkins Corners when Eldon Curry had been brought to headquarters and had even been able to talk a little with the old man himself. He'd been able to tell Grandpap that he was acquainted with Thresh and assure him that he was alright and reinforce his loyalty. At that time, he'd gained a favorable impression of the old man and was convinced of his reliability. His notion of twenty-two hundred troops in the Forrest Brigade just didn't square with the estimated numbers provided by others. Captain Logan's impression of Colonel Robert Ingersoll was that he tended to be a bit on the dramatic side and may be given to exaggeration, especially if the exaggeration served to diminish his sense of insult from his loss, as at Judkins Corners. Though Jesse had left Judkins Corners and been on his way back to Jackson when the attack had occurred, he still didn't see how Forrest could have doubled the size of his brigade in the course of fifteen miles over sparsely populated country.

Nevertheless, whatever his numbers, Forrest was a force to be dealt with. After spending a short time threatening to gobble up General Sullivan's brigade, he turned north, and by Christmas Eve was threatening Columbus, Kentucky with its vast depots and warehouses brimming with supplies that were prepared for Grant's move on Vicksburg. In this event, he had actually gained numbers along the way, as he'd not only been able to recruit, but there were other small regiments of Confederate cavalry operating in the area that had been combined for Forrest's purposes.

General Sullivan had remained at Jackson, Tennessee the whole time. Though Grant's instructions had been for him either to run Forrest aground and destroy him or at least keep him on the run, Sullivan could do neither. He didn't have the cavalry to match Forrest, and his infantry was only able to stand and fight, and then not in the numbers sufficient to be at any one place where Forrest would confront them. By December 30, however, with Forrest wreaking havoc almost a hundred miles to the north, Sullivan pulled up stakes at Jackson and started north in pursuit. Again, he left small detachments at some of the more important towns, Lexington, Jacks Creek, and Clarksburg, to try to head Forrest off, if he tried to recross the Tennessee River, but his main effort by now was to confront the man directly. He had word that the river was well patrolled, that all ferries and bridges had been destroyed, and, in his own words, he told Grant in a dispatch on December 31, that he had, "Forrest in a tight place ... My troops are moving on him ... I hope with success."

Though the weather had turned stormy and the rivers were high, there was still much to be done and many miles to be covered before the noose around "Old Bedford" could be brought up snug. A general confrontation did develop at Parkers Cross Roads on New Years Day, in which Forrest was attacked by no less than three of General Sullivan's pursuing regiments and in which both sides suffered severe losses, both as to prisoners captured and men killed. Then, despite General Sullivan's claims of victory, Forrest proceeded south to his original point of debarkation, preparing to cross back over the Tennessee on the same boats that had brought him west.

Forrest's last sortie west of the Tennessee involved Colonel Englemann's cavalry regiment of about sixteen hundred, garrisoned at Judkins Corners near where the flat boats had been anchored. Logan had persuaded General Sullivan to allow the small detachment to focus a search on the river front along the bank of the Tennessee to try to find the boats they knew were hidden somewhere along that stretch of river-bank and he had been allowed to take a scouting party of 120 cavalrymen to accompany Colonel Englemann to Judkins Corners and scout from there.

Logan was allowed in on the preparations when this whole thing was being mapped out and though it went counter to the general's plan, Colonel Englemann was ultimately assigned to set up an encampment at Judkins Corners, monitoring the fortifications at night and scouting the countryside during the daylight hours.

The last day General Forrest was to be on the western side of the river, the Union regiment was dug in at Judkins Corners as Forrest was about to head back across the river. Logan had been trying to get Colonel Englemann to venture out and look for Forrest's transport boats, but the colonel was more concerned with protecting his flanks than exploring uncharted territory, chasing a ghost. As he told Logan and the five lieutenants assigned to the regiment, "I'm convinced Forrest has at his disposal an army of five or six thousand and will just eat us up."

As it happened, Colonel Englemann did venture out for a short excursion toward the river, but his small troop, consisting of himself, Logan, and four troopers, encountered an advance scout of thirteen of Forrest's men, mounted and apparently prepared to fight. In their haste to return to the entrenchments at Judkins Corners, Colonel Englemann's horse stumbled, throwing him off putting him completely out of service. It appeared he had suffered a broken arm and perhaps some cracked ribs, and was treated by the regiment's doctor, who gave him some laudanum, rendering him completely senseless.

Shortly thereafter, Forrest and his brigade attacked Judkins Corners as though he was going to sweep the regiment into the river but being well entrenched, they were ready for him and managed to hold him off. It was about three o'clock in the afternoon when Forrest's brigade struck. Logan wondered later what reason he had for the attack, as Forrest was on his way back to the river and had no cause to take another outpost. In their reflections on the attack, Logan and the other command officers speculated that he must have figured the Englemann Regiment had ammunition or equipment that he could take back across with him. They also had two rifled cannons, which they knew Forrest would have liked to take with him as a prize.

Logan was the only officer left above the rank of lieutenant, and in Colonel Ingersoll's absence, the command fell to him for the time. Forrest started the attack on the north side of the town, and then, just as quickly changed his approach to east. Owing to the well-structured entrenchments that had been started earlier by Colonel Ingersoll the men were ready as they heard that this was one of Forrest's tactics and held him off on that side, too. Soon he attacked from the north again found the Federals were still holding pretty well over there.

After a brief lull in the melee, Forrest set up a white flag and sent in a messenger to tell the embattled Union troops that they were surrounded and should give up, in order to, as he termed it, "... avoid any unnecessary bloodshed." The Federals hadn't lost even one man, unless you could count

Colonel Englemann, and Logan found it odd that Forrest wanted the Federals to surrender, but he received the messenger, nevertheless. According to his reports, Forrest might have lost one man killed and one or two wounded, but that was all. It wasn't much of a battle until then.

The messenger came in and while they were talking, they saw a troop coming in from the south as though they had just ridden in to give Forrest some extra reinforcements, and at that juncture Logan got a little worried. Still talking to the messenger, though, and no sooner had the first troop of "reinforcements" ridden off toward the west, there was another big bunch coming in from the south even though, as Jesse thought, there hadn't been much fighting down south and he couldn't understand why they'd be down there at all. Another thing he noticed was that one of the battle flags they were flying was identical to one that the troop just before them had been flying and even some of the horses looked very similar. It began to dawn on him that the whole thing was a bluff.

The messenger, a lieutenant in the worst looking rags Logan had ever seen on a man, was telling him, "Old Bedford has about forty thousand troops or more and he'll just wipe you'uns out if you'uns was to resist. Bedford ain't a'playin' games and you'uns had better surrender if y'all knew what was good fer y'all."

Logan told him he'd go talk to the colonel and to just wait there. He went back behind some sheds that were nearby and waited a few minutes, then went back and told the lieutenant that Colonel Englemann felt the regiment was better off to just hold tight. The lieutenant just nodded and kind of looked sad and asked if he couldn't talk to Colonel Englemann. Logan told him the colonel would negotiate with Forrest, but not with a lieutenant and he was lucky to get to talk to a captain, so he went back to his brigade without accomplishing much.

The next thing you know, Bedford was on them from the west, and they had their hands full but held him off again and lost only one man killed, but they did have one other man wounded who later died. Bedford lost fifteen men in that attack, four killed, four wounded, and seven captured. He also lost somewhere around eight or nine horses, and though they breached the Federal line at one point it seemed to Logan to be more of a feint, and it was there that the seven Confederates were captured. Forrest's men were all on horseback, of course, and fighting from the ground Englemann's troops had the advantage, even though the Rebels could move fast, the Federals could stay low and shoot them out of the saddle.

The Union men having captured seven of the Rebels, it seemed to Logan that that may have made Bedford think a little about the wisdom of pursuing the attack further. He talked to two of the prisoners and they pretty well agreed that Forrest had the advantage in numbers. One of the prisoners said ten thousand, and the other didn't know but he thought it looked pretty bad for the Federals. Jesse reflected that all this was sort of funny, him standing talking to this man as a prisoner and being told that his own regiment of Union troops were in trouble.

Even so, Forrest sent in another messenger, this time a captain, giving Logan the same story. "Either surrender or suffer overwhelming defeat," He said. He also wanted to talk to the colonel and was told the same thing as was told the lieutenant; that it appeared to Logan that they were in pretty good shape and the colonel felt the same way. The messenger, obviously experienced in such negotiations, continued at some length, telling the Union captain how silly it was for them to stand and fight when they were so badly outnumbered but Jesse held his ground.

After a few minutes of listening, Jesse said to the officer, "Well, Captain, let's look at it this way. We have killed or captured your troopers ten to one over those we have lost and my colonel, if you must know, is just spoiling for a fight. He gave me an order to hold you as our prisoner to see if doing that might get your regiment to come on in and try us out. I told him that would be a violation of trust, but he wants me to take you in right now."

The man turned white and was, Logan observed, sidling over toward his horse to try to make a getaway. Jesse decided to just let him go, as he'd come in under a flag of truce. He got on his horse and made it out of camp as fast as the animal would take him. Logan was a little worried that Bedford would take what he'd said as an insult and really try to make them pay, but he didn't.

When the captain left, there was one more half-hearted attack, but then things got pretty quiet. The Confederates didn't attack again after that, despite Logan's concerns. It had gotten dark by then and Forrest's men set up camp around the perimeter of the town. By this time Colonel Englemann had recovered his senses somewhat and Logan told him what had happened. They took a tour of the works and the colonel had a chance to look at all of Forrest's campfires and duck a few of the bullets they were sending in, and told Jesse they'd have to surrender the next morning. He wanted to send a messenger out right then but Jesse stalled him so they could at least burn the stores. The men of the regiment were all on foot, with the cavalry horses secured in the center of town, but it really looked as though they were surrounded and there wasn't any way to break out. They could see troops moving around, between them and the enemy's campfires and it even looked like there were other reinforcements coming in.

Colonel Englemann gave orders to spike the cannons and burn the stores, but before the orders could be passed on, he again passed out. The colonel slept like a baby all night and Logan was reluctant to abandon what he perceived as a secure entrenchment. The firing from the enemy lines faded away toward dawn, and when it got light the men in blue looked out on an empty field. The Rebels had completely disappeared, leaving their campfires burning. Logan was alternately disgusted, amused, and relieved. He'd spent the whole night walking around trying to keep the spirits of the men up, and didn't get a wink of sleep, and Colonel Englemann got up the next morning, bright eyed and bushy tailed and saw that the field was clear. Nor did he even remember that he'd given orders to spike the cannon and burn the stores. He sent back a report to General Sullivan that they'd received the enemy and handled him roughly and that Forrest had left the field taking his wounded with him.

That was all. It was typical Forrest. When he couldn't bluff you out of your trenches, he just went away. *"The man"*, thought Jesse, *"is a genius."*

———⟫•⟨⟩•⟪———

For several days Generals Sullivan and Grenville Dodge, who had come to his aid, directed a search of the bottomlands along the west side of the Tennessee River trying to find the remnants of Forrest's 'defeated' army. The only trace they could find of his having been there were a trail of dead soldiers and some horse and wagon tracks leading to the river.

General Grant was forced to rethink the assignment of General Sullivan to a field unit and chose to place him in a position he thought more suited to his capabilities. After the wild goose chase along the Tennessee River, Jeremiah Sullivan was recalled and given the role of Inspector General on Grant's staff. Captain Jesse Logan was also reassigned. At the request of General Rosecrans, replacing General Don Carlos Buell, Jesse was sent east to the Army of the Cumberland, then headquartered near Nashville.

The pursuit of Nathan Bedford Forrest was abandoned for the time being.

21

NASHVILLE, 1863

The state capitol of Tennessee had been in Federal hands for most of the previous year, with Andrew Johnson appointed as War Governor by President Lincoln. The sentiments of the people of the area, as elsewhere in Tennessee, were mixed. Eastern Tennessee had been adamant about their desire to stay with the union, and the western part of the state had been just as adamant about secession. Following the capture of Fort Donelson and Fort Henry by General Grant in February 1862, western Tennessee was now largely in the hands of the Federals and the eastern part of the state was largely occupied by the men in butternut. In general, however the people of Nashville and the surrounding area were accepting of the Federal occupancy, especially when the city was host to Federal troops and the real money that they brought with them. The city was largely untouched by the ravages of war in spite of the contested status of the state, and offered the image of a bustling and rather undisturbed city, except for the endless movement of men, materials, and supplies of war that passed through daily, supplying Federal money in the bargain.

Business was brisk. Investment by the Union army brought with it greenbacks, which were much more spendable, even in the south, than the currency circulated by the Confederate government or southern banks. On the outskirts of the city, however, were entrenchments and cannon, row after row of cannon, looking south and reminding anyone in doubt that there was indeed a war going on.

Captain Logan had been transferred from the west upon General Sullivan's reassignment, and was simply told to report to army headquarters, without specific assignment of his own. On locating the general office of the Army of the Cumberland, an imposing building not far from the state capitol, he entered a door that was marked "Quartermaster" and inquired with the sergeant who was sitting behind a desk in the first office he came to.

"I'm Captain Logan," he informed the man at the desk. "I've been told to report here for assignment."

The sergeant, a man who Jesse estimated as being about forty, but who, though clean shaven, looked older than his years, pushed back from the desk, his chair scraping harshly on the tiled floor as he reached for a pair of crutches. "I'll tell the capt'n you're here, Captain," he said without any sign of recognition. "I don't have no information on your comin' here, but that ain't unusual. They don't tell me nothin' around here and I have to find out most of it for myself. What's your firs' name, Captain?"

"It's Jesse," came a voice from the next room. "It's Captain Jesse Logan, and we've been expecting you, Sir."

Before the sergeant at the desk could rise, Frank Davis came quickly from the rear office with his right hand extended in greeting. He looked much as he had when Jesse had seen him last, but thinner and older than Jesse remembered. "Captain Logan! My land, how are you? How did you happen to draw this assignment? It's certainly good to see you, Sir. It looks as though the climate out west has agreed with you. You certainly haven't lost any weight. I'd never expected to run into you in this part of the country."

The bond between the two men that had been established two thousand miles away in the hills of Wyoming and reinforced during their campaign through western Virginia was instantly rekindled. Frank Davis had been Jesse's mentor and friend through many struggles and trials. Jesse, on the other hand, younger by almost twenty years, had proven himself again and again in Davis' eyes, and the respect they had for each other ran both directions. Davis, having prepared himself for this meeting, was doing all the talking. Jesse was silent for several minutes before getting a chance to speak. "It's good to see you, too, Captain. How did you draw this desk assignment, anyway?"

"Well, I got a little wound, just after you left Virginia, and I'm doing desk duty until it heals up completely. Your friend John Goodin and I got into an argument and without so much as a 'How d'y do', he took a shot at me. 'Hit me in the side, he did, and I thought I was a goner. But Sergeant Hawkins was just outside the tent and heard what was going on. He come running to my rescue just in time to catch Goodin scurrying out o' the tent like some kind of a rat. Goodin took a shot at Lige, too, but missed. So Lige already had his revolver out and took two shots at Goodin. Hit him right there," he said pointing to his left shoulder section, "Bam, bang! Just like that. There's something wrong with that man, Jesse. You and I talked about it the last time we were together. I think it was back in Lewiston, wasn't it? We both felt like we were sitting ducks for old Goodin's wrath."

"Well, I never —," Jesse muttered. "Captain, I just never thought Goodin was that kind of a man, in spite of the fact that he took a dislike for me. What do you suppose got into him? Did Lige kill him?"

"No. he didn't. Pity, somehow, but taking the lives of our own men is not what we're supposed to do, as you may recall, but that man must have a charmed life. He's taken three or four hits, now, and has still survived. You remember, we talked a little, a few days before this happened, and then after you left, he was talking as though he was some kind of a hero for that little incident where Colonel Abernathy and he cooked up that escape plot. Well, he didn't think I knew about his conniving to get Abernathy cut loose. And then, when you got transferred, he was strutting around the camp like the town peacock when I called him in to tell him he was likely to be arrested and was there anything he wanted me to know, you know, and that sort of thing. I was trying to get something out of him, and he must have figured maybe I was the only other person than yourself that knew the facts. He just turned white as a sheet. All the blood drained out of his face and he turned around without saying a word and walked out. Then, a few minutes later, he came into my tent and called me some names and then just took a shot at me. That was it. I ducked sideways and hit the dirt, but if I hadn't he'd of got me for sure."

"Say, Jesse, why don't you come on over to my house, tonight. I was able to bring my wife, Mary and my two young'uns down here whilst I recover. I have a little house just a few blocks over, here, and I'd like you to meet her. I've told you all about her, but you never met her and I'd like you to. You know she's from the part of the country where you grew up. You and her might have a lot to talk about."

"Frank, I'd like that. It's been some time since I've visited a real home here or anywhere else. The idea that anyone in this world can even have a home is hard for me to imagine, what with everything going on around us, the war and all. You told me you were married to the most beautiful woman in these United States, but this is the first time you even told me her name."

"Well, I'll tell you this much, Captain Logan. This woman is not only beautiful, she's got a head on her shoulders. She's put together just a beautiful little place out of scraps and pieces, and is busy all the time with those two kids of mine. She's organized the other wives of the officers into a sewing society, although I think they spend more time talking than they do sewing. She's even befriended some of the local ladies, even some who were leaning toward secession, and has included them in the 'society'. She's just a natural-born organizer."

"It seems General Rosecrans and Governor Johnson are pretty confident about our ability to hold on to Nashville, doesn't it?" Jesse mused. "Are there many families here right now?"

"About twenty or thirty of the officers have their families here, Jesse. I think I'm the only one below the rank of colonel, though. When I was reassigned after Goodin took that shot at me, General Rosecrans suggested I bring my wife and children down to help me get back on my feet. By the way, what happened to Jere Sullivan, anyway? I thought he was pretty well liked in a field position, and here he is working in the adjutant's office for General Grant."

"If I have the picture right, General Grant got a little miffed with General Sullivan when he failed to run Bedford Forrest to ground." Jesse scratched his nose and looked at the floor. "When Old Bedford came across the Tennessee back last month, he didn't have anything going for him. He only had a little over two thousand troops, and they weren't very well armed, at that. His horses weren't in the best of shape, and even getting across the river was touchy. If we'd had sense enough to listen to some of the reports that were coming in about the possibility of his coming across the river down at Clifton, he never would have made it across. At least not as soon and as easy as he did."

Jesse went over to a window and looked out at the fading daylight. "We had a boy in one of our battalions who was from River Bend, just across the river from Clifton, and his grandpa got word to us about Bedford crossing the river. We had a couple of other sources right there in Clifton that told us he was in the region, too, but as good as General Sullivan has always been about sorting out intelligence, he didn't show much horse sense on this one. Rumors about the size of Bedford's brigade were running anywhere from five to ten thousand and he just reckoned old Bedford had a larger army than he really did. General Grant knew Forrest was going to try to disrupt our supply trains, and he had given General Sullivan strict and positive orders — very specific — to track that man down and put him out of commission. General Sullivan just has his own way of doing things and this time he miscalculated."

By the time Jesse had finished his story, they were standing before a small house and Frank turned up the walk. "Come on, Jesse, Mary's waiting and I'm sure there will be plenty of food for all of us. She usually feeds the children earlier and they'll be in the other room, but I do want them to meet you. I've told them all about you, you know."

Frank Davis' wife was indeed at the door and waiting for him. He went in the door and gave her an affectionate hug and a kiss on the cheek and then turned to introduce her to Jesse. Mary Davis had already looked past her husband at the tall soldier standing behind him and the color drained from her face. Logan also stepped back in surprise.

In 1855 Sergeant Frank Davis had gone west in response to orders from General Harney to show the strength of the United States army and convince the Indians that warfare against an army such as that was futile. Part of his mission took him as far as Eagle Station, Nevada, where he met a young lady with whom he immediately became infatuated and, after a short time, married. The young lady was locally known as Spanish Mary and had gone the few miles north from Genoa to try the market at Eagle Station.

"Jesse, I want you to meet my bride of almost seven years," Frank was saying. "This is the most devoted wife a man could have and I want you to look around this house. As little as she's had to work with, she has made this place a Home Sweet Home. Mary," he said turning to her, "This is Captain Jesse Logan, the man I've told you about. He's from out your way and I'm sure you two have a lot in common."

Mary had regained her composure, somewhat, and Frank failed to perceive any reaction on her part on meeting a man who, of all people, had shared some of her past and with whom she indeed, had "— a lot in common." She smiled as Jesse took her hand and the old Spanish Mary Jesse had known as a young man of fifteen was there before him. She was a little heavier than he remembered, but her figure hadn't suffered a bit from the passage of time and the baring of two children. She was vintage Mary, poised, controlled, and very becoming.

"How do you do?" Mary said in a voice only slightly reminiscent of her Spanish heritage. "It's so nice to meet you Captain. Captain Davis has indeed told me a lot about you, but he didn't mention you were so tall." Her voice was low and musical, and she almost seemed to be mocking Jesse as she stood before him.

"Mrs. Davis," Jesse said with a low bow and in a voice that mirrored hers, "the pleasure is all mine. I hope I haven't inconvenienced you by coming here this way. If it will be any inconvenience at all, I assure you I can certainly go back to camp and be perfectly comfortable. I might offer to take you and Captain Davis to a hotel for supper, but I understand you have two little children and it would probably be something of a difficulty taking them out at this hour."

"Not at all," she said. "There is plenty of food right here at our house. I'll just tell the girl to set another place." The home was small but there appeared to be three rooms that Jesse could identify. One, the front room also had dining arrangements set up. The other two were probably the kitchen off to the left and rear of the home and the bedroom on the right behind the main room. A black woman in her mid forties emerged from the kitchen and Mary turned and spoke in a low voice to her, whereupon "Sarah" turned back into the kitchen and immediately returned with an additional place setting for supper.

"So, it's — Captain — Logan," Mary said tentatively. "Frank has never mentioned you by name, Captain, only that you had been friends for many years and he had been disappointed that you'd been transferred west before I had a chance to meet you. There was a Logan family in Genoa before I left. I assume you are a member of that family."

"Yes, Ma'am, that's my family, the ones in Genoa — it was Mormon Station when I lived there," he said with a smile. "That was a long time ago. It seems so far back in time, yet there are a few things that happened back then that are still fresh in my memory." He let the import of the comment settle for a moment, then continued. "Had you lived in Mormon Station, Mrs. Davis?"

The unspoken agreement was sealed. Neither was going to reveal, at least in present company, the events of the past that had brought Mary and Jesse together in their younger years. So far as their present situation was concerned, they were meeting for the first time and anything that had happened in the past would remain in the past.

"Will you excuse me for a moment?" Frank Davis was saying. "I want to take off my boots and say hello to the children." He turned toward the bedroom and disappeared.

As he left the room, Mary reached out a hand toward Jesse and, with a pleading look in her eyes, mouthed the words, "Thank you." Jesse gazed at her with rapt interest. His mind went back to the day along Silver Creek when he first enjoyed the intimacy of a woman's touch and he envisioned Mary in the state of undress in which he'd seen her at that time.

"Won't you have a seat, Captain Logan?" Mary was asking him in a calm controlled voice. "It will be a few minutes before we have supper, and perhaps you'd care to rest. Have you been traveling long, today? Where have you come from, just now? Would you care to meet our two children?"

"Yes, I'd like to meet your children, Mrs. Davis. The captain has told me so much about them and also about you. I just came up from Columbia, today. I had been given orders to report to the Army of the Cumberland headquarters, but without specific assignment. I still don't know where I'll be assigned."

Sarah, overhearing the conversation, brought the children out of the kitchen where they had been eating supper, just as Frank emerged from the bedroom.

"Papa!" they screamed, almost in unison. "Papa, what did you bring us?" they cried. They clung to his legs, sitting on his slippered feet, and making it difficult for him to walk.

"How are my two urchins, today?" Frank asked in a loud voice, reaching down and picking up first one and then the other of the two children. His actions were somewhat pained, but his face was beaming. "Have you ever seen two such beautiful children in your life, Captain Logan?" he asked, holding them in his arms. The children were both fair-haired, the girl having the dark eyes of her mother and the boy with hazel colored eyes, like Frank's side of the family. The girl, Rachel, was about five, Jesse guessed, and the boy, Timothy, was probably only a year younger. They were indeed handsome children, Jesse agreed.

Mary went over and took Timothy from Frank's arms and held him closely. "These are my two twin prizes for having to put up with my wandering husband. He had a promising job with his father in Indiana before the war, but he just couldn't stay still. He had to get right in and fight for Mr. Lincoln, as soon as the word went out. But fortunately, he left me with these two and I was quite comfortable in Indiana. I'll probably return there before long, if conditions are fair for traveling. I just don't like to have the children so close to the fighting, even though it also keeps them close to their father. He'll be fully recovered from his gunshot wound, soon, and I don't think it's good that we stay here."

"Do you think there is that immediate a danger, Mrs. Davis?" Jesse inquired. "Mrs. Johnson has come here to live with the governor, and I understand there are several wives who are now staying with their husbands. I am inclined to feel that Nashville is very important to the Union and that it will be held at all hazards, if Mr. Lincoln has anything to say about the matter."

"Mrs. Johnson had the dubious choice of living here or remaining in Greenville, which is still in Rebel control," Mary raising her voice with a slight show of emotion. "Mrs. Johnson was a prisoner in her own home and it was only as a result of some very shrewd negotiations that Governor Johnson was able to secure her release. I hear it was through the good offices of Mr. John Bell that he was able to bring her here. She is indeed a lucky woman to have been released from the clutches of that renegade band. And as for Nashville being an important prize for the Union, it would be equally important to the Confederacy if they were to be able to occupy this town. My friends tell me there is great psychological value to whoever owns the city of Nashville, as well as being a shipping center. I don't think all Tennesseans realize the importance of this state to both sides in this war. It is almost the equal of Virginia in that regard."

Jesse was impressed with the authority and knowledge Mary demonstrated in the discussion of politics. "Have you had an opportunity to talk to Mrs. Johnson?" he asked.

"Oh, yes, I have," Mary responded, enthusiastically. "She's a very gracious lady and has had the officers' wives to tea on several occasions. I consider myself awfully lucky to be here at this time. It is truly the opportunity of a lifetime to be able to meet with someone so knowledgeable on political affairs. This little girl from away out west is extremely flattered to have been able to engage with such highly placed people as the Governor and his wife."

"You know, Ma — ah — Mrs. Davis," Jesse said catching himself, "Governor Johnson was not always the highly placed person we now know him to be. He started his career as a tailor in Greenville and it's been widely rumored that Mrs. Johnson, after their marriage, was even the one who taught him to read. Where I lived for several years after I moved from Nevada, I was a friend of the Johnsons' daughter, Mary, and her husband Dan Stover. I had an opportunity to talk to the Governor during those years and I reckon I was just as impressed by Mr. and Mrs. Johnson, as you are. They are my idea of the kind of people that this country really needs to keep us on a stable and peaceful path. Unfortunately, they seem to be in the minority in the south."

Sarah had been quietly setting food on the table just behind where Frank had been sitting. She tapped Mary on the shoulder and murmured something in her ear to let her know supper was ready for them. The children were removed to the bedroom and instructed to prepare for bed. Mary rose, announced supper, and graciously took Jesse's arm, as though they were engaged in a procession to the dining hall of some grand mansion. Frank joined them, held the chair for his wife, and seated himself at the head of their small dining table.

Jesse was amazed at the cultivated manners of his hostess. He knew she had been well trained as a young girl in the home of a rather affluent family in the west, but his earlier association with her had given him no indication of her ability to absorb and integrate into her own personality the customs and attitudes of her current environment. His impression of Mary Davis as a young wife, mother and figure in the community in which she found herself grew moment by moment as he watched her deal with her various duties. From Maria, the governess to Spanish Mary to Mrs. Frank Davis was a transition of profound proportion. Jesse found himself thinking that whatever dimensions and characteristics she had displayed that afternoon almost eight years ago beside the banks of Silver Creek, the characteristics she was now demonstrating were just as attractive.

As they walked the few steps to the dining table in the Davis home, her grasp on his arm told him they were still friends, but how that friendship would be played out was something upon which he didn't dare to speculate. His mind took him back in time to those magic moments in Nevada, and he found himself every bit as attracted to Mary Davis as he had been back then to Spanish Mary.

Supper with Frank and Mary Davis was congenial and cordial, if somewhat restrained. The supper table was a place for polite exchange and conversation and the Davis home was certainly well adapted to those pleasantries.

After supper, Jesse took his leave and, on Frank's directions, rode to a camp that had been set out for transient officers and men. He checked in with an orderly and, after seeing that his horse was secure, he found the tent he had been assigned, laid out his bedroll and retired for the night.

The following day dawned cold and wet and Jesse was up at dawn, more to stay dry than to return to headquarters. After rising and finding that there was a mess tent staffed by local help, he headed for army headquarters, only to be met by a contingent of eight or ten officers and their aids all bent on the same thing. The squad was riding into town, covered by ponchos and gum blankets to shield them from the elements. When their leader spotted Jesse, he hailed him, asking to be directed to the quartermaster's tent or office, as the case may be, as they were looking for Captain Davis. After a brief conversation, Jesse recognized some of the officers. It was the command staff of the First Tennessee Cavalry (USA) that had just ridden into town from up around Glasgow, Kentucky.

The colonel of the regiment was Bob Johnson, the governor's son, whom Jesse had known from their visits at the home of Dan Stover, over in Carter's Station, and whom Jesse recognized immediately. Robert, after recognizing Jesse, struck up a cordial conversation, although he looked frail and complained that his health seemed to be failing him. The lieutenant colonel was none other than Jim Brownlow, son of the Editor of the Knoxville Whig newspaper, Parson William Brownlow who was almost as famous as Bob Johnson's father. Jim, younger than Jesse by two years, had had a reputation as something of a reckless youth, and although hailing from Knoxville, he had been born in Jonesborough, and been as far east as Elizabethton on several occasions before the war. Jim Brownlow was well known in all of East Tennessee.

Though his father, William Brownlow was a Whig and the governor a Democrat, the two younger men got along well, especially in the present event. They worked together to develop a reputation for the First Tennessee almost as fearsome as Bedford Forrest had done for his regiment fighting on the side of the Confederacy.

Other men with whom Jesse had been well acquainted were also with the regiment. John Feathers, only a few years older than Jesse, was a private in Company "L", whose captain was Jim Colville, another friend from the Watauga Valley. Chaplain for the regiment was Captain John Holtsinger, a tall, spare man, and a Presbyterian minister from Greenville. Jesse and his family had sat in many a church meeting listening to the messages Reverend Holtsinger had delivered, and Jesse felt a real sense of comfort when he saw him ride up with the staff of the First Tennessee. He knew the regiment was in good hands with so many distinguished men for whom he had had such respect in the earlier days.

"Bully for the First Tennessee! Bully for the 'old flag'! Hurrah for the U. S. of America!" Jesse shouted as he and the regimental staff rode on toward headquarters. "With a force like this, the cause of freedom is secure!"

Colonel Johnson grinned broadly, but his manner was subdued. "I don't think the First Tennessee can win the war by itself, Captain," he commented. "We've done our share of winning the few skirmishes we've been part of, but Little Joe Wheeler and old Bedford have done their share, too."

"I know, Colonel," Logan responded. "I was just over west when Bedford was stirring things up the other side of the Tennessee, and I'm here to tell you he's a smart one. He had us running in circles like a dog chasing his tail. Then just when we figured we had him in a standoff, he'd disappear and show up forty miles away, just as sassy."

"Well, maybe we can learn something from that old fox." Bob Johnson commented. "We fight a little different from the way he does, but some of his tactics are sure to be useful to us. You know how he feints and dodges and then comes at you from the back? Well, we tried that up on the Salt River against John Morgan, and we beat him up pretty good. After that, ol' John H. left Kentucky, and I hope for good. We just came in from up there, and I want you to know there wasn't much of a Rebel force left to fight. That's why we were ordered south. By the way, Captain, what is your assignment here in Nashville? I thought you were working with General Sullivan out west of here."

"General Sullivan has been reassigned to General Grant's staff, I think to handle a lot of the scouting and secret information work the general has for him out there. I'm told that General Grant has it in his mind to capture

Vicksburg, Mississippi, and there's no way those Rebs are going to keep him from it. They can make it awful miserable for him on the way, but I'll tell you, gentlemen, General Grant will be in Vicksburg by summer."

"Why didn't you go with him?" Jim Colville inquired. "You were his adjutant, weren't you, Jesse?"

"Yes — yes, I was, but I got the idea that it was only the general, General Sullivan that Grant wanted." Logan took off his hat and scratched his head. "General Sullivan has a nose for news, and he can put two and two together and come up with four when everyone else is saying 'six'. He's pretty cute in coming up with the best slant on what's happening on the other side. The only time he's missed, that I know of, is when we were up against old Bedford. That Forrest caught General Sullivan looking the other way every time he moved. It was uncanny how that man could outguess his opponents, and I mean all of us."

About that time, a young lieutenant in a well-fitting uniform rode up. "I'm looking for Captain Logan," he announced, then turning toward Jesse, he did a classic double take. "Jesse, is that you?" the young man asked incredulously. It was one of Jesse's old schoolmates, Alf Gahagan, who, back in Elizabethton, had been friends with both Jesse, Paul Venable, and Tom Singleton, and also with Eli Morgan and Sid Coster, the men who were instrumental in Jesse's capture by the Rebels the preceding year, as well as Adam Gainfield, the Confederate corporal who had finally sealed Logan's fate at Doe River Cove.

Alf, as Jesse recalled, had been one of the better students at Elizabethton Grammar School, and after graduation, had been expected to go to some school like Virginia Military Institute, but the war intervened. In October 1861, he had eluded conscription by the Confederate authorities only by hiding and running, and when he encountered Dan Ellis, he imposed upon him to include him in his next trip through the Cumberland Gap to the security of Kentucky. He and many of the others in the regiment had made their way to Flat Lick, where it had been rumored there would be a regiment of Tennessee volunteers formed up in a short while. Then, when Robert Johnson arrived a few days later, the Fourth Tennessee Volunteer Infantry, USA was formed with Johnson as its colonel and Alf as a First Lieutenant, Company "D". Later that year, the need for Cavalry became urgent, and as the men from the Fourth were mostly all from East Tennessee and skilled horsemen by nature, the regiment was renamed and equipped as the First Tennessee Cavalry (USA).

"Jesse, ah — Captain Logan, I mean," Alf said with a smile and a quick salute, "orders from General Rosecrans." He held out his hand with a piece of paper in it. Alf Gahagan looked much younger than his years, and, at twenty-two, appeared to be about seventeen. He carried himself well, though, and with a keen intelligence and quick wit, he was well liked and respected by his company, even the older members of the troop. He and Jesse had been closely associated in both debate and mathematics back home, and had a strong respect for the other's abilities.

Jesse unfolded the written order and studied it for a few moments before his face broke out in a smile. "Well, wouldn't you know it? The general has given me a temporary assignment with some obscure regiment of cavalry called the First Tennessee," he said with mock disgust, "whoever they are."

"Well, I'll be hanged," Bob Johnson said with equal disdain. "It's not enough I have to bear up under the burden of the likes of Jim Colville and Alf Gahagan, now they want me to take on a Jesse Logan to compound my misery. What will the general think of next? It looks like Carter County is going to take over the First Tennessee."

⸺⸺ ◈ ⸺⸺

The next few days were spent getting acquainted with the duties of command. Abraham Hammond, who had been a captain with Company "I", had been promoted to major and there was need for a captain to fill his place. Lieutenant William Kidwell had been selected for promotion but owing to ill health had been furloughed for a time. It was not known how long Captain Logan would be with the unit and Colonel Johnson thought it a wise move to use Jesse to fill that temporary vacancy.

The First Tennessee was a close-knit group and Jesse sensed some reservation on the part of the men in accepting this newcomer. His old friends from the Watauga Valley, John Armitage, Abner Bible, A. J. Davis, and others often came to Jesse's aid and made the job much easier. William Kidwell was a popular choice for captain and even after he received his furlough and prior to leaving to stay with family in Kentucky he spent enough time around camp to reinforce Jesse's acceptance. Colonel Johnson and Lieutenant Colonel Brownlow were also in evidence and gave Jesse considerable credibility with the men. Colonel Johnson continued to show signs of poor health and the men in the ranks were turning more and more to Colonel Brownlow. It seemed to be owing to his support that established Jesse's credibility with the troops.

It was not long before Jesse's leadership was tested. The Rebels were threatening at Franklin, about fifteen miles to the south, and on February first, Colonel Brownlow was directed to take a small reconnaissance company to test their strength. Company "I" and a contingent from Company "C" were selected for the raid. After crossing the Harpeth River, the unit entered directly into the town of Franklin and found it full of Confederate officers and men, spending leisure time with the local townspeople. It reminded Jesse a little of the small town of Port Republic on the Shenandoah River when he and a small cavalry troop had uprooted Stonewall Jackson, but this time the invasion was on a smaller scale.

The Rebel soldiers were totally unprepared for the presence of the invaders, but were there in such numbers that it was also something of a surprise to Jim Brownlow and his men. As it was late in the day, and preparations for a pitched battle had not been made on either side, the First Tennessee, after a brief council and reconnaissance, grabbed up about fifteen prisoners and made their way back across the river to safety. They had accomplished their purpose, that of testing the enemy presence in the area and banging their heads a bit to give General Bragg something to think about, and were content to return to Nashville to report their findings. It was a classic Bedford Forest raid and served the purpose of rattling the composure of the Rebel command. The Federals lost one man in the skirmish.

The following morning there was a general council of commanders to assess the results of the raid and to plan for future attacks. Colonel Johnson had also called the commanders together for an important announcement.

"Gentlemen," Bob Johnson began, "You all know I haven't been in the best of health trying to lead you in some of the battles and skirmishes we've been in these last few months. This last ride down here from Louisville was pretty hard on me and I don't see me staying in the saddle for much longer."

There was a murmur among the twenty-five or so commanders attending the meeting. Jesse had been only vaguely aware of any health problems with Colonel Johnson, but he'd not been with the troop all that long, anyway.

Johnson continued, "Now that we've come all the way as far as Nashville, I'm reluctant to leave the regiment at such a propitious juncture. But at the same time, I've been talking to my father and he has suggested I could still be of use to the Union in a less demanding role, here at the capitol."

There was nodding and the exchange of glances among the commanders. There had been general discussion among those same commanders as to the strength of their colonel and the strain their lifestyle places on one who is not completely sound and fit for the rigors of that type of activity. Living in the saddle, changing camps almost nightly, and trying to hold up under the severe rigors of command was a test of strength for anyone. Jesse's uncle, Dr. Pleasant Logan from Elizabethton, had been Regimental Surgeon up until December, and even he had finally concluded it would not do for him to continue in that capacity. He'd decided to take his chances and return to East Tennessee and resume practice there, rather than continue the severe and demanding life of an army surgeon. The combination of mental and physical strain took its toll on a man's constitution.

"You men all know," Johnson continued, "that Jim Brownlow had carried much of the weight of command for the past several weeks and has done so with great distinction. The raid last night down in Franklin was an example of his skill at leading the regiment and doing maximum damage to the enemy while at the same time minimizing our own exposure. I know we lost one man in that raid, Jim Chanaberry from Company "C". Private Chanaberry was a brave soldier as well as a true patriot and he will be missed in the ranks. Nevertheless, our brave men killed at least three of the enemy and took fifteen prisoners, and on balance, we did more damage to them than they did to us. Besides, the psychological damage of raiding a town where they had no idea — absolutely no inkling — that we were anywhere in the area, that's the kind of warfare that takes its toll on an enemy. Just ask Captain Logan how it feels to have an enemy sniping at you from behind every bush when you didn't even know there was a bush to snipe from." Bob Johnson grinned at the obtuse reference, but then continued.

"At any rate, I've recommended Jim Brownlow's promotion to Colonel to take over command of the regiment and I'll be reassigned to Headquarters, most likely in a Quartermaster role. That'll give me a wide range of activity to try to help organize the occupation of Nashville and help keep the peace among the citizenry here. To replace Jim, I've submitted the name of Captain Dyer for promotion to Lieutenant Colonel."

A round of vocal approval and light applause went up at the announcement. Calvin Dyer was popular with the officers and men of the First Tennessee, and the promotion was considered to be well deserved. He had risen through the ranks in Company "H" from the time the regiment was formed almost a year ago and had performed honorably and bravely throughout the assignment. Jesse thought to himself that the First Tennessee was more like a family or a village on the move where everyone knew everyone else than any unit he had belonged to before. Though he was well acquainted with many of the men in the regiment, he still felt a little like a stranger, as so many of them had been through a great deal of marching, fighting, and suffering, almost as brothers.

Colonel Johnson continued, "The regiment has been ordered south and we'll be moving out day after tomorrow, so let's get our affairs in order and be ready to move at four in the morning. I know you'll work as hard for Jim Brownlow as you have for me this past year, and will demonstrate the will and worth of the mountaineers from East Tennessee. That's all, Men. Good luck and may God be with you all the way."

Jesse went back to his tent with anticipation. He'd be moving out with a regiment of men whom he'd known for a long time, even though he wasn't with them at the start. He wondered about fate and luck and how the least incident in a man's life could shape the events for a long time to come. Tom Singleton and Jesse had been schoolmates with many of the men of the First Tennessee, and had been as anxious to get into the army as many of their friends had. Yet, Tom was over somewhere in Kentucky with an entirely different army and Jesse had taken a long, long road to finally get to soldier with his friends from Carter County. Grandpa Kellar had often used the phrase; "— play the hand you're dealt," alluding to a person's obligation to make the most of his circumstances, whatever they may be. Grandpap was the closest thing Jesse had to a father that he could remember, and he was eternally grateful to the old man for the wisdom he had imparted in the few short years he'd lived at Kellars Crossing. Jesse found himself riding over toward the offices where Frank Davis was assigned and talk a little to Frank and perhaps bid him goodbye. He didn't know how long he'd be gone and Frank might be reassigned before he could return.

The smooth-shaven sergeant was at his desk as Jesse walked in and looked up with a bored indifference.

"Is Captain Davis in?" Jesse asked.

"No, Sir, Captain," the sergeant replied, "He was in earlier, but I think he's gone for the day. It's something about a reassignment and he has to get Mrs. Davis ready to go back home, I think."

Jesse turned and left the office and rode the short distance to the Davis' home. He went up the walk and knocked at the door. Mary answered.

"Hello, Mrs. Davis," Jesse began, "is the captain in?"

"Jesse, come in," Mary said with a slight smile. "No, Frank is away at the livery with the children and won't be back for a few minutes. Anyway, I've wanted to talk to you and this will give us an opportunity before he gets back."

"I shouldn't stay, Mary. It isn't proper for me to be here and you have a reputation to consider. I'll come back later when Frank gets back. When do you think that will be?"

"Jesse, please stay. There's no harm in our just sitting down for a few minutes and talking until the captain gets back. I've so much to say to you and it isn't anything I can say in front of the children or Frank. I want you to know that I appreciate your silence when we first met a few days ago, but Frank knows of my past and we have long since put that behind us. He doesn't know, though, that you and I were as close as we'd been. The names and faces of those I'd been friends with in Nevada are gone and forgotten, all but one. I don't think Frank would take it lightly if he knew you and I had been sweethearts."

When she said the words "... you and I had been sweethearts", Mary lowered her eyes and her voice as though she was savoring the memory. Then she looked up into Jesse's face and the light in her eyes was just as it had been back there along the banks of Silver Creek.

"Jesse," Mary said with deep emotion in her voice, "this isn't easy for me to say, but bear me out. When I called after you that day that I was your girl, I committed myself to a lifetime of just that. If you want me today, I'm yours and if you want me to stay in Nashville, I'll stay, no matter where they send Frank. I've been good and chaste and proper and dignified and all that an officer in the United States Army could want of a wife, but I haven't been fooling myself. I'm Jesse Logan's girl, the same as I was when we met in front of Parkers' Store in Genoa, and your mother read the look on my face. That week after that I stayed out of sight for your sake, but when you left Nevada, my heart went with you. I'll go with you wherever you go, if you just say the word."

"Mary, don't talk like that," Jesse admonished, but by now they had both stood up and moved together. "You know you have a good life and a good husband and those beautiful children. What would happen to all of that if you stayed here? Even if you stayed, I'm moving out with the troop in a couple of days and you'd be alone with nothing more than a heap of regrets for having walked out on Frank."

Mary had moved close to Jesse and was fumbling with his belt buckle. She had unbuttoned the front of her bodice and her breasts were visible beneath the thin camisole she wore as an undergarment. Jesse took her by the shoulders and held her back away from him. "Mary, we're going to have to figure this thing out," he heard himself saying. "We can't just stop the war and go off and live together without a plan. Please, Mary, let's give ourselves some time to work out some details on this thing before we ruin the lives of your children and possibly our own lives in the process."

Jesse's mind was racing. He had no idea as to when Frank Davis might return and this was certainly not the time to start a free-for-all that would virtually ruin all it touched. If he could get some time to separate himself from her, as lovely and inviting as she had made herself, he was confident she would calm down and return to the role she had chosen for herself those many years ago back in Eagle Station. The prospect of recreating the passion he had experienced as a young man was like a magnet drawing him to this woman, but caution, usually not a big consideration in Jesse's life, was now restraining him.

"Mary, let's talk about this," Jesse said again, still trying to buy time. "Even if we could work out a way to be together, we have to first think of other people; your husband and children. Frank married you and brought you out of a very wild and primitive environment, and you have committed your life to him. Don't you agree?"

Then he said sternly, "Button up your dress. If the captain sees you in this state, he'll think I was trying to rape you. I have to go out and walk this thing off. I'm in no condition to discuss this situation rationally. I'll go out as though I'm looking for Frank and he and I will come back together when I find him." He was buying time and trying to give Mary some opportunity to regain her composure. He knew that if Frank and the children came home at that moment, her lack of self-control might erupt again and the whole matter would be out of hand. He picked up his hat and backed out the door. She was a lovely woman, there was no denying that. He wondered about the sanity of a man who would leave such an invitation and walk away, and his mind went back to the afternoon at Silver Creek when he looked back at her, totally nude and just as inviting as she was right now. But he had a friendship and a war to consider and this was no time for indulging one's passions when the stakes were so high.

He clapped his hat on his head, mounted his horse and rode toward where he thought the livery would be. After riding only a few hundred feet, he could see Frank Davis and the children in the distance. He rode quickly toward them and when they were close enough to speak in low tones, Jesse invited Frank to get down from the carriage he was driving. Jesse dismounted and went over to the head of the carriage horse as though to adjust its bridle. Frank followed, not quite understanding what Jesse had in mind.

"Frank, I just came from your house, looking for you and Mrs. Davis seemed awfully upset. Is she okay?"

"Well, I just left her about an hour ago and she seemed just fine. Did she say anything to you?"

Jesse tried to be indirect but place a logical interpretation on the matter. "I think she's upset about leaving Nashville, Frank. I went over to Headquarters looking for you and they said they thought you were going to take Mrs. Davis and the children to the station and send her back home. When I went to your house, I said something to that effect to her, she got quite upset and, well, — emotional. Do you think it's the safest thing to do, sending her back by herself? I'm sure you could get some time off to take her back to Indiana and then come on back. That train ride can be tough on a woman and even hazardous."

"I'll see what is going on Jesse, and may take your advice. If I do go back on furlough, though, I'll need someone to leave my things with here. Can you come on by the house and sort of see us off?"

"I'd rather not, Frank. As I said, Mrs. Davis seemed quite upset, and I think she looked at me as the villain. I don't want to upset her again, if I can help it. If you wouldn't mind, don't even tell her you saw me. I told her I was going to look for you, but I'd rather not let her know we even had this conversation. Can you do that for me?"

"Why, of course, Jess. I can keep your name out of the discussion if you think it best, but why? You know the children will let her know that we've seen each other."

"Well, I reckon you're right about that, so I suppose you'll have to tell her we met, but try to play down this conversation, anyway. As I say, partner, I have the idea she looks at me as a snake in the grass, and there's no need to bring up this thing if you can avoid it, okay?"

"Sure, but that means I won't be seeing you until I get back. Do you know where you'll be going from here?"

The conversation continued for a few moments more as the two friends said their good-byes, and they then went their separate ways.

As Jesse rode back toward the saddlery station to get his horse checked for shoes, he reflected on what had happened. It had been over a year ago, back in Coalwood, that Frank Davis, then a sergeant had laughingly given Jesse an order to '— stay away from women.' And now, he'd come precariously close to violating both the order and the friendship that they had fostered for so many years. The old affair between him and Spanish Mary and his first encounter with Frank Davis had been within six weeks of each other, and that had been over seven years ago. Now, the whole scenario was being replayed in a totally different fashion, and Jesse wondered at a fate so whimsical as to put the three of them together in such bizarre circumstances, and in a setting so far from their first encounter that it was almost impossible to grasp.

22

FORT DICK ROBINSON

E arly in February, 1863 the First Tennessee had received orders to join with the Fourteenth Corps, under the command of General James Steedman, whom Jesse had known from his service in 1861 at Philippi and Beverly in western Virginia, when he had first mustered into the army. Steedman was a large man of about forty-five and was well liked and respected by his officers and men. Though not schooled in military tactics, he had been Director of Public Works in Ohio before the war, and seemed to be a natural leader. His size and manner instilled confidence in his men and he had distinguished himself gallantly at many engagements, particularly the Battle of Perryville.

General Steedman's division was ordered to move south from Nashville to reconnoiter and anchor the right wing of the Union Army and to try to maintain a balance with the Confederate cavalry under the command of CSA General Joe Wheeler. The division was augmented by the addition of a second regiment, the Fifth Tennessee Cavalry, under Lieutenant Colonel Robert Galbraith. The Fifth was sometimes known as the First Middle Tennessee Cavalry, and sometimes erroneously, the First Tennessee Cavalry, confusing the records and often damaging the reputation of Colonel Brownlow's regiment, as the Fifth was something of a rowdy group. They had been recruited from the counties surrounding Nashville and Murfreesboro, during the summer of 1862, and though they had a reputation for gallantry in the battles in which they had been involved, their command had not been able to pull them together as a disciplined fighting unit in the short time since their mustering in.

Colonel Jim Brownlow was not particularly pleased at the assignment of the additional regiment, though they were small in number, only about 750 men. They were difficult to contain and were often found abandoning their units in small numbers and returning to their homes, which were scattered throughout the region. Individually, some of the men in the regiment had personal grudges with some of the other families in the area, and didn't hesitate to take out their hostilities on the people they disliked. General Steedman, Governor Johnson, and particularly, General Rosecrans took a dim view of the lack of discipline that characterized the Fifth Tennessee, but they were fighting men and it was fighting men that were needed in the Cumberland Valley in 1863.

Since the First Tennessee was the only regiment of cavalry in General Steedman's division, they were kept on the move constantly, trying to scout and counter the effect of the Rebels. The regiment, at the time was composed of only about three thousand officers and men, including the Fifth Tennessee, as opposed to the forces under Confederate General Joe Wheeler amounting to almost three times that number. By the end of February, General Steedman's division had moved as far south as Concord Church and was pressing toward Triune. The weather was severe, and the men of the First Tennessee were having a difficult time, but the same weather affected the men in gray and the Federals were able to push their line steadily south. By March 1, they were ensconced at Triune, Tennessee, about twenty-five miles south of Nashville. While the Rebels gave way reluctantly, the northern forces were all-in-all better equipped, and within a few days, General Steedman was able to move his whole division to Triune, where they stayed until the first part of June.

Still, the First Tennessee was kept busy with scouting, picket duty, small raids, and patrols, and very few nights were spent in their beds or even within sight or sound of their camp. It was during this bivouac that Captain Will Kidwell, having recovered somewhat from the illness that had prevented him from taking command of Company "Eye", returned to duty. His health was not the greatest, but his sense of dedication had brought him back to his assignment. Jesse worked with the regiment without command and for several days he simply accompanied Company "I" on some of its raids and patrols. Toward the end of June, he was ordered to Division Headquarters where he was summoned to General Steedman's office. General Steedman and Colonel Whitaker were there to meet him.

"Captain," the general said, after introductions had been exchanged, "since you are without command right now with the First Tennessee, and as you are fairly well acquainted with the region around the Watauga Valley, I'd like to propose a mission for you that'll take you through some pretty wild country, but will also put you quite near your home, if you succeed.

"It's about two hundred and fifty miles from here to Elizabethton, and there is very little to make one think this trip would be anything short of insanity, but here's the story —. The governor's wife has a cousin, or friend, or some such — I'm not quite sure —, who is still in that area and she, Mrs. Johnson, is worried sick that the woman will be killed or worse by the rebels. She has gotten word back that this young woman has lost her family and is now living on the generosity of friends, and has been threatened by the Rebs because of the loyalty of her father and brother, both of whom having been killed. It is well known, both among her friends and the Confederate regiment occupying that area that she has been doing some scouting and organizing and such for the Union, and the governor just doesn't think she'll last long if she stays in the Watauga Valley."

"Tennessee is fairly secure all the way from here by way of southern Kentucky almost to the Cumberland Gap, so taking that route your passage that far would be safe enough, but beyond that for a hundred miles, you'd be on your own. We could send one or two men with you, if that's what you'd want to do, but it will still be risky, getting a young woman back through the lines and all. What do you think?"

Jesse hesitated for a moment before he responded. "General, I'm a little at a loss for words. I never expected such an assignment, and though — well — I — ah — I would welcome the chance to get back to my kinfolk, you know, I'm not much of a scout or that sort of thing. Are you sure this is the job for someone like me? I know the country around Elizabethton and all, but mightn't there be someone else in the regiment who is more suited for the job? I'm perfectly willing to go, but, well, Sir, the success of such an assignment depends on how well prepared the leader is, and there must be others who are more familiar with the territory than I am. And General, what are we doing sending a captain on a scouting mission?"

"Captain," the general responded in his most congenial tone of voice, "to tell you the truth, the governor, and Colonel Johnson, both brought up your name in connection with the assignment. It's not as though I just — I just picked your name out of the hat. You know, I was with the 14th Ohio in West Virginia when we were sweeping the Rebs through that part of the country. You have quite a reputation for resourcefulness with the Army of the Cumberland and even before that, when you were with the Sixth Indiana. To put that with the fact that you're from that area makes you the first choice of several people around here. The governor doesn't want to lose you, but he isn't getting much peace of mind these days, what with Mrs. Johnson so worried and all. Give it some thought, Son. You're free to turn it down, but it would make a lot of people feel better if it was you, and not someone they don't have a lot of faith in, that was to take the job."

The message was clear. Jesse was well aware that to turn his back on Governor and Mrs. Johnson would cause some real consternation and concern, and with ties as close to the governor as his family had, it would not do to walk away from such a request. "General," he said after a few seconds pause, "I'll be glad to take the job. When do I start?"

"I'm glad you see it that way, Captain. Get your gear together and report to Captain Davis at Headquarters in Nashville as soon as you can. You'll have to go see the governor for specifics, but Headquarters will supply you with anything you need for the trip. Is there anyone especially you want to go with you?"

"Sir, let me think on that for a little bit. If I'm not mistaken, I think I can get to Fort Dick Robinson all right, by train most of the way, and then I may be able to pick up someone from Carter County, maybe even Dan Ellis, who'll help me get back to Watauga Valley. After that, I'll try to fetch some of the local boys who probably would like to be making their way out of the valley, anyway, maybe even some other kinfolk of this woman, whoever she is. Did you know her name or anything?" Jesse was formulating a plan even as he was concluding the conversation with General Steedman, and only needed to fill in a few names to flesh out the details.

"Governor Johnson didn't include that information in his message, Captain, but you should be able to see him in Nashville tomorrow and find all that out."

"Fine, Sir, I only need to get a few of my things and I'll be off for Nashville right away. I should be there by evening." Jesse saluted.

———— ◦((◦))◦ ————

Jesse got his small poke of personal property together, mounted his horse, and was in Nashville along toward twilight. He went directly to Headquarters, but because of the hour, Frank Davis had left for the day. Jesse thought he knew where to find him, so he went directly to the house where the Davises had been living. The place was dark and appeared to be abandoned. Jesse knocked several times, but got no response. He tried the door which was not locked and let himself in. In the waning light of day, it looked as though the house was not in use, but he struck a match and looked for a lamp, finding one on the table in the middle of the room. After lighting the lamp, he looked around. The thought struck him that this would be as convenient a place as any to spend the night, as long as no one else was living there. He walked toward the room that he'd remembered as the bedroom and opened the door. Inside the room he could see that there was a lighted lamp on a table near a bed, but the flame was turned so low that it gave virtually no light to the room. As Jesse swung his own lamp out in front of him, he could make out the figure of Frank Davis on the bed, fully clothed, but apparently asleep.

Jesse was puzzled by the sight, but decided it was just as well to let Davis go on sleeping, and pursue any questions the following day. He went outside, unsaddled his horse, which he removed to the little stable at the rear of the house, and went back into the house. In the front room, he made up a bed out of his saddle and bedroll and retired for the night.

The next day, Jesse woke before daylight and looked about the small room. There was nothing to indicate the place was used for meals, except that there were two empty liquor bottles on the sideboard where the family kept their washbowl. Frank Davis, so far as Jesse knew, had not been a heavy drinker, and the two bottles looked out of place. He got a fire started in the stove and began to look around for some food, but found none, not even Army rations. As he moved about the room, the door to the bedroom opened and Frank Davis emerged. His clothes were rumpled and his beard, usually neatly trimmed, was long and disheveled. He looked ten years older than he had, only a few weeks before, when Jesse had seen him last. He was even thinner than Jesse remembered, having lost weight at that time from the effects of the gunshot wound he'd received, from which he had seemed to be recovering.

Jesse tried to sound cheerful, despite the uncertain circumstances. "Hello, Frank. I'm sorry to have dropped in on you unannounced, but you were sleeping so soundly last night I didn't want to wake you."

Frank Davis looked at Jesse for several seconds, his eyes trying to focus and his brain trying to grasp the reality of the situation. Finally, he spoke, "What're you doing here, Logan? Shouldn't you be out on the town with your girlfriend? Shouldn't you be playing the big-time hero with somebody's wife? Why did you come here? There's nobody here that you can bed. My 'wife', as she likes to call herself, has gone back to my family where heaven only knows who she's with right now. Why don't you get on up to Indiana? You might be able to catch up with her and give her a good time. That's what you're here for, ain't it?"

"Frank, what're you talking about? I come here to see you and find you in the most desiccated condition I've ever seen a man. What have you done to yourself? What has happened to you? You seemed to be getting over your wounds and now I find you looking like death warmed over. What on earth has happened to you?"

"As if you didn't know, 'ch Captain? As if you didn't know all about my wife and you making a fool out of me. You didn't think I'd figure it out, did you, Captain Logan? You didn't think I'd realize you and my wife were lovers behind my back. My best friend and my wife! What a sad state of affairs! Well, I'm not going to let it go with just a nod, you know. Logan, I'm going to kill you and then I'm going to kill that cheating bitch of a wife, then — then —," Davis lowered his head for a moment and turned back into the bedroom. In a few seconds he returned with a revolver in his hand, weaving and unsteady but obviously determined to use the gun on Jesse. He cocked the hammer and leveled the gun at Jesse's head. He pulled the trigger but the hammer just snapped on an uncapped nipple, giving Jesse just enough time to lunge across the room and grab the revolver by the frame, freezing the cylinder and preventing it from being turned to rearm or fire. With his free hand, Jesse pushed Frank back against the wall. In his dazed and weakened condition, Davis was no match for Jesse's size and strength and he immediately buckled and fell to the floor.

"What's got into you, Frank?" Jesse shouted, wrenching the gun from his hand. "What are you raving about?"

Logan was shaken by the attempt on his life. It had been less than a year since the well publicized confrontation between two Union generals, William Nelson and Jefferson C. Davis had resulted in Nelson's death, and that had been in a public setting in a hotel in Louisville, Kentucky. Reports of conflicts between fellow soldiers were common in the tense conditions of war, and Logan had just experienced, first hand, how such things could happen. His hands were shaking as he dislodged the percussion caps from the cylinder of Frank Davis's revolver.

Davis was not only weak from the effects of his old gunshot wound, he was also debilitated from the effects of the alcohol he had been consuming and the lack of food and rest, of which he'd been depriving himself since Mary had left for their home up north. He sat on the floor with his knees pulled up, his forearms resting on his knees and his head down. He didn't speak for several minutes and his body seemed to convulse with silent sobbing, but Jesse watched him intently on the chance that he was carrying a second gun. Finally, he lifted his head. "I trusted you, Logan," he said in a muffled voice. "I relied on you, I treated you like a brother, I recommended you for promotion, I welcomed you into my house, and this is the thanks I get."

"Frank, I still have no idea what you're talking about. What is it that I'm supposed to have done to get you so riled up? Last time I saw you, we were discussing your wife going back home and I told you at the time I thought, maybe, she was angry with me, but I don't know what it was I did to make her angry, or you, either."

The idea was beginning to sink in that Mary had made some comments to Frank about their old affair, but he wasn't going to do or say anything that might disclose any of the confidences he and she had shared when they were both young. Frank might be focused on something entirely different from that old flame, and Jesse needed time to sort out the pieces. He was stalling for time and the chance to learn more about his predicament.

"I'm not saying I'm any kind of angel, Frank, but I haven't done anything to you to get you so riled up. I know you've been really good to me. You covered for me with John Goodin, when he was after my hide, and you've taught me how to soldier and you trusted me as a sharpshooter. Sometimes I think I haven't deserved all you have done for me since we met back there in Wyoming, but I swear I don't know what you're talking about and if I did, maybe we could straighten this thing out."

"I'm talking about your trying to get my wife to run away with you, Logan. That's what I'm talking about. When I got back to the house with the children after I saw you up at the livery, she was in such a state, I thought she was going to walk out on me and the kids right there. I calmed her down some and she told me all about you and her, back — back there in Nevada. All about how you had been sweethearts and all and how you left town 'cause you thought she might set up a ruckus with your family. What a low trick! When I met you, you convinced me you were nothing but a quiet country boy with no more malice in you than a bluebird. Then when we were working together back there in Virginia, you started chasing all the women you could get close to, that Miss Livingston and the girl in Coalwood, and then, how about the Pryor girl? Were you sparking her, too? And now I find you're coming around behind my back trying to get my Mary away from me. What kind of a man are you, anyway?"

Logan was dumfounded. It looked as though Davis had been taking notes since they had last seen each other and had made some assumptions about Jesse's personal life that went beyond reality, if not beyond speculation. Davis was the best friend he had in this part of the country, and he didn't need any enemies behind the lines. There were enough Rebels to satisfy that requirement, but at least most of them were where you could keep an eye on them and you knew them by the color of their uniforms.

It was apparent that Captain Davis had abused his health since his wife had gone north and undoubtedly blamed Jesse for her being upset as well as for her leaving, though that had been planned before he had showed up in Nashville. The thing that was so surprising was that she had appeared so contained and in control when he had first gone to the Davis home, and how distraught she seemed when he had seen her the second time, just before she left Nashville. However, this was not the time to try to analyze human behavior. He had a friendship to recover and a mission to pursue at the request of the governor.

"Frank, I have to get on over to see Governor Johnson this morning, but first I want you and me to go get something to eat. Can we put this thing about Mrs. Davis aside for a little while and talk about it later? You're right about her and me being friends when we were young, but believe me, Captain, she was way beyond my hope and dreams as a sweetheart. She was a year or two older than I was, and — well — you remember how attractive she was when you first met her. She was just out of my range, Frank, and I knew it. She lived with my folks for a while, and I knew her as a friend but any idea of us being more than that was just a wild dream on my part. Listen, she was such a beauty that she could have had any man in the territory, but she picked you. Don't ask me why," he tried a weak joke without visible effect.

"She must have been upset about having to leave you, but I swear I didn't say anything improper to her when I talked to her. You know, I didn't recognize her when you first introduced me to her, and I won't say I wasn't smitten by her beauty even then. But don't ever, ever think I'd do something to try to get your wife away from you. I may be a pushover for a pretty face, but your friendship means too much to me for us to get crossways. Now, how about going with me to get something to eat?"

The entire time Logan was talking he wandered about the small living room of the house, assessing the condition and contents but keeping one eye on Captain Davis with the idea that he still might try to attack him. He got the other man onto his feet and persuaded him to splash some water in his face. Then they went to a nearby hotel and into the restaurant. They talked in low tones and as the meal progressed, Jesse thought he could see Frank's disposition improving. After breakfast, Jesse suggested that they both go next door to the barbershop to do something about their rough appearance. Jesse was intent on getting Frank to go to see the governor with him and then try to get him furloughed for a short period to return to Indiana and set things straight with Mary. The more he talked, the better the idea began to sound to Davis and by the time they were at the capitol building he seemed pretty well subdued. They went to the governor's office and spoke to the secretary, a man whom Captain Davis knew on a friendly basis.

"The governor will only be a few minutes, Captain," the sergeant at the desk said, mostly to Davis. "I think he's expecting Captain Logan, but I'm sure he'd be glad to see you, too."

Presently a man came out of the office whom Jesse thought he recognized, but there was no recognition on the other man's part. Jesse turned to Davis and said in a low tone of voice, "Isn't that John Bell, the fellow who ran for President back in '60?"

"Hanged if I know, Jesse. What makes you think I'm possum with the kind of people that run for president?" Davis responded in what Jesse thought was a much more relaxed manner than he'd seen his friend earlier in the day.

They went on in to the governor's office and were greeted by Andrew Johnson. He was a rather short man, a little on the heavy side, but he carried himself well, standing as tall as he could. He was a man who had been through many personal trials and struggles and it was apparent that he was no stranger to confrontation. His face was serious, even when he tried to smile, and the bags under his eyes gave evidence that he had missed lots of sleep since his appointment to the governor's post in war-torn Tennessee. As always, Governor Johnson was impeccably dressed, living up to his reputation as one tailor who did not neglect his own appearance. The office was simple but fastidiously clean. There was a desk in the center of the room and a couch along one of the walls, near a window that looked out on the street in front of the capitol building. Straight back chairs were the rule in the governor's office, except for the couch and one lightly padded swivel chair behind the desk. The desk was clear of papers, with nothing but an inkwell and a small cigar box resting upon its polished surface.

"Come in, Gentlemen," Governor Johnson greeted them. "Please take a seat. I'll be right with you as soon as I take care of a couple of details with Mr. Pipkin." He went into the outer office and spoke to the secretary for a few moments, returning with an air of relief and perhaps some resignation. "The man you passed in the outer office was — ah — John Bell, whom I knew before this thing started. He was the Whig candidate for President, you know, although he ran on what he and his supporters styled the 'Constitutional Union' ticket. Captain Logan, I'm sure you recall Mr. Bell, as he was a friend of your grandfather and relied a great deal on his support in the Watauga Valley when he ran for the senate in — what was it? — 1847, I think. We were never very close, he being a Whig and such, but he's done me several favors these last few months. It was him who helped Mrs. Johnson gain her freedom from those people over in Greenville. Terrible thing — those people. To think they'd persecute an innocent woman just because of the political views of her husband. They call that a free country, gentlemen, but I'll tell you it's been anything but freedom for the people of these regions if they don't entertain the views of the Rebel class."

"Yes, Sir, I thought that was who that was, but he's changed some since I saw him back in Doe River Cove. I recall his talking some to my grandpa about the election. I'm thinking it was him my grandpa voted for that year."

"Yes, I suppose it was. Your grandfather was a tried and true Whig, as I recall, and I'm sure that his voting for me on the Democrat ticket was often hard for him to swallow, but I know he supported me both in my run for Senate and also for governor in 1853 and '55. Well — those were the days — we didn't know how peaceful and serene life was, then. We thought we were living in turbulent times, then, but we didn't have any inkling of how turbulent they were to become." The governor shook his head and chuckled to himself. "None at all! Well, I supported Douglas in the 1860 election, but I do think John Bell would have done more to keep the Union together than any one in that election. I don't know. I just don't know."

The governor looked more tired than Jesse had ever seen him. He hung his head and massaged his forehead. Then he continued to describe a difficult situation that had been reported to him about a young lady in Elizabethton. "Perhaps you recall Steven Venable who lived there in Elizabethton. Well, he had a son and a daughter, both of whom shared his dedication to the cause of the Union, and when Steven and his son were killed, his daughter —,"

"Sir, excuse me. You say both Mr. Venable and Paul have been killed? How did this happen? I was at their home last year just before the Rebs captured me and sent me to Richmond to prison. In fact, it was as I was leaving the Venable home that I was captured. Also, in a way it was Mr. Venable who started things off that allowed me to escape from Libby Prison."

"You know, I think, Captain, it was because of their political inclinations that both Steven and his son were assassinated. — 'Terrible thing. Those people, they say they want to be free from an oppressive government but still they do these things to innocent people whose only transgression is their sense of loyalty to the best government on earth. It just isn't right. Even that fellow, Parson Brownlow, with whom I have had a few disagreements in our time, has been seized by the Rebels and thrown in prison, for no reason other than the Secesh thought he might be capable of stirring up resentment toward their 'cause'. Well, you know this isn't the time or place to discuss these matters, I suppose, but that is the reason I called you in here. Mrs. Venable died last year, it was in the summer, I think, and then, last fall, Steven and his son — wasn't it Paul, or something like that?"

"Yes, Sir. Paul. I went to school with him."

"Yes, that was it, anyway, he and his father were trying to keep the business together, and Paul, of course was — well — he was working with my son-in-law Colonel Stover, to try to keep some of the local people there from starving, and —," the governor's voice trailed off.

"I reckon they were in pretty bad shape after that bridge affair at Zollicoffer, weren't they, Governor?" Jesse inquired.

"Yes, they were, but you know, the Venables didn't have anything to do with that. They were just there in Elizabethton at the time, and, I think, maybe Steven may have had something to do with supplying some of the materials for that affair. At least that's what the Secesh thought."

"Anyway, you know, Steven and the boy were out one night, apparently after curfew. They were right there at their house on Johnson Street when the Rebs — a patrol of the garrison there, or some of their home guard — challenged them right there on the street by their house and when they saw who it was, they just shot them both. Just shot them both! And that was something like — what?— six or seven months after the bridge thing."

"Sir, what happened to Lily — the girl?" Jesse asked with some concern. It had been Lily to whom he had written the note from prison and who had helped instigate the events that had resulted in his escape from prison.

"Well, the girl — Lily, yes that's her name, she's — uh — related through her mother to Sam Angel, and his mother is a cousin of Mrs. Johnson. Sam is now in Kentucky working to form up another Tennessee Regiment, and — ah — he's been telling Mrs. Johnson how this girl is living like a fox in a den, hiding in the daytime and scouting at night or whenever she can to help the Union. Dan Ellis — you know Dan, I think — he knows about her but hasn't been able to get in touch with her and try to bring her out. She seems to have — like, — well, just vanished into the hills there and nobody can talk her into leaving. The Secesh are trying to find her and lock her up and the Unionists are trying find her to persuade her to leave for her own safety, and it has my wife in such a state I can't do anything to calm her down." Andrew Johnson recounted about all he recalled of the recent events of east Tennessee in one breath.

"And you think I can locate her and bring her out, Governor?"

"Son, before Steven and the boy were killed, it was well known that the girl had been instrumental in helping you get out of that jail down in Richmond, and there was talk that after that happened, she sort of changed. She got the idea in her head that she was some kind of "Joan of Arc" and she took it on herself to get into these little scouting sorties and help the Union in any way she could."

"She made a couple of trips through the Union lines to carry messages on the movement of the Rebs and even helped pilot some of our people through the lines, something like Dan Ellis is doing. At first, she was acting kind of friendly with the Rebs and being sweet and all, and getting information from some of them, but they got wise to her game and when they tried to trap her, she dropped out of sight and just disappeared. We were hoping that when you got back into the country, she'd hear about it and come out of hiding."

Up until this time, Frank Davis had been just sitting and listening to what was being said. Finally, he spoke, "Governor, I'm scheduled to return to my old unit, the Seventh Ohio and I was supposed to go with Captain Logan as far as Camp Dick Robinson and try to give him some support. It also happens that I'm a little bit familiar with that region. We've been a pretty good team in the past and I might just be of some help if I were to go on to Elizabethton with him."

Logan was shocked at the comment. Captain Davis knew nothing of the region of East Tennessee and though they'd been friends for many years in several different situations, it didn't seem to Jesse that Davis was particularly suited for this mission. He was not prepared for this turn of events and hesitated before commenting.

Davis continued, "Captain Logan and I have known each other since '55, and have always been able to work well together. This doesn't seem to me to be a one-man job. He's going to need someone to back him up. I'd certainly like to be able to help."

As strange as the idea sounded to Logan, he did feel that Captain Davis might be of some minor assistance, but the idea of putting him through what promised to be a grueling and arduous journey was a discouragement. Neither did Logan like the idea of having the older man slow him down on his way toward Elizabethton. His physical condition was deteriorated. He had obviously neglected his health with some excessive drinking, and he was not accustomed to strenuous activity, having been working in an office for several months. Besides, this was not the way orders should be formulated; first submitting suggestions to the governor. If he approved the idea, who among the generals would dare to countermand him?

Logan turned toward Davis with a surprised look. "Are you sure you can keep up with the stress of a hundred miles of mountain wilderness, Captain? I'm not even sure of the trail I'll be taking, and it's very likely going to be really rugged. I expect we'll travel most of the way from Camp Dick Robinson on foot, and it'll be a hard journey. Besides, we came here to try to arrange a furlough for you to get back your health and perhaps spend some time with your family and eventually back to your unit. I'd have to question the wisdom of sending two captains out on a scouting mission that could be as easily handled by a sergeant and a private."

Frank Davis smiled broadly, a warm, friendly look coming over his haggard face as though he was contemplating a vacation trip with an old friend. He nodded slowly toward Logan and then raised his eyes gazing out the window into the distance as though he was watching some far away scene. "Captain, this is something I've been trained for and have wanted to do for some time. You remember when we first met, I was in charge of a squad of scouts living off of the land and making our way west by sheer will power and intuition, dealing with hostile Indians and we never lost a man. You know, I think we can make this trip and you can be back here in probably less than two weeks and be about your business. We've worked well together in the past and should have no problems here, what with your knowledge of the geography and people and my ability to plan and execute such a mission. It should be no trouble at all."

Jesse thought back to the time out west when he first encountered Frank Davis and reflected on what had transpired between them. One of the things he recalled clearly was that while Davis was certainly a good leader, he wasn't even prepared to bring down game to feed his own men. Logan had been the marksman who fed the troop when he was with them. It seemed as though Captain Davis was trying to convince the governor to let him lead a mission of which he knew little, and was ill prepared and poorly equipped to participate in, much the less lead. Even so, this was not the time or place to challenge a fellow officer who was volunteering to go along on what could prove to be a dangerous assignment. Reflecting on the tirade Davis had caused earlier in the day, Jesse wondered if there might be some other motive in his volunteering for the proposed trip. He had tried to shoot Logan that morning and though he had apparently calmed down, his behavior didn't imply any regret or change of heart over his outburst.

Governor Johnson watched the exchange intently and had obviously warmed to the idea of sending both Davis and Logan on the mission. "If you think this is best, Captain Davis, I'll arrange to have you released from duty here so you can make the trip. What do you think, Captain Logan?"

Logan was speechless. To recommend against Davis' plan would be something of an insult, but to endorse it just didn't make sense. The urgency that the governor had placed on the mission gave him no time to stall for intervention from someone else who could shed a different perspective on the matter and it looked as though he was just going to have to make the best of a bad situation. "It promises to be a tough mission, Governor Johnson, but I suppose we can get in and out without too much trouble, that is if Captain Davis thinks he's up to it."

Jesse was embarrassed. He had not expected such a turn of events.

He knew that Frank Davis, as the senior officer, would logically and legally assume command of the mission, and yet it was he, Logan, who had been selected to take the job because of his experience and familiarity with the people and region. This was the army, though. One did not question or challenge the position of one's superior officer, however illogical, especially in the presence of the governor of the state.

"I'm in as good a shape as I've been for many a month, Captain," Davis smiled. "and I'll bet I can still put you through your paces."

———— ((()) ————

They traveled by rail from Nashville to Louisville and on to Nicholasville, Kentucky, and then rode their horses the rest of the way to Camp Dick Robinson. From there they would assess their route south to reach their final destination.

Cumberland Gap, through which they would have to pass to get from southeastern Kentucky to East Tennessee, was in the hands of the Rebels at the time. It's strategic value to both sides of the conflict was considerable. More so to the Federal forces as a means of protecting eastern Kentucky and its availability as a staging point to offer military assistance to any expedition by the Federals into East Tennessee, but at present, its value to the Rebs was to prevent a federal invasion of East Tennessee, and it was the Rebs who had the upper hand at the moment. This was owing to General Bragg and often to the work of Colonel John Hunt Morgan and his diverse and sudden raids throughout the eastern part of Kentucky and south-western Virginia.

———— ((()) ————

At Camp Dick Robinson, the nature of their mission changed. Up until this time they had been traveling by railroad through friendly territory, usually with a number of fellow soldiers and in relatively comfortable circumstances. Now, they would have to go some sixty miles south to Barboursville by horseback but then probably a trip of about a hundred miles through some country that was pretty wild and liberally salted with Rebel scouting parties. The few people that occupied the region were primarily in sympathy with the North, but the Secesh government was clinging to the country tenaciously, much for its value as a food source but also as a buffer between the Federal forces in Kentucky and strategic east Tennessee.

Logan had hoped to find Dan Ellis somewhere in Southeast Kentucky to scout them through the lines, but such was not the case. He had been for a time at Camp Dick, but had left for the Watauga Valley just a few days previously. They were not completely on their own, however. Though Ellis was not in the region at the time, Logan did encounter Sid Coster, whom he had most recently seen in New Castle and who had returned to the Holston Valley with Ellis after that meeting. Sid was working as a scout by this time, helping with the job of piloting people and mail between the Watauga Valley and eastern Kentucky. He was assigned to Headquarters Company but was primarily freelancing to help pilot people over the Cumberland Ridge or, at times, Poors Ridge to the safety of Kentucky.

They arrived at the camp on a bright July morning and spent the better part of that day there, gathering what little information was available about the region and also about the Confederate strength to the south and east. Rumors were rampant about all sorts of military movements. There was furious activity in the camp, in itself a small city, reflecting the rumor that General Ambrose Burnside had been ordered south from Cincinnati to try to occupy a section around Knoxville and to relieve some of the pressure General Rosecrans was experiencing at Chattanooga.

The stories they heard ran all the way from an impending raid across the Ohio River into Ohio and Indiana by John Hunt Morgan from Kentucky to a movement by General Burnside from the north, finally taking note of President Lincoln's urging to invest the East Tennessee region and kick the Confederates out of the Knoxville area. The latter would make military sense, as the seizure of Knoxville would then simplify the retention of Nashville, and the occupation of Chattanooga and constriction of Rebel military traffic from Richmond to the western front. Jesse suggested they go the few miles north to Camp Nelson and see if they could join that march, if it truly existed, but Captain Davis rejected that idea.

Frank Davis, over the two-day train ride from Nashville to Lexington had been relaxed and congenial, somewhat different from the man Logan had come to know as a leader and organizer of troops, but also strangely different from the agitated attitude he had displayed when he suspected Logan of a romantic relationship with his wife, Mary. It almost appeared to Jesse that the matter of his concern for his wife had been completely forgotten. Logan did, on one occasion, bring up her name during the four days it had taken them to arrive at Camp Dick Robinson, but Frank Davis dismissed the subject immediately. As a matter of fact, Davis seemed more preoccupied with talking over old times, the scenery, politics in the army, and anything else of an abstract nature that came to hand.

Something that had bothered Logan, however, was the fact that Davis had not even broached the subject of preparations for the last leg of their trip, the portion they were now facing. As the senior officer, Davis, by military protocol, was authorized to command the mission and he'd not even mentioned preparations during the trip. Jesse had obtained a Sharps carbine and cleaned and oiled his own Colt Navy revolver, as well as the Smith and Wesson revolver he had obtained from Bert Oakley in New Castle. He had also obtained a telescope and a compass, some rope, and blankets, as well as extra sox and a new belt knife, but it looked as though Davis had only a bedroll, a knife and his revolver in preparation for the trip. It began to look as though he was not really giving so much thought to the trip and was expecting something far different from that which Logan was contemplating. Logan brought up the subject of preparations a time or two but obtained little satisfaction. It was as though Captain Davis was on furlough and hadn't a care in the world. Logan dismissed the matter as evidence that Davis was planning to allow the younger captain to proceed with the mission alone, allowing him to resume his old command with the Seventh Ohio, or continue on to Indiana to reconnect with his wife.

During their stop at the garrison at Camp Dick Robinson, Logan wandered about a bit, occupying himself with the usual pastime of a soldier when arriving in a new situation, that of looking for any old friends and particularly for Lieutenant Sam Angel, who was supposed to be a source of much of the information he had received concerning Lily Venable. The men at the garrison were mostly from the Midwest; Ohio, Indiana, Michigan, and Wisconsin, but while they were interested in the visiting captains and though they tried to be helpful there was just not much information on what they could expect on the next leg of their trip. They did find their old regiment, the Seventh Ohio, but were surprised to find Company "H" completely decimated. Nothing was left of their old company but a skeleton crew consisting of Lieutenant Goodin, Sergeant Hawkins, Corporal Martin Mason, and eleven men. Neither could they discover the reason for such a reduced staffing. Goodin received them coldly and evaded all questions as to the reason for the reduced condition of the company.

Leaving Davis and Goodin alone, Logan wandered off, joining a group of officers at the headquarters tent early in the day, he sat down at a camp table, watching a game of checkers between two lieutenants. There were two or three other officers nearby, but when the game ended, they drifted off, as did the loser of the game.

"Want to lose a little money?" the winner of the game said to Jesse in a friendly manner. "Or maybe you can help provision your trip south at the expense of 'Old Sam.' I'm not the best checker player in the world, but I been whupping the likes of these fellers fer the past two weeks. Maybe your style of checkers can teach me some new tricks."

Logan sat down at the table and watched as 'Old Sam" spread the pieces across the board.

"You're on your way south to rescue that-there little flea that's been pestering the Rebs around Elizabethton, ain't'cha?" Sam asked. The information on their mission was no secret about the camp, and no one was treating it as such.

"Yes, I reckon we're the ones who got the big job all right. I'm not sure the governor was doing us any favors, but orders is orders, and that's what we all do, here, just follow orders."

"How'r ye fixed fer ammunition? I hear the Rebs are pretty well dug in down there at the Gap and around Knoxville, and you may have to fight yer way in and out."

"We aren't goin' through Knoxville, if we can help it. I think we can go around to the east and avoid most of the Rebel patrols. What d'you think? By the way, my name is Logan, Jesse Logan," he said putting out his hand.

"I know yer name. You can just call me Sam," the other man responded, "Sam Angel. I know a little about the situation down there."

Having never met Lieutenant Sam Angel and knowing of him only through his reputation, Jesse was surprised and pleased. "Well, I reckon you do! You're the man I wanted to see about Lily. I understand she's a cousin of yours and Mrs. Johnson's, and I'd like to know why in tarnation you don't just go back down there yourself and bring her out. It would surely save the governor a lot of grief and settle Mrs. Johnson down a bit on the way."

Angel laughed, a short snort of a chuckle, rather than anything resembling mirth, "Captain, I don't know what Andy Johnson has been telling you, but I want to tell you that that girl is not bothered by what the Governor, the President, the Rebels, or you or I want to do. She's her own law. You remember the old sayin' we used to have down there in the valley; — There's two theories on winnin' an argument with a woman. — Neither one works."

Sam Angel went on. "I have a job to do, here, and I'm going to stay with it. Your job is to follow orders, just like mine, and I know you'll have to make the best of it. I can tell you a little bit about what to expect when you get down to the Watauga, but I can't give you much advice on how to get there. I think it's possible there's a feller over at Company 'B', name's Travis, that kin maybe fill you in on some of the goin's on down there and also the best track to take getting there. Another one is Sid Coster, the feller you've been talking to. He can do you some good, too. I understand he's from your part of the country and has just traveled some with Dan Ellis back to them parts, not long back. You kin find the both of them right over through them trees, on the far side by that big pine that's down on the ground. Do you want to play checkers, or am I just wasting my time?"

"I'm sorry, Sam, my mind just wouldn't be much on the game, with this little run looking at me tomorrow. Maybe I'd better go over there and look for Travis."

"Before you go, though, Captain, is that other captain, that older feller, is he the one that's supposed to be goin' with you on this run?'

"Frank Davis? Is he the one you're talkin' about? Yes, he's my partner in this job, but I'm not sure he's going with me."

"Watch him. I don't know how well you know the man, but to me he seems a little shifty. You know what I mean? He jus' don't seem to have any mind about this-here trip ye'r on, but he's more interested in is there any kind of places a feller kin hide out, kin he live off'n the country fer a time, what kind of country ye'll be goin' through, and that sort of thing. Not that there's anything wrong with hidin' out, but it appears the particulars of the trip, or how does a feller find Lily, are less important to him than how many people are livin' along the way an' what's the best escape ef things go sour on the trip. Does that strike you queer at all, or am I just imagining things?"

Logan thought over the comments for a few moments. "You know, I just never gave it any thought, Sam. I've known Frank Davis for a long time, and he's always seemed to have his mind on the job, but now that you mention it, he doesn't seem to be thinking the same way as most people would when they'd be looking to make a hundred-mile trot through some really tough country. I don't know about his looking for places to hide out, but maybe that has something to do with what you're talking about. Well, we'll see. I'm going to look for that other fellow, Travis, I reckon. 'Nice meetin' you. You take care, now, and thanks for your help."

"You take care, too. I jus' ain't sure if that partner of yours is the one I'd like to have lookin' out for me. His mind just don't seem to be on the job, that's all."

Logan went over to where Sam Angel had indicated he might find the man named Travis, and asked if anyone there knew such a man. He was directed to a man sitting by himself on the fallen pine tree, as Sam had pointed out.

"Are you Sergeant Travis?" Logan asked, noting the chevrons on the man's sleeves.

"Yes, sir, I am," the man replied, "What can I do for you, Captain?"

Logan and Travis discussed some of the particulars and pitfalls of the impending journey, and Travis expressed some questions about the governor's reasoning in trying to get the girl, Lily Venable, out of the Elizabethton region.

"She's doing quite a job down there, from what I hear, and I ain't so sure she'd want to leave if you was to find her, anyhow," Travis complained. "What's the gov'nor want with trying to get her out?"

"Well, she's kinfolk, and Mrs. Johnson thinks she's in some kind of great danger back there, and is all upset and giving the governor fits till he does something about it. I know the girl, and she helped get me out of prison back last year. I don't think she especially intended it that way, but that's what she did. She seems to be doing alright, down there, from what I hear, but when the governor, or maybe I should say the 'Mrs. Governor' puts out an order, we just do what we're told."

"And that other captain, that older fella, is your partner in all this? Do you think he's the man for the job? I was talking to some fellers a little while ago, and they thought he was a little p'culiar, what with sort of a — well I don't know — sort of a disconnected attitude toward the whole thing. Is he in charge of the trip? He just don't seem to have anything in mind except where a man can hide out along the way, or which way to go if he was to get off'n the trail, or how to get out of the mountains without getting caught. Is it him or you going to be in charge?"

Jesse was getting a picture with which he was uncomfortable. Frank Davis, so far as he was concerned, was not well suited for this task to begin with but had talked himself onto the mission, without Jesse's particular approval. Then, it was the fact that Frank, throughout the trip, had dismissed the recent falling-out he and Jesse had gone through concerning his wife, Mary. And now, it had been his feeling, reinforced by what he'd heard from several others that Davis had no particular interest in the trip, but was more concerned with the geography than the purpose of their mission.

"I'll give you somethin' of a little map so's you'll kind of know where you are and where you need to be, but that's all it is. I know these parts pretty good, but I don't know all the names of the roads and such." With that Travis pulled out a piece of brown paper from his pocket and proceeded to draw.

"This here is where we are right now. You can follow the wagon road as far as Walnut Flat and then maybe catch a supply train as far as London. Then it's about fifteen miles on a good road to Barboursville an' a little old salt train line on to Cumberlan' Ford. H'it's only about five miles then to Cumberlan' Gap, but the Rebs have that Gap pretty well guarded, so you'll have to go east through Cranks Gap into Virginia. You've got to do it in the daylight, though, else you'll miss it. H'it's hard to see when it's dark and you have to be lookin' for it, even in the daytime. If you could take that feller, Coster with you, you'd have a better chance of makin' it. He's been that way before, a couple of times, I think. There's a sort of a road in some places, but there's Reb patrols aroun' an' you'll have to keep yer head down."

Travis continued to detail the features he'd drawn on the map and finally concluded, "If'n you go on to the south from Crank's Gap, you'll cross a couple of small streams, an' then you hit the Powell River Valley. If you kin stay away from the patrols, the people are right friendly in those parts and you shouldn't have too much trouble gettin' across that little valley an' there's a road up the valley that'll take you to Mulberry Gap. Go south from there an' that road goes right through Sneedsville an' across the Clinch River, down to Rogersville. H'it's about twenty miles from Cranks Gap to Sneedsville an' another twenty to Rogersville. I reckon you'll perty well know the way after that."

They talked for another ten minutes and finally Logan thanked Travis and headed for the quartermaster tent. When he got to the tent, he stood around for a few minutes, until most of the other men had drifted away and he then walked over to a sergeant who was issuing supplies. "Sergeant, do you happen to have an extra cylinder for a Navy Colt? He asked.

"Yes, sir, Captain, I think we do. What company are you with?" he asked as a matter of routine.

"I'm with the First Tennessee Cavalry, but I'm transient, working out of the Governor's office in Nashville, and am on a special mission. I don't have a requisition for the cylinder, but I am willing to sign anything you may need. Isn't it possible that I could just get one as an expendable?"

"Well, yes, I suppose so. We put these things out all the time, whenever someone needs one. Are you going out right away?" the sergeant asked without any particular interest.

"Yes, probably in the next two - three days, I think."

Logan went back to the headquarters tent where he'd left his bedroll and took out the powder and shot from his knap sack. He took the new cylinder and 'short loaded' it with only enough powder to push the lead ball out the end of the barrel of the gun, but not enough to do any damage, nor even hit what the shooter intended. He put the new cylinder into his ditty bag. He put the ditty bag away in his bedroll and went toward the mess tent to get something to eat; what he thought might be his last good meal for about the next week.

At the mess tent, reflecting on the various possibilities and probabilities he would be encountering when he reached the Watauga Valley, Jesse's mind kept drifting back to his feelings for Olivia Livingston and how he'd felt when, after a glorious night together and the fulfillment of a long-standing attraction he'd felt for her, he had just ridden out of town without so much as a goodbye. He had written to her several times during his assignments in western Tennessee but without any response. He had no way of knowing whether any of his letters had been received or not. It was entirely possible that she had been so upset with him and his impulsive behavior that she had simply torn the letters up, with or without reading them. It was also possible that she had answered the letters but those answers had not caught up with him.

He decided to try one more time, this time addressing the letter to her in care of Bert Oakley at New Castle.

August 13, 1863
Dear Miss Livingston,
When we parted at Lewisburg, I had no idea that my life would take on such a change, and change it has. I now find myself in Kentucky at Camp Dick Robinson and about to set out on a scouting mission for the purpose of trying to rescue a person who, according to my best information, doesn't even want to be rescued.
You recall hearing about the young woman to whom I'd written a letter from Libby Prison and who was partly responsible for my escape from that place? It seems that she is without family in Elizabethton, the other members of her family having died of various causes. It also seems that she is related to Governor Johnson's wife, who is so worried about her that she (Mrs. Johnson) engineered a campaign to get up a scouting party to rescue her and the choice of scouts fell upon Capt. Davis and me! Two Captains! I was ordered and Capt. Davis volunteered.
What has all this to do with you? You ask.
I've written several letters to you, Olivia, all expressing my devotion. For whatever reason, I've not heard back from you. I hope and pray nothing has happened to change your feelings toward me and that our communication difficulties have merely been caused by a failing on the part of the mail service, but I'm nevertheless anxious, awfully anxious.
I have no idea as to the potential success of this mission, but when it is finished, being relatively near to my old home in Doe River Cove and to western Virginia, my plans are first to visit my family, and then to seek you out. I truly hope and trust that your feelings will be in agreement, or at least in acceptance of these plans.
While I can't predict the actual dates, I expect that I will be able to visit my family, either during the scouting mission or, as noted, shortly

following its conclusion. Should you find it impossible or inadvisable for me to try to contact you, I ask that you send me such a letter either agreeing or disagreeing with this proposal. Then you might send that letter to my family, Mr. and Mrs. Henry Kellar, at Kellars Crossing, Doe River Cove, Tenn. with a request to hold it there for me.

I'm sure you probably think of me as being insensitive of the need to be more attentive to the relationship we had developed, and I can't argue with that. I'm also aware of the idea that my actions have appeared self-serving, as I did receive a sudden promotion incidental to my assignment with Gen'l. Sullivan. I assure you, my dearest, that my fondest desire, other than to be with you, is to see this war finished, and I plan to do whatever I can to assist wherever I can in facilitating both of those objectives.

Incidentally, the enclosed poetry is something I've put together in scattered idle moments, and, having no one else to burden with it, I'm sending it along to you. We can discuss it when we again meet, which I hope will be soon. It reflects some of the thoughts we have shared since we first met. Please give this idea favorable consideration. I miss you, I long for you, and yes, I love you.

Sincerely and affectionately,

Jesse K. Logan, Capt.

United States Army

Camp Dick Robinson

Finishing the letter after about an hour's thought, Jesse enclosed the poem he had written.

Poem

We joined this fight, mere boys without aim
*   With neither purpose, nor cause, nor love,*
But each man knew he'd see great fame
*   If only given a chance to prove.*
To prove that he, yes, he alone,
*   Could win for his side the victory craved,*
A vict'ry so vague none could've known,
*   If one scrap of honor could still be saved.*

We marched away to drum and fife
*   Fair ladies at us kisses blew.*
Each felt he'd waited all his life

To see this great, brave dream come true.

Now we are soldiers, in the field
 We've seen the foe and found him strong.
He fires from tree, from stone, and shield.
 'Feels he is right and we are wrong.

We know not what the 'morrow may bring,
 But only that the enemy is near.
And that his cannons loudly ring
 From the crests of hills for all to hear.

As we through mud, through dust, and mire
 Trudge onward, toward the battle thrown.
That future youth we may inspire,
 To fix their gaze above our own.

For could it be, we're here on earth
 To settle forever mankind's test?
That timeless query "What's each man's worth?
 Is not the lowest as dear as the best?"

"Is not the plainest just as good,
 In the eyes of God, and those of man,
As he who in all his fine'ry stood,
 And donned a crown when his time began?"

Is it I, O' Lord, who has in his breast,
 The truth and all that with it goes?
Or is it that one, who across the crest,
 Fires back at me, the meanest of foes?

Oh, grant that we more than soldiers may be,
 But liberators of a captive race.
That in this year or two or three
 May we, with destiny keep pace.

And when the guns of war are stilled
 And from the field, the cannons gone,
May we go home, if God's so willed,

And hear, "Well done, my boy, well done."

23

A HILL TOWARD HOME

Jesse stood up from where he was sitting and looked about. Frank Davis was sitting at one of the tables nearby, so Jesse went to the mess line, got a plate of food and a cup of coffee and took a spot across the table from him.

"Where've you been, Logan?" Davis asked congenially.

"I've just been out bumming around, trying to find out anything I could about this run we're going to have to make tomorrow."

"Tomorrow, is it?" Davis asked in surprise, his mood suddenly souring. "What made you think we'd have to start tomorrow? Where'd you get that idea?"

"Captain, we've now been out eight days and I calculate we have at least another four-day travel to get to Watauga Valley, and you told the Governor we'd be back in two weeks. Add to that score, that we'll have to scout out that young lady as soon as we get down there, and that'll take us a few days and then it's who-knows-how-long to make the return trip. You're the senior officer, here, but don't you think we'd better get moving?"

"You're right, Captain, I am the senior officer on this mission and it'll be me that makes the decisions as to when we move and when we wait. Now just you settle your bones for a time, because I'm not ready to move just yet. I'll be sure to let you know when I am."

After a few minutes of strained silence, Jesse said, in what he hoped was a more congenial tone, "Frank, have you given any thought to going back to Indiana, to your wife and kids for a time? This business of using two captains to do the work of maybe a sergeant and maybe a private or two is ridiculous. I can see them sending me, 'cause I know the territory, I know the people, and I know the woman that we're supposed to locate, and Governor Johnson has it in his head that all that is important. As valuable as you've been to the Federal Army, they owe you a furlough and you owe your wife some time together, away from the army. This is a waste of a good captain's time. You're too good a man to go chasing off through the hills on no more than the whim of Mrs. Johnson. I'm following orders. I'm committed. You can call off your part in this thing at any time, without any recriminations from anybody."

As Jesse talked, Davis just sat motionless, staring at his plate of food. When Logan paused, Captain Davis looked up from the table. Thoughts, hostile thoughts, were going through his mind, but he held his tongue, knowing their situation in the midst of thirty or forty people was not the best place to express himself as he would have liked.

Then, leaning forward across the table toward Jesse, he said in a low, strained voice, "Logan, maybe you don't realize it, but they're sending me on this mission, first, to see to it that you don't screw the thing up, as you've done a dozen times since you joined the army, and secondly to protect the reputation of the U. S. Army. Governor Johnson knows all about you and your inclination to bed every pretty woman you meet, and he agreed to your taking this assignment, partly to get you out of Nashville so's he could maintain a little credibility with the citizens there. I'm going along now, just to keep you from messing up. Just to protect the reputation of the U. S. Army. Now, you just settle down for a time and we'll go when I'm ready to go."

It was clear to Jesse that Frank Davis had conjured up a set of circumstances in his mind that had no relationship to reason or reality. Jesse hadn't even been in Nashville when summoned to the Governor's office, and he certainly had had no close contact with any woman for the past several months. He was dumfounded, but realized that his suspicions were justified as to Davis's motives for pursuing this trip.

Following Frank Davis's outburst, Jesse ate his meal in silence, got up to clean off his plate and put it back on the line. He walked out of the mess tent without looking around, but he could feel Frank Davis's eyes burning a hole in his back. Without a word to anyone, he walked back to the tent where he'd left his bedroll, picked it up along with his other gear, checked his weapons for readiness, and started for the saddlery. He first went over to the camp where he'd first met Sid Coster. "Sid, get your stuff together. We're leavin' town," he said gruffly. "We can't waste any more time, and we're not makin' any money just sittin' around this place."

Logan had disobeyed orders before, and he'd probably hear about this one, but he'd been sent out on a mission and the likes of a messed-up Captain Davis was not going to keep him from doing what he was ordered to do. As soon as Sid came out of his tent with a knapsack and bed-roll, the two men went to the saddlery, where Jesse checked out his regular horse, Bob, and signed a voucher for a horse for Sid. They immediately started south and soon cleared the company street, looking for the wagon road to Barboursville. As they left camp, Logan looked back over his shoulder just in time to see Davis coming out of the mess area. Davis hadn't spotted them and their passage was secure, at least for a short time, but they would have to be on the lookout to be sure. He spurred Bob into a trot with Sid matching him, and they were soon well off, on the road to Barboursville.

They reached the little town of Crab Orchard by sundown, and went into the general store, there, purchasing a freshly decapitated chicken and some potatoes. Proceeding some three or four miles south, they stopped for the night and cooked supper.

"What's got into you, Jesse?" Sid asked, as they settled in for the night. "Why are we taking off at this time? Wasn't that other captain supposed to go with you? What's going on?"

"I can't wait on him, Sid. I don't know what's got into that man. I don't think he even intends to make this trip and is just stalling to see if there's some way to avoid it. Maybe he knows something I don't, but he isn't telling me anything except, 'Wait until I say the word'. I got orders from the governor and from my general to go down to Elizabethton and try to find Lily, and that's what I'm gonna to do, Davis or no."

"You know, Jess, Captain Davis got me aside this morning and asked me a lot of odd questions about the trail down to the Watauga, and also what I knew about you, and were you reliable, and how long I'd known you, if I'd ever seen you in a gunfight, and stuff like that. It was sort of strange, because I know you two have been friends as long as you've been in the army, and he just seemed to be pumping me for information like what you'd do if him and you were to get into a fight or something. I told him about that fight in New Castle, an' I think he might be skeer'd of you, Jesse."

Logan turned, looking Sid Coster in the eye. "He was asking you about what you thought about him and me getting into a fight?"

"That's the idea I got, when he tracked me down. I told him I was about to head back south and see what was going on down in the Watauga, and he said he might be wanting me to pilot him through the pass, but it didn't sound like you were going. And now here we are, heading out and he's still sitting there. Who's in charge, here, Jesse, him or you?"

Logan had entertained misgivings about Captain Davis's real motives in going along on the journey, and his most recent confrontation with Davis had confirmed those concerns. He had short loaded that revolver cylinder on the possibility that he and Davis were bound for an out-and-out fight, one that he thought might lead to Davis trying to kill him. He'd planned to secretly switch the cylinder on Davis's revolver if opportunity presented itself, to avoid the possibility that Davis might ambush him, and it now looked as though he was on the right track.

"Sid, I don't know what Davis has in mind, but the way he's been acting lately, I got the idea he might be trying to set a trap for me, and was just delaying this trip south to try to gain some kind of angle on how to go about it. We had a little falling out a couple of weeks ago and he was so mad he tried to kill me at that time, but I thought he'd cooled down. Maybe not."

"A little falling out and he was going to kill you? I'd hate to see what he'd do over a really big scrap. What did you do to him to make him so mad?"

"It was nothing at all. He had the idea that I was interested in his wife, and he just went sideways. I'd known his wife, Mary, when I was a kid and when she told him about it, he took it to mean I was sweet on her, and he went nuts. There was nothing to it, but he didn't believe me when I told him that."

"Was she from the valley?" Sid asked in reference to the Watauga Valley.

"No, I'd known her before I came back to the valley, out in Nevada. We were good friends, but I hadn't seen her for a long time until I met her at his house. She was a real beauty then and is now, and I can hardly blame Frank for trying to protect his interests, but my dedication to him was more important to me than a flirtation with his wife."

"Did you make a play for her? Did it look like you had her in your sights? I never told you this, but a lot of the girls back home thought you were pretty hot stuff, what with your white hair and about seven feet tall. That could shake a man's confidence if it looked like you were about to move in on him and walk off with his sweetie."

"No, Sid, I didn't even give her a serious look," Jesse said with a half-smile, "but I suspect she might have said something to him that made him suspicious, and it must have set him off."

"Hey, Indian Fighter," Coster used the old sobriquet Eli Morgan had pinned on Jesse when they were in school, "you can't keep your notions to yourself, and you know it. I've seen that 'innocent' look you have when you look at a girl. It's like a fox hangin' around the back door of the hen house. No wonder Davis was mad."

The following morning, they cooked some bacon, eggs, and coffee they had bought at Crab Orchard, and got back on the road. The discussion didn't change from the previous day, and after about ten miles, Coster pulled up.

"Jesse," he said, "I'm thinking we should go back, get Captain Davis, and bring him along. This just isn't right, leaving him behind and splitting up the team, when the Governor thought it would be the two of you going after Lily, and he's the senior officer, and was actually counting on us, you and me, to help him get her out."

"Tell me what that would accomplish, Sid," Jesse inquired. "Davis doesn't know Lily, he doesn't know the valley, he doesn't know how to get there, he came on this trip like nothing more than a volunteer without reason, so what could possibly have prompted him to put himself to the trouble of following us through this wild country, just to talk to a girl he doesn't even know? I really think he is doing it to get me out in the woods, to put me out of the picture, and eliminate me as competition for his wife. And, listen. — Don't think for one minute, Pal, that he won't kill you, too, just to eliminate any witnesses."

"I'll tell you what," Jesse continued. "If including Frank Davis in this mission means so much to you, why don't I just go on ahead. I have the map that Travis gave me. You go back and pick Davis up at the camp, and we can meet some place over the ridge. I really don't think it's wise for us to put ourselves in a dangerous spot by getting together out there in the mountains without anyone else around. You've been this way, before. Where do you think would be a safe place to meet up and go on down to the Watauga Valley?"

Coster thought for a moment. "Rogersville is probably the first town of any size. Why don't we meet there?" On that note, the two old friends parted, with Logan heading east and Coster going back toward Camp Dick Robinson.

Jesse spent the next night again in the open, the stars overhead for a roof, but the night was clear and the weather fair, and when he stopped to rest, he simply sat down by a tree and went to sleep. About dawn, he found himself lying sideways, almost in the same position he'd been in when he nodded off, and stiff from having moved so little in the night. After getting up and stretching, he walked stiffly over to where Bob was tethered, saddled him, and rode east for an hour before stopping to brew some coffee and fry some bacon. At a small nearby stream, he filled his canteen, washed his face, and sat down to contemplate his route.

He was still on the north side of Poors Ridge and if Sid got back to Camp Dick Robinson, he and Davis could start out that day and be just a couple of days behind. Not knowing the way as well as Sid, Jesse knew he would be somewhat slower in his trip over the ridge, but he wanted to be sure he was in a populated area when Sid and Frank Davis caught up with him.

Logan left the stream beside which he had been seated and began to climb toward the summit and seek out Cranks Gap as Sergeant Travis and Sid had directed.

Late in the afternoon, he reached what he felt was Poors Ridge and without much trouble spotted the gap, crossing the gap by about sundown. Cane Creek was just as Travis had indicated on his map and Logan started down the south side of the ridge, crossing the creek, feeling he'd been either pretty lucky or pretty smart, but he wasn't sure which.

That evening he stopped again, tethered Bob in a grassy clearing, cooked some salt-pork and potatoes, and slept.

————⸖«◉»⸖————

Davis spent the remainder of the afternoon at his tent, cleaning his revolver. He hadn't noticed the absence of the junior captain as he went back to his tent from lunch. He was not so much interested in Logan's whereabouts as he was as to how he would go about killing the man whom he perceived as nothing more than an interloper, trying to come between him and the one person in the world who made his life worth living. In his confused and distorted thinking, Frank Davis had ruminated endlessly on what had gone on in the past between Logan and Mary and had come to the conclusion that for the sake of his happiness and, for that matter, Mary's also, he was going to have to eliminate the man he'd befriended so many years ago.

When he had encountered Logan at his house in Nashville almost two weeks previously, Davis had been in a state of hopelessness, but then he began to focus on what he had to do to get his life back in order. He considered himself a fairly young man, with a promising future both in the army and afterward as well, and he wasn't going to let old friendships stand in his way. If he could get Logan into an out-of-the-way situation where he could quietly kill him without suspicion or recrimination, he'd solve his problem. If, by chance, Logan should detect his plans and he, himself were killed, then Mary would be happy enough with her substitute lover. It was a small price to pay for peace of mind.

It had all been worked out in his plans and all he needed now was the resolve and opportunity to kill the man who had been a friend for these many years, almost like a younger brother, and yet had developed into what Davis perceived as 'evil personified'. The few days between Nashville and Camp Dick Robinson had not changed his perception, but had simply given him time to clarify his thinking on the matter. He was confident Logan suspected nothing, and he, Davis, had given him no reason for suspicion.

He had been the epitome of friendliness and congeniality, except for that little confrontation at lunch, and he felt that even that little breach of good favor was necessary to assert his authority. Logan had a habit of thinking for himself at times and it was important to bring him back into line occasionally.

Yes, they would start out for the Watauga Valley within the next couple of days, but it would be Davis, not Logan who would be the leader, determine the pace, and set the direction. Everything was in order. He sat down in the waning light of the day and penned a letter to Mary.

My dear and loving wife,

I must let you know, my dear, that I have been sent on a scouting mission to rescue a young woman who is the relative of your friend Mrs. Johnson and for whom Mrs. Johnson is sorely concerned. While I have little information about the mission, suffice it to say that the trip was engineered by none other than your old friend, Jesse Logan. I believe I've been commissioned to accompany Captain Logan, perhaps to keep him from resuming some of his old habits, that of gaining the confidence of young women for his own romantic purposes.

This is not an easy letter to write. While Captain Logan and I have been close in the past, it has come to my attention that he has developed some promiscuous tendencies, and as we discussed before you left for our home, he has insinuated himself more than once on the good graces of some poor young woman, only to leave her distraught and heartbroken. I don't intend for that to happen, even if it means taking the life of that man, as I consider him to be totally unsuited to wear the uniform of a Federal Officer.

On the way south from this place, our trip will take us for a distance of possibly one hundred miles, and I intend to confront Captain Logan along that way with the gravity of his propensities. Knowing his quick temper, I don't expect he will take this confrontation as anything but an insult and a threat, and I expect him to react violently.

I will be prepared, my Dear Mary, and will do all I can to protect myself, even to the death, to defend your honor, as well as the honor of the United States army. It is entirely possible that one of us may die, but rest assured that if it be my fate to be left out on that mountain, I will have died for the sake of protecting my loving wife and dear children and perhaps even the honor of the woman whom we are commissioned to rescue.

If I am not fated to see your lovely face again, Dear Mary, please kiss the

children for me and let them know their father died in their service, and
the service of their country.
Ever your loving husband and obedient servant,
Frank Davis, Cap't, United States Army
Camp Dick Robinson, Kentucky

The following morning, Davis arose in good humor. His plans were firm and he had every hope of success. He thought it would be appropriate for him to get a few provisions together, just for show, and to start the trek into the mountains. He also thought it might be wise to remain in the mountains a few days after he caught and eliminated his adversary, so he secured enough food for that additional time. He then left his tent and went to get some water to wash up and prepare himself for the events of the day. On his way to the latrine, he passed the tent where he knew Logan to have been staying, and he rapped several times with the handle of his knife on the tent post. "Get up, Logan. We have work to do." He stuck his head in the tent and looked around. Neither Logan nor any of his belongings were in the tent. It was vacant!

There was an orderly not far from the tent and Captain Davis addressed him, a little perturbed. "Have you seen anything of our Captain Logan, Corporal?"

"Not since two days ago at about noon, Captain," the orderly responded.

"What do you mean? Were you here the whole time?"

"Yes, Sir, I've been in and out of this part of the camp since the last couple of days, Sir, and the last time I saw that officer, he was carrying his bed roll and walking thataway," he said pointing toward the saddlery.

"Did he say anything to anybody?"

"No, Sir, he just kind of had his head down and was a'walkin' like he was on his way somewheres. He had that scout, that what's-his-name, Coster, with him."

Davis was furious. This was typical Logan, disobeying orders and going off on his own. He'd hear about this insubordination, if he lived through the confrontation Davis had planned when he caught him. "Corporal, get me a mount," he hissed.

"Captain, I don't think the saddler will just issue me a horse on my own hook. I'm going to need orders to get one, I think."

"Never mind, I'll do it myself," Davis snapped as he turned and walked at a fast pace toward the saddlery.

As a captain, Davis had little trouble obtaining a horse and saddle, and without so much as reporting back to garrison, he belted on his revolver and canteen, strapped his knapsack and bed roll behind his saddle, mounted the horse, and started south.

An hour out of camp, Davis was lost. He tried to follow a southerly path, but the terrain became precipitously steep and rocky and he had to retrace his steps several times. He headed back for camp reflecting bitterly on all the misery Logan had put him through.

As he approached Camp Dick Robinson, he encountered Sid Coster, with whom he'd had a brief conversation about the trail south. It suddenly occurred to him that this was a man who was familiar with the countryside and had been employed as a scout from the Watauga Valley. It was a stroke of luck. As earlier anticipated, Davis would enlist the man's aid and possibly get far enough ahead of Logan to catch him unawares along the trail and kill him, right then and there. If it became necessary, Davis might also have to eliminate Coster, but he would make that decision in due time.

Sid Coster recognized the captain and hailed him. "Captain Davis, I was just comin' to look for you. I've just left Captain Logan. I'd known him before the war you know, and we'd set out together for the Watauga Valley, but after a time, we agreed that it might be better if I came back and took you through the Gap and on down to the valley, you not being quite so familiar with the way."

Davis had to think a moment. If this man had been a friend of Logan's and the two of them had worked out a plan to bring him and Logan back together somewhere in that vastly unsettled region to the southeast, it only meant one thing; that they were conspiring to kill him. Coster was his best means of finding Logan, but was also part of a threat. His mind worked feverishly. He was caught in an extremely delicate situation, but Frank Davis was an extremely resourceful man. He had to make it look to Coster as though he was anxious to reach Logan, but would also have to avoid the trap they were setting.

"Where, pray tell, is Captain Logan, and why has he not come back here with you? This is very strange, but I appreciate your coming back to fetch me. I'm anxious to go with Captain Logan on this mission and it's strange that he's sought to strike out on his own, now isn't it?"

"Captain, we left Tuesday with the idea that there was some urgency in getting down into the valley, but after talkin' it over, we agreed that you should be included in any further decisions, since you are the senior officer. Captain Logan will be waiting for us in Rogersville, sir. We thought it would be better to have me come back and guide you through the mountains."

"I see. Captain Logan decided that it would better suit his purposes to have you guide me through the mountains, but he will be able to negotiate this strange country on his own. Is that about the way you see it, young man?"

Coster was perplexed. He could tell he had a long way to go to assuage this man's doubts, but his options were limited. "Yes, sir. Captain Logan felt — well, I felt — an' we talked about the fact that we — err — he — well, no."

"We had set off maybe a little hastily, and — well — it seemed as though I should come back and see to it that you got through the mountains safely and then you and him could get back together at Rogersville. Then, — well —, Captain, could we just get started, sir, and talk this thing over along the way?" Sid Coster began to wonder why he had bothered to come all this way back to fetch a man who was, in essence, nothing more than an unnecessary player in the whole scheme, and was clearly at odds with the purpose of the mission.

Davis, on the other hand, could see that these two amateurs had set about to get him out into the mountains and ambush him. This man, Coster, didn't have a very plausible story to present, to get him into a compromising situation. He needed the man to get to Logan, but he'd have to eliminate them both, if for no other reason, than they were both conspiring to kill him. The trick was to get to the fatal rendezvous without being the fatality.

"I'm ready when you are, Mr. Coster, and as you say, we can talk this over on the way."

⟫⟪⟨⟩⟫⟪

Logan crawled out of his bed in the cedar thicket at about 4:30 in the morning and was cautiously making his way south toward Rogersville. He found that the trail he'd been on crossed a small creek, and was undoubtedly the one Sergeant Travis had told him about. It was summer and the creek was not at a particularly high level, making his crossing fairly easy. As directed, he followed the trail and then found a trail leading uphill. At about noon, he stopped and dismounted, eating some of the salt pork he had cooked the day before. He was at the top of a ridge and could see several miles in all directions, but was also in some pretty good cover. He sat down next to a tree, got out the map Sergeant Travis had drawn, and studied it for a time.

The next thing Logan knew, he was awakened by the sense that there was someone nearby, almost standing over him. He tried to look and see who was there without appearing to have wakened, but the man standing over him spoke, indicating he was aware of Jesse's having awakened.

"Takin' a little nap, was ye, young feller?" the voice was cracking and aged, and when Logan looked up, he could see why. The owner of the voice was one of the most ancient looking people he had ever seen. He was stooped and arthritic, and his beard hung down past his waste. He had a wretched looking hat on his head from which protruded a mop of tangled white hair and his teeth were brown when he smiled, which he did, quite often. His clothing was patched and torn and his shoes were moccasins, obviously homemade, as they didn't show the skills of any Indian tribe in their construction.

"How's come you to be in these parts, sonny," the old man queried. "Wherever you come from, you come a long way, I'd 'low. Air you running from or to?"

"I'm just passing through here on my way to the Watauga Valley, mister," Logan offered. "I've got some business down there and I've been looking for the shortest way to get there. Am I on the right track?"

"I reckon ye'r on the right road, but how's come you to be out here all alone, though? Usually, old Dan is the one who's been he'ping folks down through these parts. Why'n't you a'goin' along with old Dan? He jes' passed through here about ten days past."

"I wasn't in time to catch him. I just got to the Cranks Gap yesterday and started out from there."

It was a tense conversation. The old man held a squirrel rifle at ready and Logan didn't dare make a move toward his weapons as any time he shifted position, the man would bring the rifle around as if to protect himself.

"I reckon you live nearby, mister," Logan offered to try to relax the conversation. He thought that perhaps he could find out a little about the old man and try to gain his confidence. It was unlikely the man would be a southern sympathizer, but he certainly didn't demonstrate any sympathy toward Logan or his uniform, either.

"Close enough," the old man offered. "I seen you a'comin' this way and reckoned you was fixin' to set down fer a bit. That's be'n about a half-hour's past, by now."

"How well do you know Dan Ellis? He's a pretty good friend of mine and has helped me out two or three times, when I needed it. He hails from my part of the country, down in the Watauga Valley."

"Good enough," the old man repeated himself. "He's a good'un fer bringing some scratch up here when I'm in need. Sometimes it's flour, and sometimes it's sugar, 'r that kind'a thing. I put him up a night 'r two when the weather gits real bad. We gits along perty good, Dan and me."

"Say, I don't even know your name," Logan said cheerfully. "My name's Jesse, Jesse Logan."

"Folks call me Enoch," the man offered, warming a little to the conversation.

"Have you lived in these parts long?"

"Long enough," Enoch said, drawing back a little from the friendly young man.

From time to time, Logan had heard of people living in the hills, and the name Enoch was one that he'd heard several times when he was younger. He recalled that Adam Gainfield, one of his friends from school, had mentioned Enoch as a brother of his grandfather and a confirmed hermit. "You're Enoch Gainfield, ain't'cha? I knew your nephew down in the valley, — Adam. He was a good friend of mine when I was livin' down in Doe River Cove," he said trying to revert to the vernacular of his encounter.

Enoch was surprise somewhat, to think that this outlander should even have been aware of his existence, much less know his name. He studied Jesse intently for a few moments. "What did you say ye'r name was?" he finally asked.

"I'm Jesse Logan. My gran'pap is Henry Kellar, and my pa was David Logan. My uncle is Pleasant Logan, down in Elizabethton. They's both doctors, 'cept my pa died a few years back."

"A long time back, I'd 'low," Enoch said slowly, as though he was sifting thoughts through his head one by one. "It was ye'r pap that fixed my poor wife and little baby Sarah when'st they was ailin' one time, and he did a right smart job of it, too. That was back in '42 or '43, as I recollect, and it wasn't but a short time later that I heerd your pap and your mammy and all the young'uns jes' packed up an' left the hills, goin' out west, 'er somethin'. They had a whole pa'ssle of young'uns, as I recall."

"Well, I'm the last of those young'uns," Jesse declared. "I was only three or four when we left these hills, and then, when I was fifteen, I came back here to live with my kinfolk. I been living here ever since, except, I joined the army back in sixty-one."

"What year is it, now?"

"Well, it's '63, Mr. Gainfield, 1863. How long has it been since you've seen your family down in the valley?"

"I'm not sure's I'd know who my family is, even. That young feller, he's 'bout your age, I think, you named him — didn't you say his name is Adam or somethin' like that? Well, he come up here and I saw him fer a little bit. He was riding a horse and was dressed jes' like you, 'cept his clo's was a little on the lighter side, and maybe not so perty, but they was jes' the same as yours. He seems like a nice young feller."

"When was that you saw Adam, Mr. Gainfield?" Logan asked, remembering that Adam Gainfield had joined the Confederate Army, and probably had been on a scouting mission.

"H'it was jes a couple of months ago, I think. Ye-ah, jes' a couple of months ago."

"Was he alright? Did he look well?"

"He looked fit enough to me, I 'low. He was with two other fellers who were dressed jes' like him. What is it with you young fellers? Does you all dress the same way? First h'it was Adam and his frien's and now here you come with these fancy duds on and I reckon ever' body in the country will be dressing that way, if'n they kin find the clo's to put on. Their clo's was a little more on the brown or sort of lightish brown side and ye'rs is more blue, but they all looked alike, and a lot like them clo's ye'r wearin'."

So Adam was still wearing a Confederate uniform. The last time Logan had seen Adam Gainfield, he had gotten the idea the young man was not happy to be in the Rebel Army, but it seemed things had not changed that much. It was also evident that the Rebs were still scouting these hills and trying to maintain control despite the rumors of General Burnside's proposed movement into the East Tennessee area.

"Mr. Gainfield, I'd be trying to get Doe River Cove, if I could, but I think it'd be best for me to go by way of Rogersville. Could you he'p me out in which way I should go to try to get there the shortest way possible?"

"Well, son, first of all, the shortest way ain't always the best way, and I don't know if you want to cross these hills direct or follow the rivers. They goes generally from the northeast, and you have to cross the ridges headin' south ever' so often to get where you wants to be. Or you could cross that there ridge, get into the Clinch Valley and get right on down to Rogersville from there. If you follow the Powell on east from here you gets into some perty steep country and it'll be hard travelin' goin' that a'way."

Logan was facing a tough choice. First, it was apparent that the old man was oblivious to the distinction in the uniforms of the northern and southern armies, and he wasn't so sure he even knew there was a war going on. He had removed any insignia of rank from his uniform, but wasn't sure it would have made any difference to the old man anyway. Besides that, he was not sure of Enoch's loyalties, or what they would be if he were aware of the conflict. Time was not of any particular consequence at the moment, but Logan had to move south, with or without Gainfield's help, but it would sure be easier to find his way if he knew the best route to avoid the Rebel patrols.

"Which way does Dan Ellis usually go from here when he heads back toward the Watauga Valley?" Jesse said, deciding circumspection was still to his advantage.

"I'd 'low Dan heads straight east an' a little south from here and when he gits to the railroad, he stays perty well with it 'til h'it gits to Clinch River, then he jes' heads up-river to the valley, wherever he wants to be. What is it with you and Dan that makes you want to take the worst way you kin?"

"I'll be honest with you, Mr. Gainfield —,"

"Folks call me Enoch, young feller," the old man growled.

"Yes, sir, Enoch. Anyway, I'm trying to get to my kinfolk in Doe River Cove, and there a lot of folks, those who are riding with Adam, your nephew, that don't want me to get down there at all. In fact, they're really after me for not joining the Rebel army, but I'm going to stay loyal to the United States and the friends I have, who are fighting for what we believe is right. You never did say whether you cotton for the north or south, but that's the way I feel, anyway. Down in the Watauga Valley there's a young woman who the governor, Governor Johnson wants to have brought out of the valley 'cause he thinks she's in danger, and he's given me the job of going down there and trying to talk her into getting back to Nashville. You might even know the woman. Her name is Lily Venable. They say she's been giving the Rebel army fits and they'd like to catch up with her and lock her up. Do you know about her?"

"What does Adam have to do with all this?"

"Adam is in the army of the Rebel gov'ment, although I don't think he really wants to be there, and them people are riled up against me and the rest of the Federal army and are doin' all they can to get Tennessee to break off from the USA."

"Adam is a'ridin' with the Rebels?" Enoch showed some political awareness.

"Yes, sir. I don't think his heart is in it, but for some reason they got him into the army and won't turn him loose. I saw him last year and he didn't seem too happy, but he seems to think he has to do it. Do you know anything about it?"

"Where does old Dan fit into all this?"

"Dan Ellis is working with th' loyal folks. He's tryin' to he'p some of them, the ones who don't want to get dragged into the Rebel army like Adam was. Dan is tryin' to get them out of the valley into Kentucky where they'll be safer. He'd take anyone that wanted out of East Tennessee up through the Gap into Kentucky, but he has to be ca'ful to stay outa' the way of them Rebel patrols, so's he don't get caught. I think they'd kill him if they'd catch up with him."

"So that's why them fellers with Adam was so interested in where Dan goes. I wondered why they was so curious with his whereabouts. I was a'wonderin' the same about you, but mister, I gets the idea you're fit enough. If'n you still wants to know which way Dan goes to get back down them hills, I'll tell you . . . "

"Down in that-there valley, Dan usually heads down this little ridge from here. H'it's headin' south right here, an' when he gits to the river, he sort of heads fer the east a piece to Mulberry Gap. Then he goes south about twenty mile or so to Rogersville. That's where you wants to go, h'ain't it?"

"Enoch, that's exactly what I want to do. I need to get a move on and make my way down out off the plateau. Come to think of it, there might be a feller followin' me, and he's just likely to have fire in his eyes, 'cause he thinks I done him wrong and he has a score to settle. He's a feller about this high, wearing this same blue uniform as me, and he has a beard, not as nice as yours, but down to about here," he gestured with his left hand striking his chest just below his collar.

"Did you do him bad, son?" Enoch asked in a fatherly manner.

"No, sir, I surely did not," came the reply. "He had trouble with his wife, and he thinks I was behind it, but it's all in his head. He's cooked up a wild notion that I'm after his wife, and I'm so busy fighting this war that I don't need a woman to fight with, too. I'd just like to be friends with this feller — his name is Frank — and get on with what the governor sent me to do, but I don't think he's going to let it rest. Anyway, I want to thank you for your help and if you see Adam, try to talk him out of stayin' with them renegades he's thrown in with. It'll only cause him grief, I swear."

"The roads is scant in these parts for the next twenty or thirty miles, son, and there ain't many people hereabouts, so's t'would probably do fer you to travel in the daytime, if'n ye're ca'ful. That's what old Dan does, anyhow. You suit yerse'f, but that's my advice. You kin stay at my place the night, and strike out in the mornin' and make just as good time. I got some possum cookin' in the pot at home, and ye're welcome to it. What do you say?"

"I'd think that's a good idea, Enoch." And with that the two new friends headed back for Enoch's shanty for some possum stew and a night's rest.

—————=((●))=—————

Earlier that day Corporal Adam Gainfield, CSA with two privates, Lemuel Worth and Willie McCorcle, were riding north from the Clinch River, scouting for the likes of the elusive Dan Ellis. The terrain was rough and steep, and they had just come over a high ridge and had found the headwaters of the Little

Powell River. The day was wearing on, and the three men knew they'd have to spend the night on the trail. Adam had been turning the matter of wearing the uniform of the Confederacy over and over in his mind, ever since he was caught in a 'recruiting' sweep back in 1861 and had resolved that this was the time to try to join with the Federal forces and satisfy his own true loyalties.

He had been a firm, though not vocal supporter of the Federal cause, and had no reason to expect to join either army, but least of all, the Confederate Army. He'd been a fair student at Elizabethton Grammar School, but when he was about sixteen, he began to work with his father and older brother Kenneth at the drayage business that his father had started when he had come to the Watauga Valley in about 1840.

Adam's father, Jeremy Gainfield, had migrated from the region of Harrisonburg, Virginia with his father and two uncles and had gone into the business of farming and hauling hay, grain, vegetables, and tobacco for other farmers in the valley. They had been moderately successful at the business but after some minor disagreements over business, one of the uncles, Enoch, having lost his wife and only daughter to an influenza epidemic, packed up his belongings and headed for the hills, effectively assuming the life of a hermit in the Cumberland Mountains, some miles north of Knoxville, and near the Virginia-Tennessee line. That had been almost fifteen years ago, and Adam's father had tried several times to locate Enoch and try to get him to return to the valley. Finally, in about 1855, he did find his Uncle, but the old man had found peace in the mountains and scorned all entreaties to reconcile.

Jeremy Gainfield had even taken Adam to see the old man at one point, but Enoch was not to be moved. Adam never forgot the experience, though, and when he was taken into a Confederate militia unit, and after he had gained the rank of corporal, he found reason to visit Enoch on scouting missions, and had at least established that he was still alive and well. Adam did not discuss with Enoch the war or the implications of Adam's wearing the uniform of a southern soldier, as his family, like most East Tennesseans, were staunchly pro-Union, and he wasn't anxious to alienate his uncle. Actually, Enoch had formed no particular loyalties in the Civil War, except that he did rely on the generosity of Dan Ellis from time to time, and had learned from Dan that there was fighting going on down the mountain, and that Dan was loyal to the Union.

Ellis had been conducting his secret trips from the Elizabethton region for many months, escorting people into Kentucky, mostly men who wanted to escape the conscription act of the Confederate Government. Adam Gainfield knew Dan Ellis from his boyhood days, and had even sought him out to gain his assistance in escaping the Rebel draft at one time, but up until now he was pretty well resigned to the fact that he'd have to stay in a Confederate uniform. He well knew that to desert and join the army of the North would mean the death penalty if he were caught, and that prospect did not sit well with him, unless he could be assured that he'd be moved to a Yankee unit far from East Tennessee.

Now Adam was as close to the Federal lines as he had been in several months, and the idea of escaping to the northern army was like a magnate, drawing him north. The two soldiers he was with were not particularly political in their inclinations. McCorcle was a little more vocal in his support for the cause of secession than Lem Worth, but neither was much more than moderately committed to the southern cause. McCorcle had joined the army to accompany an older brother, and Worth had joined to get away from an impoverished home life. This scouting mission, for them, was more like an outing in the woods that an assignment of war.

The countryside through which they were riding was only vaguely familiar to Gainfield, and not at all to the others. Gainfield was at the head of the group, and was leading the others toward where he remembered his uncle Enoch to be living. The trio suddenly came to a steep drop in the terrain; the small stream that would feed the Powell River, falling about forty feet to some rocks at the bottom of a steep gorge. The stream was low, as there had been little rain for several weeks, but the streambed demonstrated that during the wet seasons there was a considerable flow over these falls, and the rocks at the bottom were well exposed.

"Hold it, men," Gainfield called out. "This piece ain't passable, and we're goin' to have to turn back. I think we can go around that rise to the east and make our way down to the river."

"Are you sure this is the Little Powell?" McCorcle inquired. "H'it ain't much more than a dribble, here. I kin spit faster than that-there trickle you call a river."

"Well, if it ain't the Little Powell, at least it'll take us down to the Powell. H'it's jes' that I wants to get up there a ways an' see my uncle. I think he might be able to tell us a little about where that Dan Ellis is."

"Well, you jes' tell us which way to go, Mr. Boone. We mus' be almos' to the Kentucky line, by now. How much farther is it to you oncle's place, anyway?"

"I reckon about five mile, by now. I 'spect we're goin' to have to spend the night out here again, an' I'd'ruther spend it with my uncle. He's a little queer, but he's real friendly an' he jes' might have some perty good fixins on the fire."

Suddenly, as Gainfield tried to turn his horse, the ground gave way and the horse started to slide toward the steep embankment that dropped away to the rocks below. Gainfield grabbed at a sapling growing nearby, and pulled himself free from the sliding horse. He managed to get his feet on the ground, still clinging with one hand to the horse's reins and the other to the small tree. The horse, using the assistance of his now dismounted rider, clamored toward safety, but the earth was soft under the cover of the forest and kept giving way beneath him. Suddenly, however, the bridle rein by which Adam was supporting the horse broke and the horse, thrashing wildly, tumbled down the embankment. He landed feet first on the boulders at the foot of the falls, but collapsed and lay for a moment. Then, in a vain effort, he tried to rise, but it was apparent that he was so badly injured that he couldn't get up.

Gainfield clamored down the cliff after his fallen horse and nearly met with a similar fate. At the last moment on his downward slide, he managed to stop by digging his heels into the dirt and rocks and grabbing a small bush. At that point, the horse tried again to right himself and it was all the young man could do to keep out of the way of flying hooves. He reached the horse's head and caught hold of the bridle, controlling the head and calming the horse somewhat. Still wide eyed and breathing in powerful gasps, the horse continued to struggle, but it was clear that he had broken at least one leg and another was cut to the bone on some of the sharp rocks and was bleeding badly. Winded, the horse lay his head to one side to try to catch his breath.

Adam Gainfield knew he was now afoot. The horse would be useless if he managed to live, and with blood streaming from the cuts on his legs and neck, it didn't look as though he would survive. Adam stood up and balanced himself on two of the boulders, looking down at his fallen mount. With resignation, he reached over and unbuckled the saddlebags from the saddle and tried to loosen the cinch. It was no use. The cinch was still under the fallen animal and the saddle was obviously broken beyond use. He pulled a broken carbine from its scabbard, looked at it briefly and threw it aside. Then he drew his revolver, checked the caps and shot the dying animal in the side of the head. He then made his way tearfully toward the place where he thought he'd be able to pick up the creek-side trail to wait for the other riders.

McCorcle and Worth, following the directions Gainfield had noted before his slide down the hill, circled the small hill off to their right and made their way down a steep slope. At the bottom of the slope, they made their way back toward where they had last seen their corporal and started calling his name. Immediately, Gainfield answered and the three soldiers were reunited. After some discussion, it was agreed that they would go on to the north and try to find Gainfield's uncle. If they could, they might be able to get a horse from him, though that was not likely. If that was not possible, perhaps it would be best if Gainfield stayed behind and the two other soldiers could go back to their company, get another horse and return. Meanwhile, the terrain was sufficiently gradual to allow Gainfield to mount on the back of McCorcle's horse and proceed, at least for a while.

It fit nicely into Gainfield's plans. Though he regretted losing his horse, if he could now dismiss the other two soldiers to return to camp and come back with a replacement mount, he could be gone when they got back, and his attempt to enlist with the Federal Army could succeed.

—————((◍))—————

Frank Davis and Sid Coster cleared Crank's Gap and started south on a vague trail, known only to a very few, and barely discernable, if at all. At times, Coster noticed evidence of the passing of a horse only a short time ago and knew that Logan had been able to follow the directions he had been given. As they traveled south, Coster tried to engage Davis in conversation and ferret out the motives behind his relentless pursuit of the younger captain.

"Captain Logan tells me you and him have known each other for a long time. He came back to live in Doe River Cove in about fifty-five and says he'd met you even before that. When we was young, he told some of us fellers about the time he was takin' a wagon to sell some hides or somethin' and he met up with you when you were only a sergeant an' had been out in the mountains chasin' wild Indians."

"Yes, that was a long time ago. I'd never of thought at the time we'd be chasin' each other around the hills of Tennessee. He seemed like a nice young man at the time and it's strange the way everything turned out."

"He _is_ a nice young man, Captain," Sid Coster declared, defensively, "I don't know about what's happened between you, but I get the idea you two are a little peeved with one another. I've known Jesse perty well for these past six or seven years and he's always seemed like a square shooter. What was it that got between you?"

"There's nothing, nothing at all. We just set out on this trip to do a job — you know — to try to get that young lady out of the Watauga Valley and

427

maybe take her back to live with her kinfolks in Nashville, and Captain Logan just — well — just decided to go off on his own without consulting me. That's all. — That just isn't the way we do it in the army. He'd been a good soldier up till now and I can't understand what got into him. He's funny when it comes to being around women, you know. I've seen him do some silly things when there's a girl involved and I'm not so sure but what he saw an opportunity to get this girl off somewhere for himself and started off without thinking. Did you ever see any of that kind of behavior when you knew him back home?"

Coster had to think for a minute. It occurred to him that Logan's 'nothing-at-all' explanation of the situation was more credible than Davis's, 'nothing-at-all'.

"Well, I know he was perty friendly with some of the girls back in the valley, and I also know that this young lady that you'uns are lookin' for had been writin' to him when he was in Libby Prison, and, so the story goes, she somehow helped him to escape. I don't know that that would mean that he's been acting silly about girls or anything."

"Don't you think he got it into his head that if he got off ahead of me that he'd be able to find this Lily and — well — spend a little time with her without having to answer to me or the governor? Didn't he send you back to look for me just so's he could get a head start on us? Why'd he do that, d'you think? Don't sell this fellow short, Mr. Coster. He's pretty cunning."

Coster was confused. Logan had not sent him back. It had been at his own suggestion that he and Logan had separated and Logan had gone on ahead. Even so, Coster's first suggestion had been for them both to return to Camp Dick Robinson and rejoin Captain Davis and Logan had complicated things by going off on his own. It didn't make sense that such a ruckus could begin merely over Logan's desire to get down into the valley just a day or two ahead of him and Captain Davis. Some of what Davis was saying made sense, in a strange way, unless one took note of the concerns Logan had expressed supporting his desire to reunite with Captain Davis in a more densely populated area than these Cumberland Mountains.

"Captain, look at this. Even if he was to get down into the valley a day or two ahead of us, he still doesn't know where to find Lily and it'd take him prob'ly more than a day or two to find out where she's hidin'."

"So, Mr. Coster, you don't think doing something like that is silly? It's like I told you, Logan doesn't always think straight when there's a pretty girl involved. Can't you get it into your head that he's not exactly in control of his own emotions when he smells romance in the air? I remember one time up in Coalwood when he was sitting in the park there with his hands all over a pretty young woman, right out in public. She ended up calling the sheriff about it and we had to send him off on a courier mission to just keep the people of the town from lynching him. That's how much of a 'straight shooter' your friend Logan is."

———》《《(》)《———

After a breakfast of bacon and biscuits, Jesse stood and prepared to set out on the trail, "I still have the rest of the day, Enoch, and I'm powerful anxious to make my way down the mountain. If I'm going to make Rogersville by nightfall, I'd better get moving."

With that, Logan packed up his bedroll and weapons, mounted his horse and started to move south on the faint trail along the ridgeline that Enoch had showed him. He turned after a few steps and looked back at the old man. "Is there anythin' I can do for you, Enoch? I don't have much food, but I can leave you a little of the army biscuits I have. You've been awful good to me."

"Get on with you, young feller. I've got all I needs right here, and old Dan takes perty good care of me when he comes through. You be ca'ful and do like I say. 'Don't have to worry 'bout travelin' in the daytime till ye gits to the Clinch. Then you'd better slow down and work at night. Good luck."

Jesse turned and headed down the faint trail along a broad ridge, following the old man's directions. He had gone not more than forty or fifty yards when he heard the sound of a horse's hooves and a voice loudly addressing Enoch. It was the voice of Frank Davis, but at that distance, he could not make out what they were saying. He immediately got off his horse, and took his carbine from its scabbard.

He fumbled in his saddle-bags for the short-loaded cylinder he had brought along, and in the process, his bedroll fell from his saddle near the trail, but he ignored it. He then tied Bob to a tree in some bushes well off the trail, and made his way cautiously back toward Enoch's camp. When he got close enough to hear what was being said, he stopped, then continued through the brush to try to gain a better position.

"Yes, sir, matter of fact, I seen a feller ridin' by this way about a hour or two ago. Big feller! He was headin' up that there ridge, seemed to be goin' east, he was," Enoch said, pointing in a direction ninety degrees from that in which Logan had left him.

"Did you talk to him? Did he say anything about where he was going?" Davis asked, dismounting from his horse to look for hoof-prints in the dirt.

"Didn't say a thing. Matter of fact, I didn't even 'proach him. He looked downright mean and determined, and I ain't in no condition to take on a big feller like that, not me. It didn't even come over me to talk to him or let him know I was anywhere around."

"Who were you talking to just now, before I rode up? I thought I heard voices."

"I reckon I was jes' talkin to myse'f. I finds myse'f doin' that from time to time, anymore. When that-there young feller went by, I reckon I conjured up some talk in my head an' I was jes' lettin' it out."

Suddenly, still unseen by Frank Davis or Enoch, a pair of horsemen came from the south, the direction from which Logan had just returned. Two of the Confederate cavalrymen, the two who had recently been riding patrol with Adam Gainfield, had been making their way to the north along the trail Jesse had intended to travel. They had spotted his discarded bedroll and, energized by the discovery, decided to seek out the owner. Adam Gainfield had dismounted from behind Willie McCorcle and had picked up the bedroll. He confirmed that it was of Federal origin by the markings and directed the other two to go on ahead and try to find out who the bedroll belonged to. They missed seeing Logan, who was concealed in the underbrush, but were heading straight for where Davis and Enoch were holding their conversation.

Davis, thinking he had located his prey, had left Sid Coster on the trail, admonishing him to wait a few minutes, as Davis wanted to 'clarify some matters', if one of the voices was, in fact, Jesse. He had then ridden ahead to investigate.

Coster, following instructions, was holding back as 'cover', but was still not sure of what was happening. He tied his horse and proceeded cautiously toward the conversation on foot. *"Jesse was right. Captain Davis wants to sneak up on Jesse, shoot him, and then come back and shoot me,"* he thought to himself.

After the brief discussion with Enoch, Davis was alerted to the sound of the Rebel horses and, sensing trouble, he quickly turned to remount his horse to try to get away or at least gain cover for a fight. The Rebel horsemen were too fast. They had the advantage of being on the move, with their quarry in sight, and Davis had no idea where to run or hide. In his effort to mount his horse, he caught his foot on the bedroll behind the saddle, and lost his balance, slowing his effort to escape. He turned and fired his revolver at the approaching horsemen, and then succeeded in remounting his horse, but his two shots had both missed hitting the Rebels. He fired again, hitting the second rider in the shoulder, but the lead rider, McCorcle, was almost upon him and had his revolver in his hand. He shot twice, one of the shots taking effect, and Davis fell from the saddle.

The second horseman, Lem Worth, had managed to pull his horse to a stop and McCorcle, after getting off his horse and looking over Davis's, apparently lifeless body, walked back and helped his companion down from his horse. "They's another Yank here, somewhere, Lem. They's two bedrolls, and only one dead Yank, and we're a'gonna have to catch th'other one. He's around here somewheres. Hey, old man, what happened to that-there other Yank who was with this one?"

"Ye're gonna have to find him without much help from me," Lem Worth, the wounded horseman said with a pained look on his face. "That shot took me perty good, and I don't know kin I even make it back to camp with this hole in me. Where did he hit me, Willie? Kin you tell?"

"Jes' you sit here fer a few minutes Lem, and take a rest. I'm gonna talk to the old man and see if he knows anythin'. Gainfield should be a'comin' up with us perty quick, and he'll he'p you out. I don't know what happened to him, but he should be along any minute. Hey, old man!" he said walking some twenty or thirty feet over toward where Enoch was standing, "Where's the other Yank? I asked you once't a'ready and I wants a answer. What happened to the other Yank?"

"What other Yank? There hasn't been a Yank in these parts sence Gen'ral Jackson brought them fellers down to fight the British, to my way of thinking."

"Don't play dumb with me, Old Timer. This here dead man is a Yankee soldier and he had someone with him. Now, where is he?"

"Wal, I reckon there was another feller with this one, but he went up that-away," he said pointing to the southeast.

"We jes' come from there and there wa'n't anybody on the trail. That's where we found a bedroll throwed down, and there has to be someone belongs to that bedroll. Come on, Old Timer, you give me some straight answers or you'll end up like your Yankee friend, toes up on the trail." With that the soldier reached out and grabbed Enoch by the beard and shook him violently. "Come on, you old buzzard, where's th'other Yank?"

Logan stepped out of his hiding place and yelled at the soldier, "Get your hands off him and get 'em up in the air. You don't have any call to get rough with that man. He's not going to give you any help. Stand clear of him or I'll blow your head off your shoulders. Stand clear, I'm tellin' you."

"You better not try it, Billie, or you'll jes' as likely hit yer shiftless friend. An' ef you don't, I'll shoot him, jes' as soon as I shoot you," the Rebel soldier said, putting his revolver to Enoch's head. "Now put your gun on the ground and step away from it."

Logan had the advantage of a large tree for cover, and he quickly ducked behind it, but he was constrained from firing at the other man for fear of hitting Enoch. In the confusion, however, Enoch pushed away and dove for the ground near where his musket lay. As soon as he moved, Logan fired his carbine, hitting the soldier dead center and killing him instantly. The other Confederate soldier, hearing the commotion, grabbed his own revolver and haltingly ran toward the sounds of fighting. He couldn't move too quickly, however, because of the pain from his wounded shoulder. As he approached the fighting, the only person he could see was Enoch, standing over his fallen companion. He took aim from a distance of about thirty yards, but before he could fire, Adam Gainfield, who had been following on foot, shot him from behind.

A screen of trees and brush had separated Adam Gainfield and Jesse Logan, but now Gainfield cleared the thicket and stood within twenty-five yards of Logan, searching for an adversary, but not sure of where the unidentified adversary was hiding. Jesse still had the cover of the large tree. He raised his revolver, but then recognized Adam across the clearing.

"Drop the gun, Adam," he called out. "Put it down, Pal. I have the advantage, this time. You don't have a chance."

"Don't be too sartin'" he heard a voice off to his left. "This-here squirrel rifle hits whatever I tell it to, and that feller you're pointin' ye'r gun at jes' happens to be my kin."

"Hold it, hold it, HOL-DIT," Adam shouted, dropping his revolver. "If that's you, Jesse Logan, jes' give me a minute or two to talk and we'll get this thing straightened out. Uncle Enoch, put down your rifle an' come on over here. We got some talkin' to do, but first, we better tend to these three fellers an' see if there's anythin' we can do fer 'em an' save their lives. Is that okay with you, Jesse?"

About this time, Sid Coster had come up, armed with only his musket and looked around the clearing. He had heard the shouting and shooting and had advanced cautiously, but hearing Jesse's voice, he showed himself along the edge of the clearing near where Frank Davis had fallen, but said nothing.

"That's fine with me, Adam," Logan responded, holstering his weapon and heading toward the fallen Frank Davis. "If you'll check the two over there, I'd like to check on this fellow. He's been pretty close to me for a long time, and I'm afraid he's not doin' too well." He went over to where Davis was lying and found him badly wounded but still alive. He glanced up when he saw the figure of Coster emerge from the edge of the clearing, "Oh, it's you, Sid. I'm afraid Captain Davis has been hit bad. Come here and let's see what we can do for him."

Jesse turned Davis's head and looked at his face, leaning close to check for breathing. There was a faint sign of labored breathing and Jesse pulled out his own canteen and moistened Davis's lips to try to revive him. Davis opened his eyes.

"Frank, thank God you're alive," Logan said to the other officer. "Just take it easy and let me see where you're hit. You'll be alright, count on it."

"Logan, I reckon you've won the prize. She's yours, but I hope you'll treat her right. I knew it was going to be either you or me, but I didn't suspect that was you in the Rebel uniform just now."

"Take it easy, Frank, you're talking crazy. What do you mean Rebel uniform? I just took my bars off my uniform in case we ran into someone that thought they might get a bigger bounty for a captain than a private. You take it easy for a minute. You'll be alright."

By that time, Sid Coster had come to Jesse's side and knelt down beside the fallen Frank Davis.

"I ain't gonna be alright and you know it," Davis whispered. "You got me good and you can go claim your prize. Mary'll be waitin' for you. You and her — you deserve each other."

Logan let Davis's head down and stood up. "Adam," he called out. "Can you give us a hand with this man? He's still alive. Sid, 'you got a canteen?"

As Gainfield approached, he was surprised to see Coster stooped over Davis's still form, and looked from Jesse to Sid a couple of times trying to understand what had happened. Logan inquired, "How are your two friends, Adam?"

"They're both gone, Jesse, how's that fella doing?" Then, looking at Coster, "Sid! Where in the world did you come from?"

"He may still be alive," Logan responded, "but I don't know how bad he's hurt."

Coster was leaning over the fallen captain and had his head down trying to determine whether Davis was still breathing. In a moment, though, he looked up, shaking his head. It was apparent that Frank Davis had died, the last words Coster had heard were those accusing Logan. His eyes were partly open but unseeing and when Sid lifted his hand and released it, it fell lifeless to his side. Jesse took off his hat and bowed his head. He'd lost a man who'd been his greatest supporter and yet enigmatically, had recently been a potential foe. The latter, he thought they could have resolved, but he'd never be able to replace the friendship and support Frank Davis had provided. He silently rendered a prayer of thanks, grief, and supplication for the life of this man, who had been almost like a father to him.

There were tears in Jesse's eyes when he put his hat back on and said in a muffled voice, "He's gone."

Then, looking about, Jesse said to Enoch, "I reckon we'd better get to burying them. Enoch, do you have any place around here that you use to bury somebody? There's no point in taking them somewhere else. This is as good a place as any."

Then, after a brief moment of reflection, he continued, "The only thing I'd particularly like to do is take my captain out to the top of the mountain and bury him facing north toward his home in Indiana. He was my sergeant and my lieutenant and then he was my captain, and the only thing he ever wanted out of this war was to get it behind him. Whenever we had any fightin' or anythin' rough to get to, he'd say something about just getting it behind us, like it was another hill we had to cross to get us home. I'd like to bury him on a hilltop where he can be always facing home. I think that's what he'd want."

Sid Coster was perplexed at Logan's show of emotion.

They gathered the horses, five of them, now, and placing the fallen soldiers each on one of the horses, they took them to a nearby mountaintop, where they buried them in separate graves. Enoch had produced an old shovel and the three younger men took turns digging shallow graves.

"Captain Davis would like it if he knew he was being buried next to soldiers from the other side of this war," Jesse declared with an air of reverence in his voice. "He was a peaceful man at heart and always thought the best of everyone, and he'd be proud to sit down with anyone and try to settle this thing without any more trouble. He was a good man, and he taught me an awful lot, not just about soldiering, but about how to live, too."

It was late afternoon by the time they finished with the little impromptu ceremony of burying their companions. Enoch had gone back down to his little shebang and had stirred up the fire under his stew pot. Jesse, Sid, and Adam were alone on the mountain for a time, just talking and reminiscing about their boyhood and about the friendships they'd shared with each other, their fallen friends, and some of their friends back home, including Lily Venable. Coster seemed to be quieter and more reflective than the other two, but joined in the conversation occasionally, contributing what he could about the events that had brought the three together. By the time they started back down the hill to the hut where Enoch was living, they had come to a pretty good understanding.

"You know, fellas," Gainfield said reflectively, "I just shot a man who depended on me. He was one of the men assigned to me for this here scouting trip, and he expected me to give him support when he needed it. He helped me when my horse got so banged up, I had to put him down.

Back up there when I lost my horse, he was awful nice to me and didn't fuss when he had to take me up behind him on the horse he was ridin'. An' I jes' now shot him. Jesse, that was the first time I ever shot anyone, an' h'it was one of my own men."

"I was itchin' to git shed of this Rebel uniform, but I shouldn't've shot one of my own men to do it, should I?" By this time, the young man was shaking and seemed to be near tears. It was evident that he was not only remorseful over what had happened, but also embarrassed at being so emotional and in pouring out his innermost feelings, especially in the presence of soldiers of the opposing army, albeit old friends.

"Adam, you just can't take it that way," Logan comforted him as they led the horses back down the hill towards Enoch's camp. "That man may have been a soldier in the same army as you, but he was about to shoot your uncle. There was nothing else you could have done. In a war, we sometimes have to take action that is painful to us at the time, but we do it to save the lives of those we choose to protect and to get this thing behind us. It's like my friend Frank always said, Adam, 'It's just another hill toward home'. If you want to go back to the valley when this thing's all over, you'd rather face your family knowing that you'd saved the life of your uncle, than to let someone kill him when he wasn't even doin' no harm to anyone. You did the right thing, Adam, and no one can fault you for it."

"Well, maybe you're right, Jesse, but h'it don't make a feller feel too good, shootin' somebody, does it? Have you ever shot anybody before today?" he asked, then reflecting on Logan's reputation as a sharpshooter from the early days of the war, Gainfield mumbled, "Well, I reckon this ain't so new to you, but h'it don't set well at first, does It?"

Captain Jesse Logan did not reply to the question. He was reflecting on the time, over two years past, out on the side of Rich Mountain when an inexperienced private with a Spencer rifle shot a Rebel captain. It had been a devastating experience, but he had faith in his leader, Sergeant Frank Davis, so much so that he did what he was told. At the time, it was all the army could do to convince their troops to shoot low enough to fatally strike the enemy soldiers. The tendency was to shoot so high that there was less chance of hitting anyone, and casualties were light on both sides. After a few fatal hits from both armies, the men finally got the idea that they themselves could be killed if they weren't effective in their use of their own weapons, but at first, the idea of taking a life, especially the life of a fellow American, was too repulsive to even consider. Jesse's experience had been a little different than most. In a skirmish with hostile Indians his desire to survive had introduced to him the concept of taking a life to protect his friends or his own life. Still, when it had happened to him at Rich Mountain, he had suffered with enormous guilt, but later, when threatened by hostile soldiers coming up the hills after him, he did not hesitate to shoot to save the lives of his friends and his own life. He tried now to use the experience to give much needed support to Adam Gainfield when he needed it.

Sid Coster had remained silent for most of the conversation. The last words he had heard from Frank Davis's lips gave him reason to think Logan had shot him, and Coster was trying to come to a resolution and perhaps some justification for such an act. He had known Logan for many years and had considered him to be a friend and a reliable companion, but now he had reason to think that he'd just taken the life of a man from their own side of the conflict. It didn't square with his sense of duty.

"Adam," Logan continued, "there's three times when a soldier takes a life. The first is when he has to, to save his own life or the life of someone with him. The second is when something happens that's an accident, and that's unfortunate but acceptable. The third is when he's following orders and we're expected to do that all the time. Back last year, when you had the drop on me down there in Doe River Cove, wouldn't you have shot me to save your own life or to save your lieutenant's life?" Logan asked. "Sometimes, when we're following orders or trying to save a life, it's just something we have to do. There's no way of getting around it, and there's no lookin' back. There's no lookin' back, Adam."

"We're soldiers, you an' me an' Sid, an' there's things that soldiers have to do whether they like it or not. It's the way the world is an' the way it's always been. Like I said back there on the top of the mountain just now, these fellows are the lucky ones. They are at peace with the world and at peace with God. It's fellows like us that has to make these intolerable decisions to go on fighting, which side we should fight for, an' who we should shoot at an' who we shouldn't. You could just as easy had your uncle take a shot at me back there, but you didn't. Why not? You made a decision to save a life rather than to take one, and you didn't hesitate. That's what soldiers do. That's what we signed up for and what we're paid for."

Sid Coster finally broke his silence. "Would somebody please tell me what happened back there? I missed all the shooting and would like to know why two Rebs and a Yank just got buried back on that hill."

Jesse and Adam filled Sid in on the sequence as they had seen it; the fact that it had been one of Adam's companions and not Jesse who had shot Captain Davis. This completely contradicted what Sid has assumed from Frank Davis' last few words. It also relieved his mind greatly, as up until that time he had been under the assumption that Davis' had been anticipating an out-and-out shooting between himself and Jesse Logan.

"Sid, I was really scared that Frank was actually going to try to bushwhack me somewhere along this trail, and when I agreed to wait for you two at Rogersville, it was to get him out of the hills and around people so he couldn't shoot me, — and shoot you too, Pal, — out here in the wilderness without no witnesses. But no, Sid. I did not kill Frank Davis."

Then, after a few moments he continued, "One thing that bothers me most is that now his wife, Mary, is a widow." I knew her back in Nevada and that was the thing, when he found it out, that must have set him off. She's a nice woman and I really feel bad that now she's just left with nothing more than possibly a widow's pension, if she's able to talk the government out of that."

Their conversation turned to Jesse's mission, and as far as Adam Gainfield could tell them, Lily Venable was still in the Watauga Valley, but he also felt that she wasn't at all inclined to leave. He had been in contact with her a time or two and had received the distinct impression that she was planning to stay in the valley, in spite of any hardships. It had been she who had been partly responsible for Gainfield's decision to assert his loyalties to the Union, despite the fact that he was in the army of the Confederacy. He confided that it had been his tentative plan, if the opportunity arose, to get away from the two soldiers who had been with him and try to get to the garrison at Camp Dick Robinson and join the Union Army.

Logan mulled the situation over in his mind and considered using Gainfield's help to get back down into the valley to try to get Lily to go with them back to Nashville. Weighing the risks, though, Logan felt such a move would be too dangerous, as Gainfield would be considered a deserter if he were caught, and most assuredly executed.

That evening, the three friends went on down to Enoch's camp and enjoyed a bowl of possum stew, and after they had spreadout their bedrolls, they spent another hour or two reminiscing by the campfire, and slept.

24

GAINFIELD

"**J**esse, I've decided to go with you. You may know the valley, but I know how to get us there." Gainfield announced as the three friends were getting out of their bedrolls.

"Adam, I thought we had this thing settled. You go back into Rebel territory and they catch you out of uniform or anything like out of uniform, they'll stand you up against a wall and shoot you. You've seen too much of the get-the-Yankee-sympathizers attitude among the gray coats to ever think you could pull something like this and live if you get caught. You're just gonna have to head up north to Camp Dick Robinson like Sid and a lot of other boys from the valley have done and check in at the garrison and tell them your story. Sam Angel — you maybe remember him — he's a lieutenant up there and is one of those people putting together a new regiment. He'll be glad to sign you up. Or, you can ask to be reassigned to a unit out west and never have to take the chance of running into anyone from these parts who'd recognize you as a deserter, 'cause that's what you are, you know. Sid knows the way better than the both of us and can get me there in fine shape."

"Listen, Jesse. You're not my boss, and I'm still technically a soldier in the Rebel army, and I'm a corporal, and when I say I'm headin' south, I'm headin' south and there's nothin' you can do to stop me. If you want to come along, that's just fine with me, but come or not, I'm going back to the valley. If it turns out that I can help you convince Lily to go back with you, then maybe I'll go along fer company."

"Mr. Gainfield," Logan said slowly, drawing his revolver from its holster on the ground where he had been sleeping, "you're my pris'ner, now, and since you say you're a corporal in the Rebel army, I'm going to have to treat you as an enemy, and I'm taking you pris'ner and I'm about to turn you in to the nearest garrison for disposition. Now, get on that horse and start movin' north."

"Take a hike, you big stretched out drink of water. You ain't takin' me nowhere. You may have to shoot me, but I'm headin' south."

"Get on that horse!"

"Go jump in the lake!"

"This is ridiculous," Logan finally said after a few moments of the two men trying to stare each other down. "You haven't changed a bit from school. You're just as pig-headed as you ever were. Let's set down a bit and see if we can't reason this out. Now, come on over here and sit down. Look at me when I talk! Look at me, Adam! How about this. — How about we do go back down the valley together, you a Rebel soldier, and us a pair of Yanks. Then, if we're caught, we can phony up a story about one of us is the other's prisoner, till we can work out the details. What is it about the valley that makes you so set on going back there?" The logic of his argument was faulty, but he was just trying various ideas to get Gainfield's participation.

"It's not so much that I want to go back down in the valley, Jesse, h'it's just that I know where ever'thin' is, an' I got a pretty good idea of where we can find Lily. Another thing; I got a few scores to settle before I goes off to the Union army."

"What kind of scores? You aren't going down there with me just to even up some grudge you have against somebody you think did somebody wrong."

"Jesse, you have no idea of what it means to be a Loyalist in a Rebel uniform. The things that them gray-backs did to the people who stayed loyal to the Union are unbelievable. I was in a squad looking for bridge burners — you know that's the big bird on all the Rebs' shoulders — Bridge Burners," he said in an exaggerated manner. "They'd take women and children out in the yard of the house and then burn the house down with the man inside. And if he stuck his head out, they'd make target practice out of him. Once't they didn't even let the woman out of the house. You know Jake Settles over at Crystal Creek? They suspected his wife Jane of packing lunch for them fellers who done the Zollicoffer Bridge and they kept her inside when they burned the house. Jake wasn't even home and they found him later and just hung him, right in downtown Zollicoffer. They was one squad, a feller name's Stance, and he had a squad of what they called Rangers, "The Holston Rangers", and they was jus' a'runnin' rampant over the likes of them folks who had any loyalty for the North. An' the military authorities, — if you can call 'em that — wasn't doin' nothin' to try to hold 'em back. They was jus' ignorin' the whole situation. 'Jus' ignorin' it."

"That's why I joined the militia. They caught me one day with my pa and Uncle Edward an' we was headin' down toward Elizabethton, an' that there bunch of peckerwoods —, 'must 'a been about twenty of 'em — they came ridin' down the road jes' as big as thunder, an' when they spotted us they come up to us on the road an' that feller Stance says to us, 'Hain't you the Gainfield clan? I heer'd you'uns is some of them that's been burnin' them bridges down on the Holston,' he says."

"An' my pa, he jes' speaks up real quick like, and he says, 'You got it wrong, Mister. We is jes' now on our way down to Elizabethton to see if'n we cain't join up with the army. Ain't that right, boys?' he says. An' we, Uncle Edward an' me —, we jes' nods our heads and agrees with ever'thing Pa says, 'cause we been hearing so much about how them 'rangers' jes' as soon string you up as look at you. Well, we went down to the place where you're supposed to join up and we all three goes in an' signs the papers, right there, 'cept my pa, — you know he has that game leg. — They wouldn't take him. They says fer him to come back some other time an' see if they's anythin' they need from him, but he never went back. Anyway, they never bothered him anymore, but they was always a kind of suspicion that hung over me an' Uncle Edward about us bein' Unionists. They transferred Uncle Edward to the Twenty-first Mississippi — I think to split us up — an' I haven't seen him since las' year."

"You know that night when I caught up with you and Sid and Eli on the road out of Doe River Cove, an' brought you back there to turn you in. I had just been appointed Corporal, just to keep me occupied, I think, an' they still didn't trust me. H'it was only just this las' few months that they's been a'lettin' me take out a squad for scoutin', and, o' course, this is the way I act." He chuckled at the thought. "Well, I guess they was right. They shouldn't 've trusted me in the firs' place."

Having spent the night at Enoch's camp and after they got up, they cleared all the signs of the struggle that had occurred on the trail that ran toward the south and on into Tennessee. In addition to the five horses they now had, there were three extra revolvers and three carbines. They divided the equipment, leaving Enoch Sid's musket, while Sid took one of the carbines and a revolver. The other carbines they also left with Enoch, having no use for them. They offered one horse to Enoch, but he declined the offer. He was comfortable enough without a horse, so the three soldiers decided to lead the extra horses down the mountains and give them to anyone they might encounter who needed them.

Logan, Gainfield and Coster sat down to a breakfast of bacon and biscuits and talked over the prospects of success of Gainfield going south with the other two. Coster was again silent throughout most of the conversation, but finally spoke his mind. "I'm of a mind to go on back to Camp Dick Robinson and join a unit. I see most of the men I've known already in an organized company and I just think it would be better if you two went on south without me. I can be more use to the cause of the Union as a soldier or just continue scouting with Dan Ellis."

"I don't agree, Sid," Logan put in. "You should be the one to take me through the hills and Adam should go on back to Camp Dick Robinson. You know the way and Adam should not be caught here in this part of the country or he'll end up shot or hung. Well, why don't we do this?"

Jesse laid out a plan for all three of the men to head on down to Rogersville, assess conditions there, and then decide their next move. Coster still would be scouting for the Union and piloting refugees back through the mountains, Logan had his own assignment, and Gainfield could settle his affairs in the Watauga Valley, assist either man as needed, and return to Camp Dick Robinson with Sid on his next trip.

Logan took Frank Davis's possessions and put them in his saddlebag to be mailed to Mary when the opportunity arose. He contemplated the task of notifying her of Davis's death and knew that the responsibility would logically fall to him. He took a little time and sat down with a pencil and paper and drafted a note, intending to formalize it with pen and ink when he got a chance.

Dear Mrs. Davis,
It is with heavy heart that I write this message to you, but as Captain Davis's friend and close associate, I must inform you of his passing. I know how devoted he was to you and you to him and the children, and this is one of the saddest moments of my life.
Frank Davis was like a brother to me, teaching me a great deal about life in general and also about the duties attached to being a good soldier. Of the last, he was an outstanding example from the time we were first assigned together in May of 1861. Many times he was offered the rank of captain in the army, but he told our colonel that he felt it his duty to be instrumental in preparing the men for the rigors of battle, and he could do that best as a sergeant. And that is exactly what he did. Later, as you know, he did accept higher rank and always filled the office to which he was assigned with highest integrity and dedication.
Without grieving you with details of Frank's untimely and unfortunate death, I must tell you that he was a brave and loyal soldier and friend right up until the end of his life. He was proud to be a captain in the

army of the United States and comported himself with gallantry and distinction and you have every right to be proud of him and the service he performed for his country.

In the event there may be some compensation due you from the government as Captain Davis' widow, I'd suggest you retain this letter as documentation of his service-connected demise.

His few belongings which he entrusted to me I am sending by courier to Camp Dick Robinson where I trust they will be mailed to you. I would like to have a few moments of your time someday to reflect and share on the value it has been to me, just knowing and following Captain Davis. Until then, I remain, etc.

He folded the note and put it into his saddlebag, to be formalized and mailed with the parcel of personal belongings which they had taken from Frank Davis' body. Then the three friends packed their gear and headed south. There was the smell of rain in the air as they prepared for their trip down the mountain. They estimated it would be a day's ride to Rogersville and then another day to Elizabethton, depending on the resistance they would meet. As they left camp, rain was starting to fall, first in random drops, large wet splashes against their gum rain blankets, and before long, in smaller, but steady drops, drenching everything that wasn't protected. They slowly descended the mountain from where they had been camped and reached the Clinch River without incident but there, they halted in their progress south. The river had risen in the storm enough to impede their progress, and the footing for their horses became so slippery that it was difficult to travel. It was a summer shower that could last a few minutes or a few days, and there was no way to tell which.

They discussed seeking shelter for a time, but nothing seemed to be available, so heading southeast, they finally happened on an abandoned cabin. There the three unlikely traveling companions paused for the remainder of the day and through the night, waiting for the storm to clear. The house was small and dusty. The windows were also very small and two of the four windows were without glass. They surmised that the house had been vacant for some time and a neighbor had helped himself to the unneeded window panes. Neither was there much left of the shakes on the roof and the three travelers had to choose their spots on the floor with care, to minimize their exposure to the rain that came in unabated. It was not a particularly comfortable night, but with the gum blankets they had brought, they managed to stay reasonably dry.

The conversation flowed between the old friends, both concerning their teenage years and also their viewpoints on the matter of the war between the states. Gainfield, though he left school a year earlier than his companions, nevertheless had gained considerable knowledge and insight on the causes and effects of the war and in addition had experienced first-hand some of the atrocities of war committed by the Rebels, particularly the Holston Rangers.

Logan, on the other hand, assured him that the southern soldiers were not alone in their inclination to ravage and pillage. "Any time a soldier is in enemy country there'll be times when he does things without apparent justification, reckoning that he's doing them out of a sense of patriotism, retaliation, or whatever comes into his head. Meanwhile, the local people look at what he's doing as acts of unjustified aggression, and hate him all the more. Then they do little things to show they're angry and to demonstrate their loyalty to their side of the argument. So the occupying army takes these little things, blows them up into signs of a local uprising, and retaliates all the more. It ain't pleasant and it ain't civilized, but it's war, just as much as two armies coming together and shooting it out."

"I saw it in West Tennessee all the time," he went on. "The difference, sometimes, is that we, — those of us in the Union Army, — we were trying to identify the friendlies from the hostiles and we didn't want to alienate the local people any more than we had to, so we tried to handle them a little more gently than maybe we would otherwise. That was all except some of the regiments that were recruited from that local part of the country. A lot of the time, they were out for revenge against anybody and everybody who they thought had been a part of their misery up until time the Feds took over."

"Well, that might be so with the Union army, but with the Rebs," Adam offered, "they thought they knew all the people who were loyal to the Union, and they took it out on them every chance they got. And that's a fact. I saw it all the time."

Logan had his doubts about what seemed to be an exaggeration on the part of the other man, but he let the matter pass. There was no point in causing an argument over which side was worse than the other. He was sure that there was enough blame to go around, whatever side you took.

The following morning dawned bright and sunny. There were birds singing in the trees around the little cabin and for all the world it appeared as though there was no hostility anywhere. Sid went out to bring in the horses for the trip down into the valley, and Logan, having long since adopted the habit of shaving whenever the opportunity presented itself, took this day as one of those opportunities. While the hair of his head was a pale blond, his beard was a fiery red and he was always shocked whenever he had allowed it to grow to any recognizable length and viewed his reflection in a glass or a pond. He couldn't accept the idea of having to meet old friends somewhere on the trail in the next day or two and subjecting them to the sight of a red bearded man that they had perhaps recalled as a tow-headed youth. He pulled his ditty bag out of his bedroll and shook out his razor and a small bar of soap while Gainfield stood leaning against the doorpost of the cabin, watching the process. Logan's captain's bars fell out onto the table amidst the other small items of personal interest.

"Did you just take those from Captain Davis?" Adam idly inquired. "I thought you'd taken all his stuff and put it in that little parcel you were going to send off to his wife. Why'd you keep those bars?"

"Those, my young friend, are my own emblem of rank," Jesse said with comic, exaggerated pride. "You didn't know it, Partner, but when you caught up with me on the road to Kellars Crossing, you launched me on a path to stardom."

"What are you talking about, Logan? When I picked you off the road last year you were on yer way to jail. What ever happened after that, I cain't take credit for. What's this all about?"

Logan went on to relate what had happened to him; the visit to the Masonic lodge in Richmond, the burning of the Confederate gun works, the sojourn with Dan Ellis, Tom Singleton and Sid Coster on his way back to his unit in Lewisburg and his adventures in the western part of the state.

Adam Gainfield was incredulous. "While I slave away at being the best Rebel soldier I can and work my way up to corporal, you ride around on a horse and get to be a captain. It just don't seem fair. Now I know why I want to join the Union Army. It's so's I kin be promoted to gen'ral. I was always smarter than you. It was just because Mr. Putnam liked you best, you an' yer western accent, like you was some kind of a cos-mo-<u>pol</u>-itan." He drew the word out as though trying to emulate a northern inflection.

"So you're a big greenhorn," he used the word in its reference to a soldier of high rank, rather than its later adaptation; that of a neophyte. "Here I thought I was the ranking member of this team and all along you're carryin' those bars around in your ditty bag, just layin' to pounce on me and subdue me with your superior rank. Well, if you're a captain, Jesse Logan, I should at least be sworn in as a major and maybe promoted the next week. And, besides, how's come Sid didn't say anythin' about you bein' a capt'n? He hasn't said a word of it. Are you sure you didn't jus' take them bars from Captain Davis to impress the home folks?"

"Don't you worry none about my bein' what I am, Adam. Have I ever steered you wrong? Would your old pal Jesse Logan do a thing like that? Have I ever lied to you? Well, have I?"

"I'm thinkin', I'm thinkin'. You're so full of bull I can't quite come up with an answer, but just give me a few minutes and I'll think of somethin'."

They saddled their horses, and continued east along the river. The ground was slippery from the recent rains and the river was still too high to cross, but the freshness bought by the summer rain, the peacefulness of the region, and the agreeable company made for a pleasant trip. The conversation and revelation at the cabin as to Logan's rank disturbed Adam Gainfield not at all, and he chatted like the old companion that he had been during their years in school. They laughed together and even broke into song a time or two.

Bleeding and wounded upon the field, two dying soldiers lay,
Bidding each other a last farewell, just at the close of day.

One thought of mother at home alone, feeble and old and gray,
One of the sweetheart he'd left in town, happy and young and gay.

One pressed a ringlet of thin gray hair, one held a lock of brown,
Bidding goodbye to the Stars and Stripes, just as the sun went down.

Gainfield didn't know much of the song at first, but he picked it up quickly and the three old friends sang lustily as they followed the old road toward Rogersville, Gainfield and Coster carrying the tune with Logan supplying the harmony, sometimes in a falsetto voice.

'Just Before the Battle, Mother,' by George Root was a favorite of Sid Coster, and they worked that song over a few times, also.

Enoch had packed them some bacon and biscuits and they were completely at peace with the world. It would have been easy to forget the kind of mission they were on, except for their military equipment and the fact that they were travelling under orders from the Wartime Governor of Tennessee.

Fording the Clinch, they crossed over the next range of mountains, and descended into the Holston Valley. They encountered a decent road for the last few miles and followed it down into the valley as dusk approached, but suddenly they heard voices from around the next bend in the road. They quickly halted their progress, seeking the shelter of a large growth of trees and blackberry vines.

"What do you think, fellas?" Logan inquired. "Maybe I'll just sneak on ahead and see what's going on. It sounds like some sort of party or something. These people aren't supposed to be laughing and singing down in these parts, not whilst the Rebels are in charge, anyway. You hold my horse a bit, Sid, and I'll walk down there and see what's goin' on." He got off his horse and proceeded toward the sound of the voices. As he approached, he stayed under the cover of the roadside bushes and moved within earshot of the voices.

"I know, I know, they's gonna be here any day — any minute now, I tell you. I heer'd it over t' Rogersville yistiday and you seen fer yer se'f how them Rebs jes' skedaddled," said one man.

Another answered, "There ain't a Reb to be had in this whole valley, I'd betcha. If'n there was, jes' let me get my han's on 'im, an' I'll give 'im a taste of 'Bonny Blue you-know-what'".

Several people laughed uproariously. Another shouted, "Hey, Johnny! Where's yer frien' Jeff Davis when you need 'im? Where's yer Braxton Bragg-ert?"

The gist of the conversation was obvious. The Confederate army had withdrawn, ostensibly in anticipation of an invasion from the Federals, but actually to reinforce Bragg's army at Chickamauga Creek. The anticipated invasion by General Burnside was merely the side-bar of a Confederate military maneuver. Jesse had heard rumors when he was at Camp Dick Robinson about plans for General Burnside to invade East Tennessee, and it appeared to him that the rumors were true.

There was general celebrating and merry-making among the loyalist population and the secessionists, if there were any in the region, were not in evidence. Logan backed away silently and hurried back to where Adam and Sid were standing with the horses. He explained what he had seen.

After a moment of reflection, Adam announced, offering his wrists as though to be shackled, "Well, Mr. Logan, I'm your prisoner. I reckon the Rebs have skedaddled and the country is in Union hands."

Then, putting his hands down he exclaimed, "You see how clever I am at picking sides? When the Rebs are in control I'm a Reb and when the Yanks are in charge, guess what! I jes' became a loyal Yankee!"

"Yes, Adam," Logan said reflecting his friend's humor, and poking him in the side, "it looks like the Rebs have taken the road south. The people here are all over the place, down there by that store, just whoopin' and hollerin' like it was Kingdom Come. Mount up, boys, we're goin' down an' help celebrate.

The three soldiers got back on their horses and proceeded south along the farm road and when they rounded the bend approaching the small roadside store, they were spotted by the people in the gathering crowd.

"There's your Reb soldier, Jerry," one of them shouted. "What did you say you'd do to him, give him a dose of Bonnie Blue whatchamacallit?"

"There's Yanks holdin' on to him, though. H'it looks like they's got him pris'ner!"

"Hey, Yank, where'd ye git the skulker. We thought all the Rebs done left town."

Logan had taken the lead in the little procession and as he approached the crowd, he held up a hand to try to silence them. "Hold on, folks, hold on. This here's a loyalist caught up in the conscription. We're partners. Don't do him no harm, please. He just hasn't had a chance to change his uniform, yet. What's all this about the Rebs leavin' the valley? We'd been up in the hills and hadn't heard anything."

"Ain't you one of Gen'r'l Burnside's men, Yank? We heer'd he was comin' but nobody's seen him yet."

And from another, "How's come you to be ahead of your comp'ny. Where's the rest of the troop?"

And still another, "H'ain't you that-there White Angel, that Logan feller? We know'd you'd be comin' back one of these days. Your oncle, Doc Pleasant's a'been tellin' us you'd be back. Where's y'r troop?"

"How's come the Reb still has his carbine? What's goin' on, here? He has his pistol, too! What're you fellers up to, Logan? Maybe we should jes' take that Reb and string him up, like they did with my cousin Everest!"

The three soldiers were still on their horses, but were trying to back away from the excited crowd, some of whom were circling around, both from curiosity and agitation. Logan was trying to explain to those within earshot what he and Adam were doing in the region, but his words were drowned in the tumultuous din arising from the crowd, which consisted of perhaps thirty men, women and children.

Then came from the crowd another voice, "Hey, wait a minute, folks. Ain't that there Jeremy Gainfield's boy? He's the one who he'ped my Oncle Jeff ease out'a that trap the Rebs set fer him down on th' Holston. He's be'n perty good to us all the time the Rebs's be'n in these parts. Don't hurt that boy."

Gradually the hostility subsided, and the soldiers began to gain some bit of assurance that they would be more hospitably received by the crowd and the shouting began to turn to more of a greeting than a threat. Jesse climbed down from his horse to establish a little better sense of communication with the people and began to ask some questions of his own. "We've just come from Camp Dick Robinson, over the ridge, and haven't been in touch with

General Burnside or his army. Can you folks tell me what you know about the Rebs and where they've gone?"

One member of the crowd stepped forward and spoke to the two travelers. "I'm Henry Janier, and all we know is that the Rebs have moved south. There was a man come ridin' through here yistiday with the word that Gen'r'l Burnside was a'comin' down the valley an' h'it spooked them Rebs so bad they jes' cleared out. He said Gen'r'l Burnside was a'fixin' to take Knoxville and the whole Holston Valley and that he had about forty thousand troops with him. The Rebs jes' lit out like a bunch o' scalded dogs."

After some fifteen or twenty minutes' conversation with the crowd, Jesse drew his companions aside to discuss what their next move should be. "We'd better move on, at least to Rogersville and see what we can find, but I don't think it would be a good idea to have Adam keep those clothes. If those folks over there hadn't recognized him, we might all three of us have been in trouble."

"Maybe I could just buy some clothes here, at least a coat, and get shed of this uniform, such as it is. The pants ain't even grey and they can pass, but this coat is pure Reb, what with th' corp'rl stripes an' all, an' it seems to be raisin' some tempers in these parts. I'd hate to have someone kill me fer a Reb, now that I'm a Yank," Adam said with a grin.

They went back to talk to some of the people in the group. "We think we'd better move on south," Logan told them, "but it would be better if first Corporal Gainfield could get a different coat. Is there anyone who might have an old coat they could let us have. We'd be glad to pay for it — an' we do have Federal greenbacks," he added with a smile, prompting a chuckle or two from the crowd. Several people stepped forward, two of them taking their coats off and offering them to Gainfield.

"H'ain't you got any at home I might use?" Gainfield asked. "I wouldn't want to just take the coat right off'n your back. I know this seems downright poetic, but I'm not sure we'll be back this way an' I'd hate to deprive anyone of their reg'lar clo'es."

One of the men said eagerly, "This ain't my best coat, Mister Gainfield. I got as better a one back home. Go ahead and take it. H'it ain't much, but it'll keep you from looking like a Reb, anyways. Take it, I don't need it."

Logan dug into his ditty bag and pulled out a Federal one-dollar note, offering it to the generous donor. "Thank you, sir. Would this cover the cost of the coat?"

The man looked at the bill with a surprised but hungry look on his face. "Oh, I jes' couldn't take all that money fer that old coat," he said, literally licking his lips. "That-there's way too much."

His wife slipped up beside him and whispered a few words in his ear and after responding to her plea in a whispered voice, he exclaimed, "Well, if you insist," and quickly snatched the note from Logan's outstretched hand. The crowd reacted with an audible cheer and some handshakes all around. Logan, Coster and Gainfield just looked at each other, the thought passing between them as to how impoverished the local people must be, to have the exchange of one dollar create such enthusiasm.

Gainfield took off his jacket with the corporal chevrons on it and gave it to the man. He took it, looked it over and passed it to a friend who did the same. The uniform jacket made the rounds among the small crowd, passing from one hand to another until all had had an opportunity to examine it with great curiosity, some looking it over several times. The children especially were awed at the coat, following it through the crowd.

Presently, the three soldiers got back on their horses and bade the revelers goodbye. They continued south for a time, hoping to gain Rogersville by evening. They spent the night along the banks of a little creek, and proceeded south through Rogersville the following morning. As they got down into the Holston Valley, they looked northeast and saw a cloud of dust.

"I'll wager that's the van of General Burnside's Army," Logan said with some assurance. "There's no doubt in my mind that that cloud of dust is a really large army and I'll give you dollars to doughnuts that it's General Burnside. Let's go see." With that they turned toward the oncoming cloud and spurred their horses into a trot. After a short ride, they could see several skirmishers in advance of the main body of soldiers, and Logan hailed them. A corporal from the vidette rode forward and when he got within twenty or thirty yards, he pulled up and saluted Captain Logan, but kept his distance, not sure of whether he was on safe ground.

"I'm Captain Logan from the First Tennessee Cavalry, Corporal, and my partners and I are on a scouting mission from Nashville. I didn't expect to find Federals in this area, but I'm certainly glad to see you. Could I trouble you to take me to your Commander?"

About a mile back from where he encountered the skirmishers, at the direction of the corporal, Captain Logan located Federal General James Shackelford, introduced himself, and explained his mission. "I'm not sure I even have a mission, now that the Union is in control here in this part of the country," Logan said, "but I'll have to report back to Governor Johnson and see what further has to be done on this situation."

"Weren't you with the Seventh Ohio, some time ago, Captain," General Shackelford inquired. "I seem to remember you as a rifleman under General Rosecrans; The White Angel," he added with a smile. "Anyway, your Company "H" is on a track out west of us and assigned to General Haskell's

Brigade. Lieutenant Goodin is the officer in charge of the company until Captain Davis gets back from 'temporary' in Nashville. Ride with me for a way and we can maybe get you back to General Haskell and see if we can't accommodate you and get you a wire so you can contact the governor. That may take a couple of days."

"Well, I'll be wanting to talk to General Haskell, anyway, as Captain Davis was recently killed, and won't be coming back. Why didn't they promote Goodin?"

Shackelford looked at Logan for a moment, as though wondering which tree he had fallen out of. "How long is it since you've been with the Seventh, Captain?"

"Well, it was last summer, just before they moved north to Franklin. I was with Captain Davis, down in Nashville, but I haven't been with the regiment since then."

"Company "H" is mostly dissolved, and what is left is just Goodin, and a couple of sergeants. General Haskell is so mad at that company he'd ship them off to Richmond or somewhere back east, if he had a chance. Goodin had a couple of the fellows shot for desertion and the whole company pert'-near mutinied over it, and then he had some of those men wheelhauled, — a bad job of it, I might say, and the men pert'-near strung him up over that. Then he put everyone in the company on report and recommended they be confined to camp for the rest of the war. As I hear it, General Haskell was just waiting for Captain Davis to get back to see if he couldn't restore order. Nothing was left when a lot of enlistments were up and about thirty men deserted, and Goodin was left in charge of that 'nothing'. Just two sergeants, and a handful of privates, as I said."

Logan looked over at Adam Gainfield. "And you were so happy to be with the Federal Army, Corporal. That's the outfit I was attached to last year."

General Shackelford offered a comment, "It was a good company when you were there, Captain, so far as we knew. Then when Captain Davis was injured and went into recuperation, it kind of fell to that fellow Goodin to keep it going and he doesn't seem to know the meaning of discipline. General Haskell may want to put you in charge, if he doesn't disband the unit."

"I'm afraid that if he were to do that, there'd be a shootout about the first day I took command, but I'll do anything the General wants. I really have to try to contact Governor Johnson, though, before I take on any new assignments."

"I'm sure we can do that as soon as the line catches up with us. We haven't had telegraph contact for the past several days, ever since before

Columbia."

"What happened there?"

"We got into it with the rear guard of the Reb Army, and kicked up a bit of a fuss. We haven't seen anything of the Rebs since then, have you?"

Logan smiled and jerked his thumb at Adam Gainfield. "This is the last one I've run into, and I've been recruiting him to the cause of truth and justice for about the past week. I think I have him convinced of the error of his ways. I should also take him back to headquarters and turn him over to the Provost for questioning. He's been with the Confederate Army for the past year or so," as he reached out and patted Adam on the shoulder.

Then, turning back to General Shackelford, "Corporal Gainfield and I have known each other for many years, and I know he'll be a great help to General Burnside in establishing the troop strength in the valley. He was conscripted against his will and finally found a way to get back to his true loyalties. Where can we find the Provost?"

"You'll just have to wait until we join up with the main body of the army and inquire, but I don't think there's much rush. You men can just ride along with me and maybe you can help give us an idea of where we're going. As I understand it, this valley leads right to Knoxville. Soldier, do you know of any Rebel troops left in the area?" he directed his last question to Gainfield.

"Sir, I was with a company of state militia, and on a scoutin' mission, sent out about eight days ago. As far as I knew, Knoxville was well garrisoned when I left. There was some talk, though of pullin' our troops south to he'p General Bragg at Chattanooga. Maybe that's what's happened."

"What kind of an army did they have here in Knoxville?"

"H'it was General Buckner's Corps, I think. You know I was still with Lieutenant Arnold over in Johnson City and Elizabethton, so I wasn't up on what they had down there. Ours was th' East Tennessee militia, so I'd reckon they're still here in the valley."

The four men were riding side by side along a fairly well-maintained road, with skirmishers out ahead and to their sides. The General summoned a lieutenant who had been riding somewhat ahead of them. "Lieutenant Simpson," he called, "call in your sergeants and let them know we're still in some possibly hostile territory, and have them keep the scouts out well in advance."

"Sir, the lieutenant responded, every house we pass, we've been asking of the people about the enemy, and they're all of the same voice. The Rebs pulled out right after we had that little set-to at Columbia, and they haven't seen a one of them since. These people are all Unionists, every last one of them."

"Well, alright, but there still may be bands of irregulars in the area, so tell the men to stay sharp. This man says there are militia companies still hereabouts." The lieutenant saluted and rode westward toward Knoxville and the lead vidette.

At Morristown, the cavalry halted and camped for the night. The following day they continued southwest toward Knoxville while the main force under General Burnside had circled further west through Kingston, routing the remaining Confederate contingents from that region. The cavalry got into Knoxville on September 1, amidst such celebration as they had never imagined. United States flags were draped from every building and smaller flags were in the hands of the children. There was shouting and singing everywhere. The Confederate forces had executed an orderly removal and no resistance was to be found anywhere.

25

KNOXVILLE

Jesse had never seen such an outpouring of emotion, or such a crowd as lined the streets of Knoxville. Commitments such as that which President Lincoln had made to W. B. Carter, a local businessman, had gone unresolved over the past two years of the war. It had been well recognized, however, that eastern Tennessee was vital to both sides of the conflict. The southern interest was strategic while the Union concern was more humanitarian. The humanitarian, once it became strategic, with the fact that Generals Thomas and Rosecrans, and eventually General Grant, with thousands of Federal troops now saw the strategy of holding the region of Chattanooga against the south, finally won the day. To reinforce the southern forces at Chattanooga under Braxton Bragg, Confederate General Simon Buckner, who had commanded the main force at Knoxville, abandoned the northeastern portion of the state under orders to go to the aid of General Bragg. General Burnside was the unwitting beneficiary of this move as coincidentally he had been sent south from Columbus, Ohio, pausing to organize his forces at Camp Nelson, and then continue on, bypassing the Rebel forces at Cumberland Gap and brushing aside several other small outposts to occupy Knoxville.

Captain Logan, riding temporarily with General Shackelford, entered the city on September 1, 1863, followed two days later by General Burnside himself, with the main body of the Army of the Cumberland. The army immediately set about assessing the potentials for defense of the city, organizing the deployment of available troops, scouting for food sufficient for the force of about thirty thousand men, and running sorties into the outlying areas to drive out any remaining Rebel forces.

While Burnside's occupying the region was the cause for loyalist celebration, his presence there was not unnoticed by General Lee or General Bragg, nor did they intend that it should be anything but temporary. Knoxville's occupation by Federal troops cut off a major supply route between the productive fields and forests of the states of Tennessee, Alabama, Mississippi and Louisiana from the population and military needs of Virginia, and the resources of the Richmond Confederacy from the military needs of Chattanooga.

Three railroads; the East Tennessee and Virginia, the East Tennessee and Georgia, and the East Tennessee and Kentucky converged at Knoxville, but were essentially useless to the Union forces, except for short runs. The E.T.&V. was under complete Rebel control from the Virginia state line north and east. and the E.T.& K. went north only a short distance into the Cumberland Mountains, and was of only little value. The East Tennessee and Georgia line led through and beyond Chattanooga, and was the best conveyance of supplies between Nashville and Knoxville. As western Virginia was still in the hands of the Confederates, any Federal provisions destined for Knoxville had to come from Louisville, Kentucky, down through Nashville, then east through Chattanooga and up the Tennessee Valley. Knoxville was situated at the end of a long, long supply line from Nashville, and they found themselves the beneficiaries of only the meager remains of what the Union forces at Chattanooga didn't grab when the supply trains came through. Fortunately, it was the fall of the year, the natives were friendly, greenbacks were highly treasured, and the Federal troops at Knoxville were not to go hungry, at least not right away.

Knoxville is situated along the north banks of the Holston (now the Tennessee) River and was defined by three small creeks, tributaries of the Holston. The three creeks were aptly named, reading from east to west, First Creek, Second Creek, and (appropriately) Third Creek. Fourth Creek was some miles to the southwest. The town of Knoxville occupied the region between First Creek and Second Creek, a distance of about a half mile, east-to-west. The city was also about a half mile wide sloping back from the banks of the Holston River on the south, to the city's rail yards on the north edge of town.

As soon as General Burnside arrived, he directed the reinforcement of existing forts and batteries and building several new ones, especially west of the city from where he expected any Confederate forces to attack. His expectations would be sound, as it was not long before General Lee ordered one of his best generals, James Longstreet, up from Chattanooga to try to take back the city and region that was so vital to the southern war effort.

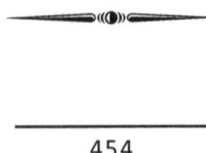

With General Burnside's permission, Logan set about immediately to make his way back to Doe River Cove and home. His mission was to contact Lily Venable and try to convince her to return with him to Nashville, if possible. With Adam Gainfield, now dressed in a new blue uniform, having explained his mission to General Shackelford, they set out across the newly rebuilt pontoon bridge at the foot of Gay Street and proceeded east. Sid Coster had already parted company at Rogersville, and headed south to Elizabethtown. They arrived at Greenville just after sunset, located a cousin of Jesse's and spent the night with her and her family. The next morning, they set out for Doe River Cove and Kellars Crossing. As they approached the location where Adam had taken Jesse prisoner almost two years earlier, they both became a little pensive.

"I reckon, Jesse — err — Captain, even then I could jus' as easy let you go and no one would have been the wiser. My thinking at that time was some mixed. I had jus' b'en promoted, an' was a trifle obligated to that lieutenant, Lieutenant Arnold. My mind jus' wasn't quite made up as to who I was loyal to an' what I was expected to do."

"I know, Adam. I know what you mean, but what you don't realize is that you probably saved my life that night. Not by catchin' me after I got away from Eli, and Sid, and Mac, and Albert, but when you were comin' down the road that night those fellas were about to string me up, and if you and your lieutenant hadn't happened along, that's just what they would've done. So you see, you saved my life, even if it did cost me some time at Libby Prison. I'm sure they would've killed me. I'm sure of it."

"It's funny how things turn out," Adam mused. "Our lives twist and turn and sometimes we end up someplace we really need to be without actually tryin' to get there in the first place. Jus' like where we are now, goin' out here to look fer Lily when she is prob'ly as safe she's ever be'n sence this war started. What're you gonna tell her if we find her?"

"Heck, I don't know. As I see it, if she didn't want to leave the Watauga before, she surely won't be inclined to leave, now. All we can do is talk to her and explain what we've been ordered to do and let her make her own mind up. I'm sure Mrs. Johnson will relax now that the valley is back in the hands of the Union. The thing that worries me is how long the Union can keep control here. This part of the country is really important to the Rebs, 'cause it has the railroads that they need to move their supplies. Although," he mused in reflection, "now that we have Chattanooga and Nashville, both, they don't have as much use for the railroad."

They arrived at the Kellar home at about 4:30 in the afternoon and Jesse walked up to the front door. He was excited. He hadn't seen his family for almost two years and had only received scattered letters from his grandparents in the time he was assigned out in the western part of the state. He knocked at the door knowing it would have been acceptable for him to have walked right in without knocking, but after twenty months' absence, he was reluctant to just barge in. He waited on the porch for what seemed an eternity but could hear voices inside, so he knew there would be someone come fairly soon. He knocked again on the screen door, this time a little more firmly. Finally, he heard footsteps approaching the door and the inner door slowly opened.

The screen door obscured his vision but he could see the form of a woman standing in the doorway. It wasn't Grandma Emma; it was someone slimmer, perhaps one of his cousins, then she spoke.

"Hello, Captain Logan, we've been expecting you." The unmistakable voice of Olivia Livingston greeted his ears. Jesse was speechless.

"What's the matter, Captain. 'Cat got your tongue?"

Jesse grabbed the handle of the screen door and jerked. It was latched from the inside. He rattled the door. "You open this door and you'll see what's got my tongue, Livingston. Open the door before I jerk it off its hinges!" He said, not believing it could actually be her.

Olivia unlatched the screen door and pushed it open. They grabbed at each other in a passionate embrace and held each other close for a couple of minutes. Then Olivia relaxed her hold and started to back away, but Jesse said, "I'm not done yet," and clung to her for almost an additional minute, murmuring sweet nothings in her ear. Grandma and Grandpa Kellar were standing in the living room watching the display of affection and finally Henry Kellar ventured a greeting.

"Ain't you gonna say anything to your family, young fella, or 'you just gonna stand there squeezin' the life out'a that poor girl?"

Jesse and Olivia stepped back from each other and Jesse grabbed Emma, his grandmother and hugged her while at the same time reaching out to shake hands with his grandfather.

Presently, Emma Kellar noticed Adam Gainfield standing off to the side on the front porch of the house. "Adam Gainfield." She said with a surprised voice, "what in the world're you doin' here, and in a Union uniform?"

"Ma'am, I'm afraid —," Gainfield began, but Jesse broke in, coming to Adam's defense.

"Adam just saved my neck again, Grandma, and decided if he was going to keep helping me out of trouble he might just as well be wearing a blue uniform," and with that he and Adam proceeded to tell a little of the events that they had been engaged in. Adam contributed to the telling of the story, as Jesse seemed to be minimizing the seriousness and exaggerating the humor of some of the events that they had been involved in. Olivia, too, broke in from time to time, clarifying things the two men overlooked. The conversation was lively and often humorous but, at times, grew serious. It was clear that Jesse and his two friends had quite a tale to tell, all involving Jesse's irrepressible inclination to act unpredictably and often — as the other two seemed to feel — a little recklessly. Henry and Emma Kellar agreed with that conclusion and admonished Jesse gently but firmly.

"It's lucky for you that you have good friends and probably a few guardian angels looking out for your hide, young man," Grandma said.

"I'm sure of that, Grandma. Both Adam and Olivia have been the best friends a man could hope for."

"Thank you for that vote of confidence," Olivia offered, "but for the past year this 'friend' has certainly been wondering what had happened to you. I hadn't heard a word from you until just a week ago. You had me worried sick, Friend."

Jesse reached over and patted Olivia's hand. "Libbie, I did write to you — several times, — and wondered what had become of you, too. I just can't believe we're here together, though. Where were you when you got this last letter?"

"I was at Bert's store in New Castle. He's married again, you know, and has his sister and her husband running the store while he and Sarah and I are on the road. By the way, do you think we could set up in Knoxville, or do the local merchants manage to supply the army's needs?"

"I don't know," Jesse responded. "I wasn't there long enough to find out. I think I should go back that way after I find Lily and we can get some ideas."

Henry Kellar broke into the conversation, "Jesse," he said, "you know you left that rifle here, and I suspect some of your old friends that're working fer the Rebs know about it and would really like to get their hands on it. Have you heard any talk about that rifle, Adam?"

"Ye're right, Mr. Kellar," Adam responded. "I know there's be'n talk around town from time to time 'bout that rifle. Eli Morgan, an' some of the others would give their eye teeth to get their han's on it. I'm s'prised he hasn't jus' come here and stole it from you."

"I suspect he's sent some of his friends by here, jus' nosing around and tryin' to figure out whether it's someplace they could get to it. Eli has never come, himself, but there's been a couple of fellas from over 't Greenville who come here askin' about work a while back, an' I know they didn't any more want work than that dog of mine. Anyway, Jesse, it's safe put away in that you-know-where cupboard, an' we can get it out any time you need it."

"Thanks, Grandpa." Jesse said with a smile, "I've thought about that rifle a lot and wished I had it sometimes. Ol' Bedford Forrest came after my battalion back out there in Judkins Corners, and really stirred things up for us. If I would've had it there, I could've made life miserable for those fellas. As it was, they didn't do much damage, but I'd've surely made it hot for them if I'd had that rifle. Of course, it's probably been safer here that ever it would've been in some of the places I've been."

After a time, Adam announced that he was going home to try to contact his father and mother. With the Federals in control of the region, it was a little safer than it had been, but there was still the possibility of the irregulars, or home guard as they liked to be called, drifting about, making trouble for the loyalist factions and families. Still Adam was determined to see his folks and share with them the fact that he was now attached to the Union Army, even though he hadn't yet been officially enrolled in any unit. Armed with the carbine he'd acquired when he was up in the mountains at Enoch's house, and his own government-issue revolver he felt safe enough to make his way home.

Emma, with Olivia's assistance, went into the house to prepare dinner and Jesse and his grandfather, Henry were left alone on the porch. Their conversation, much like hundreds of conversations over their earlier years, ranged from dogs and horses to politics and the war. It was unbelievably peaceful and comfortable for Jesse to be sitting there with his grandfather, sometimes with a dog at his knee, sometimes just quietly gazing out across the field that separated the house from the mill. Three men were still working the mill. A person could clearly hear the chugging of the steam engine that powered the saws and also the rising and fading scream of the saws.

The conversation had a dream-like quality about it. They both had a lot of catching up to do, as to events that the other had been exposed to and involved in. They both treasured the health, welfare, and very presence, each of the other. It was good to be home.

At dinner the conversation turned to Olivia and her plans for the future. She had left Bert Oakley and his wife in Lewiston, as soon as she could break away after receiving Jesse's letter. With the address he had provided for her to write to him, she immediately set out for Doe River Cove, driving a closed wagon on the sides of which was painted 'Bert Oakley Enterprises'. She had been dressed like a man, with her hair pulled up under a hat and often with a smudged face to hide her femininity. Her description of herself, salted liberally with some descriptive comments by Henry and Emma, drew quite a laugh from Jesse.

They agreed that Logan's first duty was to find Lily Venable and settle the matter of her plans. Then he'd return to Knoxville where the telegraph would undoubtedly be working, and obtain new orders, if any were to be issued.

━━━━⊸«(●)»⊶━━━━

Eli Morgan had not been idle during Jesse's absence from the Watauga Valley. While he initially regaled in the notoriety he had claimed for the capture of 'Corporal' Logan, word had gotten back to him that the results of his 'heroic' efforts were nothing less than a godsend for Logan and nothing more than a parenthetical and often humorous acknowledgment from a few of Morgan's close associates that he had launched the rocket that had led to 'Captain' Logan's success. It had also been discussed around the valley how Jesse's unwitting communication with Lily Venable had sparked a series of events that had essentially reversed any of the negative effects that Eli had anticipated.

Morgan had become something of a prominent figure in the Watauga Valley scene. Twice he had joined, or perhaps more accurately, had been 'conscripted' into the Confederate Army, and both times, when the opportunity had presented itself, he quietly walked away from his regiment and resumed his chosen way of life; that of a 'home guardsman'. He led a small group of irregulars which, at one time included both Sid Coster and his brother Albert, as well as Mac McMurray, Eli's brother Arthur, and several others, depending on the purpose and need of whatever mischief they could devise at the time. Sid Coster had abandoned that group and had left the valley, planning to sign up with the Federal army.

To Morgan's credit, in the incident in which Steven Venable and his son Paul were killed, the fatal action was the work of one of the irregular bands that roamed the valley and had it not been for the intervention of Eli, Lily Venable would have most certainly have died in the attack. When Steven, Paul and Lily were returning home one evening from a meeting, there had been a plan afoot to capture, or kill if necessary, the entire Venable family. Steven had assumed a pivotal role as one of the leaders in the Unionist movement, and with the assistance of a number of loyalists, including his son and daughter, he had created an underground resistance ring that included a periodic newsletter, reinforcing the resolve of the region to resist the control of the Confederate forces. With Parson

Brownlow in jail, or just recently 'exiled' to Cincinnati, Ohio, part of the resistance movement was to keep contact with him and continue publishing the words of encouragement and resolve he furnished from his prison or, as now was the case, his exile.

Ordinarily Lily was the editor of the newsletter, and with her connections throughout the region she was able to persist in supporting the unionist sentiment and supply encouraging information and news from that perspective, so lacking in the southern press. Also, through her friendship with Dan Ellis, she had access to northern publications that kept that news fresh. And, as a skilled horsewoman, she was capable of avoiding capture, even though her editorial skills put her high on the list of people the Rebels would like to neutralize.

It was Lily's equestrian skills that had attracted the admiration of Eli Morgan, not to speak of her attractiveness as an example of young, outdoor female pulchritude. They had engaged in some minor races at various events of the region and Lily never failed to place high in whatever the race involved. Eli had admired her from afar, but admired her nevertheless. Lily, knowing Eli's Rebel inclinations, engaged him in conversation from time to time, hoping to ferret some intelligence from him as to the rebel activities in the region. Most of the conversations were futile but occasionally he would confirm or deny certain information that she would then pass on to Dan Ellis or other Unionist contacts that she used.

There existed a friendly competition between the two of them, stemming largely from their involvement in the fate of Jesse Logan. Eli, while he had done what he could to capture Logan, accepted in good humor the fact that his best efforts had been negated by an innocent communication Lily had passed on to her father. Ignoring the fact that her actions were essentially innocent, he still gave her generous credit for Jesse's escape from Libby Prison.

Eli, like Jesse, had joined the local Masonic lodge shortly after Jesse's capture and was aware of the circumstances that led to Jesse's advancement to the 'Third Degree' in Randolph Lodge in Richmond. Political discussion was ordinarily avoided at all times and though the political leanings of various members were well known, it was an unwritten rule that, in the lodge, politics, like religion were to be considered strictly taboo.

Since the death of her father and brother, Lily had redoubled her activity in support of the Union and had also left her home in Elizabethton to assume the lifestyle of a fugitive. Through her contacts with Eli Morgan which she maintained infrequently, she was able to keep current as to any information she might be able to glean from him. Also, so it seemed to her, his attitude of hostility toward the Union cause was softening. At times, he even sought her out to warn her of Rebel activity that he felt might threaten her safety.

Now their roles took a reversal. Lily and her close associates were the ones who could expect the protection of the local military authorities and Eli would have to either modify his behavior or at least steer clear of the scrutiny of the military. He was uncertain as to what he should do. The freedom with which the members of the small home-guard bands had been operating was a result of their having been virtually ignored by the Confederate military. There was now a new attitude among the people of the valley. Small incidents of harassment begrudgingly tolerated in the past, were no longer accepted as just a way of life, but were met with active and sometimes armed resistance. Now it was no longer necessary to keep one's pro-Union sympathies secret. The Stars and Stripes were displayed from porches and poles without restraint and there were a surprising number of such banners coming out in the open.

Lily had adopted the region of Cedar Mountain as her hiding place before the investment of the Federal forces. It was a rough and wooded area that offered some shelter and security and the few people who occupied the region were friendly as well as close-mouthed. She was able to move from place to place as she found necessary and was able to access the more populated areas of Carter County without much trouble.

Now it was Eli's turn to find Lily and seek her assistance and advice. She was the closest thing to a unionist that he thought he could talk to and who would talk to him. His activities for the past two years had certainly been in support of the Confederate cause, but he could think of nothing that would subject him to the outrage of the Union authorities for retribution or prosecution. Nothing major, that is, except the incident that took the lives of Steven and Paul Venable, but that had been the work of 'Captain' Stance and his little band, and Eli had even been instrumental in saving Lily's life when that took place. He needed to talk to her and get her assurance in supporting his claim of innocence, if the thing were to come to the attention of the authorities.

Eli saddled his horse and struck a trail for Cedar Mountain.

Captain Jesse Logan also had business with Lily Venable. He discussed his plans with his grandfather and with Olivia, and though the scene had changed and his efforts would probably be brought to naught, he was nonetheless committed. He was a soldier on an assignment and that pretty well sealed his fate. From the local sources and from information through Henry Kellar, he knew where he might find Lily. Jesse packed a lunch, saddled his old horse, Max, kissed Olivia goodbye, and also set off for Cedar Mountain.

While both Eli and Jesse were roughly familiar with the roads and farms in the vicinity of Cedar Mountain, such as they were, there was a vast territory of timber that was sparsely explored and virtually unoccupied.

From Kellars Crossing, Jesse was able to stay with a trail that took him to the home of John Kellar, his uncle. From there, after getting his Uncle John's advice, he would take the directions he received, perhaps augmented by other locals, and do whatever needed to find the girl. As much from sentimental attachment as from anticipated need, he took his old Spencer rifle.

Eli, on the other hand, didn't have the advantage of friendly relatives or even friendly residents, as his past was no secret, and cooperation would be hard to come by. He had taken a canteen and about two days' food, but he had no idea whether any of that would be enough. He was looking especially for hoof prints or, if he was lucky, the signs of a camp, though he knew from previous conversations that Lily was in the habit of changing camp sites as often as she felt necessary. She also had access to printing resources, but Morgan was totally confounded as to their whereabouts.

About noon, Eli rode into what appeared to be a recently lumbered out patch of ground and decided to take a break. He got off his horse, tied him to one of the small remaining trees, and walked about a bit, stretching his legs, getting the circulation back into his stiff limbs, and checking the ground for any signs of recent activity. Then he pulled some food from his saddle bag walked over to a stump and sat down. After consuming a portion of the food, Eli slid off the stump, pulled his hat down a bit, and promptly dozed off.

He woke with a start. Someone had ridden into the clearing and was in the process of dismounting from his horse. He knew from the person's size that it wasn't Lily and on second glance saw it was a large man, dressed in a Federal uniform. The man was Jesse Logan. Jesse had seen Eli slumped down asleep beside the stump, but didn't recognize him. Then, as he got off his horse, Jesse heard the rustling of Eli's getting to his feet and drew his revolver. Eli had left his holstered revolver hanging on the pommel of his saddle and was making his way to retrieve it when Jesse yelled at him. "Hold it right there, Partner. You can't outrun a bullet."

Eli froze. He had no gun, no cover, and no choice but to comply. He simply turned and faced Logan with his hands out, but instead of putting his hands in the air, he almost instinctively made a gesture which is taught in Masonic lodges as a sign of distress. Logan was dumfounded.

"You — what?" Jesse immediately demanded. "Eli Morgan, don't stand there and tell me you had the good sense to go out and join a lodge." he said with a grin, putting his revolver back in its holster. "This is too much for me to imagine."

"Well, if it ain't the famous Indian fighter hisself." Seeing Logan put his revolver away, Eli had the presence of mind to resurrect his old taunt. The unwritten and often understated bond of trust between members of the organization of Freemasons surfaced immediately between the two men who had been less than intimately friendly in their school days and had assumed opposing sides in the war. "Of course, I wouldn't let the fact that you're a Mason get in the way of me joinin'. I joined the lodge jus' after we sent you away. How was I to know the Masons down there in Richmond would let you go?"

"So, 'Brother' Eli, what brings you out here in the deep woods? There aren't many honest citizens out here for you to harass. Or maybe you came up here to hide out from the legal authorities."

"There ain't no legal authorities left in the valley sence you 'n' yer blue-jacket buddies showed up. — But I guess I'd ought'r level with you, Jesse," Eli said sobering a little, "I've been friends with Lily Venable for a time, and I'm kind of lookin' to see what she might think about what I ought'r do now that the Unionists are takin' over the valley. She's a perty smart lady, an' I thought she might give me some ideas. She's out in the woods here somewheres, and I'm tryin' to find her. 'You got any ideas?"

Jesse just laughed. "You're lookin' for Lily?" he said incredulously, "So'm I. The army sent me all the way up from Nashville to keep her from falling into the hands of those bad, bad Rebs, and now you tell me she's a friend of yours. Whose side're you on, Eli?"

"I'm not quite sure, Jesse. I started out strong fer secession, but the more I see of what's a'goin' on, the more I wonder whether I ought'r jus' set this thing out an' let you an' them fight it out." Eli went on to tell Jesse about the raid that Evan Stance's Rangers had pulled on the Venable home, and how he managed to save Lily from the trap they had set. His demeanor gave indication that his original loyalties for the Confederacy were becoming doubtful and his impression that the cause of secession, if not illogical, was probably not worth the cost.

"I r'member some of the talks that you an' Sid an' Alf Gahagan had with Mr. Putnam, an' I jus' wonder whether we done the right thing." he said recalling their school days.

"Who you been talkin' to, Eli? You're beginnin' to make sense."

"I guess it's the Lily influence, Jesse," Eli said with a grin. "Sometimes she makes sense when there's no sense to be made."

"Well, sitting here talking isn't getting us anywhere, is it Eli? Do you have any idea as to where we should be looking for that young lady?"

"You prob'ly know these woods better 'n I do. Jess. Yer uncle works this part of the country. Have you talked at all to him?"

"Yup. I was talking to him about an hour ago. That's why I was out in this section. He says there hasn't been any cuttin' goin' on in these parts for a couple of years and if anyone wanted to hide, there'd be less chance of someone spottin' them in through here. There's these little patches of new-growth cedars scattered around and they make good little camp spots, and the open spaces give the grass a chance to grow pretty good for their horses. I think we're in about the right area, but Lily may just be of a different mind."

As the two men stood discussing their next move, Lily Venable approached the edge of the clearing, pausing to observe and listen to the conversation. She unobtrusively sat down on a stump near a clump of low-growing cedars and listened. Finally, she spoke up.

"If you two were lookin' to get bushwhacked," she said in a loud voice, "you couldn't have picked a better place. What is it about this war that makes two sworn enemies stand out in the middle of nowhere an' talk over old times like long lost brothers?"

"Lily!" the two men cried in concert, rushing over to her and, as she stood up, both throwing their arms around her with considerable enthusiasm. She and Eli, at nearer the same height, were wrapped together within the embrace of the larger man. Somehow, any past friction among the three faded into dim memories, and the relief of reunion dominated the encounter. Lily was the center of concern for both men and her safety was paramount in their minds.

"Well." Jesse exhaled when the emotions were spent a bit. "This sure turned out to be one of the shortest man — er, ah — woman-hunts in history. Lily we both came out here to Cedar Mountain looking for you for our own reasons and never expected to meet up with each other, or with you, so easily." The two men then went on to relate why they were there in the forest.

Lily looked at both men for a minute or so before speaking. "Let me just set this question to rest, Jesse. In spite of what Eliza Johnson or anyone else thinks, I'm not leaving Watauga Valley, at least not in the near future. I feel I have a purpose here, and here is where I expect to spend the rest of the war, if it takes the next ten years. You can go back and tell Cousin Eliza that I'm perfectly safe and happy here. I appreciate her concern, but we all have a purpose in life, and I'm not going to let the death of my brother and dear father go unheeded and unanswered. Eli was my hero when he saved my life, and I really think God put him where he was to preserve that life, and I'm determined to make it count for something. He went against what his friends thought was right, but made at least one friend in doing it. I'm deeply indebted to him."

With that, she tenderly patted Eli's shoulder, unaware of the effect that gesture would have for the remainder of the war.

"I guess it's time for me to make some decisions," Jesse mused. "I was sent here to rescue this poor girl from the clutches of the occupying army and after all this trouble I find she doesn't want or even need to be rescued. Several people along my way here told me just that; they said you were happy here and I shouldn't trouble myself, but now that I get the word straight from the source, I have to decide what to do. On one hand, I could kidnap you, Lily, but I don't think that would solve anything. I guess I'll just go back to Knoxville and report to Governor Johnson and see what he says."

"I'm sorry you had to come all this way, Jesse," Lily said, "but Mrs. Johnson knows how I feel. She's a good friend as well as being kinfolk, but the last time we talked I told her what I was doing and how I felt."

"No, it's nothing you have to apologize for, Lily. It's just the way the system works and I think we can straighten things out without any more trouble. I'll just get back to Knoxville and work things out from there. Eli. What are your plans?"

"I don't have no plans whatsomever," Eli admitted. "This thing about the Federals bein' here in the valley has me kinda over a barrel. I think the best thing for me is jus' to lay low, go back to workin' with my pa, and hope fer the best. Anyhow, I ain't got much of a stomach fer tryin' to keep up this fight with the unionists here in the valley. Fer one thing I'd be putting my neck in the noose an' fer another, I kind'a lost interest in this fightin' fer the south when the reasons we had fer fightin' like that don't really make that much sense, anymore. I think it's time fer me to let go of the tiger's tail."

―――――――(((●)))―――――――

It was September 9th, and Jesse knew it was time to return to the Union lines and report back to General Steedman and Governor Johnson that which he had accomplished in his contacts with Lily Venable. He needed to know what the army wanted of him, now that he had completed his assignment. He'd been given tentative orders to join with the 1st Tennessee Cavalry, but they were probably still in the Nashville region. His old unit, the 7th Ohio was in Knoxville and it was possible that he would be expected to rejoin them.

At home in Kellars Crossing, he took a day to get his affairs in order and return to Knoxville. Olivia was at his Grandparents' home and though he was reluctant to leave her again, he was still in the army and she knew as well as he did what was expected of him. He spent some time with her, expressing concern as to the dangers of the mission she had chosen for herself and trying to persuade her to give up such a hazardous line of work.

"You know, Libbie, you're much better off just staying here in Doe River Cove or even going back to Frederick. Do you really think it's wise to try to keep up with this double agent thing? What have you accomplished in the past few months? Who is your contact now that Captain Davis is dead?"

"I don't have a contact right now, Jesse. I haven't had one since Goodin shot Frank Davis and he was reassigned to Quartermaster in Nashville. Maybe I could come to Knoxville with you and try for a firmer relationship with the command there."

"Here's another thought, though, Sweetheart," Jesse mused. "If we were to get married, you could just stay here in the valley, and at least I'd know where to find you. I'm sure my folks would be glad to have you here and we could at least start some semblance of a life together."

"Do you really want to marry me, knowing all I've been through, Jesse? I'm not the sweet little Olivia you thought you were falling in love with back in the Alleghanies. You also recall that I committed adultery back there in Lewiston, too, don't you?"

"How'd you like to try it again, Ma'am?" Jesse teased her, not completely in jest.

"Be careful what you wish for, Captain. You might just be in danger of ruining your good Doe River reputation."

"If we were married, we could have it all; reputation, connubial bliss, the works."

"Oh, you make it sound so wonderful, Jesse, but I do think we should take some time to think about it."

"I know you're right, Libbie, but don't you think you could stay here a while and see what develops? I'm not sure whether the Rebs are going to sit still and allow the Feds to keep this region without a fight. We may be less secure here than we think, but I would feel better with you here.

The Rebs tend to let Grandpa Kellar alone, as he is supplying some much-needed material to their cause; those railroad ties and the other lumber, and Grandpa and Grandma Kellar would be happy to have you stay here, I'm sure."

Olivia jumped to her feet. "Let's go ask them."

26

LITTLE JOE WHEELER

Reaching Knoxville on the 12th of September, Logan found that only a small holding force was in the city and that General Burnside had concentrated his forces at Sweetwater, some sixty miles to the west, and was seeking instructions on how he could aid Rosecrans' Army of the Cumberland which was under siege by Bragg at Chattanooga. Ordered to hold his position unless Rosecrans called for aid, Burnside would remain at Sweetwater to keep Longstreet from moving back to Chickamauga Creek.

When Logan returned to Knoxville, and after communicating with General Steedman in Nashville by telegraph, he found that he had been reassigned to his old company, Company "H", with the 7th Ohio Volunteer Infantry, under Colonel Mike Patterson and General Milo Haskell, but he was now the company commander. As he had learned earlier, the old company had been all but wiped out, and he suspected its retention was only owing to the fact that no other unit wanted to accept Lieutenant John Goodin. Seeking out the small company, Logan found that there were only twelve privates left. He immediately called a meeting with its top staff of three; Goodin, Sergeant Lige Hawkins, and a new sergeant he had not met, Ralph Suttles.

"We're have our work cut out for us, men," he said, as he seated himself before his assigned tent. "It seems we are expected to fill our recruit complement from this area and then go on up to Camp Nelson for training. Lieutenant, I know you've been in command of the company for several months, and I'd like some time with you to find out just why you think it's been reduced to such small numbers, but that can wait. I know you men aren't familiar with this country and since our job is to do some scouting, recruiting, and securing supplies from the local folks, I may just have to leave you three here in camp to handle the administrative end of our work and I'll take what is left of the unit and do the scouting. Depending on how long we stay here we may use some of the new recruits to work with me as much as needed."

He went on to discuss the various duties he expected of Goodin and the two sergeants and presently he dismissed Hawkins and Suttles to lay out the grounds for the encampment with the aid of the other men.

"Lieutenant, I need to have a few words with you," he said as Lige Hawkins and Ralph Suttles were leaving. "I need to hear from you what has been going on in the company and what you would recommend for our future mission. If we are successful here in recruiting a proper number, we'll probably be reassigned to Camp Nelson or Dick Robinson for training before we can be effective." He purposely avoided any reference to the friction he had experienced with Goodin, saving that discussion for an appropriate time, later.

Goodin was silent for a moment. He had expected to be 'called on the carpet' immediately, and here he was, sitting with an old adversary being treated as a trusted friend, albeit now subordinate to a man, as he well knew, to whom he had been less than considerate when their roles were reversed. He studied the face of his newly assigned captain for some indication of malice, but saw none. Logan acted as though they had enjoyed a comfortable working relationship ever since they had known each other and he didn't know where to start.

"Captain," he finally began, "I don't know how much you know about the workings of the unit since you were with us, but I've tried my best to keep it together. We lost most of our men when their enlistments were up and top command failed to replace them, but we also lost some from desertions. I was told to just sit tight and wait for Captain Davis's return. What would you expect of me?"

"What did you think the reasons for those desertions were, John? How many were there?" He used Goodin's given name for the first time in conversation, hoping to relax the mood.

Here it came! Since he had first met him, Goodin had felt that Logan was the root of the discontent in the ranks of Company "H", prompting disobedience and desertion, and now he was expected to give some phony reason for the problem to the very man who had been its cause. Whether scouting, sniping, performing as the company's second lieutenant, or away from the unit in prison or burning down a gun factory, Jesse had been the subject of discussion and inspiration among his fellow soldiers, even with the amusement they enjoyed at his expense when he got into trouble with Daisy Morton in Coalwood.

For months, Goodin's private moments had been spent dwelling on those very issues, and his own lack of promotion, and now he was face to face with the cause of his distress. And the man had the unmitigated gall to address him by his first name like some kind of a friend.

"I don't know, Captain," Goodin said, his face assuming a ruddy glow, with the old scarring standing out in pale contrast, "Sergeant Hawkins and I have discussed the problem many times and we even disciplined some of the men we managed to recapture, but the desertions only seemed to get worse. There were probably around thirty or forty in all. Beside that there were absolutely no reenlistments in the company when their terms ran out. I couldn't just kidnap them, now could I?"

The conversation was not going as Logan had hoped. What he planned as a discussion of his expectation for the unit had descended into a confrontation over what he clearly perceived as Goodin's lack of leadership.

"Calm down, John," Logan said, trying to control his temper. "In my opinion, you've always, been the kind of officer who is well schooled in the rules and regulations of the army, and able to apply a solution to the problem at hand. I'd like to see you promoted for these qualities, but sometimes I think you overreact to minor infractions when you, and the troop, would be better served to simply ignore them, or just note them in the Company Log."

Then, after a long pause he continued. "Let's do some thinking as to how we can prevent the problem in the future. I'm going over to General Haskell's tent and make arrangements as to when he expects me to go out. I see Adam Gainfield, who I picked up back in the mountains last month, is still here with the army, and I think I'll ask to have him assigned with us and help me recruit. He was with a Rebel unit, as you know, but his contacts back in the Watauga Valley might be helpful. By the way, Lieutenant, what do you know about the rumor that there are a bunch of flat-boats banked up the river east of here?"

"It's only a rumor, as far as I know, just idle talk around the camp. Sergeant Hawkins told me about them, but you can't believe everything you hear, here in the army."

During the early part of the Union presence at Knoxville a company of Michigan infantry had built a fleet of about forty flat-boats up-river from the city, intending to use them to transport food down to the occupying forces, but with other options available and other matters pressing, the plan was abandoned. The boats were left along the banks of the Holston and French Broad rivers and all but forgotten.

The idea of using these boats for supplying the army and townspeople with food was a long shot, since the surrounding region had been stripped of available supplies first by the presence of the Rebel army and then by the newly ensconced Federals. As time went by, Confederate patrols were able to effectively seal the perimeter of the town enough that there was only a small stretch of riverbank accessible to land any supplies, and that short stretch was under periodic surveillance from across the Holston River.

General Haskell had introduced Logan to two other captains who were also native to east Tennessee. Captain George Doughty, who was originally from Knox County, but had lived for some years in Georgia, was assigned a similar mission as Logan's, but concentrating in and around the Knox and Sevier Counties. He knew of the flat boats and it was he who had suggested using them for their originally intended purpose. Captain Peter Justice with the First Tennessee Mounted Infantry and a native of Sullivan County, would work that area, and Jesse would work Carter, Hawkins, and Johnson Counties. He would then meet upriver with Justice and Doughty whenever they had purpose and opportunity.

Getting the boats down the river promised to be the most hazardous part of the operation, but Captain Justice devised a plan requiring one steersman and one pilot on each of the boats, poling the boats to the north side of the river at night, when darkness and the rain and mist concealed them from the roving Rebel riders. The boats were then landed along a short section of the riverbank between First Creek and the Gay Street pontoon bridge. The boats were then either dismantled and the lumber used for fortifications or, in a few cases, towed upriver against the current to be reused. The process served not only to supply food to the army and the city's occupants, but also to provide recreation for the troops in maintaining a positive activity and the knowledge that they were 'outsmarting' the Rebels.

On November 19, with Private Adam Gainfield, eight men from the Company "H", and three from other units, Logan started out again for the Watauga Valley, a distance of about a hundred miles. They camped the first night just outside Greenville without incident. Late the second day, they approached Kellars Crossing. Except for the few local men, the troops would bed down in the lumber mill and Jesse would be able to sleep at home.

Olivia was still at Kellars Crossing when Jesse arrived. She mentioned that she had discussed with Jesse's grandparents the various options for their future. Emma Kellar had enthusiastically supported the idea of their marriage, but Henry, Olivia observed, had been a bit more reserved. He expressed concern over the progress of the war and of Jesse's chances of survival. What he didn't mention were his doubts about Olivia's loyalties to the Union. This was of little consequence in the young couple's thinking by now, however, and they planned to proceed with wedding plans, albeit at a deliberate pace.

The people around Carter County were enthusiastic over the presence of General Burnside in Knoxville. Even though the remaining Confederate irregulars were still making their presence in the region known, those troops were now much less aggressive than they were when the region was under total Rebel control.

Jesse personally tried to contact as many farmers as he could, and the response was amazing. The year's harvest had been a good one and the farmers, hoping for such a situation as had developed, had hidden their bounty from the Rebels as much as possible. And, to sweeten the deal even more, General Burnside paid real Federal money for the crops. Cured meat, vegetables, corn, wheat, potatoes, cattle, hogs, sheep, poultry, and countless other commodities found their way to the river for the relief of the troops in Knoxville. Food came by wagons, handcarts, wheelbarrows, buckets, boxes, and as for the livestock, they came on foot. The flatboats were mostly beached near Mooresburg and Morristown, a somewhat remote region, and the Rebel troops had not discovered the deception.

⸻ ⸙ ⸻

At Chickamauga Creek, Confederate General Braxton Bragg had badly miscalculated his opponent and was stalemated by General Rosecrans. As these events were unfolding, dissent spread through his Army of Tennessee. Many of his subordinates were unhappy with his leadership. To rectify the situation, President Jefferson Davis went to Dalton, Georgia where they were bivouacked and met with the parties involved. While there, he suggested that Lieutenant General James Longstreet's corps, recently arrived from General Robert E. Lee's Army of Northern Virginia to assist in the Chickamauga campaign, be sent against Burnside at Knoxville. General Longstreet received orders to move northeast, being promised later support by a 5,000-man cavalry under Major General Joseph Wheeler.

Both Longstreet and Bragg were strong willed commanders and James Longstreet had his own ideas as to how the war along the Tennessee River should be conducted. Nevertheless, he was a soldier in the army of the Confederacy, and his Commander in Chief had given him an order which he was expected to obey.

At first, General Longstreet intended to start his march during the first week of November, hoping to use rail transport as far as Sweetwater, but he met with some insurmountable obstacles. The trains ran late, sufficient fuel was unavailable, and many of the engines lacked the power to climb the steeper grades through these mountains. This was East Tennessee, and some of the citizens were not quite convinced of the necessity of cooperating with the Confederate authorities. As a result, it was not until November 12th that his men finally arrived at their destination. Less than enthusiastic over being sent from the scene of action at Chickamauga, General Longstreet was also upset with the situation he encountered in his Knoxville campaign, but he plodded on.

Meanwhile, alerted to Confederate intentions, President Lincoln and General Grant were initially concerned about Burnside's exposed position, but calming their fears, Burnside successfully argued for a plan that would see his men slowly withdraw to the east toward Knoxville, using the strategy General Rosecrans had developed at Corinth, and preventing Longstreet from taking part in future fighting around Chattanooga. To do this it would be necessary to hold a position some distance southwest of Knoxville and he chose what he judged a defensible ground on the north bank of the Tennessee, just across the river from Sweetwater.

After arriving at Sweetwater, Longstreet started after the slowly retreating Burnside. On November 16, the two sides met at the key crossroads of Campbell's Station. Though the Confederates attempted a pincer attack, the Union troops succeeded in holding their position, repulsing Longstreet. Withdrawing later in the day, Burnside reached the safety of Knoxville's fortifications on the 17th. During his absence, the entrenchments there had been substantially enhanced under the eye of his chief engineer, Captain Orlando Poe.

In an effort to gain more time for strengthening the city's defenses, newly commissioned Brigadier General William Sanders, Burnside's cavalry commander, engaged the Confederates in a delaying action along the Kingston Road on November 18. Though his efforts were successful, Sanders, one of Burnsides more promising young commanders, was mortally wounded in the fighting.

Arriving just west of the city, Longstreet commenced a siege despite lacking heavy guns. Though he planned to assault Burnside's works on November 20, he elected to delay, to await reinforcements led by Generals Bushrod Johnson and Joe Wheeler. The postponement frustrated his officers as they recognized that every hour that passed allowed Union forces to strengthen their fortifications. Assessing the city's defenses and receiving word that General Joe Wheeler was enroute to support him, Longstreet proposed an assault against Fort Sanders for November 29. Located on the western edge of the Knoxville fortifications, Fort Sanders was named in honor of the recently killed cavalry commander. The fort extended out from the main defensive line and was seen by Longstreet as the most vulnerable point in the Union defenses.

Frustration and delay besieged Longstreet in his attack on Knoxville. His experience with General Burnside at Fredericksburg back in December of '62, convinced him that Burnside should be an easy target, but this was not the case. His reconnaissance of the region was contradictory. He had a map of the region that had been given him by General Simon Buckner, but intelligence from some of the local people, supposedly loyal to the interests of the Confederate forces, did not agree with the map. He chose to trust his fellow general as his experience with some locals had left him suspicious of their reliability. Unfortunately, portions of the map were inaccurate.

General Danville Leadbetter, who had been instrumental in the building of the Knoxville fortifications when it was in the hands of the Confederacy, arrived on November 25 and consulted with Longstreet, supplying his knowledge of the fortifications from the year before. For two days Longstreet, with his subordinates and Leadbetter, reconnoitered the Union lines around Knoxville. After a second look at Fort Sanders, the most prominent feature of the Federal defenses, Leadbetter recommended the attack be made at that point, and Longstreet agreed.

During the delay by Longstreet, Captain Poe had prepared the approach to Fort Sanders which entailed, first of all, a broad sloping hillside which the Rebels would have to ascend, from its southwestern edge to the fort. The distance was about 500 yards with tree stumps liberally dotting the landscape. The federals spent the better part of two nights stringing telegraph wire between these stumps, making any attempt by the Rebels to run up the hill in the dark extremely difficult without tripping and tumbling. During the early-morning hours, the randomly strung wire would make any quick ascent almost impossible.

At the crest of the hill, along the walls of the fort, the federals had dug a six-to-ten-foot deep moat which they nicknamed 'the ditch'. The ditch was conveniently partly full of water from the recent rains, and was far deeper than Longstreet's reconnaissance had calculated. He had watched some of the preparations through field glasses, and had seen Union soldiers walking easily across the ditch. What he hadn't seen were the plank bridges the soldiers were using and which were taken up at night.

On the night of November 28/29, Longstreet assembled around 4,000 men at the foot of the hill below Fort Sanders. He intended to have them surprise the defenders and storm the fort shortly before dawn. Preceded by a brief artillery bombardment, three Confederate brigades advanced as planned. Slowed considerably by the wire entanglements where they were brutally mauled by Union rifle and cannon fire, the attackers pressed on towards the fort's walls. Reaching 'the ditch', the attack broke down as the Confederates, lacking ladders, were unable to scale the fort's steep walls. Though flanking fire pinned down some of the Union defenders, Confederate forces in the ditch and surrounding areas quickly sustained heavy losses. After approximately twenty minutes, Longstreet abandoned the attack having sustained 813 casualties against only 8 men killed and 5 wounded for the Federals.

Longstreet withdrew his troops and debated his options, and as he did, word arrived that, on November 25, Bragg had been finally crushed at Chickamauga Creek and forced to retreat south. With the Army of Tennessee (CSA) badly battered, Longstreet received orders to return south to reinforce Bragg. Believing these orders to be impracticable he instead proposed a siege of Knoxville for as long as possible to prevent Burnside from joining Grant at Chicamauga for a combined offensive against Bragg and possibly to starve Burnside's army into surrender.

On November 29th, following Longstreet's stalemate, Confederate General Joe Wheeler finally arrived and was thereafter instrumental in supporting Longstreet's siege, cutting off the food supply to the city by any ordinary means. Something was going to have to be done to relieve the shortage or the Union army would be forced to surrender to General Longstreet. Wheeler and his brigade of cavalry were a formidable force during those days following Longstreet's occupation of the Knoxville area. They seemed to be everywhere. General Wheeler, while perhaps not a cavalry commander on the order of a Bedford Forrest or Jeb Stewart, was well known for his tenacity and bravery. He deployed his troops wisely and trained them to support each other in combat. When Longstreet invested the Knoxville area, Wheeler infested the surrounding countryside. At times, his men gave their attention to harassing the Federals within the boundaries of the Knoxville fortifications, and at other times they canvassed the countryside searching for food to supply the Rebels and deny the Federals.

One small factor benefitting the Federals was Longstreet's mistrust of the information provided by the local 'friendlies', but General Buckner's old map was inaccurate. The map misidentified a small stream, Little Creek, as the French Broad River and Longstreet gave Wheeler orders to limit his activities to that tributary.

Little Creek drained into the Holston River from the south very near the western boundary of Knoxville and the French Broad joined the Holston several miles farther east, but Longstreet ordered General Wheeler to stop at that line, the more westerly creek. In the confusion, there was a stretch of the city's south boundary that was not closely guarded from the opposite side of the Holston River by Wheeler's cavalry.

It was not impossible for members of the small Union cavalry contingent to escape the confines of the fortified city from time to time. Once outside those fortifications, however, the Yankees often faced roving bands of Rebel horsemen in dominating numbers, especially after November 29 when Joe Wheeler's cavalry brigade arrived.

———⊷((◍))⊶———

Returning to Knoxville on November 26th from his first scouting mission, Captain Logan was directed to suspend that activity and report to Colonel Daniel Cameron at Armstrong's Hill, on the south bank of the Holston. It appeared that General Longstreet was trying to set up a battery on Cherokee Heights south of the river, and just across the river from Fort Sanders to bombard the fort. The range was over a mile, but with rifled canon, the Rebels could do considerable flanking damage. The recent concentration of grey-clad troops opposing the Union fortifications west of Knoxville alerted Burnside that Longstreet was about to attack the city and that fort Sanders was to be the primary target. From General Longstreet's perspective, Fort Sanders was the most vulnerable point in the Federal line, and an easy access to the fortified grounds surrounding the city. Cherokee Heights would be a valuable area from which to bombard Knoxville, as well as a distraction to Burnside's efforts to protect the city's western front.

Logan and his two companion captains, Justice and Doughty, were to lend support for Cameron's infantry brigade consisting of three regiments from Kentucky, Illinois, and Ohio. First, they were to establish a skirmish line in a broad valley between Armstrong's Hill and Cherokee Heights. In the past few days the Confederates had made several feints, both north and south of the river, and by the 28th of November, when the 'Justice Regiment', as it was called, was deployed, no one quite knew where the main attack would be staged, but Fort Sanders stood out as the most attractive target. Captain Poe had improved, enhanced, and groomed the defenses approaching Fort Sanders, and it was almost as though General Burnside was sending out a formal invitation to the Rebs that, 'This is where the ball will begin. All are invited'. Longstreet responded to the invitation.

The weather had been wet for several days, and when Company "H" dismounted about a mile back from their established skirmish line, Captain Logan called them together for some much-needed instruction and indoctrination. Company "H" amounted to only 20 men by this time, but they were now part of the Justice Regiment, and were there to fight. And here they were, about to line up do battle with a veteran corps of Confederate Regulars.

After Sergeants Hawkins and Suttles had supervised the removal of essential equipage from the horses, they lined the men up in a column of twos, and put them at ease. Captain Logan approached the group.

"Men, most of you are veterans of the Allegheny campaign, and know the rules of combat. The first rule of working a skirmish line is 'stay alive'. The second rule is 'keep your companions in sight'. We're not out here to win the war, but just to work as a warning and delay line to test the enemy's numbers and strength. I'll be with you on the line as will Lieutenant Goodin and Sergeants Hawkins and Suttles. You're now well-armed and know how to shoot, but I don't expect you to stand off the whole Rebel army. That's not why you're here. The Rebs aren't as well armed as we are, but they will have the advantage of firing down-hill. One other thing I'll promise you, that if the Rebs attack in numbers, I will pull you out of harm's way plenty early. We'll probably have a fence to fire from, but I'm not too sure about that."

"Another thing — I'm not even sure the Rebs will come out of their trenches, and if our troops from our rear decide to advance, I want you men to give way and let them go by, without joining the advance. When they approach, we just get out of their way and take a reserve position. Depending on what happens out there, we will be a back-up company. Any questions?"

"Will you be mounted, Captain?" the question came from one of the newer men.

"No, I plan to be on foot, today, 'same as you."

"Who should we take orders from, Captain? There's only about sixteen of us and four of you'uns. Which of you'uns should we listen to fer orders?"

"'Good question. We'll keep the company together under the direction of Sergeant Suttles. Sergeant Hawkins, Lieutenant Goodin and I will be present, but in reserve. You'll take your orders from Sergeant Suttles.

"When we back up into our reserve position, will we be able to get back here and get our horses?" a third question.

"That depends on the circumstances, but I think we will, just so we can defend the left flank of the main line. It all depends on how rapidly the battle line moves."

Logan then directed Lieutenant Goodin to take command of the company and, riding ahead, set out the ground he would have them occupy. In agreement with Captain Justice, who was nominally in command of the small regiment, Company "H" was placed on the left end of the line. As Jesse had predicted, the skirmish line was in a broad valley, divest of any major foliage, and through which ran a heavy rail fence, from north to south, offering very little protection, but giving definition to their positioning.

As it turned out, distribution of the three companies put the men about twenty yards apart all along the line, and that was about what the three captains had hoped for. Logan's Company "H" were armed with the Spencer carbines, and it gave them excellent fire power. The other two companies were similarly equipped and orders were given that there was plenty of ammunition to go around and the men were free to use as much of it as they felt they needed, the only cautionary directive being, "Shoot low, men. Use your sights and remember that those people across that field would gladly kill you if they get close enough."

Logan had his old scoped Spencer rifle and when he had the men deployed, he made a point of posting himself along the line in various places, demonstrating the skill that had earned him his nick-name. The grey-clad members of the opposing army ranged out in plain sight on the crest of Cherokee Heights at first, watching the men in blue being posted along the skirmish line and sending a few ineffective shots down the hill, but after several well-placed shots from Logan's Spencer, they seemed to think better of such rash behavior. The 'Yanks' along the line cheered heartily at their captain's show of fire-power.

The remainder of the day was spent by Company "H" getting used to their surroundings. There had been a bit of fighting in the area in days past, and some of the men occupied their time looking for cast-off articles as souvenirs. As the fortunes of war would have it, the Rebels, too, had sharpshooters, prompting the Federals to seek the protection of improvised barricades of stacked fence rails. Moving about, if one was quick, was not too dangerous, but it was unwise to stand still without cover for more than a few seconds. Shovels were brought out and the men went to work immediately digging protective earthworks.

The following day, November 29, early in the morning, it was obvious that north of the river there was a battle raging. The firing started at first light and intensified for about twenty or thirty minutes, but then seemed to fade. Meanwhile the Rebel forces posted on Cherokee Heights had assembled and were moving down the slope of the hill toward the valley. Their move was preceded by a brisk cannon fire from a battery placed above and behind them, which did very little damage because of its elevation, but announced the attack. Logan was proud of his small troop's resilience. He watched his troops methodically pick off the descending forces, causing them to slow their assault and give Colonel Cameron's brigade time to establish a position behind them to the east.

Presently, the Rebel troops began their advance and it was time for the skirmishers to retire. On orders from their squad leaders, Company "H" moved south out of the field of fire, taking up a defensive position to protect Cameron's left flank. Logan called his sergeants together and, over the din of battle, directed the next move, which was to be to follow the main body of the brigade either east or west, whichever direction the battle took them, but to remain on the flank. The squad was to remain intact for control purposes.

Long after the battle on the north side of the river seemed to be fading, the fight for Cherokee heights continued, with Confederate General Evander Law, a seasoned strategist, directing the Rebel army, but gradually giving way to the strength of the Union brigade under Colonel Daniel Cameron. The Rebels finally settled for their original position on the crest of Cherokee Heights, and Cameron's troops dug in where Justice's skirmishers had been.

Toward the end of the day, General Longstreet called in his generals for a review of the day's efforts and for their opinion as to what to do next. Fort Sanders it seemed, and by extension Knoxville, was impregnable. A siege was in order.

The following days, Captain Logan, along with his companions, Captains Justice and Doughty, returned to their scouting duties in the productive counties of East Tennessee.

The siege by General Longstreet only lasted a few days, but his presence and that of the Wheeler Cavalry essentially sealed the city's perimeter, necessitating the use of the 'flat-boat fleet'. On December 4th, however, learning that General William Sherman had been dispatched from Chattanooga, Longstreet abandoned the siege, vacated his position, and moved northeast toward Virginia, wintering at Russellville. General Wheeler's regiment returned immediately to the Army of the Cumberland (CSA) in northern Georgia reducing northeast Tennessee's Confederate presence significantly.

The 'Justice Regiment' was released for their old scouting duties.

Captain Logan, again scouting the Carter County area for possible recruits and for supplies to feed the hungry Knoxville garrison, had been unaware of the Rebel withdrawal. Then, one day in early December, they happened to encounter Lily Venable on the road between Elizabethton and Cedar Mountain and learned the good news. Lily had developed a working friendship with Olivia Livingston and her presence and activity in the valley had become much more public under the protection of the Federal occupancy. Adam Gainfield, who had been acting as a courier for the company, was riding ahead of the squad when Lily appeared at a bend in the road.

"Hey, Adam, have you heard the latest news?" Lily called out when she saw him. "I hear you're about the only Rebel left in the valley."

"Latest news be durned, Lily. Cain't you tell the diff'rence between Rebel rags and the fine garments of a Union so'jur? What is it you're so anxious to tell us?"

"Wheeler, Longstreet, all those old buddies of yours have left the country. Longstreet just gave up and seems to be heading back for Virginia."

By this time, Captain Logan and the rest of the squad had caught up and Lily repeated her message. "Jesse, the Rebels have skedaddled! Three days ago, they up and headed east and today I was told General Wheeler and his troops just mounted up and headed back towards Chattanooga."

"What the —. How do you know all this, Lily?" Jesse demanded in amazement.

"Eli Morgan was down near Carters Depot and saw Longstreet's men moving east, bag and baggage. They must have crossed down there at the Confederate ferry and took off south of the river. Then, this morning I was over t' Elizabethton and there was that little company of General Wheeler's cavalry. I talked to one of the troopers and he says that they had orders to go back to General Bragg, down there at the Chickamauga."

Logan's squad, hearing the news, was, to a man, amazed. "Here we've been, scouring the countryside for provisions and hiding out from some big bad troopers from Little Joe's army and they just sneak off in the night. Well, we must have scared them off," one of the men from the squad remarked.

"Lige, let's talk this over," Captain Logan muttered, getting down from the saddle. The two of them, with Adam and Lily gathered and discussed their situation.

"Well, without any orders to the contrary, I think we'll just continue to scout, but I want to hear it from General Haskell as to how we should handle this thing." Then, turning back to the men of the squad, he said, "Let's turn around, Men. We need to check with the general as to what we've got to do. It's a two-day ride back to camp and we'd better get started."

As they rode toward Knoxville, they encountered a small group of men among which they recognized Eli Morgan. Lily, riding with the Logan group, greeted him warmly and immediately began to tease him about his touted friend, General Longstreet.

"Well," Eli replied with resignation, "I tried to tell him how to handle this mess and just wipe out the whole town of Knoxville, but he jes' wouldn't listen. What is it about these officer types that make a man deef? Oh, hello, there Capt'n Logan. I didn't see you settin' there. Have you found any Injuns to run off, lately?"

"No, Eli, I've been busy keeping the people of the valley safe from all those renegades you 'n' your gang have been scoutin' for. When are you going to join a real army and do the people around here proud?"

"Don't hold yer breath waitin' fer that day, Injun Fighter. I'm jes' a peaceable citizen of the great state of Tennessee an' don't want any part of this war."

"C'm'on, Eli," Lily chided. "Every one of our old gang have seen the light and gone over to the right side. Look at Adam, here. What is it about killing innocent civilians that makes you want to stay with the losing side?"

The comment made Eli Morgan shrink back into his small group. He knew what Lily was referring to and it shamed him to have been associated with the deaths of her father and brother. He rode over to where she was sitting on her horse and took her hand. "Lily, please don't bring that up," he said out of hearing by the others. "I know you must be heartbroken, and I cain't blame you, but I've apologized a dozen times and there's not much more I kin say about it."

"I know, Eli. I'm sorry I mentioned it, but their deaths have been on my mind, lately with this back-and-forth of the troops in the valley, and frankly, dear boy, I do wish you'd reconsider your idea to stay away from the Union army. You'd make a good trooper with their side and you know it."

"Well, maybe I should," he replied. "I be'n thinkin' about it an' 'cept fer the fact that I'm officially conscripted by th' Rebs, I'd be inclined to do it. They'd shoot me on sight ef they ever caught me."

Logan had ridden over to where Lily and Eli were talking. "I reckon I'll head back for camp, Lily. Eli, you take care of yourself, and if you ever decide to sign up with the North, I imagine I'll be around for a week or two, and if you do decide to join, just come in and look me up. I'd be proud to have you in my company."

Morgan smiled. "Jesse, the only thing keepin' me from joinin' fer the north is that I'd have to listen to you all day barkin' orders an' struttin' around like you know'd what you was doin'. Ef I was to join, could I be callin' you Cap'n Injun Fighter, or would y'r high-falutin' frien's git after me fer that?"

"No, Eli, I'd just take you out behind the barn and give you a whupin', just like I used to do in school."

"You never —. You and whose army? You'd need the whole regiment to do that little job."

"Will you two get serious?" Lily asked impatiently. "Jesse, Eli thinks that since he's officially a member of a Confederate unit and he'd be treated like a deserter, if he were caught in a Union uniform. What about that?"

"You know, that may be true, but the chances are very remote as to it actually happening. Adam, here, is in the same predicament, and so are a whole lot of Carter County men. And you know I'm an escaped prisoner from a Confederate prison, and in the same boat."

"Thanks fer remindin' me," Eli said with a grin. "I'll jes' note that in my book an' hold it over yer head ef we ever git caught together." He pulled from his pocket a small notebook and a stub of a pencil and scribbled something in the book.

"Well, Private Morgan, as long as we're holding people accountable, an' as you just told me you are officially a member of the Rebel army, I'm taking you prisoner. Mister, you're on your way to jail."

"I said stop fooling around, you two," Lily repeated.

As the conversation had assumed a more public turn, both groups, the military and the civilian, were enjoying the exchange. Adam Gainfield was a little perplexed, as he'd known for years that Jesse and Eli hadn't been particularly friendly, but there was no mistaking the relaxed humor that accompanied this little debate.

"Captain," Sergeant Hawkins finally asked, "don't you think we'd better get started? Otherwise, we'll be spending the next two nights on the road."

"You're right, Lige," Jesse said getting back onto his horse. "Eli, I have a feeling we'll be spending at least the next few days here around Knoxville, so give my idea some thought. Even if we're reassigned, they'll at least let me come back a day or two to say goodbye to my family, and I'll come and see you."

<hr />

Back in Knoxville two days later, Logan was called to General Haskell's tent. "Captain, we're ordered to establish winter quarters, here in Knoxville, and I want you to continue your efforts recruiting and scouting, but also purchasing provisions for the occupation. We won't be able to depend entirely on the generosity of the local population, but feel there is a mutual benefit in using their services as much as possible, as we will pay them in Federal dollars and bolster their economy. Besides, we know President Lincoln has expressed a great concern for the people of East Tennessee, and we hope — actually we expect to be able to hold this part of the state for the balance of the conflict. In due time, the quartermaster will assume the responsibility of securing provisions, but you are familiar with the region, and that day may be later than we think. Have you any questions?"

Logan thought for a moment, "General, do we have any idea as to how long it will be before the company, Company "H", will have to return to Camp Nelson? Recruiting has been rather good, but we certainly don't have a full complement of men. I am also wondering about staff. We've talked a time or two about the qualifications of my first lieutenant, and I don't have the fullest confidence in him or his abilities. Is there a possibility of adding another lieutenant?"

He went on, "And the men I seem to be adding to my unit are all horsemen. Would it be possible to convert the unit to a company of mounted infantry?"

"Hold on, Captain. You've only been assigned to the company for a month and already you're recreating the unit into your perfect plan. Let's take the questions one at a time. As to the return to Camp Nelson, — I don't know. It all depends on how soon you've reached complement. It may not happen any time before spring. The lieutenant matter — I've given that some thought and I'll allow it with your recommendation. I won't give my approval to the conversion to a company of mounted infantry until after training. No promises, Captain. Anything Else?"

"Yes, Sir. Also, there are possible charges pending against Lieutenant Goodin and I'd like to know how the army wants me to proceed."

"Put that matter on hold, Captain. As you must know, that man has family ties to people in the office of the General in Chief, and we may just be biting off more than we can chew if we level charges against him right now. I'm sorry."

"Yes, Sir. Will there be anything else?"

"One other thing, Captain. I must tell you I'm impressed with your abilities. This is your first real command position since your promotion, but you seem to have taken to the job like a duck takes to water. Keep up the good work. You'll do well in the army."

"Thank you, Sir," Jesse said with a salute. And with that he turned and left the tent.

"Lieutenant Goodin," Jesse said to his assistant the morning following his conversation with General Haskell. "Let's take a ride. Meet me over at the saddlery and take a ride with me."

After securing mounts, the two officers left the breastwork west on the Kingston road. When they had gone far enough to be reasonably certain they were not overheard, Logan turned to his lieutenant. "I feel sometimes as though we are total strangers, Lieutenant. We've worked together on and off for the past three years, and I don't know anything about you. Where are you from? Do you have family at home? 'Any brothers? Sisters? What do your father and mother think of you being in the army? What did you do before the war? What does your father do for a living?"

Goodin was speechless. He had never cared for Jesse Logan nor had he trusted him any more than he trusted anyone else in the army, yet here he was, being grilled as to his past in a manner ostensibly calculated to generate good relationships. Though the man had apparently saved his life, it was no more than a soldier should be able to expect of a fellow soldier. When the incident occurred, Logan was a corporal and Goodin, was a lieutenant. Had Logan lured him out to that hillside just to get him killed, but then saw an opportunity to be a hero?

"I'm from Ohio, Captain, and I don't have any sisters or brothers. My father is a railroad employee and he and my uncle got me to enlist, much against my better judgment, and — well, that's about it."

"Any other kinfolk in the military?" Jesse asked, knowing the answer.

"Yes, my uncle; the man I mentioned who got me into this."

"I talked to General Haskell yesterday and asked him if we'd be able to get a second lieutenant assigned. He didn't commit himself, but if they do give us authorization, is there anyone in the company you'd recommend for the job?"

"I can't think of anyone, Captain," Goodin replied.

Jesse thought the response was a little odd, as his impression of Elijah Hawkins was favorable, and there were only a handful of other men in the unit who had been there for more than a few weeks.

"What do you think about Hawkins?" he asked.

"I suppose he'd be alright. He doesn't stand out in my mind as command material, but he's at least familiar with the unit."

"Have you done any more thinking as to how we can keep so many of the men from deserting?"

"I don't have any idea. I tried to keep the company together after they gave me command, but, like I said, some of the enlistments were up and the men just wanted to go home. When other men saw what was happening, I suppose they wanted to go home, too, and so they deserted. That's my guess."

"Do you think you may have been a little hard on the men? I understand you used the wheel-haul on some of them."

"Well, that was in lieu of having them shot! What is this, some kind of an interrogation, CAPTAIN? I was doing my job, just as I was assigned, and no one has questioned me until you came back."

"Maybe it's time someone did question you about your practices. Whether we like it or not, Lieutenant, I'm the man who has to answer for the performance and discipline of this company and I need to understand what has happened since I left, and — perhaps, just perhaps, avoid similar problems in the future. If you don't know why the men were deserting in the past, then you probably don't know how to prevent future desertions. Does that make sense to you?"

"Whatever you say, Captain. I'm going back to camp, SIR, unless you want to order me to stay and enjoy any more of this friendly conversation."

Logan remained silent and Goodin turned his horse around and spurred him into a gallop, back toward the Knoxville compound.

Jesse Logan was stymied and dejected. Planned discussions turned into arguments. Suggestions were resented and perceived as orders. Sullenness and childish pouting were common responses to friendly comments. He knew he was partly to blame because he was inclined to respond to Goodin's surliness with obvious irritation. He felt that what was needed was a second lieutenant on whom he could rely and sidetrack Goodin into a position where he could do less harm. Obtaining that lieutenant was likely to be difficult, in view of the fact that the company then consisted of only twenty-seven men, including the officers.

The following day, after reporting to regiment command, Logan selected some of his new Carter County recruits, along with Adam Gainfield, and started for the Watauga Valley.

Lige Hawkins caught up with him as he was about to leave. "How about it, Captain, could I go along?"

Taking Hawkins aside, he confided, "Lige, I need you here. Lieutenant Goodin has me concerned and I need some stability in the company and also a pair of loyal eyes to help keep me informed. The dozen or so I've left behind are from the old company, and know the routine, and I'm taking the native sons along for their contacts with the people in Carter County."

Hawkins just looked at Jesse for a moment. "That makes sense, now that I think of it. I reckon that's why you're the captain, Captain."

"Just promise me one thing, Sarge. Please, no desertions until I get back," he said with a glint in his eye.

Hawkins turned and walked away with his head lowered, laughing softly to himself.

The men in the troop had been supplied with four days' rations, but knew well that they wouldn't need them. The people of Carter County were all their friends and relatives, and food would be no problem.

Their second day on the road, the troop stopped for the night in the small town of Spurgeon, where Jesse's father's family had first settled around 1820. Jesse's distant cousin, Alfred Spurgeon was still living there, having maintained the family's grist mill near the mouth of Muddy Creek.

'Fred' Spurgeon had been an active recruiter in the area and had eight men signed up for recruitment into the Union army and, after a short talk with the small group, Jesse and his squad collected the eight men and directed them to go with two members of his troop back to Knoxville to be sworn in. He then spent a few minutes with his cousin and his family, and with his remaining squad, left for the Watauga Valley, arriving there at dusk. The men in the squad scattered for their respective homes and Jesse immediately went to Kellars Crossing and his grandparents' home. Olivia was there.

"Hello, beautiful lady," Jesse greeted her.

Olivia had been working in the kitchen preparing supper for the hired men. "I don't feel very beautiful, this evening, my dear, but thank you for your thoughts. What have you found out about your future here in East Tennessee?"

"Well, I have some good news and some bad news. The good news is that Company "H" will probably be garrisoned in this area for some time, and the bad news is that nobody's killed John Goodin, yet."

"Is he still as obnoxious as ever, Jesse? What has he done, now?"

Jesse went on to describe his most recent encounters with Goodin, and how frustrated he was becoming in not being able to penetrate the man's shell of hostility. He also shared with Olivia the political barriers he had encountered when he proposed disciplining him for his involvement in Colonel Abernathy's escape attempt and the shooting of Frank Davis.

"I'm convinced he had planned to kill both Frank Davis and me to prevent us from charging him with that escape attempt. I can't reform him, I can't discipline him, and I can't get rid of him."

"Jesse, I have faith in you. You'll think of something."

"If I could only put him in a situation where I could convince him I'm his friend — but I reckon saving his life back there in Virginia wasn't enough. I know he resents my promotion to Company Commander, but there's not much I can do about that. When I try to draw him into a discussion about running the company, he just gives me the 'I-don't-know' or a 'what-would-you-expect' response, and it gets under my skin. 'Trouble is, I let it show."

Jesse spent the night at his grandparents' home and shortly after eight o'clock the next morning he met in Elizabethton with the men he had brought from Knoxville. Five other men had joined the group. One of them was Eli Morgan.

"Good morning, Mister Morgan," Logan said genially. "Don't tell me I've persuaded you to join up with us."

'Don't flatter yerse'f, Cap'n," Eli grinned. "I jes' thought it was time fer someone with some sense to go down there to Knoxville and show 'em how a army should be run."

"Nice of you, Mr. Morgan. We can use all the help we can get. General Longstreet tried for a month to show us some clever military tactics, but then I reckon he got discouraged and headed back east."

"While we're talkin', though Jesse, I got four other fellers that I think might be interested in joinin'. You r'member Billie Waldron, an' Steven Rathsburg, an' Ivan Winniger, an' —." Eli scratched his head and looked back at his companions, "oh, an' Emanuel Mayton."

"Alright, Eli. Then with you five —," and turning to the other men with Eli, "Are you men all interested?"

"Oh, yes, Sir," they responded, almost in chorus.

"Alright! With the eight in Spurgeon and seven here, we now have fifteen men to add to our company."

"What'll you give me to make it an even twenty?" Eli interjected.

"Do you really think you could rustle up five more souls from these parts to join up with us, Eli?"

"Cap'n, I knows these parts like a gopher knows a garden, an' I know who's on which side of the fence. What do you think I ben doin' these past months? Ef I kin ketch 'em, I'm sure I kin sign 'em up."

The 'gopher-knows-a garden' phrase rang a bell with Jesse, though Eli probably didn't make the connection with the night Jesse was captured and sent to prison. Nevertheless, Jesse had to chuckle at the turn of events.

Eli was true to his word. Before the day was over, he had teamed up with Lily Venable, and together they had rounded up six more men from around Elizabethton and the Watauga Valley, and the other members of the squad added fourteen more. Lily was partly responsible, as she had maintained constant contact with the loyalists in the valley and Jesse was sure it had been much to her credit that Eli Morgan even considered such a move. The other members of Jesse's small squad also contributed their familiarity with the local population, and the fact that General Burnside had been so successful in his quick defeat of General Longstreet's attack and siege was also a consideration.

The following day Captain Logan, with twenty-seven new recruits, headed west for the signing of enlistment papers. The group bivouacked for one night enroute, and though they weren't dressed as soldiers, they mostly considered themselves part of the Union army. Someone had brought a banjo, another man had a jews harp, and a few others a variety of spirits, and the scene around the campfires was festive, to say the least. The men from Logan's original squad told army stories of which even their captain was skeptical, but he said nothing to dampen the mood. He didn't bother to tell them of some of his own exploits.

As the troop approached the Knoxville enclosure, Logan halted them near a small grove of trees and directed them to sit down and rest for a bit. When they had settled, he addressed the group with a few words of advice, telling them what they could expect in their first few days as soldiers.

"You may not all get well-fitting uniforms the first few days or even weeks, but that will change as time goes by. We are a little over half-way to achieving our full complement of one hundred men, but when we get to that number, you can expect a long march to Camp Nelson Kentucky for training, and then it's up to the army where we go from there."

"I expect that I will be your captain through the course of your enlistment, unless the army has other ideas. Though many of you know me from my days living up there in the valley, my official name is Captain Logan, and it will be necessary for you to address me that way, at least when within earshot of people outside our company. Discipline is king in the army." Then Jesse smiled and confided, "In personal conversation, call me whatever comes to mind;

Jesse, Whitey, Injun Fighter, or whatever we used, back in the days —. Don't call me White Angel, though, unless you really want to irritate me."

"While you are here and when we go to Camp Nelson you will be marching and drilling until you hate the very words, but, believe me, men, discipline and the ability to react responsively will — I repeat will — save lives in tight situations. It has done it for me and it has done it for some of my friends."

"Your assignment is Company "H", 7th Regiment, Ohio Volunteer Infantry, but look around you. This is a company of East Tennesseans, and we will become well known, I'm sure, as those 'loyalists from East Tennessee' and our reputation as a fighting unit will rise or fall depending on the determination and strength of character of men from East Tennessee."

"Folks from the Great Smokies and from Watauga Valley have two things in common. They are hunters and they are horsemen, and I'd be proud if this company could become recognized as a company of sharpshooters and even — and I've already brought this up with the high command — even a company of mounted infantry whose specialty is to hit and run to keep the enemy guessing as to where we will attack them next. I've had experience with such a unit on the other side — General Bedford Forrest, and though I don't support his political views, I surely think the man is a genius and a tactical wizard."

"As you get settled into the army routine, you'll run into people you don't agree with or don't even like. I'm letting you know because I've been in the same predicament a time or two. Hold onto your temper if this happens to you. We'll have plenty of fighting out on the battle line without our fighting with the other men in camp. Losing your temper is a quick and easy way to get into trouble or get yourself killed. Believe me!"

"Alright, on your feet, men. I'll not ask you to try to march into camp. Some of you, I know, would do well marching, and some wouldn't. The trouble is that to try to match the two groups will make us look like a herd of monkeys in a circus parade."

As the squad entered the fortified enclosure the impression was electric. Logan rode at the head of the column, and could feel the eyes of the various work details scanning his entourage. He rode up to General Haskell's Tent and as the general came out, Logan rendered a sharp salute. "Company "H", short-time recruits reporting in, Sir."

"Very good, Captain," the general said returning the salute. "How long have you been out?"

"One week, Sir, since last Thursday."

"Where did you collect this fine-looking group of men?"

"In and around Elizabethton, Sir."

"You went all the way to Elizabethton and picked up all these — how many men are there, here?"

"Twenty-seven, Sir. We sent in eight more from Spurgeon four or five days ago with two of the men from my company."

General Haskell turned and spoke to one of his sergeants. "Sergeant, please escort these men to the recruiting desk and then have them report to the quartermaster."

27

NORTHWESTERN GEORGIA

On his return to the company, Captain Logan was met by Sergeants Hawkins and Suttles. Lige Hawkins was wide-eyed. "Captain," he said breathlessly, "it happened. We've had another desertion."

"Oh, come on, Lige, are you sure?"

"I'm pretty sure, Captain. It was Johnson, Sidney, one of the men who has been with the Company since '61. He got into an argument with Lieutenant Goodin a few days ago and then on Wednesday he didn't report for roll-call. Lieutenant Goodin reported it to Major Weller and we sent out a searching party, but he's gone. We couldn't find him."

"Rats! I think Johnson was from Ohio and he'll have a tough time making it back home, so we may just be able to track him. If he's heading up the river, which is what I'd expect, he's going to run into General Longstreet around Russellville. That won't be good for him and it certainly isn't good for us."

"I'm sorry, Captain. I know you were joking when you told me not to allow any desertions, and I should have taken some time to calm him down after the lieutenant got after him, but I didn't think he would take it so hard."

"What was the argument all about?"

"Something about Johnson's posture in formation. You know he had that injured shoulder from when he'd been wounded last summer, and Lieutenant Goodin has been riding him about holding his head up straight, and that's what happened."

"Thanks, Lige." Jesse said. "I'll go talk to Lieutenant Goodin."

Logan looked about the camp and finally found John Goodin at the mess tent, drinking coffee.

"Well, I'm back, Lieutenant," he said in an even tone. "How've things been going since I've been gone?"

"Nothing out of the ordinary, Captain, except one of our men is, — ah — is in the brig for being AWOL."

"Really? Who's that?"

"It's a man you probably don't know, Captain. His name is Johnson, I think."

"Oh, yes. Sidney Johnson, is it? Was he gone long?"

Goodin hesitated, "Just a couple of days. Last week he didn't report for roll-call, didn't report for work detail, and skipped evening roll-call and the next day I placed him under detention for you to review."

"Would you mind coming with me to talk to him? This doesn't seem right. We need to know what he was doing during that time."

"I have some work back at the camp to take care of, Captain. Could it wait?"

"No, Lieutenant Goodin. Johnson needs to know that we work as a team, and we take these things seriously. I want you there to support me, and to confirm or refute his story."

Goodin sat for a moment, apparently trying to think up an excuse for not going with the captain. Then he stood and without a word, and just looked at Logan, as though resigned to accompanying him to the city's jail which had been serving the army's needs for a detention facility. They rode the distance into the center of Knoxville and entered the court building. A police officer was at the desk of the jail.

"I'm Captain Logan and I understand you have a man named Johnson from Company "H", 7th Ohio here."

The officer looked at a log book. "Sorry, Captain, there's no such name on the books."

"Is it possible he has been here the last couple of days, but has been released or transferred somewhere?"

The policeman turned a page and examined the names listed. "Not by that name, Captain."

"I wonder if we could look over the men you have in custody. He may have been listed by a different name," Captain Logan was becoming suspicious. The accounts he had received from Lieutenant Goodin and Sergeant Hawkins differed significantly and he was anxious to clear up the confusion.

"Certainly, Sir, but the only two army men that are here have been formally charged by their company commanders and misidentification is virtually impossible."

Lieutenant Goodin had become obviously nervous and addressed the officer, "Officer, is there any other holding facility within the area of occupation? Are there any neighboring towns or villages with a jail?"

"Not that I know of, Lieutenant."

About that time the police chief emerged from an adjoining office. "Can I help you, Sir?" he asked, addressing Logan.

"Yes, Chief, I was told there's a man here who's been arrested for absence without leave, but he doesn't seem to be in your lock-up." Then turning to Goodin, he asked, "Lieutenant, who was it that brought him in?"

"It was, — it was Sergeant Hawkins, who I told personally to bring the man here, Captain."

"We're sorry to have bothered you, Chief, Officer," Logan said, addressing them in turn. "I reckon we'll go back and verify this story with the sergeant responsible for bringing the man in."

By this time, Lieutenant Goodin's face was flushed and he was sweating profusely. "Damn that Hawkins. I knew I shouldn't have trusted him with that prisoner. He probably let him go. I know him and Johnson have been awfully friendly over the past few weeks, and I'll just bet that he didn't even lock the man up."

"What do you mean, 'let him go'? Before I found you, I talked to Sergeant Hawkins when I first rode into camp and it was he who informed me that Johnson had deserted. He didn't say anything about him returning and being detained."

Goodin was astounded. He looked at Captain Logan in disbelief. He was caught in a lie that was completely unnecessary, except to serve the purpose of avoiding criticism for his harassing Johnson. "Hawkins is lying, Captain. He must have let Johnson go just to discredit me."

"This just isn't like Hawkins to disobey a direct order," Logan muttered. "But the police officer at the jail said they haven't got Johnson on record at all."

They rode back to the company camp, where Sergeant Hawkins was standing out in front of the headquarters tent with a second man. It was Private Sidney Johnson.

"Captain," Hawkins said, "Private Johnson decided to come back on his own. He said he started east, but it occurred to him after a couple of days that he was better off here, even facing discipline for AWOL."

"Johnson," Captain Logan said without conveying any threat, as he dismounted from his horse, "you probably realize you're going to draw some time in the brig, but I'd like a word with you before we go any further. Come on over here with me." He led the man toward his tent.

"Captain," Goodin said nervously, "I really need to talk to you before you get involved in this."

"I'll only be a few minutes, Lieutenant. I need to talk to this man immediately. Just give me a moment or two."

"Don't you see what's happening?" Goodin exclaimed. "There's more here than meets the eye, Captain, and you'll need to hear me out."

Logan walked over to where John Goodin was standing, put one hand on Goodin's shoulder and said quietly, "Lieutenant Goodin, stand down. I'll be with you momentarily."

Upon entering the tent and seating the private, Logan turned and went back outside, looking for Lieutenant Goodin. "Where's the lieutenant?" he asked Hawkins.

"I think you'll find him out behind your tent, Captain," Hawkins said with a faint smile.

Jesse stepped around the tent only to see Goodin's back, disappearing past a tent nearby. He shook his head in disgust, and returned to the front of the tent. "Sergeant, find Lieutenant Goodin and tell him to be at my tent in fifteen minutes."

He went back inside and sat down near the nervous soldier. "How long do you reckon you've been away, Soldier?" was his first question.

"I reckon it's been about five or six days, Captain. I'm really sorry, I just wasn't thinking, I guess."

Logan questioned Private Johnson for about fifteen minutes, confirming the version of his absence conveyed by Sergeant Hawkins. Johnson explained that he had left the camp via the pontoon bridge and had headed east through Greenville and Elizabethton, where he had stopped, looking for some sort of way to support himself during the journey. At Elizabethton, he had encountered an elderly couple whom he found to be friendly and they had fed him and allowed him to sleep in their barn for the night. The name of the couple was McIlroy, and Johnson had recalled a George McIlroy having just joined their company from Elizabethton.

"Well," Johnson concluded in his account of his adventure, "those folks know you, an' said they had a lot of respect for you, Captain, and were so kindly, I suppose I had a change of heart an' decided to come back to camp an' jus' face the music. The idea of two or three months dodgin' both armies on my way home didn't look near as good by then."

Logan had known the McIlroys in the past and the story was not only believable but verifiable, and, after calming Johnson's fears, he told him to report back to Sergeant Hawkins, but remain close by for further questioning. Goodin was waiting outside the tent by then, and Jesse invited him into the tent and asked him to have a seat.

After a couple of minutes, Jesse, in as calm a voice as he could manage, said, "Now, Lieutenant, what was it that you were going to tell me?"

"What did that man tell you?" Goodin asked immediately. "You know he and Hawkins were pretty close for the past few weeks and I can just bet they've cooked up a story between them that makes this thing look like it's all my fault."

"Why did you tell me Johnson was in the brig? He hadn't come back in last Thursday at all, had he? He said he got as far as Elizabethton and met a family I know up there, and decided to come back on his own. What got into your head to lead me off on that, 'in the brig' story, John? I just can't figure you out."

"Are you calling me a liar, Captain?"

"Well, let's go back over this story and maybe you can tell me who's lying, Lieutenant. When I got back into camp, Hawkins tells me one story, Johnson tells me essentially the same story, and you give me an entirely different version. What's going on?"

Goodin was flustered, "I told you that those two have been real cozy for the past few weeks, and I have an idea Hawkins let Johnson cut out for his own personal reasons and didn't think I'd find out. Then, when I checked the roll-call he cooked up a phony story to hide his own crime."

"Then what was that 'in-the-brig' story all about? Here we have an insignificant little matter of a man going AWOL for five or six days, and you make up a cock-and-bull story, and for what reason? What were you thinking? You and I have danced around this thing, now, for the past two or three hours just because you couldn't bear to tell me the truth. On its face it looks like you've just created a lie out of some personal concern, but, giving a bit, just a bit of credibility, you and I are going back to Elizabethton to check out Johnson's story."

"Another thing, Lieutenant, why were you hanging around the back of my tent back there, when Johnson and I were sitting down to talk? And, what was it that you had to tell me that was so important when I wanted to talk to Johnson? What was that all about, Lieutenant?" Logan was gratified that he had controlled his temper in this, just one of the many confrontations that had erupted between him and John Goodin.

Goodin jumped to his feet and looked down at Logan sitting in his camp chair. "I'll not be treated like some kind of liar, Mister Logan. If you want to bring charges against me, I'll face you anytime in a court martial, but it's clear you've just been out to get me ever since you came back to the company, and I want a hearing. That's all, I want a hearing!"

Logan knew that a matter of an officer lying about a man going AWOL for six days did not deserve a court martial. He stood and moved between Goodin and the front flap of the tent, blocking any inclination Goodin might entertain as to walking out on the confrontation.

"No, Lieutenant, there will be no court martial. This matter will just go on company record as one more thing you've done contrary to good discipline, and the penalty will just be recorded as a verbal warning. You're free to ask for a transfer to another company, if you feel you've been unfairly treated, but it's not worth pursuing outside this tent at the moment. Now, you go tell Sergeant Hawkins and Private Johnson I want to see them."

Goodin, already angry, bristled at being ordered to perform a menial task that the captain could have done for himself, if he'd just turn around, step out of the tent, and call the two men over, but he maintained his composure and left the tent. Hawkins and Johnson were a few yards away, talking together.

"The captain wants to see you two," he mumbled as he walked past them.

When the two soldiers entered the captain's tent and stood waiting for him to speak, the air was electric with tension. "Sergeant, I want you to put this man on report for failing to respond for roll-call the days he was absent. There will be no further disciplinary action taken at this time, but Johnson, I want you to know that this behavior is not to be tolerated in this company, and it is only owing to the good graces of your sergeant and lieutenant that you're not facing more severe punishment. You're dismissed!"

Johnson had been in the army for over two years, long enough to know that he had been subject of some sort of special leniency for reasons he didn't quite understand, but he wasn't complaining. He saluted and left the tent. Sergeant Hawkins remained.

"Captain, was there anything more you needed of me?" he inquired.

"No," Jesse settled back in his camp chair and smiled. "I think we've settled the matter successfully. "Submit a report on the incident, and note that it resulted in a verbal reprimand. And, Lige, keep this whole thing confidential, just between us. I want to see what kind of rumors circulate around the camp."

Lieutenant Goodin had gone back to his own tent in a dark mood. He had been caught in a lie and blamed his captain for the entrapment. Logan had bested him again, and John Goodin was sure that the whole scenario had been contrived between Logan, Hawkins, and possibly Private Johnson. If there were some way to get rid of Logan, he could resume command of the company and, if engineered right, perhaps even get a set of captain's bars for himself. He would have to be a little more subtle, however, than he had been when he shot Captain Frank Davis. Making a habit of shooting one's captain was not the way to gain a promotion.

Two days later, it was time for the recruitment squad to go back to Carter County and Washington County to resume their efforts. After discussing the matter with Lieutenant Goodin, Jesse directed Sergeant Suttles to gather a squad of the newer recruits to go with him. He noted to the sergeant that he would like him to see that Privates Adam Gainfield, Billie Waldron, Steven Rathsburg, Eli Morgan, and George McIlroy were part of the squad. The long trip, made on horseback required a day and a half, and the men and horses in the squad were well worn when they reached the town of Elizabethton. Again, they went their separate ways to their respective homes, but before parting, Jesse called Eli aside.

"I think we're having 'lodge', tonight, Eli," Jesse confided, "and I'm gonna go. 'You going?"

"Holy cats! I'd plum forgotten about lodge, Jesse. Sure, I'll see you there. Do you think they'll have supper, before?"

"They always do. 'About six o'clock."

Kennedy Masonic Lodge was located on the second floor of a downtown building owned by John Mundolf, and was well heated when Jesse and Eli met at the door. "We'll just walk in together and see the looks on those fellows' faces when they see you in a blue uniform." Jesse said.

The reaction was predictable. Surprise was registered on the faces of all but a very few of the men in the dining room.

Turner Carnahan, president of a local bank and a subdued secessionist, was one of the first to greet the two men. He just shook his head. "Will wonders never cease?" he said with mock disgust. "What have I done to deserve such disappointment? One of my own trusted allies now wearing the regalia of a foreign government! Brother Logan, when we asked to have those fellows in Richmond give you your third degree, we should have conditioned it with the promise that you wouldn't go converting loyal sons of the Confederacy to your devious Union philosophy."

"Brother Turner," Jesse responded in like humor, "Brother Eli's conversion started the day he joined the lodge. Yours should be taking effect any day, now."

Other members of the lodge gathered around to shake hands with the two men, and wish them both well. Two of the younger members of the lodge, having been unaware of the fact that both Jesse and Eli were members, were eager to talk to them and learn what they could about the presence of the Union forces in the valley.

After supper the men attended the formal business meeting of the lodge and the two long-time missing members were duly introduced. Both Jesse and Eli stood for a few moments and thanked the lodge for their warm welcome, and sat down. After the meeting was concluded, the two younger members approached Eli and inquired as to how they could join the army.

"That's what we come to town fer," he said in a friendly manner, "but let's wait till t'morrow and we'll work on signin' you'uns up."

Over a period of four days between Johnson, Washington, Sullivan, and Carter counties, the squad had recruited another nineteen men and their goal was almost achieved. Jesse calculated the strength of Company "H" was then about eighty-two. They returned to Knoxville with their new recruits and Sergeant Suttles escorted them over to the recruitment station where they were sworn in.

Logan and Eli Morgan had enjoyed their association during the recruitment ride, and Jesse was gratified that any old hostilities that had haunted them in the past were, in fact, passed. On their ride, they had had a chance to discuss some of the problems of the company, and Eli demonstrated a keen awareness of the delicacy of Jesse's situation, but also the discretion to keep it confidential. Captain Logan had also gone with Private McIlroy to his grandparent's home and confirmed the account Sidney Johnson had delivered as to his activities during his absence from the company.

On his return to Knoxville, Logan was summoned to regimental headquarters and General Haskell's office, where he received orders to fill any vacancies in his ranks from other partial companies and report to Fort Nelson for recruit training. Company "H", and four other companies had acquired enough new recruits to justify what would be a rather difficult march back through Cumberland Gap, especially in early March.

"Would it be possible for me to go home for a day to Carter County and tell my family what is happening?" Logan asked.

"Certainly, Captain. Contact Captain Justice, "M" Company, and tell him to watch over your unit and prepare them for departure in your absence, and I'll confirm it with him in due time."

The 'home-for-a-day' would require almost a week with travel time, and Jesse went back to his command and explained the orders to Lieutenant Goodin.

"You'll report to Captain Justice, "M" Company, for the next few days, Lieutenant. He'll provide you with the needed information to fill out our complement. It will only be about eighteen or nineteen men, from what I see on the roster. I expect we'll be leaving shortly after I get back. See to it that we have sufficient mounts for the two of us, and provisions for the trip. Oh, and Lieutenant, see if it would be possible for us to take the cars through Chattanooga and Nashville, otherwise the men will have to march most of the way."

"Does this mean I'm relieved of my command, Captain? I have served well and faithfully until you came to the company as its new commander, and I see little reason why it will be necessary for me to answer to another commander with no more experience than I have and very little more than you."

"Lieutenant, I'm not going to quibble with you about this. We are going to have to trade some of our seasoned men for some new recruits, and there are other matters that will need coordination with other companies. Captain Justice is prepared to deal with these matters, and I'm asking you to cooperate with him. Is that too much to ask?"

Put in those terms, Goodin was ill prepared to object. "Whatever you want, Captain," he replied.

As Logan was leaving camp which was on the west side of Knoxville, he rode through the town, on his approach to the pontoon bridge across the Holston River at the east end of town. Though he had visited the town occasionally several times, his familiarity with Knoxville was sketchy and he found himself riding along Cumberland Street, instead of his usual route along Main Street. As he surveyed the buildings, he noticed one which displayed the name of the business as 'Wilkins Insurance and Real Estate', bringing back the memory of his encounter with a Mr. Wilkins, when he was enroute to Cairo, back in 1861.

"*I wonder —*," Jesse said to himself. He got off his horse, tied it to the available hitching rail, and went through the front door of the shop. Sure enough, there sat the man who had befriended him on the steamboat to Clifton, Tennessee before the war started.

"Yes, Sir, can I be of service?" Steven Wilkins asked, rising from behind a desk. "What can I do for you, — err Captain?"

"Yes, Mr. Wilkins, if you would be so kind, you might tell me when the Masons meet this month," Jesse said, removing his hat.

Wilkins said nothing for a few moments, examining his guest with an obvious look of perplexity. Then Jesse's height and fair hair pricked his memory. "You're the young man on the boat," he said. "You're that young man, — that Logan, that I met back before the war, aren't you? My land, Man, it's good to see you! You're the one who asked about joining the Masons and, if I recall, promised to notify me when you were to receive your 'third degree'. Am I right?"

"Well, yes, Steven, you're right, but when I received my third degree, the timing and conditions were against my notifying any of my friends, and the circumstances were a little, well, — a little unusual." Jesse went on the describe the meeting at Randolph Lodge in Richmond and the conferral of his 'third degree'.

The two old friends sat in the real estate office and, for the period of thirty minutes, got reacquainted.

⸺⸻≫‹‹()››≪⸻⸺

After Logan had left camp, Lieutenant Goodin called Eli Morgan into his tent. There was the old rumor circulating about the camp that it had been partly owing to Morgan's efforts that Logan had been captured and sent to prison, back in 1862.

After some small talk about Morgan's experiences over the past months, Goodin broached the subject of Morgan's feelings toward Logan. Having been aware of the tension within the company, Morgan was uneasy and somewhat noncommittal in his response.

"I have always had a soft spot in my heart as to the plight of the southern people being unwillingly subjected to the abuse of authority by the abolitionists up north," Goodin confided. "I appreciate the fact that you've joined the Union army to try to end this war, but I'm sure you share my views as to the unfairness of it all."

Morgan said nothing, but nodded his head, ostensibly in agreement with the lieutenant's argument.

"Now, you've probably seen the way the captain, Captain Logan, often abuses his authority and demeans some of his subordinates in the course of the day, and I'd like your feelings as to how we might relieve the tension in the ranks. With your experience as a member of the Confederate army as well as this one, you must have some ideas."

"Well, Lieutenant, I never gave it much thought up till now," Morgan was stalling for time, as he hadn't seen anything remotely comparable to that which the lieutenant was suggesting. "How d'you think I'd be able to he'p? I'm jes' a buck private and my word don't carry much weight."

Goodin thought for a few moments. He had never been privy to the history that had prevailed between Logan and Private Morgan, or the friendship that had developed between them. "I'd like you to keep track, if you will, of any observations you may have as to the captain's handling of the affairs of the company and report back to me if you see anything questionable going on. The 'general' has commissioned me to keep an eye on Captain Logan and report any questionable activity or abuse of authority," he lied, "and I'll need someone in the ranks with some military experience to help."

Eli was dumfounded. In the first place, he had no interest in the disagreements among the higher officers, but in the second place, he had come to admire the company commander, starting with his friendship with Lily, Sid Coster, Adam Gainfield, George McIlroy, and most of the other Carter County recruits, and thirdly, he was dismayed at the disloyalty the lieutenant had demonstrated toward his captain. And in all events, Jesse was his friend.

Eli didn't blink an eye. "Lieutenant, I'll do my best. I wasn't too happy in th' Rebel army, and I ain't be'n in this one long enough to draw up any c'nclusions, but I'll keep my eyes open, I will. I surely will keep my eyes open."

It was as noncommittal a response as Eli could have fabricated, but Goodin interpreted it as a full investment in his plot. "Thank you, Private Morgan. I won't forget this. Your service to the cause is much appreciated. I'll mention your offer to help to the general."

"What cause? What general?" Morgan thought to himself. *"This man is out of his mind. I think he's just too big for his britches; just another Napoleon Comapart like we used to have back in my Rebel days."*

⸺◦《◉》◦⸺

On Jesse's return to Knoxville, he found that there would be no railroad train available, and the new training regiment would have to make their way on foot. The march north was, as expected a grueling and uncomfortable one. Major Chase had been placed in charge of the expedition, and a train of twenty-two wagons had been detailed to carry the needed supplies. It was February, the roads through Cumberland Gap were spotty and, in places, washed out, and the men were, at times, required to contribute to maintaining them so that the wagons could pass. Picks and shovels were the introduction by the Army of the Ohio to their new recruits.

Major Chase was not excessively demanding of the soldiers, so the progress was understandably slow. They arrived at Camp Nelson on the eighth of March, it being the designated training ground for the XXIII Corps.

Eli Morgan had intended to share with his captain the conversation he'd had with Lieutenant Goodin, but discretion and lack of opportunity had prevented it. Morgan kept the matter to himself, uncertain as to the loyalties of his fellow soldiers, though the sentiment in the ranks seemed to favor Captain Logan unanimously. Logan was not only a fair man, but also had a reputation as one who would risk his life for a cause to which he was committed, and that kind of a reputation scored high in the minds of his men.

Major Chase's command, now a training regiment, would be staying at Camp Nelson for anywhere from two to four weeks before being assigned to the field. Captain Logan, after settling in to an assigned encampment, called his three subordinates together on the second morning of their stay.

"Gentlemen, you recall the techniques employed by this command when we were first sworn in, and we trained under Captain Sullivan and Sergeant Davis and — of course — Lieutenant Goodin, and I thought at the time we were being overworked and abused by all the marching and drilling we were being subjected to. I think Lieutenant Goodin can attest to the fact that I, for one, was not always the epitome of submission to the rigors of training, but I assure you, Lieutenant, that training paid off in the long run."

"Sergeant Hawkins, you remember the time those bushwhackers ambushed us when we were coming in from scouting, and we both dove for cover without hesitation? That was mostly from our reacting to the training we were given under Sergeant Davis. That's the kind of thinking I want to instill in these men. I'll tell you men right now that we will have to temper strict discipline with personal concern for the welfare and concerns of the men, but that is all part of the same package. Get to know your men and let them know you are interested in keeping them alive."

"When Captain Davis was a sergeant, he had a saying I'll never forget. 'It's just another hill towards home', he'd tell us when we set out on a mission, and that's the attitude I want you to convey toward our troops. Your concern for their welfare isn't just settling arguments, teaching maneuvers, or helping write a letter home, it's also teaching the value of teamwork and being alert in times of stress and danger, and — of course, — marching in step on the parade ground, which is sometimes the toughest part of our job."

Turning to Lieutenant Goodin, Jesse asked, "Lieutenant, do you have any thoughts you'd care to express? Any questions?"

"No, Sir," Goodin quickly responded as though he was totally bored with the conversation.

"Do you two sergeants have anything you'd like to say?'

"Yes, Captain," Sergeant Hawkins responded, "we're going to need some non-commissioned officers in the troop, and I think we should be discussing qualifications. There's a couple of men, especially the more senior members, that I'd like to propose for promotion to corporal. Also, that man Morgan, Eli Morgan, has shown some initiative during our march. He might be someone to consider."

"You know," Jesse said, "it might not be a bad idea to promote one or two of the Carter County men. Are there any other of those men who have shown some smarts, someone other than a former Rebel? Lieutenant Goodin, what do you think?"

"Yes, Sir," Goodin replied. "That man, Morgan might be a good choice."

The four men discussed several options and presently settled on four names. Eli Morgan and Adam Gainfield were among those named.

The Army of the Ohio of 4,500 men, in which Logan's Company "H" had been serving had just been reassigned to Major General John Schofield's XXIII Corps, Army of the Ohio, bringing it to 15,000. It was General Grant's plan to give General William Sherman command of that corps, along with Major General George Thomas's Army of the Cumberland (50,000 men) and the Army of the Tennessee (35,000 men) under Major General James McPherson.

General Sherman was then assigned the mission of pursuing Confederate General Joseph Johnston's forces throughout the south and decimating them wherever and whenever possible. Particularly, Sherman was to work toward the conquest of Atlanta and eventually Savannah, Georgia.

The XXIII was still positioned at Knoxville, but by the first week of April, 1864, the four 'training companies' were ready for duty and the XXIII Corps was ready to move south.

In the process of preparing the company for the move, Logan encountered Eli Morgan during an idle moment, and Morgan mentioned he'd like a few minutes of the captain's time. Unobserved, Logan and Morgan walked off away from the hearing of the other members of the unit.

"Jesse, I be'n needin' to talk to you ever sence we left Knoxville," were Morgan's first words when they found themselves alone. "That-there Lieutenant Goodin, he ain't yer fren', you know. I think he's a-gunnin' fer yer hide."

"What are you talkin' about, Eli? Ever since we got here t' Camp Nelson, he's been pretty good. He was somewhat out o' sorts a time back, but we've been getting along pretty well since we got here." He was uncomfortable sharing his relationships with fellow officers in this manner, but Eli had become a trusted friend and he decided to hear him out.

"What I'm talkin' about is this, Jesse. When I first got in, he calls me out an' says t' me I should keep an eye on you an' let him know ef I ever thought you was out of line, doin' somethin' you shouldn't or bein' mean to th' men, an' he says th' gen'r'l wants to know about all y'r're doin' that ain't right, an' well, you get the picture."

"Did he tell you who the general was?"

"No, he didn't. He jes' says he was grateful fer my service to th' cause, whatever that is, and fer me t' keep my eye on you. I said I would, an' I have be'n, you know," and with that, Eli grinned, reminiscent of the day he and Jesse had first met.

Morgan went on, "In the Rebel army we had a name fer them fellers; Napoleon Comaparts, we'd call 'em. Allus got some kind of angle to git some of the other fellers in trouble."

"That son-of-a-gun," Jesse murmured, half to himself, then, "Eli, just keep this to yourself. I reckon I don't need to tell you that, 'cause you've been doing it anyway, but don't let it bother you. If the lieutenant asks you, just string him along. But, thanks for the warning, anyway. — I thought I had him coming around. Well, we'll see. What'd you call him, Napoleon Come-apart?"

※

At Camp Nelson, Company "H" received an additional lieutenant, Charles Connant. Connant was a newly commissioned lieutenant, having distinguished himself at the battle of Fort Sanders. Logan had recommended Elijah Hawkins for the position but regimental command had their own way of handling the matter.

Though retaining their original title and still assigned to the 7th Ohio Volunteer Infantry Regiment, Company "H" was commissioned a mounted infantry company as Jesse had planned, and had also explained to some of the men when they signed in. They were issued the new version Spencer carbines, and often referred to themselves as 'dragoons'. Independent of the cavalry, their main job was to harass the enemy infantry and their picket lines with hit-and-run attacks.

From Knoxville, Schofield's XXIII Corps moved southwest, pausing at Cleveland, Tennessee May 4th and 5th, where Schofield spent time conferring with his generals and with General Sherman, and they then moved south into Georgia. The Army of Tennessee, CSA, under Joseph Johnston, numbered a little over seventy thousand as opposed to the northern forces at almost one hundred thousand, but tactically, since it was Johnston's job to defend and Sherman's to attack, the northern numerical advantage was somewhat neutralized. Johnston was dug in at Dalton, Georgia, and it was there Sherman proposed to attack.

Sherman originally placed Schofield's corps on the left, or northeastern end of the battle line, Thomas, with his fifty thousand took the center, with McPherson holding the right. At times, they would use the XXIII Corps as a strike force, wherever needed, as that army was, by design, much more mobile than the other two, often using the cavalry under General Stoneman as well as several companies of mounted infantry similar to Captain Logan's.

Approaching Dalton, Major General Schofield was ordered to march on Varnell's Station, with directions to feel toward his right to maintain contact with the left wing of General O. O. Howard's fourth Corps of the Army of the Cumberland, under Thomas, and with Colonel E. M. McCook's cavalry connecting the two. Captain Logan was to coordinate with Colonel McCook in the gap between the two corps, and especially seek out and neutralize southern pickets, cavalry units, and videttes.

General Sherman was confident. After a winter of planning, his forces were on the move, well supplied and very strong. What was more, Confederate General Joe Johnston was seemingly idle, save for the usual light skirmishing by his cavalry in Schofield's front. On the early days of the campaign, Sherman's aggressiveness, the Northern army's superior numbers, and Johnston's seemingly lack of activity, were already evident and working, promising Union success.

Confederate General Johnston had established breastwork along the long, high mountain of Rocky Face Ridge and eastward across Crow Valley. Sherman decided to demonstrate against that position with his two northeastern columns while he sent McPherson's Army of the Tennessee south through Snake Creek Gap to the right, to hit at Resaca and the Western & Atlantic Railroad and sent General Joe Hooker's XX Corps around his army's left to the north to attack Confederate General Hood at Dalton.

On May 9, McPherson, passed through Snake Creek Gap, advanced to the outskirts of Resaca, where he found Confederates strongly entrenched, and pulled his column back to the gap.

On May 10, after consultation with his three commanding generals, Sherman decided to take most of his men and join McPherson to take Resaca. The next morning, discovering the Union Army retiring from their positions in front of Rocky Face Ridge, Joe Johnston moved his Rebel forces south in order to strengthen his entrenchments at Resaca. General Johnston was one of Jefferson Davis's most skilled generals, and defensive tactics were his specialty, but with only 70,000 troops as opposed to Sherman's 100,000, his skills were constantly tested.

And so the waltz went on. The Battle of Resaca lasted two days, May 14th and 15th, followed by a small skirmish at Armuchee Creek, with Joe Johnston performing predictably, wearing his attackers down little by little, as Ambrose Burnside had done between Sweetwater and Knoxville, and William Rosecrans at Corinth. Unfortunately for him, though, this was not as fast as he was depleting his own forces, which he could ill afford to do.

On July 17, 1864, Jefferson Davis relieved Johnston with John Bell Hood.

Hood was a different type of general. He was impulsive and often over confident, but he had convinced President Davis that he was capable of stopping Sherman. Hood often attacked when he should have dug in or even retreated. He often underestimated his adversaries and, even when his odds were in his favor, he sometimes failed to give due attention to the entrenchments and field preparations of his own forces, or those of his opponent, but he was a soldier's soldier. He was an inspiration to his men. His unflinching courage had cost him the use of an arm at Gettysburg and the loss of a leg at Chickamauga, and it was necessary for him to be strapped into the saddle to ride, but he was a gallant warrior.

By July 28 Sherman's army stretched in a crescent around the northern defenses of Atlanta. He also planned to cut off the railroad supply lines from Macon, Georgia, into Atlanta, thus forcing the defending army to withdraw without a direct assault. To accomplish this, Sherman directed what was one of his easternmost armies, under Maj. Gen. Oliver O. Howard, to move to the west, completely around the rest of the Union lines to the far southwestern side of Atlanta where the railroad entered the city.

Hood, anticipating General Howard's maneuver, rearranged his troops to oppose the Union army. He planned to intercept them and catch them enroute and unprepared. Although he was outnumbered by the main Union army, he felt that a surprise attack against an isolated portion of the enemy could succeed.

The armies met on the afternoon of July 28 at a place near Ezra Church. Unfortunately for Hood, the maneuver was no surprise for General Howard, who had hurriedly established a defensive position at Ezra Church and was dug in by 11:00 a.m. His troops were waiting in their trenches when Hood arrived.

Also, Hood had not done enough reconnaissance. He underestimated the number of Union troops against him and ordered what turned out to be an uncoordinated attack, failing as it assaulted the Union army's breastwork. Although the Rebel army managed to stop Howard from reaching the railroad line, they were sorely defeated. In all, they lost almost 3,000 on the Confederate side versus 642 on the Union side.

After failing to envelop Hood's left flank at the Battle of Ezra Church, Sherman still wanted to extend his right flank to hit the railroad between Macon and Atlanta. He moved General Schofield's XXIII Corps from his left to his right flank and sent him around to the north bank of Utoy Creek along with General John Palmer's XIV Corps from George Thomas's Army of the Cumberland.

On the morning of the August 7th, the Federals again began to advance on the entrenched Confederates at Utoy Creek. They encountered no resistance and found the Confederate works empty, withdrawn from the lines overnight. The victorious federals happily took their place in the line of defensive works, that now stretched from the defensive perimeter around Atlanta, ranging to the southwest, to protect the railroads at East Point.

The mounted infantry companies were kept moving constantly. When General Schofield's army was held in reserve, the mounted units were used to locate and suppress the enemy picket lines and to act as scouting units. When Schofield's XXIII Corps was deployed, the mounted infantry companies were used as scouts, and advanced vidette forces. Their losses were minimal, as they made use of the range and rapid fire that the Spencer carbines furnished them, staying clear of the less well-armed Rebel forces, with few exceptions.

For newly recruited soldiers, Company "H" was recognized as a unit contributing a great deal to the success of the army. As a point of pride, the men adopted the unofficial title of 'Logan's Dragoons', initially among themselves, though the nick-name quickly spread among the other mounted infantries, who adopted similar titles.

Captain Logan rode with the men in the company, and his old scoped Spencer allowed him even longer range than the issue carbines the men carried. Esprit d' corps was strong among the men, most of them hailing from East Tennessee now, and the few others virtually adopting that region as their nominal home. Eli Morgan and Adam Gainfield, both corporals by then, were often called upon to lead small scouting parties.

28

FRANKLIN

By September 1864, after Sherman had seized Atlanta, Confederate President Davis, senior military strategist for the Confederacy, seeing an opportunity try to take pressure off his Army of Tennessee and also to possibly take back control of the middle Tennessee and its rich agricultural land and vital rail lines, reassigned General Joe Johnston to protect the Atlantic states, and moved General John Bell Hood back into the interior to attack the Nashville area.

General Grant, no amateur at strategy himself, consulting with General Sherman decided that Sherman had sufficient forces to proceed north through the Carolinas and sent General George Thomas' Army of the Cumberland back to Nashville to occupy the already strong defenses there. Then, after due consideration, Grant dispatched, his Army of the Ohio consisting of the XXIII Corps under Major General John Schofield, and the VI Corps under Major General David Stanley to Franklin, Tennessee, to protect that region and eventually unite with General Thomas. Sherman didn't think much of General Hood, and considered him an impulsive commander, acting without due restraint and caution, and assured General Grant that those three generals, with the aid of Major General George Stoneman's 3,000-man cavalry corps, could handle Hood without much trouble.

Unfortunately, as often occurs in the military, Major Generals John Schofield and David Stanley, both of whose ranks dated from November 29, 1862, found themselves constantly bickering. Though General Sherman had assigned to Schofield the senior command responsibility, David Stanley, three years older, and having graduated from West point a year earlier that Schofield, considering himself the senior officer, often challenged Schofield's orders and a counterproductive argument ensued. General George Thomas in Nashville, senior to both men, was frequently called upon to settle some petty argument.

As the scene played out, Cavalry Commander George Stoneman had also been promoted to Major General effective that same date, but he had the good sense to recognize and accept John Schofield's assigned authority.

As Confederate General Hood's reassignment to Tennessee was originally his own idea, he was eager to make the move, feeling that there were literally thousands of loyal Rebels in Tennessee to bolster his army. He had, at that time, somewhere around 35,000 men, and felt he could not only distract Sherman's march north, but also retake a vital portion of the former Confederacy. He started a move back north through Dalton along the route the two armies had taken only months earlier as Sherman was pursuing the Rebels south from Chattanooga, but Sherman chased him farther west into Alabama.

Hood entered Florence, Alabama in mid-November and immediately started north. His objective was to get across the Duck River at Columbia and position his Army of Tennessee (CSA) between Schofield and Thomas to interrupt Schofield's supply line and prevent his and George Thomas' armies from uniting.

After Sherman had pushed Hood's 35,000 man army into Alabama, he assigned that pursuit to Schofield and returned to Atlanta, giving up his own supply line from Chattanooga to press on to Savannah. There he would be able to use the navy for supplying his needs through that port. Keeping for his campaign 60,000 men divided into two armies, Sherman struck off for Savanah, his men foraging as they went, and 'living off the land', prompting the song by Henry Clay Work, "Marching Thru Georgia", in 1865.

Captain Jesse Logan's Company "H", with the rest of the regiment, headed for Pulaski, Tennessee, one of Hood's new targets. A skirmish at Pulaski slowed Hood, but other than that did little to stop him or change his objectives. He managed to survive the Pulaski confrontation with little damage and move north. The next encounter with General Schofield's 23,000-man army was at Columbia, which was fought November 24–25. Schofield was seriously outnumbered but was fighting a retreating strategy and executed it wisely.

The battle included a Confederate diversion as part of a maneuver designed to cross the Duck River further east of Columbia, to circle around and intercept the Union's line of communications with Nashville. As Hood's army advanced northeastward from Florence, though, General Schofield's force quickly withdrew from Pulaski to Columbia, arriving on November 24, just ahead of Maj. Gen. Nathan Bedford Forrest's newly arrived Confederate cavalry.

The Federals built two lines of earthworks south of Columbia, while skirmishing with enemy cavalry on November 24 and 25. Confederate

General Hood advanced his infantry on the following day but did not assault. To organize his forces and gain strength, he made demonstrations along the front while marching two corps of his army to Davis Ford, some five miles eastward on the Duck River. Schofield correctly anticipated Hood's moves, but foul weather prevented him from crossing to the north bank of the Duck until November 28, leaving Columbia to the Confederates. The next day, both armies marched north for Spring Hill. Schofield had slowed Hood's movement but failed to stop him.

On November 29, Hood nearly cornered Schofield's force near Spring Hill, but Schofield was able to extricate his men from that trap and reach Franklin, a distance of about ten miles. Seeing that he was all but trapped, Schofield executed a daring night march to try to skirt Hood's army. The attempt would probably have been doomed to failure had it not been for the fact that Hood, suffering residual pain from his old injuries, had consumed a strong dose of laudanum that evening and passed out for the night. His commanders, aware of the movement of the Feds heading north, tried unsuccessfully to wake General Hood, and were reluctant to act without his direction allowing the Federals to pass unmolested. Schofield's army made the ten-mile trip without incident, and at times the marching men were even close enough to Hood's forces to see their campfires.

Upon arriving at Franklin, Schofield occupied and improved some old fortifications on the southern outskirts of town, with the army's rear protected by the Harpeth River.

Gaining confidence as he chased the Federals north, General Hood arrived the following day and launched a massive frontal assault on the Union lines. The attack was repulsed with heavy casualties including six Confederate generals killed, including Hiram Granbury, John Adams, States Rights Gist, and Patrick Cleburne. Cleburne, in particular represented a severe loss for the Confederacy, as his skill and daring as a general had been instrumental in several southern victories during the course of the war.

Captain Logan's Company "H", with several other companies of Mounted Infantry, was reassigned to the Union cavalry brigade, under Major General Stoneman, to be deployed east of the main battlefield, where Confederate General Forrest was again attempting to turn the Union left flank. The opposing cavalry units were almost equal in size and intense fighting occurred throughout the day. At times, Logan would have his men dismount when they had the opportunity to repel some of the raiding Rebel horsemen, and just as quickly, they would again mount up and make an attack on some isolated Confederate cavalry position, either mounted or on the ground. Logan used Corporal Adam Gainfield as banner bearer and had him stay close to give his troopers some semblance of organization, as the confusion on the field was intense. He also directed his two lieutenants to be immediately available to convey directives to the squads and communicate with higher command.

That evening, as the members of the troop straggled back into camp, Logan called his lieutenants and sergeants together for a strategy meeting. John Goodin had not yet returned to camp, and Logan found it odd, as Goodin had been fairly close to him throughout most of the day. Nevertheless, he proceeded with the meeting, intending to brief Goodin in person when he arrived back in camp.

It was after eleven o'clock when Goodin came riding into camp, and after he had secured his horse, he retired to his tent without talking to anyone. Captain Logan went to the lieutenant's tent and rapped on the tent-poll. Goodin didn't respond, and Logan was puzzled. He rapped again, a little more firmly, and this time, Goodin came to the front of the tent and pulled the flap back. "What do you want, — Captain?" he inquired in what Logan interpreted as something of dismissive tone.

"Are you alright, John?" Logan inquired. "When you disappeared this afternoon, I was worried. I thought maybe you'd been thrown from your horse, or something."

"I'm fine. I just took a wrong turn coming in, and it took me a little bit out of the way. I'm fine."

"Alright. Get some rest. I need to set out some plans for tomorrow, but it can wait till morning."

The following morning, Goodin remained in his tent and out of contact with the rest of the company, and Logan proceeded to set the company's mission for the day without him. Presently, when the horses were saddled and the men mounted, Goodin emerged from his tent, apparently prepared to ride with the company, but giving no explanation or apology for his tardiness.

Mid-day on the 30th, the Company was out on patrol when Lieutenant Goodin directed Captain Logan's attention to a wooded hill some half a mile from their location. He said he'd seen what appeared to be some activity at the fringe of the grove of trees. Captain Logan, calling his lieutenants together laid out a strategy to investigate Goodin's suspicions; the hill where he felt a portion of the Confederate cavalry would possibly be sequestered. He sent Lieutenant Goodin and Sergeant Suttles with six troopers ahead to survey the field. The bulk of the company would then follow and proceed according to the lieutenant's recommendation as to whether the move was safe, and how best to attack if, in fact, an attack was indicated. He also sent two messengers to report to the regimental commander as to where they were planning to attack.

After about twenty minutes, Logan led the company in the direction of the objective grove. Catching sight of his scouting party, he rode in their direction. He found Sergeant Suttles and the six privates out in the middle of a cotton field, waiting as he had ordered, but Goodin was nowhere to be seen.

"Where's your lieutenant?" Captain Logan inquired.

"I don't know, Captain," Sergeant Suttles replied, "He told me he was going to look over that grove of trees and rode off. I don't know where he went. He told us to stay here."

The grove Sergeant Suttles pointed out was almost a quarter-mile away, and appeared too small to hide any sizeable force. After learning from Suttles what he knew of the wooded hill, he directed Lieutenant Connant to wait in place with the company for reinforcements.

With Corporal Morgan and Private Parsons, Logan rode off toward the grove. He didn't like being separated from his company but was worried that Goodin may be in trouble. Nor did he think it wise to dispatch a soldier of a lower rank, since Goodin seemed to have set off on his own as though he didn't want an escort, and sending a corporal or private would be counterproductive. Logan began to suspect a plot.

Riding toward the little grove of trees and vines, Logan couldn't see any movement. When they were within about 75 yards, he motioned for a halt. Examining the scene, he learned nothing.

"Do either of you fellows see anything?" he asked.

Receiving a negative reply from both men, Logan said in a low tone of voice, "Well, let's ride over to the right a little way and try to get in a little closer."

No sooner had he spoken, when a shot from the grove rang out, and Parsons cried, "Hey, I'm hit!"

The three men tumbled from their horses and Logan demanded, "Where are you hit, Parsons?"

Feeling his upper left arm, Parsons replied, "I don't think it did any damage and I don't feel any blood, so the bullet must have just clipped my arm. It surely hurts, though"

Logan and the other two men knelt on the ground. "Here, take the horses, Parsons, and move back out of range. Eli, you come with me, but stay down."

The two men crawled toward where the shot had come from, anticipating further shooting, but none came. Jesse had pulled his rifle from its scabbard and now peered through the scope to try to get a better idea of who had fired the shot. Another shot sounded, but the two men were low enough in the dried cotton stalks that it missed them completely.

"Eli," Jesse said, "you take my rifle and move over to the right, there, and when you get out twenty feet or so, scope that grove, and see if you can spot whoever's shootin' at us. Stay low, though. I'll try to decoy them from here and you take them out if you can."

Morgan did as he was told, and when he was fifteen or twenty yards away, Jesse saw his cap appear just above the dry cotton. Nothing! No shot, no movement in the grove. Logan moved a bit through the cotton stalks, partially revealing himself, but there still was no reaction from the grove.

Meanwhile, Lieutenant Connant, watching the action through binoculars from a low hill, 200 yards in the rear, sent Sergeant Hawkins and a squad of eight troopers in the direction of the shooting. "Stop short about fifty yards," he told the men, "then go in on foot and try to contact the captain and find out what he knows."

As Hawkins rode off with his small squad, a cavalry unit of about 120 riders came across the hills from the west and their leader, Captain Kittleman, pulled up where Lieutenant Connant was standing.

"We've been sent up to give you a hand, Lieutenant. Where's your captain?"

"He's just over that low rise to the east, Captain, He went out to look for one of our riders and it looks like he ran into one or two hostiles. I just sent a squad over to check on his welfare. He ordered me to stay here and wait for reinforcements, and if you think we should, I'd recommend we go over there and try to take that little grove where the shooting seems to be coming from."

The newly arrived captain, after examining the grove with his binoculars, ordered his own company to divide into two squads, one skirting the grove to the right, one going around to the left, and what remained of Company "H", about seventy-five men, would charge the grove head on.

The right-hand squad would set up a perimeter south of the grove, the frontal squad would ride in directly, with the left-hand squad holding the eastward and northward escape. Connant's company, being the most familiar with the scene would take the van and pick up Captain Logan and the forward scouts on the way. The attack was designed for speed, as it was felt that surprise and an aggressive approach would be the safest. It was also decided to use plenty of noise by the frontal squad to alert the scouts and distract those in the grove as to the presence of the flanking squads.

As the attack commenced, with plenty of shouting, Jesse Logan, realizing what was going on, kept watch over the grove of trees for any defensive movements. He ran back to where Parsons was holding his horse and waited for his company of reinforcements unit to catch up.

Watching the grove, Logan caught sight of just one man in a blue uniform skirting the tree line. He jumped onto his horse just as the frontal attack squad approached, and waving his arms, motioned for them to stop. Lieutenant Conant and the lead group pulled up at Logan's signal.

"What's going on, Captain," Lieutenant Connant immediately inquired.

"Our shooter looks like none other than "H" Company's own first lieutenant, I think," he replied. "Let's go on in and check him out. There may be some Rebels with him in those woods."

At a slower pace, the company rode on toward the grove of trees to seek out the missing lieutenant. For a short time, all seemed quiet, and then the woods erupted with gunfire. Jesse was struck in the left shoulder, and two horses went down, also hit by rifle fire. One other trooper from Company "H" was struck and killed instantly. At that moment, Captain Kittleman, the commander of the reinforcement squad came forward.

"Company, dismount," he ordered. "Form a front. Take cover. Captain, you're hit. How bad is it?"

Logan had managed to stay on his horse, but was dazed by the shot. "I don't know, Captain. Take my command, if you will. I seem to be losing a lot of blood."

"I agree. You'd better get back to the infirmary. We'll send a couple of your men back with you as an escort. We can handle this thing."

Logan knew he was in trouble, but didn't want to take the time to have his wound looked at out on the field when there was a battle brewing. "Thank you, Captain. I'm sure I can make it alright."

Then, as a second wave of nausea swept over him, he said, "Well, maybe that would be a good idea, and a good idea to have a couple of men with me."

Meanwhile, Eli Morgan had been watching the woods from where the firing had come and spotted a figure in a blue uniform crouching just inside the tree line, where he appeared to be conversing with a grey-clad soldier. Morgan had a clear shot at the man in blue and didn't hesitate. Taking deliberate aim, he fired the Spencer and the man collapsed. He recharged the rifle's chamber and fired again as the second man, trying to duck behind some trees, was also hit and fell to the ground.

"Two for two," Eli muttered, "courtesy of a converted Reb. That's fer my fren' Jesse Logan."

Inspired by Morgan's marksmanship, the men from Company "H" rose without orders and charged on foot toward the wooded hill. The small Rebel force of about forty men was outnumbered, and on seeing the Federal company rushing their position, they turned and ran, some on their horses and some on foot. The divided Union forces from behind the grove gave them no place to go, and whoever was not killed or captured within the woods was rounded up as they fled.

By the end of the day, Bedford Forrest retired and General Stoneman called the Union cavalry commanders together to assess their losses and plan for the next day's fight. The meeting held a positive tone, with only about fourteen casualties reported, including Captain Logan, wounded, and the death of Lieutenant Goodin and the other trooper from Company "H". Logan was still at the infirmary and Lieutenant Connant attended the meeting in his place. It appeared that General Schofield had decimated his opponent through well positioned fortifications and the gallantry of 23,000 men.

General Hood's losses were astounding, but he was a fighter and refused to stand down. Despite the battered condition of his army, he followed Schofield north arriving outside Nashville on December 2.

The fortifications south of the city were much as Logan remembered, but realigned by General Thomas's diligence and skill. Safe in the city's defenses, always deliberate and cautious, he slowly prepared for the upcoming battle. Under pressure from General Grant to finish him off, Thomas finally attacked Hood on December 15. After two days of battle, Hood's army crumbled. As a fighting force, John Bell Hood's army was relegated to history.

As Christmas approached, the army was ordered to establish a bivouac northeast of the city, and Captain Logan was able to return to duty, his collar bone having been broken and the subclavian artery ruptured, he was extremely weak, but otherwise his mobility was unimpaired. His prompt return to the regimental infirmary had probably saved his life. The days were occupied in reassessing the army's losses and waiting for orders for further assignments. General Grant didn't take long to make his decision as to the Army's mission.

By late December, General Stoneman, commander of the Army of the Ohio's cavalry corps, was detailed to proceed to South Carolina and report to General Sherman, who was moving north in pursuit of General Joseph Johnston's Army of Tennessee, (CSA). Stoneman's destination would be Columbia, South Carolina, but it was clear that General Sherman's army was moving rapidly north. By this time, it appeared that General Johnston's intent was not so much to stop Sherman as it was to join with General Lee, and either defend Richmond or the Confederate government, if it should be forced to relocate.

The route the Union corps was to take would be bifurcated. The main portion, under General Stoneman, would go east through Georgia, while General James Wilson would take a smaller brigade of about 2000 up the Tennessee Valley, to mop up any vestiges of Confederate troops, go through Knoxville, Greenville, and Elizabethton, and up the Watauga Valley to eventually reach Boone, North Carolina, where they would reconnoiter and make further plans. With General Wilson's permission, Jesse would go ahead of the regiment, stop at Doe River Cove, and rejoin them as they marched through the valley. When some of the soldiers learned of Captain Logan's plan, they requested leave to do the same, and received the general's permission.

The soldiers took the train as far as Morristown, and then, obtaining their horses which had also been sent by the same train, rode on to their homes, agreeing to reassemble at Elizabethton six days later.

On the train there were several officers, and while they seemed to gravitate toward one another, they also made sure they spent time with the men of their various companies. Jesse, while uncomfortable from his shoulder injury, managed to engage in conversation with his men and also some of the other east Tennessee men that he knew.

Talking to a group of the Company "H" men, Jesse and a few others managed to get together. Eli Morgan took Jesse aside at one point and, in a tone of confidence, said, "Capt'n, I s'pose you knew it was me, shot that Lootinant. That Napoleon Come-apart."

"Yes, Eli, there were plenty of men who saw what was going on back there. I reckon there were a few of them who would have been inclined to do the same thing, but from that distance they probably weren't sure who it was. Anyway, in a situation like that, it could just as easily have been a Rebel in a Yankee uniform. Why — why are you concerned?"

"Well, he was one of our'n, an' I was a'wonderin' if I could get into any trouble fer shootin' 'im."

"Put it out of your mind, Eli. From what I was told he was lookin' like he was pretty possum with a Rebel officer when you took them down. Like I said, from that distance I'm surprised you even knew it was him."

"With that telescope sight you got on that rifle, Capt'n, I knew what I was doin'."

"Well, don't worry about it. Eli. The army has plenty of other stuff to spend time wondering about without bothering about who shot who out there in the woods,"

29

WATAUGA VALLEY, 1865

"That shot I took from the Rebs, or whoever it was that shot me, didn't even knock me off my horse but I feel like the whole Rebel army just used my body for a parade field." Jesse complained to his grandfather the morning after he had arrived home, while he and Henry Kellar watched as the first real snow of the season fell on the 31st of December.

"Who do you think you are, Jesse?" Henry Kellar responded. "Adam told me you were losing blood in a steady stream. He said your uniform was soaked all the way down to your knees, and then some. You're lucky to be alive. You can't lose that much blood and bounce back like you just got a cut finger. You take it easy, Son. Your grandma's cooking and Olivia's nursing will get you back in shape so's you can get back to fightin', though it looks like there won't be much more, if what I hear is true."

"Well, it's nice to be home, anyway."

Olivia had come into the room and tried to appear cheerful for Jesse's sake. "I'm so happy to have you here where I can keep an eye on you. With all you've been through it surprises me that you've survived as long as you have. I was talking to Eli Morgan and he told me what happened. By the way, you and he seem to be the best of friends these days. I thought it was he that threatened to string you up when he captured you back in —. What was it — three years ago?"

Jesse grinned, "Grandpa knows," he said. "Did I tell you back there on the road to New Castle, Libbie, that being a member of the Masons makes a good man better? Well, Eli is an example of that old saw. We ran into each other up on Cedar Mountain, and when we learned we were both members of the Masons, we managed to strike up a conversation that has changed Eli from an uncertain Rebel to a get-out of-my-way Yankee."

"Just how did you find out he's a Mason?"

"I can't tell you. It's a deep dark secret."

"Oh, you and your Masonic secrets! Grandpa, you can tell me, can't you?"

Grandpa Kellar held out his hands as though defending himself from an unpleasant subject. "I don't know what you're talking about, Olivia. I don't know any secrets," he replied with a sly smile on his face.

"Men!" Olivia exclaimed in mock disgust. "You're all the same." And with that, she stalked back to the kitchen.

Jesse changed the subject. "Grandpap, how has business been since the Feds are here in east Tennessee?" he asked. "I see you've got quite a stack of railroad ties and I hear the wagon-spoke mill working. How is the market?"

When harvesting hardwood for the production of wagon spokes, it was necessary to cut and stack the logs to season for a period of two or three years, then cut and split them down, following the grain of the wood, into pieces of suitable size to be 'turned' on the spoke mills. Unfortunately, stacking the lumber in the forest left it subject to theft. The favored process to avoid such losses was to leave the harvested logs in their original large size, making theft difficult, but there was always a period of a few weeks, when the owner was cutting the logs into short sections, making them attractive to thieves. Henry Kellar had experienced occasional thefts of lumber from his forests, which he then found necessary to buy back from different sources to keep his mills operating. This was annoying, frustrating, and expensive, but was often the only way he was able to operate.

"I now have a market for both the ties and the wagon spokes, Jesse," Henry Kellar said. "Dan Stover had some contacts with the Federal government and before he died he put me in touch with an agent who says they're willing to buy all I can produce. I've had to change some of the knives on the spoke mill, but that was no trouble, and the nice part about it is, I'm getting paid in real money. While that siege, or whatever you call it, was going on, my Confederate market dried up completely, but it all worked out for the better. Now I have a big stack of ties and hardwood, and I should be getting a good price, to boot. How's that for good luck?"

"God is watching over you, Grandpa. He's brought you through some tough times and now you're reaping the rewards."

"I think you're right, Son, but I think the same goes for you."

Grandpa Kellar got up and stoked the fire in the fireplace and when he looked back toward his companion, Jesse had fallen asleep in his rocking chair.

Olivia had slipped back into the front room where Jesse and his grandfather were sitting. "Grandpa," she said in a low voice, "I've sent word for Lily Venable to come over for a bit, this morning. Do you think it would be alright to wake Jesse? We've been doing some checking around and she's identified the leaders of some of the home guard companies, and I was thinking it might be a good idea to talk things over with Jesse and see what he thinks we ought to do with the information."

"Of course, Honey," Grandpa Kellar responded. "Jesse would be upset if you didn't wake him up. He'll just need some quiet time every so often to get his strength back."

As if on cue, Lily Venable rode into the front yard of the Kellar home with Daniel, the hired hand Olivia had sent to fetch her. She got off her horse, tied it to the hitching rail, brushed the snow off her shoulders, and greeted Olivia, who had gone to the front porch to meet her. By the time they returned to the living room, Jesse had wakened from his nap and gone to the door. Greetings were exchanged and the three friends sat down to talk. Henry Kellar excused himself, but Olivia and Lily invited him to stay.

"You'd be lots of help, here, Grandpa," Olivia protested. "You may have more to contribute on this subject than you think."

The conversation focused on the fact that, though the regular Confederate army had vacated the area of East Tennessee, there were remaining, many irregular units functioning in and about the several counties. With the help of Eli and Adam, Lily had put together a list identifying Owen White, The Jackson Home Guards, as one company; J. M. Crumley, commanding a second; James Witcher, The Zollicoffer Mounted Rifles, as the third; M. H. Morrell, the fourth; and J. F. Trevitt, commanding the fifth company. Evan Stance, and The Holston Rangers, was the sixth and The Harris Guards, whose leader she didn't know, the seventh.

There was also the East Tennessee Mounted Militia, Company "B", the only 'militia' company in uniform. They were mostly Sullivan County men, but it had been Company "B" that Adam Gainfield had been assigned to and he had identified G. R. McClellan as the current commander of that unit. Jesse knew some of the names, but considered the list very useful, as Lily had also noted the counties or regions where the bands operated.

This last, Company "B", seemed to be by far the largest, and the most well organized and recognized unit. They had uniforms and enjoyed the closest connection to Confederacy's overall command, but all, or mostly all, of the home guard companies operated essentially independent of any attempt to consolidate or organize them by the Confederate government. From the first part of the war Confederate General Buckner, then General

Bragg and President Davis accepted this situation, as they posed little interference with the regular army and were very little financial burden on the government.

When the region was under Confederate control, these irregular companies could sustain themselves with seizures of loyalist property which they managed to then resell, or also with extortive demands on some of the businesses in the area for 'protection from depredations', real or imagined, inflicted by similar groups of 'Lincolnite' militia. Individually, the members of these companies were farmers, laborers, drovers, tradesmen, and the like, who could partially support themselves individually, but with the presence of Federal authority, their lifestyle was suffering without help from the spoils of war they had become accustomed to.

'Captain' Evan Stance, commanding the Holston Rangers was a man extremely hostile to the Federal government in general and to General Grant in particular. He had fought under Grant during the Mexican-American War, and developed a strong dislike for then-Captain Sam Grant. Stance was now simmering with a burning hate toward the occupying Union forces and to the 'Lincolnite' population that he saw as benefitting therefrom.

Throughout the years of Confederate occupation, Stance had assembled a mounted company of about fifty men and, like the other home guard forces, had managed to terrorize the local loyal population while avoiding any serious conflict with the regular Confederate forces. It was his band that had killed Lily's father and brother.

"General Tillson is still at Knoxville, as far as I know," Jesse mused. "And the Fourth Tennessee is with him there. I know Colonel Mike Patterson, who's been in command of the Fourth since Dan Stover died, and I'm thinking we can interest him in chasing down some of these renegade companies of Rebel home guard and get them out of our hair." The First, Fourth, and Thirteenth Tennessee Cavalry Regiments were made up of men almost exclusively from Carter, Johnson, and Sullivan counties' original East Tennessee (USA) Militia, and were especially useful in ferreting out local irregulars of the residual Secessionist population.

Early in January, Jesse, accompanied by about ten of his company from the Watauga Valley, made the two-day ride to Knoxville. While his shoulder seemed to be healing nicely, he was still weak from loss of blood and the ride was far different from those he'd made the previous year scouting for the army's food supply.

At Knoxville, he learned that the Fourth Tennessee was scheduled to be sent to hold the mountain passes into North Carolina until East Tennessee was sufficiently relieved of the presence of the Confederate forces. The irregular Rebel forces were still strong enough to constitute a considerable threat to the Union Army as well as the civilian population. Logan supplied Colonel Patterson with the intelligence he'd gained through the efforts of Eli, Adam, Olivia, and Lily, as to the local Rebel irregulars.

"This information will be of considerable help," Mike Patterson admitted, "I'll pass it along to General Tillson. As a matter of fact, I have to go see the general this morning, and I'd suggest you come along. I know he'd be happy to spend a few minutes with you, as you seem to be fairly well informed on the Rebel activities hereabouts. We have been discussing placing a small regiment in and around Elizabethton, and it might be that this would work in with keeping you there, perhaps in command. It would probably require a commander with the rank of Lieutenant Colonel, and you'd fill the position nicely."

Logan didn't know what to say. He was anxious to renew active duty, but assuming command of a garrison was somewhat intimidating.

"We could promote Lieutenant Connant," Patterson continued, "to take command of Company H, and, as for an adjutant, — well, we'll have to talk that one over."

Sid Coster, after having worked as a guide for almost a year with Dan Ellis, had formally joined the Union army as a lieutenant with Company A, 13th Regiment, Tennessee Volunteer Cavalry, and it occurred to Logan that Sid might be available, as the 13th was at Knoxville at that time. He broached the idea to Colonel Patterson.

"Colonel," he said, "You may know Lieutenant Sidney Coster with the 13th Tennessee. I've worked with Lieutenant Coster in the past, and I might suggest he be put in charge of Company "H", my old unit, then give me Connant, as adjutant. What would you think of that idea?"

Mike Patterson thought a moment. "Do you think he has the experience to handle the job, Colonel?"

Logan didn't miss the obvious allusion to a possible promotion, but his only reaction was a trace of a smile. "I've known the man for many years, Sir, and, for one thing, he's a logical and mature thinker. For another thing, I've seen him in action, and there's no one I'd trust more with my life than Lieutenant Coster. I think he'd do well in command of a company."

"What if we would give you Coster as your adjutant and keep Connant in charge of Company H? Connant, being familiar with the company could be well suited to that position. How does that sound? The other two companies would also consist of local men under the command of George Johnson and Geoffrey Hazzard, both east Tennessee natives."

————————)(()(————————

It was January 8th, and Logan, despite his feeling of fatigue, proceeded with enthusiasm to execute Colonel Patterson's plans. The Fourth Tennessee Regiment was scheduled to deploy toward various assigned mountain passes but the new team of garrison command worked feverishly to assemble their own working unit. By the next day they had put the Elizabethton unit in shape on paper, and would use the time in transit to organize the three companies that would constitute the garrison there. They managed to get started on the morning of the tenth, Logan riding in an ambulance, as riding his horse would be both excessively tiring as well as making his paperwork awkward. As with their trip west, they stopped two nights in Morristown and in Greenville, and arrived late in the afternoon at Elizabethton.

In Elizabethton there was a small community hall which they could use for an armory and two neighboring buildings that were empty. The town council, with the consent of the owners of the two buildings, readily agreed to assign the buildings to the garrison, for which General Tillson had agreed to commit to a nominal rent. After tending to the necessary work of seeing his regiment situated, Jesse mounted his horse, and rode the few miles to Kellars Crossing. It was approaching evening at the Kellar house, lamps were lit, and there was obvious activity inside the house. He got off Max, tied him to the hitching rail and, bracing himself against the rail and the porch handrail, he paused a moment, then started up the steps into the house. Olivia saw him getting off his horse, and when she noticed his hesitant pace, she rushed out of the house.

"Jesse! Sweetheart," she cried. "Are you alright?"

"Madam," he said with feigned seriousness, standing as erect as his fatigued condition would allow, "if you don't mind, you will kindly address me with due respect using my proper title, 'Lieutenant Colonel Logan', and not just nicknames like 'darling' or 'sweetheart', or stuff like that."

In her haste, Olivia had not noticed the silver leaves on his shoulders, and when he mentioned his new rank, she stepped back and examined them. "Jesse Logan, you rascal! What in the world happened? You keep disappearing from my sight one day and come back a week later with a promotion. Are they sending you off to Petersburg, or some other dangerous assignment?"

Jesse proceeded to tell Olivia, along with Henry Kellar as well as Jesse's Uncle John Kellar, and Jesse's two cousins, Frederick and John, Jr., who happened to be at the mill that day, about his experiences the past week, and what it portended for their future.

Then, in a tone of desperation, he said to her, "Now, Miss Olivia, — you wouldn't marry a lowly private or corporal, you wouldn't marry me when I was a lieutenant, or a captain, so now, will you marry this-here Lieutenant Colonel? Please?"

The audience, who by then included Jesse's Grandmother Emma, was enthralled and broke out with some clapping and encouraging comments.

Olivia was speechless for a few moments, then she threw her arms around her fiancé and whispered in his ear, "I thought you'd given up on me. Of course I'll marry you, Darling, — ahhh, I mean — Lieutenant Colonel Logan."

The wedding took place January 21st and was held at the armory, as the small church the Kellar family attended couldn't handle the crowd. Jesse's stamina had substantially returned and he made a handsome groom. Olivia, in a pink gown, was stunning. Sid Coster was best man and Lily was Olivia's bride's maid. It was a military style wedding, complete with an Honor Guard. The street passing in front of the armory was closed and virtually the whole town of Elizabethton turned out.

Elijah Simerly, erstwhile colonel in the 13th East Tennessee Regiment and former sheriff of Carter County, had built a grand new home in Doe River Cove the past year, and invited the new couple to occupy his guest house as a honeymoon suite. The honeymoon lasted two days.

—((•))—

The Holston Rangers had been well aware of the developments in the Watauga Valley, so far as the Logan Regiment was concerned. One of their members, Judd Spurgeon, attended the marriage ceremony as Lily and Eli had observed, and they made sure Colonel Logan was introduced to Spurgeon, a blacksmith from Watauga Flats. Spurgeon was properly solicitous and complimentary toward Logan, wishing him well in his marriage as well as his ventures in the valley. Privately, he was also somewhat impressed by the

Elizabethton crowd that was in attendance, as well as the appearance of the military presence.

The Spurgeon family had been in east Tennessee since shortly after the American Revolution, having been awarded territorial land as a reward for their patriotism in that conflict. The family was now liberally distributed over the entire region. Jesse Logan's fraternal grandmother was Lilia Spurgeon, and it was probable that he and Judd were related somehow, but in their brief conversation neither man brought the subject up. Eli had briefed Jesse on the fact that Spurgeon was working with Evan Stance and was undoubtedly at the wedding for the purpose of gathering intelligence.

———— ◆ ————

On Monday, January 23, Lieutenant Colonel Logan called a meeting with Captain Coster, the three company commanders, and their lieutenants for the purpose of laying out the expectations and objectives of their occupation of the valley. At the top of his list was the capture and control of the irregular Confederate home guard companies remaining in the region. There was still a Union garrison in Knoxville, but that was a hundred miles away and the irregulars were active in all the eastern counties of the state and into North Carolina. He was also concerned with establishing a more permanent camp site as well as the guarding and policing of the current bivouac area, but his main objective was to suppress the guerilla activity in the region.

After some introductory comments Logan started the meeting with what he saw as the regiment's main duty. "We have a lot of talent in this room, I think, both as to the duties expected of us and also as to the identity and tactics of the people we're looking for," he began, and then proceeded to explore the question of the difference between civil and military violations.

"Since the irregulars, as they are called, are of a paramilitary stripe. How do we treat them if they are caught, — say, — in the commission of some kind of offense against the civilian population? Do we have the authority to take the action normally expected of the civil policing authorities, or do we really care about that? We're commissioned to capture and control military units — organizations — companies, or whatever you call them, but these little bands are essentially crooks; civilians in or out of uniform."

He was greeted with blank looks around the room, so he continued. "I wonder if we should work out an arrangement with the sheriff, Ben Sheppard, and if we do catch some of these men in the commission of a civil crime, we should try to have them prosecuted as civilians as well as imprisoning them as hostile enemy soldiers. In the absence of civil authority, a military tribunal can legally deal with any offense that affects our presence, here."

Logan then proceeded around the room soliciting comments from each officer. He introduced the list of companies and their commanders he'd had compiled and encouraged discussion as to any information anyone had on these people, as well as any additional Rebels any of his staff might be aware of. He had assigned Lieutenant Hawkins to take minutes of the meeting and watched as Hawkins filled page after page with notes and names.

At twelve o'clock, Jesse could see the officers were exhausted, and so was he. At times, there was order and decorum in the meeting but at other times it was all confusion, which he was obligated to control.

"Can I ask you men to come back tomorrow morning after Captain Coster and Lieutenant Hawkins and I sort out his notes? I think we've made a lot of progress, but I want to look over these minutes before I make assignments."

With that he dismissed the group and suggested they get some lunch. They broke into groups, mostly of those from each company and moved to the mess tent. Logan invited his four Captains and Lieutenant Hawkins to join him at lunch. After getting their food trays and coffee, the six men went to the table reserved for the regimental command staff.

"I have an idea rattling around in my brain that I'd like some feed-back on," he began. "My grandpap mentioned one day that he'd had several wagonloads of hardwood stolen and a few weeks later he learned about some fellow who had some similar loads up for sale. It turns out this man, as Grandpap learned later, was connected with Evan Stance."

"It's customary to let this type of lumber season for a couple of years or more, but with the constant need for spokes for the wheels of the wagons and caissons that are being used up so fast, the stuff has become quite important to the war effort. Grandpap says he leaves the logs in the forest to season, but when he starts to cut them into short lengths, it really becomes attractive to thieves. He can't afford to put guards on the stacks, as the thieves work in large numbers, and would most likely overpower and kill the guards."

He took a bite of the stew from his plate and a swallow of coffee, and continued, "Suppose there was a load of short-length hardwood out in a remote part of the country, — as sort of a bait, with a company of our men hidden in the underbrush. It would have to be well planned, but I think we could pull it off. What do you men think?"

The subject went around the table for a few minutes. It would be, as Jesse had mentioned, a civil crime but, if his notion was valid, executed by an irregular band of Confederate soldiers. Even if the sheriff wouldn't handle the civil crime, the army would have a goodly number of prisoners, possibly wipe out at least one of the companies of home guard, and make the others think twice before trying such a thing in the future.

"What if we took the sheriff with us and he could verify the fact that there was an actual civil crime committed? Then he could act on that crime." Sid Coster suggested.

Jesse scratched his jaw. "Alright, but do we really want civil prosecution? That only carries a few months in jail, and with the number of Rebels we are contemplating as being involved, the jails couldn't contain them. But, if we took them as military prisoners, we could ship them off for the rest of the war, anyway. But then, — if it turned out to be really just a small band of civilian thieves, we could still turn them over to the sheriff. So maybe you're right, Sid, maybe we should have the sheriff along."

Jesse and Sid visited Sheriff Benjamin F. Sheppard in his office and explained their plan. Sheppard agreed to send one or two of his deputies with the troopers, but Jesse cautioned him, "Please don't assign me a deputy yet, Sheriff, or even tell any of your men what we have in mind. You never can tell who's toady with whom in these parts, and to let the cat out of the bag too early could sour the whole deal. We're all kinfolk in these parts and you tell one person, he tells his wife or brother, and there goes our dainty idea."

The sheriff smiled, "I know what you mean, Colonel. I'll keep this thing under my hat for now, and when you're ready, just let me know when and I'll send a man out with you and you can fill him in on the details as you ride out to the spot."

Jesse had discussed his idea with Henry Kellar who suggested what he felt would be a suitable site in the forest about four miles south of Kellars Crossing along the Little Doe River. The site was a flat area on a tributary stream and surrounded by dense timber. It was accessible by a rough wagon road and the sides of the canyon were steep enough to make escape difficult. The bait was hardwood which John Kellar had felled two years previously, and was currently cutting into lengths of between two and four feet, suitable to be shaped into spokes, fellows, doubletrees, and other parts for wagons or caissons. The short sections made the material not only suited for wagon parts, but easy enough for thieves to handle, making it all the more attractive. John Kellar, Jesse's uncle, had hired several men outside his regular crew to cut and sort the lumber. He had also contacted a local teamster to move the stack to the Kellar mill the following week, giving a measure of public awareness to the fact that the lumber was in a condition to be moved.

So far, owing partially to the fact that, if stolen, the lumber would have to be hauled through a populated part of the county, it had remained intact, but that could change any moonless night.

It was late January, and on the 28th, a dance was scheduled at the armory, attracting many locals. The weather was clear, but there would be a new moon and the timing favored an attempt to execute a theft.

"Conditions are set in place," Jesse told his captains, "so as to make a theft as attractive as possible, without sending out invitations. Holding that party in the armory will make it look like many of our men will be tied up there, but I think we can get local civilians to handle the party."

Catching any such thieves would require a small squad hidden at the entrance to the canyon, with a company or two out of sight, but within striking distance. Then, after discussing the idea with Captain Connant, Logan decided that tying up two companies of his small garrison would not only be hard to maintain, but assigning extra companies might also alert the irregulars, so he felt he'd have to entrust the task to just one company.

The night of January 28, Captain Charlie Connant sequestered about thirty mounted men in a large vacant barn about half a mile south of the wagon road that led into the cutting site. The remainder of Company "H" he distributed on foot, hidden a short distance from the canyon entrance. He cautioned the men to equip themselves with warm clothing, as they may have to wait most of the night for the irregulars to emerge from the canyon with what the colonel had estimated to be four or five loaded wagons of stolen lumber. The closer to dawn the event occurred, the easier it would be to apprehend the main portion of the renegades.

A small squad of sentries was hidden closer to the entrance to the canyon, and when the irregulars entered the canyon, if that were to happen that night, those at the mouth of the canyon would alert the foot soldiers and send word to the mounted troops. The actual capture would occur as the irregulars emerged from the canyon.

Jesse had sent Eli Morgan to watch the house of Mack MacMurray, who was now a member of the Holston Rangers, to verify their suspicion that the theft would actually be attempted that night. Eli came back to the company at about seven o'clock with the report that MacMurray and three other horsemen had left Elizabethton shortly after dark. The men in the squad turned down their lamps and waited.

The hunch was good. The night was moonless and at about ten o'clock, two horsemen appeared with lanterns turned low. The squad of sentries held their concealment, but could hear the riders talking.

"I know this is the road. I he'ped ol' man Kellar when they was cuttin' this load, an' I was over here yistid'y. I knows this is the place," one rider said.

"Did you git in to see if'n the lumber is still there?

"Yep, it's still there, at least it was there yistid'y. H'it don't look like they posted no guard here-abouts, anyways. You wait here an' I'll go git th' company." With that, one of the riders rode off in the direction of Elizabethton. The other rider got off his horse, squatted on the ground, and lit a pipe.

Half an hour went by, and about forty riders and four wagons came from the direction of Elizabethton. They stopped at the mouth of the canyon. The voice of Evan Stance could be heard giving orders, directing those whom he expected to stay near the main road. The Federals had not expected him to post guards at the mouth of the canyon, and the pickets hidden nearby knew they would find it hard to get away to summon help. Adam Gainfield was one of the pickets, and when the main body of irregulars had ridden into the canyon, he hand-signaled the others in the squad that he was going to try to notify the squad of foot-soldiers and start the process moving.

His attempt was successful. He got away unnoticed, and the company began to execute Colonel Logan's plan. Stance had left four guards at the main road and they were quickly and silently subdued and led off to be tied to some trees some quarter-mile distant with two soldiers to watch over them. The Company "H" men on foot were deployed and half of the mounted soldiers moved quietly into the mouth of the canyon hiding in the trees just a few yards off the main road. The other mounted soldiers were kept in reserve. Logan had orchestrated the event so as to stop the Stance group as they emerged from the canyon and try for a complete capture, but he also gave instructions to the riders outside the canyon to watch for those trying to escape, and particularly Evan Stance, if he could be identified.

Three slow hours passed before sounds from up the canyon could be heard, announcing the approach of the irregulars. Logan had posted himself near the mouth of the canyon where the four guards had been left. As the irregulars approached with Stance in the lead, they stopped just short of the main road and Stance rode cautiously forward.

"Manny?" he called. "Manny are you out there?"

"Over here," Jesse responded in what he hoped was a voice similar to Manny's.

As Stance rode toward Logan, three riders closed in behind him but not being able to see them clearly, he assumed that they were his own men. Nevertheless, he had drawn his revolver. One of the trailing men turned up his kerosene lantern, and illuminated the scene enough for Stance to see what was happening. He immediately fired his gun in the direction of Jesse Logan, but missed. Jesse held his fire, concerned with hitting one of his own men, but Lige Hawkins had the presence of mind to spur his horse toward Stance, knocking him off balance. Stance vaulted to the ground and whirled to try another shot at his would-be captors, but both Hawkins and Logan had clear shots by then and fired simultaneously. Stance fell to the ground and lay lifeless. Lige immediately jumped from his horse and kicked Stance's revolver out of reach, and satisfied that Stance was lifeless, got back on his horse. Logan, in as loud a voice as he could summon ordered the Holston Rangers to drop their weapons.

"You're completely surrounded, men, and we don't want to kill anyone if we don't have to. Get off your horses and get over here, close to those wagons."

It was four o'clock in the morning and still dark. The only lanterns that had been lit were in the hands of the Union men, and most of the Rebels had no intention of being either killed or captured. The mouth of the canyon was obviously well blocked, making escape by horseback extremely risky. Almost as a man, the men of the Holston Rangers, vaulted from their horses and ran for the woods, but a small number, valuing their horses and tack more than their freedom, came forward and surrendered. Several more were captured as they left the cover of the forest, trying to escape on foot. Meanwhile, on orders from their Colonel, the Federals, as methodically as possible, searched the area for the fugitives, caught up the riderless horses, and tied them to any handy trees. Catching a strange horse in the dark with a lantern in one's hand is no easy task, and the process took till daylight to finish. Except for the nine who turned themselves in, the five caught trying to flee on foot, and the four guards previously captured, none of the Rangers were apprehended.

When the prisoners and horses were secured, Company "H" gathered around the captured wagons.

"Congratulations, men," Jesse announced. "We have a few chores to finish this morning and I'll have Captain Connant and Sergeant Suttles organize the company into squads. I know only about half of the irregulars were caught, but I think we made a serious dent in their operation."

Twelve of the troopers were assigned to drive the wagons to Kellars Crossing and secure the teams of horses. Two more, Barnaby Sloat and Adam Gainfield, were directed to borrow a buggy or wagon from Henry Kellar and move the body of Evan Stance to the town morgue. There would be reports made to Knoxville, and prisoners to care for. Deputy Sheriff McCaffrey, one of Sheriff Sheppard's most trusted deputies, was included in the activity as much as possible, in order to participate in any potential civilian prosecution.

Lily Venable was at the Kellar home when Jesse rode into the yard. She and Olivia came out to meet him.

"Jesse," Lily said with tears in her eyes, "Barnaby Sloat told me what happened back there. I know it's bad manners to thank a person for killing someone, but I'm certainly grateful to you for bringing that man to justice. It not only relieved my mind but it also took a load off my shoulders. I had planned to kill him myself."

"Oh, Lily," Jesse replied, getting off his horse and putting his arms around her, "that's nice of you to say, but it isn't your job to kill people. We're soldiers, and taking a life in the performance of our duties is expected of us, but it just isn't the job of a civilian, especially a nice person like you."

He then went over to his wife, hugged her tightly, and greeted her with a kiss.

"You survived another adventure, Colonel," she said with affectionate resignation.

———————⟫•((◦))•⟪———————

Lieutenant Colonel Logan's grand scheme netted him just one man deceased, eighteen prisoners, fifty-four horses, and four wagons filled with the bulk of John Kellar's hardwood. The next day the regiment was divided into three groups. Logan selected several volunteers from the regiment who would do the clerical work under the direction of Sergeant Shelby Smith. They would formulate an official report, try to identify the irregulars who escaped, and inventory the captured horses and equipment. The second group would tend the horses, tack, and any other property left behind, and the third group would be released to Sergeant Suttles for routine garrison duties, and might be called on to assist as needed. From the last group he also assigned four men to assist Sheriff Sheppard as needed.

Sheriff Sheppard had come to the armory asking what he was expected to do with his eighteen new prisoners. Logan greeted him and invited him into a small office, where there was a coffee pot on a small wood stove.

"Here's my problem, Sheriff," Logan explained. "These are local men, not legally attached to any recognized military unit, caught in the commission of a crime against a civilian that I, an army officer, virtually anticipated, even to the time and day. Secondly, they were acting under the direction of their leader, even though they were not, essentially, part of any official military unit. Thirdly, if charged with a civil crime they would stand trial before a jury of their friends and neighbors. 'Number four, I was so sure they would take my bait, I probably assigned more federal troopers than I really needed to catch about forty crooks, but only managed to bring in nineteen, and one of those died in the capture. Another thing, — the victim of this crime is not only a civilian, he's my own uncle.

I'm in a poor position as an accuser. Unless you object, we'll just release the whole bunch until we have had a chance to talk to the state's attorney."

The sheriff was smiling by the time Logan finished describing his dilemma, but then added, "You know, of course, Colonel, that these men and the ones that escaped can be charged with murder. Any time there is a death occurring during the commission of a felony, the people committing the original crime are also guilty of murder. That man, Stance, was killed trying to escape, and, as I understand, had also taken a shot at you or one of your men. Am I right?"

Logan thought for a moment, "You're right, Sheriff. That was all part of the crime, wasn't it? It was all part of the same crime."

"But here's another question," Jesse went on. "Suppose those men were part of a regular army unit. Would what they did qualify as nothing more than a military skirmish, and them just trying to commandeer materials necessary to supply their national interests and aims? The Confederate government could easily declare them to be regulars and neutralize any civilian charges, if they found out."

"You're out of my realm, Colonel, but I think your question could start a whole new discussion on military protocol."

It was time to pay another visit to General Tillson.

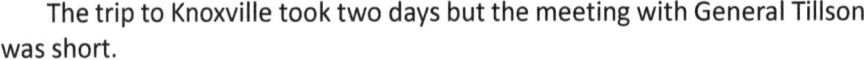

The trip to Knoxville took two days but the meeting with General Tillson was short.

"First, Colonel Logan," the general said after learning the reason for the visit, "my compliments on capturing Stance. He has been a source of consternation since the beginning of this war. Secondly, though, — I'd recommend that you parole the men that you captured, identify and arrest the others, parole them, and move on. We don't have the time or resources to pursue the prosecution process. The men you've caught, as you mentioned, are common citizens with families and occupations, and we need all the good will we can generate. With Stance out of our hair the Holston Rangers will, most likely, just cease to exist, especially if you can keep an eye on them individually. Can you do that?"

Logan had given the process considerable thought during his trip, and responded enthusiastically, "Of course I can, General. Many of those we caught as well as those who escaped are well known to various men from my regiment. One of them was a cousin of mine. It will be no trouble to neutralize them, I'm sure. I'm also quite certain we can secure promises of non-participation from most of them. And as for a murder charge against the entire irregular company, it was one of my lieutenants and I who actually shot and killed him. I don't see a murder charge holding up under those conditions."

"That will work alright, then, Colonel. Incidentally, the wire between here and Elizabethton is just about repaired and operating. That should save you considerable time and trouble. And one other thing, — you're Regimental Commander, now, and I'll trust you to use your own discretion handling matters such as this. Just keep me informed. That's all I ask."

"Thank you, General," Logan said rising from his chair. "Will that be all, Sir?"

"That's all, Colonel. Congratulations on bringing those men in, and have a Happy New Year."

—⫸⫷(❂)⫸⫷—

It was February 3, when Jesse arrived back home, and, after checking with his captains at Elizabethton, he rode out to Kellars Crossing. Daniel, the hired man, was at the mill and walked over to the Kellar home to take charge of Jesse's horse.

"You certainly have been busy, lately, Jesse," Daniel remarked. "But now, with those rascals caught up, things might slow down a bit around here. You know, though, I might be able to put you on to some of them as got away. I got folks all around the county, an' they'd be tickled pink to give you some names."

"Thanks, Daniel, but let me ask you something. You have a line on the men who made up Captain Stance's Rangers, and what do you think they'll do as a group now that Stance is dead?"

"I really think they'll jus' disband an' go back to their old jobs, that's what I think. What d'you think?"

"I have to agree. I've been thinking we could just catch 'em up, twist their tails a little bit, and tell 'em to knock off the funny business and get back to work. You know I have all their horses and saddles."

"Yep, I know. I he'ped put 'em away."

"I don't want to be too easy on them, Dan," Jesse continued, "but I really think we can work out something to neutralize 'em and maybe, just maybe, neutralize some of the other home guard companies around the region."

"'Big order, Jesse," Daniel said, shaking his head. "I really gotta give you credit for puttin' that bunch out'a commission. It was just last year, those guys done stole a couple of loads o' lumber from your granddad, an' then came an' sold 'em back to him an' there was nothin' he could do but play along."

"I know. That's what gave me the idea we pulled off the other night."

Jesse called a meeting of his officers, directing them to seek out those in their respective companies who had knowledge, no matter how remote, on the membership of the various little home guard companies around the valley. The week before, he'd had Sid Coster and Lige Hawkins organize the information that had been gained from questioning the eighteen surviving prisoners and from the searches made of the captured saddles and wagons. That information was used to identify as many of the Holston Rangers as possible, contact them, and gain additional information as to any other members of any of the companies. The fact that the Federals were holding fifty-four horses and four wagons was strong incentive for the escaped rangers to surrender.

The process became a virtual canvassing campaign. Word spread that the Federal troops posed no particular threat to the freedom of the irregulars, and as they were all east Tennessee men, gossip became a helpful tool, and information came into the headquarters without much trouble.

There were a number of holdouts among the most recalcitrant, but by the time the campaign had run throughout the month of February, about two-hundred of the irregulars from several companies had been arrested, interviewed, and paroled, after signing a promise to refrain from any further hostile activity.

The results were promising. News of the Confederate reversals in Virginia and the Carolinas helped persuade the hold-out secesh population that their hopes for independence were dimming, and cooperation with Logan, the garrison commander, being a local man, was not such a bad idea, after all. There were still isolated hostilities, but they were more often between men who, two months ago, had been die-hard secessionists, and currently had taken up opposing viewpoints on the matter of submission.

Rumors were rampant, one being that someone in the Stance camp had tipped off the Logan Regiment about the theft and lured Stance into a position where he fell into that fatal trap, while his cohorts escaped. Judd Spurgeon, the cousin who had attended Jesse's wedding, was suspected as the tipster, with the theory that he wanted to take over the Holston Rangers and this was his opportunity. Judd sought out Jesse at Elizabethton and asked to be locked up.

"Colonel," Judd said, after he and Jesse went into Jesse's office and Jesse had poured them each a hot cup of coffee, "You maybe didn't know it, but your grandma and my grandpa were brother and sister. Another thing you maybe don't know was that I be'n a part of the Holston Rangers fer about two years. Another thing you maybe —."

"Hold it, Mr. Spurgeon, —, or, maybe I should call you Cousin Judd, I do know all that, but what is this visit all about? Surely this isn't just a social call or a review of family history."

Spurgeon went on to relate what he'd heard of the rumor and that he feared for his life. "I'd think it would be safer fer me right now to be locked up in the county jail, rather than out there where I'd run up ag'in' someone who believed that baloney. I'm turnin' myse'f in, is what I'm doin'."

"Judd, we're not takin' prisoners. It's not our job to take civilians as prisoners of war, unless they're caught up in a pitched battle, and that thing out at Doe River, even though one man was killed, just doesn't measure up. Were you there that night?" he asked, knowing the answer.

"Oh, yes, I was there, an' when you hollered out to put down our guns, I was jus' a little bit behind the — the first wagon. You'uns got my best horse an' saddle an' my favorite huntin' rifle. I jumped off ol' Steamer an' took to the woods."

"Well, I'd let you have him back, but I don't think it would help your reputation any to be seen going back home with your best horse and all," Jesse smiled. "Tell you what I'll do. I'll give the town paper a story about that thing the other night, how I expected what happened, and how I don't want to cause any more grief in the valley. And I'll tell the folks they can get their horses back if they come in an' sign a promise not to do any more fightin', an' for them to break up their home guard companies. You know that's what we're doing anyway, and I'll just make it official. How do you think that would set?"

"Then, what about my horse?" Judd asked.

"Come back in a week or so, Judd, and we'll turn him back to you. It'll look better that way."

Spurgeon had calmed considerably with the assurance that his situation would be explained in the newspaper, and presently he finished his coffee and stood to leave. "You sure you couldn't lock me up for a day or two, just till the paper comes out, Colonel?" he asked, rising from his chair.

"Well, I'll tell you. You can work around here for a couple of days if you want to, and make it look like you're in jail, or you can go see Sheriff Sheppard and ask him. I don't run the jail, you know. But what you can do is go see my clerk an' sign a promise not to do any more fightin'. I should be gettin' a promise like that from all the irregulars I can, an' you could help if you'd talk to some of the men from your old company an' have them come on in an' make that move."

The two men shook hands and exchanged goodbyes. As an afterthought, Spurgeon offered, "I'm proud to meet you, ag'in, cousin. I be'n wonderin' what you was like, an' you're a alright guy, fer a Yankee."

"I'll take that as a compliment, Judd, but I wouldn't go around letting people know we're related. It still might not set so well with some of them."

While the story in the newspaper did not please some of the more radical loyalists in the region, it did resolve much of the hostility between neighbors and had an overall calming effect with the general population.

30

GENOA

A t 24, Jesse Logan had become a responsible and respected figure in his home town, the valley where he was born and where he had spent some of his most formative years as a teenager, studying under the watchful eye of his grandparents and of Mr. Putnam, his school teacher.

Returning to the valley as a Lieutenant Colonel in the Federal army, he encountered Mr. Putnam once or twice on the streets of Elizabethton, and his former teacher also attended Jesse's wedding in January. There they had an opportunity to chat for a few minutes. Mr. Putnam was impressed, if somewhat amused with Jesse's success in the army. "Mr. Logan, when you were in school, I was unsure as to whether you'd turn out to be the town clown or one of its more distinguished citizens. What has motivated you thus far in your young life to rise to such a responsible rank as Lieutenant Colonel? I'd guess you're one of the youngest colonels in the army, aren't you? You've probably passed up all the competition."

"Oh, no, not at all. There's a general named Custer who's probably about my age, and my friend Jim Brownlow is younger than I am, and he's a full colonel. But in this army, Mr. Putnam, I don't think there's any competition with anyone else, except a man's own capabilities. The thought often occurred to me that I would like to move ahead in the army and try to accomplish more than I could at whatever grade I held at the time, but I can't think of anyone that I felt that I was competing with. I think it was you who introduced me to the term, 'C'est le guerre', and that's been the rule, I think, as to who gets promoted and who doesn't."

"My first promotion was a result of my ability as a marksman, I reckon. I was assigned as a rifleman, partly because my brother David had given me a very accurate rifle when I joined the army and partly because I'd also developed some shooting skills as a hunter in Nevada. and here in Tennessee. 'Funny, it really made me uneasy to just shoot people, even enemy soldiers, because of my upbringing, I suppose. Even now, I don't like to think about it. I'm glad I'm a colonel, now, because that means I don't have to shoot at people for a living."

"You know, my principle reading material when I was in Nevada was the Bible, and in the first few chapters of Proverbs, it says that killing is not only wrong, it's foolish. I couldn't get that out of my head as a sharpshooter and it gave me some sleepless nights."

"The second promotion, I suppose, was because I burned down a gun factory in Lynchburg. The army needed a lieutenant and I was available. Then I managed to capture a Rebel colonel, and they made me a captain, and on it went from there."

Putnam laughed, "You haven't changed a bit, Mr., — err — Colonel Logan. I'll never forget the explanation you delivered in class about the 1794 Whiskey Rebellion, and I thought at the time I had some kind of exceptional person on my hands, and, as you may recall, after that we spent some extra time together to try to instill some wisdom and understanding into your thinking process. I do believe it worked, or at least I'd like to take some credit for your success. Even so, I see you haven't lost your sense of humor."

Olivia, seeing Jesse with the older man and seemingly enjoying his conversation, approached them, perhaps seeking an introduction.

"Mr. Putnam, I'd like to introduce you to my wife, Olivia, my confidant, and a profound influence in my life. Darling, this is Mr. Putnam, my school teacher and also a great influence in my late teenage years. It was Mr. Putnam's wisdom that gave me the basis for my attitude toward the follies of secession and slavery."

"Mr. Putnam, I'm delighted to meet you," Olivia said enthusiastically. "I suspect it was due partly to your influence, then, that Jesse became such an advocate for the cause of human freedom," and with those words, she withdrew from her handbag the poem that Jesse had sent her on his reflections about the war.

Putnam read the poem, "This is impressive, Colonel, may I publish it?" he asked.

"I'd rather that it not be published," Jesse said. "I'm trying to maintain an image of moderation here in the valley, and, as I recall, this little piece is a bit altruistic."

The three smiled as Putnam returned the poem to Olivia.

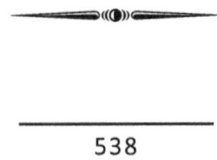

Now Logan was settling into what he perceived as a new chapter in his life; that of a married man with attending responsibilities, and a stable assignment managing a large contingent of men, with the stated objective of essentially controlling the residual Rebel resistance there in the Watauga Valley.

His presence in the valley was not un-noticed. Though his late-teen years had passed without particular notice, his notoriety as the 'White Angel' had been revived to a small degree with his returning to his home town. Also, his capture of the Holston Rangers brought him a certain celebrity standing. His days were filled with visits by citizens with grievances, some petty and some significant, as to what they perceived as the depredations of a four-year occupation by a foreign government. They wanted redress, if not revenge. Some days he might have four or five people come to his office with complaints against the Rebel element. Each person would be interviewed courteously, questioned as to the identity, associations, activities, and residence of the subjects of their complaint, with notes taken. Sometimes the information was valuable, sometimes not, but the person complaining always went away with a feeling that their concerns were not being ignored.

As part of his information-gathering Logan encountered Reverend Holtsinger, whom he had known before the war, and had also known when Holtsinger had been chaplain with the First Tennessee Volunteer Cavalry during the few short weeks Logan had also been assigned with that Regiment. John Holtsinger was again living in Greenville. He had been in the valley for many years, and was active in community affairs, and was a wealth of information. He came to Elizabethton occasionally and at this time came to Jesse's office.

Jesse escorted the minister into his office and offered him some coffee. After some preliminary remarks, they got down to business. Holtsinger was extremely helpful in his knowledge of the home guard units throughout the region, and Colonel Logan had to take notes to update his own knowledge of the problems in the valley.

"You know, Chaplain," Jesse commented, "sometimes I get the feeling we're chasing our tails on this venture. We identify some of the hostiles, track them down, bring them in, ostensibly convince them of the futility of their resistance, parole them, and turn them loose, and for what? I'm afraid they may just go back to their old habits, agitating and terrorizing the Unionists and giving us grief. What do you think?"

"Well, you may be right, Colonel, at least in part, but I know there's been a bit of a change in Greenville, even in my congregation. There are at least two men who have contacted me with the story that they are giving up their association with the home guard. Of course, they are well aware of my commitment to the Union, and their seriousness may be questionable, but I tend to believe them. Though I try to avoid the issues of slavery and secession in my exposure to my congregation, I feel that my parishioners are pretty well unanimous in their political persuasion and these two men are now attending church fairly regularly. I've been preaching on the Books of Kings, the difference between knowledge and wisdom, between intelligence and common sense, and they may be taking heed. I'm hoping for more, and if you were to attend some Sunday morning, I'm sure it would have a salutary effect."

"That sounds like a good idea, Reverend, I'll be over in the next couple of weeks. But, if you wouldn't mind, don't announce my coming. There's no need to attract trouble, as might be the case if word got around that the source of some people's trouble would be occupying a pew in your congregation."

Jesse had a cousin in Greenville, a woman a few years his senior. She had married a horse doctor whose veterinary service had kept him from conscription. Jesse wrote Rose a letter and asked if he and Olivia might stay with her and her husband Stanley for two nights, as the sixty-mile round-trip from Doe River Cove would tax their horse's endurance, if they tried to do it in one day. Rose wrote back with an enthusiastic invitation.

Jesse and Olivia set out on February 25, 1865 in the small one-horse coupe that the Kellar Family owned. They reached the home of Rose and Stanley Fletcher in Greenville about sundown. The Fletcher family consisted of Doctor Fletcher, Rose, his wife, two boys, eleven and twelve, and a daughter, Sylvia, sixteen. When Jesse and Olivia arrived, Rose and Sylvia were in the process of preparing dinner and the doctor met the Logans in the front yard of the home, invited them in, and directed the boys to tend to the care of Jesse's horse. After introductions, Olivia accompanied the other two women into the Kitchen and Jesse sat down with Stanley, joined presently by the boys, Edward and Earl.

Though they had met Jesse a year or two ago, the boys were fascinated, listening to their cousin, a Lieutenant Colonel in the United States Army. The previous week, they had been told by their father that Jesse and his wife were expected, and were admonished to keep the matter in confidence, to which they both agreed, but were not quite sure why. It was a matter of pride to be related to the commanding officer of the near-by garrison.

The following morning, the weather was clear, but cold, and the two families walked the short distance to the Presbyterian Church and met Reverend Holtsinger at the door of the church. He greeted them warmly and asked Jesse if he would care to deliver a few words to the congregation, to which Jesse agreed. He then had one of the ushers to escort them to a pew toward the front of the sanctuary.

About midway through the service, Jesse was introduced and invited to address the congregation. After thanking the pastor and congregation for allowing him to talk, he first spoke for a few moments about his own faith. Then he told the people about how important it had been to him, personally and professionally, that the "Church", without any reference to denomination, remain influential, a symbol of strength, sacrifice, and morality, in the lives of the American people, but especially during the stressful time of war.

The following morning, Jesse and Olivia thanked their host and hostess and left for home. Jesse had removed his gun-belt for comfort, but placed his revolver on the seat next to him. About an hour out of Greenville, the road passed through a section of low hills and was flanked by heavy tree growth. Suddenly they saw, coming over a hill about a quarter of a mile ahead, four masked horsemen riding hard in their direction. The lead rider had a revolver in his right hand. Jesse stopped his horse and tried to turn the buggy around, but the road was too narrow to make the turn an easy maneuver. By the time he had the buggy halfway reversed, the horsemen were almost upon them. The lead man shouted for Logan to stop, leveled his pistol at them, and fired. His shot went wide, and Jesse, pulling out his own gun, shot the man out of the saddle.

Meanwhile, Olivia had taken a single-shot Allen pistol out of her purse, and shot the second rider, knocking him off his horse, also. Seeing this, the two surviving riders, deciding they would like to live to fight another day, pulled up sharply and reversed their direction, as fast as they had come.

"That was nice shooting, Libbie," Jesse exclaimed as he hugged his wife. "I didn't have much faith in that little Allen you carry, but you certainly made it work for you, this time. When those other two guys saw they were facing two-against-two, they kind of lost interest."

"Jesse, Darling," she said in a surprisingly calm voice, "you'd better check those two men and see if they're still alive, don't you think?"

"First things first, My Love," he said, hugging her again. "I'm more concerned with your welfare than theirs. Are you alright?"

"Colonel, — go do your soldierly duty! The one I hit seems to be coming around."

"Yes, Dear," Logan said, as he stepped down from the coupe. Then, almost to himself, he muttered, "Always the concerned care-giver, even in the heat of battle."

Libbie's .32 caliber pistol was hardly powerful enough to do more than knock the rider unconscious. The bullet had hit him in the head, and the shot, somewhat cushioned by his hat-band, only penetrated the skin and traveled a few inches, exiting toward the rear of his skull. He was sitting up on the road when Jesse reached his side, with blood running down his face. He had drawn his revolver in the attack, and it was now lying some ten or twelve feet away from him. His horse had stopped and was grazing beside the road. He was a young man, about Jesse's age, and the look on his face was sheer confusion.

"Sit still, Mister," Logan said to him. "Let's see if you're alright."

The man looked blankly at Jesse, but did as he was told. Olivia had climbed down from the buggy and had torn several strips of cloth from one of her undergarments to serve as bandages. She knelt beside the dazed man and proceeded to wrap his head with the strips of cloth, while Jesse went to check on the other assailant. He was dead.

Jesse returned to where Olivia and the surviving attacker were kneeling and sitting. "What do you think, Libbie? Is he injured, other than that head wound?"

"I don't think so, Hon." Then turning to the man on the ground, she asked, "Do you feel any pain, Mister, other than your head?"

The man looked at Olivia, looked about in confusion, then back to Olivia, "Am I in heaven?" he asked.

Olivia smiled, glanced up at Jesse, and replied, "Do you think you belong in heaven? Do you remember what you were doing a few minutes ago?"

"What was I doing? Where am I? Who are you?"

"I'm Olivia. What's your name?"

"Joshua. J-O-S-H-U-A. My name is Joshua. Where are we? Are you sure you're not an angel?"

"Yes, she is, but you're not in Heaven," Jesse offered. "Can you stand up, Joshua?" he asked, trying to help the man to his feet.

Joshua stood up unsteadily and looked up at Jesse's face, some eight or ten inches above his own. "Who are you? Why are you so big?"

"Do you remember anything, Joshua? Do you know where we are?" Jesse asked.

"No. Where are we?"

Jesse and Olivia looked at each other. "I'll catch up the horses and put that other man's body on his horse. Then, if you can ride Joshua's horse, we'll put him in the seat beside me and go back to Greenville," he said. "I'd rather drive the buggy with him beside me than take a chance on him coming around and causing trouble with you up there in the buggy."

By the time they got back to Greenville, it was after 12:00 noon, and a light snow had started to fall. They took their two 'captives' to the town marshal's office and explained their situation. The marshal simply locked Joshua in the town's two-cell jail, and proceeded to fill out some preliminary papers on Logan's report. He detailed his deputy to take the body of the dead assailant to the town's undertaker and morgue for possible identification and burial. Olivia drove the buggy to the Fletcher home and asked Rose if they might stay another night.

That evening, before supper, Jesse sat down in the front room with Dr. Fletcher and the two boys. "I think those four men knew who I was and where I'd be and I'm wondering how the word got around. The reason we wanted to keep my coming here a secret, boys, was to try to avoid what happened, today. We have to remember that there is still a war going on in these parts, and there are still Rebels trying their best to win. What do you boys know? Did you tell anyone about my coming to Greenville?"

Edward and Earl looked at each other with bewildered expressions. Then the younger boy, Earl, lowered his eyes and murmured, "You know, one day we were just talkin' b'tween ourselves when our frien', Henry came up and he may have heard what we were talkin' about. Then, we saw him in church yesterday, and he said he knew about Cousin Jesse being in town. Do you think it may have been him that let the cat out of the bag, Pa?"

"That's possible, I reckon," Dr Fletcher said. "It doesn't make much difference, now, because it may have been Cousin Jesse's just being in church that tipped the Rebels off, but a man got killed because the word got out. It could have happened, even without your friend, Henry, overhearing you, but it teaches us all a lesson. The war still isn't over and we all have to be careful who we talk to and what we say, don't we?"

The following day, after checking with the town marshal, Jesse and Olivia again set out for Elizabethton and home. Toward sundown, they reached the Elizabethton armory and Jesse checked in to let Captain Coster know he was back and to learn about any recent developments.

"It's nice to have you back, Colonel, and yes, things have been busy. There was a raid up in Union, yesterday. We think it was the Hadley Company, and three civilians were killed. Captain Hazzard's company was up there, and drove the Rebs off, but it looks like it was something of a revenge attack. You know, — they just changed the name of that town back to 'Union' from 'Zollicoffer', and of the three men that were killed, two of them were members of the town council."

"Did you notify General Tillson, Sid?"

"I did, yes, and he's responded, inquiring as to whether we need any assistance. Do you think we do, Colonel?"

"Let's talk about it tomorrow at staff, and work out a response. I think we can handle it ourselves."

On Tuesday, February 28th, Lieutenant Colonel Logan sat down with his captains, again with Lieutenant Hawkins as a note-taker, and discussed a strategy. "The irregulars seem to be up in the Iron Mountain Range, mostly, and are taking advantage of the cover that those mountains provide. They're just coming into the valley occasionally to restock their supplies and, as this was the case, to take revenge on David McClellan's old political opponents. He owned half that town, lock, stock, and barrel, before he died back at Shiloh in '62, and prob'bly David's cousin, "GR" and Hadley resented fact that the town council has assumed its earlier name, especially the name of "Union". So I'd reckon "GR" and Hadley came out of hiding just to get revenge. Now, the question is, 'What next?' What do you fellows think?"

Captain Hazzard, who, with his '3rd Company', was garrisoned at the town of Union when the raid occurred, was responsible for chasing the Rebel force back into the mountains, was first to speak. "This was mostly Hadley's raid, though I know him and McClellan are pretty cozy, but what I noticed was that they didn't raid any of the army's stores or supplies. I think they would have, though, if we hadn't run them off. It's been some time since they've restocked their supplies, and I wouldn't be surprised if they try another raid pretty soon, to do just that."

"What do you other fellows think of that?" Logan asked. "We don't have much of a warehouse in Union, even though it's on the E.T. & V. Rail Line. Do you think they'll come down as far as Elizabethton, try for Morristown or Rogersville, or maybe wait for a train to come through?"

Captain Coster spoke next, "Elizabethton is too strong. I think they'll wait for a train and take their chances."

"I agree," Logan said, "and here's what I propose." He went on to lay out what he calculated to be a battle plan that would capture at least a large portion of the two Rebel companies involved in the raids.

With Captain Coster and Lieutenant Hawkins, he gathered together several of the members of the company, including Eli Morgan, Adam Gainfield, George McIlroy, and three men from Blountville, all of whom he trusted to provide geographic details of the small Iron Mountain Range, just east of Union. Raiding parties were said to be using the mountains to hide from his troops, but he didn't know which access canyon or canyons they were using. He even contacted his cousin, Dan Spurgeon and picked his brain a bit. Dan and his father, Ozzie, had livery stables in Union and Blountville, and Logan didn't want to miss any chance to gain advantage over the raiders.

As a distraction, Logan dispatched his troops in several directions for the next few days, ostensibly looking for the Rebels who had raided the town of Union. Also, he contacted Knoxville to find out when the next supply train would be coming through. It would be March 9th, just over a week away. He gave that information to the "News", the local newspaper. General Tillson, in Knoxville wired Logan to ask if he needed additional troops, but Jesse replied that additional troops would simply signal his intent to mount a campaign against the irregulars, and defeat his purpose. There should be the usual squadron of guard troops on the train, but no extraordinary military presence.

The train would approach Union from the southwest, pass through a forested range of hills and then negotiate about three miles of open farmland before stopping at the town. Heading on east, the train would again pass through some five miles of open land along the foot of Iron Mountain, and it was there that Logan expected the Rebels would attempt their raid, giving them optimum access to their choice of canyons back up into the mountains.

On March 9th, Logan posted Captain Hazzard's company in Union, concealing them among barns, stables and warehouses. The engineer of the train was to deliver three short blasts on the whistle when he was departing from the train station in Union. The troops were then to assemble, follow the train from a respectable distance and, if possible, ride in on the raiders, should a raid actually occur, which it did.

After the train left Union, right on cue, the Hazzard Company followed it at a distance so as not to discourage a Rebel raid, but closed in, just as the train slowed to clear an obstruction on the tracks and Hadley's Rebel troops had begun to surround it. The Rebels initially showed their intent to stop the train with an opening salvo of gun-fire, which was answered by the troops on the train, but then, seeing Hazzard's troopers, the irregulars quickly fled east and south toward the mountains, about a mile away. It was a long race, but Captain Hazzard had been instructed not to try to overtake the Rebels, as it was Logan's plan to follow them into which ever canyon the Rebels would use as their escape.

Rebel Captain GR McClellan, of course, had other plans. On the chance that the Federal troops would follow the irregulars into the canyon, he hid his own Rebel company beside the road to close in behind them, creating the classic ambush. The Bluecoats would be trapped.

The trap might have worked for the irregulars if Colonel Logan hadn't placed signalmen on hills near the entrances of the three canyons that he felt the Rebs would most likely use, and placed his other two companies close enough to be able to close in on the canyon that was selected. He had sent out his scouts during the previous week and, with the aid and advice of the local members of the regiment, they had narrowed the probabilities down to just three canyons.

The battle was brief. It was mid-day and the distinction of the blue uniforms, as opposed to the mostly plain clothing of the irregulars, minimized the confusion. The two reserve Union companies had spread out when entering the mouth of the canyon to sweep up stragglers, and the surrender was almost 100 percent.

The irregulars, having heard of Lieutenant Colonel Logan's reputation for leniency, gave little resistance, especially when outnumbered and trapped. The loss was four Federals and three Rebels wounded, and one broken leg when one of the Rebels was thrown from his horse. He and the other wounded were promptly picked up and taken to Union, where there was a doctor.

When the Rebels were rounded up and subdued by the Federal troops, the sorting and screening process took place. This was conducted in a casual manner, probably more like a gathering of old friends than an encounter between victor and vanquished. Greetings were exchanged, friendships were renewed, and news of other battles was discussed impersonally, as though they had occurred in some distant time and country. Personal property was left in the hands of the owners and any government property was either seized or destroyed, depending on its value to the Logan Regiment. Both of the Rebel commanders were interviewed and instructed to be at the Elizabethton armory the following day, pending a disposition decision from Colonel Logan's superiors.

<hr />

The following weeks were somewhat routine, with patrols picking up individuals and small bands of renegades, questioning them, arresting them, and bringing them into Elizabethton, only to be paroled. Surprisingly, very few repeats were encountered. Peaceful coexistence seemed to be more attractive than the continuation of what had come to be considered a futile conflict. Capture and parole by the Federal army seemed to put a seal on many of the would-be secessionists' aspirations for a separate country, at least in East Tennessee.

On the first of April word had come from Knoxville that General Grant had ordered all "available forces not essential to active operations," to relocate to Petersburg, Virginia. Grant was contemplating a strategic assault on the Confederate forces there, extending the Federal lines to try to turn General Lee's lines and take Richmond from the west. He particularly wanted cavalry companies, and the Logan Regiment qualified. General Tillson wired Lieutenant Colonel Logan to collapse his Elizabethton operation down and proceed as quickly as possible via Roane Mountain and Boone, North Carolina to Lynchburg, Virginia and wait there for further orders. There was still a considerable Confederate presence in and around Bristol, Virginia, the railroad route, so that the mountain route, while slower and more difficult, was much less likely to encounter Rebel resistance.

Logan had recovered sufficiently from his shoulder injury to lead the force, and he made immediate preparations. They started east on April 3. He and Olivia had just rented a small house in Elizabethton, and their goodbyes were quick.

"You will be careful, won't you, Jesse?" she admonished him. "We've only been married two months and here you are, setting off on a mission that seems as dangerous as any you've been involved in, and I don't want to lose you."

"My Love, I now have everything in the world to motivate me to stay well, and I'll just have to trust God to keep me healthy. I'd like to tell you not to worry, but thinking of how I'd feel if you were to start off on one of your old excursions to Richmond or wherever you would go off to, worrying is in our nature, isn't it?"

They hugged for a few more minutes, kissed tenderly, and Jesse climbed on his horse, Bob, for the ride over the Smokies, followed by 310 fresh mounted troops.

They bivouacked just west of the mountain pass, the first night, and set out early the next day. They encountered no resistance on the way, the pass being held by Brigadier General Mike Patterson's troops. He found General Patterson at that camp and they discussed the call for troops, which did not seem to apply to Patterson's Fourth Brigade, and the Logan Regiment moved on.

Their next night was at Sparta, North Carolina, no more than a few houses and a grocery store operated by a man named Parks, who was one of the many loyalists in the mountains. Jesse calculated that they were within another two-day ride from Roanoke, but in fact the ride was three days, owing to some token resistance from roving Rebel horsemen and the need to secure feed for their horses. Logan went to the railroad depot in Roanoke for any message from higher command, but found nothing of the sort, owing partially to the adverse reception he received from the station agent and partly because the telegraph system was intermittently malfunctioning. He decided to continue east.

The farther east the regiment rode, the more they encountered random Rebel horsemen who were detached and seemingly confused. Then on the evening of Sunday, April 9th. As they were settling down in a burned-over area just south of Lynchburg, a group of riders in tattered Rebel uniforms rode into camp as though they intended to stay the night. Lige Hawkins escorted the Rebs over to where Logan and his captains were settling down for the evening.

"Colonel, these men have some news that you might find interesting," Lige announced.

"Colonel," one of the men, a lieutenant, stepped forward with a casual salute, "we jus' come from Appomattox an' maybe you'uns don't know it, but the war is over, — at least down 't Richmond. Your Gen'r'l Grant an' our Bobby Lee jus' signed an agreement to end th' fightin' there. I don't know where you'uns were fixin' to go, but they ain't no fightin' goin' on hereabouts. Gen'r'l Grant jus' counted noses an' sent us home. He jes' let us keep our horses an' han'-guns, took away our long guns, an' turned us loose."

Logan looked over the group and turned to Captain Connant. "Captain do we have enough provisions to help these men out?" Then turning back to the spokesman of the group, he said, "You and your troop are welcome to stay the night with us, soldier. We'll feed you and you'll be free to go your way, tomorrow, if you want to. We'll have to get on east to find General Grant, and find out where we have to go from here."

As they gave the Rebels directions to the mess tent and a place where they could bed down, several more vagrant Rebels showed up, mostly on horseback, or leading horses. Lieutenant Colonel Logan instructed his men to welcome the visitors into camp, feed them and their horses, and make them comfortable. Then he called his staff together for a brief conference. He decided they should look for army command and obtain further instructions.

At Appomattox, the next day, they found General Grant, and Lieutenant Colonel Logan approached him seeking instructions.

"So you're our White Angel," General Grant said, after introductions were accomplished. "Your brother David owns a leather shop out in Cairo, doesn't he? He told me all about you, and you should know he seems to think very highly of you. I know he won't be disappointed judging from the silver leaves you're wearing."

"You know my brother, General? Have you seen him recently? How's he doing?"

The look of fatigue that had occupied General Grant's face was gone. He smiled broadly, probably the first smile that had crossed his face in many months. "I haven't seen David in years, but if you see him any time soon, tell him I haven't forgotten the seven dollars I owe him for the liniment and saddle bags."

Then, seeing the puzzled look on Jesse's face, he said, "Never mind, Colonel, I'll be returning out that way soon and it would give me great pleasure to give him the money, myself. Incidentally, though, Colonel, I hear you neutralized my old sergeant, Evan Stance. How did you manage that?"

The two men talked for a few minutes, the general authorizing the Logan Regiment's return to Knoxville and resume activities there.

"General Sherman seems to have things pretty well in hand, down in the Tidewater," General Grant said, "and I understand there are still some renegade troops in your state that need to be brought under control. As I now see it, you can probably take the train through Bristol back to Elizabethton, as resistance seems to be diminishing along that part of the rail line."

————((◉))————

Back in the Holston Valley, Logan was surprised to find black crepe draping the public buildings. President Lincoln had been killed, and the perpetrator was on the loose. A few days later, however, the assassin, an actor named John Wilkes Booth, was captured in rural Maryland and was shot and killed in the process of arrest. The news was devastating, and also cast a cloud of uncertainty over the question of peace.

In Doe River Cove, Jesse and his grandfather discussed the tragedy of President Lincoln's death and speculated on how it would affect the conflict.

"It gives a person a different view of life, Jesse," Henry Kellar remarked. "Do you realize that the man who is now president of these United States has been a guest in this very home? What do you think of that?"

"Grandpa, sometimes I say to myself, 'Well,' — and then sometimes I don't know what to say." Jesse said, recalling an old saw his grandfather had used in past years. "I think it's a crazy world, that's what I think."

Jesse and his regiment settled back into a routine of tracking and identifying small bands of Rebels, but the need obviously diminished as the country converted to the acceptance of the inevitable and small groups of 'reformers' or 'carpetbaggers', as they were eventually called, began to assert their influence over the political and social systems. As East Tennessee had only a minimal number of slaves, the number of carpetbaggers was also small, compared to some other regions.

Jesse got restless. In June, he applied for release from the army. The application worked its way through the Federal bureaucracy and in August the day after he turned 25, Jesse Logan returned to civilian life. Olivia was ecstatic.

Jesse and Olivia had discussed this day for many weeks. Neither of them thought that his staying in the army was an attractive idea, and the two options left him were either joining with his uncles and cousins in the lumber business in the Watauga Valley, or heading west to Nevada. Gold and silver having been discovered in Storey county and elsewhere in the state in 1859, Nevada had become a state in 1862, and business was booming. The sheep, hog, and beef-cattle market was prospering, and Jesse's brothers had written him with the suggestion that he would be a welcome addition to the family work force. The prospect was inviting.

"What do you think you could do, out there in the west, Jesse?" Olivia asked, as they were discussing his options. "You only have experience in ordering people around, riding around on your horse, and shooting people. That only qualifies you for robbing banks or stage coaches."

"Not a bad idea, Dear, but maybe I could become a Sheriff, or something. That sounds just a bit more respectable, and maybe safer than being a bank robber."

"But, Libbie, one thing that has been bothering me is this gold watch I've been carrying since this whole thing began," he mused, patting the pocket where the watch was kept. "You know it belonged to a Rebel soldier and I'd like to get it back to his family, or his Masonic Lodge. What would you think about taking the cars up through Lexington and Staunton and then on up through Baltimore and west from there? We might even be able to visit some of your family, there in Frederick."

They spent a little time discussing Jesse's early assignment as a rifleman and the circumstances surrounding his acquiring the watch. "I really felt bad about just helping myself to a nice watch that had belonged to a soldier from the Rebel army, but over time, I got used to the idea of the swapping that was going on between the two sides."

Having saved a respectable amount of money, they packed their meager belongings and headed to the railroad station in Union. The train-trip, which could accommodate their horses, Max and Bob, could take them as far as Cairo, Illinois.

It was a day's trip to Lexington, where they got off the train and took their horses to the local livery stable and checked in at a nearby hotel. There they asked for directions to the Masonic Lodge to try to find the family of the owner of the watch which Jesse, in his words, "had been entrusted with." Arriving at the lodge at about six o'clock in the evening, they found the building dark.

The next morning, they again went to the lodge building where they met a man, who informed them he was the 'Tiler' and caretaker of the premises. Asking about the family of the former member Alfred Stearman, Jesse received a look of surprise from the young man.

"What is it you want to know about Captain Stearman?" the man asked. "He's been dead for four years. The Yanks killed him back in '61 just after the war started, out in the Tygart Valley. He was my father. He was with the Seventh Virginia, an' was killed by one of the Union snipers."

The color drained from Jesse's face and he felt a wave of nausea, suspecting that the owner of the prized watch was probably the first victim of his marksmanship as a Union rifleman. He looked over at his wife with bewilderment in his eyes. The burden of taking the life of another person, a soldier in the opposing army, came flooding back. Jesse was back on the hillside of Rich Mountain, wiping sweat from his eyes and following orders, firing at a captain in the Rebel army.

"Mr. Stearman," he muttered, "I'm so sorry. I was a soldier in the Union Army, and I was prob'ly in that same battle. I know what it's like to lose someone so close to you, and so does my wife. It's devastating, and we want to express our sincere condolences." What Jesse didn't have the heart to tell the young man was his own role the tragedy.

"This watch," he said, taking it out of his pocket, "was found on the battlefield after the fight, and my sergeant gave it to me to keep until the war ended. I think the lodge gave it to your father in honor of his service. It has his name inside the cover, and I want to give it to you, if you want it. I'm a Mason, myself, and I —," his voice trailed off.

Olivia, with tears in her eyes, also offered her condolences. "Mr. Stearman, it makes me so sad to think about friends, really brothers, fighting each other and some of them losing their lives. It just makes me so sad. Were you with your father at Beverly?"

"No, Ma'am. I had jus' joined up an' was at Manassas with Jackson. Then I spent the whole war, pert'near, marchin' up an' down the Shenandoah Valley, an' never got a scratch."

The three former enemies stood near the front of the Masonic building and talked for the period of half an hour. Jesse and Olivia had planned to go to the Stearman home and give the watch to Captain Stearman's widow, but thought better of the idea, as they were both afraid that Jesse's involvement in the captain's death would become apparent and destroy any trust thus far established. They wished the young man well and took their leave, back to the railroad station.

From Lexington, the rail line went directly to Baltimore and on the trip, they explored the thought of seeking out some of Olivia's relatives in Frederick. She was not particularly enthusiastic about the idea, as she had no close relatives left in the area, her parents having both died.

They changed trains in Baltimore and proceeded west. Three days later, they changed trains in Vandalia, Illinois and then on south to Cairo. With his new wife, Jesse visited his brother David, a comfortably established merchant in Cairo, but with thoughts of relocating to more attractive marketing areas, such as St. Joseph or Scotts Bluff, as he predicted the leather market in Cairo would diminish with the ending of the war. Jesse made sure David was informed of General Grant's promise to pay him the seven dollars he owed him, and after David related the details of the event, they enjoyed a laugh at the story of the saddlebags.

From Cairo, the couple took a river boat to St. Louis and then on up the Missouri River to St. Joseph, Missouri. There, Jesse hired a local coach to take him and Olivia to the place that he remembered his mother's boarding house to have been, but either his memory was faulty or the house had been torn down and replaced by a hotel; he wasn't quite sure which. Anyway, the couple spent the night in the suspect hotel, the last really comfortable bed they would occupy for almost five weeks.

It was decision time. Their options were to board a stagecoach from St. Joseph for the trip west, or take a small flat-bottom sternwheeler as far up the river as Rulo, Nebraska and then board a stagecoach west. Either trip would be about a thousand miles and two to three weeks, to Salt Lake City, where Jesse and Olivia thought about spending the winter, if necessary.

Since this was, in a way, their honeymoon, and Rulo was reputed to have a rather luxurious hotel, they decided in favor of that town, now boasting almost 500 residents, a new grammar school, a fine blacksmith shop, and a nearby range of hills from the summit of which one could view three states; Nebraska, Kansas and Missouri, as well as many beautiful miles of the Missouri River.

On their arrival, they found all the described features were in place, except the hotel. Instead, they had to settle for a rather run-down boarding house that doubled as a brothel, with one 'bathroom' serving the four upstairs bedrooms, and half-naked women plying the hallway. Jesse was amused, Olivia was scandalized.

It was a two-night stay at Rulo, waiting for the weekly stagecoach, but the intervening day, after breakfast with two of the very friendly female residents, the couple spent their time walking the main street, with a side trip to the vaunted hill, where they enjoyed, not only the view, but a picnic lunch as well.

"Those were certainly handsome ladies, back there at breakfast," Olivia said during their lunch. "That one in the blue dress had quite a figure; as they say, one that would stop an army."

"Yes," Jesse agreed with a sly smile, "and a face that would stop a clock."

Olivia found his comment hilarious, but said quietly, "Jesse, you're not being very kind."

"No, I suppose you're right, my love. I shouldn't have said that. In fact, in all probability, that face would only slow a clock down."

"You nasty thing," she said, whereupon her husband reached over and, laying her back on the grass, kissed her passionately.

"I love you," he said.

"Well, isn't that nice? It just so happens that I love you, too."

———— ◦((◦))◦ ————

The next day, the west-bound stagecoach was empty, except for the usual mail bags, and the couple were free to choose the forward-facing seats. Though the trip west seemed tortuously slow, Jesse assured his wife that the forty or fifty miles a day they were traveling were much better than what he remembered as twenty miles on a good day and as few as five or six on a not-so-good day.

Their most pressing problem was the dust! September, after a dry summer across the Nebraska plains, makes for a dry, dusty trip. Olivia had the foresight to bring a veil which she draped over her head during the day and washed faithfully at their nightly stage-stops which, as luck would have it, were mostly situated along small creeks or lakes, so refreshing water was readily available. The stage-stops were not much more than long, low buildings with two or three apartments and a small dining room. There would also be a near-by corral, and usually a barn, for the teams that were required to pull the coaches and any saddle-horses belonging to the passengers. It was a developing business and not all the glitches had been worked out at the stops. The railroad was still just a dream in the minds of politicians and business moguls, and the stage lines were more a nightmare developed by necessity.

The first major stop on the route, one where the trail merged with the old Oregon Trail, was Fort Kearny along the Platte River. Jesse was anxious to visit the fort, as he knew several men who had served there, and he was curious to see if there was anyone at the fort that he might know. He was not disappointed. The stage stopped at a station just outside the gate of Fort Kearny, and Jesse, after asking the stage driver if he might take a few minutes visiting the fort, started for the front gate.

"Take all the time you want, Mister," the driver said. "This-here, is our night stop. We'll be leavin' again at six AM."

He inquired of the sentry where he might find the commanding officer and was directed to a low building off to his right. Entering the door of the building, Jesse saw a man sitting at a desk who, when he looked up, Jesse immediately recognized. It was Lieutenant Tom Singleton, Jesse's long-time class-mate, hunting partner, fellow soldier, neighbor, and friend, and Jesse was speechless. Tom looked up from his work and stared at the visitor, and then stood up. The two men ran toward each other and collided in a bear hug in the middle of the room.

"What in the world are you doing here, Tom?" Jesse exclaimed.

"I might ask you the same question, Jesse, though I suspect you're on your way back to Nevada, aren't you? When the war was winding down, I had the choice of either getting out of the army or coming west, and the result is what stands here before your eyes."

"What happened to you after we split up at Lewiston? I completely lost track of you. Where did you go? But wait a minute. I have to go get my wife."

Logan went back out the gate as the driver was sorting the mail and Olivia was just getting down from the coach. Jesse was just in time to help her down. "You'll never guess who I just ran into, Libbie. Come on in and meet an old friend."

They obtained their carpet bags from the coach and Jesse carried them into the fort. Tom had come out of his office and approached the couple. "Well, well, well," he remarked. "Mr. and Mrs. Logan. Why didn't you invite me to the wedding?"

"I told you. I had completely lost track of you, Tom. Where have you been all this time?"

"Well," he said, after greeting and congratulating Olivia, "after we split up, I went on to Camp Dick Robinson, and joined a training company there. They'd lost one of their instructors and apparently were desperate enough to keep me on, with the training staff. I had just worked my way up to sergeant, when last June, I had an opportunity to transfer out west to fill a vacancy here at Fort K. Well, no sooner had I got here, the First Lieutenant died and they needed a replacement, one who could read and write, so here I am. You remember when we were young, we used to talk about joining the army and seeing new places, and there I was at Camp Dick, teaching 'left-right-left'."

Fort Kearny could hardly be considered a fort, as it had no fortified enclosure, but consisted of a parade ground, surrounded by a ring of buildings; barracks, offices, barns, stables, corrals, and storage sheds. It apparently existed more for its service as a supply depot and staging facility for the army, the natives, and the settlers, than for its defensibility. It had the enviable reputation of being the only American fort that had never experienced an attack.

The camp had comfortable guest quarters, and, though Jesse complained about the one-person cots which the Army provided, at least they were able to share a room. That evening, the three old friends stayed up till two in the morning, drinking some terrible red wine and talking. The next day, they were up dutifully at five o'clock, with Olivia frantic about the condition of her hair. After some quick goodbyes with Tom Singleton, they got onto the stage at six o'clock, sharp, and in about three minutes after the stage left town, its only two passengers were asleep.

The stagecoach made good time, considering the circumstances, often as much as sixty miles a day on the plains of Nebraska, but as the terrain began to rise, the pace slowed and the stops to change horses became more frequent, each one requiring ten minutes or more, even though the attendants were obviously skilled at their jobs. It was twelve days from Fort Kearny to Salt Lake City, with Jesse conducting the equivalent of a narrated tour for his partner as they made their way along the trail.

At Salt Lake City, Jesse found that he was still listed on the rolls of the Mormon Church, but spending the winter in the city would present a problem. The couple, not having been married in the Mormon Church, would not be allowed to share quarters within the church's jurisdiction.

They talked the matter over. They had two choices; either they could marry according to Mormon tradition, which would require several days of instruction and counselling, or they could brave the weather and proceed to Genoa. They chose the latter. The stages were still running regularly, and the trip would only take them some eleven or twelve more days. Though they were both tired of traveling, the lure of home, family, and stable surroundings was irresistible.

Jesse and Olivia again boarded the Overland Stage and started west across the Great Salt Desert. The trip from Salt Lake City to Humboldt Wells was, as Jesse described it, four days of sheer monotony and the stage stops were spartan. The horses were never driven faster than a fast walk, as the change stations were then about twenty-five miles apart. At the last stop leaving Salt Lake City, the stage was loaded with as much hay and grain as it could carry. It was not the job of the Overland Stage Company to transport feed for the livestock, but it served them well to take as much feed along as possible, should space on the coach allow.

The young couple tried to lighten the tedium by playing children's games telling stories about their childhoods and singing songs. A recent song that was circulating in those days was "Sweet Betsy from Pike", which Jesse had learned over the years during the war. Another was a ditty he'd learned from his grandfather.

'Doodly, Doodly sat on a rail,
A-pickin' the feathers that grew in his tail.
Along came a redheaded girl with a gun,
And shot poor Doodly-do.'

"What is that supposed to be all about?" Olivia asked.

"It doesn't mean anything," Jesse replied. "It's just a song. I think Doodly-do must be a rooster. I don't know. It's just a song, Libbie. 'You want to hear it again?"

"Maybe some other time, Darling, I'll let you know."

As the days wore on, the conversation between the two newlyweds varied from the weather, the scenery, their childhoods, their aspirations and plans, and just about anything else that came to mind. At Humboldt Wells the stage line assumed the course of the Humboldt River, and the travel became a little more comfortable. They followed the river past the site where Jesse, Hoke Blackstone, and Fall had gotten into the fight with the Indians, and Jesse lapsed into a pensive mood, relating some of the experiences he'd had with his two friends. He described to Olivia how much he had learned from Fall and reflected on the profound influence his association with the dark-skinned cowboy had his life.

At a lull in the conversation, Olivia broached a subject that she had been avoiding, ever since they had reunited in Doe River Cove.

"Jesse," she said thoughtfully, "what happened to Jed Abernathy? I know you went after that transportation caravan, that day in Lewiston, and all that was ever said to me was that he was killed in an escape attempt and that you had caught up with the convoy and were somehow involved. Do you know what happened?"

"That was a long time ago, Libbie. I reckon I should tell you the story, but I just don't know where to start. He was not what I'd call a very nice man, but he didn't deserve to die, at least not then and there." Jesse then went on to relate the circumstances surrounding the death of Colonel Abernathy, including the feeling of remorse he'd experienced over the incident.

"I know I should probably have told you what happened, but I just couldn't seem to summon the resolve to tell you that I had caused the death of the husband of the woman with whom I was, and am, in love. One thing that really weighed on my mind was that comment I had made to him about snapping his neck if it would serve my interests. What a strange world we live in! I disliked the man! I disrespected him, I distrusted him, but I didn't mean to kill him, even though in a strange way it was to my own benefit that it happened." He went on to tell her of the circumstances surrounding Colonel Abernathy's death.

"Darling," she said after he recounted the story, "the door was closed on any feeling, good or bad, that I had for that man. I told you that, when we had him as a prisoner in Lewisburg and he claimed he wanted to see his 'wife'. I didn't hate him, but I certainly didn't want to have anything more to do with him. He was a millstone around my neck, you know. I didn't know where he was or whether he was even still living, but I also knew that I was bound to him by marriage and couldn't legally pursue a normal life without somehow getting shed of those marriage bonds. And think about this, Jesse. Had it not been for Jed Abernathy, my life would have been entirely different and I might never have met that corporal from Company H."

The conversation continued for another fifteen minutes, and Jesse finally turned to his wife, hugged her closely, and confessed that he was much relieved, having shared the sad secret that had been haunting him for two years.

Eleven days after leaving Salt Lake City, on November 3rd, 1865, Jesse and Olivia Logan stepped off the stagecoach in Genoa, Nevada and into a new life, adorned with 57 years of marital bliss, eight children, 22 grandchildren and who-knows-how-many 'greats' after that.

At the stage-stop, Jesse's mother, his brothers George, John, and Will, three of his sisters, all married now, Ben Jones, his wife Jane, and their son Dick, and Hoke Blackstone were there to greet the young couple. There were hugs and hand-shakes all around, and one of the last was Ben, a foot shorter than Jesse.

Ben Jones, the diminutive Welsh blacksmith who had been Jesse's mentor through his early life, the man who was most like a father to him before he left Genoa, extended his left arm as though he wanted to hug Jesse, and Jesse leaned over to accommodate their difference in height. With right-hands clasped they embraced each other and as they did, Ben murmured in Jesse's ear, "Well done, my boy, well done."